Praise for

Fire & Blood

"*Fire & Blood* is Martin Unbound . . . and I couldn't put it down. . . . There's an addictive quality to the prose that's outright gossipy. . . . The obvious comparison here is J.R.R. Tolkien's *The Silmarillion*. . . . Writing centuries after the events he's describing, the Gyldayn voice complicates this game of thrones with a clash of perspectives and a storm of debatable facts. . . . Heavy stuff, but *Fire & Blood* flies."

—*Entertainment Weekly*

"A masterpiece of popular historical fiction."

—*The Sunday Times*

"[George R. R.] Martin is still a powerfully gifted, inventive writer. . . . [*Fire & Blood*] has hundreds of fascinating anecdotes, ranging from the cruel fate of a jester named Tom Turnip to a dragon that, tellingly, refuses to venture beyond the Wall. . . . *Fire & Blood* is a lavish object, with charts, family trees, and stunning illustrations by comic book artist Doug Wheatley. . . . In this sense it fits into a venerable tradition, from J.R.R. Tolkien in his *Silmarillion* to Diana Gabaldon in her companion to the Outlander series."

—*USA Today*

"The saga is a rich and dark one, full of both the title's promised elements. . . . It's hard not to thrill to the descriptions of dragons engaging in airborne combat, or the dilemma of whether defeated rulers should 'bend the knee,' 'take the black' and join the Night's Watch, or simply meet an inventive and horrible end."

—*The Guardian*

"Lean and efficient and slyly seductive and instructive . . . The text is filled with such a wealth of incident and so many colorful characters."

—*Locus*

"The overall narrative of the book is wonderfully fluid. . . . *Fire & Blood* was a great surprise to me. I found myself becoming deeply emotionally invested in the Targaryens, thrilling when they achieved great victories and lamenting when they succumbed to their more idiotic desires. (And they have a *lot* of idiotic desires.) This book *feels* like A Song of Ice and Fire. And you know how I know? Because I want the next book right away."

—*Tor.com*

"[There are] treasures hidden in this new Targaryen history."

—*Vanity Fair*

"The world of ice and fire only gets more fascinating the more we learn about it."

—*Mashable*

"[*Fire & Blood*] explores the dragon-fueled secrets upon which the current saga is built."

—*Hollywood Reporter*

"Martin has done it again. . . . [*Fire & Blood* is] a beautiful weaving of the wars, marriages, deaths, dragons, and politics that shape the world Martin has created, leaving the reader feeling like this is a true history rather than a piece of fantasy. This is a masterpiece of world-building. . . . Beyond Martin's legions of fans, anyone with a taste for richly, even obsessively detailed historical fiction or fantasy about royalty will enjoy this extraordinary work."

—*Booklist* (starred review)

"Filled with fascinating facts about House Targaryen . . . *Fire & Blood* is an absolutely irresistible, dragon-filled delight."

—*Bustle*

"Fantasy master Martin provides backstory for the world of Westeros, extending the story of the Targaryens centuries into the past. . . . There are plenty of fierce dragons, impaled bodies, and betrayals to keep the storyline moving along briskly. A splendid exercise in worldbuilding and a treat for Martin's legions of fans."

—*Kirkus Reviews* (starred review)

By George R. R. Martin

A Song of Ice and Fire

Book One: A Game of Thrones
Book Two: A Clash of Kings
Book Three: A Storm of Swords
Book Four: A Feast for Crows
Book Five: A Dance with Dragons

The Lands of Ice & Fire
The World of Ice & Fire: The Untold History of Westeros and the Game of Thrones
A Knight of the Seven Kingdoms
Fire & Blood

Dying of the Light
Windhaven (with Lisa Tuttle)
Fevre Dream
The Armageddon Rag
Dead Man's Hand (with John J. Miller)

Graphic Novels

A Game of Thrones, Volumes 1–4
A Clash of Kings, Volumes 1–4
The Mystery Knight
Windhaven
Starport

Short Story Collections

Dreamsongs: Volume I
Dreamsongs: Volume II
A Song for Lya and Other Stories
Songs of Stars and Shadows
Sandkings
Songs the Dead Men Sing
Nightflyers
Tuf Voyaging
Portraits of His Children
Quartet

Edited by George R. R. Martin

New Voices in Science Fiction, Volumes 1–4
The Science Fiction Weight-Loss Book (with Isaac Asimov and Martin Harry Greenberg)
The John W. Campbell Awards, Volume 5
Night Visions 3
Wild Cards I–XXII

Co-edited with Gardner Dozois

Warriors I–III
Songs of the Dying Earth
Down These Strange Streets
Old Mars
Dangerous Women
Rogues
Old Venus

Fire & Blood

Fire & Blood

George R. R. Martin

Bantam Books
New York

2022 Bantam Books Trade Paperback Tie-in Edition

Published in the United States by Bantam Books, an imprint of Random House, a division of Penguin Random House LLC, New York.

BANTAM BOOKS is a registered trademark and the B colophon is a trademark of Penguin Random House LLC.

Originally published in hardcover in the United States by Bantam Books, an imprint of Random House, a division of Penguin Random House LLC, in 2018.

ISBN 978-0-593-59800-9
Ebook ISBN 978-1-5247-9629-7

Printed in the United States of America on acid-free paper

randomhousebooks.com

1st Printing

Book design by Virginia Norey

for Lenore, Elias, Andrea, and Sid,
the Mountain Minions

Contents

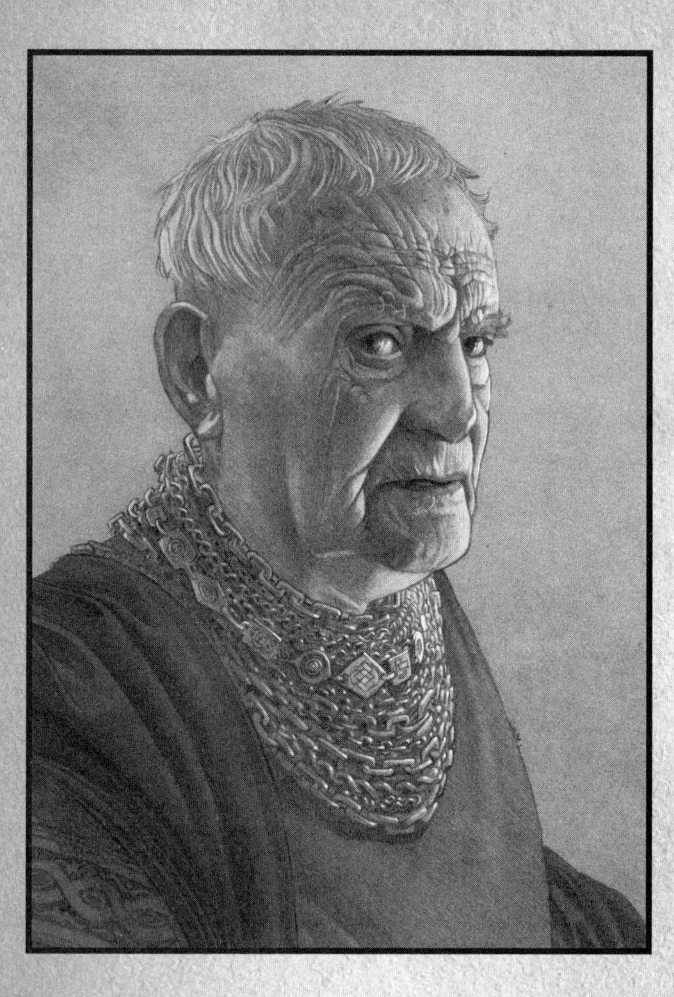

Fire & Blood

Being a History of the Targaryen Kings of Westeros

Volume One

from Aegon I (the Conqueror)

to

the Regency of Aegon III (the Dragonbane)

by Archmaester Gyldayn

of the Citadel of Oldtown

(here transcribed by George R. R. Martin)

Aegon's Conquest

The maesters of the Citadel who keep the histories of Westeros have used Aegon's Conquest as their touchstone for the past three hundred years. Births, deaths, battles, and other events are dated either AC (After the Conquest) or BC (Before the Conquest).

True scholars know that such dating is far from precise. Aegon Targaryen's conquest of the Seven Kingdoms did not take place in a single day. More than two years passed between Aegon's landing and his Oldtown coronation . . . and even then the Conquest remained incomplete, since Dorne remained unsubdued. Sporadic attempts to bring the Dornishmen into the realm continued all through King Aegon's reign and well into the reigns of his sons, making it impossible to fix a precise end date for the Wars of Conquest.

Even the start date is a matter of some misconception. Many assume, wrongly, that the reign of King Aegon I Targaryen began on the day he landed at the mouth of the Blackwater Rush, beneath the three hills where the city of King's Landing would eventually stand. Not so. The day of Aegon's Landing was celebrated by the king and his descendants, but the Conqueror actually dated the start of his reign from the day he was crowned and anointed in the Starry Sept of Oldtown by the High Septon of the Faith. This coronation took place two years after Aegon's Landing, well after all three of the major battles of the Wars of Conquest had been fought and won. Thus it can be seen that most of Aegon's actual conquering took place from 2–1 BC, Before the Conquest.

The Targaryens were of pure Valyrian blood, dragonlords of ancient lineage. Twelve years before the Doom of Valyria (114 BC), Aenar Targaryen sold his holdings in the Freehold and the Lands of the Long Summer, and moved with all his wives, wealth, slaves, dragons, siblings, kin, and children to Dragonstone, a bleak island citadel beneath a smoking mountain in the narrow sea.

At its apex Valyria was the greatest city in the known world, the center of civilization. Within its shining walls, twoscore rival houses vied for power and glory in court and council, rising and falling in an endless, subtle, oft savage struggle for dominance. The Targaryens were far from the most powerful of the dragonlords, and their rivals saw their flight to Dragonstone as an act of surrender, as cowardice. But Lord Aenar's maiden daughter Daenys, known forever afterward as Daenys the Dreamer, had foreseen the destruction of Valyria by fire. And when the Doom came twelve years later, the Targaryens were the only dragonlords to survive.

Dragonstone had been the westernmost outpost of Valyrian power for two centuries. Its location athwart the Gullet gave its lords a stranglehold on Blackwater Bay and enabled both the Targaryens and their close allies, the Velaryons of Driftmark (a lesser house of Valyrian descent) to fill their coffers off the passing trade. Velaryon ships, along with those of another allied Valyrian house, the Celtigars of Claw Isle, dominated the middle reaches of the narrow sea, whilst the Targaryens ruled the skies with their dragons.

Yet even so, for the best part of a hundred years after the Doom of Valyria (the rightly named Century of Blood), House Targaryen looked east, not west, and took little interest in the affairs of Westeros. Gaemon Targaryen, brother and husband to Daenys the Dreamer, followed Aenar the Exile as Lord of Dragonstone, and became known as Gaemon the Glorious. Gaemon's son Aegon and his daughter Elaena ruled together after his death. After them the lordship passed to their son Maegon, his brother Aerys, and Aerys's sons, Aelyx, Baelon, and Daemion. The last of the three brothers was Daemion, whose son Aerion then succeeded to Dragonstone.

The Aegon who would be known to history as Aegon the Conqueror and Aegon the Dragon was born on Dragonstone in 27 BC. He was the only son, and second child, of Aerion, Lord of Dragonstone, and Lady Valaena of House Velaryon, herself half Targaryen on her mother's side. Aegon had two trueborn siblings; an elder sister, Visenya, and a younger sister, Rhaenys. It had long been the custom amongst the dragonlords of Valyria to wed brother to sister, to keep the bloodlines pure, but Aegon took both his sisters to bride. By tradition, he would have been expected to wed only his older sister, Visenya; the inclusion of Rhaenys as a second wife was unusual, though not without precedent. It was said by some that Aegon wed Visenya out of duty and Rhaenys out of desire.

All three siblings had shown themselves to be dragonlords before they wed. Of the five dragons who had flown with Aenar the Exile from Valyria, only one survived to Aegon's day: the great beast called Balerion, the Black Dread. The dragons Vhagar and Meraxes were younger, hatched on Dragonstone itself.

A common myth, oft heard amongst the ignorant, claims that Aegon Targaryen had never set foot upon the soil of Westeros until the day he set sail to conquer it, but this cannot be truth. Years before that sailing, the Painted Table had been carved and decorated at Lord Aegon's command; a massive slab of wood, some fifty feet long, carved in the shape of Westeros, and painted to show all the woods and rivers and towns and castles of the Seven Kingdoms. Plainly, Aegon's interest in Westeros long predated the events that drove him to war. As well, there are reliable reports of Aegon and his sister Visenya visiting the Citadel of Oldtown in their youth, and hawking on the Arbor as guests of Lord Redwyne. He may have visited Lannisport as well; accounts differ.

The Westeros of Aegon's youth was divided into seven quarrelsome kingdoms, and there was hardly a time when two or three of these kingdoms were not at war with one another. The vast, cold, stony North was ruled by the Starks of Winterfell. In the deserts of Dorne, the Martell princes held sway. The gold-rich westerlands were ruled by the Lannisters of Casterly Rock, the fertile Reach by the Gardeners of Highgarden. The

Vale, the Fingers, and the Mountains of the Moon belonged to House Arryn . . . but the most belligerent kings of Aegon's time were the two whose realms lay closest to Dragonstone, Harren the Black and Argilac the Arrogant.

From their great citadel, Storm's End, the Storm Kings of House Durrandon had once ruled the eastern half of Westeros, from Cape Wrath to the Bay of Crabs, but their powers had been dwindling for centuries. The Kings of the Reach had nibbled at their domains from the west, the Dornishmen harassed them from the south, and Harren the Black and his ironmen had pushed them from the Trident and the lands north of the Blackwater Rush. King Argilac, last of the Durrandon, had arrested this decline for a time, turning back a Dornish invasion whilst still a boy, crossing the narrow sea to join the great alliance against the imperialist "tigers" of Volantis, and slaying Garse VII Gardener, King of the Reach, in the Battle of Summerfield twenty years later. But Argilac had grown older; his famous mane of black hair had gone grey, and his prowess at arms had faded.

North of the Blackwater, the riverlands were ruled by the bloody hand of Harren the Black of House Hoare, King of the Isles and the Rivers. Harren's ironborn grandsire, Harwyn Hardhand, had taken the Trident from Argilac's grandsire, Arrec, whose own forebears had thrown down the last of the river kings centuries earlier. Harren's father had extended his domains east to Duskendale and Rosby. Harren himself had devoted most of his long reign, close on forty years, to building a gigantic castle beside the Gods Eye, but with Harrenhal at last nearing completion, the ironborn would soon be free to seek fresh conquests.

No king in Westeros was more feared than Black Harren, whose cruelty had become legendary all through the Seven Kingdoms. And no king in Westeros felt more threatened than Argilac the Storm King, last of the Durrandon, an aging warrior whose only heir was his maiden daughter. Thus it was that King Argilac reached out to the Targaryens on Dragonstone, offering Lord Aegon his daughter in marriage, with all the lands east of the Gods Eye from the Trident to the Blackwater Rush as her dowry.

Aegon Targaryen spurned the Storm King's proposal. He had two wives, he pointed out; he did not need a third. And the dower lands being offered had belonged to Harrenhal for more than a generation. They were not Argilac's to give. Plainly, the aging Storm King meant to establish the Targaryens along the Blackwater as a buffer between his own lands and those of Harren the Black.

The Lord of Dragonstone countered with an offer of his own. He would take the dower lands being offered if Argilac would also cede Massey's Hook and the woods and plains from the Blackwater south to the river Wendwater and the headwaters of the Mander. The pact would be sealed by the marriage of Argilac's daughter to Orys Baratheon, Lord Aegon's childhood friend and champion.

These terms Argilac the Arrogant rejected angrily. Orys Baratheon was a baseborn half-brother to Lord Aegon, it was whispered, and the Storm King would not dishonor his daughter by giving her hand to a bastard. The very suggestion enraged him. Argilac had the hands of Aegon's envoy cut off and returned to him in a box. "These are the only hands your bastard shall have of me," he wrote.

Aegon made no reply. Instead he summoned his friends, bannermen, and principal allies to attend him on Dragonstone. Their numbers were small. The Velaryons of Driftmark were sworn to House Targaryen, as were the Celtigars of Claw Isle. From Massey's Hook came Lord Bar Emmon of Sharp Point and Lord Massey of Stonedance, both sworn to Storm's End, but with closer ties to Dragonstone. Lord Aegon and his sisters took counsel with them, and visited the castle sept to pray to the Seven of Westeros as well, though he had never before been accounted a pious man.

On the seventh day, a cloud of ravens burst from the towers of Dragonstone to bring Lord Aegon's word to the Seven Kingdoms of Westeros. To the seven kings they flew, to the Citadel of Oldtown, to lords both great and small. All carried the same message: from this day forth there would be but one king in Westeros. Those who bent the knee to Aegon of House Targaryen would keep their lands and titles. Those who took up arms against him would be thrown down, humbled, and destroyed.

Accounts differ on how many swords set sail from Dragonstone with Aegon and his sisters. Some say three thousand; others number them only in the hundreds. This modest Targaryen host put ashore at the mouth of the Blackwater Rush, on the northern bank where three wooded hills rose above a small fishing village.

In the days of the Hundred Kingdoms, many petty kings had claimed dominion over the river mouth, amongst them the Darklyn kings of Duskendale, the Masseys of Stonedance, and the river kings of old, be they Mudds, Fishers, Brackens, Blackwoods, or Hooks. Towers and forts had crowned the three hills at various times, only to be thrown down in one war or another. Now only broken stones and overgrown ruins remained to welcome the Targaryens. Though claimed by both Storm's End and Harrenhal, the river mouth was undefended, and the closest castles were held by lesser lords of no great power or military prowess, and lords moreover who had little reason to love their nominal overlord, Harren the Black.

Aegon Targaryen quickly threw up a log-and-earth palisade around the highest of the three hills, and dispatched his sisters to secure the submission of the nearest castles. Rosby yielded to Rhaenys and golden-eyed Meraxes without a fight. At Stokeworth a few crossbowmen loosed bolts at Visenya, until Vhagar's flames set the roofs of the castle keep ablaze. Then they too submitted.

The Conquerors' first true test came from Lord Darklyn of Duskendale and Lord Mooton of Maidenpool, who joined their power and marched south with three thousand men to drive the invaders back into the sea. Aegon sent Orys Baratheon out to attack them on the march, whilst he descended on them from above with the Black Dread. Both lords were slain in the one-sided battle that followed; Darklyn's son and Mooton's brother thereafter yielded up their castles and swore their swords to House Targaryen. At that time Duskendale was the principal Westerosi port on the narrow sea, and had grown fat and wealthy from the trade that passed through its harbor. Visenya Targaryen did not allow the town to be sacked, but she did not hesitate to claim its riches, greatly swelling the coffers of the Conquerors.

This perhaps would be an apt place to discuss the differing characters of Aegon Targaryen and his sisters and queens.

Visenya, eldest of the three siblings, was as much a warrior as Aegon himself, as comfortable in ringmail as in silk. She carried the Valyrian longsword Dark Sister, and was skilled in its use, having trained beside her brother since childhood. Though possessed of the silver-gold hair and purple eyes of Valyria, hers was a harsh, austere beauty. Even those who loved her best found Visenya stern, serious, and unforgiving; some said that she played with poisons and dabbled in dark sorceries.

Rhaenys, youngest of the three Targaryens, was all her sister was not, playful, curious, impulsive, given to flights of fancy. No true warrior, Rhaenys loved music, dancing, and poetry, and supported many a singer, mummer, and puppeteer. Yet it was said that Rhaenys spent more time on dragonback than her brother and sister combined, for above all things she loved to fly. She once was heard to say that before she died she meant to fly Meraxes across the Sunset Sea to see what lay upon its western shores. Whilst no one ever questioned Visenya's fidelity to her brother-husband, Rhaenys surrounded herself with comely young men, and (it was whispered) even entertained some in her bedchambers on the nights when Aegon was with her elder sister. Yet despite these rumors, observers at court could not fail to note that the king spent ten nights with Rhaenys for every night with Visenya.

Aegon Targaryen himself, strangely, was as much an enigma to his contemporaries as to us. Armed with the Valyrian steel blade Blackfyre, he was counted amongst the greatest warriors of his age, yet he took no pleasure in feats of arms, and never rode in tourney or melee. His mount was Balerion the Black Dread, but he flew only to battle or to travel swiftly across land and sea. His commanding presence drew men to his banners, yet he had no close friends, save Orys Baratheon, the companion of his youth. Women were drawn to him, but Aegon remained ever faithful to his sisters. As king, he put great trust in his small council and his sisters, leaving much of the day-to-day governance of the realm to them . . . yet did not hesitate to take command when he found it necessary. Though he dealt harshly with rebels and traitors, he was open-handed with former foes who bent the knee.

This he showed for the first time at the Aegonfort, the crude wood-and-earth castle he had raised atop what would henceforth and forever be known as Aegon's High Hill. Having taken a dozen castles and secured the mouth of the Blackwater Rush on both sides of the river, he commanded the lords he had defeated to attend him. There they laid their swords at his feet, and Aegon raised them up and confirmed them in their lands and titles. To his oldest supporters he gave new honors. Daemon Velaryon, Lord of the Tides, was made master of ships, in command of the royal fleet. Triston Massey, Lord of Stonedance, was named master of laws, Crispian Celtigar master of coin. And Orys Baratheon he proclaimed to be "my shield, my stalwart, my strong right hand." Thus Baratheon is reckoned by the maesters the first King's Hand.

Heraldic banners had long been a tradition amongst the lords of Westeros, but such had never been used by the dragonlords of old Valyria. When Aegon's knights unfurled his great silken battle standard, with a red three-headed dragon breathing fire upon a black field, the lords took it for a sign that he was now truly one of them, a worthy high king for Westeros. When Queen Visenya placed a Valyrian steel circlet, studded with rubies, on her brother's head and Queen Rhaenys hailed him as, "Aegon, First of His Name, King of All Westeros, and Shield of His People," the dragons roared and the lords and knights sent up a cheer . . . but the smallfolk, the fishermen and fieldhands and goodwives, shouted loudest of all.

The seven kings that Aegon the Dragon meant to uncrown were not cheering, however. In Harrenhal and Storm's End, Harren the Black and Argilac the Arrogant had already called their banners. In the west, King Mern of the Reach rode the ocean road north to Casterly Rock to meet with King Loren of House Lannister. The Princess of Dorne dispatched a raven to Dragonstone, offering to join Aegon against Argilac the Storm King . . . but as an equal and ally, not a subject. Another offer of alliance came from the boy king of the Eyrie, Ronnel Arryn, whose mother asked for all the lands east of the Green Fork of the Trident for the Vale's support against Black Harren. Even in the North, King Torrhen Stark of Winterfell sat with his lords bannermen and counselors late into the night, discussing what was to be done about this would-be conqueror. The whole realm waited anxiously to see where Aegon would move next.

Within days of his coronation, Aegon's armies were on the march again. The greater part of his host crossed the Blackwater Rush, making south for Storm's End under the command of Orys Baratheon. Queen

Rhaenys accompanied him, astride Meraxes of the golden eyes and silver scales. The Targaryen fleet, under Daemon Velaryon, left Blackwater Bay and turned north, for Gulltown and the Vale. With them went Queen Visenya and Vhagar. The king himself marched northwest, to the Gods Eye and the newly completed Harrenhal, the gargantuan fortress that was the pride and obsession of King Harren the Black.

All three of the Targaryen thrusts faced fierce opposition. Lords Errol, Fell, and Buckler, bannermen to Storm's End, surprised the advance elements of Orys Baratheon's host as they were crossing the Wendwater, cutting down more than a thousand men before fading back into the trees. A hastily assembled Arryn fleet, augmented by a dozen Braavosi warships, met and defeated the Targaryen fleet in the waters off Gulltown. Amongst the dead was Aegon's admiral, Daemon Velaryon. Aegon himself was attacked on the south shore of the Gods Eye, not once but twice. The Battle of the Reeds was a Targaryen victory, but they suffered heavy losses at the Wailing Willows when two of King Harren's sons crossed the lake in longboats with muffled oars and fell upon their rear.

In the end, though, Aegon's enemies had no answer for his dragons. The men of the Vale sank a third of the Targaryen ships and captured near as many, but when Queen Visenya descended upon them from the sky, their own ships burned. Lords Errol, Fell, and Buckler hid in their familiar forests until Queen Rhaenys unleashed Meraxes and a wall of fire swept through the woods, turning the trees to torches. And the victors at the Wailing Willows, returning across the lake to Harrenhal, were ill prepared when Balerion fell upon them out of the morning sky. Harren's longboats burned. So did Harren's sons.

Aegon's foes also found themselves plagued by other enemies. As Argilac the Arrogant gathered his swords at Storm's End, pirates from the Stepstones descended on the shores of Cape Wrath to take advantage of their absence, and Dornish raiding parties came boiling out of the Red Mountains to sweep across the marches. In the Vale, young King Ronnel had to contend with a rebellion on the Three Sisters, when the Sistermen renounced all allegiance to the Eyrie and proclaimed Lady Marla Sunderland their queen.

Yet these were but minor vexations compared to what befell Harren the

Black. Though House Hoare had ruled the riverlands for three generations, the men of the Trident had no love for their ironborn overlords. Harren the Black had driven thousands to their deaths in the building of his great castle of Harrenhal, plundering the riverlands for materials, and beggaring lords and smallfolk alike with his appetite for gold. So now the riverlands rose against him, led by Lord Edmyn Tully of Riverrun. Summoned to the defense of Harrenhal, Tully declared for House Targaryen instead, raised the dragon banner over his castle, and rode forth with his knights and archers to join his strength to Aegon's. His defiance gave heart to the other riverlords. One by one, the lords of the Trident renounced Harren and declared for Aegon the Dragon. Blackwoods, Mallisters, Vances, Brackens, Pipers, Freys, Strongs . . . summoning their levies, they descended on Harrenhal.

Suddenly outnumbered, King Harren the Black took refuge in his supposedly impregnable stronghold. The largest castle ever raised in Westeros, Harrenhal boasted five gargantuan towers, an inexhaustible source of fresh water, huge subterranean vaults well stocked with provisions, and massive walls of black stone higher than any ladder and too thick to be broken by any ram or shattered by a trebuchet. Harren barred his gates and settled down with his remaining sons and supporters to withstand a siege.

Aegon of Dragonstone was of a different mind. Once he had joined his power with that of Edmyn Tully and the other riverlords to ring the castle, he sent a maester to the gates under a peace banner, to parley. Harren emerged to meet him; an old man and grey, yet still fierce in his black armor. Each king had his banner bearer and his maester in attendance, so the words that they exchanged are still remembered.

"Yield now," Aegon began, "and you may remain as Lord of the Iron Islands. Yield now, and your sons will live to rule after you. I have eight thousand men outside your walls."

"What is outside my walls is of no concern to me," said Harren. "Those walls are strong and thick."

"But not so high as to keep out dragons. Dragons fly."

"I built in stone," said Harren. "Stone does not burn."

To which Aegon said, "When the sun sets, your line shall end."

It is said that Harren spat at that and returned to his castle. Once inside, he sent every man of his to the parapets, armed with spears and bows and crossbows, promising lands and riches to whichever of them could bring the dragon down. "Had I a daughter, the dragonslayer could claim her hand as well," Harren the Black proclaimed. "Instead I will give him one of Tully's daughters, or all three if he likes. Or he may pick one of Blackwood's whelps, or Strong's, or any girl born of these traitors of the Trident, these lords of yellow mud." Then Harren the Black retired to his tower, surrounded by his household guard, to sup with his remaining sons.

As the last light of the sun faded, Black Harren's men stared into the gathering darkness, clutching their spears and crossbows. When no dragon appeared, some may have thought that Aegon's threats had been hollow. But Aegon Targaryen took Balerion up high, through the clouds, up and up until the dragon was no bigger than a fly upon the moon. Only then did he descend, well inside the castle walls. On wings as black as pitch Balerion plunged through the night, and when the great towers of Harrenhal appeared beneath him, the dragon roared his fury and bathed them in black fire, shot through with swirls of red.

Stone does not burn, Harren had boasted, but his castle was not made of stone alone. Wood and wool, hemp and straw, bread and salted beef and grain, all took fire. Nor were Harren's ironmen made of stone. Smoking, screaming, shrouded in flames, they ran across the yards and tumbled from the wallwalks to die upon the ground below. And even stone will crack and melt if a fire is hot enough. The riverlords outside the castle walls said later that the towers of Harrenhal glowed red against the night, like five great candles . . . and like candles, they began to twist and melt as runnels of molten stone ran down their sides.

Harren and his last sons died in the fires that engulfed his monstrous fortress that night. House Hoare died with him, and so too did the Iron Islands' hold on the riverlands. The next day, outside the smoking ruins of Harrenhal, King Aegon accepted an oath of fealty from Edmyn Tully, Lord of Riverrun, and named him Lord Paramount of the Trident. The other riverlords did homage as well, to Aegon as king and to Edmyn Tully as their liege lord. When the ashes had cooled enough to allow men to enter the castle safely, the swords of the fallen, many shattered or melted or twisted into ribbons of steel by dragonfire, were gathered up and sent back to the Aegonfort in wagons.

South and east, the Storm King's bannermen proved considerably more loyal than King Harren's. Argilac the Arrogant gathered a great host about him at Storm's End. The seat of the Durrandons was a mighty fastness, its great curtain wall even thicker than the walls of Harrenhal. It too was thought to be impregnable to assault. Word of King Harren's end soon reached the ears of his old enemy King Argilac, however. Lords Fell and Buckler, falling back before the approaching host (Lord Errol had been killed), had sent him word of Queen Rhaenys and her dragon. The old warrior king roared that he did not intend to die as Harren had, cooked inside his own castle like a suckling pig with an apple in his mouth. No stranger to battle, he would decide his own fate, sword in hand. So Argilac the Arrogant rode forth from Storm's End one last time, to meet his foes in the open field.

The Storm King's approach was no surprise to Orys Baratheon and his men; Queen Rhaenys, flying Meraxes, had witnessed Argilac's departure from Storm's End and was able to give the Hand a full accounting of the enemy's numbers and dispositions. Orys took up a strong position on the hills south of Bronzegate, and dug in there on the high ground to await the coming of the stormlanders.

As the armies came together, the stormlands proved true to their name. A steady rain began to fall that morning, and by midday it had turned into a howling gale. King Argilac's lords bannermen urged him to delay his attack until the next day, in hopes the rain would pass, but the Storm King outnumbered the Conquerors almost two to one, and had almost four times as many knights and heavy horses. The sight of the Targaryen banners flapping sodden above his own hills enraged him, and the battle-seasoned old warrior did not fail to note that the rain was blowing from the south, into the faces of the Targaryen men on their hills. So Argilac the Arrogant gave the command to attack, and the battle known to history as the Last Storm began.

The fighting lasted well into the night, a bloody business and far less one-sided than Aegon's conquest of Harrenhal. Thrice Argilac the Arrogant led his knights against the Baratheon positions, but the slopes were steep and the rains had turned the ground soft and muddy, so the warhorses struggled and foundered, and the charges lost all cohesion and momentum. The stormlanders fared better when they sent their spearmen up the hills on foot. Blinded by the rain, the invaders did not see them climbing until it was too late, and the wet bowstrings of the archers made their bows useless. One hill fell, and then another, and the fourth and final charge of the Storm King and his knights broke through the Baratheon center . . . only to come upon Queen Rhaenys and Meraxes. Even on the ground, the dragon proved formidable. Dickon Morrigen and the Bastard of Blackhaven, commanding the vanguard, were engulfed in dragonflame, along with the knights of King Argilac's personal guard. The warhorses panicked and fled in terror, crashing into riders behind them, and turning the charge into chaos. The Storm King himself was thrown from his saddle.

Yet still Argilac continued to battle. When Orys Baratheon came down the muddy hill with his own men, he found the old king holding off half a dozen men, with as many corpses at his feet. "Stand aside," Baratheon commanded. He dismounted, so as to meet the king on equal footing, and offered the Storm King one last chance to yield. Argilac cursed him instead. And so they fought, the old warrior king with his streaming white hair and Aegon's fierce, black-bearded Hand. Each man took a wound from the other, it was said, but in the end the last of the Durrandon got his wish, and died with a sword in his hand and a curse on his lips. The death of their king took all heart out of the stormlanders, and as the word spread that Argilac had fallen, his lords and knights threw down their swords and fled.

For a few days it was feared that Storm's End might suffer the same fate as Harrenhal, for Argilac's daughter Argella barred her gates at the approach of Orys Baratheon and the Targaryen host, and declared herself the Storm Queen. Rather than bend the knee, the defenders of Storm's End would die to the last man, she promised when Queen Rhaenys flew Meraxes into the castle to parley. "You may take my castle, but you will win only bones and blood and ashes," she announced . . . but the soldiers of the garrison proved less eager to die. That night they raised a peace

banner, threw open the castle gate, and delivered Lady Argella gagged, chained, and naked to the camp of Orys Baratheon.

It is said that Baratheon unchained her with his own hands, wrapped his cloak around her, poured her wine, and spoke to her gently, telling her of her father's courage and the manner of his death. And afterward, to honor the fallen king, he took the arms and words of the Durrandon for his own. The crowned stag became his sigil, Storm's End became his seat, and Lady Argella his wife.

With both the riverlands and stormlands now under the control of Aegon the Dragon and his allies, the remaining kings of Westeros saw plainly that their own turns were coming. At Winterfell, King Torrhen called his banners; given the vast distances in the North, he knew that assembling an army would take time. Queen Sharra of the Vale, regent for her son Ronnel, took refuge in the Eyrie, looked to her defenses, and sent an army to the Bloody Gate, gateway to the Vale of Arryn. In her youth Queen Sharra had been lauded as "the Flower of the Mountain," the fairest maid in all the Seven Kingdoms. Perhaps hoping to sway Aegon with her beauty, she sent him a portrait and offered herself to him in marriage, provided he named her son Ronnel as his heir. Though the portrait did finally reach him, it is not known whether Aegon Targaryen ever replied to her proposal; he had two queens already, and Sharra Arryn was by then a faded flower, ten years his elder.

Meanwhile, the two great western kings had made common cause and assembled their own armies, intent on putting an end to Aegon for good and all. From Highgarden marched Mern IX of House Gardener, King of the Reach, with a mighty host. Beneath the walls of Castle Goldengrove, seat of House Rowan, he met Loren I Lannister, King of the Rock, leading his own host down from the westerlands. Together the Two Kings commanded the mightiest host ever seen in Westeros: an army fifty-five thousand strong, including some six hundred lords great and small and more than five thousand mounted knights. "Our iron fist," boasted King Mern. His four sons rode beside him, and both of his young grandsons attended him as squires.

The Two Kings did not linger long at Goldengrove; a host of such size must remain on the march, lest it eat the surrounding countryside bare.

The allies set out at once, marching north by northeast through tall grasses and golden fields of wheat.

Advised of their coming in his camp beside the Gods Eye, Aegon gathered his own strength and advanced to meet these new foes. He commanded only a fifth as many men as the Two Kings, and much of his strength was made up of men sworn to the riverlords, whose loyalty to House Targaryen was of recent vintage, and untested. With the smaller host, however, Aegon was able to move much more quickly than his foes. At the town of Stoney Sept, both his queens joined him with their dragons—Rhaenys from Storm's End and Visenya from Crackclaw Point, where she had accepted many fervent pledges of fealty from the local lords. Together the three Targaryens watched from the sky as Aegon's army crossed the headwaters of the Blackwater Rush and raced south.

The two armies came together amongst the wide, open plains south of the Blackwater, near to where the goldroad would run one day. The Two Kings rejoiced when their scouts returned to them and reported Targaryen numbers and dispositions. They had five men for every one of Aegon's, it seemed, and the disparity in lords and knights was even greater. And the land was wide and open, all grass and wheat as far as the eye could see, ideal for heavy horse. Aegon Targaryen would not command the high ground, as Orys Baratheon had at the Last Storm; the ground was firm, not muddy. Nor would they be troubled by rain. The day was cloudless, though windy. There had been no rain for more than a fortnight.

King Mern had brought half again as many men to the battle as King Loren, and so demanded the honor of commanding the center. His son and heir, Edmund, was given the vanguard. King Loren and his knights would form the right, Lord Oakheart the left. With no natural barriers to anchor the Targaryen line, the Two Kings meant to sweep around Aegon on both flanks, then take him in the rear, whilst their "iron fist," a great wedge of armored knights and high lords, smashed through Aegon's center.

Aegon Targaryen drew his own men up in a rough crescent bristling with spears and pikes, with archers and crossbowmen just behind and light cavalry on either flank. He gave command of his host to Jon Mooton, Lord of Maidenpool, one of the first foes to come over to his cause.

The king himself intended to do his fighting from the sky, beside his queens. Aegon had noted the absence of rain as well; the grass and wheat that surrounded the armies was tall and ripe for harvest . . . and very dry.

The Targaryens waited until the Two Kings sounded their trumpets and started forward beneath a sea of banners. King Mern himself led the charge against the center on his golden stallion, his son Gawen beside him with his banner, a great green hand upon a field of white. Roaring and screaming, urged on by horns and drums, the Gardeners and Lannisters charged through a storm of arrows down unto their foes, sweeping aside the Targaryen spearmen, shattering their ranks. But by then Aegon and his sisters were in the air.

Aegon flew above the ranks of his foes upon Balerion, through a storm of spears and stones and arrows, swooping down repeatedly to bathe his foes in flame. Rhaenys and Visenya set fires upwind of the enemy and behind them. The dry grasses and stands of wheat went up at once. The wind fanned the flames and blew the smoke into the faces of the advancing ranks of the Two Kings. The scent of fire sent their mounts into panic, and as the smoke thickened, horse and rider alike were blinded. Their ranks began to break as walls of fire rose on every side of them. Lord Mooton's men, safely upwind of the conflagration, waited with their bows and spears, and made short work of the burned and burning men who came staggering from the inferno.

The Field of Fire, the battle was named afterward.

More than four thousand men died in the flames. Another thousand perished by sword and spear and arrow. Tens of thousands suffered burns, some so bad that they would remain scarred for life. King Mern IX was amongst the dead, together with his sons, grandsons, brothers, cousins, and other kin. One nephew survived for three days. When he died of his burns, House Gardener died with him. King Loren of the Rock lived, riding through a wall of flame and smoke to safety when he saw the battle lost.

The Targaryens lost fewer than a hundred men. Queen Visenya took an arrow in one shoulder, but soon recovered. As the dragons gorged themselves on the dead, Aegon commanded that the swords of the slain be gathered up and sent downriver.

Loren Lannister was captured the next day. The King of the Rock laid his sword and crown at Aegon's feet, bent the knee, and did him homage. And Aegon, true to his promises, lifted his beaten foe back to his feet and confirmed him in his lands and lordship, naming him Lord of Casterly Rock and Warden of the West. Lord Loren's bannermen followed his example, and so too did many lords of the Reach, those who had survived the dragonfire.

Yet the conquest of the west remained incomplete, so King Aegon parted from his sisters and marched at once for Highgarden, hoping to secure its surrender before some other claimant could seize it for his own. He found the castle in the hands of its steward, Harlan Tyrell, whose forebears had served the Gardeners for centuries. Tyrell yielded up the keys to the castle without a fight and pledged his support to the conquering king. In reward Aegon granted him Highgarden and all its domains, naming him Warden of the South and Lord Paramount of the Mander, and giving him dominion over all House Gardener's former vassals.

It was King Aegon's intent to continue his march south and enforce the submission of Oldtown, the Arbor, and Dorne, but whilst at Highgarden word of a new challenge came to his ears. Torrhen Stark, King in the North, had crossed the Neck and entered the riverlands, leading an army of savage northmen thirty thousand strong. Aegon at once started north to meet him, racing ahead of his army on the wings of Balerion, the Black Dread. He sent word to his two queens as well, and to all the lords and knights who had bent the knee to him after Harrenhal and the Field of Fire.

When Torrhen Stark reached the banks of the Trident, he found a host half again the size of his own awaiting him south of the river. Riverlords, westermen, stormlanders, men of the Reach . . . all had come. And above their camp Balerion, Meraxes, and Vhagar prowled the sky in ever-widening circles.

Torrhen's scouts had seen the ruins of Harrenhal, where slow red fires still burned beneath the rubble. The King in the North had heard many accounts of the Field of Fire as well. He knew that the same fate might await him if he tried to force a crossing of the river. Some of his lords bannermen urged him to attack all the same, insisting that northern valor would carry the day. Others urged him to fall back to Moat Cailin and make his stand there on northern soil. The king's bastard brother Brandon Snow offered to cross the Trident alone under cover of darkness, to slay the dragons whilst they slept.

King Torrhen did send Brandon Snow across the Trident. But he crossed with three maesters by his side, not to kill but to treat. All through the night messages went back and forth. The next morning, Torrhen Stark himself crossed the Trident. There upon the south bank of the Trident, he knelt, laid the ancient crown of the Kings of Winter at Aegon's feet, and swore to be his man. He rose as Lord of Winterfell and Warden of the North, a king no more. From that day to this day, Torrhen Stark is remembered as the King Who Knelt . . . but no northman left his burned bones beside the Trident, and the swords Aegon collected from Lord Stark and his vassals were not twisted nor melted nor bent.

Now Aegon Targaryen and his queens parted company. Aegon turned south once again, marching toward Oldtown, whilst his two sisters mounted their dragons—Visenya for the Vale of Arryn and Rhaenys for Sunspear and the deserts of Dorne.

Sharra Arryn had strengthened the defenses of Gulltown, moved a strong host to the Bloody Gate, and tripled the size of the garrisons in Stone, Snow, and Sky, the waycastles that guarded the approach to the Eyrie. All these defenses proved useless against Visenya Targaryen, who rode Vhagar's leathery wings above them all and landed in the Eyrie's inner courtyard. When the regent of the Vale rushed out to confront her, with a dozen guards at her back, she found Visenya with Ronnel Arryn seated on her knee, staring at the dragon, wonder-struck. "Mother, can I go flying with the lady?" the boy king asked. No threats were spoken, no angry words exchanged. The two queens smiled at one another and exchanged courtesies instead. Then Lady Sharra sent for the three crowns (her own regent's coronet, her son's small crown, and the Falcon Crown of Mountain and Vale that the Arryn kings had worn for a thousand years), and surrendered them to Queen Visenya, along with the swords of her garrison. And it was said afterward that the little king flew thrice about the summit of the Giant's Lance, and landed to find himself a little lord.

Thus did Visenya Targaryen bring the Vale of Arryn into her brother's realm.

Rhaenys Targaryen had no such easy conquest. A host of Dornish spearmen guarded the Prince's Pass, the gateway through the Red Mountains, but Rhaenys did not engage them. She flew above the pass, above the red sands and the white, and descended upon Vaith to demand its submission, only to find the castle empty and abandoned. In the town beneath its walls, only women and children and old men remained. When asked where their lords had gone, they would only say, "Away." Rhaenys followed the river downstream to Godsgrace, seat of House Allyrion, but it too was deserted. On she flew. Where the Greenblood met the sea, Rhaenys came upon the Planky Town, where hundreds of poleboats, fishing skiffs, barges, houseboats, and hulks sat baking in the sun, joined together with ropes and chains and planks to make a floating city, yet only a few old women and small children appeared to peer up at her as Meraxes circled overhead.

Finally the queen's flight took her to Sunspear, the ancient seat of House Martell, where she found the Princess of Dorne waiting in her abandoned castle. Meria Martell was eighty years of age, the maesters tell us, and had ruled the Dornishmen for sixty of those years. She was very fat, blind, and almost bald, her skin sallow and sagging. Argilac the Arrogant had named her "the Yellow Toad of Dorne," but neither age nor blindness had dulled her wits.

"I will not fight you," Princess Meria told Rhaenys, "nor will I kneel to you. Dorne has no king. Tell your brother that."

"I shall," Rhaenys replied, "but we will come again, Princess, and the next time we shall come with fire and blood."

"Your words," said Princess Meria. "Ours are *Unbowed, Unbent, Unbroken.* You may burn us, my lady . . . but you will not bend us, break us, or make us bow. This is Dorne. You are not wanted here. Return at your peril."

Thus queen and princess parted, and Dorne remained unconquered.

To the west, Aegon Targaryen met a warmer welcome. The greatest city in all of Westeros, Oldtown was ringed about with massive walls, and ruled by the Hightowers of the Hightower, the oldest, richest, and most

powerful of the noble houses of the Reach. Oldtown was also the center of the Faith. There dwelt the High Septon, Father of the Faithful, the voice of the new gods on earth, who commanded the obedience of millions of devout throughout the realms (save in the North, where the old gods still held sway), and the blades of the Faith Militant, the fighting order the smallfolk called the Stars and Swords.

Yet when Aegon Targaryen and his host approached Oldtown, they found the city gates open and Lord Hightower waiting to make his submission. As it happened, when word of Aegon's landing first reached Oldtown, the High Septon had locked himself within the Starry Sept for seven days and seven nights, seeking the guidance of the gods. He took no nourishment but bread and water, and spent all his waking hours in prayer, moving from one altar to the next. And on the seventh day, the Crone had lifted up her golden lamp to show him the path ahead. If Oldtown took up arms against Aegon the Dragon, His High Holiness saw, the city would surely burn, and the Hightower and the Citadel and the Starry Sept would be cast down and destroyed.

Manfred Hightower, Lord of Oldtown, was a cautious lord and godly. One of his younger sons served with the Warrior's Sons, and another had only recently taken vows as a septon. When the High Septon told him of the vision vouchsafed him by the Crone, Lord Hightower determined that he would not oppose the Conqueror by force of arms. Thus it was that no men from Oldtown burned on the Field of Fire, though the Hightowers were bannermen to the Gardeners of Highgarden. And thus it was that Lord Manfred rode forth to greet Aegon the Dragon as he approached, and to offer up his sword, his city, and his oath. (Some say that Lord Hightower also offered up the hand of his youngest daughter, which Aegon declined politely, lest it offend his two queens.)

Three days later, in the Starry Sept, His High Holiness himself anointed Aegon with the seven oils, placed a crown upon his head, and proclaimed him Aegon of House Targaryen, the First of His Name, King of the Andals, the Rhoynar, and the First Men, Lord of the Seven Kingdoms, and Protector of the Realm. ("Seven Kingdoms" was the style used, though Dorne had not submitted. Nor would it, for more than a century to come.)

Only a handful of lords had been present for Aegon's first coronation at the mouth of the Blackwater, but hundreds were on hand to witness his second, and tens of thousands cheered him afterward in the streets of Oldtown as he rode through the city on Balerion's back. Amongst those at Aegon's second coronation were the maesters and archmaesters of the Citadel. Perhaps for that reason, it was this coronation, rather than the Aegonfort crowning on the day of Aegon's landing, that became fixed as the start of Aegon's reign.

Thus were the Seven Kingdoms of Westeros hammered into one great realm, by the will of Aegon the Conqueror and his sisters.

Many thought that King Aegon would make Oldtown his royal seat after the wars were done, whilst others thought he would rule from Dragonstone, the ancient island citadel of House Targaryen. The king surprised them all by proclaiming his intent to make his court in the new town already rising upon the three hills at the mouth of the Blackwater Rush, where he and his sisters had first set foot on the soil of Westeros. King's Landing, the new town would be called. From there Aegon the Dragon would rule his realm, holding court from a great metal seat made from the melted, twisted, beaten, and broken blades of all his fallen foes, a perilous seat that would soon be known through all the world as the Iron Throne of Westeros.

Reign of the Dragon

The Wars of King Aegon I

The long reign of King Aegon I Targaryen (1 AC–37 AC) was by and large a peaceful one . . . in his later years, especially. But before the Dragon's Peace, as the last two decades of his kingship were later called by the maesters of the Citadel, came the Dragon's wars, the last of which was as cruel and bloody a conflict as any ever fought in Westeros.

Though the Wars of Conquest were said to have ended when Aegon was crowned and anointed by the High Septon in the Starry Sept of Oldtown, not all of Westeros had yet submitted to his rule.

In the Bite, the lords of the Three Sisters had taken advantage of the chaos of Aegon's Conquest to declare themselves a free nation and crown Lady Marla of House Sunderland their queen. As the Arryn fleet had largely been destroyed during the Conquest, the king commanded his Warden of the North, Torrhen Stark of Winterfell, to end the Sistermen's Rebellion, and a northern army departed from White Harbor on a fleet of hired Braavosi galleys, under the command of Ser Warrick Manderly. The sight of his sails, and the sudden appearance of Queen Visenya and Vhagar in the skies above Sisterton, took the heart out of the Sistermen; they promptly deposed Queen Marla in favor of her younger brother.

Steffon Sunderland renewed his fealty to the Eyrie, bent the knee to Queen Visenya, and gave his sons over as hostages for his good behavior, one to be fostered with the Manderlys, the other with the Arryns. His sister, the deposed queen, was exiled and imprisoned. After five years, her tongue was removed, and she spent the remainder of her life with the silent sisters, tending to the noble dead.

On the other side of Westeros, the Iron Islands were in chaos. House Hoare had ruled the ironmen for long centuries, only to be extinguished in a single night when Aegon unleashed Balerion's fires on Harrenhal. Though Harren the Black and his sons perished in those flames, Qhorin Volmark of Harlaw, whose grandmother had been a younger sister of Harren's grandsire, declared himself the rightful heir "of the black line," and assumed the kingship.

Not all ironborn accepted his claim, however. On Old Wyk, under the bones of Nagga the Sea Dragon, the priests of the Drowned God placed a driftwood crown on the head of one of their own, the barefoot holy man Lodos, who proclaimed himself the living son of the Drowned God and was said to be able to work miracles. Other claimants arose on Great Wyk, Pyke, and Orkmont, and for more than a year their adherents battled one another on land and sea. It was said that the waters between the islands were so choked with corpses that krakens appeared by the hundreds, drawn by the blood.

Aegon Targaryen put an end to the fighting. He descended on the islands in 2 AC, riding Balerion. With him came the war fleets of the Arbor, Highgarden, and Lannisport, and even a few longships from Bear Island dispatched by Torrhen Stark. The ironmen, their numbers diminished by a year of fratricidal war, put up little resistance . . . indeed, many hailed the coming of the dragons. King Aegon slew Qhorin Volmark with Blackfyre, but allowed his infant son to inherit his father's lands and castle. On Old Wyk, the priest-king Lodos, purported son of the Drowned God, called upon the krakens of the deep to rise and drag down the invaders' ships. When that failed to happen, Lodos filled his robes with stones and walked into the sea, "to seek my father's counsel." Thousands followed. Their bloated, crab-eaten bodies washed up on the shores of Old Wyk for years to come.

Afterward, the issue arose as to who should rule the Iron Islands for the king. It was suggested that the ironmen be made vassals of the Tullys of Riverrun or the Lannisters of Casterly Rock. Some even urged that they be given over to Winterfell. Aegon listened to each claim, but in the end decided that he would allow the ironborn to choose their own lord paramount. To no one's surprise, they chose one of their own: Vickon Greyjoy, Lord Reaper of Pyke. Lord Vickon did homage to King Aegon, and the Dragon departed with his fleets.

Greyjoy's writ extended only to the Iron Islands, however; he renounced all claim to the lands House Hoare had seized upon the mainland. Aegon granted the ruined castle of Harrenhal and its domains to Ser Quenton Qoherys, his master-at-arms on Dragonstone, but required him to accept Lord Edmyn Tully of Riverrun as his liege lord. The new-made Lord Quenton had two strong sons and a plump grandson to assure the succession, but as his first wife had been carried off by spotted fever three years earlier, he further agreed to take one of Lord Tully's daughters as his bride.

With the submission of the Three Sisters and the Iron Islands, all of Westeros south of the Wall was now ruled by Aegon Targaryen, save Dorne alone. So it was to Dorne that the Dragon next turned his attention. Aegon first attempted to win the Dornishmen with words, dispatching a delegation of high lords, maesters, and septons to Sunspear to treat with Princess Meria Martell, the so-called Yellow Toad of Dorne, and persuade her of the advantages of joining her realm to his. Their negotiations continued for the best part of a year, but achieved nothing.

The start of the First Dornish War is generally fixed at 4 AC, when Rhaenys Targaryen returned to Dorne. This time she came with fire and blood, just as she had threatened. Riding Meraxes, the queen descended out of a clear blue sky and set the Planky Town ablaze, the fires leaping from boat to boat until the whole mouth of the Greenblood was choked with burning flotsam, and the pillar of smoke could be seen as far away as Sunspear. The denizens of the floating town took to the river for refuge from the flames, so fewer than a hundred died in the attack, and most of those from drowning rather than dragonfire. But first blood had been shed.

Elsewhere, Orys Baratheon led one thousand picked knights up the Boneway, whilst Aegon himself marched through the Prince's Pass at the head of an army thirty thousand strong, led by near two thousand mounted knights and three hundred lords and bannermen. Lord Harlan Tyrell, the Warden of the South, was heard to say that they had more than enough power to smash any Dornish army that tried to stand before them, even without Aegon and Balerion.

No doubt he had the right of that, but the issue was never proved, for the Dornishmen never offered battle. Instead they withdrew before King Aegon's host, burning their crops in the field and poisoning every well. The invaders found the Dornish watchtowers in the Red Mountains slighted and abandoned. In the high passes, Aegon's vanguard found its way barred by a wall of sheep carcasses, shorn of all wool and too rotted to eat. The king's army was already running short of food and fodder by the time they emerged from the Prince's Pass to face the Dornish sands. There Aegon divided his forces, sending Lord Tyrell south against Uthor Uller, Lord of the Hellholt, whilst he himself turned eastward, to besiege Lord Fowler in his mountain fastness Skyreach.

It was the second year of autumn, and winter was thought to be close at hand. In that season, the invaders hoped, the heat in the deserts would be less, water more plentiful. But the Dornish sun proved unrelenting as Lord Tyrell marched toward Hellholt. In such heat, men drink more, and every waterhole and oasis in the army's path had been poisoned. Horses began to die, more every day, followed by their riders. The proud knights discarded their banners, their shields, their very armor. Lord Tyrell lost a quarter of his men and almost all his horses to the Dornish sands, and when at last he reached the Hellholt, he found it abandoned.

Orys Baratheon's attack fared little better. His horses struggled on the stony slopes of the narrow, twisting passes, but many balked completely when they reached the steepest sections of the road, where the Dornish had chiseled steps into the mountains. Boulders rained down on the Hand's knights from above, the work of defenders the stormlanders never saw. Where the Boneway crossed the river Wyl, Dornish archers suddenly appeared as the column was making its way across a bridge, and arrows rained down by the thousands. When Lord Orys ordered his men to fall back, a massive rockfall cut off their retreat. With no way forward and no way back, the stormlanders were butchered like hogs in a pen. Orys Baratheon himself was spared, along with a dozen other lords thought worth the ransom, but they found themselves captives of Wyl of Wyl, the savage mountain lord called Widow-lover.

King Aegon himself had more success. Marching eastward through the foothills, where runoff from the heights provided water and game was plentiful in the valleys, he took the castle Skyreach by storm, won Yronwood after a brief siege. The Lord of the Tor had recently died, and his steward surrendered without a fight. Farther east, Lord Toland of Ghost Hill sent forth his champion to challenge the king to single combat. Aegon accepted and slew the man, only to discover afterward that he had not been Toland's champion, but his fool. Lord Toland himself was gone.

As was Meria Martell, the Princess of Dorne, when King Aegon descended upon Sunspear on Balerion, to find his sister Rhaenys there before him. After burning the Planky Town, she had taken Lemonwood, Spottswood, and Stinkwater, accepting obeisances from old women and children, but nowhere finding an actual enemy. Even the shadow city outside the walls of Sunspear was half-deserted, and none of those who remained would admit to any knowledge of the whereabouts of the Dornish lords and princess. "The Yellow Toad has melted into the sands," Queen Rhaenys told King Aegon.

Aegon's answer was a declaration of victory. In the great hall at Sunspear, he gathered together what dignitaries remained and told them that Dorne was now part of the realm, that henceforth they would be his leal subjects, that their former lords were rebels and outlaws. Rewards were offered for their heads, particularly that of the Yellow Toad, Princess Meria Martell. Lord Jon Rosby was named Castellan of Sunspear and Warden of the Sands, to rule Dorne in the king's name. Stewards and castellans were named for all the other lands and castles the Conqueror had taken. Then King Aegon and his host departed back the way they had come, west along the foothills and through the Prince's Pass.

They had hardly reached King's Landing before Dorne erupted behind them. Dornish spearmen appeared from nowhere, like desert flowers after a rain. Skyreach, Yronwood, the Tor, and Ghost Hill were all recaptured within a fortnight, their royal garrisons put to the sword. Aegon's castellans and stewards were allowed to die only after long torment. It was said that the Dornish lords had a wager over who could keep their captive alive the longest whilst dismembering them. Lord Rosby, Castellan of Sunspear and Warden of the Sands, had a kinder end than most. After the Dornishmen swarmed in from the shadow city to retake the castle, he was bound hand and foot, dragged to the top of the Spear Tower, and thrown from a window by none other than the aged Princess Meria herself.

Soon only Lord Tyrell and his host remained. King Aegon had left Tyrell behind when he departed. Hellholt, a strong castle on the river Brimstone, was thought to be well situated to deal with any revolts. But the river was sulfurous, and the fish taken from it made the Highgardeners sick. House Qorgyle of Sandstone had never submitted, and Qorgyle spearmen cut down Tyrell's foraging parties and patrols whenever they strayed too far west. The Vaiths of Vaith did the same to the east. When word of the Defenestration of Sunspear reached the Hellholt, Lord Tyrell gathered his remaining strength and set off across the sands. His announced intention was to capture Vaith, march east along the river, retake Sunspear and the shadow city, and punish Lord Rosby's murderers. But somewhere east of the Hellholt amidst the red sands, Tyrell and his entire army disappeared. No man of them was ever seen again.

Aegon Targaryen was not a man to accept defeat. The war would drag on for another seven years, though after 6 AC the fighting degenerated into an endless bloody series of atrocities, raids, and retaliations, broken up by long periods of inactivity, a dozen short truces, and numerous murders and assassinations.

In 7 AC, Orys Baratheon and the other lords who had been taken captive on the Boneway were ransomed back to King's Landing for their weight in gold, but on their return it was found that the Widow-lover had lopped off each man's sword hand, so they might never again take up swords against Dorne. In retaliation, King Aegon himself descended on the mountain fastnesses of the Wyls with Balerion, and reduced half a dozen of their keeps and watchtowers to heaps of molten stone. The Wyls took refuge in caves and tunnels beneath their mountains, however, and the Widow-lover lived another twenty years.

In 8 AC, a very dry year, Dornish raiders crossed the Sea of Dorne on ships provided by a pirate king from the Stepstones, attacking half a dozen towns and villages along the south shore of Cape Wrath and setting fires that spread through half the rainwood. "Fire for fire," Princess Meria is reported to have said.

This was not something the Targaryens would allow to go unanswered. Later that same year, Visenya Targaryen appeared in the skies of Dorne, and Vhagar's fires were loosed upon Lemonwood, Ghost Hill, and the Tor.

In 9 AC, Visenya returned again, this time with Aegon himself flying beside her, and Sandstone, Vaith, and the Hellholt burned.

The Dornish answer came the next year, when Lord Fowler led an army through the Prince's Pass and into the Reach, moving so swiftly that he was able to burn a dozen villages and capture the great border castle Nightsong before the marcher lords realized the foe was upon them. When word of the attack reached Oldtown, Lord Hightower sent his son Addam with a strong force to retake Nightsong, but the Dornish had anticipated just that thing. A second Dornish army under Ser Joffrey Dayne came down from Starfall and attacked the city. Oldtown's walls proved too strong for the Dornish to overcome, but Dayne burned fields, farms, and villages for twenty leagues around the city, and slew Lord Hightower's younger son, Garmon, when the boy led a sortie against him. Ser Addam Hightower reached Nightsong only to find that Lord Fowler had put the castle to the torch and its garrison to the sword. Lord Caron and his wife and children had been carried back to Dorne as captives. Rather than pursue, Ser Addam returned at once to Oldtown to relieve the city, but Ser Joffrey and his army had melted back into the mountains as well.

Old Lord Manfred Hightower died soon after. Ser Addam succeeded his father as the Lord of the High Tower, as Oldtown cried out for vengeance. King Aegon flew Balerion to Highgarden to take counsel with his Warden of the South, but Theo Tyrell, the young lord, was most reluctant to contemplate another invasion of Dorne after the fate that had befallen his father.

Once again the king unleashed his dragons against Dorne. Aegon himself fell upon Skyreach, vowing to make the Fowler seat "a second Harrenhal." Visenya and Vhagar brought fire and blood to Starfall. And Rhaenys and Meraxes returned once more to the Hellholt . . . where tragedy struck. The Targaryen dragons, bred and trained to battle, had flown through storms of spears and arrows on many occasions, and suffered little harm. The scales of a full-grown dragon were harder than steel, and even those arrows that struck home seldom penetrated enough to do more than enrage the great beasts. But as Meraxes banked above the Hellholt, a defender atop the castle's highest tower triggered a scorpion, and a yard-long iron bolt caught the queen's dragon in the right eye. Meraxes did not die at once, but came crashing to earth in mortal agony, destroying the tower and a large section of the Hellholt's curtain wall in her death throes.

Whether Rhaenys Targaryen outlived her dragon remains a matter of dispute. Some say that she lost her seat and fell to her death, others that she was crushed beneath Meraxes in the castle yard. A few accounts claim the queen survived her dragon's fall, only to die a slow death by torment in the dungeons of the Ullers. The true circumstances of her demise will likely never be known, but Rhaenys Targaryen, sister and wife to King Aegon I, perished at the Hellholt in Dorne in the 10th year After the Conquest.

The next two years were the years of the Dragon's Wroth. Every castle in Dorne, save Sunspear, was burned thrice over, as Balerion and Vhagar returned time and time again. The sands around the Hellholt were fused into glass in places, so hot was Balerion's fiery breath. The Dornish lords were forced into hiding, but even that did not buy them safety. Lord Fowler, Lord Vaith, Lady Toland, and four successive Lords of the Hellholt were murdered, one after the other, for the Iron Throne had offered a lord's ransom in gold for the head of any Dornish lord. Only two of the killers lived to collect their rewards, however, and the Dornishmen took their reprisals, repaying blood with blood. Lord Connington of Griffin's Roost was killed whilst hunting, Lord Mertyns of Mistwood poisoned with his whole household by a cask of Dornish wine, Lord Fell smothered in a brothel in King's Landing.

Nor were the Targaryens themselves exempt. The king was attacked thrice, and would have fallen on two of those occasions but for his guards. Queen Visenya was set upon one night in King's Landing. Two of her escorts were slain before Visenya herself cut down the last attacker with Dark Sister.

The most infamous act of that bloody age occurred in 12 AC, when Wyl of Wyl, the Widow-lover, arrived uninvited at the wedding of Ser Jon Cafferen, heir to Fawnton, to Alys Oakheart, daughter to the Lord of Old Oak. Admitted through a postern gate by a treacherous servant, the Wyl attackers slew Lord Oakheart and most of the wedding guests, then made the bride look on as they gelded her husband. Afterward they took turns raping Lady Alys and her handmaids, then carried them off and sold them to a Myrish slaver.

By then Dorne was a smoking desert, beset by famine, plague, and blight. "A blasted land," traders from the Free Cities called it. Yet House Martell still remained *Unbowed, Unbent, Unbroken,* as their words avowed. One Dornish knight, brought before Queen Visenya as a captive, insisted that Meria Martell would sooner see her people dead than slaves to House Targaryen. Visenya replied that she and her brother would be glad to oblige the princess.

Age and ill health finally did what dragons and armies could not. In 13 AC, Meria Martell, the Yellow Toad of Dorne, died abed (whilst having intimate relations with a stallion, her enemies insisted). Her son Nymor succeeded her as Lord of Sunspear and Prince of Dorne. Sixty years old, his health already failing, the new Dornish prince had no appetite for further slaughter. He began his reign by sending a delegation to King's Landing, to return the skull of the dragon Meraxes and offer King Aegon terms of peace. His own heir, his daughter Deria, led the embassy.

Prince Nymor's peace proposals encountered strong opposition in King's Landing. Queen Visenya was hard set against them. "No peace without submission," she declared, and her friends on the king's council echoed her words. Orys Baratheon, who had grown bent and bitter in his later years, argued for sending Princess Deria back to her father less a hand. Lord Oakheart sent a raven, suggesting that the Dornish girl be sold into "the meanest brothel in King's Landing, till every beggar in the city has had his pleasure of her." Aegon Targaryen dismissed all such proposals; Princess Deria had come as an envoy under a banner of peace and would suffer no harm under his roof, he vowed.

The king was weary of war, all men agreed, but granting the Dornishmen peace without submission would be tantamount to saying that his beloved sister Rhaenys had died in vain, that all the blood and death had been for naught. The lords of his small council further cautioned that any such peace could be seen as a sign of weakness and might encourage fresh rebellions, which would then need to be put down. Aegon knew that the Reach, the stormlands, and the marches had suffered grievously during the fighting, and would neither forgive nor forget. Even in King's Landing, the king dared not let the Dornish outside the Aegonfort without a strong escort, for fear that the smallfolk of the city would tear them to pieces. For all these reasons, Grand Maester Lucan wrote later, the king was on the point of refusing the Dornish proposals and continuing the war.

It was then that Princess Deria presented the king with a sealed letter from her father. "For your eyes only, Your Grace."

King Aegon read Prince Nymor's words in open court, stone-faced and silent, whilst seated on the Iron Throne. When he rose afterward, men said, his hand was dripping blood. He burned the letter and never spoke of it again, but that night he mounted Balerion and flew off across the waters of Blackwater Bay, to Dragonstone upon its smoking mountain. When he returned the next morning, Aegon Targaryen agreed to the terms proposed by Nymor. Soon thereafter he signed a treaty of eternal peace with Dorne.

To this day, no one can say with certainty what might have been in Deria's letter. Some claim it was a simple plea from one father to another, heartfelt words that touched King Aegon's heart. Others insist it was a list of all those lords and noble knights who had lost their lives during the war. Certain septons even went so far as to suggest that the missive was ensorceled, that it had been written by the Yellow Toad before her death, using a vial of Queen Rhaenys's own blood for ink, so that the king would be helpless to resist its malign magic.

Grand Maester Clegg, who came to King's Landing many years later, concluded that Dorne no longer had the strength to fight. Driven by desperation, Clegg suggested, Prince Nymor might have threatened that, should his peace be refused, he would engage the Faceless Men of Braavos to kill King Aegon's son and heir, Queen Rhaenys's boy, Aenys, then but six years old. It may be so . . . but no man will ever truly know.

Thus ended the First Dornish War (4–13 AC).

The Yellow Toad of Dorne had done what Harren the Black, the Two Kings, and Torrhen Stark could not; she had defeated Aegon Targaryen and his dragons. Yet north of the Red Mountains, her tactics earned her only scorn. "Dornish courage" became a mocking name for cowardice amongst the lords and knights of Aegon's kingdoms. "The toad hops into her hole when threatened," wrote one scribe. Another said, "Meria fought like a woman, with lies and treachery and witchery." The Dornish "victory" (if victory it was) was seen to be dishonorable, and the survivors of the fight, and the sons and brothers of those who had fallen, promised one another that another day would come, and with it a reckoning.

Their vengeance would need to wait for a future generation, and the accession of a younger, more bloodthirsty king. Though he would sit the Iron Throne for another twenty-four years, the Dornish conflict was Aegon the Conqueror's last war.

Three Heads Had the Dragon

Governance Under King Aegon I

Aegon I Targaryen was a warrior of renown, the greatest Conqueror in the history of Westeros, yet many believe his most significant accomplishments came during times of peace. The Iron Throne was forged with fire and steel and terror, it is said, but once the throne had cooled, it became the seat of justice for all Westeros.

The reconciliation of the Seven Kingdoms to Targaryen rule was the keystone of Aegon I's policies as king. To this end, he made great efforts to include men (and even a few women) from every part of the realm in his court and councils. His former foes were encouraged to send their children (chiefly younger sons and daughters, as most great lords desired to keep their heirs close to home) to court, where the boys served as pages, cupbearers, and squires, the girls as handmaidens and companions to Aegon's queens. In King's Landing, they witnessed the king's justice at first hand, and were urged to think of themselves as leal subjects of one great realm, not as westermen or stormlanders or northmen.

The Targaryens also brokered many marriages between noble houses from the far ends of the realm, in hopes that such alliances would help tie the conquered lands together and make the seven kingdoms one. Aegon's queens, Visenya and Rhaenys, took a special delight in arranging these matches. Through their efforts, young Ronnel Arryn, Lord of the Eyrie, took a daughter of Torrhen Stark of Winterfell to wed, whilst Loren Lannister's eldest son, heir to Casterly Rock, married a Redwyne girl from the Arbor. When three girls, triplets, were born to the Evenstar of Tarth, Queen Rhaenys arranged betrothals for them with House Corbray, House Hightower, and House Harlaw. Queen Visenya brokered a double wedding between House Blackwood and House Bracken, rivals whose history of enmity went back centuries, matching a son of each house with a daughter of the other to seal a peace between them. And when a Rowan girl in Rhaenys's service found herself with child by a scullion, the queen found a knight to marry her in White Harbor, and another in Lannisport who was willing to take on her bastard as a fosterling.

Though none doubted that Aegon Targaryen was the final authority in all matters relating to the governance of the realm, his sisters Visenya and Rhaenys remained his partners in power throughout his reign. Save perhaps for Good Queen Alysanne, the wife of King Jaehaerys I, no other queen in the history of the Seven Kingdoms ever exercised as much influence over policy as the Dragon's sisters. It was the king's custom to bring one of his queens with him wherever he traveled, whilst the other remained at Dragonstone or King's Landing, oft as not seated on the Iron Throne, ruling on whatever matters came before her.

Though Aegon had designated King's Landing as his royal seat and installed the Iron Throne in the Aegonfort's smoky longhall, he spent no more than a quarter of his time there. Full as many of his days and nights were spent on Dragonstone, the island citadel of his forebears. The castle below the Dragonmont had ten times the room of the Aegonfort, with considerably more comfort, safety, and history. The Conqueror was once heard to say that he even loved the scent of Dragonstone, where the salt air always smelled of smoke and brimstone. Aegon spent roughly half the year at his two seats, dividing his time between them.

The other half he devoted to an endless royal progress, taking his court from one castle to another, guesting with each of his great lords in turn. Gulltown and the Eyrie, Harrenhal, Riverrun, Lannisport and Casterly Rock, Crakehall, Old Oak, Highgarden, Oldtown, the Arbor, Horn Hill, Ashford, Storm's End, and Evenfall Hall had the honor of hosting His

Grace many times, but Aegon could and would turn up almost anywhere, sometimes with as many as a thousand knights and lords and ladies in his train. He journeyed thrice to the Iron Islands (twice to Pyke and once to Great Wyk), spent a fortnight at Sisterton in 19 AC, and visited the North six times, holding court thrice in White Harbor, twice at Barrowton, and once at Winterfell on his very last royal progress in 33 AC.

"It is better to forestall rebellions than to put them down," Aegon famously said, when asked the reason for his journeys. A glimpse of the king in all his power, mounted on Balerion the Black Dread and attended by hundreds of knights glittering in silk and steel, did much to instill loyalty in restless lords. The smallfolk needed to see their kings and queens from time to time as well, the king added, and know that they might have the chance to lay their grievances and concerns before him.

And so they did. Much of every royal progress was given over to feasts and balls and hunts and hawking, as every lord attempted to outdo the others in splendor and hospitality, but Aegon also made a point of holding court wherever he might travel, whether from a dais in some great lord's castle or a mossy stone in a farmer's field. Six maesters traveled with him, to answer any questions he might have on local law, customs, and history, and to make note of such decrees and judgments as His Grace might hand down. A lord should know the land he rules, the Conqueror later told his son Aenys, and through his travels Aegon learned much and more about the Seven Kingdoms and its peoples.

Each of the conquered kingdoms had its own laws and traditions. King Aegon did little to interfere with those. He allowed his lords to continue to rule much as they always had, with all the same powers and prerogatives. The laws of inheritance and succession remained unchanged, the existing feudal structures were confirmed, lords both great and small retained the power of pit and gallows on their own land, and the privilege of the first night wherever that custom had formerly prevailed.

Aegon's chief concern was peace. Before the Conquest, wars between the realms of Westeros were common. Hardly a year passed without someone fighting someone somewhere. Even in those kingdoms said to be at peace, neighboring lords oft settled their disputes at swordpoint. Aegon's accession put an end to much of that. Petty lords and landed knights

were now expected to take their disputes to their liege lords and abide by their judgments. Arguments between the great houses of the realm were adjudicated by the Crown. "The first law of the land shall be the King's Peace," King Aegon decreed, "and any lord who goes to war without my leave shall be considered a rebel and an enemy of the Iron Throne."

King Aegon also issued decrees regularizing customs, duties, and taxes throughout the realm, whereas previously every port and every petty lord had been free to exact however much they could from tenants, smallfolk, and merchants. He also proclaimed that the holy men and women of the Faith, and all their lands and possessions, were to be exempt from taxation, and affirmed the right of the Faith's own courts to try and sentence any septon, Sworn Brother, or holy sister accused of malfeasance. Though not himself a godly man, the first Targaryen king always took care to court the support of the Faith and the High Septon of Oldtown.

King's Landing grew up around Aegon and his court, on and about the three great hills that stood near the mouth of the Blackwater Rush. The highest of those hills had become known as Aegon's High Hill, and soon enough the lesser hills were being called Visenya's Hill and the Hill of Rhaenys, their former names forgotten. The crude motte-and-bailey fort that Aegon had thrown up so quickly was neither large enough nor grand enough to house the king and his court, and had begun to expand even before the Conquest was complete. A new keep was erected, all of logs and fifty feet high, with a cavernous longhall beneath it, and a kitchen, made of stone and roofed with slate in case of fire, across the bailey. Stables appeared, then a granary. A new watchtower was raised, twice as tall as the older one. Soon the Aegonfort was threatening to burst out of its walls, so a new palisade was raised, enclosing more of the hilltop, creating space enough for a barracks, an armory, a sept, and a drum tower.

Below the hills, wharves and storehouses were rising along the riverbanks, and merchants from Oldtown and the Free Cities were tying up beside the longships of the Velaryons and Celtigars, where only a few fishing boats had previously been seen. Much of the trade that had gone through Maidenpool and Duskendale was now coming to King's Landing. A fish market sprung up along the riverside, a cloth market between the hills. A customs house appeared. A modest sept opened on the Blackwater, in the hull of an old cog, followed by a stouter one of daub-and-wattle on the shore. Then a second sept, twice as large and thrice as grand, was built atop Visenya's Hill, with coin sent by the High Septon. Shops and homes sprouted like mushrooms after a rain. Wealthy men raised walled manses on the hillsides, whilst the poor gathered in squalid hovels of mud and straw in the low places between.

No one planned King's Landing. It simply grew . . . but it grew quickly. At Aegon's first coronation, it was still a village squatting beneath a motte-and-bailey castle. By his second, it was already a thriving town of several thousand souls. By 10 AC, it was a true city, almost as large as Gulltown or White Harbor. By 25 AC, it had outgrown both to become the third most populous city in the realm, surpassed only by Lannisport and Oldtown.

Unlike its rivals, however, King's Landing had no walls. It needed none, some of its residents were known to say; no enemy would ever dare attack the city so long as it was defended by the Targaryens and their dragons. The king himself might have shared these views originally, but the death of his sister Rhaenys and her dragon, Meraxes, in 10 AC and the attacks upon his own person undoubtedly gave him cause . . .

And in the 19th year After the Conquest, word reached Westeros of a daring raid in the Summer Isles, where a pirate fleet had sacked Tall Trees Town and carried off a thousand women and children as slaves, along with a fortune in plunder. The accounts of the raid greatly troubled the king, who realized that King's Landing would be similarly vulnerable to any enemy shrewd enough to fall upon the city when he and Visenya were elsewhere. Accordingly, His Grace ordered the construction of a ring of walls about King's Landing, as high and strong as those that protected Oldtown and Lannisport. The task of building them was conferred upon Grand Maester Gawen and Ser Osmund Strong, the Hand of the King. To honor the Seven, Aegon decreed that the city would have seven gates, each defended by a massive gatehouse and defensive towers. Work on the walls began the next year and continued until 26 AC.

Ser Osmund was the king's fourth Hand. His first had been Lord Orys Baratheon, his bastard half-brother and companion of his youth, but Lord Orys was taken captive during the Dornish War and suffered the loss of his sword hand. When ransomed back, his lordship asked the king to be relieved of his duties. "The King's Hand should have a hand," he said. "I will not have men speaking of the King's Stump." Aegon next called on Edmyn Tully, Lord of Riverrun, to take up the Handship. Lord Edmyn served from 7–9 AC, but when his wife died in childbed, he decided that his children had more need of him than the realm, and begged leave to return to the riverlands. Alton Celtigar, Lord of Claw Isle, replaced Tully, serving ably as Hand until his death from natural causes in 17 AC, after which the king named Ser Osmund Strong.

Grand Maester Gawen was the third in that office. Aegon Targaryen had always kept a maester on Dragonstone, as his father and father's father had before him. All the great lords of Westeros, and many lesser lords and landed knights, relied upon maesters trained in the Citadel of Oldtown to serve their households as healers, scribes, and counselors, to breed and train the ravens who carried their messages (and write and read those messages for lords who lacked those skills), help their stewards with the household accounts, and teach their children. During the Conquest, Aegon and his sisters each had a maester serving them, and afterward the king sometimes employed as many as half a dozen to deal with all the matters brought before him.

But the wisest and most learned men in the Seven Kingdoms were the archmaesters of the Citadel, each of them the supreme authority in one of the great disciplines. In 5 AC, King Aegon, feeling that the realm might benefit from such wisdom, asked the Conclave to send him one of their own number to advise and consult with him on all matters relating to the governance of the realm. Thus was the office of Grand Maester created, at King Aegon's request.

The first man to serve in that capacity was Archmaester Ollidar, keeper of histories, whose ring and rod and mask were bronze. Though exceptionally learned, Ollidar was also exceptionally old, and he passed from this world less than a year after taking up the mantle of Grand Maester. To fill his place, the Conclave selected Archmaester Lyonce, whose ring and rod and mask were yellow gold. He proved more robust than his predecessor, serving the realm until 12 AC, when he slipped in the mud, broke his hip, and died soon thereafter, whereupon Grand Maester Gawen was elevated.

The institution of the king's small council did not come into its full bloom until the reign of King Jaehaerys the Conciliator, but that is not to suggest that Aegon I ruled without the benefit of counsel. He is known to have consulted often with his various Grand Maesters, and his own household maesters as well. On matters relating to taxation, debts, and incomes, he sought the advice of his masters of coin. Though he kept one septon at King's Landing and another at Dragonstone, the king more oft wrote to the High Septon of Oldtown on religious issues, and always made a point of visiting the Starry Sept during his yearly circuit. More than any of these, King Aegon relied upon the King's Hand, and of course upon his sisters, the Queens Rhaenys and Visenya.

Queen Rhaenys was a great patron to the bards and singers of the Seven Kingdoms, showering gold and gifts on those who pleased her. Though Queen Visenya thought her sister frivolous, there was a wisdom in this that went beyond a simple love of music. For the singers of the realm, in their eagerness to win the favor of the queen, composed many a song in praise of House Targaryen and King Aegon, and then went forth and sang those songs in every keep and castle and village green from the Dornish Marches to the Wall. Thus was the Conquest made glorious to the simple people, whilst Aegon the Dragon himself became a hero king.

Queen Rhaenys also took a great interest in the smallfolk, and had a special love for women and children. Once, when she was holding court in the Aegonfort, a man was brought before her for beating his wife to death. The woman's brothers wanted him punished, but the husband argued that he was within his lawful rights, since he had found his wife abed with another man. The right of a husband to chastise an erring wife was well established throughout the Seven Kingdoms (save in Dorne). The husband further pointed out that the rod he had used to beat his wife was no thicker than his thumb, and even produced the rod in evidence. When the queen asked him how many times he had struck his wife, however, the husband could not answer, but the dead woman's brothers insisted there had been a hundred blows.

Queen Rhaenys consulted with her maesters and septons, then rendered her decision. An adulterous wife gave offense to the Seven, who had created women to be faithful and obedient to their husbands, and therefore must be chastised. As god has but seven faces, however, the punishment should consist of only six blows (for the seventh blow would be for the Stranger, and the Stranger is the face of death). Thus the first six blows the man had struck had been lawful . . . but the remaining ninety-four had been an offense against gods and men, and must be punished in kind. From that day forth, the "rule of six" became a part of the common law, along with the "rule of thumb." (The husband was taken to the foot of the Hill of Rhaenys, where he was given ninety-four blows by the dead woman's brothers, using rods of lawful size.)

Queen Visenya did not share her sister's love of music and song. She was not without humor, however, and for many years kept her own fool, a hirsute hunchback called Lord Monkeyface whose antics amused her greatly. When he choked to death on a peach pit, the queen acquired an ape and dressed it in Lord Monkeyface's clothing. "The new one is cleverer," she was wont to say.

Yet there was darkness in Visenya Targaryen. To most of the world, she presented the grim face of a warrior, stern and unforgiving. Even her beauty had an edge to it, her admirers said. The oldest of the three heads of the dragon, Visenya was to outlive both of her siblings, and it was rumored that in her later years, when she could no longer wield a sword, she delved into the dark arts, mixing poisons and casting malign spells. Some even suggest that she might have been a kinslayer and a kingslayer, though no proof has ever been offered to support such calumnies.

It would be a cruel irony if true, for in her youth no one did more to protect the king. Visenya twice wielded Dark Sister in Aegon's defense when he was set upon by Dornish cutthroats. Suspicious and ferocious by turns, she trusted no one but her brother. During the Dornish War, she took to wearing a shirt of mail night and day, even under her court clothes, and urged the king to do the same. When Aegon refused, Visenya grew furious. "Even with Blackfyre in your hand, you are only one man," she told him, "and I cannot always be with you." When the king pointed out that he had guardsmen around him, Visenya drew Dark Sister and slashed him across the cheek so quickly the guards had no time to react. "Your guards are slow and lazy," she said. "I could have killed you as easily as I cut you. You require better protection." King Aegon, bleeding, had no choice but to agree.

Many kings had champions to defend them. Aegon was the Lord of the Seven Kingdoms; therefore, he should have seven champions, Queen Visenya decided. Thus did the Kingsguard come into being; a brotherhood of seven knights, the finest in the realm, cloaked and armored all in purest white, with no purpose but to defend the king, giving up their own lives for his if need be. Visenya modeled their vows on those of the Night's Watch; like the black-cloaked crows of the Wall, the White Swords served for life, surrendering all their lands, titles, and worldly goods to live a life of chastity and obedience, with no reward but honor.

So many knights came forward to offer themselves as candidates for the Kingsguard that King Aegon considered holding a great tourney to determine which of them was the most worthy. Visenya would not hear of it, however. To be a Kingsguard knight required more than just skill at arms, she pointed out. She would not risk placing men of uncertain loyalty about the king, regardless of how well they performed in a melee. She would choose the knights herself.

The champions she selected were young and old, tall and short, dark and fair. They came from every corner of the realm. Some were younger sons, others the heirs of ancient houses who gave up their inheritances to serve the king. One was a hedge knight, another bastard born. All of them were quick, strong, observant, skilled with sword and shield, and devoted to the king.

These are the names of Aegon's Seven, as written in the White Book of the Kingsguard: Ser Richard Roote; Ser Addison Hill, Bastard of Cornfield; Ser Gregor Goode; Ser Griffith Goode, his brother; Ser Humfrey the Mummer; Ser Robin Darklyn, called Darkrobin; and Ser Corlys Velaryon, Lord Commander. History has confirmed that Visenya Targaryen chose well. Two of her original seven would die protecting the king, and all would serve with valor to the end of their lives. Many brave men have followed in their footsteps since, writing their names in the White Book and donning the white cloak. The Kingsguard remains a synonym for honor to this day.

Sixteen Targaryens followed Aegon the Dragon to the Iron Throne, before the dynasty was at last toppled in Robert's Rebellion. They numbered amongst them wise men and foolish, cruel men and kind, good men and evil. Yet if the dragon kings are considered solely on the basis of their legacies, the laws and institutions and improvements they left behind, the name of King Aegon I belongs near the top of the list, in peace as well as war.

The Sons of the Dragon

King Aegon I Targaryen took both of his sisters to wife. Rhaenys and Visenya were dragonriders, with the silver-gold hair, purple eyes, and beauty of true Targaryens. Elsewise, the two queens were as unlike each other as any two women could be . . . save in one other respect. Each of them gave the king a son.

Aenys came first. Born in 7 AC to Aegon's younger wife, Rhaenys, the boy was small at birth and sickly. He cried all the time, and it was said that his limbs were spindly, his eyes small and watery, and that the king's maesters feared for his survival. He would spit out the nipples of his wet nurse, and give suck only at his mother's breasts, and rumors claimed that he screamed for a fortnight when he was weaned. So unlike King Aegon was he that a few even dared suggest that His Grace was not the boy's true sire, that Aenys was some bastard born of one of Queen Rhaenys's many handsome favorites, the son of a singer or a mummer or a mime. And the prince was slow to grow as well. Not until he was given the young dragon Quicksilver, a hatchling born that same year on Dragonstone, did Aenys Targaryen begin to thrive.

Prince Aenys was three when his mother, Queen Rhaenys, and her dragon, Meraxes, were slain in Dorne. Her death left the boy prince inconsolable. He stopped eating, and even began to crawl as he had when he was one, as if he had forgotten how to walk. His father despaired of him, and rumors flew about the court that King Aegon might take another wife, as Rhaenys was dead and Visenya childless and perhaps barren. The king kept his own counsel on these matters, so no man could say what thoughts he might have entertained, but many great lords and noble knights appeared at court with their maiden daughters, each more comely than the last.

All such speculation ended in 11 AC, when Queen Visenya suddenly announced that she was carrying the king's child. A son, she proclaimed confidently, and so he proved to be. The prince came squalling into the world in 12 AC. No newborn was ever more robust than Maegor Targaryen, maesters and midwives agreed; his weight at birth was almost twice that of his elder brother.

The half-brothers were never close. Prince Aenys was the heir apparent, and King Aegon kept him close by his side. As the king moved about the realm from castle to castle, so did the prince. Prince Maegor remained with his mother, sitting by her side when she held court. Queen Visenya and King Aegon were oft apart in those years. When he was not on a royal progress, Aegon would return to King's Landing and the Aegonfort, whilst Visenya and her son remained on Dragonstone. For this reason, lords and commons alike began to refer to Maegor as the Prince of Dragonstone.

Queen Visenya put a sword into her son's hand when he was three. Supposedly the first thing he did with the blade was butcher one of the castle cats, men said . . . though more like this tale was a calumny devised by his enemies many years later. That the prince took to swordplay at once cannot be denied, however. For his first master-at-arms his mother chose Ser Gawen Corbray, as deadly a knight as could be found in all the Seven Kingdoms.

Prince Aenys was so oft in his sire's company that his own instruction in the chivalric arts came largely from the knights of Aegon's Kingsguard, and sometimes the king himself. The boy was diligent, his instructors agreed, and did not want for courage, but he lacked his sire's size and strength, and was never more than adequate as a fighter, even when the king pressed Blackfyre into his hands, as he did from time to time. Aenys would not disgrace himself in battle, his tutors told one another, but no songs would ever be sung about his prowess.

Such gifts as this prince possessed lay elsewhere. Aenys was a fine singer himself, as it happened, with a strong sweet voice. He was courteous and charming, clever without being bookish. He made friends easily, and young girls seemed to dote on him, be they highborn or low. Aenys loved to ride as well. His father gave him coursers, palfreys, and destriers, but his favorite mount was his dragon, Quicksilver.

Prince Maegor rode as well, but showed no great love for horses, dogs, or any animal. When he was eight, a palfrey kicked him in the stables. Maegor stabbed the horse to death . . . and slashed half the face off the stableboy who came running at the beast's screams. The Prince of Dragonstone had many companions through the years, but no true friends. He was a quarrelsome boy, quick to take offense, slow to forgive, fearsome in his wroth. His skill with weapons was unmatched, however. A squire at eight, he was unhorsing boys four and five years his elder in the lists by the time he was twelve, and battering seasoned men-at-arms into submission in the castle yard. On his thirteenth nameday in 25 AC, his mother, Queen Visenya, bestowed her own Valyrian steel blade, Dark Sister, upon him . . . half a year before his marriage.

The tradition amongst the Targaryens had always been to marry kin to kin. Wedding brother to sister was thought to be ideal. Failing that, a girl might wed an uncle, a cousin, or a nephew, a boy a cousin, aunt, or niece. This practice went back to Old Valyria, where it was common amongst many of the ancient families, particularly those who bred and rode dragons. *The blood of the dragon must remain pure,* the wisdom went. Some of the sorcerer princes also took more than one wife when it pleased them, though this was less common than incestuous marriage. In Valyria before the Doom, wise men wrote, a thousand gods were honored, but none were feared, so few dared to speak against these customs.

This was not true in Westeros, where the power of the Faith went unquestioned. The old gods were still worshipped in the North and the Drowned God in the Iron Islands, but in the rest of the realm there was a single god with seven faces, and his voice upon this earth was the High

Septon of Oldtown. And the doctrines of the Faith, handed down through centuries from Andalos itself, condemned the Valyrian marriage customs as practiced by the Targaryens. Incest was denounced as a vile sin, whether between father and daughter, mother and son, or brother and sister, and the fruits of such unions were considered abominations in the sight of gods and men. With hindsight, it can be seen that conflict between the Faith and House Targaryen was inevitable. Indeed, many amongst the Most Devout had expected the High Septon to speak out against Aegon and his sisters during the Conquest, and were most displeased when the Father of the Faithful instead counseled Lord Hightower against opposing the Dragon, and even blessed and anointed him at his second coronation.

Familiarity is the father of acceptance, it is said. The High Septon who had crowned Aegon the Conqueror remained the Shepherd of the Faithful until his death in 11 AC, by which time the realm had grown accustomed to the notion of a king with two queens, who were both wives and sisters. King Aegon always took care to honor the Faith, confirming its traditional rights and privileges, exempting its wealth and property from taxation, and affirming that septons, septas, and other servants of the Seven accused of wrongdoing could only be tried by the Faith's own courts.

The accord between the Faith and the Iron Throne continued all through the reign of Aegon I. From 11 AC to 37 AC, six High Septons wore the crystal crown; His Grace remained on good terms with each of them, calling at the Starry Sept each time he came to Oldtown. Yet the question of incestuous marriage remained, simmering below the courtesies like poison. Whilst the High Septons of King Aegon's reign never spoke out against the king's marriage to his sisters, neither did they declare it to be lawful. The humbler members of the Faith—village septons, holy sisters, begging brothers, Poor Fellows—still believed it sinful for brother to lie with sister, or for a man to take two wives.

Aegon the Conqueror had fathered no daughters, however, so these matters did not come to a head at once. The sons of the Dragon had no sisters to marry, so each of them was forced to seek elsewhere for a bride.

Prince Aenys was the first to marry. In 22 AC, he wed the Lady Alyssa, the maiden daughter of the Lord of the Tides, Aethan Velaryon, King Aegon's lord admiral and master of ships. She was fifteen, the same age as the prince, and shared his silvery hair and purple eyes as well, for the Velaryons were an ancient family descended from Valyrian stock. King Aegon's own mother had been a Velaryon, so the marriage was reckoned one of cousin to cousin.

It soon proved both happy and fruitful. The following year, Alyssa gave birth to a daughter. Prince Aenys named her Rhaena, in honor of his mother. Like her father, the girl was small at birth, but unlike him she proved to be a happy, healthy child, with lively lilac eyes and hair that shone like beaten silver. It was written that King Aegon himself wept the first time his granddaughter was placed in his arms, and thereafter doted upon the child . . . mayhaps in some part because she reminded him of his lost queen, Rhaenys, in whose memory she had been named.

As the glad tidings of Rhaena's birth spread across the land, the realm rejoiced . . . save, perhaps, for Queen Visenya. Prince Aenys was the unquestioned heir to the Iron Throne, all agreed, but now an issue arose as to whether Prince Maegor remained second in the line of succession, or should be considered to have fallen to third behind the newborn princess. Queen Visenya proposed to settle the matter by betrothing the infant Rhaena to Maegor, who had just turned eleven. Aenys and Alyssa spoke against the match, however . . . and when word reached the Starry Sept, the High Septon sent a raven, warning the king that such a marriage would not be looked upon with favor by the Faith. His High Holiness proposed a different bride for Maegor: his own niece, Ceryse Hightower, maiden daughter to the Lord of Oldtown, Manfred Hightower (not to be confused with his grandsire of the same name). King Aegon, mindful of the advantages of closer ties with Oldtown and its ruling house, saw wisdom in the choice and agreed to the match.

Thus it came to pass that in 25 AC, Maegor Targaryen, Prince of Dragonstone, wed Lady Ceryse Hightower in the Starry Sept of Oldtown, with the High Septon himself performing the nuptials. Maegor was thirteen, the bride ten years his senior . . . but the lords who bore witness to the bedding all agreed that the prince made a lusty husband, and Maegor himself boasted that he had consummated the marriage a dozen times that night. "I made a son for House Targaryen last night," he proclaimed as he broke fast.

The son came the next year . . . but the boy, named Aegon after his grandsire, was born to Lady Alyssa and fathered by Prince Aenys. Once again, celebrations swept the Seven Kingdoms. The little prince was robust and fierce and had "a warrior's look about him," declared his grandsire, Aegon the Dragon himself. While many still debated whether Prince Maegor or his niece, Rhaena, should have precedence in the order of succession, it seemed beyond question that Aegon would follow his father, Aenys, just as Aenys would follow Aegon.

In the years that followed, other children came one after the other to House Targaryen . . . to the delight of King Aegon, if not necessarily that of Queen Visenya. In 29 AC, Prince Aegon acquired a baby brother when Alyssa gave Prince Aenys a second son, Viserys. In 34 AC, she gave birth to Jaehaerys, her fourth child and third son. In 36 AC came another daughter, Alysanne.

Princess Rhaena was thirteen when her little sister was born, but Grand Maester Gawen observed that "the girl delighted so in the babe that one might think she was the mother herself." The eldest daughter of Aenys and Alyssa was a shy, dreamy child, who seemed to be more comfortable with animals than other children. As a little girl, she often hid behind her mother's skirt or clung to her father's leg in the presence of strangers . . . but she loved to feed the castle cats, and always had a puppy or two in the bed. Though her mother provided her with a succession of suitable companions, the daughters of lords great and small, Rhaena never seemed to warm to any of them, preferring the company of a book.

At the age of nine, however, Rhaena was presented with a hatchling from the pits of Dragonstone, and she and the young dragon she named Dreamfyre bonded instantly. With her dragon beside her, the princess slowly began to grow out of her shyness; at the age of twelve she took to the skies for the first time, and thereafter, though she remained a quiet girl, no one dared to call her timid. Not long after, Rhaena made her first true friend in the person of her cousin Larissa Velaryon. For a time the two girls were inseparable . . . until Larissa was suddenly recalled to Driftmark to be wed to the second son of the Evenstar of Tarth. The young are nothing if not resilient, however, and the princess soon found a new companion in the Hand's daughter, Samantha Stokeworth.

It was Princess Rhaena, legend says, who put a dragon's egg in Princess Alysanne's cradle, just as she had for Prince Jaehaerys two years earlier. If those tales be true, from those eggs came the dragons Silverwing and Vermithor, whose names would be writ so large in the annals of the years to come.

Princess Rhaena's love for her siblings, and the realm's joy at each new Targaryen princeling, was not shared by Prince Maegor or his mother, Queen Visenya, for each new son born to Aenys pushed Maegor farther down in the line of succession, and there were still those who claimed he stood behind Aenys's daughters too. And all the while Maegor himself remained childless, for Lady Ceryse did not quicken in the years that followed their marriage.

On tourney ground and battlefield, however, Prince Maegor's accomplishments far exceeded those of his brother. In the great tourney at Riverrun in 28 AC, Maegor unhorsed three knights of the Kingsguard in successive tilts before falling to the eventual champion. In the melee, no man could stand before him. Afterward he was knighted on the field by his father, who dubbed him with no less a blade than Blackfyre. At ten-and-six, Maegor became the youngest knight in the Seven Kingdoms.

Other feats followed. In 29 AC and again in 30 AC, Maegor accompanied Osmund Strong and Aethan Velaryon to the Stepstones to root out the Lysene pirate king Sargoso Saan, and fought in several bloody affrays, showing himself to be both fearless and deadly. In 31 AC, he hunted down and slew a notorious robber knight in the riverlands, the so-called Giant of the Trident.

Maegor was not yet a dragonrider, however. Though a dozen hatchlings had been born amidst the fires of Dragonstone in the later years of Aegon's reign, and were offered to the prince, he refused them all. When his young niece Rhaena, in only her twelfth year, took to the sky astride Dreamfyre, Maegor's failure became the talk of King's Landing. Lady Alyssa teased him about it one day in court, wondering aloud whether "my good-brother is afraid of dragons." Prince Maegor darkened in rage at the jape, then replied coolly that there was only one dragon worthy of him.

The last seven years of the reign of Aegon the Conqueror were peaceful ones. After the frustrations of his Dornish War, the king accepted the continued independence of Dorne, and flew to Sunspear on Balerion on the tenth anniversary of the peace accords to celebrate a "feast of friendship" with Deria Martell, the reigning Princess of Dorne. Prince Aenys accompanied him on Quicksilver; Maegor remained on Dragonstone. Aegon had made the seven kingdoms one with fire and blood, but after celebrating his sixtieth nameday in 33 AC, he turned instead to brick and mortar. Half of every year was still given over to a royal progress, but now it was Prince Aenys and his wife, Lady Alyssa, who journeyed from castle to castle, whilst the aging king remained at home, dividing his days between Dragonstone and King's Landing.

The fishing village where Aegon had first landed had grown into a sprawling, stinking city of a hundred thousand souls by that time; only Oldtown and Lannisport were larger. Yet in many ways King's Landing was still little more than an army camp that had swollen to grotesque size: dirty, reeking, unplanned, impermanent. And the Aegonfort, which had spread halfway down Aegon's High Hill by that time, was as ugly a castle as any in the Seven Kingdoms, a great confusion of wood and earth and brick that had long outgrown the old log palisades that were its only walls.

It was certainly no fit abode for a great king. In 35 AC, Aegon moved with all his court back to Dragonstone and gave orders that the Aegonfort be torn down, so that a new castle might be raised in its place. This time, he decreed, he would build in stone. To oversee the design and construction of the new castle, he named the King's Hand, Lord Alyn Stokeworth (Ser Osmund Strong had died the previous year), and Queen Visenya. (A jape went about the court that King Aegon had given Visenya charge of building the Red Keep so he would not have to endure her presence on Dragonstone.)

Aegon the Conqueror died of a stroke on Dragonstone in the 37th year After the Conquest. His grandsons Aegon and Viserys were with him at his death, in the Chamber of the Painted Table; the king was showing them the details of his conquests. Prince Maegor, in residence at Dragonstone at the time, spoke the eulogy as his father's body was laid upon a funeral pyre in the castle yard. The king was clad in battle armor, his mailed hands folded over the hilt of Blackfyre. Since the days of Old Valyria, it had ever been the custom of House Targaryen to burn their dead, rather than consigning their remains to the ground. Vhagar supplied the flames to light the fire. Blackfyre was burned with the king, but retrieved by Maegor afterward, its blade darker but elsewise unharmed. No common fire can damage Valyrian steel.

The Dragon was survived by his sister Visenya; his sons, Aenys and Maegor; and five grandchildren. Prince Aenys was thirty years of age at his father's death, Prince Maegor five-and-twenty.

Aenys had been at Highgarden on his progress when his father died, but Quicksilver returned him to Dragonstone for the funeral. Afterward he donned his father's iron-and-ruby crown, and Grand Maester Gawen proclaimed him Aenys of House Targaryen, the First of His Name, King of the Andals and the Rhoynar and the First Men, Lord of the Seven Kingdoms, and Protector of the Realm. The lords who had come to Dragonstone to bid their king farewell knelt and bowed their heads. When Prince Maegor's turn came, Aenys drew him back to his feet, kissed his cheek, and said, "Brother, you need never kneel to me again. We shall rule this realm together, you and I." Then the king presented his father's sword, Blackfyre, to his brother, saying, "You are more fit to bear this blade than me. Wield it in my service, and I shall be content."

(This bequest would prove to be most unwise, as later events would demonstrate. Since Queen Visenya had previously gifted her son with Dark Sister, Prince Maegor now possessed both of the ancestral Valyrian steel swords of House Targaryen. From this date forward, however, he would wield only Blackfyre, whilst Dark Sister hung on the walls of his chambers on Dragonstone.)

After the funeral rites had been completed, the new king and his entourage sailed to King's Landing, where the Iron Throne still stood amidst mounds of rubble and mud. The old Aegonfort had been torn down, and pits and tunnels pockmarked the hill where the cellars and foundations of the Red Keep were being dug, but the new castle had not yet begun to rise.

Nonetheless, thousands came to cheer King Aenys as he claimed his father's seat for his own.

Thereafter His Grace set out for Oldtown to receive the blessing of the High Septon. Though he could have made the journey in a few short days on Quicksilver, Aenys preferred to travel by land, accompanied by three hundred mounted knights and their retinues. Queen Alyssa rode beside him, together with their three eldest children. Princess Rhaena was fourteen years of age, a beautiful young girl who stole the heart of every knight who saw her; Prince Aegon was eleven, Prince Viserys eight. (Their younger siblings, Jaehaerys and Alysanne, were deemed too young for such an arduous journey and remained on Dragonstone.) After setting out from King's Landing, the king's party made its way south to Storm's End, then west across the Dornish Marches to Oldtown, guesting at each castle on the way. His return would be by way of Highgarden, Lannisport, and Riverrun, it was decreed.

All along the route the smallfolk appeared by the hundreds and thousands to hail their new king and queen and cheer the young princes and princess. But whilst Aegon and Viserys relished in the cheers of the crowds and the feasts and frolics put on at every castle to entertain the new monarch and his family, Princess Rhaena reverted to her former shyness. At Storm's End, Orys Baratheon's maester went so far as to write, "The princess did not seem to want to be there, nor did she approve of anything she saw or heard. She scarce seemed to eat, would not hunt or hawk, and when pressed to sing—for she is said to have a lovely voice—she refused rudely and returned to her chambers." The princess had been most loath to be parted from her dragon, Dreamfyre, and her latest favorite, Melony Piper, a red-haired maiden from the riverlands. It was only when her mother, Queen Alyssa, sent for Lady Melony to join them on the progress that Rhaena finally put aside her sullenness to join the celebrations.

At the Starry Sept, the High Septon anointed Aenys Targaryen as his predecessor had once anointed his father, and presented him with a crown of yellow gold with the faces of the Seven inlaid in jade and pearl. Yet even as Aenys was receiving the blessing of the Father of the Faithful, others were casting doubt on his fitness to sit the Iron Throne. Westeros required a warrior, they whispered to one another, and Maegor was plainly the stronger of the Dragon's two sons. Foremost amongst the whisperers was the Dowager Queen Visenya Targaryen. "The truth is plain enough," she is reported to have said. "Even Aenys sees it. Why else would he have given Blackfyre to my son? He knows that only Maegor has the strength to rule."

The new king's mettle would be tested sooner than anyone could have imagined. The Wars of Conquest had left scars throughout the realm. Sons now come of age dreamed of avenging long-dead fathers. Knights remembered the days when a man with a sword and a horse and a suit of armor could slash his way to riches and glory. Lords recalled a time when they did not need a king's leave to tax their smallfolk or kill their enemies. "The chains the Dragon forged can yet be broken," the discontented told one another. "We can win our freedoms back, but now is the time to strike, for this new king is weak."

The first stirrings of revolt were in the riverlands, amidst the colossal ruins of Harrenhal. Aegon had granted the castle to Ser Quenton Qoherys, his old master-at-arms. When Lord Qoherys died in a fall from his horse in 9 AC, his title passed to his grandson Gargon, a fat and foolish man with an unseemly appetite for young girls who became known as Gargon the Guest. Lord Gargon soon became infamous for turning up at every wedding celebrated within his domains so that he might enjoy the lord's right of the first night. A more unwelcome wedding guest can scarce be imagined. He also made free with the wives and daughters of his own servants.

King Aenys was still on his progress, guesting with Lord Tully of Riverrun on his way back to King's Landing, when the father of a maid whom Lord Qoherys had "honored" opened a postern gate at Harrenhal to an outlaw who styled himself Harren the Red and claimed to be a grandson of Harren the Black. The brigands pulled his lordship from his bed and dragged him to the castle godswood, where Harren sliced off his genitals and fed them to a dog. A few leal men-at-arms were killed; the rest agreed to join Harren, who declared himself Lord of Harrenhal and King of the Rivers (not being ironborn, he did not claim the islands).

When word reached Riverrun, Lord Tully urged the king to mount Quicksilver and descend on Harrenhal as his father had. But His Grace,

perhaps mindful of his mother's death in Dorne, instead commanded Tully to summon his banners and lingered at Riverrun as they gathered. Only when a thousand men were assembled did Aenys march . . . but when his men reached Harrenhal, they found it empty but for corpses. Harren the Red had put Lord Gargon's servants to the sword and taken his band into the woods.

By the time Aenys returned to King's Landing the news had grown even worse. In the Vale, Lord Ronnel Arryn's younger brother Jonos had deposed and imprisoned his loyal sibling, and declared himself King of Mountain and Vale. In the Iron Islands, another priest king had walked out of the sea, announcing himself to be Lodos the Twice-Drowned, the son of the Drowned God, returned at last from visiting his father. And high in the Red Mountains of Dorne, a pretender called the Vulture King appeared and called on all true Dornishmen to avenge the evils visited on Dorne by the Targaryens. Though Princess Deria denounced him, swearing that she and all leal Dornishmen wanted only peace, thousands flocked to his banners, swarming down from the hills and up out of the sands, through goat tracks in the mountains into the Reach.

"This Vulture King is half-mad, and his followers are a rabble, undisciplined and unwashed," Lord Harmon Dondarrion wrote to the king. "We can smell them coming fifty leagues away." Not long after, that selfsame rabble stormed and seized his castle of Blackhaven. The Vulture King personally sliced off Dondarrion's nose before putting Blackhaven to the torch and marching away.

King Aenys knew these rebels had to be put down, but seemed unable to decide where to begin. Grand Maester Gawen wrote that the king could not comprehend why this was happening. The smallfolk loved him, did they not? Jonos Arryn, this new Lodos, the Vulture King . . . had he wronged them? If they had grievances, why not bring them to him? "I would have heard them out." His Grace spoke of sending messengers to the rebels, to learn the reasons for their actions. Fearing that King's Landing might not be safe with Harren the Red alive and near, he sent Queen Alyssa and their younger children to Dragonstone. He commanded his Hand, Lord Alyn Stokeworth, to take a fleet and army to the Vale to put down Jonos Arryn and restore his brother Ronnel to the lordship. But when the ships were about to sail, he countermanded the order, fearing that Stokeworth's departure would leave King's Landing undefended. Instead he sent the Hand with but a few hundred men to hunt down Harren the Red, and decided he would summon a great council to discuss how best to put down the other rebels.

Whilst the king prevaricated, his lords took to the field. Some acted on their own authority, others in concert with the Dowager Queen. In the Vale, Lord Allard Royce of Runestone assembled twoscore loyal bannermen and marched against the Eyrie, easily defeating the supporters of the self-styled King of Mountain and Vale. But when they demanded the release of their rightful lord, Jonos Arryn sent his brother to them through the Moon Door. Such was the sad end of Ronnel Arryn, who had flown thrice about the Giant's Lance on dragonback.

The Eyrie was impregnable to any conventional assault, so "King" Jonos and his die-hard followers spat down defiance at the loyalists, and settled in for a siege . . . until Prince Maegor appeared in the sky above, astride Balerion. The Conqueror's younger son had claimed a dragon at last: none other than the Black Dread, the greatest of them all.

Rather than face Balerion's fires, the Eyrie's garrison seized the pretender and delivered him to Lord Royce, opening the Moon Door once again and serving Jonos the kinslayer as he had served his brother. Surrender saved the pretender's followers from burning, but not from death. After taking possession of the Eyrie, Prince Maegor executed them to a man. Even the highest born amongst them were denied the honor of dying by sword; traitors deserved only a rope, Maegor decreed, so the captured knights were hanged naked from the walls of the Eyrie, kicking as they strangled slowly. Hubert Arryn, a cousin to the dead brothers, was installed as Lord of the Vale. As he had already sired six sons by his lady wife, a Royce of Runestone, the Arryn succession was seen to be secure.

In the Iron Islands, Goren Greyjoy, Lord Reaper of Pyke, brought "King" Lodos (Second of That Name) to a similar swift end, marshalling a hundred longships to descend on Old Wyk and Great Wyk, where the pretender's followers were most numerous, and putting thousands of them to the sword. Afterward he had the head of the priest king pickled in brine and sent to King's Landing. King Aenys was so pleased by the gift that he offered Greyjoy any boon he might desire. This proved unwise. Lord Goren, wishing to prove himself a true son of the Drowned God, asked the king for the right to expel all the septons and septas who had come to the Iron Islands after the Conquest to convert the ironborn to the worship of the Seven. King Aenys had no choice but to agree.

The largest and most threatening rebellion remained that of the Vulture King along the Dornish Marches. Though Princess Deria continued to issue denunciations from Sunspear, there were many who suspected that she was playing a double game, for she did not take the field against the rebels and was rumored to be sending them men, money, and supplies. Whether that was true or not, hundreds of Dornish knights and several thousand seasoned spearmen had joined the Vulture King's rabble, and the rabble itself had swelled enormously, to more than thirty thousand men. So large had his host become that the Vulture King made an ill-considered decision and divided his strength. Whilst he marched west against Nightsong and Horn Hill with half the Dornish power, the other half went east to besiege Stonehelm, seat of House Swann, under the command of Lord Walter Wyl, the son of the Widow-lover.

Both hosts met with disaster. Orys Baratheon, known now as Orys One-Hand, rode forth from Storm's End one last time, to smash the Dornish beneath the walls of Stonehelm. When Walter Wyl was delivered into his hands, wounded but alive, Lord Orys said, "Your father took my hand. I claim yours as repayment." So saying, he hacked off Lord Walter's sword hand. Then he took his other hand and both his feet as well, calling them his "usury." Strange to say, Lord Baratheon died on the march back to Storm's End, of the wounds he himself had taken during the battle, but his son Davos always said he died content, smiling at the rotting hands and feet that dangled in his tent like a string of onions.

The Vulture King himself fared little better. Unable to capture Nightsong, he abandoned the siege and marched west, only to have Lady Caron sally forth behind him, to join up with a strong force of marchers led by Harmon Dondarrion, the mutilated Lord of Blackhaven. Meanwhile Lord Samwell Tarly of Horn Hill suddenly appeared athwart the Dornish line of march with several thousand knights and archers. Savage Sam, that lord was called, and so he proved in the bloody battle that ensued, cutting down dozens of Dornishmen with his great Valyrian steel blade Heartsbane. The Vulture King had twice as many men as his three foes combined, but most were untrained and undisciplined, and when faced with armored knights at front and rear, their ranks shattered. Throwing down their spears and shields, the Dornish broke and ran, making for the distant mountains, but the marcher lords rode after them and cut them down, in what became known after as "the Vulture Hunt."

As for the rebel king himself, the man who called himself the Vulture King was taken alive and tied naked between two posts by Savage Sam Tarly. The singers like to say that he was torn to pieces by the very vultures from whom he took his style, but in truth he perished of thirst and exposure, and the birds did not descend on him until well after he was dead. (In later years, several other men would take the title Vulture King, but whether they were of the same blood as the first, no man can say.) His death is generally accounted as the end of the Second Dornish War, though that is somewhat of a misnomer, since few Dornish lords ever took the field, and Princess Deria continued to vilify the Vulture King until his end and took no part in his campaigns.

The first of the rebels proved to be the last as well, but Harren the Red was at last brought to bay in a village west of the Gods Eye. The outlaw king did not die meekly. In his last fight, he slew the King's Hand, Lord Alyn Stokeworth, before being cut down by Stokeworth's squire, Bernarr Brune. A grateful King Aenys conferred knighthood on Brune, and rewarded Davos Baratheon, Samwell Tarly, No-Nose Dondarrion, Ellyn Caron, Allard Royce, and Goren Greyjoy with gold, offices, and honors. The greatest plaudits he bestowed on his own brother. On his return to King's Landing, Prince Maegor was hailed as a hero. King Aenys embraced him before a cheering throng, and named him Hand of the King. And when two young dragons hatched amidst the firepits of Dragonstone at the end of that year, it was taken for a sign.

But the amity between the Dragon's sons did not long endure.

It may be that conflict was inevitable, for the two brothers had very different natures. King Aenys loved his wife, his children, and his people, and wished only to be loved in turn. Sword and lance had lost whatever appeal they ever had for him. Instead His Grace dabbled in alchemy, astronomy, and astrology, delighted in music and dance, wore the finest silks, samites, and velvets, and enjoyed the company of maesters, septons, and wits. His brother, Maegor, taller, broader, and fearsomely strong, had no patience for any of that, but lived for war, tourneys, and battle. He was rightly regarded as one of the finest knights in Westeros, though his savagery in the field and his harshness toward defeated foes was oft remarked upon as well. King Aenys sought always to please; when faced with difficulties, he would answer with soft words, whereas Maegor's reply was ever steel and fire. Grand Maester Gawen wrote that Aenys trusted everyone, Maegor no one. The king was easily influenced, Gawen observed, swaying this way and that like a reed in the wind, like as not to heed whichever counselor last had his ear. Prince Maegor, on the other hand, was rigid as an iron rod, unyielding, unbending.

Despite such differences, the sons of the Dragon continued to rule together amicably for the best part of two years. But in 39 AC, Queen Alyssa gave King Aenys yet another heir, a girl she named Vaella, who sadly died in the cradle not long after. Perhaps it was this continued proof of the queen's fertility that drove Prince Maegor to do what he did. Whatever the reason, the prince shocked the realm and the king both when he suddenly announced that Lady Ceryse was barren, and he had therefore taken a second wife in Alys Harroway, daughter of the new Lord of Harrenhal.

The wedding was performed on Dragonstone, under the aegis of the Dowager Queen Visenya. As the castle septon refused to officiate, Maegor and his new bride were joined in a Valyrian rite, "wed by blood and fire." The marriage took place without the leave, knowledge, or presence of King Aenys. When it became known, the two half-brothers quarreled bitterly. Nor was His Grace alone in his wroth. Manfred Hightower, father of Lady Ceryse, made protest to the king, demanding that Lady Alys be put aside. And in the Starry Sept at Oldtown, the High Septon went even further, denouncing Maegor's marriage as sin and fornication, and calling the prince's new bride "this whore of Harroway." No true son or daughter of the Seven would ever bow to such, he thundered.

Prince Maegor remained defiant. His father had taken both of his sisters to wife, he pointed out; the strictures of the Faith might rule lesser men, but not the blood of the dragon. No words of King Aenys could heal the wound his brother's words thus opened, and many pious lords throughout the Seven Kingdoms condemned the marriage, and began to speak openly of "Maegor's Whore."

Vexed and angry, King Aenys gave his brother a choice: put Alys Harroway aside and return to Lady Ceryse, or suffer five years of exile. Prince Maegor chose exile. In 40 AC he departed for Pentos, taking Lady Alys, Balerion his dragon, and the sword Blackfyre with him. (It is said that Aenys requested that his brother return Blackfyre, to which Prince Maegor replied, "Your Grace is welcome to try and take her from me.") Lady Ceryse was left abandoned in King's Landing.

To replace his brother as Hand, King Aenys turned to Septon Murmison, a pious cleric said to be able to heal the sick by the laying on of hands. (The king had him lay hands on Lady Ceryse's belly every night, in the hopes that his brother might repent his folly if his lawful wife could be made fertile, but the lady soon grew weary of the nightly ritual and departed King's Landing for Oldtown, where she rejoined her father in the Hightower.) No doubt His Grace the king hoped the choice would appease the Faith. If so, he was wrong. Septon Murmison could no more heal the realm than he could make Ceryse Hightower fecund. The High Septon continued to thunder, and all through the realm the lords in their halls spoke of the king's weakness. "How can he rule the Seven Kingdoms when he cannot even rule his brother?" they said.

The king remained oblivious to the discontent in the realm. Peace had returned, his troublesome brother was across the narrow sea, and a great new castle had begun to rise atop Aegon's High Hill: built all in pale red stone, the king's new seat would be larger and more lavish than Dragonstone, with massive walls and barbicans and towers capable of withstanding any enemy. The Red Keep, the people of King's Landing named it. Its building had become the king's obsession. "My descendants shall rule from here for a thousand years," His Grace declared. Perhaps thinking of those descendants, in 41 AC Aenys Targaryen made a disastrous blunder and announced his intention to give the hand of his daughter Rhaena in marriage to her brother Aegon, heir to the Iron Throne.

The princess was eighteen, the prince fifteen. They had been close since childhood, playmates when young. Though Aegon had never claimed a dragon of his own, he had ascended into the skies more than once with his sister, on Dreamfyre. Lean and handsome and growing taller every year, Aegon was said by many to be the very image of his grandsire at the same age. Three years of service as a squire had sharpened his prowess with sword and axe, and he was widely regarded as the best young lance in all the realm. Of late, many a young maiden had cast her eye upon the prince, and Aegon was not indifferent to their charms. "If the prince is not wed," Grand Maester Gawen wrote the Citadel, "His Grace may soon have a bastard grandchild to contend with."

Princess Rhaena had many a suitor as well, but unlike her brother she gave encouragement to none of them. She preferred to spend her days with her siblings, her dogs and cats, and her newest favorite, Alayne Royce, daughter to the Lord of Runestone . . . a plump and homely girl, but so cherished that Rhaena sometimes took her flying on the back of Dreamfyre, just as she did her brother Aegon. More often, though, Rhaena took to the skies by herself. After her sixteenth nameday, the princess declared herself a woman grown, "free to fly where I will."

And fly she did. Dreamfyre was seen as far away as Harrenhal, Tarth, Runestone, Gulltown. It was whispered (though never proved) that on one of these flights Rhaena surrendered the flower of her maidenhead to a lowborn lover. A hedge knight, one story had it; others named him a singer, a blacksmith's son, a village septon. In light of these tales, some have suggested that Aenys might have felt a need to see his daughter wed as soon as possible. Regardless of the truth of that surmise, at eighteen Rhaena was certainly of an age to marry, three years older than her mother and father had been when they were wed.

Given the traditions and practices of House Targaryen, a match between his two eldest children must have seemed the obvious course to King Aenys. The affection between Rhaena and Aegon was well-known, and neither raised any objection to the marriage; indeed, there is much to suggest that both had been anticipating just such a partnership since they had first played together in the nurseries of Dragonstone and the Aegonfort.

The storm that greeted the king's announcement took them all by surprise, though the warning signs had been plain enough for those with the wit to read them. The Faith had condoned, or at the very least ignored, the marriage of the Conqueror and his sisters, but it was not willing to do the same for their grandchildren. From the Starry Sept came a blistering condemnation, denouncing the marriage of brother to sister as an obscenity. Any children born of such a union would be "abominations in the sight of gods and men," the Father of the Faithful proclaimed, in a declaration that was read by ten thousand septons throughout the Seven Kingdoms.

Aenys Targaryen was infamous for his indecision, yet here, faced with the fury of the Faith, he stiffened and grew stubborn. The Dowager Queen Visenya advised him that he had but two choices; he must abandon the marriage and find new matches for his son and daughter or mount his dragon, Quicksilver, to fly to Oldtown to burn the Starry Sept down around the High Septon's head. King Aenys did neither. Instead he simply persisted.

On the day of the wedding, the streets outside the Sept of Remembrance—built atop the Hill of Rhaenys, and named in honor of the Dragon's fallen queen—were lined with Warrior's Sons in gleaming silver armor, making note of each of the wedding guests as they passed by, afoot, ahorse, or in litters. The wiser lords, perhaps expecting that, had stayed away.

Those who did come to bear witness saw more than a wedding. At the feast afterward, King Aenys compounded his misjudgment by granting the title Prince of Dragonstone to his presumptive heir, Prince Aegon. A hush fell over the hall at those words, for all present knew that title had hitherto belonged to Prince Maegor. At the high table, Queen Visenya rose and stalked from the hall without the king's leave. That night she mounted Vhagar and returned to Dragonstone, and it is written that when her dragon passed before the moon, that orb turned as red as blood.

Aenys Targaryen did not seem to comprehend the extent to which he had roused the realm against him. Eager to win back the favor of the smallfolk, he decreed that the prince and princess would make a royal progress through the realm, no doubt thinking of the cheers that had greeted him everywhere he went on his own progress. Wiser perhaps than her father, Princess Rhaena asked his leave to bring her dragon, Dreamfyre, with them, but Aenys forbade it. As Prince Aegon had not yet ridden a dragon, the king feared that the lords and commons might think his son unmanly if they saw his wife on dragonback and him upon a palfrey.

The king had grossly misjudged the temper of the kingdom, the piety of his people, and the power of the High Septon's words. From the first day they set out, Aegon and Rhaena and their escort were jeered by crowds of the Faithful wherever they went. At Maidenpool, not a single septon could be found to pronounce a blessing at the feast Lord Mooton threw in their honor. When they reached Harrenhal, Lord Lucas Harroway refused to admit them to his castle unless they agreed to acknowledge his daughter Alys as their uncle's true and lawful wife. Their refusal won them no love from the pious, only a cold wet night in tents beneath the towering walls of Black Harren's mighty castle. At one village in the riverlands, several Poor Fellows went so far as to pelt the royal couple with clods of dirt. Prince Aegon drew his sword to chastise them and had to be restrained by his own knights, for the prince's party was greatly outnumbered. Yet that did not stop Princess Rhaena from riding up to them to say, "You are fearless when facing a girl on a horse, I see. The next time I come, I will be on a dragon. Throw dirt on me then, I pray you."

Elsewhere in the realm, matters went from bad to worse. Septon Murmison, the King's Hand, was expelled from the Faith in punishment for performing the forbidden nuptials, whereupon Aenys himself took quill in hand to write to the High Septon, asking that His High Holiness restore "my good Murmison," and explaining the long history of brother-sister marriages in old Valyria. The High Septon's reply was so venomous that His Grace went pale when he read it. Far from relenting, the Shepherd of the Faithful addressed Aenys as "King Abomination," declaring him a pretender and a tyrant, with no right to rule the Seven Kingdoms.

The Faithful were listening. Less than a fortnight later, as Septon Murmison was crossing the city in his litter, a group of Poor Fellows came swarming from an alley and hacked him to pieces with their axes. The Warrior's Sons began to fortify the Hill of Rhaenys, turning the Sept of Remembrance into their citadel. With the Red Keep still years away from completion, the king decided that his manse atop Visenya's Hill was too vulnerable and made plans to remove himself to Dragonstone with Queen Alyssa and their younger children. That proved a wise precaution. Three days before they were to sail, two Poor Fellows scaled the manse's walls and broke into the king's bedchamber. Only the timely intervention of the Kingsguard saved Aenys from an ignoble death.

His Grace was trading Visenya's Hill for Visenya herself. On Dragonstone the Queen Dowager famously greeted him with, "You are a fool and a weakling, nephew. Do you think any man would ever have dared speak so to your father? You have a dragon. Use him. Fly to Oldtown and make this Starry Sept another Harrenhal. Or give me leave, and let me roast this pious fool for you." Aenys would not hear of it. Instead he sent the Queen Dowager to her chambers in Sea Dragon Tower and ordered her to remain there.

By the end of 41 AC, much of the realm was deep in the throes of a full-fledged rebellion against House Targaryen. The four false kings who had arisen on the death of Aegon the Conqueror now seemed like so many posturing fools against the threat posed by this new rising, for these rebels believed themselves soldiers of the Seven, fighting a holy war against godless tyranny.

Dozens of pious lords throughout the Seven Kingdoms took up the cry, pulling down the king's banners and declaring for the Starry Sept. The Warrior's Sons seized the gates of King's Landing, giving them control over who might enter and leave the city, and drove the workmen from the unfinished Red Keep. Thousands of Poor Fellows took to the roads, forcing travelers to declare whether they stood with "the gods or the abomination," and remonstrating outside castle gates until their lords came forth to denounce the Targaryen king. In the westerlands, Prince Aegon and Princess Rhaena were forced to abandon their progress and take shelter in Crakehall castle. An envoy from the Iron Bank of Braavos, sent to Oldtown to treat with Martyn Hightower, the new Lord of the Hightower and voice of Oldtown (his father, Lord Manfred, having died a few moons earlier), wrote home to say that the High Septon was "the true king of Westeros, in all but name."

The coming of the new year found King Aenys still on Dragonstone, sick with fear and indecision. His Grace was but thirty-five years of age, but it was said that he looked like a man of sixty, and Grand Maester Gawen reported that he oft took to his bed with loose bowels and stomach cramps. When none of the Grand Maester's cures proved efficacious, the Dowager Queen took charge of the king's care, and Aenys seemed to improve for a time . . . only to suffer a sudden collapse when word reached him that thousands of Poor Fellows had surrounded Crakehall, where his son and daughter were reluctant "guests." Three days later, the king was dead.

Like his father, Aenys Targaryen, the First of His Name, was given over to the flames in the yard at Dragonstone. His funeral was attended by his sons Viserys and Jaehaerys, twelve and seven years of age respectively, and his daughter Alysanne, five. His widow, Queen Alyssa, sang a dirge for him, and his own beloved Quicksilver set his pyre alight, though it was recorded that the dragons Vermithor and Silverwing added their own fire to hers.

Queen Visenya was not present. Within an hour of the king's death, she had mounted Vhagar and flown east across the narrow sea. When she returned, Prince Maegor was with her, on Balerion.

Maegor descended on Dragonstone only long enough to claim the crown; not the ornate golden crown Aenys had favored, with its images of the Seven, but the iron crown of their father set with its blood-red rubies. His mother placed it on his head, and the lords and knights gathered there knelt as he proclaimed himself Maegor of House Targaryen, First of His Name, King of the Andals, the Rhoynar, and the First Men, Lord of the Seven Kingdoms, and Protector of the Realm.

Only Grand Maester Gawen dared object. By all the laws of inheritance, laws that the Conqueror himself had affirmed after the Conquest, the Iron Throne should pass to King Aenys's son Aegon, the aged maester said. "The Iron Throne will go to the man who has the strength to seize it," Maegor replied. Whereupon he decreed the immediate execution of the Grand Maester, taking off Gawen's old grey head himself with a single swing of Blackfyre.

Queen Alyssa and her children were not on hand to witness King Maegor's coronation. She had taken them from Dragonstone within hours of her husband's funeral, crossing to her lord father's castle on nearby Driftmark. When told, Maegor gave a shrug . . . then retired to the Chamber of the Painted Table with a maester, to dictate letters to lords great and small throughout the realm.

A hundred ravens flew within the day. The next day, Maegor flew as well. Mounting Balerion, he crossed Blackwater Bay to King's Landing, accompanied by the Dowager Queen Visenya upon Vhagar. The return of the dragons set off riots in the city, as hundreds tried to flee, only to find the gates closed and barred. The Warrior's Sons held the city walls, the pits and piles of what would be the Red Keep, and the Hill of Rhaenys, where they had made the Sept of Remembrance their own fortress. The Targaryens raised their standards atop Visenya's Hill and called for leal men to gather to them. Thousands did. Visenya Targaryen proclaimed that her son Maegor had come to be their king. "A true king, blood of Aegon the Conqueror, who was my brother, my husband, and my love. If any man questions my son's right to the Iron Throne, let him prove his claim with his body."

The Warrior's Sons were not slow to accept her challenge. Down from the Hill of Rhaenys they rode, seven hundred knights in silvered steel led by their grand captain, Ser Damon Morrigen, called Damon the Devout. "Let us not bandy words," Maegor told him. "Swords will decide this matter." Ser Damon agreed; the gods would grant victory to the man whose cause was just, he said. "Let each side have seven champions, as it was done in Andalos of old. Can you find six men to stand beside you?" For Aenys had taken the Kingsguard to Dragonstone, and Maegor stood alone.

The king turned to the crowd. "Who will come and stand beside his king?" he called. Many turned away in fear or pretended that they did not hear, for the prowess of the Warrior's Sons was known to all. But at last one man offered himself: no knight, but a simple man-at-arms who called himself Dick Bean. "I been a king's man since I was a boy," he said. "I mean to die a king's man."

Only then did the first knight step forward. "This bean shames us all!" he shouted. "Are there no true knights here? No leal men?" The speaker was Bernarr Brune, the squire who had slain Harren the Red and been knighted by King Aenys himself. His scorn drove others to offer their swords. The names of the four Maegor chose are writ large in the history of Westeros: Ser Bramm of Blackhull, a hedge knight; Ser Rayford Rosby; Ser Guy Lothston, called Guy the Glutton; and Ser Lucifer Massey, Lord of Stonedance.

The names of the seven Warrior's Sons have likewise come down to us. They were: Ser Damon Morrigen, called Damon the Devout, Grand Captain of the Warrior's Sons; Ser Lyle Bracken; Ser Harys Horpe, called Death's Head Harry; Ser Aegon Ambrose; Ser Dickon Flowers, the Bastard of Beesbury; Ser Willam the Wanderer; and Ser Garibald of the Seven Stars, the septon knight. It is written that Damon the Devout led a prayer, beseeching the Warrior to grant strength to their arms. Afterward the Queen Dowager gave the command to begin. And the issue was joined.

Dick Bean died first, cut down by Lyle Bracken mere instants after the combat began. Thereafter accounts differ markedly. One chronicler says that when the hugely fat Ser Guy the Glutton was cut open, the remains of forty half-digested pies spilled out. Another claims Ser Garibald of the Seven Stars sang a paean as he fought. Several tell us that Lord Massey hacked off the arm of Harry Horpe. In one account, Death's Head Harry tossed his battle-axe into his other hand and buried it between Lord Massey's eyes. Other chroniclers suggest Ser Harys simply died. Some say the fight went on for hours, others that most of the combatants were down and dying in mere moments. All agree that great deeds were done and mighty blows exchanged, until the end found Maegor Targaryen standing alone against Damon the Devout and Willam the Wanderer. Both of the Warrior's Sons were badly wounded, and His Grace had Blackfyre in his hand, but even so, it was a near thing. Even as he fell, Ser Willam dealt the king a terrible blow to the head that cracked his helm and left him insensate. Many thought Maegor dead until his mother removed his broken helm. "The king breathes," she said. "The king lives." The victory was his.

Seven of the mightiest of the Warrior's Sons were dead, including their commander, but more than seven hundred remained, armed and armored and gathered about the crown of the hill. Queen Visenya commanded her son be taken to the maesters. As the litter-bearers bore him down the hill, the Swords of the Faith dropped to their knees in submission. The Dowager Queen ordered them to return their fortified sept atop the Hill of Rhaenys.

For twenty-seven days Maegor Targaryen lingered at the point of death, whilst maesters treated him with potions and poultices and septons prayed above his bed. In the Sept of Remembrance, the Warrior's Sons prayed as well, and argued about their course. Some felt the order had no choice but to accept Maegor as king, since the gods had blessed him with victory; others insisted that they were bound by oath to obey the High Septon and fight on.

The Kingsguard arrived from Dragonstone in the nonce. At the behest of the Dowager Queen, they took command of the thousands of Targaryen loyalists in the city and surrounded the Hill of Rhaenys. On Driftmark, the widowed Queen Alyssa proclaimed her own son Aegon the true king, but few heeded her call. The young prince, just shy of manhood, remained at Crakehall half a realm away, trapped in a castle surrounded by Poor Fellows and pious peasants, most of whom considered him an abomination.

In the Citadel of Oldtown, the archmaesters met in conclave to debate the succession and choose a new Grand Maester. Thousands of Poor Fellows streamed toward King's Landing. Those from the west followed the hedge knight Ser Horys Hill, those from the south a gigantic axeman called Wat the Hewer. When the ragged bands encamped about Crakehall left to join their fellows on the march, Prince Aegon and Princess Rhaena were finally able to depart. Abandoning their royal progess, they made their way to Casterly Rock, where Lord Lyman Lannister offered them his protection. It was his wife, Lady Jocasta, who first discerned that Princess Rhaena was with child, Lord Lyman's maester tells us.

On the twenty-eighth day after the Trial of Seven, a ship arrived from Pentos upon the evening tide, carrying two women and six hundred sellswords. Alys of House Harroway, Maegor Targaryen's second wife, had returned to Westeros . . . but not alone. With her sailed another woman, a pale raven-haired beauty known only as Tyanna of the Tower. Some said the woman was Maegor's concubine. Others named her Lady Alys's paramour. The natural daughter of a Pentoshi magister, Tyanna was a tavern dancer who had risen to be a courtesan. She was rumored to be a poisoner and sorceress as well. Many queer tales were told about her . . . yet as soon as she arrived, Queen Visenya dismissed her son's maesters and septons and gave Maegor over to Tyanna's care.

The next morning, the king awoke, rising with the sun. When Maegor appeared on the walls of the Red Keep, standing between Alys Harroway and Tyanna of Pentos, the crowds cheered wildly, and the city erupted in celebration. But the revels died away when Maegor mounted Balerion and descended upon the Hill of Rhaenys, where seven hundred of the Warrior's Sons were at their morning prayers in the fortified sept. As dragonfire set the building aflame, archers and spearmen waited outside for those who came bursting through the doors. It was said the screams of the burning men could be heard throughout the city, and a pall of smoke lingered over King's Landing for days. Thus did the cream of the Warrior's Sons meet their fiery end. Though other chapters remained in Oldtown, Lannisport, Gulltown, and Stoney Sept, the order would never again approach its former strength.

King Maegor's war against the Faith Militant had just begun, however. It would continue for the remainder of his reign. The king's first act upon ascending the Iron Throne was to command the Poor Fellows swarming toward the city to lay down their weapons, under penalty of proscription and death. When his decree had no effect, His Grace commanded "all leal lords" to take the field and disperse the Faith's ragged hordes by force. In response, the High Septon in Oldtown called upon "true and pious children of the gods" to take up arms in defense of the Faith, and put an end to the reign of "dragons and monsters and abominations."

Battle was joined first in the Reach, at the town of Stonebridge. There nine thousand Poor Fellows under Wat the Hewer found themselves caught between six lordly hosts as they attempted to cross the Mander. With half his men north of the river and half on the south, Wat's army was cut to pieces. His untrained and undisciplined followers, clad in boiled leather, roughspun, and scraps of rusted steel, and armed largely with woodsmen's axes, sharpened sticks, and farm implements, proved utterly unable to stand against the charge of armored knights on heavy horses. So grievous was the slaughter that the Mander ran red for twenty leagues, and thereafter the town and castle where the battle had been

fought became known as Bitterbridge. Wat himself was taken alive, though not before slaying half a dozen knights, amongst them Lord Meadows of Grassy Vale, commander of the king's host. The giant was delivered to King's Landing in chains.

By then Ser Horys Hill had reached the Great Fork of the Blackwater with an even larger host; close on thirteen thousand Poor Fellows, their ranks stiffened by the addition of two hundred mounted Warrior's Sons from Stoney Sept, and the household knights and feudal levies of a dozen rebel lords from the westerlands and riverlands. Lord Rupert Falwell, famed as the Fighting Fool, led the ranks of the pious who had answered the High Septon's call; with him rode Ser Lyonel Lorch, Ser Alyn Terrick, Lord Tristifer Wayn, Lord Jon Lychester, and many other puissant knights. The army of the Faithful numbered twenty thousand men.

King Maegor's army was of like size, however, and His Grace had almost twice as much armored horse, as well as a large contingent of longbowmen, and the king himself riding Balerion. Even so, the battle proved a savage struggle. The Fighting Fool slew two knights of the Kingsguard before he himself was cut down by the Lord of Maidenpool. Big Jon Hogg, fighting for the king, was blinded by a sword slash early in the battle, yet rallied his men and led a charge that broke through the lines of the Faithful and put the Poor Fellows to flight. A rainstorm dampened Balerion's fires but could not quench them entirely, and amidst smoke and screams King Maegor descended again and again to serve his foes with flame. By nightfall victory was his, as the remaining Poor Fellows threw down their axes and streamed away in all directions.

Triumphant, Maegor returned to King's Landing to seat himself once more upon the Iron Throne. When Wat the Hewer was delivered to him, chained yet still defiant, Maegor took off his limbs with the giant's own axe, but commanded his maesters to keep the man alive "so he might attend my wedding." Then His Grace announced his intent to take Tyanna of Pentos as his third wife. Though it was whispered that his mother, the Queen Dowager, had no love for the Pentoshi sorceress, only Grand Maester Myros dared speak against her openly. "Your one true wife awaits you in the Hightower," Myros said. The king heard him out in silence, then descended from the throne, drew Blackfyre, and slew him where he stood.

Maegor Targaryen and Tyanna of the Tower were wed atop the Hill of Rhaenys, amidst the ashes and bones of the Warrior's Sons who had died there. It was said that Maegor had to put a dozen septons to death before he found one willing to perform the ceremony. Wat the Hewer, limbless, was kept alive to witness the marriage.

King Aenys's widow, Queen Alyssa, was present as well, with her younger sons, Viserys and Jaehaerys, and her daughter Alysanne. A visit from the Dowager Queen and Vhagar had persuaded her to leave her sanctuary on Driftmark and return to court, where Alyssa and her brothers and cousins of House Velaryon did homage to Maegor as the true king. The widowed queen was even compelled to join the other ladies of the court in disrobing His Grace and escorting him to the nuptial chamber to consummate his marriage, a bedding ceremony presided over by the king's second wife, Alys Harroway. That task done, Alyssa and the other ladies took their leave of the royal bedchamber, but Alys remained, joining the king and his newest wife in a night of carnal lust.

Across the realm in Oldtown, the High Septon was loud in his denunciations of "the abomination and his whores," whilst the king's first wife, Ceryse of House Hightower, continued to insist that she was Maegor's only lawful queen. And in the westerlands, Aegon Targaryen, Prince of Dragonstone, and his wife, Princess Rhaena, remained defiant as well.

All through the turmoil of Maegor's ascension, King Aenys's son and the princess, his wife, had remained at Casterly Rock, where Rhaena grew great with child. Most of the knights and young lordlings who had set out with them on their ill-fated progress had abandoned them, rushing off to King's Landing to bend their knees to Maegor. Even Rhaena's handmaids and companions had found excuses to absent themselves, save for her friend Alayne Royce and a former favorite, Melony Piper, who arrived at Lannisport with her brothers to swear the loyalty of their house.

All his life Prince Aegon had been considered the heir presumptive to the Iron Throne, but now, suddenly, he found himself reviled by the pious and abandoned by many he had thought to be his leal friends. Maegor's supporters, who seemed more numerous every day, were not shy in saying that Aegon was "his father's son," suggesting that they saw in him the same weakness that had brought down King Aenys. Aegon had never ridden a dragon, they pointed out, whereas Maegor had claimed Balerion, and the prince's own bride, Princess Rhaena, had been flying Dreamfyre since the age of twelve. Queen Alyssa's attendance at Maegor's wedding was trumpeted as proof that Aegon's own mother had abandoned his cause. Though Lyman Lannister, Lord of Casterly Rock, stood firm when Maegor demanded that Aegon and his sister be returned to King's Landing "in chains, if need be," even he would not go so far as to pledge his sword to the youth who now found himself being called "the pretender" and "Aegon the Uncrowned."

And thus it was there at Casterly Rock that Princess Rhaena gave birth to Aegon's daughters, twins they named Aerea and Rhaella. From the Starry Sept came another blistering proclamation. These children too were abominations, the High Septon proclaimed; fruits of lust and incest, accursed of the gods. The maester at Casterly Rock who helped deliver the children tells us that afterward Princess Rhaena begged the prince her husband to take them all across the narrow sea to Tyrosh or Myr or Volantis, anywhere beyond their uncle's reach, for "I would gladly give up my own life to make you king, but I will not put our girls at risk." But her words fell on stony ears and her tears were shed in vain, for Prince Aegon was determined to claim his birthright.

The dawn of the year 43 AC found King Maegor in King's Landing, where he had taken personal charge of the construction of the Red Keep. Much of the finished work was now undone or changed, new builders and workmen were brought in, and secret passages and tunnels crept through the depths of Aegon's High Hill. As the red stone towers rose, the king commanded the building of a castle within the castle, a fortified redoubt surrounded by a dry moat that would soon be known to all as Maegor's Holdfast.

In that same year, Maegor made Lord Lucas Harroway, father of his wife Queen Alys, his new Hand . . . but it was not the Hand who had the king's ear. His Grace might rule the Seven Kingdoms, men whispered, but he himself was ruled by the three queens: his mother, Queen Visenya; his paramour, Queen Alys; and the Pentoshi witch, Queen Tyanna. "The mistress of whispers," Tyanna was called, and "the king's raven," for her black hair. She spoke with rats and spiders, it was said, and all the vermin of

King's Landing came to her by night to tell tales of any fool rash enough to speak against the king.

Meanwhile, thousands of Poor Fellows still haunted the roads and wild places of the Reach, the Trident, and the Vale; though they would never again assemble in large numbers to face the king in open battle, the Stars fought on in smaller ways, falling upon travelers and swarming over towns, villages, and poorly defended castles, slaying the king's loyalists wherever they found them. Ser Horys Hill had escaped the battle at Great Fork, but defeat and flight had tarnished him, and his followers were few. The new leaders of the Poor Fellows were men like Ragged Silas, Septon Moon, and Dennis the Lame, hardly distinguishable from outlaws. One of their most vicious captains was a woman called Poxy Jeyne Poore, whose savage followers made the woods between King's Landing and Storm's End all but impassable to honest travelers.

Meanwhile, the Warrior's Sons had chosen a new grand captain in the person of Ser Joffrey Doggett, the Red Dog of the Hills, who was determined to restore the order to its former glory. When Ser Joffrey set out from Lannisport to seek the blessing of the High Septon, a hundred men rode with him. By the time he arrived in Oldtown, so many knights and squires and freeriders had joined him that his numbers had swollen to two thousand. Elsewhere in the realm, other restless lords and men of faith were gathering men as well, and plotting ways to bring the dragons down.

None of this had gone unnoticed. Ravens flew to every corner of the realm, summoning lords and landed knights of doubtful loyalty to King's Landing to bend the knee, swear homage, and deliver a son or daughter as a hostage for their obedience. The Stars and Swords were outlawed; membership in either order would henceforth be punishable by death. The High Septon was commanded to deliver himself to the Red Keep, to stand trial for high treason.

His High Holiness responded from the Starry Sept, commanding the king to present himself in Oldtown to beg the forgiveness of the gods for his sins and cruelties. Many of the Faithful echoed his defiance. Some pious lords did travel to King's Landing to do homage and present hostages, but more did not, trusting to their numbers and the strength of their castles to keep them safe.

King Maegor let the poisons fester for almost half a year, so engrossed was he in the building of his Red Keep. It was his mother who struck first. The Dowager Queen mounted Vhagar and brought fire and blood to the riverlands as once she had to Dorne. In a single night, the seats of House Blanetree, House Terrick, House Deddings, House Lychester, and House Wayn were set aflame. Then Maegor himself took wing, flying Balerion to the westerlands, where he burned the castles of the Broomes, the Falwells, the Lorches, and the other "pious lords" who had defied his summons. Lastly he descended upon the seat of House Doggett, reducing it to ash. The fires claimed the lives of Ser Joffrey's father, mother, and young sister, along with their sworn swords, serving men, and chattel. As pillars of smoke rose all through the westerlands and the riverlands, Vhagar and Balerion turned south. Another Lord Hightower, counseled by another High Septon, had opened the gates of Oldtown during the Conquest, but now it seemed as if the greatest and most populous city in Westeros must surely burn.

Thousands fled Oldtown that night, streaming from the city gates or taking ship for distant ports. Thousands more took to the streets in drunken revelry. "This is a night for song and sin and drink," men told one another, "for come the morrow, the virtuous and the vile burn together." Others gathered in septs and temples and ancient woods to pray they might be spared. In the Starry Sept, the High Septon railed and thundered, calling down the wroth of the gods upon the Targaryens. The archmaesters of the Citadel met in conclave. The men of the City Watch filled sacks with sand and pails with water to fight the fires they knew were coming. Along the city walls, crossbows, scorpions, spitfires, and spear-throwers were hoisted onto the battlements in hopes of bringing down the dragons when they appeared. Led by Ser Morgan Hightower, a younger brother of the Lord of Oldtown, two hundred Warrior's Sons spilled forth from their chapterhouse to defend His High Holiness, surrounding the Starry Sept with a ring of steel. Atop the Hightower, the great beacon fire turned a baleful green as Lord Martyn Hightower called his banners. Oldtown waited for the dawn, and the coming of the dragons.

And the dragons came. Vhagar first, as the sun was rising, then Balerion, just before midday. But they found the gates of the city open, the battlements unmanned, and the banners of House Targaryen, House Tyrell, and House Hightower flying side by side atop the city walls. The Dowager Queen Visenya was the first to learn the news. Sometime during the blackest hour of that long and dreadful night, the High Septon had died.

A man of three-and-fifty, as tireless as he was fearless, and to all appearances in robust good health, this High Septon had been renowned for his strength. More than once he had preached for a day and a night with-

out taking sleep or nourishment. His sudden death shocked the city and dismayed his followers. Its causes are debated to this day. Some say that His High Holiness took his own life, in what was either the act of a craven afraid to face the wroth of King Maegor, or a noble sacrifice to spare the goodfolk of Oldtown from dragonfire. Others claim the Seven struck him down for the sin of pride, for heresy, treason, and arrogance.

Many and more remain certain he was murdered . . . but by whom? Ser Morgan Hightower did the deed at the command of his lord brother, some say (and Ser Morgan was seen entering and leaving the High Septon's privy chambers that night). Others point to the Lady Patrice Hightower, Lord Martyn's maiden aunt and a reputed witch (who did indeed seek an audience with His High Holiness at dusk, though he was alive when she departed). The archmaesters of the Citadel are also suspected, though whether they made use of the dark arts, an assassin, or a poisoned scroll is still a matter of some debate (messages went back and forth between the Citadel and the Starry Sept all night). And there are still others who hold them all blameless and lay the High Septon's death at the door of another rumored sorceress, the Dowager Queen Visenya Targaryen.

The truth will likely never be known . . . but the swift reaction of Lord Martyn when word reached him at the Hightower is beyond dispute. At once he dispatched his own knights to disarm and arrest the Warrior's Sons, amongst them his own brother. The city gates were opened, and Targaryen banners raised along the walls. Even before Vhagar's wings were sighted, Lord Hightower's men were rousting the Most Devout from their beds and marching them to the Starry Sept at spearpoint to choose a new High Septon.

It required but a single ballot. Almost as one, the wise men and women of the Faith turned to a certain Septon Pater. Ninety years old, blind, stooped, and feeble, but famously amiable, the new High Septon almost collapsed beneath the weight of the crystal crown when it was placed upon his head . . . but when Maegor Targaryen appeared before him in the Starry Sept, he was only too pleased to bless him as king and anoint his head with holy oils, even if he did forget the words of the blessing.

Queen Visenya soon returned to Dragonstone with Vhagar, but King Maegor remained in Oldtown for almost half the year, holding court and presiding over trials. To the captive Swords of the Warrior's Sons, a choice was given. Those who renounced their allegiance to the order would be permitted to travel to the Wall and live out their days as brothers of the Night's Watch. Those who refused could die as martyrs to their faith. Three-quarters of the captives chose to take the black. The remainder died. Seven of their number, famous knights and the sons of lords, were given the honor of having King Maegor himself remove their heads with Blackfyre. The rest of the condemned were beheaded by their own former brothers-in-arms. Of all their number, only one man received a full royal pardon: Ser Morgan Hightower.

The new High Septon formally dissolved both the Warrior's Sons and the Poor Fellows, commanding their remaining members to lay down their arms in the name of the gods. The Seven had no more need of warriors, proclaimed His High Holiness; henceforth the Iron Throne would protect and defend the Faith. King Maegor granted the surviving members of the Faith Militant till year's end to surrender their weapons and give up their rebellious ways. After that, those who remained defiant would find a bounty on their heads: a gold dragon for the head of any unrepentant Warrior's Son, a silver stag for the "lice-ridden" scalp of a Poor Fellow.

The new High Septon did not demur, nor did the Most Devout.

During his time at Oldtown, the king was also reconciled with his first wife, Queen Ceryse, the sister of his host, Lord Hightower. Her Grace agreed to accept the king's other wives, to treat them with respect and honor and speak no further ill against them, whilst Maegor swore to restore to Ceryse all the rights, incomes, and privileges due her as his wedded wife and queen. A great feast was held at the Hightower to celebrate their reconciliation; the revels even included a bedding and a "second consummation," so all men would know this to be a true and loving union.

How long King Maegor might have lingered at Oldtown cannot be known, for in the latter part of 43 AC another challenge to his throne arose. His Grace's long absence from King's Landing had not gone unnoticed by his nephew, and Prince Aegon was quick to seize his chance. Emerging at last from Casterly Rock, Aegon the Uncrowned and his wife, Rhaena, raced across the riverlands with a handful of companions and entered the city concealed beneath sacks of corn. With so few followers, Aegon dared not seat himself upon the Iron Throne, for he knew he could not hold it. They were there for Rhaena's Dreamfyre . . . and so the prince might claim his father's dragon, Quicksilver. In this bold endeavor, they were aided by friends in Maegor's own court who had grown weary of the king's cruelties. The prince and princess entered King's Landing in a wagon pulled by mules, but when they made their departure it was on dragonback, flying side by side.

From there, Aegon and Rhaena returned to the westerlands to assemble an army. As the Lannisters of Casterly Rock were still reluctant to openly espouse Prince Aegon's cause, his adherents gathered at Pinkmaiden Castle, seat of House Piper. Jon Piper, Lord of Pinkmaiden, had pledged his sword to the prince, but it was widely believed that it was his fiery sister Melony, Rhaena's girlhood friend, who won him to the cause. It was there at Pinkmaiden that Aegon Targaryen, mounted on Quicksilver, descended from the sky to denounce his uncle as a tyrant and usurper, and call upon all honest men to rally to his banners.

The lords and knights who came were largely westermen and riverlords; the Lords Tarbeck, Roote, Vance, Charlton, Frey, Paege, Parren, Farman, and Westerling were amongst them, together with Lord Corbray of the Vale, the Bastard of Barrowton, and the fourth son of the Lord of Griffin's Roost. From Lannisport came five hundred men under the banner of a bastard son of Lyman Lannister, Ser Tyler Hill, by which ploy the cunning Lord of Casterly Rock lent supporters to the young prince whilst still keeping his own hands clean, should Maegor prevail. The Piper levies were led not by Lord Jon or his brothers, but by their sister Melony, who donned man's mail and took up a spear. Fifteen thousand men had joined the rebellion as Aegon the Uncrowned began his march across the riverlands to stake his claim to the Iron Throne, led by the prince himself on King Aenys's beloved dragon, Quicksilver.

Though their ranks included seasoned commanders and puissant knights, no great lords had rallied to Prince Aegon's cause . . . but Queen Tyanna, mistress of whisperers, wrote to warn Maegor that Storm's End, the Eyrie, Winterfell, and Casterly Rock had all been in secret communication with his brother's widowed queen, Alyssa. Before declaring for the

Prince of Dragonstone, they wished to be convinced he might prevail. Prince Aegon required a victory.

Maegor denied him that. From Harrenhal came forth Lord Harroway, from Riverrun Lord Tully. Ser Davos Darklyn of the Kingsguard marshalled five thousand swords in King's Landing and struck out west to meet the rebels. Up from the Reach came Lord Peake, Lord Merryweather, Lord Caswell, and their levies. Prince Aegon's slow-moving host found armies closing from all sides; each smaller than their own force, but so many that the young prince (still but seventeen) did not know where to turn. Lord Corbray advised him to engage each foe separately before they could join their powers, but Aegon was loath to divide his strength. Instead he chose to march on toward King's Landing.

Just south of the Gods Eye, he found Davos Darklyn's Kingslanders athwart his path, sitting on high ground behind a wall of spears, even as scouts reported Lords Merryweather and Caswell advancing from the south, and Lords Tully and Harroway from the north. Prince Aegon commanded a charge, hoping to break through the Kingslanders before the other loyalists fell upon his flanks, and mounted Quicksilver to lead the attack himself. But scarce had he taken wing when he heard shouts and saw his men below pointing to where Balerion the Black Dread had appeared in the southern sky.

King Maegor had come.

For the first time since the Doom of Valyria, dragon contended with dragon in the sky, even as battle was joined below.

Quicksilver, a quarter the size of Balerion, was no match for the older, fiercer dragon, and her pale white fireballs were engulfed and washed away in great gouts of black flame. Then the Black Dread fell upon her from above, his jaws closing round her neck as he ripped one wing from her body. Screaming and smoking, the young dragon plunged to earth, and Prince Aegon with her.

The battle below was nigh as brief, if bloodier. Once Aegon fell, the rebels saw their cause was doomed and ran, discarding arms and armor as they fled. But the loyalist armies were all around them, and there was no escape. By day's end, two thousand of Aegon's men had died, against a hundred of the king's. Amongst the dead were Lord Alyn Tarbeck, Denys

Snow the Bastard of Barrowton, Lord Ronnel Vance, Ser Willam Whistler, Melony Piper and three of her brothers . . . and the Prince of Dragonstone, Aegon the Uncrowned of House Targaryen. The only notable loss amongst the loyalists was Ser Davos Darklyn of the Kingsguard, slain at the hands of Lord Corbray with Lady Forlorn. Half a year of trials and executions followed. Queen Visenya persuaded her son to spare some of the rebellious lords, but even those who kept their lives lost lands and titles and were forced to give up hostages.

One notable name could be found neither amongst the dead nor the captive: Rhaena Targaryen, sister and wife to Prince Aegon, had not joined the host. Whether that was by his command or her own choice is still debated to this day. All that is known for certain is that Rhaena remained at Pinkmaiden Castle with her daughters when Aegon marched . . . and with her, Dreamfyre. Would the addition of a second dragon to the prince's host have made a difference when battle was joined? We shall never know . . . though it has been pointed out, and rightly, that Princess Rhaena was no warrior, and Dreamfyre was younger and smaller than Quicksilver, and certainly no true threat to Balerion the Black Dread.

When word of the battle reached the west and Princess Rhaena learned that both her husband and her friend Lady Melony had fallen, it is said she heard the news in a stony silence. "Will you not weep?" she was asked, to which she replied, "I do not have the time for tears." Whereupon, fearing her uncle's wroth, she gathered up her daughters, Aerea and Rhaella, and fled farther, first to Lannisport and then across the sea to Fair Isle, where the new lord Marq Farman (whose father and elder brother had both perished in the battle, fighting for Prince Aegon) gave her sanctuary and swore no harm would come to her beneath his roof. For the best part of a year, the people of Fair Isle watched the east in dread, fearing the sight of Balerion's dark wings, but Maegor never came. Instead the victorious king returned to the Red Keep, where he grimly set about getting himself an heir.

The 44th year After the Conquest was a peaceful one compared to what had gone before . . . but the maesters who chronicled those times wrote that the smell of blood and fire still hung heavy in the air. Maegor I Targaryen sat the Iron Throne as his Red Keep rose around him, but his court was grim and cheerless, despite the presence of his three queens . . . or perhaps because of it. Each night he summoned one of his wives to his bed, yet still he remained childless, with no heir but for the sons and daughters of his brother, Aenys. "Maegor the Cruel," he was called, and "kinslayer" as well, though it was death to say either in his hearing.

In Oldtown, the ancient High Septon died, and another was raised up in his place. Though he spoke no word against the king or his queens, the enmity between King Maegor and the Faith endured. Hundreds of Poor Fellows had been hunted down and slain, their scalps delivered to the king's men for the bounty, but thousands more still roamed the woods and hedges and the wild places of the Seven Kingdoms, cursing the Targaryens with their every breath. One band even crowned their own High Septon, in the person of a bearded brute named Septon Moon. And a few Warrior's Sons still endured, led by Ser Joffrey Doggett, the Red Dog of the Hills. Outlawed and condemned, the order no longer had the strength to meet the king's men in open battle, so the Red Dog sent them out in the guise of hedge knights, to hunt and slay Targaryen loyalists and "traitors to the Faith." Their first victim was Ser Morgan Hightower, late of their order, cut down and butchered on the road to Honeyholt. Old Lord Merryweather was the next to die, followed by Lord Peake's son and heir, Davos Darklyn's aged father, even Blind Jon Hogg. Though the bounty for the head of a Warrior's Son was a golden dragon, the smallfolk and peasants of the realm hid and protected them, remembering what they had been.

On Dragonstone, the Dowager Queen Visenya had grown thin and haggard, the flesh melting from her bones. Queen Alyssa remained on the island as well, with her son Jaehaerys and her daughter Alysanne, prisoners in all but name. Prince Viserys, the eldest surviving son of Aenys and Alyssa, was summoned to court by His Grace. A promising lad of fifteen years, beloved of the commons, Viserys was made squire to the king . . . with a Kingsguard knight for a shadow, to keep him well away from plots and treasons.

For a brief while in 44 AC, it seemed as if the king might soon have that son he desired so desperately. Queen Alys announced she was with child, and the court rejoiced. Grand Maester Desmond confined Her

Grace to her bed as she grew great with child, and took charge of her care, assisted by two septas, a midwife, and the queen's sisters Jeyne and Hanna. Maegor insisted that his other wives serve his pregnant queen as well.

During the third moon of her confinement, however, Lady Alys began to bleed heavily from the womb and lost the child. When King Maegor came to see the stillbirth, he was horrified to find the boy a monster, with twisted limbs, a huge head, and no eyes. "This cannot be my son!" he roared in anguish. Then his grief turned to fury, and he ordered the immediate execution of the midwife and septas who had charge of the queen's care, and Grand Maester Desmond as well, sparing only Alys's sisters.

It is said that Maegor was seated on the Iron Throne with the head of the Grand Maester in his hands when Queen Tyanna came to tell him he had been deceived. The child was not his seed. Seeing Queen Ceryse return to court, old and bitter and childless, Alys Harroway had begun to fear that the same fate awaited her unless she gave the king a son, so she had turned to her lord father, the Hand of the King. On the nights when the king was sharing a bed with Queen Ceryse or Queen Tyanna, Lucas Harroway sent men to his daughter's bed to get her with child. Maegor refused to believe. He told Tyanna she was a jealous witch, and barren, throwing the Grand Maester's head at her. "Spiders do not lie," the mistress of the whisperers replied. She handed the king a list.

Written there were the names of twenty men alleged to have given their seed to Queen Alys. Old men and young, handsome men and homely ones, knights and squires, lords and servants, even grooms and smiths and singers; the King's Hand had cast a wide net, it seemed. The men had only one thing in common: all were men of proven potency known to have fathered healthy children.

Under torture, all but two confessed. One, a father of twelve, still had the gold paid him by Lord Harroway for his services. The questioning was carried out swiftly and secretly, so Lord Harroway and Queen Alys had no inkling of the king's suspicions until the Kingsguard burst in on them. Dragged from her bed, Queen Alys saw her sisters killed before her eyes as they tried to protect her. Her father, inspecting the Tower of the Hand, was flung from its roof to smash upon the stones below. Harroway's sons, brothers, and nephews were taken as well. Thrown onto the spikes that lined the dry moat around Maegor's Holdfast, some took hours to die; the simpleminded Horas Harroway lingered for days. The twenty names on Queen Tyanna's list soon joined them, and then another dozen men, named by the first twenty.

The worst death was reserved for Queen Alys herself, who was given over to her sister-wife Tyanna for torment. Of her death we will not speak, for some things are best buried and forgotten. Suffice it to say that her dying took the best part of a fortnight, and that Maegor himself was present for all of it, a witness to her agony. After her death, the queen's body was cut into seven parts, and her pieces mounted on spikes above the seven gates of the city, where they remained until they rotted.

King Maegor himself departed King's Landing, assembling a strong force of knights and men-at-arms and marching on Harrenhal to complete the destruction of House Harroway. The great castle on the Gods Eye was lightly held, and its castellan, a nephew of Lord Lucas and cousin to the late queen, opened his gates at the king's approach. Surrender did not save him; His Grace put the entire garrison to the sword, along with every man, woman, and child he found to have any drop of Harroway blood. Then he marched to Lord Harroway's Town on the Trident and did the same there.

In the aftermath of the bloodletting, men began to say that Harrenhal was cursed, for every lordly house to hold it had come to a bad and bloody end. Nonetheless, many ambitious king's men coveted Black Harren's mighty seat, with its broad and fertile lands . . . so many that King Maegor grew weary of their entreaties, and decreed that Harrenhal should go to the strongest of them. Thus did twenty-three knights of the king's household fight with sword and mace and lance amidst the blood-soaked streets of Lord Harroway's Town. Ser Walton Towers emerged victorious, and Maegor named him Lord of Harrenhal . . . but the melee had been a savage affray, and Ser Walton did not live long enough to enjoy his lordship, dying of his wounds within the fortnight. Harrenhal passed to his eldest son, though its domains were much diminished, as the king granted Lord Harroway's Town to Lord Alton Butterwell, and the rest of the Harroway holdings to Lord Darnold Darry.

When at last Maegor returned to King's Landing to seat himself again upon the Iron Throne, he was greeted with the news that his mother, Queen Visenya, had died. Moreover, in the confusion that followed the death of the Queen Dowager, Queen Alyssa and her children had made their escape from Dragonstone, with the dragons Vermithor and Silverwing . . . to where, no man could say. They had even gone so far as to steal Dark Sister as they fled.

His Grace ordered his mother's body burned, her bones and ashes interred beside those of the Conqueror. Then he sent his Kingsguard to seize his squire, Prince Viserys. "Chain him in a black cell and question him sharply," Maegor commanded. "Ask him where his mother has gone."

"He may not know," protested Ser Owen Bush, a knight of Maegor's Kingsguard. "Then let him die," the king answered famously. "Perhaps the bitch will turn up for his funeral."

Prince Viserys did not know where his mother had gone, not even when Tyanna of Pentos plied him with her dark arts. After nine days of questioning, he died. His body was left out in the ward of the Red Keep for a fortnight, at the king's command. "Let his mother come and claim him," Maegor said. But Queen Alyssa never appeared, and at last His Grace consigned his nephew to the fire. The prince was fifteen years old when he was killed, and had been much loved by smallfolk and lords alike. The realm wept for him.

In 45 AC, construction finally came to an end on the Red Keep. King Maegor celebrated its completion by feasting the builders and workmen who had labored on the castle, sending them wagonloads of strongwine and sweetmeats, and whores from the city's finest brothels. The revels lasted for three days. Afterward, the king's knights moved in and put all the workmen to the sword, to prevent them from ever revealing the Red Keep's secrets. Their bones were interred beneath the castle that they had built.

Not long after the completion of the castle, Queen Ceryse was stricken with a sudden illness and passed away. A rumor went around the court that Her Grace had given offense to the king with a shrewish remark, so he had commanded Ser Owen to remove her tongue. As the tale went, the queen had struggled, Ser Owen's knife had slipped, and the queen's throat had been slit. Though never proven, this story was widely believed at the time; today, however, most maesters believe it to be a slander concocted by the king's enemies to further blacken his repute. Whatever the truth, the death of his first wife left Maegor with but a single queen, the black-haired, black-hearted Pentoshi woman Tyanna, mistress of the spiders, who was hated and feared by all.

Hardly had the last stone been set on the Red Keep when Maegor commanded that the ruins of the Sept of Remembrance be cleared from the top of Rhaenys's Hill, and with them the bones and ashes of the Warrior's Sons who had perished there. In their place, he decreed, a great stone "stable for dragons" would be erected, a lair worthy of Balerion, Vhagar, and their get. Thus commenced the building of the Dragonpit. Perhaps unsurprisingly, it proved difficult to find builders, stonemasons, and laborers to work on the project. So many men ran off that the king was finally forced to use prisoners from the city's dungeons as his workforce, under the supervision of builders brought in from Myr and Volantis.

Late in the year 45 AC, King Maegor took the field once again to continue his war against the outlawed remnants of the Faith Militant, leaving Queen Tyanna to rule King's Landing together with the new Hand, Lord Edwell Celtigar. In the great wood south of the Blackwater, the king's forces hunted down scores of Poor Fellows who had taken refuge there, sending many to the Wall and hanging those who refused to take the black. Their leader, the woman known as Poxy Jeyne Poore, continued to elude the king until at last she was betrayed by three of her own followers, who received pardons and knighthoods as their reward.

Three septons traveling with His Grace declared Poxy Jeyne a witch, and Maegor ordered her to be burned alive in a field beside the Wendwater. When the day appointed for her execution came, three hundred of her followers, Poor Fellows and peasants all, burst from the woods to rescue her. The king had anticipated this, however, and his men were ready for the attack. The rescuers were surrounded and slaughtered. Amongst the last to die was their leader, who proved to be Ser Horys Hill, the bastard hedge knight who had escaped the carnage at the Great Fork three years earlier. This time he proved less fortunate.

Elsewhere in the realm, however, the tide of the times had begun to turn against the king. Smallfolk and lords alike had come to despise him for his many cruelties, and many began to give help and comfort to his enemies. Septon Moon, the "High Septon" raised up by the Poor Fellows against the man in Oldtown they called the High Lickspittle, roamed the riverlands and Reach at will, drawing huge crowds whenever he emerged from the woods to preach against the king. The hill country north of the Golden Tooth was ruled in all but name by the Red Dog, Ser Joffrey Doggett, self-proclaimed Grand Captain of the Warrior's Sons. Neither Casterly Rock nor Riverrun seemed inclined to move against him. Dennis the Lame and Ragged Silas remained at large, and wherever they roamed, smallfolk helped keep them safe. Knights and men-at-arms sent out to bring them to justice oft vanished.

In 46 AC, King Maegor returned to the Red Keep with two thousand skulls, the fruits of a year of campaigning. They were the heads of Poor Fellows and Warrior's Sons, he announced, as he dumped them out beneath the Iron Throne . . . but it was widely believed that many of the grisly trophies belonged to simple crofters, fieldhands, and swineherds guilty of no crime but faith.

The coming of the new year found Maegor still without a son, not even a bastard who might be legitimized. Nor did it seem likely that Queen Tyanna would give him the heir that he desired. Whilst she continued to serve His Grace as mistress of whisperers, the king no longer sought her bed.

It was past time for him to take a new wife, Maegor's counselors agreed . . . but they parted ways on who that wife should be. Grand Maester Benifer suggested a match with the proud and lovely Lady of Starfall, Clarisse Dayne, in the hopes of detaching her lands and house from Dorne. Alton Butterwell, master of coin, offered his widowed sister, a stout woman with seven children. Though admittedly no beauty, he argued, her fertility had been proved beyond a doubt. The King's Hand, Lord Celtigar, had two young maiden daughters, thirteen and twelve years of age respectively. He urged the king to take his pick of them, or marry both if he preferred. Lord Velaryon of Driftmark advised Maegor to send for his niece Rhaena, the widow of Aegon the Uncrowned. By taking her to wife, Maegor could unite their claims, prevent any fresh rebellions from gathering around her, and acquire a hostage against any plots her mother, Queen Alyssa, might foment.

King Maegor listened to each man in turn. Though in the end he scorned most of the women they put forward, some of their reasons and arguments took root in him. He would have a woman of proven fertility, he decided, though not Butterwell's fat and homely sister. He would take more than one wife, as Lord Celtigar urged. Two wives would double his chances of getting a son; three wives would triple it. And one of those wives should surely be his niece; there was wisdom in Lord Velaryon's counsel. Queen Alyssa and her two youngest children remained in hiding (it was thought that they had fled across the narrow sea, to Tyrosh or perhaps Volantis), but they still represented a threat to Maegor's crown, and any son he might father. Taking Aenys's daughter to wife would weaken any claims put forward by her younger siblings.

After the death of her husband and her flight to Fair Isle, Rhaena Targaryen had acted quickly to protect her daughters. If Prince Aegon had truly been the king, by law his eldest daughter, Aerea, stood his heir, and might therefore claim to be the rightful Queen of the Seven Kingdoms . . . but Aerea and her sister, Rhaella, were barely a year old, and Rhaena knew that to trumpet such claims would be tantamount to condemning them to death. Instead, she dyed their hair, changed their names, and sent them from her, entrusting them to certain powerful allies, who would see them fostered in good homes by worthy men who would have no inkling of their true identities. Even their mother must not know where the girls were going, the princess insisted; what she did not know she could not reveal, even under torture.

No such escape was possible for Rhaena Targaryen herself. Though she could change her name, dye her hair, and garb herself in a tavern wench's roughspun or the robes of a septa, there was no disguising her dragon. Dreamfyre was a slender, pale blue she-dragon with silvery markings who had already produced two clutches of eggs, and Rhaena had been riding her since the age of twelve.

Dragons are not easily hidden. Instead the princess took them both as far from Maegor as she could, to Fair Isle, where Marq Farman granted her the hospitality of Faircastle, with its tall white towers rising high above the Sunset Sea. And there she rested, reading, praying, wondering how long she would be given before her uncle sent for her. Rhaena never doubted that he would, she said afterward; it was a question of *when,* not *if.*

The summons came sooner than she would have liked, though not as soon as she might have feared. There was no question of defiance. That would only bring the king down on Fair Isle with Balerion. Rhaena had grown fond of Lord Farman, and more than fond of his second son, Androw. She would not repay their kindness with fire and blood. She mounted Dreamfyre and flew to the Red Keep, where she learned that she must marry her uncle, her husband's killer. And there as well Rhaena met her fellow brides, for this was to be a triple wedding.

Lady Jeyne of House Westerling had been married to Alyn Tarbeck, who had died with Prince Aegon in the Battle Beneath the Gods Eye. A few months later, she had given her late lord a posthumous son. Tall and slender, with lustrous brown hair, Lady Jeyne was being courted by a younger son of the Lord of Casterly Rock when Maegor sent for her, but this meant little and less to the king.

More troubling was the case of Lady Elinor of House Costayne, the wife of Ser Theo Bolling, a landed knight who had fought for the king in his last campaign against the Poor Fellows. Though only nineteen, Lady Elinor had already given Bolling three sons when the king's eye fell upon her. The youngest boy was still at her breast when Ser Theo was arrested by the Kingsguard and charged with conspiring with Queen Alyssa to murder the king and place the boy Jaehaerys on the Iron Throne. Though Bolling protested his innocence, he was found guilty and beheaded the same day. King Maegor gave his widow seven days to mourn, in honor of the gods, then summoned her to tell her they would marry.

At the town of Stoney Sept, Septon Moon denounced King Maegor's wedding plans, and hundreds of townfolk cheered wildly, but few others dared to raise their voices against His Grace. The High Septon took ship at Oldtown, sailing to King's Landing to perform the marriage rites. On a warm spring day in the 47th year After the Conquest, Maegor Targaryen took three wives in the ward of the Red Keep. Though each of his new

queens was garbed and cloaked in the colors of her father's house, the people of King's Landing called them "the Black Brides," for all were widows.

The presence of Lady Jeyne's son and Lady Elinor's three boys at the wedding ensured that they would play their parts in the ceremony, but there were many who expected some show of defiance from Princess Rhaena. Such hopes were quelled when Queen Tyanna appeared, escorting two young girls with silver hair and purple eyes, clad in the red and black of House Targaryen. "You were foolish to think you could hide them from me," Tyanna told the princess. Rhaena bowed her head and spoke her vows in a voice as cold as ice.

Many queer and contradictory stories are told of the night that followed, and with the passage of so many years it is difficult to separate truth from legends. Did the three Black Brides share a single bed, as some claim? It seems unlikely. Did His Grace visit all three women during the night and consummate all three unions? Perhaps. Did Princess Rhaena attempt to kill the king with a dagger concealed beneath her pillows, as she later claimed? Did Elinor Costayne scratch the king's back to bloody ribbons as they coupled? Did Jeyne Westerling drink the fertility potion that Queen Tyanna supposedly brought her, or throw it in the older woman's face? Was such a potion ever mixed or offered? The first account of it does not appear until well into the reign of King Jaehaerys, twenty years after both women were dead.

This we know. In the aftermath of the wedding, Maegor declared Rhaena's daughter Aerea his lawful heir "until such time as the gods grant me a son," whilst sending her twin, Rhaella, to Oldtown to be raised as a septa. His nephew Jaehaerys, the rightful heir by all the laws of the Seven Kingdoms, was expressly disinherited in the same decree. Queen Jeyne's son was confirmed as Lord of Tarbeck Hall, and sent to Casterly Rock to be raised as a ward of Lyman Lannister. Queen Elinor's elder boys were similarly disposed of, one to the Eyrie, one to Highgarden. The queen's youngest babe was turned over to a wet nurse, as the king found the queen's nursing irksome.

Half a year later, Edwell Celtigar, the King's Hand, announced that Queen Jeyne was with child. Hardly had her belly begun to swell when the king himself revealed that Queen Elinor was also pregnant. Maegor showered both women with gifts and honors, and granted new lands and offices to their fathers, brothers, and uncles, but his joy proved to be short-lived. Three moons before she was due, Queen Jeyne was brought to bed by a sudden onset of labor pains, and was delivered of a stillborn child as monstrous as the one Alys Harroway had birthed, a legless and armless creature possessed of both male and female genitalia. Nor did the mother long survive the child.

Maegor was cursed, men said. He had slain his nephew, made war against the Faith and the High Septon, defied the gods, committed murder and incest, adultery and rape. His privy parts were poisoned, his seed full of worms, the gods would never grant him a living son. Or so the whispers ran. Maegor himself settled on a different explanation, and sent Ser Owen Bush and Ser Maladon Moore to seize Queen Tyanna and deliver her to the dungeons. There the Pentoshi queen made a full confession, even as the king's torturers readied their implements: she had poisoned Jeyne Westerling's child in the womb, just as she had Alys Harroway's. It would be the same with Elinor Costayne's whelp, she promised.

It is said that the king slew her himself, cutting out her heart with Blackfyre and feeding it to his dogs. But even in death, Tyanna of the Tower had her revenge, for it came to pass just as she had promised. The moon turned and turned again, and in the black of night Queen Elinor too was delivered of a malformed and stillborn child, an eyeless boy born with rudimentary wings.

That was in the 48th year After the Conquest, the sixth year of King Maegor's reign, and the last year of his life. No man in the Seven Kingdoms could doubt that the king was accursed now. What followers still remained to him began to melt away, evaporating like dew in the morning sun. Word reached King's Landing that Ser Joffrey Doggett had been seen entering Riverrun, not as a captive but as a guest of Lord Tully. Septon Moon appeared once more, leading thousands of the Faithful on a march across the Reach to Oldtown, with the announced intent of bearding the Lickspittle in the Starry Sept to demand that he denounce "the Abomination on the Iron Throne," and lift his ban on the military orders. When Lord Oakheart and Lord Rowan appeared before him with their levies, they came not to attack Moon, but to join him. Lord Celtigar resigned as King's Hand, and returned to his seat on Claw Isle. Reports from the Dornish Marches suggested that the Dornishmen were gathering in the passes, preparing to invade the realm.

The worst blow came from Storm's End. There on the shores of Shipbreaker Bay, Lord Rogar Baratheon proclaimed young Jaehaerys Targaryen to be the true and lawful king of the Andals, the Rhoynar, and the First Men, and Prince Jaehaerys named Lord Rogar Protector of the Realm and Hand of the King. The prince's mother, Queen Alyssa, and his sister Alysanne stood beside him as Jaehaerys unsheathed Dark Sister and vowed to end the reign of his usurping uncle. A hundred banner lords and stormland knights cheered the proclamation. Prince Jaehaerys was fourteen years old when he claimed the throne; a handsome youth, skilled with lance and longbow, and a gifted rider. More, he rode a great bronze-and-tan beast called Vermithor, and his sister Alysanne, a maid of twelve, commanded her own dragon, Silverwing. "Maegor has only one dragon," Lord Rogar told the stormlords. "Our prince has two."

And soon three. When word reached the Red Keep that Jaehaerys was gathering his forces at Storm's End, Rhaena Targaryen mounted Dreamfyre and flew to join him, abandoning the uncle she had been forced to wed. She took her daughter Aerea . . . and Blackfyre, stolen from the king's own scabbard as he slept.

King Maegor's response was sluggish and confused. He commanded the Grand Maester to send forth his ravens, summoning all his leal lords and bannermen to gather at King's Landing, only to find that Benifer had taken ship for Pentos. Finding Princess Aerea gone, he sent a rider to Oldtown to demand the head of her twin sister, Rhaella, to punish their mother for her betrayal, but Lord Hightower imprisoned his messenger instead. Two of his Kingsguard vanished one night, to go over to Jaehaerys, and Ser Owen Bush was found dead outside a brothel, his member stuffed into his mouth.

Lord Velaryon of Driftmark was amongst the first to declare for Jaehaerys. As the Velaryons were the realm's traditional admirals, Maegor woke to find he had lost the entire royal fleet. The Tyrells of Highgarden followed, with all the power of the Reach. The Hightowers of Oldtown, the Redwynes of the Arbor, the Lannisters of Casterly Rock, the Arryns of the Eyrie, the Royces of Runestone . . . one by one, they came out against the king.

In King's Landing, a score of lesser lords gathered at Maegor's command, amongst them Lord Darklyn of Duskendale, Lord Massey of Stonedance, Lord Towers of Harrenhal, Lord Staunton of Rook's Rest, Lord Bar Emmon of Sharp Point, Lord Buckwell of the Antlers, the Lords Rosby, Stokeworth, Hayford, Harte, Byrch, Rollingford, Bywater, and Mallery. Yet they commanded scarce four thousand men amongst them all, and only one in ten of those were knights.

Maegor brought them together in the Red Keep one night to discuss his plan of battle. When they saw how few they were, and realized that no great lords were coming to join them, many lost heart, and Lord Hayford went so far as to urge His Grace to abdicate and take the black. His Grace ordered Hayford beheaded on the spot and continued the war council with his lordship's head mounted on a lance behind the Iron Throne. All day the lords made plans, and late into the night. It was the hour of the wolf when at last Maegor allowed them to take their leave. The king remained behind, brooding on the Iron Throne as they departed. Lord Towers and Lord Rosby were the last to see His Grace.

Hours later, as dawn was breaking, the last of Maegor's queens came seeking after him. Queen Elinor found him still upon the Iron Throne, pale and dead, his robes soaked through with blood. His arms had been slashed open from wrist to elbow on jagged barbs, and another blade had gone through his neck to emerge beneath his chin.

Many to this day believe it was the Iron Throne itself that killed him. Maegor was alive when Rosby and Towers left the throne room, they argue, and the guards at the doors swore that no one entered afterward, until Queen Elinor made her discovery. Some say it was the queen herself who forced him down onto those barbs and blades, to avenge the murder of her first husband. The Kingsguard might have done the deed, though that would have required them to act in concert, as there were two knights posted at each door. It might also have been a person or persons unknown, entering and leaving the throne room through some hidden passage. The Red Keep has its secrets, known only to the dead. It might also

be that the king tasted despair in the dark watches of the night and took his own life, twisting the blades as needed and opening his veins to spare himself the defeat and disgrace that surely awaited him.

The reign of King Maegor I Targaryen, known to history and legend as Maegor the Cruel, lasted six years and sixty-six days. Upon his death his corpse was burned in the yard of the Red Keep, his ashes interred afterward on Dragonstone beside those of his mother. He died childless, and left no heir of his body.

Prince into King

The Ascension of Jaehaerys I

Jaehaerys I Targaryen ascended the Iron Throne in 48 AC at the age of fourteen and would rule the Seven Kingdoms for the next fifty-five years, until his death of natural causes in 103 AC. In the later years of his reign, and during the reign of his successor, he was called the Old King, for obvious reasons, but Jaehaerys was a young and vigorous man for far longer than he was an aged and feeble one, and more thoughtful scholars speak of him reverently as "the Conciliator." Archmaester Umbert, writing a century later, famously declared that Aegon the Dragon and his sisters conquered the Seven Kingdoms (six of them, at least), but it was Jaehaerys the Conciliator who truly made them one.

His was no easy task, for his immediate predecessors had undone much of what the Conqueror had built, Aenys through weakness and indecision, Maegor with his bloodlust and cruelty. The realm that Jaehaerys inherited was impoverished, war-torn, lawless, and riven with division and mistrust, whilst the new king himself was a green boy with no experience of rule.

Even his claim to the Iron Throne was not wholly beyond question. Although Jaehaerys was the only surviving son of King Aenys I, his older brother Aegon had claimed the kingship before him. Aegon the Uncrowned had died at the Battle Beneath the Gods Eye whilst trying to unseat his uncle Maegor, but not before taking to wife his sister Rhaena and siring two daughters, the twins Aerea and Rhaella. If Maegor the Cruel were accounted only a usurper with no right to rule, as certain maesters argued, then Prince Aegon had been the true king, and the succession by rights should pass to his elder daughter, Aerea, not his younger brother.

The sex of the twins weighed against them, however, as did their age; the girls were but six at Maegor's death. Furthermore, accounts left us by contemporaries suggest that Princess Aerea was a timid child when young, much given to tears and bed-wetting, whilst Rhaella, the bolder and more robust of the pair, was a novice serving at the Starry Sept and promised to the Faith. Neither seemed to have the makings of a queen; their own mother, Queen Rhaena, conceded as much when she agreed that the crown should go to her brother Jaehaerys rather than her daughters.

Some suggested that Rhaena herself might have the strongest claim to the crown, as the firstborn child of King Aenys and Queen Alyssa. There were even some who whispered that it was Queen Rhaena who had somehow contrived to free the realm from Maegor the Cruel, though by what means she might have arranged his death after fleeing King's Landing on her dragon, Dreamfyre, has never been successfully established. Her sex told against her, however. "This is not Dorne," Lord Rogar Baratheon said when the notion was put to him, "and Rhaena is not Nymeria." Moreover, the twice-widowed queen had come to loathe King's Landing and the court, and wished only to return to Fair Isle, where she had found a measure of peace before her uncle had made her one of his Black Brides.

Prince Jaehaerys was still a year and a half shy of manhood when he first ascended the Iron Throne. Thus it was determined that his mother, the Dowager Queen Alyssa, would act as regent for him, whilst Lord Rogar served as his Hand and the Protector of the Realm. Let it not be thought, however, that Jaehaerys was merely a figurehead. Right from the first, the boy king insisted upon having a voice in all decisions made in his name.

Even as the mortal remains of Maegor I Targaryen were consigned to a funeral pyre, his young successor faced his first crucial decision: how to deal with his uncle's remaining supporters. By the time Maegor was found dead upon the Iron Throne, most of the great houses of the realm and many lesser lords had abandoned him . . . but *most* is not *all.* Many of those whose lands and castles were near King's Landing and the crownlands had stood with Maegor until the very hour of his death, amongst them the Lords Rosby and Towers, the last men to see the king alive. Others who had rallied to his banners included the Lords Stokeworth, Massey, Harte, Bywater, Darklyn, Rollingford, Mallery, Bar Emmon, Byrch, Staunton, and Buckwell.

In the chaos that had followed the discovery of Maegor's body, Lord Rosby drank a cup of hemlock to join his king in death. Buckwell and Rollingford took ship for Pentos, whilst most of the others fled to their own castles and strongholds. Only Darklyn and Staunton had the courage to remain with Lord Towers to yield up the Red Keep when Prince Jaehaerys and his sisters, Rhaena and Alysanne, descended upon the castle on their dragons. The court chronicles tell us that as the young prince slid from the back of Vermithor, these "three leal lords" bent their knees before him to lay their swords at his feet, hailing him as king.

"You come late to the feast," Prince Jaehaerys reportedly told them, though in a mild tone, "and these same blades helped slay my brother Aegon beneath the Gods Eye." At his command, the three were immediately put in chains, though some of the prince's party called for them to be executed on the spot. In the black cells they were soon joined by the King's Justice, the Lord Confessor, the Chief Gaoler, the Commander of the City Watch, and the four knights of the Kingsguard who had remained beside King Maegor.

A fortnight later, Lord Rogar Baratheon and Queen Alyssa arrived at King's Landing with their host, and hundreds more were seized and imprisoned. Be they knights, squires, stewards, septons, or serving men, the charge against them was the same; they were accused of having aided and abetted Maegor Targaryen in usurping the Iron Throne and in all the crimes, cruelties, and misrule that followed. Not even women were exempt; those ladies of noble birth who had attended the Black Brides were

arrested as well, together with a score of lowborn trulls named as Maegor's whores.

With the dungeons of the Red Keep full to bursting, the question arose as to what should be done with the prisoners. If Maegor were to be counted as usurper, then his entire reign was unlawful and those who had supported him were guilty of treason and must needs be put to death. Such was the course urged by Queen Alyssa. The Dowager Queen had lost two sons to Maegor's cruelty and was of no mind to grant the men who had carried out his edicts even the dignity of a trial. "When my boy Viserys was tortured and slain, these men stood by silently and spoke no word of protest," she said. "Why should we listen to them now?"

Against her fury stood Lord Rogar Baratheon, Hand of the King and Protector of the Realm. Whilst his lordship agreed that Maegor's men were surely deserving of punishment, he pointed out that should their captives be executed, the usurper's remaining loyalists would be disinclined to bend the knee. Lord Rogar would have no choice but to march on their castles one by one and winkle each man out of his stronghold with steel and fire. "It can be done, but at what cost?" he asked. "It would be a bloody business, one that might harden hearts against us." Let Maegor's men stand trial and confess their treason, the Protector urged. Those found guilty of the worst crimes could be put to death; for the remainder, let them tender hostages to ensure their future loyalty, and surrender some of their lands and castles.

The wisdom of Lord Rogar's approach was plain to most of the young king's other supporters, yet his views might not have prevailed had not Jaehaerys himself taken a hand. Though only ten-and-four, the boy king proved from the first that he would not be content to sit by meekly whilst others ruled in his name. With his maester, his sister Alysanne, and a handful of young knights by his side, Jaehaerys climbed the Iron Throne and summoned his lords to attend him. "There will be no trials, no torture, and no executions," he announced to them. "The realm must see that I am not my uncle. I shall not begin my reign by bathing in blood. Some came to my banners early, some late. Let the rest come now."

Jaehaerys as yet had neither been crowned nor anointed, and was still shy of his majority; his pronouncement therefore had no legal force, nor did he have the authority to overrule his council and regent. Yet such was the power of his words, and the determination he displayed as he sat looking down upon them all from the Iron Throne, that Lords Baratheon and Velaryon at once gave the prince their support, and the rest soon followed. Only his sister Rhaena dared say him nay. "They will cheer you as the crown is placed upon your head," she said, "as once they cheered our uncle, and before him our father."

In the end, the question rested with the regent . . . and whilst Queen Alyssa desired vengeance for her own sake, she was loath to go against her son's wishes. "It would make him seem weak," she is reported to have said to Lord Rogar, "and he must *never* seem weak. That was his father's downfall." And thus it was that most of Maegor's men were spared.

In the days that followed, the dungeons of King's Landing were largely emptied. After being given food and drink and clean raiment, the captives were escorted to the throne room seven at a time. There, before the eyes of gods and men, they renounced their allegiance to Maegor and did homage to his nephew Jaehaerys from their knees, whereupon the young king bade each man rise, granted him pardon, and restored his lands and titles. It must not be thought that the accused escaped without punishment, however. Lords and knights alike were compelled to send a son to court to serve the king and stand as hostages; from those who had no sons, a daughter was required. The wealthiest of Maegor's lords surrendered certain lands as well, Towers, Darklyn, and Staunton amongst them. Others purchased their pardons with gold.

The royal clemency did not extend to all. Maegor's headsman, gaolers, and confessors were all adjudged to be guilty of abetting Tyanna of the Tower in the torture and death of Prince Viserys, who had so briefly been Maegor's heir and hostage. Their heads were delivered to Queen Alyssa,

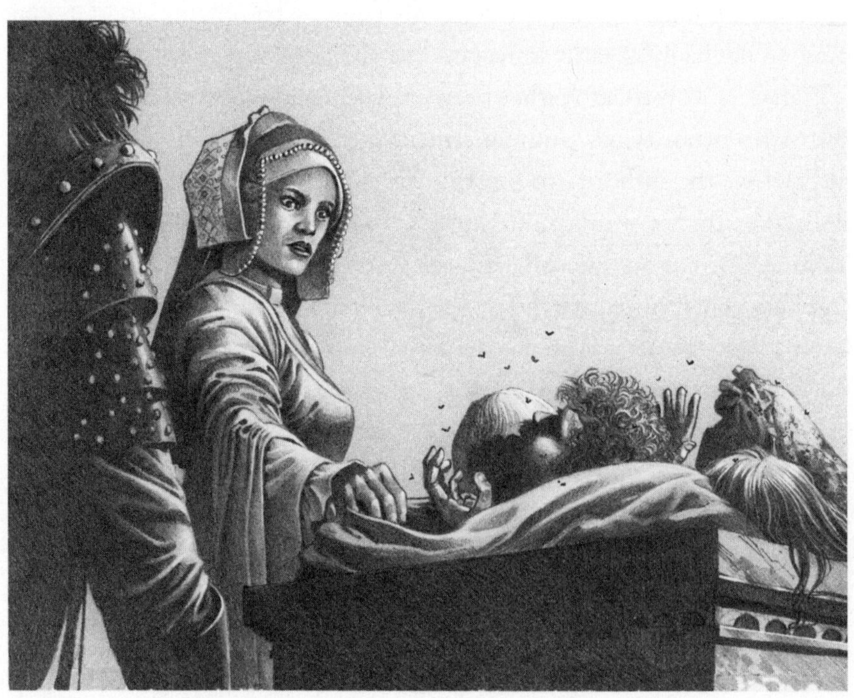

together with the hands they had dared raise against the blood of the dragon. Her Grace pronounced herself "well pleased" with the tokens.

One other man also lost his head: Ser Maladon Moore, a Kingsguard knight, who was accused of having held Ceryse Hightower, Maegor's first queen, whilst his Sworn Brother, Ser Owen Bush, removed her tongue, during which Her Grace's struggles caused the blade to slip, bringing about her death. (Ser Maladon, it should be noted, insisted the whole tale was a fabrication, and said Queen Ceryse died of "shrewishness." He did, however, admit to delivering Tyanna of the Tower to King Maegor's hands and standing witness as he slew her, so he had a queen's blood on his hands regardless.)

Five of Maegor's Seven yet survived. Two of those, Ser Olyver Bracken and Ser Raymund Mallery, had played a part in the late king's fall by turning their cloaks and going over to Jaehaerys, but the boy king observed rightly that in doing so they had broken their vows to defend the king's life with their own. "I will have no oathbreakers at my court," he proclaimed. All five Kingsguard were therefore sentenced to death . . . but at the urging of Princess Alysanne, it was agreed that they might be spared if they would exchange their white cloaks for black by joining the Night's Watch. Four of the five accepted this clemency and departed for the Wall; along with Ser Olyver and Ser Raymund, the turncloaks, went Ser Jon Tollett and Ser Symond Crayne.

The fifth Kingsguard, Ser Harrold Langward, demanded a trial by battle. Jaehaerys granted his wish and offered to face Ser Harrold himself in single combat, but in this he was overruled by the Queen Regent. Instead a young knight from the stormlands was sent forth as the Crown's champion. Ser Gyles Morrigen, the man chosen, was a nephew to Damon the Devout, the Grand Captain of the Warrior's Sons, who had led them in their Trial of Seven against Maegor. Eager to prove his house's loyalty to the new king, Ser Gyles made short work of the elderly Ser Harrold, and was named Lord Commander of Jaehaerys's Kingsguard soon after.

Meanwhile, word of the prince's clemency spread throughout the realm. One by one, the remainder of King Maegor's adherents dismissed their hosts, left their castles, and made the journey to King's Landing to swear fealty. Some did so reluctantly, fearing that Jaehaerys might prove to be as weak and feckless a king as his father . . . but as Maegor had left no heirs of the body, there was no plausible rival around whom opposition might gather. Even the most fervent of Maegor's supporters were won over once they met Jaehaerys, for he was all a prince should be; fair-spoken, open-handed, and as chivalrous as he was courageous. Grand Maester Benifer (newly returned from his self-imposed exile in Pentos) wrote that he was "learned as a maester and pious as a septon," and whilst some of that may be discounted as flattery, there was truth to it as well. Even his mother, Queen Alyssa, is reported to have called Jaehaerys "the best of my three sons."

It must not be thought that the reconciliation of the lords brought peace to Westeros overnight. King Maegor's efforts to exterminate the Poor Fellows and the Warrior's Sons had set many pious men and women against him, and against House Targaryen. Whilst he had collected the heads of hundreds of Stars and Swords, hundreds more remained at large, and tens of thousands of lesser lords, landed knights, and smallfolk sheltered them, fed them, and gave them aid and comfort wherever they could. Ragged Silas and Dennis the Lame commanded roving bands of Poor Fellows who came and went like wraiths, vanishing into the greenwood whenever threatened. North of the Golden Tooth, the Red Dog of the Hills, Ser Joffrey Doggett, moved between the westerlands and riverlands at will, with the support and connivance of Lady Lucinda, the pious wife of the Lord of Riverrun. Ser Joffrey, who had taken upon himself the mantle of the Grand Captain of the Warrior's Sons, had announced his intention to restore that once-proud order to its former glory, and was recruiting knights to its banners.

Yet the greatest threat was in the south, where Septon Moon and his followers camped beneath the walls of Oldtown, defended by Lord Oakheart and Lord Rowan and their knights. A massive hulk of a man, Moon had been blessed with a thunderous voice and an imposing physical presence. Though his Poor Fellows had proclaimed him "the true High Septon," this septon (if indeed he was such) was no picture of piety. He boasted proudly that *The Seven-Pointed Star* was the only book he had ever read, and many questioned even that, for he had never been known to quote from that holy tome, and no man had ever seen him read nor write.

Barefoot, bearded, and possessed of immense fervor, the "Poorest Fellow" could speak for hours, and often did . . . and what he spoke about was sin. "I am a sinner," were the words with which Septon Moon began every sermon, and so he was. A creature of immense appetites, a glutton and a drunkard renowned for his lechery, Moon lay each night with a different woman, impregnating so many of them that his acolytes began to say that his seed could make a barren woman fertile. Such was the ignorance and folly of his followers that this tale became widely believed; husbands began to offer him their wives and mothers their daughters. Septon Moon never refused such offers, and after a time some of the hedge knights and men-at-arms amongst his rabble began to paint images of the "Cock o' the Moon" on their shields, and a brisk trade grew up in clubs, pendants, and staffs carved to resemble Moon's member. A touch with the head of these talismans was believed to bestow prosperity and good fortune.

Every day Septon Moon went forth to denounce the sins of House Targaryen and the Lickspittle who permitted their abominations, whilst inside Oldtown the true Father of the Faithful had become a virtual prisoner in his own palace, unable to set forth outside the confines of the Starry Sept. Though Lord Hightower had closed his gates against Septon Moon and his followers and refused to allow them entrance to his city, he showed no eagerness to take up arms against them, despite repeated entreaties from His High Holiness. When pressed for reasons, his lordship cited a distaste for shedding pious blood, but many claimed the real reason was his unwillingness to offer battle to Lords Oakheart and Rowan, who had granted Moon their protection. His reluctance earned him the name Lord Donnel the Delayer from the maesters of the Citadel.

The long conflict between King Maegor and the Faith had made it imperative that Jaehaerys be anointed king by the High Septon, Lord Rogar and the Queen Regent agreed. Before that could happen, however, Septon Moon and his ragged horde must needs be dealt with, so the prince could travel safely to Oldtown. It had been hoped that the news of Maegor's death would be sufficient to persuade Moon's followers to disperse, and some had done just that . . . but no more than a few hundred in a host that numbered close to five thousand. "What can the death of one dragon matter when another rises up to take its place?" Septon Moon declared to his throng. "Westeros will not be clean again until all the Targaryens have been slain or driven back into the sea." Every day he preached anew, calling upon Lord Hightower to deliver Oldtown to him, calling upon the High Lickspittle to leave the Starry Sept and face the wroth of the Poor Fellows he had betrayed, calling upon the smallfolk of the realm to rise up. (And every night he sinned anew.)

Across the realm in King's Landing, Jaehaerys and his counselors considered how to rid the realm of this scourge. The boy king and his sisters, Rhaena and Alysanne, all had dragons, and some felt the best way to deal with Septon Moon was the way Aegon the Conqueror and his sisters had dealt with the Two Kings on the Field of Fire. Jaehaerys had no taste for such slaughter, however, and his mother, Queen Alyssa, flatly forbade it, reminding them of the fate of Rhaenys Targaryen and her dragon in Dorne. Lord Rogar, the King's Hand, said, with some reluctance, that he would lead his own host across the Reach and disperse Moon's men by force of arms . . . though it would mean pitting his stormlanders, and whatever other forces he might gather, against Lords Rowan and Oakheart and their knights and men-at-arms, as well as the Poor Fellows. "Like as not, we will win," the Protector said, "but not without cost."

Mayhaps the gods were listening, for even as the king and council argued in King's Landing the problem was resolved in a most unexpected way. Dusk was falling outside of Oldtown when Septon Moon retired to his tent for his evening meal, exhausted by a day of preaching. As always he was guarded by his Poor Fellows, huge strapping axemen with unshorn beards, but when a comely young woman presented herself at the septon's tent with a flagon of wine that she wished to give to His Holiness in return for his help, they admitted her at once. They knew what sort of help the woman required; the sort that would put a babe inside her belly.

A short time passed, during which the men outside the tent heard only occasional gusts of laughter from Septon Moon, inside. But then, suddenly, there was a groan, and a woman's shriek, followed by a bellow of rage. The tent flap was thrown open and the woman burst out, half-naked and barefoot, and dashed away wide-eyed and terrified before any of the Poor Fellows could think to stop her. Septon Moon himself followed a moment later, naked, roaring, and drenched in blood. He was holding his neck, and blood was leaking between his fingers and dripping down into his beard from where his throat had been slit open.

It is said that Moon staggered through half the camp, lurching from campfire to campfire in pursuit of the doxy who had cut him. Finally even his great strength failed him; he collapsed and died as his acolytes pressed around him, wailing their grief. Of his slayer there was no sign; she had vanished into the night, never to be seen again. Angry Poor Fellows tore the camp apart for a day and a night in search of her, knocking over tents, seizing dozens of women, and beating any man who tried to stand in their way . . . but the hunt came up empty. Septon Moon's own guards could not even agree on what his killer had looked like.

The guards did recall that the woman had brought a flagon of wine with her as a gift for the septon. Half the wine still remained in the flagon when the tent was searched, and four of the Poor Fellows shared it as the sun was coming up, after carrying the corpse of their prophet back to his own bed. All four were dead before noon. The wine had been laced with poison.

In the aftermath of Moon's death, the ragged host that he had led to Oldtown began to disintegrate. Some of his followers had already slipped away when word of King Maegor's death and Prince Jaehaerys's ascension reached them. Now that trickle became a flood. Before the septon's corpse had even begun to stink, a dozen rivals had come forward to claim his mantle, and fights began to break out amongst their respective followers. It might have been thought that Moon's men would turn to the two lords amongst them for leadership, but nothing could be further from the truth. The Poor Fellows especially were no respectors of nobility . . . and the reluctance of Lords Rowan and Oakheart to commit their knights and men-at-arms to an assault on the walls of Oldtown had made them suspicious of the two lords.

The possession of Moon's mortal remains became itself a bone of contention between two of his would-be successors, the Poor Fellow known as Rob the Starvling and a certain Lorcas, called Lorcas the Learned, who boasted of having committed all of *The Seven-Pointed Star* to memory. Lorcas claimed to have had a vision that Moon would yet deliver Oldtown into the hands of his followers, even after death. After seizing the septon's body from Rob the Starvling, this "learned" fool strapped it atop a destrier, naked, bloody, and rotting, to storm the gates of Oldtown.

Fewer than a hundred men joined in the attack, however, and most of them died beneath a rain of arrows, spears, and stones before they got within a hundred yards of the city walls. Those who did reach the walls were drenched in boiling oil or set afire with burning pitch, Lorcas the Learned himself amongst them. When all his men were dead or dying, a dozen of Lord Hightower's boldest knights rode forth from a sally port, seized Septon Moon's body, and removed his head. Tanned and stuffed, it would later be presented to the High Septon in the Starry Sept as a gift.

The abortive attack proved to be the last gasp of Septon Moon's crusade. Lord Rowan decamped within the hour, with all his knights and men-at-arms. Lord Oakheart followed the next day. The remainder of the host, hedge knights and Poor Fellows and camp followers and tradesmen, streamed away in all directions (looting and pillaging every farm, village, and holdfast in their path as they went). Fewer than four hundred remained of the five thousand that Septon Moon had brought to Oldtown when Lord Donnel the Delayer at last bestirred himself and rode forth in force to slaughter the stragglers.

Moon's murder removed the last major obstacle to the accession of Jaehaerys Targaryen to the Iron Throne, but from that day to this, debate has raged as to who was responsible for his death. No one truly believed that the woman who attempted to poison the "sinful septon" and ended by cutting his throat was acting on her own. Plainly she was but a catspaw . . . but whose? Did the boy king himself send her forth, or was she mayhaps an agent of his Hand, Rogar Baratheon, or his mother, the Queen Regent? Some came to believe that the woman was one of the Faceless Men, the infamous guild of sorcerer-assassins from Braavos. In support of this claim, they cited her sudden disappearance, the way she seemed to "melt into the night" after the murder, and the fact that Septon Moon's guards could not agree on what she looked like.

Wiser men and those more familiar with the ways of the Faceless Men give this theory little credence. The very clumsiness of Moon's murder speaks against it being their work, for the Faceless Men take great care to make their killings appear as natural deaths. It is a point of pride with them, the very cornerstone of their art. Slitting a man's throat and leaving him to stagger forth into the night screaming of murder is beneath them. Most scholars today believe that the killer was no more than a camp follower, acting at the behest of either Lord Rowan or Lord Oakheart, or mayhaps the both of them. Though neither dared desert Moon whilst he lived, the alacrity with which the two lords abandoned his cause after his death suggests that their grievance had been with Maegor, not with House Targaryen . . . and, indeed, both men would soon return to Oldtown, penitent and obedient, to bend the knee before Prince Jaehaerys at his coronation.

With the way to Oldtown clear and safe once more, that coronation took place in the Starry Sept in the waning days of the 48th year After the Conquest. The High Septon—the High Lickspittle that Septon Moon had hoped to displace—anointed the young king himself, and placed his father Aenys's crown upon his head. Seven days of feasting followed, during which hundreds of lords great and small came to bend their knees and swear their swords to Jaehaerys. Amongst those in attendance were his sisters, Rhaena and Alysanne; his young nieces, Aerea and Rhaella; his mother, the Queen Regent Alyssa; the King's Hand, Rogar Baratheon; Ser Gyles Morrigen, the Lord Commander of the Kingsguard; Grand Maester Benifer; the assembled archmaesters of the Citadel . . . and one man no one could have expected to see: Ser Joffrey Doggett, the Red Dog of the Hills, self-proclaimed Grand Captain of the outlawed Warrior's Sons. Doggett had arrived in the company of Lord and Lady Tully of Riverrun . . . not in chains, as most might have expected, but with a safe conduct bearing the king's own seal.

Grand Maester Benifer wrote afterward that the meeting between the boy king and the outlaw knight "set the table" for all of Jaehaerys's reign to follow. When Ser Joffrey and Lady Lucinda urged him to undo his

uncle Maegor's decrees and reinstate the Swords and Stars, Jaehaerys refused firmly. "The Faith has no need of swords," he declared. "They have my protection. The protection of the Iron Throne." He did, however, rescind the bounties that Maegor had promised for the heads of Warrior's Sons and Poor Fellows. "I shall not wage war against my own people," he said, "but neither shall I tolerate treason and rebellion."

"I rose against your uncle just as you did," replied the Red Dog of the Hills, defiant.

"You did," Jaehaerys allowed, "and you fought bravely, no man can deny. The Warrior's Sons are no more and your vows to them are at an end, but your service need not be. I have a place for you." And with these words, the young king shocked the court by offering Ser Joffrey a place by his side as a knight of the Kingsguard. A hush fell then, Grand Maester Benifer tells us, and when the Red Dog drew his longsword there were some who feared he might be about to attack the king with it . . . but instead the knight went to one knee, bowed his head, and laid his blade at Jaehaerys's feet. It is said that there were tears upon his cheeks.

Nine days after the coronation, the young king departed Oldtown for King's Landing. Most of his court traveled with him in what became a grand pageant across the Reach . . . but his sister Rhaena stayed with them only as far as Highgarden, where she mounted her dragon, Dreamfyre, to return to Fair Isle and Lord Farman's castle above the sea, taking her leave not only of the king, but of her daughters. Rhaella, a novice sworn to the Faith, had remained at the Starry Sept, whilst her twin, Aerea, continued on with the king to the Red Keep, where she was to serve as a cupbearer and companion to the Princess Alysanne.

Yet a curious thing befell Queen Rhaena's girls after the king's coronation, it was observed. The twins had ever been mirror images of each other in appearance, but not in temperament. Whereas Rhaella was said to be a bold and willful child and a terror to the septas who had been given charge of her, Aerea had been known as a shy, timid creature, much given to tears and fears. "She is frightened of horses, dogs, boys with loud voices, men with beards, and dancing, and she is terrified of dragons," Grand Maester Benifer wrote when Aerea first came to court.

That was before Maegor's fall and Jaehaerys's coronation, however. Afterward, the girl who remained at Oldtown devoted herself to prayer and study, and never again required chastisement, whereas the girl who returned to King's Landing proved to be lively, quick-witted, and adventurous, and was soon spending half her days in the kennels, the stables, and the dragon yards. Though nothing was ever proved, it was widely believed that someone—Queen Rhaena herself, mayhaps, or her mother, Queen Alyssa—had used the occasion of the king's coronation to switch the twins. If so, no one was inclined to question the deception, for until such time as Jaehaerys sired an heir of the body, Princess Aerea (or the girl who now bore that name) was the heir to the Iron Throne.

All reports agree that the king's return from Oldtown to King's Landing was a triumph. Ser Joffrey rode by his side, and all along the route they were hailed by cheering throngs. Here and there Poor Fellows appeared, gaunt unwashed fellows with long beards and great axes, to beg for the same clemency that had been granted the Red Dog. This Jaehaerys granted them, on the condition that they agreed to journey north and join the

Night's Watch at the Wall. Hundreds swore to do so, amongst them no less a personage than Rob the Starvling. "Within a moon's turn of being crowned," Grand Maester Benifer wrote, "King Jaehaerys had reconciled the Iron Throne to the Faith and put an end to the bloodshed that had troubled the reigns of his uncle and father."

The Year of the Three Brides

49 AC

The 49th year after Aegon's Conquest gave the people of Westeros a welcome respite from the chaos and conflict that had gone before. It would be a year of peace, plenty, and marriage, remembered in the annals of the Seven Kingdoms as the Year of the Three Brides.

The new year was but a fortnight old when news of the first of the three weddings came out of the west, from Fair Isle by the Sunset Sea. There, in a small swift ceremony under the sky, Rhaena Targaryen wed Androw Farman, the second son of the Lord of Fair Isle. It was the groom's first marriage, the bride's third. Though twice widowed, Rhaena was but twenty-six. Her new husband, just ten-and-seven, was notably younger, a comely and amiable youth said to be utterly besotted with his new wife.

Their wedding was presided over by the groom's father, Marq Farman, Lord of Fair Isle, and conducted by his own septon. Lyman Lannister, Lord of Casterly Rock, and his wife, Jocasta, were the only great lords in attendance. Two of Rhaena's former favorites, Samantha Stokeworth and Alayne Royce, made their way to Fair Isle in some haste to stand with the widowed queen, together with the groom's high-spirited sister, the Lady Elissa. The remainder of the guests were bannermen and household knights sworn to either House Farman or House Lannister. King and court remained entirely ignorant of the marriage until a raven from the Rock brought word, days after the wedding feast and the bedding that sealed the match.

Chroniclers in King's Landing report that Queen Alyssa was deeply offended by her exclusion from her daughter's wedding, and that relations between mother and child were never as warm afterward, whereas Lord Rogar Baratheon was furious that Rhaena had dared remarry without the Crown's leave . . . the Crown in this instance being himself, as the young king's Hand. Had leave been asked, however, there was no certainty it would have been granted, for Androw Farman, the second son of a minor lord, was thought by many to be far from worthy of the hand of a woman who had been twice a queen and remained the mother of the king's heir. (As it happened, the youngest of Lord Rogar's brothers remained unwed as of 49 AC, and his lordship had two nephews by another brother who were also of a suitable age and lineage to be considered potential mates for a Targaryen widow, facts which might well explain both the Hand's anger and the secrecy with which Queen Rhaena wed.) King Jaehaerys himself and his sister Alysanne rejoiced at the tidings, dispatching gifts and congratulations to Fair Isle and commanding that the Red Keep's bells be rung in celebration.

Whilst Rhaena Targaryen was celebrating her marriage on Fair Isle, back in King's Landing King Jaehaerys and his mother, the Queen Regent, were busy selecting the councillors who would help them rule the realm for the next two years. Conciliation remained their guiding principle, for the divisions that had so recently torn Westeros apart were far from healed. Rewarding his own loyalists and excluding Maegor's men and the Faithful from power would only exacerbate the wounds and give rise to new grievances, the young king reasoned. His mother agreed.

Accordingly, Jaehaerys reached out to the Lord of Claw Isle, Edwell Celtigar, who had been Hand of the King under Maegor, and recalled him to King's Landing to serve as lord treasurer and master of coin. For lord admiral and master of ships, the young king turned to his uncle Daemon Velaryon, Lord of the Tides, Queen Alyssa's brother and one of the first great lords to abandon Maegor the Cruel. Prentys Tully, Lord of Riverrun, was summoned to court to serve as master of laws; with him came his redoubtable wife, the Lady Lucinda, far famed for her piety. Command of the City Watch, the largest armed force in King's Landing, the king entrusted to Qarl Corbray, Lord of Heart's Home, who had fought beside Aegon the Uncrowned beneath the Gods Eye. Above them all stood Rogar Baratheon, Lord of Storm's End and Hand of the King.

It would be a mistake to underestimate the influence of Jaehaerys Targaryen himself during the years of his regency, for despite his youth the boy king had a seat at most every council (but not all, as will be told shortly) and was never shy about letting his voice be heard. In the end, however, the final authority throughout this period rested with his mother, the Queen Regent, and the Hand, a redoubtable man in his own right.

Blue-eyed and black-bearded and muscled like a bull, Lord Rogar was the eldest of five brothers, all grandsons of Orys One-Hand, the first Baratheon Lord of Storm's End. Orys had been a bastard brother to Aegon the Conqueror and his most trusted commander. After slaying Argilac the Arrogant, last of the Durrandon, he had taken Argilac's daughter to wife. Lord Rogar could thus claim that both the blood of the dragon and that of the storm kings of old flowed in his veins. No swordsman, his lordship preferred to wield a double-bladed axe in battle . . . an axe, he oft said, "large and heavy enough to cleave through a dragon's skull."

Those were dangerous words during the reign of Maegor the Cruel, but if Rogar Baratheon feared Maegor's wroth, he hid it well. Men who knew him were unsurprised when he gave shelter to Queen Alyssa and her children after their flight from Dragonstone, and when he was the first to proclaim Prince Jaehaerys king. His own brother Borys was heard to say that Rogar dreamed of facing King Maegor in single combat and cutting him down with his axe.

That dream fate denied him. Instead of a kingslayer, Lord Rogar became a kingmaker, delivering to Prince Jaehaerys the Iron Throne. Few questioned his right to take his place at the side of the young king as Hand; some went so far as to whisper that it would be Rogar Baratheon who ruled the realm henceforth, for Jaehaerys was a boy and the son of a weak father, whilst his mother was only a woman. And when it was announced that Lord Rogar and Queen Alyssa were to marry, the whispers grew louder . . . for what is a queen's lord husband, if not a king?

Lord Rogar had been married once before, but his wife had died young, taken off by a fever less than a year after their wedding. The Queen Regent Alyssa was forty-two years old, and thought to be past her childbearing years; the Lord of Storm's End, ten years her junior. Writing some years later, Septon Barth tells us that Jaehaerys was opposed to the marriage; the young king felt that his Hand was overreaching himself, motivated more by a desire for power and position than a true affection for his mother. He was angry that neither his mother nor her suitor had sought his leave as well, Barth said . . . but as he had raised no objections to his sister's marriage, the king did not believe he had the right to prevent his mother's. Jaehaerys thus held his tongue and gave no hint of his misgivings save to a few close confidants.

The Hand was admired for his courage, respected for his strength, feared for his military prowess and skill at arms. The Queen Regent was loved. *So beautiful, so brave, so tragic,* women said of her. Even such lords as might have balked at a woman ruling over them were willing to accept her as their liege, secure in the knowledge that she had Rogar Baratheon standing beside her, and the young king little more than a year away from his sixteenth nameday.

She had been a beautiful child, all men agreed, the daughter of the mighty Aethan Velaryon, Lord of the Tides, and his lady wife Alarra of House Massey. Her line was ancient, proud, and rich, her mother esteemed as a great beauty, her grandsire amongst the oldest and closest friends of Aegon the Dragon and his queens. The gods blessed Alyssa herself with the deep purple eyes and shining silvery hair of Old Valyria, and gave her charm and wit and kindness as well, and as she grew suitors flocked around her from every corner of the realm. There was never any true question of whom she would wed, however. For a girl such as her, only royalty would suffice, and in the year 22 AC she married Prince Aenys Targaryen, the unquestioned heir to the Iron Throne.

Theirs was a happy and fruitful marriage. Prince Aenys was a gentle and attentive husband, warm-natured, generous, and never unfaithful. Alyssa bore him five strong, healthy children, two daughters and three sons (a sixth child, another daughter, died in her cradle shortly after birth), and when his sire died in 37 AC, the crown passed to Aenys, and Alyssa became his queen.

In the years that followed, she saw her husband's reign crumble and turn to ash, as enemies rose up all around him. In 42 AC he died, a broken man and despised, only five-and-thirty years of age. The queen scarce had time to grieve for him before his brother seized the throne that rightly belonged to her eldest son. She saw her son rise up against his uncle and die, together with his dragon. A short while later, her second son followed him to the funeral pyre, tortured to death by Tyanna of the Tower. Together with her two youngest children, Alyssa was made a prisoner in all but name of the man who had brought about the death of her sons, and was made to bear witness when her eldest daughter was forced into marriage to that same monster.

The game of thrones takes many a queer turn, however, and Maegor himself had fallen in turn, in no small part thanks to the courage of the widowed Queen Alyssa, and the boldness of Lord Rogar, who had befriended her and taken her in when no one else would. The gods had been good to them and granted them victory, and now the woman who had been Alyssa of House Velaryon was to be given a second chance at happiness with a new husband.

The wedding of the King's Hand and the Queen Regent was to be as splendid as that of the widowed Queen Rhaena had been modest. The High Septon himself would perform the marriage rites, on the seventh day of the seventh moon of the new year. The site would be the half-completed Dragonpit, still open to the sky, whose rising tiers of stone benches would allow for tens of thousands to observe the nuptials. The celebrations would include a great tourney, seven days of feasts and frolics, and even a mock sea battle to be fought in the waters of Blackwater Bay.

No wedding half so magnificent had been celebrated in Westeros in living memory, and lords great and small from throughout the Seven Kingdoms and beyond gathered to be part of it. Donnel Hightower came up from Oldtown with a hundred knights and seventy-seven of the Most Devout, escorting His High Holiness the High Septon, whilst Lyman Lannister brought three hundred knights from Casterly Rock. Brandon Stark, the ailing Lord of Winterfell, made the long journey down from the North with his sons Walton and Alaric, attended by a dozen fierce northern bannermen and thirty Sworn Brothers of the Night's Watch. Lords Arryn, Corbray, and Royce represented the Vale, Lords Selmy, Dondarrion, and Tarly the Dornish Marches. Even from beyond the borders of the realm the great and mighty came; the Prince of Dorne sent his sister, the Sealord of Braavos a son. The Archon of Tyrosh crossed the narrow sea himself with his maiden daughter, as did no fewer than twenty-two magisters from the Free City of Pentos. All brought handsome gifts to bestow on the Hand and Queen Regent; the most lavish came from those who had only lately been Maegor's men, and from Rickard Rowan and Torgen Oakheart, who had marched with Septon Moon.

The wedding guests came ostensibly to celebrate the union of Rogar Baratheon and the Dowager Queen, but they had other reasons for attendance, it should not be doubted. Many wished to treat with the Hand, who was seen by many as the true power in the realm; others wished to take the measure of their new boy king. Nor did His Grace deny them that opportunity. Ser Gyles Morrigen, the king's champion and sworn shield, announced that Jaehaerys would be pleased to grant audience to any lord or landed knight who wished to meet with him, and sixscore accepted his invitation. Eschewing the great hall and the majesty of the Iron Throne, the young king entertained the lords in the intimacy of his solar, attended only by Ser Gyles, a maester, and a few servants.

There, it is said, he encouraged each man to speak freely and share his views on the problems of the realm and how they might best be overcome. "He is not his father's son," Lord Royce told his maester afterward; grudging praise mayhaps, but praise all the same. Lord Vance of Wayfarer's Rest was heard to say, "He listens well, but says little." Rickard Rowan found Jaehaerys gentle and soft-spoken, Kyle Connington thought him witty and good-humored, Morton Caron cautious and shrewd. "He laughs often and freely, even at himself," Jon Mertyns said approvingly, but Alec Hunter thought him stern, and Torgen Oakheart grim. Lord Mallister pronounced him wise beyond his years, whilst Lord Darry said he promised to be "the sort of king any lord should be proud to kneel to." The most profound praise came from Brandon Stark, Lord of Winterfell, who said, "I see his grandsire in him."

The King's Hand attended none of these audiences, but it should not be thought that Lord Rogar was an inattentive host. The hours his lordship spent with his guests were devoted to other pursuits, however. He hunted with them, hawked with them, gambled with them, feasted with them, and "drank the royal cellars dry." After the wedding, when the tourney began, Lord Rogar was present for every tilt and every melee, surrounded by a lively and oft drunken coterie of great lords and famous knights.

The most notorious of his lordship's entertainments occurred two days before the ceremony, however. Though no record of it exists in any court chronicle, tales told by servants and repeated for many years thereafter amongst the smallfolk claim that Lord Rogar's brothers had brought seven virgins across the narrow sea from the finest pleasure houses of Lys. Queen Alyssa had surrendered her own maidenhood many years before to Aenys Targaryen, so there could be no question of Lord Rogar deflowering her on their wedding night. The Lysene maidens were meant to make up for that lack. If the whispers heard about court afterward were true, his lordship supposedly plucked the flowers of four of the girls before exhaustion and drink did him in; his brothers, nephews, and friends did for the other three, along with twoscore older beauties who had sailed with them from Lys.

Whilst the Hand roistered and King Jaehaerys sat in audience with the lords of the realm, his sister Princess Alysanne entertained the highborn women who had come with them to King's Landing. The king's elder sister, Rhaena, had chosen not to attend the nuptials, preferring to remain on Fair Isle with her own new husband and her court, and the Queen Regent Alyssa was busy with preparations for the wedding, so the task of playing hostess to the wives, daughters, and sisters of the great and mighty fell to Alysanne. Though she had only recently turned thirteen, the young princess rose to the challenge brilliantly, all agreed. For seven days and seven nights, she broke her fast with one group of highborn ladies, dined with a second, supped with a third. She showed them the wonders of the Red Keep, sailed with them on Blackwater Bay, and rode with them about the city.

Alysanne Targaryen, the youngest child of King Aenys and Queen Alyssa, had been little known amongst the lords and ladies of the realm before then. Her childhood had been spent in the shadow of her brothers and her elder sister, Rhaena, and when she was spoken of at all it was as "the little maid" and "the other daughter." She was little, this was true; slim and slight of frame, Alysanne was oft described as pretty but seldom as beautiful, though she was born of a house renowned for beauty. Her eyes were blue rather than purple, her hair a mass of honey-colored curls. No man ever questioned her wits.

Later, it would be said of her that she learned to read before she was weaned, and the court fool would make japes about little Alysanne dribbling mother's milk on Valyrian scrolls as she tried to read whilst suckling at her wet nurse's teat. Had she been a boy she would surely have been sent to the Citadel to forge a maester's chain, Septon Barth would say of her . . . for that wise man esteemed her even more than her husband, whom he served for so long. That was far in the future, however; in 49 AC, Alysanne was but a girl of thirteen years, yet all the chronicles agree that she made a powerful impression on those who met her.

When the day of the wedding finally arrived, more than forty thousand smallfolk ascended the Hill of Rhaenys to the Dragonpit to bear witness to the union of the Queen Regent and the Hand. (Some observers put the count even higher.) Thousands more cheered Lord Rogar and Queen Alyssa in the streets as their procession made its way across the city, attended by hundreds of knights on caparisoned palfreys, and columns of septas ringing bells. "Never has there been such a glory in all the annals of Westeros," wrote Grand Maester Benifer. Lord Rogar was clad head to heel in cloth-of-gold beneath an antlered halfhelm, whilst his bride wore a greatcloak sparkling with gemstones, with the three-headed dragon of House Targaryen and the silver seahorse of the Velaryons facing one another on a divided field.

Yet for all the splendor of the bride and groom, it was the arrival of Alyssa's children that set King's Landing to talking for years to come. King Jaehaerys and Princess Alysanne were the last to appear, descending from a bright sky on their dragons, Vermithor and Silverwing (the Dragonpit still lacked the great dome that would be its crowning glory, it must be recalled), their great leathern wings stirring up clouds of sand as they came down side by side, to the awe and terror of the gathered multitudes. (The oft-told tale that the arrival of the dragons caused the aged High Septon to soil his robes is likely only a calumny.)

Of the ceremony itself, and the feast and bedding that followed in due course, we need say little. The Red Keep's cavernous throne room hosted the greatest of the lords and the most distinguished of the visitors from across the sea; lesser lords, together with their knights and men-at-arms, celebrated in the yards and smaller halls of the castle, whilst the smallfolk of King's Landing made merry in a hundred inns, wine sinks, pot shops, and brothels. Notwithstanding his purported exertions two nights prior, it is reliably reported that Lord Rogar performed his husbandly duties with vigor, cheered on by his drunken brothers.

Seven days of tourney followed the wedding, and kept the gathered lords and the people of the city enthralled. The tilts were as hard-fought and thrilling as had been seen in Westeros in many a year, all agreed . . . but it was the battles fought afoot with sword and spear and axe that truly excited the passions of the crowd on this occasion, and for good reason.

It will be recalled that three of the seven knights who served as Maegor the Cruel's Kingsguard were dead; the remaining four had been sent to the Wall to take the black. In their places, King Jaehaerys had thus far named only Ser Gyles Morrigen and Ser Joffrey Doggett. It was the Queen Regent, Alyssa, who first put forward the idea that the remaining five vacancies be filled through test of arms, and what better occasion for it than the wedding, when knights from all over the realm would gather? "Maegor had old men, lickspittles, cravens, and brutes about him," she declared. "I want the knights protecting my son to be the finest to be found anywhere in Westeros, true honest men whose loyalty and courage is unquestioned. Let them win their cloaks with deeds of arms, whilst all the realm looks on."

King Jaehaerys was quick to second his mother's notion, but with a practical twist of his own. Sagely, the young king decreed that his would-be protectors should prove their prowess afoot, not in the joust. "Men who would do harm to their king seldom attack on horseback with lance in hand," His Grace declared. And so it was that the tilts that followed his mother's wedding yielded pride of place to the wild melees and bloody duels the maesters would dub the War for the White Cloaks.

With hundreds of knights eager to compete for the honor of serving in the Kingsguard, the combats lasted seven full days. Several of the more colorful competitors became favorites of the smallfolk, who cheered them raucously each time they fought. One such was the Drunken Knight, Ser Willam Stafford, a short, stout, big-bellied man who always appeared so intoxicated that it was a wonder he could stand, let alone fight. The commons named him "the Keg o' Ale," and sang "Hail, Hail, Keg o' Ale" whenever he took the field. Another favorite of the commons was the Bard of Flea Bottom, Tom the Strummer, who mocked his foes with ribald songs before each bout. The slender mystery knight known only as the Serpent in Scarlet also had a great following; when finally defeated and unmasked, "he" proved to be a woman, Jonquil Darke, a bastard daughter of the Lord of Duskendale.

In the end, none of these would earn a white cloak. The knights who did, though less madcap, proved themselves second to none in valor, chivalry, and skill at arms. Only one was the scion of a lordly house; Ser Lorence Roxton, from the Reach. Two were sworn swords; Ser Victor the Valiant, from the household of Lord Royce of Runestone, and Ser Willam the Wasp, who served Lord Smallwood of Acorn Hall. The youngest champion, Pate the Woodcock, fought with a spear instead of a sword, and some questioned whether he was a knight at all, but he proved so skillful with his chosen weapon that Ser Joffrey Doggett settled the matter by dubbing the lad himself, whilst hundreds cheered.

The eldest champion was a grizzled hedge knight named Samgood of Sour Hill, a scarred and battered man of three-and-sixty who claimed to have fought in a hundred battles "and never you mind on what side, that's for me and the gods to know." One-eyed, bald, and almost toothless, the knight called Sour Sam looked as gaunt as a fencepost, but in battle he displayed the quickness of a man half his age, and a vicious skill honed through long decades of battles great and small.

Jaehaerys the Conciliator would sit the Iron Throne for fifty-five years, and many a knight would wear a white cloak in his service during that long reign, more than any other monarch could boast. But it was rightly said that never did any Targaryen possess a Kingsguard who could equal the boy king's first Seven.

The War for the White Cloaks marked the end of the festivities of what soon became known as the Golden Wedding. As the visitors took their leaves to wend their way home to their own lands and keeps, all agreed that it had been a magnificent event. The young king had won the admiration and affection of many lords both great and small, and their sisters, wives, and daughters had only praise for the warmth shown them by Princess Alysanne. The smallfolk of King's Landing were pleased as well; their boy king seemed to have every sign of being a just, merciful, and chivalrous ruler, and his Hand, Lord Rogar, was as open-handed as he was bold in battle. Happiest of all were the city's innkeeps, taverners, brewers, merchants, cutpurses, whores, and brothel keepers, all of whom had profited mightily from the coin the visitors brought to the city.

Yet though the Golden Wedding was the most lavish and far-famed of the nuptials of 49 AC, the third of the marriages made in that fateful year would prove to be the most significant.

With their own wedding now safely behind them, the Queen Regent and the King's Hand next turned their attention to finding a suitable match for King Jaehaerys . . . and, to a lesser extent, for his sister Princess Alysanne. So long as the boy king remained unwed and without issue, the daughters of his sister Rhaena would remain his heirs . . . but Aerea and

Rhaella were still children, and, it was felt by many, manifestly unfit for the crown.

Moreover, Lord Rogar and Queen Alyssa both feared what might befall the realm should Rhaena Targaryen return from the west to act as regent for a daughter. Though none dared speak of it, it was plain that discord had arisen between the two queens, for the daughter had neither attended her mother's wedding nor invited her to her own. And there were some who went further and whispered that Rhaena was a sorceress, who had used the dark arts to murder Maegor upon the Iron Throne. Therefore it was incumbent upon King Jaehaerys to marry and beget a son as soon as possible.

The question of *who* the young king might marry was less easily resolved. Lord Rogar, who was known to harbor thoughts of extending the power of the Iron Throne across the narrow sea to Essos, put forward the notion of forging an alliance with Tyrosh by wedding Jaehaerys to the Archon's daughter, a comely girl of fifteen years who had charmed all at the wedding with her wit, her flirtatious manner, and her blue-green hair.

In this, however, his lordship found himself opposed by his own wife, Queen Alyssa. The smallfolk of Westeros would never accept a foreign girl with dyed tresses as their queen, she argued, no matter how delightful her accent. And the pious would oppose the girl bitterly, for it was known that the Tyroshi kept not the Seven, but worshipped Red R'hllor, the Patternmaker, three-headed Trios, and other queer gods. Her own preference was to look to the houses who had risen in support of Aegon the Uncrowned in the Battle Beneath the Gods Eye. Let Jaehaerys wed a Vance, a Corbray, a Westerling, or a Piper, she urged. Loyalty should be rewarded, and by making such a match the king would honor Aegon's memory, and the valor of those who fought and died for him.

It was Grand Maester Benifer who spoke loudest against such a course, pointing out that the sincerity of their commitment to peace and reconciliation might be doubted if they were seen to favor those who had fought for Aegon over those who had remained with Maegor. A better choice, he felt, would be a daughter of one of the great houses that had taken little or no part in the battles between uncle and nephew; a Tyrell, a Hightower, an Arryn.

With the King's Hand, the Queen Regent, and the Grand Maester so divided, other councillors felt emboldened to put forward candidates of their own. Prentys Tully, the royal justiciar, nominated a younger sister of his own wife, Lucinda, famed for her piety. Such a choice would surely please the Faith. Daemon Velaryon, the lord admiral, suggested that Jaehaerys might marry the widowed Queen Elinor, of House Costayne. How better to show that Maegor's supporters had been forgiven than by taking one of his Black Brides to queen, mayhaps even adopting her three sons by her first marriage. Queen Elinor's proven fertility was another point in her favor, he argued. Lord Celtigar had two unwed daughters, and had famously offered Maegor his choice of them; now he offered the same girls again for Jaehaerys. Lord Baratheon was having none of it. "I have seen your daughters," Rogar said to Celtigar. "They have no chins, no teats, and no sense."

The Queen Regent and her councillors discussed the question of the king's marriage time and time again over most of a moon's turn, but came no closer to reaching a consensus. Jaehaerys himself was not privy to these debates. On this Queen Alyssa and Lord Rogar agreed. Though Jaehaerys might well be wise beyond his years, he was still a boy, and ruled by a boy's desires, desires that on no account could be allowed to overrule the good of the realm. Queen Alyssa in particular had no doubt whatsoever about whom her son would choose to marry were the choice left to him: her youngest daughter, his sister the Princess Alysanne.

The Targaryens had been marrying brother to sister for centuries, of course, and Jaehaerys and Alysanne had grown up expecting to wed, just as their elder siblings Aegon and Rhaena had. Morever, Alysanne was only two years younger than her brother, and the two children had always been close and strong in their affection and regard for one another. Their father, King Aenys, would certainly have wished for them to marry, and once that would have been their mother's wish as well . . . but the horrors she had witnessed since her husband's death had persuaded Queen Alyssa to think elsewise. Though the Warrior's Sons and Poor Fellows had been disbanded and outlawed, many former members of both orders remained at large in the realm and might well take up their swords again if provoked. The Queen Regent feared their wroth, for she had vivid memories of all that had befallen her son Aegon and her daughter Rhaena when their marriage was announced. "We dare not ride that road again," she is reported to have said, more than once.

In this resolve she was supported by the newest member of the court, Septon Mattheus of the Most Devout, who had remained in King's Landing when the High Septon and the rest of his brethren returned to Oldtown. A great whale of a man, as famed for his corpulence as for the magnificence of his robes, Mattheus claimed descent from the Gardener kings of old, who had once ruled the Reach from their seat at Highgarden. Many regarded him as a near certainty to be chosen as the next High Septon.

The present occupant of that holy office, whom Septon Moon had derided as the High Lickspittle, was cautious and complaisant, so there was little to no danger of any marriage being denounced from Oldtown so long as he continued to speak for the Seven from his seat in the Starry Sept. The Father of the Faithful was not a young man, however; the journey to King's Landing to officiate at the Golden Wedding had almost been the end of him, men said.

"If it should fall to me to don his mantle, His Grace of course would have my support in any choice he might make," Septon Mattheus assured the Queen Regent and her advisors, "but not all of my brethren are so inclined, and . . . dare I say . . . there are other Moons out there. Given all that has occurred, to marry brother to sister at this juncture would be seen as a grievous affront to the pious, and I fear for what might happen."

Their queen's misgivings thus confirmed, Rogar Baratheon and the other lords put aside all consideration of Princess Alysanne as a bride for her brother Jaehaerys. The princess was three-and-ten years of age, and had recently celebrated her first flowering, so it was thought desirable to see her wed as soon as possible. Though still far apart as regarded a suitable match for the king, the council settled swiftly on a partner for the princess; she would be married on the seventh day of the new year, to Orryn Baratheon, the youngest of Lord Rogar's brothers.

Thus it was settled by the Queen Regent and the King's Hand and their lords councillors and advisors. But like many such arrangements through the ages, their plan was soon undone, for they had grievously underestimated the will and determination of Alysanne Targaryen herself, and her young king, Jaehaerys.

No announcement had yet been made of Alysanne's betrothal, so it is not known how word of the decision reached her ears. Grand Maester Benifer suspected a servant, for many such had come and gone whilst the lords debated in the queen's solar. Lord Rogar himself was suspicious of Daemon Velaryon, the lord admiral, a prideful man who might well have believed that the Baratheons were overreaching themselves in hopes of displacing the Lords of the Tide as the second house in the realm. Years later, when these events had passed into legend, the smallfolk would tell each other that "rats in the walls" had overheard the lords talking and rushed to the princess with the news.

No record survives of what Alysanne Targaryen said or thought when first she learned that she was to be wed to a youth ten years her senior, whom she scarcely knew and (if rumor can be believed) did not like. We know only what she did. Another girl might have wept or raged or run pleading to her mother. In many a sad song, maidens forced to wed against their will throw themselves from tall towers to their deaths. Princess Alysanne did none of these things. Instead she went directly to Jaehaerys.

The young king was as displeased as his sister at the news. "They will be making wedding plans for me as well, I do not doubt," he deduced at once. Like his sister, Jaehaerys did not waste time with reproaches, recriminations, or appeals. Instead he acted. Summoning his Kingsguard, he instructed them to sail at once for Dragonstone, where he would meet them shortly. "You have sworn me your swords and your obedience," he reminded his Seven. "Remember those vows, and speak no word of my departure."

That night, under cover of darkness, King Jaehaerys and Princess Alysanne mounted their dragons, Vermithor and Silverwing, and departed the Red Keep for the ancient Targaryen citadel below the Dragonmont. Reportedly the first words the young king spoke upon landing were, "I have need of a septon."

The king, rightly, had no trust in Septon Mattheus, who would surely have betrayed their plans, but the sept on Dragonstone was tended by an old man named Oswyck, who had known Jaehaerys and Alysanne since their births, and instructed them in the mysteries of the Seven throughout their childhood. As a younger man, Septon Oswyck had ministered to King Aenys, and as a boy he had served as a novice in the court of Queen Rhaenys. He was more than familiar with the Targaryen tradition of sibling marriage, and when he heard the king's command, he assented at once.

The Kingsguard arrived from King's Landing by galley a few days later. The following morning, as the sun rose, Jaehaerys Targaryen, the First of His Name, took to wife his sister Alysanne in the great yard at Dragonstone, before the eyes of gods and men and dragons. Septon Oswyck performed the marriage rites; though the old man's voice was thin and tremulous, no part of the ceremony was neglected. The seven knights of the Kingsguard stood witness to the union, their white cloaks snapping in the wind. The castle's garrison and servants looked on as well, together with a good part of the smallfolk of the fishing village that huddled below Dragonstone's mighty curtain walls.

A modest feast followed the ceremony, and many toasts were drunk to the health of the boy king and his new queen. Afterward Jaehaerys and Alysanne retired to the bedchamber where Aegon the Conqueror had once slept beside his sister Rhaenys, but in view of the bride's youth there was no bedding ceremony, and the marriage was not consummated.

That omission would prove to be of great importance when Lord Rogar and Queen Alyssa arrived belatedly from King's Landing in a war galley, accompanied by a dozen knights, forty men-at-arms, Septon Mattheus, and Grand Maester Benifer, whose letters give us the most complete accounting of what transpired.

Jaehaerys and Alysanne met them inside the castle gates, holding hands. It is said that Queen Alyssa wept when she saw them. "You foolish children," she said. "You know not what you've done."

Then up spoke Septon Mattheus, his voice thunderous as he berated the king and queen and prophesized that this abomination would once

more plunge all of Westeros into war. "They shall curse your incest from the Dornish Marches to the Wall, and every pious son of the Mother and the Father shall denounce you as the sinners you are." The septon's face grew red and swollen as he raved, Benifer tells us, and spittle sprayed from his lips.

Jaehaerys the Conciliator is rightly honored in the annals of the Seven Kingdoms for his calm demeanor and even temper, but let no man think that the fire of the Targaryens did not burn in his veins. He showed it then. When Septon Mattheus finally paused for a breath, the king said, "I will accept chastisement from Her Grace my mother, but not from you. Hold your tongue, fat man. If another word passes your lips, I will have them sewn shut."

Septon Mattheus spoke no more.

Lord Rogar was not so easily cowed. Blunt and to the point, he asked only if the marriage had been consummated. "Tell me true, Your Grace. Was there a bedding? Did you claim her maidenhead?"

"No," the king replied. "She is too young."

At that Lord Rogar smiled. "Good. You are not wed." He turned to the knights who had accompanied him from King's Landing. "Separate these children, gently if you please. Escort the princess to Sea Dragon Tower and keep her there. His Grace shall accompany us back to the Red Keep."

But as his men moved forward, the seven knights of Jaehaerys's Kingsguard stepped up and drew their swords. "Come no closer," warned Ser Gyles Morrigen. "Any man who lays a hand upon our king and queen shall die today."

Lord Rogar was dismayed. "Sheath your steel and move aside," he commanded. "Have you forgotten? I am the King's Hand."

"Aye," old Sour Sam answered, "but we're the Kingsguard, not the Hand's guard, and it's the lad who sits the chair, not you."

Rogar Baratheon bristled at Ser Samgood's words, and answered, "You are seven. I have half a hundred swords behind me. A word from me and they will cut you to pieces."

"They might kill us," replied young Pate the Woodcock, brandishing his spear, "but you will be the first to die, m'lord, you have my word upon that."

What might have happened next no man can say, had not Queen Alyssa chosen that moment to speak. "I have seen enough death," she said. "So have we all. Put up your swords, sers. What is done is done, and now we all must needs live with it. May the gods have mercy on the realm." She turned to her children. "We shall go in peace. Let no man speak of what happened here today."

"As you command, Mother." King Jaehaerys pulled his sister closer and put his arm around her. "But do not think that you shall unmake this marriage. We are one now, and neither gods nor men shall part us."

"Never," his bride affirmed. "Send me to the ends of the earth and wed me to the King of Mossovy or the Lord of the Grey Waste, Silverwing will always bring me back to Jaehaerys." And with that she raised herself onto her toes and lifted her face to the king, and he kissed her full upon the lips whilst all looked on.*

When the Hand and the Queen Regent had made their departure, the king and his young bride closed the castle gates and returned to their chambers. Dragonstone would remain their refuge and their residence for the remainder of Jaehaerys's minority. It is written that the young king and queen were seldom apart during that time, sharing every meal, talking late into the night of the green days of their childhood and the challenges ahead, fishing and hawking together, mingling with the island's smallfolk in dockside inns, reading to one another from dusty leatherbound tomes they found in the castle library, taking lessons together from Dragon-

* Or so the confrontation at the gates of Dragonstone was set down by Grand Maester Benifer, who was there to witness it. From that day to this, the tale has been a favorite of lovesick maidens and their squires throughout the Seven Kingdoms, and many a bard has sung of the valor of the Kingsguard, seven men in white cloaks who faced down half a hundred. All of these tellings overlook the presence of the castle garrison, however; such records as have come down to us indicate that twenty archers and as many guardsmen were stationed on Dragonstone at this time, under the command of Ser Merrell Bullock and his sons Alyn and Howard. Where their loyalties lay at this time and what part they might have played in any conflict shall never be known, but to suggest the king's Seven stood alone mayhaps presumes too much.

stone's maesters ("for we still have much to learn," Alysanne is said to have reminded her husband), praying beside Septon Oswyck. They flew together as well, all around the Dragonmont and oft as far as Driftmark.

If servants' tales may be believed, the king and his new queen slept naked and shared many long and lingering kisses, abed and at table and at many other times throughout the day, yet never consummated their union. Another year and a half would pass before Jaehaerys and Alysanne would finally join as man and woman.

Whenever lords and council members traveled to Dragonstone to consult with the young king, as they did from time to time, Jaehaerys received them in the Chamber of the Painted Table where his grandsire had once planned his conquest of Westeros, with Alysanne ever by his side. "Aegon had no secrets from Rhaenys and Visenya, and I have none from Alysanne," he said.

Though it might well have been that there were no secrets between them during these bright days in the morning of the marriage, their union itself remained a secret to most of Westeros. Upon their return to King's Landing, Lord Rogar instructed all those who had accompanied them to Dragonstone to speak no word of what had transpired there, if they wished to keep their tongues. Nor was any announcement made to the realm at large. When Septon Mattheus attempted to send word of the match to the High Septon and Most Devout in Oldtown, Grand Maester Benifer burned his letter rather than dispatch a raven, on orders from the Hand.

The Lord of Storm's End wanted time. Angry at the disrespect he felt the king had shown him and unaccustomed to defeat, Rogar Baratheon remained determined to find a way to part Jaehaerys and Alysanne. So long as their marriage remained unconsummated, he believed, a chance remained. Best then to keep the wedding secret, so it might be undone without anyone being the wiser.

Queen Alyssa wanted time as well, though for a different reason. *What is done is done,* she had said at the gates of Dragonstone, and so she believed . . . but memories of the bloodshed and chaos that had greeted the marriage of her other son and daughter still haunted her nights, and the

Queen Regent was desperate to find some way to ascertain that history would not be repeated.

Meanwhile, she and her lord husband still had a realm to rule for the best part of a year, until Jaehaerys attained his sixteenth nameday and took the power into his own hands.

And so matters stood in Westeros as the Year of the Three Brides drew to an end, and gave way to a new year, the 50th since Aegon's Conquest.

A Surfeit of Rulers

All men are sinners, the Fathers of the Faith teach us. Even the noblest of kings and the most chivalrous of knights may find themselves overcome by rage and lust and envy, and commit acts that shame them and tarnish their good names. And the vilest of men and the wickedest of women likewise may do good from time to time, for love and compassion and pity may be found in even the blackest of hearts. "We are as the gods made us," wrote Septon Barth, the wisest man ever to serve as the Hand of the King, "strong and weak, good and bad, cruel and kind, heroic and selfish. Know that if you would rule over the kingdoms of men."

Seldom was the truth of his words seen as clearly as during the 50th year after Aegon's Conquest. As the new year dawned, all across the realm plans were being made to mark a half century of Targaryen rule over Westeros with feasts, fairs, and tourneys. The horrors of King Maegor's rule were receding into the past, the Iron Throne and the Faith were reconciled, and the young King Jaehaerys I was the darling of smallfolk and great lords alike from Oldtown to the Wall. Yet unbeknownst to all but a few, storm clouds were gathering on the horizon, and faintly in the distance wise men could hear a rumble of thunder.

A realm with two kings is like a man with two heads, the smallfolk are wont to say. In 50 AC, the realm of Westeros found itself blessed with one king, a Hand, and three queens, as in King Maegor's day . . . but whereas Maegor's queens had been consorts, subservient to his will, living and dying at his whim, each of the queens of the half-century was a power in her own right.

In the Red Keep of King's Landing sat the Queen Regent Alyssa, widow of the late King Aenys, mother to his son Jaehaerys, and wife to the King's Hand, Rogar Baratheon. Just across Blackwater Bay on Dragonstone, a younger queen had arisen when Alyssa's daughter Alysanne, a maid of thirteen years, had pledged her troth to her brother King Jaehaerys, against the wishes of her mother and her mother's lord husband. And far to the west on Fair Isle, with the whole width of Westeros separating her from both mother and sister, was Alyssa's eldest daughter, the dragonrider Rhaena Targaryen, widow of Prince Aegon the Uncrowned. In the westerlands, riverlands, and parts of the Reach, men were already calling her the Queen in the West.

Two sisters and a mother, the three queens were bound by blood and grief and suffering . . . and yet between them lay shadows old and new, growing darker by the day. The amity and unity of purpose that had enabled Jaehaerys, his sisters, and their mother to topple Maegor the Cruel had begun to fray, as long-simmering resentments and divisions made themselves felt. For the remainder of the regency the boy king and his little queen would find themselves deeply at odds with the King's Hand and the Queen Regent, in a rivalry that would continue into Jaehaerys's own reign and threaten to plunge the Seven Kingdoms back into war.*

* It should be noted, lest we be charged with omission, that there was a fourth queen in Westeros in 50 AC. The twice-widowed Queen Elinor of House Costayne, who had found King Maegor dead upon the Iron Throne, had departed King's Landing after Jaehaerys's ascent. Dressed in the robes of a penitent and accompanied only by a handmaid and one leal man-at-arms, she made her way to the Eyrie in the Vale of Arryn to visit the eldest of her three sons by Ser Theo Bolling, and thence to Highgarden in the Reach, where her second son had been fostered to Lord Tyrell. Once satisfied of their well-being, the former queen reclaimed her youngest boy and repaired to her father's seat at Three Towers in the Reach, where she declared she would live quietly for the remainder of her life. Fate, and King Jaehaerys, had other plans for her, as we shall relate later. Suffice it to say that Queen Elinor played no role in the events of 50 AC.

The immediate cause of the tension was the king's sudden and secret marriage to his sister, which had taken the Hand and the Queen Regent unawares and thrown their own plans and schemes into disarray. It would be a mistake to believe that was the sole cause of the estrangement, however; the other weddings that had made 49 AC the Year of the Three Brides had also left scars.

Lord Rogar had never asked Jaehaerys for leave to wed his mother, an omission the boy king took for a sign of disrespect. Moreover, His Grace did not approve of the match; as he would later confess to Septon Barth, he valued Lord Rogar as a counselor and friend, but he did not need a second father, and thought his own judgment, temperament, and intelligence to be superior to his Hand's. Jaehaerys also felt he should have been consulted about his sister Rhaena's marriage, though he felt that slight less keenly. Queen Alyssa, for her part, was deeply hurt that she had neither been advised of nor invited to Rhaena's wedding on Fair Isle.

Away in the west, Rhaena Targaryen nursed her own grievances. As she confided to the old friends and favorites she had gathered around her, Queen Rhaena neither understood nor shared her mother's affection for Rogar Baratheon. Though she honored him grudgingly for rising in support of her brother Jaehaerys against their uncle Maegor, his inaction when her own husband, Prince Aegon, faced Maegor in the Battle Beneath the Gods Eye was something she could neither forget nor forgive. Also, with the passage of time Queen Rhaena grew ever more resentful that her own claim to the Iron Throne, and that of her daughters, had been disregarded in favor of that of "my baby brother" (as she was wont to call Jaehaerys). She was the firstborn, she reminded those who would listen, and had been a dragonrider before any of her siblings, yet all of them and "even my own mother" had conspired to pass her over.

Looking back now with the benefit of hindsight, it is easy to say that Jaehaerys and Alysanne had the right of it in the conflicts that arose during the last year of their mother's regency, and to cast Queen Alyssa and Lord Rogar as villains. That is how the singers tell the tale, certainly; the swift and sudden marriage of Jaehaerys and Alysanne was a romance unequaled since the days of Florian the Fool and his Jonquil, to hear them sing of it. And in songs, as ever, love conquers all. The truth, we submit, is a deal less simple. Queen Alyssa's misgivings about the match grew out of genuine concern for her children, the Targaryen dynasty, and the realm as a whole. Nor were her fears without foundation.

Lord Rogar Baratheon's motives were less selfless. A proud man, he had been stunned and angered by the "ingratitude" of the boy king he had regarded as a son, and humiliated when forced to back down at the gates of Dragonstone before half a hundred of his men. A warrior to the bone, Rogar had once dreamed of facing Maegor the Cruel in single combat, and could not stomach being shamed by a lad of fifteen years. Lest we think too harshly of him, however, we would do well to remember Septon Barth's words. Though he would do some cruel, foolish, and evil things during his last year as Hand, he was not a cruel or evil man at heart, nor even a fool; he had been a hero once, and we must remember that even as we look at the darkest year of his life.

In the immediate aftermath of his confrontation with Jaehaerys, Lord Rogar could think of little else but the humiliation he had suffered. His lordship's first impulse was to return to Dragonstone with more men, enough to overwhelm the castle garrison and resolve the situation by force. As for the Kingsguard, Lord Rogar reminded the council that the White Swords had sworn to lay down their lives for the king and "I shall be pleased to give them that honor." When Lord Tully pointed out that Jaehaerys could simply close the gates of Dragonstone against them, Lord Rogar was undeterred. "Let him. I can take the castle by storm if need be." In the end only Queen Alyssa could reach his lordship through his wroth and dissuade him from this folly. "My love," she said softly, "my children ride dragons, and we do not."

The Queen Regent, no less than her husband, wished to have the king's rash marriage undone, for she was convinced that word of it would once again set the Faith against the Crown. Her fears were fanned by Septon Mattheus; once away from Jaehaerys, and secure in the knowledge that his lips would not be sewn shut, the septon found his tongue again, and spoke of little else but how "all decent folk" would condemn the king's incestuous union.

Had Jaehaerys and Alysanne returned to King's Landing in time to celebrate the new year, as Queen Alyssa prayed ("They will come to their senses and repent this folly," she told the council), reconciliation might have been possible, but that did not happen. When a fortnight came and went and then another, and still the king did not reappear at court, Alyssa announced her intention to return to Dragonstone, this time alone, to beg her children to come home. Lord Rogar angrily forbade it. "If you go crawling back to him, the boy will never listen to you again," he said. "He has put his own desires ahead of the good of the realm, and that cannot be allowed. Do you want him to end as his father did?" And so the queen bent to his will and did not go.

"That Queen Alyssa wished to do the right thing, no man should doubt," Septon Barth wrote years later. "Sad to say, however, she oft seemed at a loss as to what that thing might be. She desired above all to be loved, admired, and praised, a yearning she shared with King Aenys, her first husband. A ruler must sometimes do things that are necessary but unpopular, however, though he knows that opprobrium and censure must surely follow. These things Queen Alyssa could seldom bring herself to do."

Days passed and turned to weeks and thence to fortnights, whilst hearts hardened and men grew more resolute on both sides of Blackwater Bay. The boy king and his little queen remained on Dragonstone, awaiting the day when Jaehaerys would take the rule of the Seven Kingdoms in his own hands. Queen Alyssa and Lord Rogar continued to hold the reins of power in King's Landing, searching for a way to undo the king's marriage and avert the calamity they were certain was to come. Aside from the council, they told no one of what had transpired on Dragonstone, and Lord Rogar commanded the men who had accompanied them to speak no word of what they had seen, at the penalty of losing their tongues. Once the marriage had been annulled, his lordship reasoned, it would be as if it had never happened so far as most of Westeros was concerned... so long as it remained secret. Until the union was consummated, it could still easily be set aside.

This would prove to be a vain hope, as we know now, but to Rogar

Baratheon in 50 AC it seemed possible. For a time he must surely have drawn encouragement from the king's own silence. Jaehaerys had moved swiftly to marry Alysanne, but having done the deed he seemed in no great haste to announce it. He certainly had the means to do so, had he so desired. Maester Culiper, still spry at eighty, had been serving since Queen Visenya's day, and was ably assisted by two younger maesters. Dragonstone had a full complement of ravens. At a word from Jaehaerys, his marriage could have been proclaimed from one end of the realm to the other. He did not speak that word.

Scholars have debated ever since as to the reasons for his silence. Was he repenting a match made in haste, as Queen Alyssa would have wished? Had Alysanne somehow offended him? Had he grown fearful of the realm's response to the marriage, recalling all that had befallen Aegon and Rhaena? Was it possible that Septon Mattheus's dire prophecies had shaken him more than he cared to admit? Or was he simply a boy of fifteen who had acted rashly with no thought to the consequences, only to find himself now at a loss as to how to proceed?

Arguments can and have been made for all these explanations, but in light of what we know now about Jaehaerys I Targaryen, they ultimately ring hollow. Young or old, this was a king who never acted without thinking. To this writer it seems plain that Jaehaerys was not repenting his marriage and had no intention of undoing it. He had chosen the queen he wanted and would make the realm aware of that in due course, but at a time of his own choosing, in a manner best calculated to lead to acceptance: when he was a man grown and a king ruling in his own right, not a boy who had wed in defiance of his regent's wishes.

The young king's absence from court did not go unnoticed for long. The ashes of the bonfires lit in celebration of the new year had scarce grown cold before the people of King's Landing began asking questions. To curtail the rumors, Queen Alyssa put out word that His Grace was resting and reflecting on Dragonstone, the ancient seat of his house . . . but as more time passed, with still no sign of Jaehaerys, lords and smallfolk alike began to wonder. Was the king ill? Had he been made a prisoner, for reasons yet unknown? The personable and handsome boy king had moved amongst the people of King's Landing so freely, seemingly delighting in mingling with them, that this sudden disappearance seemed unlike him.

Queen Alysanne, for her part, was in no haste to return to court. "Here I have you to myself, day and night," she told Jaehaerys. "When we go back, I shall be fortunate to snatch an hour with you, for every man in Westeros will want a piece of you." For her, these days on Dragonstone were an idyll. "Many years from now when we are old and grey, we shall look back upon these days and smile, remembering how happy we were."

Jaehaerys himself no doubt shared some of these sentiments, but the young king had other reasons for remaining on Dragonstone. Unlike his uncle Maegor, he was not prone to bursts of rage, but he was more than capable of anger, and he would never forget nor forgive his deliberate exclusion from the council meetings wherein his marriage and that of his sister were being discussed. And whilst he would always remain grateful to Rogar Baratheon for helping him to the Iron Throne, Jaehaerys did not intend to be ruled by him. "I had one father," he said to Maester Culiper during those days on Dragonstone, "I do not require a second." The king recognized and appreciated the virtues of the Hand, but he was aware of his flaws as well, flaws that had become very apparent in the days leading up to the Golden Wedding, when Jaehaerys himself had sat in audience with the lords of the realm whilst Lord Rogar was hunting, drinking, and deflowering maidens.

Jaehaerys was aware of his own shortcomings too—shortcomings he intended to rectify before he sat the Iron Throne. His father, King Aenys, had been slighted as weak, in part because he was not the warrior that his brother Maegor was. Jaehaerys was determined that no man would ever question his own courage or skill at arms. On Dragonstone he had Ser Merrell Bullock, commander of the castle garrison, his sons Ser Alyn and Ser Howard, a seasoned master-at-arms in Ser Elyas Scales, and his own Seven, the finest fighters in the realm. Every morning Jaehaerys trained with them in the castle yard, shouting at them to come at him harder, to press him, harry him, and attack him in every way they knew. From sunrise till noon he worked with them, honing his skills with sword and spear and mace and axe whilst his new queen looked on.

It was a hard and brutal regimen. Each bout ended only when the king himself or his opponent declared him dead. Jaehaerys died so often that the men of the garrison made a game of it, shouting "The king is dead" every time he fell, and "Long live the king" when he struggled to his feet. His foes began a contest, wagering with one another to see which of them could kill the king the most. (The victor, we are told, was young Ser Pate the Woodcock, whose darting spear purportedly gave His Grace fits.) Jaehaerys was oft bruised and bloody by evening, to Alysanne's distress, but his prowess improved so markedly that near the end of his time on Dragonstone, old Ser Elyas himself told him, "Your Grace, you will never be a Kingsguard, but if by some sorcery your uncle Maegor himself were to rise from the grave, my coin would be on you."

One evening, after a day in which Jaehaerys had been severely tested and battered, Maester Culiper said to him, "Your Grace, why do you pun-

ish yourself so harshly? The realm is at peace." The young king only smiled and replied, "The realm was at peace when my grandsire died, but scarcely had my father climbed onto the throne than foes rose up on every side. They were testing him, to learn if he was strong or weak. They will test me as well."

He was not wrong, though his first trial, when it came, was to be of a very different nature, one that no amount of training in the yards of Dragonstone could possibly have prepared him for. For it was his worth as a man, and his love for his little queen, that were to be put to the test.

We know very little about the childhood of Alysanne Targaryen; as the fifthborn child of King Aenys and Queen Alyssa, and a female, observers at court found her of less interest than her older siblings who stood higher in the line of succession. From what little has come down to us, Alysanne was a bright but unremarkable girl; small but never sickly, courteous, biddable, with a sweet smile and a pleasing voice. To the relief of her parents, she displayed none of the timidity that had afflicted her elder sister, Rhaena, as a small child. Neither did she exhibit the willful and stubborn temperament of Rhaena's daughter Aerea.

As a princess of the royal household, Alysanne would of course have had servants and companions from an early age. As an infant certainly she would have had a wet nurse; like most noble women, Queen Alyssa did not give suck to her own children. Later a maester would have taught her to read and write and do sums, and a septa would have instructed her in piety, deportment, and the mysteries of the Faith. Girls of common birth would have served as her maids, washing her clothing and emptying her chamberpot, and in good time she would certainly have taken ladies of a like age and noble blood as companions, to ride and play and sew with.

Alysanne did not choose these companions for herself; they were selected for her by her mother, Queen Alyssa, and they came and went with some frequency, to ascertain that the princess did not grow too fond of any of them. Her sister Rhaena's penchant for showering an unseemly amount of affection and attention on a succession of favorites, some of whom were considered less than suitable, had been the source of much whispering at court, and the queen did not want Alysanne to be the subject of similar rumors.

All this changed when King Aenys died on Dragonstone and his brother, Maegor, returned from across the narrow sea to seize the Iron Throne. The new king had little love and less trust for any of his brother's children, and he had his mother, the Dowager Queen Visenya, to enforce his will. Queen Alyssa's household knights and servants were dismissed, together with the servants and companions of her children, and Jaehaerys and Alysanne were made wards of their great-aunt, the fearsome Visenya. Hostages in all but name, they spent their uncle's reign being shuttled between Driftmark, Dragonstone, and King's Landing at the will of others, until Visenya's death in 44 AC offered Queen Alyssa an opportunity to escape, a chance she seized with alacrity, fleeing Dragonstone with Jaehaerys, Alysanne, and the blade Dark Sister.

No reliable accounts of Princess Alysanne's life after the escape survive to this day. She does not appear again in the annals of the realm until the final days of Maegor's bloody reign, when her mother and Lord Rogar rode forth from Storm's End at the head of an army, whilst Alysanne, Jaehaerys, and their sister, Rhaena, descended on King's Landing with their dragons.

Undoubtedly Princess Alysanne had handmaids and companions in the days that followed Maegor's death. Their names and particulars have not come down to us, unfortunately. We do know that none of them came with the princess when she and Jaehaerys fled the Red Keep on their dragons. Aside from the seven knights of the Kingsguard and the castle garrison, cooks, stablehands, and other servants, the king and his bride were unattended on Dragonstone.

That was hardly proper for a princess, let alone for a queen. Alysanne must have her household, and in that her mother, Alyssa, saw an opportunity to undermine, and mayhaps undo, her marriage. The Queen Regent resolved to dispatch to Dragonstone a carefully selected company of companions and servants to see to the young queen's needs. The plan, Grand Maester Benifer assures us, was Queen Alyssa's . . . but it was one that Lord Rogar assented to gladly, for he saw at once a way to twist it to his own ends.

The aged Septon Oswyck, who had performed the wedding rites for Jaehaerys and Alysanne, kept the sept on Dragonstone, but a young lady of royal birth required one of her own sex to see to her religious instruction. Queen Alyssa sent three; the formidable Septa Ysabel, and two wellborn novices of Alysanne's own age, Lyra and Edyth. To take charge of the serving girls and maids of Alysanne's household, she dispatched Lady Lucinda Tully, the wife of the Lord of Riverrun, whose fierce piety was renowned through all the land. With her came her younger sister, Ella of House Broome, a modest maid whose name had briefly been offered as a match for Jaehaerys. Lord Celtigar's daughters, so recently scorned by the Hand as being chinless, breastless, and witless, were included as well. ("We had as well get some use of them," Lord Rogar supposedly told their father.) Three other girls of noble birth made up the remainder of the company, one each from the Vale, the stormlands, and the Reach: Jennis of House Templeton, Coryanne of House Wylde, and Rosamund of House Ball.

Queen Alyssa wanted her daughter attended by suitable companions of her own age and station, no doubt, but that was not her sole motivation in sending these ladies to Dragonstone. Septa Ysabel, the novices Edyth and Lyra, and the deeply pious Lady Lucinda and her sister had a further charge. It was the hope of the Queen Regent that these fiercely righteous women might impress upon Alysanne, and mayhaps even Jaehaerys, that for brother to lie with sister was an abomination in the eyes of the Faith. "The children" (as Alyssa persisted in calling the king and queen) were not evil, only young and willful; suitably instructed, they might see the error of their ways and repent their marriage before it tore the realm apart. Or so she prayed.

Lord Rogar's motives were baser. Unable to rely on the loyalty of the castle garrison or the knights of the Kingsguard, the Hand needed eyes and ears on Dragonstone. All that Jaehaerys and Alysanne said and did was to be reported back to him, he made clear to Lady Lucinda and the others. He was especially anxious to learn if and when the king and queen intended on consummating their marriage. That, he stressed, must be prevented.

And mayhaps there was more.

And now unfortunately we must give some consideration to a certain distasteful book that first appeared in the Seven Kingdoms some forty years after the events presently being discussed. Copies of this book still pass from hand to hand in the low places of Westeros, and may oft be found in certain brothels (those catering to patrons able to read) and the libraries of men of low morals, where they are best kept under lock and key, hidden from the eyes of maidens, goodwives, children, and the chaste and pious.

The book in question is known under various titles, amongst them *Sins of the Flesh, The High and the Low, A Wanton's Tale,* and *The Wickedness of Men,* but all versions bear the subtitle *A Caution for Young Girls.* It purports to be the testimony of a young maid of noble birth who surrendered her virtue to a groom in her lord father's castle, gave birth to a child out of wedlock, and thereafter found herself partaking of every sort of wickedness imaginable during a long life of sin, suffering, and slavery.

If the author's tale is true (parts of it strain credulity), during the course of her life she found herself a handmaid to a queen, the paramour of a young knight, a camp follower in the Disputed Lands of Essos, a serving wench in Myr, a mummer in Tyrosh, the plaything of a corsair queen in the Basilisk Isles, a slave in Old Volantis (where she was tattooed, pierced, and ringed), the handmaid of a Qartheen warlock, and finally the mistress of a pleasure house in Lys . . . before ultimately returning to Oldtown and the Faith. Purportedly she ended her life as a septa in the Starry Sept, where she set down this story of her life to warn other young maids not to do as she had done.

The lascivious details of the author's erotic adventures need not concern us here. Our only interest is in the early part of her sordid tale, the story of her youth . . . for the alleged author of *A Caution for Young Girls* is none other than Coryanne Wylde, one of the girls sent to Dragonstone as a companion to the little queen.

We have no way to ascertain the veracity of her story, nor even whether she was in truth the author of this infamous book (some argue plausibly that the text is the product of several hands, for the style of the prose varies greatly from episode to episode). Lady Coryanne's early history, however, is confirmed in the accounts of the maester who served at the

Rain House during her youth. At the age of thirteen, he records, Lord Wylde's younger daughter was indeed seduced and deflowered by a "surly lad" from the stables. In *A Caution for Young Girls,* this lad is described as a handsome boy her own age, but the maester's account differs, painting the seducer as a pox-scarred varlet of thirty years distinguished only by a "male member as stout as a stallion's."

Whatever the truth, the "surly lad" was gelded and sent to the Wall as soon as his deed was known, whilst Lady Coryanne was confined to her chambers to give birth to his baseborn son. The boy was sent away soon after birth, to Storm's End, where he would be fostered by one of the castle stewards and his barren wife.

The bastard boy was born in 48 AC, according to the maester's journals. Lady Coryanne was carefully watched afterward, but few beyond the walls of the Rain House knew of her shame. When the raven came to summon her to King's Landing, her lady mother told her sternly that she was never to speak of her child or her sin. "In the Red Keep, they will take you for a maiden." But as the girl made her way to the city, escorted by her father and a brother, they stopped for the night at an inn on the south bank of the Blackwater Rush, beside the ferry landing. There she found a certain great lord awaiting her arrival.

And here the tale grows even more tangled, for the identity of the man at the inn is a matter of some dispute, even amongst those who accept *A Caution for Young Girls* to contain a modicum of truth.

Over the years and centuries, as the book was copied and recopied, many changes and emendations crept into the text. The maesters who labor at the Citadel copying books are rigorously trained to reproduce the original word for word, but few mundane scribes are so disciplined. Such septons, septas, and holy sisters as copy and illuminate books for the Faith oft strike out or alter any passages they believe to be offensive, obscene, or theologically unsound. As virtually the whole of *A Caution for Young Girls* is obscene, it was not like to have been transcribed by either maesters or septons. Given the number of copies known to exist (hundreds, though as many more were burned by Baelor the Blessed), the scribes responsible were most likely septons expelled from the Faith for drunkenness, theft, or fornication, failed students who left the Citadel without a chain, hired quills from the Free Cities, or mummers (the worst of all). Lacking the rigor of maesters, such scribes oft feel free to "improve" on the texts they are copying. (Mummers in particular are prone to this.)

In the case of *A Caution for Young Girls,* such "improvements" largely consisted of adding ever more episodes of depravity and changing the existing episodes to make them even more disturbing and lascivious. As alteration followed alteration over the years, it became ever more difficult to ascertain which was the original text, to the extent that even maesters at the Citadel cannot agree as to the title of the book, as has been noted. The identity of the man who met Coryanne Wylde in the inn by the ferry, if indeed such a meeting ever took place, is another matter of contention. In the copies entitled *Sins of the Flesh* and *The High and the Low* (which tend to be the older versions, and the shortest), the man at the inn is identified as Ser Borys Baratheon, eldest of Lord Rogar's four brothers. In *A Wanton's Tale* and *The Wickedness of Men,* however, the man is Lord Rogar himself.

All these versions agree on what happened next. Dismissing Lady Coryanne's father and brother, the lord commanded the girl to disrobe so he might inspect her. "He ran his hands over every part of me," she wrote, "and bade me turn this way and that and bend and stretch and open my legs to his gaze, until at last he pronounced himself satisfied." Only then did the man reveal the purpose of the summons that had brought her to King's Landing. She was to be sent to Dragonstone, a supposed maid, to serve as one of Queen Alysanne's companions, but once there she was to use her wiles and her body to beguile the king into bed.

"Jaehaerys is a man-maid like as not, and besotted with his sister," this man supposedly told her, "but Alysanne is but a child and you are a woman any man would want. Once His Grace tastes your charms he may come to his senses and abandon this folly of a marriage. He may even choose to keep you afterward, who can say? There can be no question of marriage, of course, but you would have jewels, servants, whatever you might want. There are rich rewards in being a king's bedwarmer. If Alysanne should discover you abed together, so much the better. She is a prideful girl and would be quick to abandon an unfaithful spouse. And if you should get with child again, you and the babe would be well taken care of, and your father and mother will be richly rewarded for your service to the Crown."*

Can we put any credence in this tale? At this late date, so far removed from the events in question, with all the principals long dead, there is no way to be certain. Beyond the testimony of the girl herself, we have no source to verify that this meeting by the ferry ever took place. And if some Baratheon did indeed meet privily with Coryanne Wylde before she reached King's Landing, we cannot know what words he might have spoken to her. He could as easily have simply been instructing her in her duties as a spy and tattle, as the other girls had been instructed.

Archmaester Crey, writing at the Citadel in the last years of King Jaehaerys's long reign, believed that the meeting at the inn was a clumsy calumny intended to blacken the name of Lord Rogar, and went so far as to attribute the lie to Ser Borys Baratheon himself, who quarreled bitterly with his brother in later life. Other scholars, including Maester Ryben, the Citadel's foremost expert on banned, forbidden, fraudulent, and obscene texts, put the story down as no more than a bawdy tale of the sort known to excite the lust of young boys, bastards, whores, and the men who partake of their favors. "Amongst the smallfolk there are always men of a lascivious character who delight in tales of great lords and noble knights despoiling maidens," Ryben wrote, "for this persuades them that their betters share their own base lusts."

Mayhaps. Yet there are certain things that we do know beyond a doubt that may allow us to draw our own conclusions. We do know that the younger daughter of Morgan Wylde, Lord of the Rain House, was deflowered at an early age and gave birth to a bastard boy. We can be reasonably certain that Lord Rogar knew of her shame; not only was he Lord Morgan's liege, but the child was placed in his own household. We know

* Certain copies of *A Wanton's Tale* include an additional amorous episode wherein Lord Rogar himself has carnal knowledge of the girl "all through the night," but these are almost certainly a later addition by some lustful scribe or depraved pander.

that Coryanne Wylde was amongst the maids who were sent to Dragonstone as companions for Queen Alysanne . . . a singularly curious choice, if a lady-in-waiting was all she was meant to be, for scores of other young girls of noble birth and suitable age were also available, girls whose maidenheads were intact and whose virtue was beyond reproach.

"Why her?" many have asked in the years since. Did she have some special gift, some particular charm? If so, no one remarked on it at the time. Could Lord Rogar or Queen Alyssa have been indebted to her lord father or lady mother for some past favor or kindness? We have no record of it. No plausible explanation for the selection of Coryanne Wylde has ever been offered, save for the simple, ugly answer proferred by *A Caution for Young Girls:* she was sent to Dragonstone not for Alysanne, but for Jaehaerys.*

Court records indicate that Septa Ysabel, Lady Lucinda, and the other women chosen for Alysanne Targaryen's household boarded the trading galley *Wise Woman* at dawn on the seventh day of the second moon of 50 AC, and left for Dragonstone on the morning tide. Queen Alyssa had sent word of their coming ahead by raven, yet even so she had some concern that the Wise Women, as they became known from that day forth, would find the gates of Dragonstone closed to them. Her fears were unfounded. The little queen and two Kingsguard met them at the harbor as they disembarked, and Alysanne welcomed each of them with glad smiles and gifts.

Before we relate what happened afterward, let us turn our gaze briefly to Fair Isle, where Rhaena Targaryen, the "Queen in the West," resided with her new husband and a court of her own.

It will be recalled that Queen Alyssa had been no more pleased by her eldest daughter's third marriage than by the one her son would soon make,

* It is said that many years later, when King Aegon IV was in his cups, someone raised the matter in his presence. His Grace supposedly laughed and stated his conviction that if Lord Rogar were no fool he would have instructed *all* of the maidens sent to Dragonstone in 50 AC to bed the young king, since the Hand could not have known which of them Jaehaerys would prefer. This infamous suggestion has taken root amongst the smallfolk, but it is unsupported by proof of any sort and may be safely dismissed.

though Rhaena's marriage was of less consequence. She was not alone in this, for in truth Androw Farman was a curious choice for one with the blood of the dragon in her veins.

The second son of Lord Farman, not even the heir, Androw was said to be a handsome boy with pale blue eyes and long flaxen hair, but he was nine years younger than the queen, and even at his own father's court there were those who scorned him as "half a girl" himself, for he was soft of speech and gentle of nature. A singular failure as a squire, he had never become a knight, having none of the martial skills of his lord father and elder brother. For a time, his sire had considered sending him to Oldtown to forge a maester's chain, until his own maester told him that the boy was simply not clever enough, and could hardly read nor write. Later, when asked why she had chosen such an unpromising spouse, Rhaena Targaryen replied, "He was kind to me."

Androw's father had been kind to her as well, offering her refuge on Fair Isle after the Battle Beneath the Gods Eye, when her uncle, King Maegor, was demanding her capture and the Poor Fellows of the realm were denouncing her as a vile sinner and her daughters as abominations. Some have put forward the suggestion that the widowed queen took Androw for her husband in part to repay his father for that kindness, for Lord Farman, himself a second son who had never expected to rule, was known to have great fondness for Androw, despite his deficiencies. Mayhaps there is some truth in that assertion, but another possibility, first put forward by Lord Farman's maester, may cut closer to the bone. "The queen found her true love on Fair Isle," Maester Smike wrote to the Citadel, "not with Androw, but with his sister, Lady Elissa."

Three years Androw's elder, Elissa Farman shared her brother's blue eyes and long flaxen hair, but elsewise she was as unlike him as a sibling could be. Sharp of wit and sharper of tongue, she loved horses, dogs, and hawks. She was a fine singer and a skilled archer, but her great love was sailing. *The Wind Our Steed* were the words of the Farmans of Fair Isle, who had sailed the western seas since the Dawn Age, and Lady Elissa embodied them. As a child, it was said that she spent more time at sea than upon the land. Her father's crews used to laugh to see her climbing the rigging like a monkey. She sailed her own boat around Fair Isle at the age of four-

and-ten, and by the time she was twenty she had voyaged as far north as Bear Island and as far south as the Arbor. Ofttimes, to the horror of her lord father and lady mother, she spoke of her desire to take a ship beyond the western horizon to learn what strange and wondrous lands might lie on the far side of the Sunset Sea.

Lady Elissa had been twice betrothed, once at twelve and once at sixteen, but she had frightened off both boys, as her own father admitted ruefully. In Rhaena Targaryen, however, she found a like-minded companion, and in her the queen found a new confidant. Together with Alayne Royce and Samantha Stokeworth, two of Rhaena's oldest friends, they became nigh inseparable, a court within the court that Ser Franklyn Farman, Lord Marq's elder son, dubbed "the Four-Headed Beast." Androw Farman, Rhaena's new husband, was admitted to their circle from time to time, but never so often as to be taken for a fifth head. Most tellingly, Queen Rhaena never took him flying with her on the back of her dragon, Dreamfyre, an adventure she shared frequently with the ladies Elissa, Alayne, and Sam (in fairness, it is more than possible that the queen invited Androw to share the sky with her only to have him decline, for he was not of an adventurous disposition).

It would be a mistake to regard Queen Rhaena's time at Faircastle as an idyll, however. Not everyone welcomed her presence, by any means. Even here on this distant isle there were Poor Fellows, angered that Lord Marq, like his father before him, had given support and sanctuary to one they regarded as an enemy of the Faith. The continued presence of Dreamfyre on the island was also creating problems. Glimpsed every few years, a dragon was a wonder and a terror to behold, and it was true that some of the Fair Islanders took pride in having "a dragon of our own." Others, however, were made anxious by the presence of the great beast, especially as she grew larger . . . and hungrier. Feeding a growing dragon is no small thing. And when it became known that Dreamfyre had produced a clutch of dragon eggs, a begging brother from the inland hills began to preach that Fair Isle would soon be overrun by dragons "devouring sheep and cows and men alike," unless a dragonslayer came forth to put an end to the scourge. Lord Farman sent forth knights to seize the man and silence him, but not before thousands had heard his prophecies. Though the preacher died in the dungeons under Faircastle, his words lived on, filling the ignorant with fear wherever they were heard.

Even within the walls of Lord Farman's own seat, Queen Rhaena had enemies, chief amongst them his lordship's heir. Ser Franklyn had fought in the Battle Beneath the Gods Eye and taken a wound there, blood shed in the service of Prince Aegon the Uncrowned. His grandsire had died upon that battlefield together with his eldest son, and it had been left to him to bring their corpses home to Fair Isle. Yet it seemed to him that Rhaena Targaryen showed little remorse for all the grief she had brought to House Farman, and little gratitude to him personally. He also resented her friendship with his sister, Elissa; instead of encouraging her in what he regarded as her wild, willful ways, Ser Franklyn thought the queen should be enjoining her to do her duty to her house by making an appropriate marriage and producing children. Nor did he appreciate the manner in which the Four-Headed Beast had somehow become the center of court life at Faircastle, whilst his lord father and himself were increasingly disregarded. In that he was well justified. More and more highborn lords from the westerlands and beyond were visiting Fair Isle, Maester Smike noted, but when they came it was to have audience with the Queen in the West, not with the minor lordling of a small isle and his son.

None of this was of great concern to the queen and her familiars so long as Marq Farman ruled in Faircastle, for his lordship was an amiable and good-natured man who loved all his children, his wayward daughter and weakling son included, and loved Rhaena Targaryen for loving them as well. Less than a fortnight after the queen and Androw Farman had celebrated the first anniversary of their union, however, Lord Marq died suddenly at his own table, choking to death upon a fish bone at the age of six-and-forty. And with his passing, Ser Franklyn became the Lord of Fair Isle.

He wasted little time. On the day after his father's funeral, he summoned Rhaena to his great hall (he would not deign to go to her), and commanded her to remove herself from his island. "You are not wanted here," he told her. "You are not welcome here. Take your dragon with you, and your friends, and my little brother, who would surely piss his breeches if he were made to stay. But do not presume to take my sister. She will remain here, and she will be wed to a man of my choosing."

Franklyn Farman did not lack for courage, as Maester Smike wrote in a letter to the Citadel. He did lack for sense, however, and in that moment he did not seem to realize how close he stood to death. "I could see the fire in her eyes," the maester said, "and for a moment I could see Faircastle burning, the white towers blackening and collapsing into the sea as flames leapt from every window and the dragon wheeled about again and again."

Rhaena Targaryen was the blood of the dragon, and far too proud to linger long where she was not wanted. She departed Fair Isle that very night, taking wing for Casterly Rock upon Dreamfyre after instructing her husband and companions to follow her by ship, "with all those who might love me." When Androw, flushed with anger, offered to face his brother in single combat, the queen quickly dissuaded him. "He would cut you to pieces, my love," she told him, "and were I to be thrice widowed, men would name me a witch or worse and hound me from Westeros." Lyman Lannister, Lord of Casterly Rock, had sheltered her before, she reminded him. Queen Rhaena was confident that he would welcome her again.

Androw Farman, Samantha Stokeworth, and Alayne Royce set out to follow the next morning, together with more than forty of the queen's friends, servants, and hangers-on, for Her Grace had gathered a sizable coterie about her as the Queen in the West. Lady Elissa was with them as well, for she had no intention of remaining behind; her ship, the *Maiden's Fancy,* had been made ready for the crossing. When the queen's party reached the docks, however, they found Ser Franklyn waiting for them. The rest of them could go, and good riddance, he announced, but his sister would remain on Fair Isle to be wed.

The new lord had brought only half a dozen men with him, however, and he had seriously misjudged the love the smallfolk bore his sister, particularly the sailors, shipwrights, fisherfolk, porters, and other denizens of the dockside districts, many of whom had known her since she was a small girl. As Lady Elissa confronted her brother, spitting defiance at him and demanding that he get out of her way, a crowd gathered around them, growing angrier by the moment. Oblivious to their mood, his lordship attempted to seize his sister . . . whereupon the onlookers rushed forward, overwhelming his men before they could draw their blades. Three of them were shoved off the docks into the water, whilst Lord Franklyn himself was thrown into a ship's hold full of fresh-caught cod. Elissa Farman and the rest of the queen's friends boarded *Maiden's Fancy* untouched and set sail for Lannisport.

Lyman Lannister, Lord of Casterly Rock, had given Rhaena and her husband Aegon the Uncrowned refuge when Maegor the Cruel was demanding their heads. His bastard son, Ser Tyler Hill, had fought with Prince Aegon under the Gods Eye. His wife, the formidable Lady Jocasta of House Tarbeck, had befriended Rhaena during her time at the Rock and had been the first to discern that she was with child. Just as the queen had expected, they welcomed her now, and when the rest of her party landed in Lannisport, the Lannisters took them in as well. A lavish feast was held in their honor, an entire stable was given over to Dreamfyre, and Queen Rhaena, her husband, and her companions of the Four-Headed Beast were assigned a regally appointed suite of apartments deep in the bowels of the Rock itself, safe from any harm. There they lingered for more than a moon's turn, enjoying the hospitality of the wealthiest house in all of Westeros.

As the days passed, however, that very hospitality grew ever more disquieting to Rhaena Targaryen. It became apparent to her that the bedmaids and servants assigned to them were tattlers and spies, bringing word of their every doing back to Lord and Lady Lannister. One of the castle septas asked Samantha Stokeworth whether the queen's marriage to Androw Farman had ever been consummated, and if so, who had witnessed the bedding. Ser Tyler Hill, Lord Lyman's comely bastard son, was openly scornful of Androw, even whilst doing all he could to ingratiate himself to Rhaena herself, regaling her with tales of his exploits at the Battle Beneath the Gods Eye and showing her the scars he had taken there "in your Aegon's service." Lord Lyman himself began to express an unseemly interest in the three dragon eggs that the queen had brought from Fair Isle, wondering how and when they might be expected to hatch. His wife, Lady Jocasta, suggested privately that one or more of the eggs would make a fine gift, if Her Grace should wish to show her gratitude to House Lannister for taking her in. When that ploy proved unsuccessful, Lord Lyman offered to buy the eggs outright for a staggering sum of gold.

The Lord of Casterly Rock wanted more than just a highborn guest, Queen Rhaena realized then. Beneath the warmth of his veneer, he was too cunning and too ambitious to settle for so little. He wanted an alliance with the Iron Throne, possibly through marriage between her and his bastard, or one of his trueborn sons; some union that would raise the Lannisters up past the Hightowers, the Baratheons, and the Velaryons to be the second house in the realm. And he wanted *dragons*. With dragonriders of their own, the Lannisters would be the equals of the Targaryens. "They were kings once," she reminded Sam Stokeworth. "He smiles, but he was raised on tales of the Field of Fire; he will not have forgotten." Rhaena Targaryen knew her history as well; the history of the Freehold of Valyria, writ in blood and fire. "We cannot remain here," she confided to her dear companions.

There we must leave Queen Rhaena for a time, whilst we cast our eyes eastward again toward King's Landing and Dragonstone, where the regent and king remained at odds.

Vexing as the issue of the king's marriage was to Queen Alyssa and Lord Rogar, it must not be thought that it was the only matter that concerned them during their regency. Coin, or rather the lack of coin, was the Crown's most pressing problem. King Maegor's wars had been ruinously expensive, exhausting the royal treasury. To refill his coffers Maegor's master of coin had raised existing taxes and imposed new ones, but these measures brought in less gold than anticipated and only served to deepen the anathema with which the lords of the realm regarded the king. Nor had the situation improved with the ascension of Jaehaerys. The young prince's coronation and his mother's Golden Wedding had both been splendid affairs that had done much to win him the love of lords and smallfolk alike, but all that had come at a cost. An even larger expense loomed ahead; Lord Rogar was determined to complete work on the Dragonpit before handing the city and the kingdom over to Jaehaerys, but the funds were lacking.

Edwell Celtigar, Lord of Claw Isle, had been an ineffectual Hand for

Maegor the Cruel. Given a second chance under the regency, he proved to be an equally ineffectual master of coin. Unwilling to offend his fellow lords, Celtigar instead decided to impose new taxes on the smallfolk of King's Landing, who were conveniently close at hand. Port fees were tripled, certain goods were to be taxed both coming into and out of the city, and new levies were asked of innkeeps and builders.

None of these measures had the desired effect of filling up the treasury vaults. Instead building slowed to a halt, the inns emptied, and trade declined notably as merchants diverted their ships from King's Landing to Driftmark, Duskendale, Maidenpool, and other ports where they might evade taxation. (Lannisport and Oldtown, the other great cities of the realm, were also included in Lord Celtigar's new taxes, but there the decrees had less effect, largely because Casterly Rock and the Hightower ignored them and made no effort to collect.) The new levies did, however, serve to make Lord Celtigar loathed throughout the city. Lord Rogar and Queen Alyssa received their share of opprobrium as well. Another casualty was the Dragonpit; the Crown no longer had the funds to pay the builders, and all work on the great dome ceased.

Storms were gathering to both north and south as well. With Lord Rogar occupied in King's Landing, the Dornishmen had grown bold, raiding more frequently into the marches, even troubling the stormlands. There were rumors of another Vulture King in the Red Mountains, and Lord Rogar's brothers Borys and Garon insisted they did not have the men and money required to root him out.

Even more dire was the situation in the North. Brandon Stark, Lord of Winterfell, had died in 49 AC, not long after his return from the Golden Wedding; the journey, the northmen said, had asked too much of him. His son Walton succeeded him, and when a sudden rebellion broke out in 50 AC amongst the men of the Night's Watch at Rimegate and Sable Hall, he gathered his strength and rode to the Wall to join the leal watchmen in putting them down.

The rebels were former Poor Fellows and Warrior's Sons who had accepted clemency from the boy king, led by Ser Olyver Bracken and Ser Raymund Mallery, the two turncloak knights who had served in Maegor's Kingsguard before abandoning him for Jaehaerys. The Lord Commander of the Watch, unwisely, had given Bracken and Mallery command of two crumbling forts, with orders to restore them; instead the two men decided to make the castles their own seats and establish themselves as lords.

Their uprising proved short-lived. For every man of the Night's Watch who joined their rebellion, ten remained true to their vows. Once joined by Lord Stark and his bannermen, the black brothers retook Rimegate and hanged the oathbreakers, save for Ser Olyver himself, who was beheaded by Lord Stark with his celebrated blade Ice. When word reached Sable Hall, the rebels there fled beyond the Wall in hopes of making common cause with the wildlings. Lord Walton pursued them, but two days north in the snows of the haunted forest, he and his men were set upon by giants. It was written afterward that Walton Stark slew two of them before he was dragged from his saddle and torn apart. His surviving men carried him back to Castle Black in pieces.

As for Ser Raymund Mallery and the other deserters, the wildlings gave them a cold welcome. Rebels or no, the free folk had no use for crows. Ser Raymund's head was delivered to Eastwatch half a year later. When asked what had befallen the rest of his men, the wildling chieftain laughed and said, "We ate them."

Brandon Stark's second son, Alaric, became the Lord of Winterfell. He would rule the North for twenty-three years, an able man though a stern one . . . but for a long while he had no good to say of King Jaehaerys, for he blamed the king's clemency for his brother Walton's death, and was oft heard to say that His Grace should have beheaded Maegor's men rather than sending them to the Wall.

Far removed from the troubles in the North, King Jaehaerys and Queen Alysanne remained in their self-imposed exile from the court, but they were anything but idle. Jaehaerys continued his rigorous training regimen with the knights of his Kingsguard every morn, and devoted his evenings to poring over accounts of the reign of his grandsire Aegon the Conqueror, on which he wished to model his own rule. Dragonstone's three maesters assisted him in these inquiries, as did the queen.

As the days passed, more and more visitors made their way to Dragonstone to talk with the king. Lord Massey of Stonedance was the first to appear, but Lord Staunton of Rook's Rest, Lord Darklyn of Duskendale, and Lord Bar Emmon of Sharp Point came hard on his heels, followed by the Lords Harte, Rollingford, Mooton, and Stokeworth. Young Lord Rosby, whose father had taken his own life when King Maegor fell, turned up as well, sheepishly pleading for the young king's forgiveness, which Jaehaerys was pleased to grant. Though Daemon Velaryon, as the Crown's lord admiral and master of ships, was in King's Landing with the regents, that did not prevent Jaehaerys and Alysanne from flying their dragons to Driftmark and touring his shipyards, escorted by his sons, Corwyn, Jorgen, and Victor. When word of these meetings reached Lord Rogar in King's Landing he grew furious and went so far as to ask Lord Daemon if the Velaryon fleet could be used to prevent these "lords lickspittle" from crawling to Dragonstone to curry favor with the boy king. Lord Velaryon's reply was blunt. "No," he said. The Hand took this as a further sign of disrespect.

Meanwhile, Queen Alysanne's new ladies-in-waiting and companions had settled in on Dragonstone, and it soon became apparent that her mother's hope that these Wise Women might persuade the little queen that her marriage was unwise and impious had gone seriously awry. Neither prayer, sermons, nor readings from *The Seven-Pointed Star* could shake Alysanne Targaryen's conviction that the gods had meant her to marry her brother Jaehaerys, to be his confidant and helpmate and the mother of his children. "He will be a great king," she told Septa Ysabel, Lady Lucinda, and the others, "and I will be a great queen." So firm was she in her belief, and so gentle and kindly and loving in all else, that the septa and the other Wise Women found they could not condemn her, and with every passing day they clove more to her side.

Lord Rogar's own plan to drive Jaehaerys and Alysanne apart fared no better. The young king and his queen were to spend their lives together, and though they would famously quarrel and part later in life, only to reunite, Septon Oswyck and Maester Culiper both tell us that never a cloud nor harsh word troubled their time together on Dragonstone before Jaehaerys reached his majority.

Did Coryanne Wylde fail to bed the king? Is it possible that she never made the attempt? Is the whole tale of the meeting at the inn mayhaps a fiction? Any of these are possible. The author of *A Caution for Young Girls* would have it otherwise, but here that infamous text becomes even more unreliable, splintering off into half a dozen contradictory versions of events, each more vulgar than the last.

It would not do for the wanton at the heart of that tale to admit that Jaehaerys had rejected her, or that she never found the opportunity to lure him into a bedchamber. Instead we are offered an assortment of lewd adventures, a veritable feast of filth. *A Wanton's Tale* insists that Lady Coryanne not only bedded the king, but also all seven members of the Kingsguard. His Grace supposedly gave her to Pate the Woodcock after he had sated his own lusts, Pate passed her to Ser Joffrey in turn, and so it went. *The High and the Low* omits these details, but tells us that Jaehaerys not only welcomed the girl into his bed, but also brought Queen Alysanne in to frolic with them in episodes most often associated with the infamous pleasure houses of Lys.

A somewhat more plausible tale is told in *Sins of the Flesh,* wherein Coryanne Wylde does indeed lure King Jaehaerys into her bed, only to find him fumbling, uncertain, and over-hasty, as many boys of his age are known to be when first abed with a maid. By that time, however, Lady Coryanne had grown to admire and respect Queen Alysanne, "as if she were my own little sister," and had developed warm feelings for Jaehaerys as well. Instead of attempting to undo the king's marriage, therefore, she took it upon herself to help make it a success by educating His Grace in the art of giving and receiving carnal pleasure, so that he might not prove incapable when the time came to bed his young wife.

This tale could well be as fanciful as the others, but it has a certain sweetness to it that has led some scholars to allow that it might, mayhaps, have happened. Lewd fables are not history, however, and history has only one sure thing to tell us about Lady Coryanne of House Wylde, the putative author of *A Caution for Young Girls.* On the fifteenth day of the sixth moon of 50 AC, she departed Dragonstone under the cover of night in the company of Ser Howard Bullock, the younger son of the commander of the castle garrison. A married man, Ser Howard left his wife behind him, though he took most of her jewelry. A fishing boat carried him and Lady Coryanne to Driftmark, where they took ship for the Free City of Pentos. From there they made their way to the Disputed Lands, where Ser

Howard signed on to a free company called, with a singular lack of inspiration, the Free Company. He would die in Myr three years later, not in battle but in a fall from his horse after a night of drinking. Alone and penniless, Coryanne Wylde moved on to the next of the trials, tribulations, and erotic adventures recounted in her book. We need hear no more of her.

By the time word of Lady Coryanne's flight with her purloined jewels and purloined husband reached the ears of Lord Rogar in the Red Keep, it had become obvious that his plan had failed, as had Queen Alyssa's. Piety and lust had both proved unable to break the bond between Jaehaerys Targaryen and his Alysanne.

Moreover, word of the king's marriage had begun to spread. Too many men had witnessed the confrontation at the castle gates, and the lords who had called at Dragonstone afterward had not failed to notice Alysanne's presence at the king's side, or the obvious affection between them. Rogar Baratheon might talk of tearing out tongues, but he was helpless against the whispers that spread throughout the land . . . and even across the narrow sea, where the magisters of Pentos and the sellswords of the Free Company were doubtless entertained by the tales Coryanne Wylde had to tell.

"It is done," the Queen Regent told her councillors when she realized the truth at last. "It is done and cannot be undone, Seven save us. We must needs live with it, and we must use all our powers to protect them from what may come." She had lost two sons to Maegor the Cruel, and a coldness lay between her and her oldest daughter; she could not bear the thought of being forever estranged from the two children who remained to her.

Rogar Baratheon could not yield as gracefully, however, and his wife's words woke in him a fury. In front of Grand Maester Benifer, Septon Mattheus, Lord Velaryon, and the rest, he spoke to her contemptuously. "You are weak," he declared, "as weak as your first husband was, as weak as your son. Sentiment may be forgiven in a mother, but not in a regent, and never in a king. We were fools to crown Jaehaerys. He thinks only of himself, and he will be a worse king than his father was. Thank the gods that it is not too late. We must act now and put him aside."

A hush fell over the chamber at those words. The Queen Regent stared at her lord husband in horror and then, as if to prove that he had spoken truly, began to weep, her tears running silent down her cheeks. Only then did the other lords find their tongues. "Have you taken leave of your senses?" asked Lord Velaryon. Lord Corbray, Commander of the City Watch, shook his head and said, "My men will never stand for it." Grand Maester Benifer exchanged a glance with Prentys Tully, the master of laws. Lord Tully said, "Do you mean to claim the Iron Throne for yourself, then?"

This Lord Rogar denied vehemently. "Never. Do you take me for a usurper? I want only what is best for the Seven Kingdoms. No harm need come to Jaehaerys. We can send him to Oldtown, to the Citadel. He is a bookish boy, a maester's chain will suit him."

"Then who shall sit the Iron Throne?" demanded Lord Celtigar.

"Princess Aerea," Lord Rogar answered at once. "There is a fire in her Jaehaerys does not have. She is young, but I can continue as her Hand, shape her, guide her, teach her all she must know. She has the stronger claim, her mother and father were King Aenys's first and secondborn, Jaehaerys was fourth." His fist slammed against the table then, Benifer tells us. "Her mother will support her. Queen Rhaena. And Rhaena has a *dragon*."

Grand Maester Benifer recorded what followed. "A silence fell, though the same words were on the lips of us all: 'Jaehaerys and Alysanne have dragons too.' Qarl Corbray had fought in the Battle Beneath the Gods Eye, had witnessed the terrible sight of dragon fighting dragon. For the rest of us, the Hand's words conjured visions of Old Valyria before the Doom, when dragonlord contended with dragonlord for supremacy. It was an awful vision."

It was Queen Alyssa who broke the spell, through her tears. "I am the Queen Regent," she reminded them. "Until my son shall come of age, all of you serve at my pleasure. Including the Hand of the King." When she turned to her lord husband, Benifer tells us that her eyes looked as hard and dark as obsidian. "Your service no longer pleases me, Lord Rogar. Leave us and return to Storm's End, and we need never speak again of your treason."

Rogar Baratheon looked at her incredulously. "Woman. You think you can dismiss *me*? No." He laughed. "*No*."

That was when Lord Corbray rose to his feet and drew his sword, the Valyrian steel blade called Lady Forlorn that was the pride of his house. "Yes," he said, and laid the blade upon the table, its point toward Lord Rogar. Then and only then did his lordship realize that he had gone too far, that he stood alone against every man in the room. Or so Benifer tells us.

His lordship said no further word. His face pale, he stood and removed the golden brooch that Queen Alyssa had given him as a token of his office, flung it at her contemptuously, and strode from the room. He took his leave of King's Landing that very night, crossing the Blackwater Rush with his brother Orryn. There he lingered for six days, whilst his brother Ronnal assembled their knights and men-at-arms for the march home.

Legend tells us that Lord Rogar awaited their coming in the selfsame inn beside the ferry where he, or his brother Borys, had met with Coryanne Wylde. When the Baratheon brothers and their levies finally set out for Storm's End, they had barely half as many men as had marched with them two years before to topple Maegor. The rest, it would seem, preferred the alleys and inns and temptations of the great city to the rainy woods, green hills, and moss-covered cottages of the stormlands. "I never lost so many men in battle as I did to the fleshpots and alehouses of King's Landing," Lord Rogar would say bitterly.

One of those lost was Aerea Targaryen. On the night of Lord Rogar's dismissal, Ser Ronnal Baratheon and a dozen of his men forced their way into her chambers in the Red Keep, intending to take her with them... only to find that Queen Alyssa had stolen a march on them. The girl was already gone, and her servants knew not where. It would be learned later that Lord Corbray had removed her, at the Queen Regent's command. Dressed in the rags of a common girl of the lowest order, with her silver-gold hair dyed a muddy brown, Princess Aerea would spend the rest of the regency working in a stable near the King's Gate. She was eight years old and loved horses; years later, she would say that this was the happiest time of her life.

Sad to say, there was to be little happiness for Queen Alyssa in the years to come. Her dismissal of her husband as the Hand of the King had destroyed any affection that Lord Rogar might ever have felt for her; from that day forth, their marriage was a ruined castle, an empty shell haunted by ghosts. "Alyssa Velaryon had survived the death of her husband and her two eldest sons, a daughter who perished in the cradle, years of terror under Maegor the Cruel, and a rift with her remaining children, but she could not survive this," Septon Barth would write, when he looked back upon her life. "It shattered her."

Contemporary reports from Grand Maester Benifer agree. With Lord Rogar gone, Queen Alyssa named her brother Daemon Velaryon as Hand of the King, dispatched a raven to Dragonstone to tell her son Jaehaerys some (but not all) of what had occurred, and then retired to her chambers in Maegor's Holdfast. For the remainder of her regency, she left the rule of the Seven Kingdoms to Lord Daemon, and took no further part in public life.

It would be pleasant to report that Rogar Baratheon, once back at Storm's End, reflected on the error of his ways, repented his mistakes, and became a chastened man. Sadly, that was not his lordship's nature. He was a man who knew not how to yield. The taste of defeat was like bile in the back of his throat. In war, he would boast, he would ne'er lay down his axe whilst life remained in his body . . . and this matter of the king's marriage had become a war to him, one he was determined to win. One last folly remained to him, and he did not shrink from it.

Thus it was that in Oldtown, at the motherhouse attached to the Starry Sept, Ser Orryn Baratheon appeared suddenly with a dozen men-at-arms and a letter bearing Lord Rogar's seal, demanding that the novice Rhaella Targaryen be turned over to them immediately. When questioned, Ser Orryn would say only that Lord Rogar had urgent need of the girl at Storm's End. The ploy might well have worked, but Septa Karolyn, who had the door of the motherhouse that day, had a spine of steel and a suspicious nature. Whilst placating Ser Orryn with the pretext of sending for the girl, she sent instead to the High Septon. His High Holiness was (mayhaps fortunately, for both the child and the realm) asleep, but his steward (a former knight, who had been a captain in the Warrior's Sons until they were abolished) was awake and wary.

In place of a frightened girl, the Baratheon men found themselves confronted by thirty armed septons under the command of the steward, Casper Straw. When Ser Orryn brandished a sword, Straw calmly informed him that twoscore of Lord Hightower's knights were on their way (a lie, as it happened), whereupon the Baratheons surrendered. Under questioning, Ser Orryn confessed the entire plot: he was to deliver the girl to Storm's End, where Lord Rogar planned to force her to confess that she was the actual Princess Aerea, not Rhaella. Then he meant to name her queen.

The Father of the Faithful, a man as gentle as he was weak of will, heard Orryn Baratheon's confession and forgave him. This did not prevent Lord Hightower, once informed, from throwing the captive Baratheons into a dungeon and dispatching a full account of the affair to both the Red Keep and Dragonstone. Donnel Hightower, who had rightly been named Donnel the Delayer for his reluctance to take the field against Septon Moon and his followers, seemed to have no fear of offending Storm's End by imprisoning Lord Rogar's own brother. "Let him come and try to prise him free," he said when his maester worried about how the former Hand might react. "His own wife took his hand and cut his balls off, and soon enough the king will have his head."

Across the width of Westeros, Rogar Baratheon fumed and raged when he learned of his brother's failure and imprisonment . . . but he did not call his banners, as many had feared. Instead he fell into despair. "I am done," he told his own maester glumly. "It is the Wall for me, if the gods are good. If not, the boy will have my head and make a gift of it to his mother." Having sired no children by either of his wives, he commanded his maester to draft a will and confession, wherein he absolved his brothers Borys, Garon, and Ronnal of having played any role in his wrongdoing, begged for mercy for his youngest brother, Orryn, and named Ser Borys as heir to Storm's End. "All I did and all I tried to do was for the good of the realm and the Iron Throne," he ended.

His lordship would not have long to wait to know his fate. The regency was almost at an end. With the former Hand and Queen Regent both wounded and silent, Lord Daemon Velaryon and the remaining members of the queen's council ruled the realm as best they could, "saying little and doing less" in the words of Grand Maester Benifer.

On the twentieth day of the ninth moon of 50 AC, Jaehaerys Targaryen reached his sixteenth nameday and became a man grown. By the laws of the Seven Kingdoms, he was now old enough to rule in his own right, with no further need of a regent. All across the Seven Kingdoms, lords and smallfolk alike waited to see what kind of king he would be.

A Time of Testing

The Realm Remade

King Jaehaerys I Targaryen returned to King's Landing alone, on the wings of his dragon, Vermithor. Five knights of his Kingsguard had come before him, arriving three days earlier to ascertain that all was in readiness for the king's arrival. Queen Alysanne did not accompany him. Given the uncertainty that surrounded their marriage and the fraught nature of the king's relationship with his mother, Queen Alyssa, and the lords of the council, it was thought prudent that she remain on Dragonstone for a time, with her Wise Women and the rest of the Kingsguard.

The day was not an auspicious one, Grand Maester Benifer tells us. The skies were grey, and a persistent drizzle had fallen half the morning. Benifer and the rest of the council awaited the king's coming in the inner yard of the Red Keep, cloaked and hooded against the rain. Elsewhere about the castle, knights and squires and stableboys and washerwomen and scores of other functionaries went about their daily chores, pausing from time to time to glance up at the sky. And when at last the sound of wings was heard, and a guardsman on the eastern walls caught sight of Vermithor's bronze scales in the distance, there came a cheer that grew and grew and grew, rolling past the Red Keep's walls, down Aegon's High Hill, across the city, and well out into the countryside.

Jaehaerys did not land at once. Thrice he swept over the city, each time lower than before, giving every man and boy and barefoot wench in King's Landing a chance to wave and shout and marvel. Only then did he bring Vermithor down in the yard before Maegor's Holdfast, where the lords were waiting.

"He had changed since last I saw him," Benifer records. "The stripling who had flown to Dragonstone was gone, and in his place was a man grown. He was taller than before by several inches, and his chest and arms had filled out. His hair was flowing loose about his shoulders, and a fine golden down covered his cheeks and chin, where before he had been clean-shaved. Eschewing all kingly raiment, he wore salt-stained leathers, garb fit for hunting or riding, with only a studded jack to protect him. But on his swordbelt, he bore Blackfyre . . . his grandsire's sword, the sword of kings. Even sheathed, the blade could be mistaken for no other. A shiver of fear went through me when I saw that sword. *Is there a warning there?* I wondered, as the dragon settled to the ground, smoke rising from between his teeth. I had fled to Pentos when Maegor died, frightened of what fate awaited me under his successors, and for an instant as I stood there in the damp I wondered whether I had been a fool to return."

The young king—a boy no longer—soon dispelled his Grand Maester's fear. As he slid gracefully from Vermithor's back, he smiled. "It was as if the sun had broken through the clouds," reported Lord Tully. The lords bowed before him, several going to their knees. Across the city, bells began to ring in celebration. Jaehaerys pulled off his gloves and tucked them into his belt, then said, "My lords. We have work to do."

One luminary had not been present in the yard to greet the king: his mother, Queen Alyssa. It fell to Jaehaerys to seek her out in Maegor's Holdfast, where she had secluded herself. What passed between mother and son when they came face-to-face for the first time since the confrontation on Dragonstone no man can say, but we are told that the queen's face was red and puffy from weeping when she appeared a short time later on the king's arm. The Dowager Queen, a regent no more, was present for the welcoming feast that evening, and at numerous other court functions in the days beyond that, but no longer did she have a seat at council sessions. "Her Grace continued to do her duty by the realm and her son," Grand Maester Benifer wrote, "but there was no joy in her."

The young king began his realm by remaking the council, keeping some men and replacing others who had proved unequal to their tasks. He confirmed his mother's appointment of Lord Daemon Velaryon as Hand of the King, and retained Lord Corbray as the Commander of the City Watch. Lord Tully was thanked for his service, reunited with his wife, Lady Lucinda, and sent home to Riverrun. To replace him as master of laws, Jaehaerys named Albin Massey, Lord of Stonedance, who had been amongst the first men to seek him out on Dragonstone. Massey had been forging a maester's chain at the Citadel only three years earlier, when a fever had carried off both his older brothers and his lord father. A twisted spine condemned him to walk with a limp, but as he said famously, "I do not limp when I read, nor when I write." For lord admiral and master of ships, His Grace turned to Manfryd Redwyne, Lord of the Arbor, who came to court with his young sons Robert, Rickard, and Ryam, squires all. It marked the first time the admiralty had gone to any man not of House Velaryon.

All King's Landing rejoiced when it was announced that Jaehaerys had also dismissed Edwell Celtigar as master of coin. The king spoke to him gently, it was said, and even praised the leal service of his daughters to Queen Alysanne on Dragonstone, going so far as to name them "two treasures." The daughters would remain with the queen thereafter, but Lord Celtigar himself left for Claw Isle at once. And with him went his taxes, every one of them struck down by royal decree three days into the young king's rule.

Finding a suitable man to take Lord Edwell's place as master of coin proved to be no easy task. Several of his advisors urged King Jaehaerys to appoint Lyman Lannister, supposedly the richest lord in Westeros, but Jaehaerys was disinclined. "Unless Lord Lyman can find a mountain of gold under the Red Keep, I do not know that he has the answer we require," His Grace said. He looked longer at certain cousins and uncles of Donnel Hightower, for the wealth of Oldtown derived from trade rather

than the ground, but the uncertain loyalties of Donnel the Delayer when faced with Septon Moon gave him pause. In the end Jaehaerys made a far bolder choice, reaching across the narrow sea for his man.

No lord, no knight, not even a magister, Rego Draz was a merchant, trader, and money-changer who had risen from nothing to become the richest man in Pentos, only to find himself shunned by his fellow Pentoshi and denied a seat in the council of magisters because of his low birth. Sick of their scorn, Draz gladly answered the king's call, moving his family, friends, and vast fortune to Westeros. To grant him equal honor with the other members of the council, the young king named him a lord. As he was a lord without lands, sworn men, or a castle, however, some wit about the castle dubbed him "the Lord of Air." The Pentoshi was amused. "If I could tax air, I would be a lord indeed."

Jaehaerys also sent off Septon Mattheus, that fat and furious prelate who had fulminated so loudly against incestuous unions and the king's marriage. Mattheus did not take his dismissal well. "The Faith will look askance at any king who thinks to rule without a septon by his side," he announced. Jaehaerys had a ready answer. "We shall have no lack of septons. Septon Oswyck and Septa Ysabel will remain with us, and there is a young man coming from Highgarden to see to our library. His name is Barth." Mattheus was dismissive, declaring that Oswyck was a doddering fool and Ysabel a woman, whilst he had no knowledge of Septon Barth. "Nor of many other things," the king replied. (Lord Massey's famous remark, that the king required three persons to replace Septon Mattheus in order to balance the scales, was likely uttered shortly after, assuming it was uttered at all.)

Mattheus departed four days later for Oldtown. Too corpulent to sit a horse, he traveled in a gilded wheelhouse, attended by six guardsmen and a dozen servants. Legend tells us that whilst crossing the Mander at Bitterbridge, he passed Septon Barth coming in the other direction. Barth was alone, riding on a donkey.

The young king's changes went well beyond the nobles who sat upon his council. He made a clean sweep of dozens of lesser offices as well, replacing the Keeper of the Keys, the chief steward of the Red Keep and all his understewards, the harbormaster of King's Landing (and in time, the harbormasters of Oldtown, Maidenpool, and Duskendale as well), the Warden of the King's Mint, the King's Justice, the master-at-arms, kennelmaster, master of horse, and even the castle ratcatchers. He further commanded that the dungeons beneath the Red Keep be cleaned and emptied out, and that all the prisoners found in the black cells be brought up into the sun, bathed, and allowed to make appeal. Some, he feared, might well be innocent men imprisoned by his uncle (in this Jaehaerys proved sadly correct, though many of those captives had gone quite mad during their years in darkness, and could not be released).

Only when all this had been done to his satisfaction and his new men were in place did Jaehaerys instruct Grand Maester Benifer to dispatch a raven to Storm's End, summoning Lord Rogar Baratheon back to the city.

The arrival of the king's letter set Lord Rogar and his brothers at odds. Ser Borys, oft considered the most volatile and belligerent of the Baratheons, proved the calmest in this instance. "The boy will have your head if you do as he bids," he said. "Go to the Wall. The Night's Watch will take you." Garon and Ronnal, the younger brothers, urged defiance instead. Storm's End was strong as any castle in the realm. If Jaehaerys meant to have his head, let him come and take it, they said. Lord Rogar only laughed at that. "Strong?" he said. "Harrenhal was strong. No. I will see Jaehaerys first and explain myself. I can take the black then if I choose, he will not deny me that." The next morning, he set off for King's Landing, accompanied only by six of his oldest knights, men who had known him since childhood.

The king received him seated on the Iron Throne with his crown upon his head. The lords of his council were present, and Ser Joffrey Doggett and Ser Lorence Roxton of the Kingsguard stood at the base of the throne in their white cloaks and enameled scale. Elsewise the throne room was empty. Lord Rogar's footsteps echoed as he made the long walk from the doors to the throne, Grand Maester Benifer tells us. "His lordship's pride was well-known to the king," he wrote. "His Grace had no wish to wound him further by forcing him to humble himself before the entire court."

Humble himself he did, however. The Lord of Storm's End fell to one knee, bowed his head, and laid his sword at the base of the throne. "Your Grace," he began, "I am here as you commanded. Do as you will with me.

I ask only that you spare my brothers and House Baratheon. All that I did, I did—"

"—for the good of the realm as you saw it." Jaehaerys raised a hand to silence Lord Rogar before he could say further. "I know what you did, and what you said, and what you planned. I believe you when you say you meant no harm to my person or to my queen . . . and you are not wrong, I would make a splendid maester. But I hope to make an even better king. Some men say that we are now enemies. I would sooner think of us as friends who disagreed. When my mother came to you seeking refuge, you took us in, at great risk to yourself. You could have easily clapped us in chains and made a gift of us to my uncle. Instead you swore your sword to me and called your banners. I have not forgotten.

"Words are wind," Jaehaerys went on. "Your lordship . . . my dear friend . . . spoke of treason, but committed none. You wished to undo my marriage, but you could not do so. You suggested placing Princess Aerea upon the Iron Throne in my place, but here I sit. You did send your brother to remove my niece Rhaella from her motherhouse, true . . . but for what purpose? Perhaps you only wished to have her for a ward, lacking any child of your own.

"Treasonous actions deserve punishment. Foolish words are another matter. If you truly desire to go to the Wall, I will not stop you. The Night's Watch needs men as strong as you. But I would sooner you remain here, in my service. I would not sit upon this throne if not for you, all the realm knows that. And I still have need of you. The *realm* has need of you. When the Dragon died and my father donned the crown, he was beset on all sides by would-be kings and rebel lords. The same may befall me, and for the same reason . . . to test my resolve, my will, my strength. My mother believes that godly men throughout the realm will rise against me when my marriage is made known. Mayhaps so. To meet these tests, I need good men around me, *warriors* willing to fight for me, to die for me . . . and for my queen, if need be. Are you such a man?"

Lord Rogar, thunderstruck at the king's words, looked up and said, "I am, Your Grace," in a voice thick with emotion.

"Then I pardon your offenses," King Jaehaerys said, "but there will be certain conditions." His voice grew stern as he listed them. "You will never speak another word against me or my queen. From this day forth, you shall be her loudest champion and suffer no word to be spoken against her in your presence. Furthermore, I cannot and will not suffer my mother to be disrespected. She will return with you to Storm's End, where you will live as husband and wife once again. In word and deed you will show her only honor and courtesy. Can you abide by these conditions?"

"Gladly," said Lord Rogar. "Might I ask . . . what of Orryn?"

That gave the king pause. "I shall command Lord Hightower to free your brother Ser Orryn and the men who went with him to Oldtown," Jaehaerys said, "but I cannot allow them to go unpunished. The Wall is forever, so instead I will sentence them to ten years of exile. They can sell their swords in the Disputed Lands, or sail to Qarth to make their fortunes, it matters not to me . . . if they survive, and commit no further crimes, in ten years' time they can come home. Are we agreed?"

"We are," Lord Rogar responded. "Your Grace is more than just." Then he asked if the king would require hostages of him, as a surety of his future loyalty. Three of his brothers had young children who could be sent to court, he pointed out.

In answer, King Jaehaerys descended the Iron Throne and bade Lord Rogar follow him. He led his lordship from the hall to the inner ward where Vermithor was being fed. A bull had been slaughtered for his morning meal and lay upon the stones charred and smoking, for dragons always burn their meat before consuming it. Vermithor was feasting on the flesh, tearing loose great chunks of meat with each bite, but when the king approached with Lord Rogar, the dragon raised his head and gazed at them with eyes like pools of molten bronze. "He grows larger every day," Jaehaerys said as he scratched the great wyrm under his jaw. "Keep your nieces and your nephews, my lord. Why would I need hostages? I have your word, that is all that I require." But Grand Maester Benifer heard the words he did not speak. "*Every man and maid and child in the stormlands is my hostage, whilst I ride him,* His Grace said without saying," wrote Benifer, "and Lord Rogar heard him plain."

Thus was the peace made between the young king and his former Hand, and sealed that night by a feast in the great hall, where Lord Rogar sat beside Queen Alyssa, man and wife once more, and raised a toast to

the health of Queen Alysanne, pledging her his love and loyalty before all the assembled lords and ladies. Four days later, when Lord Rogar departed to return to Storm's End, Queen Alyssa went with him, escorted by Ser Pate the Woodcock and a hundred men-at-arms to see them safe through the kingswood.*

In King's Landing, the long reign of Jaehaerys I Targaryen began in earnest. The young king faced a score of problems when he assumed the rule of the Seven Kingdoms, but two loomed larger than all the rest: the treasury was empty and the Crown's debt was mounting, and his "secret" marriage, which grew less secret with every passing day, sat like a jar of wildfire on a hearth, waiting to explode. Both questions needed to be dealt with, and quickly.

The immediate need for gold was resolved by Rego Draz, the new master of coin, who reached out to the Iron Bank of Braavos and its rivals in Tyrosh and Myr to arrange not one but three substantial loans. By playing each bank against the others, the Lord of Air negotiated as favorable terms as might be hoped for. The securing of the loans had one immediate effect; work on the Dragonpit was able to resume, and once again a small army of builders and stonemasons swarmed over the Hill of Rhaenys.

Lord Rego and his king both realized that the loans were a stopgap measure at best, however; they might slow the bleeding but they would not stanch the wound. Only taxes could accomplish that. Lord Celtigar's taxes would not serve; Jaehaerys had no interest in raising port fees or bleeding innkeeps. Nor would he simply demand gold from the lords of the realm, as Maegor had. Too much of that, and the lords would rise up.

* Ser Orryn Baratheon never did return to Westeros. Together with the men who had accompanied him to Oldtown, he crossed to the Free City of Tyrosh, where he took service with the Archon. A year later, he married the Archon's daughter, the very maid his brother Rogar had hoped to wed to King Jaehaerys as a means of securing an alliance between the Iron Throne and the Free City. A buxom maid with blue-green hair and a winsome manner, Ser Orryn's wife soon gave him a daughter, though there was some doubt whether the girl was truly his, for like many women of the Free Cities she was free with her favor. When her father's term as Archon ended, Ser Orryn lost his position as well and was forced to leave Tyrosh for Myr, where he joined the Maiden's Men, a free company with an especially unsavory reputation. He was killed soon afterward in the Disputed Lands, during a battle with the Men of Valor. We have no knowledge of the fate of his wife and daughter.

"Nothing is so costly as putting down rebellions," the king declared. The lords would pay, but of their own free will; he would tax the things they wanted, fine and costly things from across the sea. Silk would be taxed, and samite; cloth-of-gold and cloth-of-silver; gemstones; Myrish lace and Myrish tapestries; Dornish wines (but not wines from the Arbor); Dornish sand steeds; gilded helms and filigreed armor from the craftsmen of Tyrosh, Lys, and Pentos. Spices would be taxed heaviest of all; peppercorns, cloves, saffron, nutmeg, cinnamon, and all the other rare seasonings from beyond the Jade Gates, already more costly than gold, would become still costlier. "We are taxing all the things that made me rich," Lord Rego japed.

"No man can claim to be oppressed by these taxes," Jaehaerys explained to the small council. "To avoid them, a man need only forgo his pepper, his silk, his pearls, and he need not pay a groat. The men who want these things desire them desperately, however. How else to flaunt their power and show the world what wealthy men they are? They may squawk, but they will pay."

The spice and silk taxes were not the end of it. King Jaehaerys also brought forth a new law on crenellations. Any lord who wished to build a new castle or expand and repair his existing seat would need to pay a hefty price for the privilege. The new tax served a dual purpose, His Grace explained to Grand Maester Benifer. "The larger and stronger a castle, the more its lord is tempted to defy me. You would think they might learn from Black Harren, but too many do not know their history. This tax will discourage them from building, whilst those who must build regardless can replenish our treasury whilst they empty theirs."

Having done what he could to repair the Crown's finances, His Grace turned his attention to the other great matter awaiting him. At long last, he sent for his queen. Alysanne Targaryen and her dragon, Silverwing, departed Dragonstone within an hour of his summons, after having been apart from the king for nigh on half a year. The rest of her household followed by ship. By this time, even blind beggars in the alleys of Flea Bottom knew that Alysanne and Jaehaerys had been wed, but for the sake of propriety the king and queen slept separately for a moon's turn, whilst preparations were made for their second wedding.

The king was not disposed to spend coin he did not have on another Golden Wedding, as splendid and popular as that event had been. Forty thousand had witnessed his mother marry Lord Rogar. A thousand came together in the Red Keep to see Jaehaerys take his sister Alysanne to wife again. This time it was Septon Barth who pronounced them man and wife, beneath the Iron Throne.

Lord Rogar Baratheon and the Dowager Queen Alyssa were amongst those standing witness this time. Together with his lordship's brothers Garon and Ronnal, they had made their way back from Storm's End to attend the ceremony. But it was another wedding guest who excited the most talk: the Queen in the West had come as well. Borne on the wings of Dreamfyre, Rhaena Targaryen had flown in to see her siblings wed . . . and to visit her daughter Aerea.

Bells rang throughout the city as the rites were concluded, and a flight of ravens took wing to every corner of the realm to proclaim "this happy union." The king's second wedding differed from his first in one other crucial respect; it was followed by a bedding. Queen Alysanne, in later years, would declare that this was at her insistence; she was ready to lose her maidenhead, and she wanted no more questions as to whether she were "truly" married. Lord Rogar himself, roaring drunk, led the men who disrobed her and carried her to the bridal bed, whilst the queen's companions Jennis Templeton, Rosamund Ball, and Prudence and Prunella Celtigar were amongst those who did the honors for the king. There, upon a canopied bed in Maegor's Holdfast in the Red Keep of King's Landing, the marriage of Jaehaerys Targaryen and his sister Alysanne was consummated at long last, sealing their union for all time before the eyes of gods and men.

With secrecy finally at an end, the king and his court waited to see how the realm would respond. Jaehaerys had concluded that the violent opposition that had greeted his brother Aegon's marriage had several causes. Their uncle Maegor's taking of a second wife in 39 AC, in defiance of both the High Septon and his own brother, King Aenys, had shattered the delicate understanding between the Iron Throne and the Starry Sept, so the marriage of Aegon and Rhaena had been seen as a further outrage. The denunciation thus provoked had lit a fire across the land, and the

Swords and Stars had taken up the torches, along with a score of pious lords who feared the gods more than their king. Prince Aegon and Princess Rhaena had been little known amongst the smallfolk, and they had begun their progress without dragons (in large part because Aegon was not yet a dragonrider), which left them vulnerable to the mobs that sprung up to attack them in the riverlands.

None of these conditions applied to Jaehaerys and Alysanne. There would be no denunciation from the Starry Sept; whilst some amongst the Most Devout still bristled at the Targaryen tradition of sibling marriage, the present High Septon, Septon Moon's "High Lickspittle," was complaisant and cautious, not inclined to wake sleeping dragons. The Swords and Stars had been broken and outlawed; only at the Wall, where two thousand former Poor Fellows now wore the black cloaks of the Night's Watch, did they have sufficient numbers to be troublesome, were they so inclined. And King Jaehaerys was not about to repeat his brother's mistake. He and his queen meant to see the land they ruled, to learn its needs firsthand, to meet his lords and take their measure, to let themselves be seen by the smallfolk, and to hear their griefs in turn . . . but wherever they went, it would be with their dragons.

For all these reasons, Jaehaerys believed that the realm would accept his marriage . . . but he was not a man to trust in chance. "Words are wind," he told his council, "but wind can fan a fire. My father and my uncle fought words with steel and flame. We shall fight words with words, and put out the fires before they start." And so saying, His Grace sent forth not knights and men-at-arms, but preachers. "Tell every man you meet of Alysanne's kindness, her sweet and gentle nature, and her love for all the people of our kingdom, great and small," the king charged them.

Seven went forth at his command; three men and four women. In place of swords and axes, they were armed only with their wits, their courage, and their tongues. Many a tale would be told of their travels, and their exploits would become legends (growing vastly larger in the process, as is the way of legends). Only one of the seven speakers was known to the common folks of the realm when they set out: no less a person than Queen Elinor herself, the Black Bride who had found Maegor dead upon the Iron Throne. Clad in her queenly raiment, which grew shabbier and more threadbare by the day, Elinor of House Costayne would travel the Reach giving eloquent testimony to the evil of her late king and the goodness of his successors. In later years, giving up all claims to nobility, she would join the Faith, rising eventually to become Mother Elinor at the great motherhouse in Lannisport.

The names of the other six who went forth to speak for Jaehaerys would in time become nigh as famous as the queen's. Three were septons; cunning Septon Baldrick, learned Septon Rollo, and fierce old Septon Alfyn, who had lost his legs years before and was carried everywhere in a litter. The women the young king chose were no less extraordinary. Septa Ysabel had been won over by Queen Alysanne whilst serving her on Dragonstone. Diminutive Septa Violante was renowned for her skills as a healer. Everywhere she went, it was said, she performed miracles. From the Vale came Mother Maris, who had taught generations of orphan girls at a motherhouse on an island in Gulltown's harbor.

In their travels throughout the realm, the Seven Speakers talked of Queen Alysanne, her piety, her generosity, and her love for the king, her brother . . . but for those septons, begging brothers, and pious knights and lords who challenged them by citing passages from *The Seven-Pointed Star* or the sermons of High Septons past, they had a ready answer, one that Jaehaerys himself had crafted in King's Landing, ably assisted by Septon Oswyck and (especially) Septon Barth. In later years, the Citadel and the Starry Sept alike would call it the Doctrine of Exceptionalism.

Its basic tenet was simple. The Faith of the Seven had been born in the hills of Andalos of old, and had crossed the narrow sea with the Andals. The laws of the Seven, as laid down in sacred text and taught by the septas and septons in obedience to the Father of the Faithful, decreed that brother might not lie with sister, nor father with daughter, nor mother with son, that the fruits of such unions were abominations, loathsome in the eyes of the gods. All this the Exceptionalists affirmed, but with this caveat: *the Targaryens were different.* Their roots were not in Andalos, but in Valyria of old, where different laws and traditions held sway. A man had only to look at them to know that they were not like other men; their eyes, their hair, their very bearing, all proclaimed their differences. *And they flew dragons.* They alone of all the men in the world had been given the power to tame those fearsome beasts, once the Doom had come to Valyria.

"One god made us all, Andals and Valyrians and First Men," Septon Alfyn would proclaim from his litter, "but he did not make us all alike. He made the lion and the aurochs as well, both noble beasts, but certain gifts he gave to one and not the other, and the lion cannot live as an aurochs, nor an aurochs as a lion. For you to bed your sister would be a grievous sin, ser . . . but you are not the blood of the dragon, no more than I am. What they do is what they have always done, and it is not for us to judge them."

Legend tells us that in one small village, the quick-witted Septon Baldrick was confronted by a burly hedge knight, once a Poor Fellow, who said, "Aye, and if I want to fuck my sister too, do I have your leave?" The septon smiled and replied, "Go to Dragonstone and claim a dragon. If you can do that, ser, I will marry you and your sister myself."

Here is a quandary every student of history must face. When looking back upon the things that happened in years past, we can say, this and this

and this were the causes of what occurred. When looking back on things that did *not* happen, however, we have only surmise. We know the realm did not rise up against King Jaehaerys and Queen Alysanne in 51 AC as it had against Aegon and Rhaena ten years earlier. The *why* of it is a good deal less certain. The High Septon's silence spoke loudly, no doubt, and the lords and common folk alike were weary of war . . . but if words have power, wind or no, surely the Seven Speakers played a part as well.

Though the king was happy in his queen, and the realm happy with their marriage, Jaehaerys had not been wrong when he foresaw that he would face a time of testing. Having remade the council, reconciled Lord Rogar and Queen Alyssa, and imposed new taxes to restore the Crown's coffers, he was faced with what would prove to be his thorniest problem yet: his sister Rhaena.

Since taking her leave of Lyman Lannister and Casterly Rock, Rhaena Targaryen and her traveling court had made their own royal progress of sorts, visiting the Marbrands of Ashemark, the Reynes of Castamere, the Leffords at the Golden Tooth, the Vances at Wayfarer's Rest, and finally the Pipers of Pinkmaiden. No matter where she turned, the same problems arose. "They are all warm at first," she told her brother, when she met with him after his wedding, "but it does not last. Either I am unwelcome or too welcome. They murmur of the cost of keeping me and mine, but it is Dreamfyre who excites them. Some fear her, more want her, and it is those who trouble me most. They lust for dragons of their own. That I will not give them, but where am I to go?"

"Here," the king suggested. "Return to court."

"And live forever in your shadow? I need a seat of my own. A place where no lord may threaten me, banish me, or trouble those I have taken under my protection. I need lands, men, a castle."

"We can find you lands," the king said, "build you a castle."

"All the lands are taken, all the castles occupied," Rhaena replied, "but there is one I have a claim to . . . a better claim than your own, brother. I am the blood of the dragon. I want my father's seat, the place where I was born. I want Dragonstone."

To that King Jaehaerys had no answer, promising only to take the matter under consideration. His council, when the question was put to them, were united in their opposition to ceding the ancestral seat of House Targaryen to the widowed queen, but none had any better solution to offer.

After reflecting on the matter, His Grace met with his sister again. "I will grant you Dragonstone as your seat," he told her, "for there is no place more fitting for the blood of the dragon. But you shall hold the island and the castle by my gift, not by right. Our grandsire made seven kingdoms into one with fire and blood, I cannot and will not make them two by carving you off a separate kingdom of your own. You are a queen by courtesy, but I am king, and my writ runs from Oldtown to the Wall . . . and on Dragonstone as well. Are we of one mind on this, sister?"

"Are you so uncertain of that iron seat that you must needs have your own blood bend the knee to you, brother?" Rhaena threw back at him. "So be it. Give me Dragonstone and one thing more, and I shall trouble you no further."

"One thing more?" Jaehaerys asked.

"Aerea. I want my daughter restored to me."

"Done," the king said . . . mayhaps too hastily, for it must be remembered that Aerea Targaryen, a girl of eight, was his own acknowledged successor, heir apparent to the Iron Throne. The consequences of this decision would not be known for years to come, however. For the nonce it was done, and the Queen in the West at a stroke became the Queen in the East.

The better part of the year continued without further crisis or test as Jaehaerys and Alysanne settled in to rule. If certain members of the small council were taken aback when the queen began to attend their meetings, they voiced their objections only to one another . . . and soon not even that, for the young queen proved to be wise, well-read, and clever, a welcome voice in any discussion.

Alysanne Targaryen had happy memories of her childhood before her uncle Maegor seized the crown. During the reign of her father, Aenys, her mother, Queen Alyssa, had made the court a splendid place, filled with song, spectacle, and beauty. Musicians, mummers, and bards competed for her favor and that of the king. Wines from the Arbor flowed like water at their feasts, the halls and yards of Dragonstone rang with laughter, and the women of the court dazzled in pearls and diamonds. Maegor's court had been a grim, dark place, and the regency had offered little change, for the memories of King Aenys's time were painful to his widow, whilst Lord Rogar was of a martial temperament and once declared mummers to be of less use than monkeys, for "they both prance about, tumble, caper, and squeal, but if a man is hungry enough, he can eat a monkey."

Queen Alysanne looked back on the short-lived glories of her father's court fondly, however, and made it her purpose to make the Red Keep glitter as it never had before, buying tapestries and carpets from Free Cities and commissioning murals, statuary, and tilework to decorate the castle's halls and chambers. At her command, men from the City Watch combed Flea Bottom until they found Tom the Strummer, whose mocking songs had amused king and commons alike during the War for the White Cloaks. Alysanne made him the court singer, the first of many who would hold that office in the decades to come. She brought in a harpist from Oldtown, a company of mummers from Braavos, dancers from Lys, and gave the Red Keep its first fool, a fat man called the Goodwife who dressed as a woman and was never seen without his wooden "children," a pair of cleverly carved puppets who said ribald, shocking things.

All this pleased King Jaehaerys, but none of it pleased him half so much as the gift that Queen Alysanne gave him several moons later, when she told him she was with child.

Birth, Death, and Betrayal Under King Jaehaerys I

Jaehaerys I Targaryen would prove to be as restless a king as ever sat the Iron Throne. Aegon the Conqueror had famously said that the smallfolk needed to see their kings and queens from time to time, so they might lay their griefs and grievances before them. "I mean for them to see me," Jaehaerys declared, when announcing his first royal progress late in 51 AC. Many more were to follow in the years and decades to come. During the course of his long reign, Jaehaerys would spend more days and nights guesting with one lord or another, or holding audience in some market town or village, than at Dragonstone and the Red Keep combined. And oft as not, Alysanne was with him, her silvery dragon soaring beside his great beast of burnished bronze.

Aegon the Conqueror had been accustomed to taking as many as a thousand knights, men-at-arms, grooms, cooks, and other servants with him on the road. Whilst undeniably grand to behold, such processions created many difficulties for the lords honored by royal visits. So many men were difficult to house and feed, and if the king wished to go hunting, nearby woods would be overrun. Even the richest lord would oft find himself impoverished by the time the king departed, his cellars drunk dry of wine, his larders empty, and half his maidservants with bastards in their bellies.

Jaehaerys was resolved to do things differently. No more than one hundred men would accompany him on any progress; twenty knights, the rest men-at-arms and servants. "I do not need to ring myself about with swords so long as I ride Vermithor," he said. Smaller numbers also allowed him to visit smaller lords, those whose castles had never been large enough to host Aegon. His intent was to see and be seen at more places, but stay at each a shorter time, so as never to become an unwelcome guest.

The king's first progress was meant to be a modest one, commencing with the crownlands north of King's Landing and proceeding only as far as the Vale of Arryn. Jaehaerys wanted Alysanne with him, but as Her Grace was with child, he was concerned that their journeys not be too taxing. They began with Stokeworth and Rosby, then moved north along the coast to Duskendale. There, whilst the king viewed Lord Darklyn's boatyards and enjoyed an afternoon of fishing, the queen held the first of her women's courts, which were to become an important part of every royal progress to come. Only women and girls were welcome at these audiences; highborn or low, they were encouraged to come forward and share their fears, concerns, and hopes with the young queen.

The journey went without incident until the king and queen reached Maidenpool, where they were to be the guests of Lord and Lady Mooton for a fortnight before sailing across the Bay of Crabs to Wickenden, Gulltown, and the Vale. The town of Maidenpool was far famed for the sweetwater pool where legend had it that Florian the Fool had first glimpsed Jonquil bathing during the Age of Heroes. Like thousands of other women before her, Queen Alysanne wished to bathe in Jonquil's pool, whose waters were said to have amazing healing properties. The lords of Maidenpool had erected a great stone bathhouse around the pool many centuries before, and given it over to an order of holy sisters. No men were allowed to enter the premises, so when the queen slipped into the sacred waters, she was attended only by her ladies-in-waiting, maids, and septas (Edyth and Lyra, who had served beside Septa Ysabel as novices, had both recently sworn their vows to become septas, consecrated in the Faith and devoted to the queen).

The goodness of the little queen, the silence of the Starry Sept, and the exhortations of the Seven Speakers had won over most of the Faithful for Jaehaerys and his Alysanne . . . but there are always some who will not be moved, and amongst the sisters who tended Jonquil's Pool were three such women, whose hearts were hard with hate. They told one another that their holy waters would be polluted forever were the queen allowed to bathe in them whilst carrying the king's "abomination" in her belly. Queen Alysanne had only slipped out of her clothing when they fell upon her with daggers they had concealed within their robes.

Blessedly, the attackers were no warriors, and they had not taken the courage of the queen's companions into account. Naked and vulnerable, the Wise Women did not hesitate, but stepped between the attackers and their lady. Septa Edyth was slashed across the face, Prudence Celtigar stabbed through the shoulder, whilst Rosamund Ball took a dagger in the belly that, three days later, proved to be the death of her, but none of the murderous blades touched the queen. The shouts and screams of the struggle brought Alysanne's protectors running, for Ser Joffrey Doggett and Ser Gyles Morrigen had been guarding the entrance to the bathhouse, never dreaming that the danger lurked within.

The Kingsguard made short work of the attackers, slaying two out of hand whilst keeping the third alive for questioning. When encouraged, she revealed that half a dozen others of their order had helped plan the attack, whilst lacking the courage to wield a blade. Lord Mooton hanged the guilty, and might have hanged the innocent as well, save for Queen Alysanne's intervention.

Jaehaerys was furious. Their visit to the Vale was postponed; instead they returned to the safety of Maegor's Holdfast. Queen Alysanne would remain within until her child was born, but the experience had shaken her and set her to pondering. "I need a protector of mine own," she told His Grace. "Your Seven are leal men and valiant, but they are men, and there are places men cannot go." The king could not disagree. A raven flew to Duskendale that very night, commanding the new Lord Darklyn to send to court his bastard half-sister, Jonquil Darke, who had thrilled the smallfolk during the War for the White Cloaks as the mystery knight known as the Serpent in Scarlet. Still in scarlet, she arrived at King's Landing a few

days later, and gladly accepted appointment as the queen's own sworn shield. In time, she would be known about the realm as the Scarlet Shadow, so closely did she guard her lady.

Not long after Jaehaerys and Alysanne returned from Maidenpool and the queen took to her bedchamber, tidings of the most wondrous and unexpected sort came forth from Storm's End. Queen Alyssa was with child. At forty-four years of age, the Dowager Queen had been thought to be well beyond her childbearing years, so her pregnancy was received as a miracle. In Oldtown, the High Septon himself proclaimed it was a blessing from the gods, "a gift from the Mother Above to a mother who had suffered much, and bravely."

Amidst the joy, there was concern as well. Alyssa was not as strong as she had been; her time as Queen Regent had taken a toll on her, and her second marriage had not brought her the happiness she had once hoped for. The prospect of a child warmed Lord Rogar's heart, however, and he cast off his anger and repented of his infidelities to stay by his wife's side. Alyssa herself was fearful, mindful of the last babe she had borne to King Aenys, the little girl Vaella who had died in the cradle. "I cannot suffer that again," she told her lord husband. "It would rip my heart apart." But the child, when he came early the following year, would prove to be robust and healthy, a big red-faced boy born with a fuzz of jet-black hair and "a squall that could be heard from Dorne to the Wall." Lord Rogar, who had long ago put aside any hopes of having children by Alyssa, named his son Boremund.

The gods give grief as well as joy. Long before her mother was brought to term, Queen Alysanne was also delivered of a son, a boy she named Aegon, to honor both the Conqueror and her lost and much lamented brother, the uncrowned prince. All the realm gave thanks, and no one more so than Jaehaerys. But the young prince had come too early. Small and frail, he died three days after birth. So bereft was Queen Alysanne that the maesters feared for her life as well. Forever after, she blamed her son's death on the women who attacked her at Maidenpool. Had she been allowed to bathe in the healing waters of Jonquil's Pool, she would say, Prince Aegon would have lived.

Discontent lay heavy upon Dragonstone as well, where Rhaena Targaryen had established her own small court. As they had with Jaehaerys before her, neighboring lords began to seek her out, but the Queen in the East was not her brother. Many of her visitors were received coldly, others turned away without an audience.

Queen Rhaena's reunion with her daughter Aerea had not gone well, either. The princess had no memory of her mother, and the queen no knowledge of her child, nor any fondness for the children of others. Aerea had loved the excitement of the Red Keep, with lords and ladies and envoys from queer foreign lands coming and going, knights training in the yards every morning, singers and mummers and fools capering by night, and all the clangor and color and tumult of King's Landing just beyond the walls. She had loved the attention lavished on her as the heir to the Iron Throne as well. Great lords, gallant knights, bedmaids, washerwomen, and stableboys alike had praised her, loved her, and vied for her favor, and she had been the leader of a pack of young girls of both high and low birth who had terrorized the castle.

All that had been taken from her when her mother carried her off to Dragonstone against her wishes. Compared to King's Landing, the island was a dull place, sleepy and quiet. There were no girls of her own age in the castle, and Aerea was not allowed to mingle with the daughters of the fisherfolk in the village beneath the walls. Her mother was a stranger to her, sometimes stern and sometimes shy, much given to brooding, and the women who surrounded her seemed to take little interest in Aerea. Of all of them, the only one the princess warmed to was Elissa Farman of Fair Isle, who told her tales of her adventures and promised to teach her how to sail. Lady Elissa was no happier on Dragonstone than Aerea herself, however; she missed her wide western seas and spoke often of returning to them. "Take me with you," Princess Aerea would say when she did, and Elissa Farman would laugh.

Dragonstone did have one thing King's Landing largely lacked: dragons. In the great citadel under the shadow of the Dragonmont, more dragons were being born every time the moon turned, or so it seemed. The eggs that Dreamfyre had laid on Fair Isle had all hatched once on Dragonstone, and Rhaena Targaryen had made certain that her daughter made their acquaintance. "Choose one and make him yours," the queen urged the princess, "and one day you will fly." There were older dragons in the yards as well, and beyond the walls wild dragons that had escaped the castle made their lairs in hidden caves on the far side of the mountain. Princess Aerea had known Vermithor and Silverwing during her time at court, but she had never been allowed too close to them. Here she could visit with the dragons as often as she liked; the hatchlings, the young drakes, her mother's Dreamfyre . . . and greatest of them all, Balerion and Vhagar, huge and ancient and sleepy, but still terrifying when they woke and stirred and spread their wings.

In the Red Keep, Aerea had loved her horse, her hounds, and her friends. On Dragonstone, the dragons became her friends . . . her only friends, aside from Elissa Farman . . . and she began to count the days until she could mount one and fly far, far away.

King Jaehaerys finally made his progress through the Vale of Arryn in 52 AC, calling at Gulltown, Runestone, Redfort, Longbow Hall, Heart's Home, and the Gates of the Moon before flying Vermithor up the Giant's Lance to the Eyrie, as Queen Visenya had done during the Conquest. Queen Alysanne accompanied him for part of his travels, but not all; she had not yet recovered her full strength after childbirth, and the grief that followed. Still, by her good offices, the betrothal of Lady Prudence Celtigar to Lord Grafton of Gulltown was arranged. Her Grace also held a women's court at Gulltown, and a second at the Gates of the Moon; what she heard and learned would change the laws of the Seven Kingdoms.

Men oft speak today of Queen Alysanne's laws, but this usage is sloppy and incorrect. Her Grace had no power to enact laws, issue decrees, make proclamations, or pass sentences. It is a mistake to speak of her as we might speak of the Conqueror's queens, Rhaenys and Visenya. The young queen did, however, wield enormous influence over King Jaehaerys, and when she spoke, he listened . . . as he did upon their return from the Vale of Arryn.

It was the plight of widows throughout the Seven Kingdoms that the women's courts had made Alysanne aware of. In times of peace especially, it was not uncommon for a man to outlive the wife of his youth, for young men most oft perish upon the battlefield, young women in the birthing bed. Be they of noble birth or humble, men left bereft suchwise would oft after a time take second wives, whose presence in the household was resented by the children of the first wife. Where no bonds of affection existed, upon the man's own death his heirs could and did expel the widow from the home, reducing her to penury; in the case of lords, the heirs might simply strip away the widow's prerogatives, incomes, and servants, reducing her to little more than a boarder.

To rectify these ills, King Jaehaerys in 52 AC promulgated the Widow's Law, reaffirming the right of the eldest son (or eldest daughter, where there was no son) to inherit, but requiring said heirs to maintain surviving widows in the same condition they had enjoyed before their husband's death. A lord's widow, be she a second, third, or later wife, could no longer be driven from his castle, nor deprived of her servants, clothing, and income. The same law, however, also forbade men from disinheriting their children by a first wife in order to bestow their lands, seat, or property upon a later wife or her own children.

Building was the king's other concern that year. Work continued on the Dragonpit, and Jaehaerys oft visited the site to see the progress with his own eyes. Whilst riding from Aegon's High Hill to the Hill of Rhaenys, however, His Grace took note of the most lamentable state of his city. King's Landing had grown too fast, with manses and shops and hovels and rat pits springing up like mushrooms after a hard rain. The streets were close and dark and filthy, with buildings so close to one another that men could clamber from one window to another. The wynds coiled about like drunken snakes. Mud, manure, and nightsoil were everywhere.

"Would that I could empty the city, knock it down, and build it all anew," the king told his council. Lacking that power, and the coin such a massive undertaking would have required, Jaehaerys did what he could. Streets were widened, straightened, and cobbled where possible. The worst styes and hovels were torn down. A great central square was carved out and planted with trees, with markets and arcades beneath. From that hub, long wide streets sprung, straight as spears: the King's Way, the Gods' Way, the Street of the Sisters, Blackwater Way (or the Muddy Way, as the smallfolk soon renamed it). None of this could be accomplished in a night; work would continue for years, even decades, but it was the year 52 AC when it began, by the king's command.

The cost of rebuilding the city was not inconsequential, and put further strain upon the Crown's treasury. Those difficulties were exacerbated by the growing unpopularity of the Lord of Air, Rego Draz. In a short time, the Pentoshi master of coin had become as widely loathed as his predecessor, though for different reasons. He was said to be corrupt, taking the king's gold to fatten his own purse, a charge Lord Rego treated with derision. "Why should I steal from the king? I am twice as rich as he is." He was said to be godless, for he did not worship the Seven. Many a queer god is worshipped in Pentos, but Draz was known to keep but one, a small household idol like unto a woman great with child, with swollen breasts and a bat's head. "She is all the god I need," was all he would say upon the matter. He was said to be a mongrel, an assertion he could not deny, for all Pentoshi are part Andal and part Valyrian, mixed with the stock of slaves and older peoples long forgotten. Most of all, he was resented for his wealth, which he did not deign to conceal but flaunted with his silken robes, ruby rings, and gilded palanquin.

That Lord Rego Draz was an able master of coin even his enemies could not deny, but the challenge of paying for the completion of the Dragonpit and the rebuilding of King's Landing strained even his talents. The taxes on silk, spice, and crenellations alone could not answer, so Lord Rego reluctantly imposed a new levy: a gate fee, required of anyone entering or leaving the city, collected by the guards on the city's gates. Additional fees were assessed for horses, mules, donkeys, and oxen, and wagons and carts were taxed heaviest of all. Given the amount of traffic that came and went from King's Landing every day, the gate tax proved to be highly lucrative, bringing in more than enough coin to meet the need . . . but at considerable cost to Rego Draz himself, as the grumbling against him increased tenfold.

A long summer, plentiful harvests, and peace and prosperity both at home and abroad helped to blunt the edge of the discontent, however, and as the year drew to a close, Queen Alysanne brought the king splendid news. Her Grace was once again with child. This time, she vowed, no enemies would come near her. Plans for a second royal progress had already been made and announced before the queen's condition became known. Though Jaehaerys decided at once that he would remain by his wife's side until the babe was born, Alysanne would not have it. He must go, she insisted.

And so he did. The coming of the new year saw the king taking to the sky again on Vermithor, this time for the riverlands. His progress began with a stay at Harrenhal as a guest of its new lord, the nine-year-old Maegor Towers. From there he and his retinue moved on to Riverrun, Acorn Hall, Pinkmaiden, Atranta, and Stoney Sept. At his queen's request, Lady Jennis Templeton traveled with the king to hold women's courts at Riverrun and Stoney Sept in her place. Alysanne remained in the Red Keep, presiding over council meetings in the king's absence, and holding audience from a velvet seat at the base of the Iron Throne.

As Her Grace grew great with child, just across Blackwater Bay by the Gullet another woman was delivered of another child whose birth, whilst less noted, would in time be of great significance to the lands of Westeros and the seas that lay beyond. On the isle of Driftmark, Daemon Velaryon's eldest son became a father for the first time when his lady wife presented him with a handsome, healthy boy. The babe was named Corlys, after the great-great-uncle who had served so nobly as the Lord Commander of the first Kingsguard, but in the years to come the people of Westeros would come to know this new Corlys better as the Sea Snake.

The queen's own child followed in due course. She was brought to bed during the seventh moon of 53 AC, and this time she gave birth to a strong and healthy child, a girl she named Daenerys. The king was at Stoney Sept when word reached him. He mounted Vermithor and flew back to King's Landing at once. Though Jaehaerys had hoped for another son to follow him upon the Iron Throne, it was plain that he doted on his daughter from the moment he first took her in his arms. The realm delighted in the little princess as well . . . everywhere, that is, save on Dragonstone.

Aerea Targaryen, the daughter of Aegon the Uncrowned and his sister Rhaena, was eleven years of age, and had been heir to the Iron Throne for as long as she could remember (but for the three days that separated Prince Aegon's birth from his death). A strong-willed, bold-tongued, fiery young girl, Aerea delighted in the attention that came with being a queen-in-waiting, and was not pleased to find herself displaced by the newborn princess.

Her mother, Queen Rhaena, likely shared these feelings, but she held her tongue and spoke no word of it even to her closest confidants. She had trouble enough in her own hall at the time, for a rift had opened between her and her beloved Elissa Farman. Denied any part of the incomes of Fair Isle by her brother Lord Franklyn, Elissa asked the Dowager Queen for gold sufficient to build a new ship in the shipyards of Driftmark, a large, swift vessel meant to sail the Sunset Sea. Rhaena denied her request. "I could not bear for you to leave me," she said, but Lady Elissa heard only, *"No."*

With the hindsight of history to guide us, we can look back and see that all the portents were there, ominous signs of difficult days ahead, but even the archmaesters of the Conclave saw none of that as they reflected on the year about to end. Not one of them realized that the year ahead would be amongst the darkest in the long reign of Jaehaerys I Targaryen, a year so marked by death, division, and disaster that the maesters and smallfolk alike would come to call it the Year of the Stranger.

The first death of 54 AC came within days of the celebrations that marked the coming of the new year, as Septon Oswyck passed in his sleep. He was an old man and had been failing for some time, but his passing cast a pall over the court all the same. At a time when the Queen Regent, the King's Hand, and the Faith had all opposed the marriage of Jaehaerys and Alysanne, Oswyck had agreed to perform the rites for them, and his courage had not been forgotten. At the king's request, his remains were interred on Dragonstone, where he had served so long and so faithfully.

The Red Keep was still in mourning when the next blow fell, though at the time it seemed an occasion for joy. A raven from Storm's End delivered an astonishing message: Queen Alyssa was once again with child, at the age of forty-six. "A second miracle," Grand Maester Benifer proclaimed when he told the king the news. Septon Barth, who had taken on Oswyck's duties after his death, was more doubtful. Her Grace had never completely recovered from the birth of her son Boremund, he cautioned; he questioned whether she still had strength enough to carry a child to term. Rogar Baratheon was elated at the prospect of another son, however, and foresaw no difficulties. His wife had given birth to seven children, he insisted. Why not an eighth?

On Dragonstone, problems of another sort were coming to a head. Lady Elissa Farman could suffer life upon the island no more. She had heard the sea calling, she told Queen Rhaena; it was time for her to take her leave. Never one to make a show of her emotions, the Queen in the East received the news stone-faced. "I have asked you to stay," she said. "I will not beg. If you would go, go." Princess Aerea had none of her mother's restraint. When Lady Elissa came to say her farewells, the princess wept and clung to her leg, pleading with her to stay, or failing that, to take her along. "I want to be with you," Aerea said, "I want to sail the seas and have adventures." Lady Elissa shed a tear as well, we are told, but she pushed the princess away gently and told her, "No, child. Your place is here."

Elissa Farman departed for Driftmark the next morning. From there she took ship across the narrow sea to Pentos. Thereafter she made her way overland to Braavos, whose shipwrights were far famed, but Rhaena Targaryen and Princess Aerea had no notion of her final destination. The queen believed she had gone no farther than Driftmark. Lady Elissa had good reason for wanting more distance between her and the queen, however. A fortnight after her departure, Ser Merrell Bullock, still commander of the castle garrison, brought three terrified grooms and the keeper of the dragon yard into Rhaena's presence. Three dragon eggs were missing, and days of searching had not turned them up. After questioning every man who had access to the dragons closely, Ser Merrell was convinced that Lady Elissa had made off with them.

If this betrayal by one she had loved wounded Rhaena Targaryen she hid it well, but there was no hiding her fury. She commanded Ser Merrell to question the grooms and stableboys more sharply. When the questioning proved fruitless, she relieved him of his command and expelled him from Dragonstone, together with his son Ser Alyn, and a dozen other men she found suspicious. She even went so far as to summon her husband, Androw Farman, demanding to know if he had been complicit in his sister's crime. His denials only goaded her to more rage, until their shouts could be heard echoing through the halls of Dragonstone. She sent men to Driftmark, only to learn that Lady Elissa had sailed to Pentos. She sent men to Pentos, but there the trail went cold.

Only then did Rhaena Targaryen mount Dreamfyre to fly to the Red Keep and inform her brother of what had transpired. "Elissa had no love for dragons," she told the king. "It was gold she wanted, gold to build a ship. She will sell the eggs. They are worth—"

"—a fleet of ships." Jaehaerys had received his sister in his solar, with only Grand Maester Benifer present to bear witness to what was said. "If those eggs should hatch, there will be another dragonlord in the world, one not of our own house."

"They may not hatch," Benifer said. "Not away from Dragonstone. The heat . . . it is known, some dragon eggs simply turn to stone."

"Then some spicemonger in Pentos will find himself possessed of three very costly stones," Jaehaerys said. "Elsewise . . . the birth of three young dragons is not a thing that can easily be kept secret. Whoever has them will want to crow. We must have eyes and ears in Pentos, Tyrosh, Myr, all the Free Cities. Offer rewards for any word of dragons."

"What do you mean to do?" his sister Rhaena asked him.

"What I must. What *you* must. Do not think to wash your hands of this, sweet sister. You wanted Dragonstone and I gave it to you, and you brought this woman there. This thief."

The long reign of Jaehaerys I Targaryen was a peaceful one, for the most part; such wars as he fought were few and short. Let no man mistake Jaehaerys for his father, Aenys, however. There was nothing weak about him, nothing indecisive, as his sister Rhaena and Grand Maester Benifer witnessed then, when the king went on to say, "Should the dragons turn up, anywhere from here to Yi Ti, we will demand their return. They were stolen from us, they are ours by right. If that demand should be denied, then we must needs go and get them. Take them back if we can, kill them if not. No hatchlings can hope to stand against Vermithor and Dreamfyre."

"And Silverwing?" asked Rhaena. "Our sister—"

"—had no part in this. I will not put her at risk."

The Queen in the East smiled then. "She is Rhaenys, and I am Visenya. I have never thought otherwise."

Grand Maester Benifer said, "You are speaking of waging war across the narrow sea, Your Grace. The costs—"

"—must needs be borne. I will not allow Valyria to rise again. Imagine what the triarchs of Volantis would do with dragons. Let us pray it never comes to that." With that His Grace ended the audience, cautioning the others not to speak of the missing eggs. "No one must know of this but we three."

It was too late for such cautions, though. On Dragonstone, the theft was common knowledge, even amongst the fisherfolk. And fisherfolk, as is known, sail to other islands, and thus the whispers spread. Benifer, acting through the Pentoshi master of coin, who had agents in every port, reached out across the narrow sea as the king had commanded . . . "paying good coin to bad men" (in the words of Rego Draz) for any news of dragon eggs, dragons, or Elissa Farman. A small host of whisperers, informers, courtiers, and courtesans produced hundreds of reports, a score of which proved to be of value to the Iron Throne for other reasons . . . but every rumor of the dragon eggs proved worthless.

We know now that Lady Elissa made her way to Braavos after Pentos, though not before taking on a new name. Having been driven from Fair Isle and disowned by her brother Lord Franklyn, she took on a bastard name of her own devising, calling herself Alys Westhill. Under that name, she secured an audience with the Sealord of Braavos. The Sealord's menagerie was far famed, and he was glad to buy the dragon eggs. The gold she received in return she entrusted to the Iron Bank, and used it to finance the building of the *Sun Chaser,* the ship she had dreamed of for many a year.

None of this was known on Westeros at the time, however, and soon enough King Jaehaerys had a fresh concern. In the Starry Sept of Oldtown, the High Septon had collapsed whilst ascending a flight of steps to his bedchamber. He was dead before he reached the bottom. All across the realm, bells in every sept sang a dolorous song. The Father of the Faithful had gone to join the Seven.

The king had no time for prayer or grieving, though. As soon as His Holiness was interred, the Most Devout would be assembling in the Starry Sept to choose his successor, and Jaehaerys knew that the peace of the realm depended on the new man continuing the policies of his predecessor. The king had his own candidate for the crystal crown: Septon Barth, who had come to oversee the Red Keep's library, only to become one of his most trusted advisors. It took half the night for Barth himself to persuade His Grace of the folly of his choice; he was too young, too little known, too unorthodox in his opinions, not even one of the Most Devout. He had no hope of being chosen. They would need another candidate, one more acceptable to his brothers of the Faith.

The king and the lords of the council were agreed on one thing, however; they must needs do all they could to make certain that Septon Mattheus was not chosen. His tenure in King's Landing had left a legacy of mistrust behind it, and Jaehaerys could neither forgive nor forget his words at the gates of Dragonstone.

Rego Draz suggested that some well-placed bribes might produce the desired result. "Spread enough gold amongst these Most Devout and they will choose me," he japed, "though I would not want the job." Daemon Velaryon and Qarl Corbray advocated a show of force, though Lord Daemon wished to send his fleet, whilst Lord Qarl offered to lead an army. Albin Massey, the bent-backed master of laws, wondered if Septon Mattheus might suffer the same fate as the High Septon who had made such trouble for Aenys and Maegor; a sudden, mysterious death. Septon Barth, Grand Maester Benifer, and Queen Alysanne were horrified by all these proposals, and the king rejected them out of hand. He and the queen would go to Oldtown at once, he decided instead. His High Holiness had been a leal servant to the gods and a staunch friend to the Iron Throne, it was only right that they be there to see him laid to rest.

The only way to reach Oldtown in time was by dragon.

All the lords of the council, even Septon Barth, were made uneasy by the thought of the king and queen alone in Oldtown. "There are still those amongst my brothers who do not love Your Grace," Barth pointed out. Lord Daemon agreed, and reminded Jaehaerys of what had befallen the queen at Maidenpool. When the king insisted that he would have the protection of the Hightower, uneasy glances were exchanged. "Lord Donnel is a schemer and a sulker," said Manfryd Redwyne. "I do not trust him. Nor should you. He does what he thinks best for himself, his house, and Oldtown, and cares not a fig for anyone or anything else. Not even for his king."

"Then I must convince him that what is best for his king is what is best for himself, his house, and Oldtown," said Jaehaerys. "I believe I can do that." So he ended the discussion and gave orders for their dragons to be brought forth.

Even for a dragon, the flight from King's Landing to Oldtown is a long one. The king and queen stopped twice along the way, once at Bitterbridge and once at Highgarden, resting overnight and taking counsel with their lords. The lords of the council had insisted that they take *some* protection at the very least. Ser Joffrey Doggett flew with Alysanne, and the Scarlet Shadow, Jonquil Darke, with Jaehaerys, so as to balance the weight each dragon carried.

The unexpected arrival of Vermithor and Silverwing at Oldtown brought thousands to the streets to point and stare. No word of their coming had been sent ahead, and there were many in the city who were frightened, wondering what this might portend . . . none, mayhaps, more than Septon Mattheus, who turned pale when he was told. Jaehaerys brought down Vermithor on the wide marble plaza outside the Starry Sept, but it was his queen who made the city gasp when Silverwing alighted atop the Hightower itself, the beating of her wings fanning the flames of its famous beacon.

Though the High Septon's funeral rites were the purported reason for their visit, His High Holiness had already been interred in the crypts beneath the Starry Sept by the time the king and queen arrived. Jaehaerys gave a eulogy nonetheless, addressing a huge crowd of septons, maesters, and smallfolk in the plaza. At the end of his remarks, he announced that he and the queen would remain in Oldtown until the new High Septon had been chosen "so we might ask for his blessing." As Archmaester Goodwyn wrote afterward, "The smallfolk cheered, the maesters nodded sagely, and the septons looked at one another and thought on dragons."

During their time in Oldtown, Jaehaerys and Alysanne slept in Lord

Donnel's own apartments at the top of the Hightower, with all of Oldtown spread out below. We have no certain knowledge of what words passed between them and their host, for their discussions took place behind closed doors without even a maester present. Years later, however, King Jaehaerys told Septon Barth all that occurred, and Barth set down a summary for the sake of history.

The Hightowers of Oldtown were an ancient family, powerful, wealthy, proud . . . and large. It had long been their custom for the younger sons, brothers, cousins, and bastards of the house to join the Faith, where many had risen high over the centuries. Lord Donnel Hightower had a younger brother, two nephews, and six cousins serving the Seven in 54 AC; the brother, one nephew, and two cousins wore the cloth-of-silver of the Most Devout. It was Lord Donnel's desire that one of them become High Septon.

King Jaehaerys did not care which house His High Holiness derived from, or whether he was of low or noble birth. His only concern was that the new High Septon be an Exceptionalist. The Targaryen tradition of sibling marriage must never again be questioned by the Starry Sept. He wanted the new Father of the Faithful to make Exceptionalism an official doctrine of the Faith. And though His Grace had no objection to Lord Donnel's brother, nor the rest of his ilk, none of them had yet spoken on the issue, so . . .

After hours of discussion, an understanding was reached, and sealed with a great feast wherein Lord Donnel praised the wisdom of the king, whilst making him acquainted with his brothers, uncles, nephews, nieces, and cousins. Across the city at the Starry Sept, the Most Devout convened to choose their new shepherd, with agents of Lord Hightower and the king amongst them, unbeknownst to most. Four ballots were required. Septon Mattheus led on the first, as anticipated, but lacked the votes necessary to secure the crystal crown. Thereafter his numbers dwindled on every ballot, whilst other men rose up.

On the fourth ballot, the Most Devout broke tradition, choosing a man who was not one of their own number. The laurel fell to the Septon Alfyn, who had crossed the Reach a dozen times in his litter on behalf of Jaehaerys and his queen. The Seven Kingdoms had no fiercer champion of

Exceptionalism than Alfyn, but he was the oldest of the Seven Speakers, and legless besides; it seemed likely the Stranger would seek him out sooner rather than later. When that befell, his own successor would be a Hightower, the king assured Lord Donnel, provided his kin aligned themselves firmly with the Exceptionalists during Septon Alfyn's reign.

Thus was the bargain struck, if Septon Barth's account can be believed. Barth himself did not question it, though he rued the corruption that made the Most Devout so easy to manipulate. "It would be better if the Seven themselves would choose their Voice on earth, but when the gods are silent, lords and kings will make themselves heard," he wrote, and added that both Alfyn and Lord Donnel's brother, who succeeded him, were more worthy of the crystal crown than Septon Mattheus could ever have been.

No one was more astonished by the selection of Septon Alfyn than Septon Alfyn himself, who was at Ashford when word reached him. Traveling by litter, it took him more than a fortnight to reach Oldtown. Whilst awaiting his coming, Jaehaerys used the time to call at Bandallon, Three Towers, Uplands, and Honeyholt. He even flew Vermithor to the Arbor, where he sampled some of that island's choicest wines. Queen Alysanne remained in Oldtown. The silent sisters hosted her in their motherhouse for a day of prayer and contemplation. Another day she spent with the septas who cared for the city's sick and destitute. Amongst the novices she met was her niece Rhaella, whom Her Grace pronounced a learned and devout young woman "though much given to stammers and blushes." For three days she lost herself in the Citadel's great library, emerging only to attend lectures on the Valyrian dragon wars, leechcraft, and the gods of the Summer Isles.

Afterward she feasted the assembled archmaesters in their own dining hall, and even presumed to lecture them. "If I had not become queen, I might have liked to be a maester," she told the Conclave. "I read, I write, I think, I am not afraid of ravens . . . or a bit of blood. There are other highborn girls who feel the same. Why not admit them to your Citadel? If they cannot keep up, send them home, the way you send home boys who are not clever enough. If you would give the girls a chance, you might be surprised by how many forge a chain." The archmaesters, loath to gainsay the queen, smiled at her words and bobbed their heads and assured Her Grace that they would consider her proposal.

Once the new High Septon reached Oldtown, stood his vigil in the Starry Sept, and had been duly anointed and consecrated to the Seven, forsaking his earthly name and all earthly ties, he blessed King Jaehaerys and Queen Alysanne at a solemn public ceremony. The Kingsguard and a company of retainers had joined the king and queen as well by that point, so His Grace decided to return by way of the Dornish Marches and the stormlands. Visits at Horn Hill, Nightsong, and Blackhaven followed.

Queen Alysanne found the last especially congenial. Though his castle was small and modest compared to the great halls of the realm, Lord Dondarrion was a splendid host and his son Simon played the high harp as well as he jousted, and entertained the royal couple by night with sad songs of star-crossed lovers and the fall of kings. So taken with him was the queen that the party lingered longer at Blackhaven than they had intended. They were still there when a raven reached them from Storm's End with dire tidings; their mother, Queen Alyssa, was at the point of death.

Once more Vermithor and Silverwing took to the skies, to bring the king and queen to their mother's side as quickly as possible. The remainder of the royal party would follow overland by way of Stonehelm, Crow's Nest, and Griffin's Roost, under the command of Ser Gyles Morrigen, Lord Commander of the Kingsguard.

The great Baratheon stronghold of Storm's End has but a single tower, the massive drum tower raised by Durran Godsgrief during the Age of Heroes to stand against the wroth of the storm god. At the top of that tower, beneath only the maester's cell and the rookery, Alysanne and Jaehaerys found their mother asleep in a bed that stank of urine, drenched in sweat and gaunt as a crone, save for her swollen belly. A maester, a midwife, and three bedmaids were in attendance on her, each grimmer than the last. Jaehaerys discovered Lord Rogar seated outside the chamber door, drunk and despairing. When the king demanded to know why he was not with his wife, the Lord of Storm's End growled, "The Stranger's in that room. I can smell him."

A cup of wine tinged with sweetsleep was all that allowed Queen Alyssa even this brief respite, Maester Kyrie explained; Alyssa had been in agony for some hours before. "She was screaming so," one of the servants added. "Every bit o' food we give her comes back up, and she's having awful pain."

"She was not due," Queen Alysanne said, in tears. "Not yet."

"Not for a moon's turn," confirmed the midwife. "This is no labor, m'lords. Something's tore inside her. Babe's dying, or will be dead soon. The mother's too old, she's no strength to push, and the babe's twisted around . . . it's no good. They'll be gone by first light, both o' them. Begging your pardons."

Maester Kyrie did not disagree. Milk of the poppy would relieve the queen's pain, he said, and he had a strong draught prepared . . . but it could kill Her Grace as easily as help her, and would almost certainly kill the child inside her. When Jaehaerys asked what could be done, the maester said, "For the queen? Nothing. She is beyond my power to save. There is a chance, a slight chance, that I could save the child. To do so I would need to cut the mother open and remove the child from her womb. The babe might live, or not. The woman will die."

His words set Queen Alysanne to weeping. The king said only, "The woman is my mother, and a queen," in a heavy tone. He stepped outside again, pulled Rogar Baratheon to his feet, and dragged him back into the birthing chamber, where he bade the maester repeat what he had just said. "She is your wife," King Jaehaerys reminded Lord Rogar. "It is for you to say the words."

Lord Rogar, we are told, could not bear to look upon his wife. Nor could he find the words until the king took him roughly by the arm and shook him. "Save my son," Rogar told the maester. Then he wrenched free and fled the room again. Maester Kyrie bowed his head and sent for his blades.

In many of the accounts that have come down to us, we are told that Queen Alyssa woke from her sleep before the maester could begin. Though wracked by pain and violent convulsions, she cried tears of joy to see her children there. When Alysanne told her what was about to happen, Alyssa gave her assent. "Save my babe," she whispered. "I will go to see my boys again. The Crone will light my way." It is pleasant to believe these were the queen's last words. Sad to say, other accounts tell us that Her Grace died without waking when Maester Kyrie opened her belly. On one point all agree: Alysanne held her mother's hand in her own from start to finish, until the babe's first squall filled the room.

Lord Rogar did not get the second son that he had prayed for. The child was a girl, born so small and weak that midwife and maester alike did not believe she would survive. She surprised them both, as she would surprise many others in her time. Days later, when he had finally recovered himself enough to consider the matter, Rogar Baratheon named his daughter Jocelyn.

First, however, his lordship had to contend with a more contentious arrival. Dawn was breaking and Queen Alyssa's body was not yet cold when Vermithor raised his head from where he had been coiled sleeping in the yard, and gave out with a roar that woke half of Storm's End. He had scented the approach of another dragon. Moments later Dreamfyre descended, silver crests flashing along her back as her pale blue wings beat against the red dawn sky. Rhaena Targaryen had come to make amends to her mother.

She came too late; Queen Alyssa was gone. Though the king told her she did not need to look upon their mother's mortal remains, Rhaena insisted, ripping away the bedclothes that covered her to gaze upon the maester's work. After a long time she turned away to kiss her brother on the cheek and embrace her younger sister. The two queens held each other for a long while, it is said, but when the midwife offered Rhaena the newborn babe to hold, she refused. "Where is Rogar?" she asked.

She found him below in his great hall with his young son, Boremund, in his lap, surrounded by his brothers and his knights. Rhaena Targaryen pushed through all of them to stand over him, and began to curse him to his face. "Her blood is on your hands," she raged at him. "Her blood is on your cock. May you die screaming."

Rogar Baratheon was outraged by her accusations. "What are you saying, woman? This is the will of the gods. The Stranger comes for all of us. How could it be my doing? What did I do?"

"You put your cock in her. She gave you one son, that should have been enough. *Save my wife,* you should have said, but what are wives to men like you?" Rhaena reached out and grabbed his beard and pulled his face to hers. "Hear this, my lord. Do not think to wed again. Take care of the whelps my mother gave you, my half-brother and half-sister. See that they want for nothing. Do that, and I will let you be. If I should hear even a whisper of your taking some other poor maid to wife, I will make another Harrenhal of Storm's End, with you and her inside it."

When she had stormed from the hall, back to her dragon in the yard, Lord Rogar and his brothers shared a laugh. "She is mad," he declared. "Does she think to frighten me? *Me?* I did not fear the wroth of Maegor the Cruel, should I fear hers?" Thereafter he drank a cup of wine, summoned his steward to make arrangements for his wife's burial, and sent his brother Ser Garon to invite the king and queen to stay on for a feast in honor of his daughter.*

It was a sadder king who returned to King's Landing from Storm's End. The Most Devout had given him the High Septon he desired, the Doctrine of Exceptionalism would be a tenet of the Faith, and he had reached an accord with the powerful Hightowers of Oldtown, but these victories had turned to ashes in his mouth with the death of his mother. Jaehaerys was not one to brood, however; as he would do so often during his long reign, the king shrugged off his sorrows and plunged himself into the ruling of his realm.

Summer had given way to autumn and leaves were falling all across the Seven Kingdoms, a new Vulture King had emerged in the Red Mountains, the sweating sickness had broken out on the Three Sisters, and Tyrosh and Lys were edging toward a war that would almost certainly engulf the Stepstones and disrupt trade. All this must needs be dealt with, and deal with it he did.

Queen Alysanne found a different answer. Having lost a mother, she found solace in a daughter. Though not quite a year and a half old, Princess Daenerys had been talking (after a fashion) since well before her first nameday, and had gone past crawling, lurching, and walking into running. "She is in a great hurry, this one," her wet nurse told the queen. The little princess was a happy child, endlessly curious and utterly fearless, a delight to all who knew her. She so enchanted Alysanne that for a time Her Grace

* Rogar Baratheon never wed again.

even began to eschew council sessions, preferring to spend her days playing with her daughter and reading her the stories that her own mother had once read to her. "She is so clever, she will be reading to me before long," she told the king. "She is going to be a great queen, I know it."

The Stranger was not yet done with House Targaryen in that cruel year of 54 AC, however. Across Blackwater Bay on Dragonstone, Rhaena Targaryen had found new griefs awaiting her when she returned from Storm's End. Far from being a joy and a comfort to her as Daenerys was to Alysanne, her own daughter Aerea had become a terror, a willful wild child who defied her septa, her mother, and her maesters alike, abused her servants, absented herself from prayers, lessons, and meals without leave, and addressed the men and women of Rhaena's court with such charming names as "Ser Stupid," "Lord Pigface," and "Lady Farts-a-Lot."

Her Grace's husband, Androw Farman, though less vocal and openly defiant, was no less angry. When word first reached Dragonstone that Queen Alyssa was failing, Androw had announced that he would accompany his wife to Storm's End. As her husband, he said, his place was at Rhaena's side, to give her comfort. The queen had refused him, however, and not gently. A loud argument had preceded her departure, and Her Grace was heard to say, "The wrong Farman ran away." Her marriage, never passionate, had become a mummer's farce by 54 AC. "And not an entertaining one," Lady Alayne Royce observed.

Androw Farman was no longer the lad that Rhaena had married five years earlier on Fair Isle, when he was ten-and-seven. The comely stripling had become puffy-faced, round-shouldered, and fleshy. Never well regarded by other men, he had found himself forgotten and ignored by their lordly hosts during Rhaena's wanderings in the west. Dragonstone proved to be no better. His wife was still a queen, but no one mistook Androw for a king, or even a lord consort. Though he sat at Queen Rhaena's side during meals, he did not share her bed. That honor went to her friends and favorites. His own bedchamber was in an altogether different tower from hers. The gossips at court said the queen told him that it was better that they slept apart, so he need not be disturbed if he should find some pretty maid to warm his bed. There is no indication that he ever did.

His days were as empty as his nights. Though he had been born upon an island and now lived upon another, Androw did not sail or swim or fish. A failed squire, he had no skill with sword nor axe nor spear, so when the men of the castle garrison trained each morning in the yard, he kept to his bed. Thinking that he might be of a bookish disposition, Maester Culiper tried to interest him in the treasures of Dragonstone's library, the ponderous tomes and Old Valyrian scrolls that had fascinated King Jaehaerys, only to discover that the queen's husband could not read. Androw rode passably well, and from time to time would have a horse saddled so he might trot about the yard, but he never passed beyond the gates to explore the Dragonmont's rocky paths or the far side of the island, nor even the fishing village and docks beneath the castle.

"He drinks a deal," Maester Culiper wrote to the Citadel, "and has been known to spend entire days in the Chamber of the Painted Table, moving painted wooden soldiers about the map. Queen Rhaena's companions are wont to say he is planning his conquest of Westeros. They do not mock him to his face for her sake, but they titter at him behind his back. The knights and men-at-arms pay him no mind whatsoever, and the servants obey him or not, as they please, with no fear of his displeasure. The children are the cruelest, as children often are, and none half so cruel as the Princess Aerea. She once emptied a chamberpot upon his head, not for anything he did, but because she was wroth with her mother."

Androw Farman's discontent on Dragonstone only grew worse after his sister's departure. Lady Elissa had been his closest friend, mayhaps his only friend, Culiper observed, and despite his tearful denials, Rhaena found it hard to accept that he had played no role in the matter of her dragon eggs. When the queen dismissed Ser Merrell Bullock, Androw had asked her to appoint him commander of the castle garrison in Bullock's place. Her Grace had been breaking her fast with four of her ladies-in-waiting at the time. The women burst into laughter at his request, and after a moment the queen had laughed as well. When Rhaena flew to King's Landing to inform King Jaehaerys of the theft, Androw had offered to accompany her. His wife refused him scornfully. "What would that serve? What could you possibly do but fall off the dragon?"

Queen Rhaena's denial of his wish to go with her to Storm's End was but the latest and the last in a long string of humiliations for Androw

Farman. By the time Rhaena returned from her mother's deathbed, he was well past any desire to comfort her. Sullen and cold, he sat silent at meals and avoided the queen's company elsewise. If Rhaena Targaryen was troubled by his sulks, she gave little sign of it. She found consolation in her ladies instead, in old friends like Samantha Stokeworth and Alayne Royce, and newer companions like her cousin Lianna Velaryon, Lord Staunton's pretty daughter Cassella, and young Septa Maryam.

Whatever peace they helped her find proved short-lived. Autumn had come to Dragonstone, as to the rest of Westeros, and with it came cold winds from the north and storms from the south raging up the narrow sea. A darkness settled over the ancient fortress, a gloomy place even in summer; even the dragons seemed to feel the damp. And as the year waned, the sickness came to Dragonstone.

It was not the sweating sickness, nor the shaking sickness, nor greyscale, Maester Culiper pronounced. The first sign was a bloody stool, followed by a terrible cramping in the gut. There were a number of diseases that could be the cause, he told the queen. Which of those might be to blame he never determined, for Culiper himself was the first to die, less than two days after he began to feel ill. Maester Anselm, who took his place, thought his age to blame. Culiper had been closer to ninety than to eighty, and not strong.

Cassella Staunton was the next to succumb, however, and she was but four-and-ten. Then Septa Maryam sickened, and Alayne Royce, and even big, boisterous Sam Stokeworth, who liked to boast that she had never been sick a day in her life. All three died the same night, within hours of one another.

Rhaena Targaryen herself remained untouched, though her friends and dear companions were being felled one by one. It was her Valyrian blood that saved her, Maester Anselm suggested; ailments that carried off ordinary men in a matter of hours could not prevail against the blood of the dragon. Males also seemed largely immune to this queer plague. Aside from Maester Culiper, only women were struck down. The men of Dragonstone, be they knights, scullions, stableboys, or singers, remained healthy.

Queen Rhaena ordered the gates of Dragonstone closed and barred. As yet there was no sickness beyond her walls, and she meant for it to stay that way, to protect the smallfolk. When she sent word to King's Landing, Jaehaerys acted at once, commanding Lord Velaryon to send forth his galleys to make certain no one escaped to spread the pestilence beyond the island. The King's Hand did as commanded, though not without grief, for his own young niece was amongst the women still on Dragonstone.

Lianna Velaryon died even as her uncle's galleys were pushing off from Driftmark. Maester Anselm had purged her, bled her, and covered her with ice, all to no avail. She died in Rhaena Targaryen's arms, convulsing as the queen wept bitter tears.

"You weep for her," Androw Farman said when he saw the tears on his wife's face, "but would you weep for me?" His words woke a fury in the queen. Lashing him across the face, Rhaena commanded him to leave her, declaring that she wanted to be alone. "You shall be," Androw said. "She was the last of them."

Even then, so lost was the queen in her grief that she did not realize what had happened. It was Rego Draz, the king's Pentoshi master of coin, who first gave voice to suspicion when Jaehaerys assembled his small council to discuss the deaths on Dragonstone. Reading over Maester Anselm's accounts, Lord Rego furrowed his brow and said, "Sickness? This is no sickness. A weasel in the guts, dead in a day . . . this is the tears of Lys."

"Poison?" King Jaehaerys said in shock.

"We know more of such things in the Free Cities," Draz assured him. "It is the tears, never doubt it. The old maester would have seen it soon enough, so he had to die first. That is how I would do it. Not that I would. Poison is . . . dishonorable."

"Only women were struck down," objected Lord Velaryon.

"Only women got the poison, then," said Rego Draz.

When Septon Barth and Grand Maester Benifer concurred with Lord Rego's words, the king dispatched a raven to Dragonstone. Once Rhaena Targaryen read his words, she had no doubt. Summoning the captain of her guards, she commanded that her husband be found and brought to her.

Androw Farman was not to be found in his bedchamber nor the queen's,

nor the great hall, nor the stables, nor the sept, nor Aegon's Garden. In Sea Dragon Tower, in the maester's chambers under the rookery, they discovered Maester Anselm dead, with a dagger between his shoulder blades. With the gates closed and barred, there was no way to leave the castle save by dragon. "My worm of a husband does not have the courage for that," Rhaena declared.

Androw Farman was located at last in the Chamber of the Painted Table, a longsword clutched in his grasp. He made no attempt to deny the poisonings. Instead he boasted. "I brought them cups of wine, and they drank. They *thanked* me, and they drank. Why not? A cupbearer, a serving man, that's how they saw me. Androw the sweet. Androw the jape. What could *I* do, but fall off the dragon? Well, I could have done a lot of things. I could have been a lord. I could have made laws and been wise and given you counsel. I could have killed your enemies, as easily as I killed your friends. *I could have given you children.*"

Rhaena Targaryen did not deign to reply to him. Instead she spoke to her guards, saying, "Take him and geld him, but staunch the wound. I want his cock and balls fried up and fed to him. Do not let him die until he has eaten every bite."

"No," Androw Farman said, as they moved around the Painted Table to grasp him. "My wife can fly, and so can I." And so saying, he slashed ineffectually at the nearest man, backed to the window behind him, and leapt out. His flight was a short one: downward, to his death. Afterward Rhaena Targaryen had his body hacked to pieces and fed to her dragons.

His was the last notable death of 54 AC, but there was still more ill to come in that terrible Year of the Stranger. Just as a stone thrown into a pond will send out ripples in all directions, the evil that Androw Farman had wrought would spread across the land, touching and twisting the lives of others long after the dragons were done feasting on his blackened, smoking remains.

The first ripple was felt in the king's own small council, when Lord Daemon Velaryon announced his desire to step down as Hand of the King. Queen Alyssa, it will be recalled, had been Lord Daemon's sister, and his young niece Lianna had been amongst the women poisoned on Dragonstone. Some have suggested that rivalry with Lord Manfryd Redwyne, who had replaced him as lord admiral, played a part in Lord Daemon's decision, but this seems a petty aspersion to cast at a man who served so ably and so long. Let us rather take his lordship at his word and accept that his advancing age and a desire to spend his remaining days with his children and grandchildren on Driftmark were the cause of his departure.

Jaehaerys's first thought was to look to the other members of his council for Lord Daemon's successor. Albin Massey, Rego Draz, and Septon Barth had all shown themselves to be men of great ability, earning the king's trust and gratitude. None, however, seemed wholly suitable. Septon Barth was suspected of having greater loyalty to the Starry Sept than to the Iron Throne. Moreover, he was of very low birth; the great lords of the realm would never allow the son of a blacksmith to speak with the king's voice. Lord Rego was a godless Pentoshi and an upjumped spicemonger, and his birth was, if anything, even lower than Septon Barth's. Lord Albin, with his limp and twisted back, would strike the ignorant as somehow sinister. "They look at me and see a villain," Massey himself told the king. "I can serve you better from the shadows."

There could be no question of bringing back Rogar Baratheon nor any of King Maegor's surviving Hands. Lord Tully's term upon the council during the regency had been undistinguished. Rodrik Arryn, Lord of the Eyrie and Defender of the Vale, was a boy of ten, having come untimely into his lordship after the deaths of his uncle Lord Darnold and his sire Ser Rymond at the hands of the wildling raiders they had unwisely pursued into the Mountains of the Moon. Jaehaerys had but recently reached an understanding with Donnel Hightower, but still did not entirely trust the man, no more than he did Lyman Lannister. Bertrand Tyrell, the Lord of Highgarden, was known to be a drunkard, whose unruly bastard sons would bring disgrace down on the Crown if turned loose upon King's Landing. Alaric Stark was best left in Winterfell; a stubborn man by all reports, stern and hard-handed and unforgiving, he would make for an uncomfortable presence at the council table. It would be unthinkable to bring an ironman to King's Landing, of course.

With none of the great lords of the realm being found suitable, Jaehaerys next turned to their lords bannermen. It was thought desirable that the Hand be an older man, whose experience would balance the king's youth. As the council included several learned men of bookish inclination, a warrior was wanted as well, a man blooded and tested in battle whose martial reputation would dishearten the Crown's enemies. After a dozen names had been put forward and bandied about, the choice finally fell to Ser Myles Smallwood, Lord of Acorn Hall in the riverlands, who had fought for the king's brother, Aegon, beneath the Gods Eye, battled Wat the Hewer at Stonebridge, and ridden with the late Lord Stokeworth to bring Harren the Red to justice during the reign of King Aenys.

Justly famed for his courage, Lord Myles wore the scars of a dozen savage fights upon his face and body. Ser Willam the Wasp of the Kingsguard, who had served at Acorn Hall, swore there was no finer, fiercer, or more leal lord in all the Seven Kingdoms, and Prentys Tully and the redoubtable Lady Lucinda, his liege lords, had naught but praise for Smallwood as well. Thus persuaded, Jaehaerys gave his assent, a raven took wing, and within the fortnight, Lord Myles was on his way to King's Landing.

Queen Alysanne played no part in the selection of the King's Hand. Whilst the king and council were deliberating, Her Grace was absent from King's Landing, having flown Silverwing to Dragonstone to be with her sister and comfort her in her grief.

Rhaena Targaryen was not a woman easily comforted, however. The loss of so many of her dear friends and companions had plunged her into a black melancholy, and even the mention of Androw Farman's name provoked her to fits of rage. Far from welcoming her sister and whatever solace she might bring, Rhaena thrice tried to send her away, even going so far as to scream at Her Grace in view of half the castle. When the queen refused to go, Rhaena retreated to her own chambers and barred the doors, emerging only to eat . . . and that less and less often.

Left to her own devices, Alysanne Targaryen set about restoring a modicum of order to Dragonstone. A new maester was sent for and installed, a new captain appointed to take charge of the castle garrison. The queen's own beloved Septa Edyth arrived to assume the place of Rhaena's much lamented Septa Maryam.

Shunned by her sister, Alysanne turned to her niece, but there too she encountered rage and rejection. "Why should I care if they're all dead? She'll find new ones; she always does," Princess Aerea told the queen. When Alysanne tried to share stories of her own girlhood, and told of how Rhaena had put a dragon's egg into her cradle and cuddled and cared for her "as if she were my mother," Aerea said, "She never gave me an egg, she just gave me away and flew off to Fair Isle." Alysanne's love for her own daughter provoked the princess to anger as well. "Why should she be queen? I should be queen, not her." It was then that Aerea broke down into tears at last, pleading with Alysanne to take her back with her to King's Landing. "Lady Elissa said that she would take me, but she went away and forgot me. I want to come back to court, with the singers and the fools and all the lords and knights. Please take me with you."

Moved by the girl's tears, Queen Alysanne could do no more than promise to take the matter up with her mother. When Rhaena next emerged from her chambers to take a meal, however, she rejected the notion out of hand. "You have everything and I have nothing. Now you would take my daughter too. Well, you shall not have her. You have my throne, content yourself with that." That same night Rhaena summoned Princess Aerea to her chambers to berate her, and the sounds of mother and daughter shouting at one another rang through the Stone Drum. The princess refused to speak to Queen Alysanne after that. Stymied at every turn, Her Grace finally returned to King's Landing, to the arms of King Jaehaerys and the merry laughter of her own daughter, Princess Daenerys.

As the Year of the Stranger neared its end, work on the Dragonpit was all but complete. The great dome in place at last, the massive bronze gates hung, the cavernous edifice dominated the city from the crown of Rhaenys's Hill, second only to the Red Keep upon Aegon's High Hill. To mark its completion and celebrate the arrival of the new Hand, Lord Redwyne proposed to the king that they stage a great tourney, the largest and grandest the realm had seen since the Golden Wedding. "Let us put our sorrows behind us and begin the new year with pageantry and celebration," Redwyne argued. The autumn harvests had been good, Lord Rego's taxes were bringing in a steady stream of coin, trade was on the increase; paying for the tourney would not be a concern, and the event would bring thousands of visitors, and their purses, to King's Landing. The rest of the council was all in favor of the proposal, and King Jaehaerys allowed that a tourney might indeed give the smallfolk something to cheer, "and help us forget our woes."

All such preparations were thrown into disarray by the sudden and unexpected arrival of Rhaena Targaryen from Dragonstone. "It may well be that dragons somehow sense, and echo, the moods of their riders," Septon Barth wrote, "for Dreamfyre came down out of the clouds like a raging storm that day, and Vermithor and Silverwing rose up and roared at her coming, suchwise that all of us who saw and heard were fearful that the dragons were about to fly at one another with flame and claw, and tear each other apart as Balerion once did to Quicksilver by the Gods Eye."

The dragons did not, in the end, fight, though there was much hissing and snapping as Rhaena flung herself off Dreamfyre and stormed into Maegor's Holdfast, shouting for her brother and her sister. The source of her fury was soon known. Princess Aerea was gone. She had fled Dragonstone as dawn broke, stealing into the yards and claiming a dragon for her own. And not just any dragon. *"Balerion!"* Rhaena exclaimed. "She took Balerion, the mad child. No hatchling for her, no, not her, she had to have the Black Dread. *Maegor's* dragon, the beast that slew her father. Why him, if not to pain me? What did I give birth to? What kind of beast? I ask you, *what did I give birth to*?"

"A little girl," Queen Alysanne said, "she is just an angry little girl." But Septon Barth and Grand Maester Benifer tell us that Rhaena did not seem to hear her. She was desperate to know where her "mad child" might have fled. Her first thought had been King's Landing, Aerea had been so eager to return to court . . . but if she was not here, where?

"We will learn that soon enough, I suspect," King Jaehaerys said, as calm as ever. "Balerion is too big to hide or pass unnoticed. And he has a fearsome appetite." He turned to Grand Maester Benifer then, and commanded that ravens be sent forth to every castle in the Seven Kingdoms. "If any man in Westeros should so much as glimpse Balerion or my niece, I want to know at once."

The ravens flew, but there was no word of Princess Aerea that day, or the day after, or the day after that. Rhaena remained at the Red Keep all the while, sometimes raging, sometimes shaking, drinking sweetwine to sleep. Princess Daenerys was so frightened by her aunt that she cried whenever she came into her presence. After seven days Rhaena declared that she could no longer sit here idle. "I need to find her. If I cannot find her, at least I can look." So saying, she mounted Dreamfyre and was gone.

Neither mother nor daughter was seen or heard from again during what little remained of that cruel year.

Jaehaerys and Alysanne

Their Triumphs and Tragedies

The accomplishments of King Jaehaerys I Targaryen are almost too many to enumerate. Chief amongst them, in the view of most students of history, are the long periods of peace and prosperity that marked his time upon the Iron Throne. It cannot be said Jaehaerys avoided conflict entirely, for that would be beyond the power of any earthly king, but such wars as he fought were short, victorious, and contested largely at sea or on distant soil. "It is a poor king who wages battle against his own lords and leaves his own kingdom burned, bloody, and strewn with corpses," Septon Barth would write. "His Grace was a wiser man than that."

Archmaesters can and do quibble about the numbers, but most agree that the population of Westeros north of Dorne doubled during the Conciliator's reign, whilst the population of King's Landing increased fourfold. Lannisport, Gulltown, Duskendale, and White Harbor grew as well, though not to the same extent.

With fewer men marching off to war, more remained to work the land. Grain prices fell steadily throughout his reign, as more acres came under the plough. Fish became notably cheaper, even for common men, as the fishing villages along the coasts grew more prosperous and more boats put to sea. New orchards were planted everywhere from the Reach to the Neck. Lamb and mutton became more plentiful and wool finer as shepherds increased the size of their flocks. Trade increased tenfold, despite the vicissitudes of wind, weather, and wars and the disruptions they caused from time to time. The crafts flourished as well; farriers and blacksmiths, stonemasons, carpenters, millers, tanners, weavers, felters, dyers, brewers, vintners, goldsmiths and silversmiths, bakers, butchers, and cheesemakers all enjoyed a prosperity hitherto unknown west of the narrow sea.

There were, to be sure, good years and bad years, but it was rightly said that under Jaehaerys and his queen the good years were twice as good as the bad years were bad. Storms there were, and ill winds, and bitter winters, but when men look back today upon the Conciliator's reign it is easy to mistake it for one long green and gentle summer.

Little of this would have been apparent to Jaehaerys himself as the bells of King's Landing rang to usher in the 55th year since Aegon's Conquest. The wounds left by the cruel year that had gone before, the Year of the Stranger, were as yet too raw . . . and king, queen, and council alike feared what might lie ahead, with the Princess Aerea and Balerion still vanished from human ken, and Queen Rhaena gone in search of them.

Having taken leave of her brother's court, Rhaena Targaryen flew to Oldtown first, in the hopes that her wayward daughter might have sought out her twin sister. Lord Donnel and the High Septon each received her courteously, but neither had any help to offer. The queen was able to visit for a time with her daughter Rhaella, so like and yet so unlike her twin, and it can be hoped that she found some balm for her pain there. When Rhaena expressed regret that she had not been a better mother, the novice Rhaella embraced her and said, "I have had the best mother any child could wish for, the Mother Above, and you are to thank for her."

Departing Oldtown, Dreamfyre took the queen northward, first to Highgarden, then to Crakehall and Casterly Rock, whose lords had welcomed her in days gone by. Nowhere had a dragon been seen, save for her own; not even a whisper of Princess Aerea had been heard. Thence Rhaena returned to Fair Isle, to face Lord Franklyn Farman once again. The years had not made his lordship any fonder of the queen, nor any wiser in how he chose to speak to her. "I had hoped my lady sister might come home to do her duty once she fled from you," Lord Franklyn said, "but we have had no word of her, nor of your daughter. I cannot claim to know the princess, but I would say she is well rid of you, as was Fair Isle. If she turns up here we shall see her off, just as we did her mother."

"You do not know Aerea, that much is true," Her Grace responded. "If she does indeed find her way to these shores, my lord, you may find she is not as forbearing as her mother. Oh, and I wish you luck if you should try to 'see off' the Black Dread. Balerion quite enjoyed your brother, by now he may desire another course."

After Fair Isle, history loses track of Rhaena Targaryen. She would not return to King's Landing or Dragonstone for the rest of the year, nor present herself at the seat of any lord in the Seven Kingdoms. We have fragmentary reports of Dreamfyre being seen as far north as the barrowlands and the banks of the Fever River, and as far south as the Red Mountains of Dorne and the canyons of the Torrentine. Shunning castles and cities, Rhaena and her dragon were glimpsed flying over the Fingers and the Mountains of the Moon, the misty green forests of Cape Wrath, the Shield Islands, and the Arbor . . . but nowhere did she seek out human company. Instead she sought the wild, lonely places, windswept moors and grassy plains and dismal swamps, cliffs and crags and mountain glens. Was she still hunting for some sign of her daughter, or was it simply solitude she desired? We shall never know.

Her long absence from King's Landing was for the good, however, for the king and his council were growing ever more vexed with her. The accounts of Rhaena's confrontation with Lord Farman on Fair Isle had appalled the king and his lords alike. "Is she mad, to speak so to a lord in his own hall?" Lord Smallwood said. "Had it been me, I would have had her tongue out." To which the king replied, "I hope you would not truly be so foolish, my lord. Whatever else she may be, Rhaena remains the blood of the dragon, and my sister, whom I love." His Grace did not take issue with Lord Smallwood's point, it should be noted, only with his words.

Septon Barth said it best. "The power of the Targaryens derives from their dragons, those fearsome beasts who once laid waste to Harrenhal and destroyed two kings upon the Field of Fire. King Jaehaerys knows this, just as his grandsire Aegon did; the power is always there, and with it the threat. His Grace also grasps a truth that Queen Rhaena does not, however; the threat is most effective when left unspoken. The lords of the realm are proud men all, and little is gained by shaming them. A wise king will always let them keep their dignity. Show them a dragon, aye. They will remember. Speak openly of burning down their halls, boast of how you fed their own kin to your dragons, and you will only inflame them and set their hearts against you."

Queen Alysanne prayed daily for her niece Aerea and blamed herself for the child's flight . . . but she blamed her sister more. Jaehaerys, who had taken little note of Aerea even during the years she had been his heir, chided himself now for that neglect, but it was Balerion who most concerned him, for well he understood the dangers of a beast so powerful in the hands of an angry thirteen-year-old girl. Neither Rhaena Targaryen's fruitless wanderings nor the storm of ravens Grand Maester Benifer sent forth had turned up any word of the princess or the dragon, beyond the usual lies, mistakes, and delusions. As the days went by and the moon turned and turned again, the king began to fear that his niece was dead. "Balerion is a willful beast, and not one to be trifled with," he told the council. "To leap upon his back, never having flown before, and take him up . . . not to fly about the castle, no, but out across the water . . . like as not he threw her off, poor girl, and she lies now at the bottom of the narrow sea."

Septon Barth did not concur. Dragons were not vagabond by nature, he pointed out. More oft than not, they find a sheltered spot, a cave or ruined castle or mountaintop, and nest there, going forth to hunt and thence returning. Once free of his rider, Balerion would surely have returned to his lair. It was his own surmise that, given the lack of any sightings of Balerion in Westeros, Princess Aerea had likely flown him east across the narrow sea, to the vast fields of Essos. The queen concurred. "If the girl were dead, I would know it. She is still alive. I feel it."

All the agents and informers that Rego Draz had engaged to hunt down Elissa Farman and the stolen dragon eggs were now given a new mission: to find Princess Aerea and Balerion. Reports soon began to come in from all up and down the narrow sea. Most proved useless, as with the dragon eggs; rumors, lies, and false sightings, concocted for the sake of a reward. Some were third- or fourth-hand, others with such paucity of detail that they amounted to little more than "I may have seen a dragon. Or something big, with wings."

The most intriguing report came from the hills of Andalos north of Pentos, where shepherds spoke in fearful tones of a monster on the prowl, devouring entire flocks and leaving only bloody bones behind. Nor were the shepherds themselves spared should they chance to stumble on this beast, for this creature's appetite was by no means limited to mutton. Those who actually encountered the monster did not live to describe him, however . . . and none of the stories mentioned fire, which Jaehaerys took to mean that Balerion could not be to blame. Nonetheless, to be certain, he sent a dozen men across the narrow sea to Pentos to try to hunt down this beast, led by Ser Willam the Wasp of his Kingsguard.

Across that selfsame narrow sea, unbeknownst to King's Landing, the shipwrights of Braavos had completed work on the carrack *Sun Chaser,* the dream Elissa Farman had purchased with her stolen dragon's eggs. Unlike the galleys that slid forth daily from the Arsenal of Braavos, she was not oared; this was a vessel meant for deep waters, not bays and coves and inland shallows. Fourmasted, she carried as much sail as the swan ships of the Summer Isles, but with a broader beam and deeper hull that would allow her to store sufficient provisions for longer voyages. When one Braavosi asked her if she meant to sail to Yi Ti, Lady Elissa laughed and said, "I may . . . but not by the route you think."

The night before she was to set sail, she was summoned to the Sealord's Palace, where the Sealord served her herring, beer, and caution. "Go with care, my lady," he told her, "but go. Men are hunting you, all up and down the narrow sea. Questions are being asked, rewards are being offered. I would not care for you to be found in Braavos. We came here to be free of Old Valyria, and your Targaryens are Valyrian to the bone. Sail far. Sail fast."

As the lady now known as Alys Westhill took leave of the Titan of Braavos, life in King's Landing continued as before. Unable to locate his lost niece, Jaehaerys Targaryen proceeded as he always would in times of trouble, and gave himself over to his labors. In the quiet of the Red Keep's

library, the king began work on what was to be one of the most significant of his achievements. With the able assistance of Septon Barth, Grand Maester Benifer, Lord Albin Massey, and Queen Alysanne—a foursome His Grace dubbed "my even smaller council"—Jaehaerys set out to codify, organize, and reform all the kingdom's laws.

The Westeros that Aegon the Conqueror had found had consisted of seven kingdoms in truth and not just name, each with its own laws, customs, and traditions. Even within those kingdoms, there had been considerable variance from place to place. As Lord Massey would write, "Before there were seven kingdoms, there were eight. Before that nine, then ten or twelve or thirty, and back and back. We speak of the Hundred Kingdoms of the Heroes, when there were actually ninety-seven at one time, one hundred thirty-two at another, and so on, the number forever changing as wars were lost and won and sons followed fathers."

Oft as not, the laws changed as well. This king was stern, this king was merciful, this one looked to *The Seven-Pointed Star* for guidance, this one held to the ancient laws of the First Men, this one ruled by whim, t'other went one way when sober and another when drunk. After thousands of years, the result was such a mass of contradictory precedents that every lord possessed of the power of pit and gallows (and some who were not) felt free to rule however he might wish on any case that came before his seat.

Confusion and disorder were offensive to Jaehaerys Targaryen, and with the help of his "smaller council," he set out to "clean the stables." "These Seven Kingdoms have one single king. It is time they had a single law as well." A task so monumental would not be one year's work, or ten's; simply gathering, organizing, and studying the existing laws would require two years, and the reforms that followed would continue for decades. Yet here is where the Great Code of Septon Barth (who in the end would contribute thrice as much as any other man to the Books of Law that resulted) began, in that autumn year of 55 AC.

The king's labors would continue for many years to come, the queen's for nine turns of the moon. Early that same year, King Jaehaerys and the people of Westeros were thrilled to learn that Queen Alysanne was once again with child. Princess Daenerys shared their delight, though she told her mother in firm terms that she wanted a little sister. "You sound a queen already, laying down the law," her mother told her, laughing.

Marriages had long been the means by which the great houses of Westeros bound themselves together, a reliable method of forging alliances and ending disputes. Just as the Conqueror's wives had before her, Alysanne Targaryen delighted in making such matches. In 55 AC she took particular pride in betrothals she arranged for two of the Wise Women who had served in her household since Dragonstone: Lady Jennis Templeton would wed Lord Mullendore of Uplands, whilst Lady Prunella Celtigar was joined in marriage to Uther Peake, Lord of Starpike, Lord of Dunstonbury, and Lord of Whitegrove. Both were considered exceptional matches for the ladies in question, and a triumph for the queen.

The tourney that Lord Redwyne had proposed to celebrate the completion of the Dragonpit was finally held at midyear. Lists were raised in the fields west of the city walls between the Lion Gate and the King's Gate, and the jousting there was said to be especially splendid. Lord Redwyne's eldest son, Ser Robert, showed his prowess with a lance against the best the realm had to offer, whilst his brother Rickard won the squire's tourney and was knighted on the field by the king himself, but the champion's laurels went to the gallant and handsome Ser Simon Dondarrion of Blackhaven, who won the love of the commons and queen alike when he crowned Princess Daenerys as his queen of love and beauty.

No dragons had been settled in the Dragonpit as yet, so that colossal edifice was chosen for the site of the tourney's grand melee, a clash of arms such as King's Landing had never seen before. Seventy-seven knights took part, in eleven teams. The competitors began ahorse, but once unhorsed continued on foot, battling with sword, mace, axe, and morningstar. When all the teams but one had been eliminated, the surviving members of the final team turned on one another, until only a single champion remained.

Though the participants bore only blunted tourney weapons, the battles were hard-fought and bloody, to the delight of the crowds. Two men were killed, and more than twoscore wounded. Queen Alysanne, wisely, forbade her favorites, Jonquil Darke and Tom the Strummer, from taking part, but the old "Keg o' Ale" once more took the field to roars of approval from the commons. When he fell, the smallfolk found a new favorite in the upjumped squire Ser Harys Hogg, whose house name and pig's head helm earned him the style of Harry the Ham. Other notables who joined the melee included Ser Alyn Bullock, late of Dragonstone, Rogar Baratheon's brothers Ser Borys, Ser Garon, and Ser Ronnal, an infamous hedge knight called Ser Guyle the Cunning, and Ser Alastor Reyne, champion of the westerlands and master-at-arms at Casterly Rock. After hours of blood and clangor, however, the last man left standing was a strapping young knight from the riverlands, a broad-shouldered blond bull called Ser Lucamore Strong.

Soon after the conclusion of the tourney, Queen Alysanne left King's Landing for Dragonstone, there to await the birth of her child. The loss of Prince Aegon after only three days of life still weighed heavily upon Her Grace. Rather than subject herself to the rigors of travel or the demands of life at court, the queen sought the quiet of the ancient seat of her house, where her duties would be few. Septa Edyth and Septa Lyra remained by Alysanne's side, together with a dozen fresh young maidens chosen from amongst a hundred who coveted the distinction of serving as a companion to the queen. Two of Rogar Baratheon's nieces were amongst those so honored, along with daughters and sisters of the Lords Arryn, Vance, Rowan, Royce, and Dondarrion, and even a woman of the North, Mara Manderly, daughter to Lord Theomore of White Harbor. To lighten their evenings, Her Grace also brought her favorite fool, the Goodwife, with his puppets.

There were some at court who had misgivings about the queen's desire to remove herself to Dragonstone. The island was damp and gloomy at the best of times, and in autumn strong winds and storms were common. The recent tragedies had only served to blacken the castle's reputation even further, and some feared that the ghosts of Rhaena Targaryen's poisoned friends might haunt its halls. Queen Alysanne dismissed these concerns as foolishness. "The king and I were so happy on Dragonstone," she told the doubters. "I can think of no better place for our child to be born."

Another royal progress had been planned for 55 AC, this time to the westerlands. Just as she had when carrying Princess Daenerys, the queen refused to let the king cancel or postpone the trip, and sent him forth alone. Vermithor carried him across Westeros to the Golden Tooth, where the rest of his retinue caught up with him. From there His Grace visited Ashemark, the Crag, Kayce, Castamere, Tarbeck Hall, Lannisport and Casterly Rock, and Crakehall. Notable by its omission was Fair Isle. Unlike his sister Rhaena, Jaehaerys Targaryen was not a man given to making threats, but he had his own ways of making his disapproval felt.

The king returned from the west a moon's turn before the queen was due, so he might be at her side when she delivered. The child came precisely when the maesters had said he would; a boy, clean-limbed and healthy, with eyes as pale as lilac. His hair, when it came in, was pale as well, shining like white gold, a color rare even in Valyria of old. Jaehaerys named him Aemon. "Daenerys will be cross with me," Alysanne said, as she put the princeling to her breast. "She was most insistent on wanting a sister." Jaehaerys laughed at that and said, "Next time." That night, at Alysanne's suggestion, he placed a dragon's egg in the prince's cradle.

Thrilled by the news of Prince Aemon's birth, thousands of smallfolk lined the streets outside the Red Keep when Jaehaerys and Alysanne returned to King's Landing a moon's turn later, in hopes of getting a glimpse of the new heir to the Iron Throne. Hearing their chants and cheers, the king finally mounted the ramparts of the castle's main gate and raised the boy over his head for all to see. Then, it was said, a roar went up so loud that it could be heard across the narrow sea.

As the Seven Kingdoms celebrated, word reached the king that his sister Rhaena had been seen again, this time at Greenstone, the ancient seat of House Estermont on the isle of the same name, off the shores of Cape Wrath. Here she decided to linger for a time. The very first of Rhaena's favorites, her cousin Larissa Velaryon, had been married to the second son of the Evenstar of Tarth, it may be recalled. Though her husband was dead, Lady Larissa had borne him a daughter, who had only recently been wed to the elderly Lord Estermont. Rather than remain on Tarth or return to Driftmark, the widow had chosen to stay with her daughter on Greenstone after the wedding. That Lady Larissa's presence drew Rhaena Targaryen to Estermont cannot be doubted, for the island was elsewise singularly lacking in charm, being damp, windswept, and poor. With her daughter lost to her and her dearest friends and favorites in the grave, it should not be surprising that Rhaena sought solace with a companion of her childhood.

It would have surprised (and enraged) the queen to know that another former favorite was passing close to her at that very moment. After stopping at Pentos to take on supplies, Alys Westhill and her *Sun Chaser* had made their way to Tyrosh, with only the narrowest part of the narrow sea betwixt them and Estermont. The perilous passage through the pirate-infested waters of the Stepstones lay ahead, and Lady Alys was hiring crossbowmen and sellswords to see her safely through the straits to open water, as many a prudent captain did. The gods in their caprice chose to keep Queen Rhaena and her betrayer ignorant of one another, however, and the *Sun Chaser* passed through the Stepstones without incident. Alys Westhill discharged her hirelings on Lys, taking on fresh water and provisions before turning west and setting sail for Oldtown.

Winter came to Westeros in 56 AC, and with it grim news out of Essos. The men that King Jaehaerys had sent to investigate the great beast prowling the hills north of Pentos were all dead. Their commander, Ser Willam the Wasp, had engaged a guide in Pentos, a local who claimed to know where the monster lurked. Instead, he had led them into a trap, and somewhere in the Velvet Hills of Andalos, Ser Willam and his men had been set upon by brigands. Though they had given a good account of themselves, the numbers were against them, and in the end they were overwhelmed and slain. Ser Willam had been the last to fall, it was said. His head had been returned to one of Lord Rego's agents in Pentos.

"There is no monster," Septon Barth concluded after hearing the sad tale, "only men stealing sheep, and telling tales to frighten other men away." Myles Smallwood, the King's Hand, urged the king to punish Pentos for the outrage, but Jaehaerys was unwilling to make war upon an entire city for the crimes of some outlaws. So the matter was put to rest, and the fate of Ser Willam the Wasp was inscribed in the White Book of the Kingsguard. To fill his place, Jaehaerys awarded a white cloak to Ser Lucamore Strong, the victor of the great melee in the Dragonpit.

More news soon came from Lord Rego's agents across the water. One report spoke of a dragon being displayed in the fighting pits of Astapor on Slaver's Bay, a savage beast with shorn wings the slavers set against bulls, cave bears, and packs of human slaves armed with spears and axes, whilst thousands roared and shouted. Septon Barth dismissed the account at once. "A wyvern, beyond a doubt," he declared. "The wyverns of Sothoryos are oft taken for dragons by men who have never seen a dragon."

Of far more interest to the king and council was the great fire that had swept across the Disputed Lands a fortnight past. Fanned by strong winds and fed by dry grasses, the blaze had raged for three days and three nights, engulfing half a dozen villages and one free company, the Adventurers, who found themselves trapped between the onrushing flames and a Tyroshi host under the command of the Archon himself. Most had chosen to die upon Tyroshi spears rather than be burned alive. Not a man of them had survived.

The source of the fire remained a mystery. "A dragon," Ser Myles Smallwood declared. "What else could it be?" Rego Draz remained unconvinced. "A lightning strike," he suggested. "A cookfire. A drunk with a torch looking for a whore." The king agreed. "If this were Balerion's doing, he would surely have been seen."

The fires of Essos were far from the mind of the woman calling herself Alys Westhill in Oldtown; her eyes were fixed upon the other horizon, on the storm-lashed western seas. Her *Sun Chaser* had come to port in the last days of autumn, yet still she lingered at dockside as Lady Alys searched for a crew to sail her. She was proposing to do what only a handful of the boldest mariners had ever dared attempt before, to sail beyond the sunset in search of lands undreamed of, and she did not want men aboard who might lose heart, rise up against her, and force her to turn back. She required men who shared her dream, and such were not easily found, even in Oldtown.

Then as now, ignorant smallfolk and superstitious sailors clung to the belief that the world was flat and ended somewhere far to the west. Some spoke of walls of fire and boiling seas, some of black fogs that went on forever, some of the very gates of hell. Wiser men knew better. The sun and moon were spheres, as any man with eyes could see; reason suggested that the world must be a sphere as well, and centuries of study had convinced the archmaesters of the Conclave there could be no doubt of that.

The dragonlords of the Freehold of Valyria had believed the same, as did the wise of many distant lands, from Qarth to Yi Ti to the isle of Leng.

The same accord did not exist as regards the size of the world. Even amongst the archmaesters of the Citadel, there was deep division on that question. Some believed the Sunset Sea to be so vast that no man could hope to cross it. Others argued it might be no wider than the Summer Sea where it stretched from the Arbor to Great Moraq; a tremendous distance, to be sure, but one that a bold captain might hope to navigate with the right ship. A western route to the silks and spices of Yi Ti and Leng could mean incalculable riches for the man who found it . . . if the sphere of the world was as small as these wise men suggested.

Alys Westhill did not believe it was. The scant writings she left behind show that even as a child Elissa Farman was convinced the world was "far larger and far stranger than the maesters imagine." Not for her the merchant's dream of reaching Ulthos and Asshai by sailing west. Hers was a bolder vision. Between Westeros and the far eastern shores of Essos and Ulthos, she believed, lay other lands and other seas waiting to be discovered: another Essos, another Sothoryos, another Westeros. Her dreams were full of sundering rivers and windswept plains and towering mountains with their shoulders in the clouds, of green islands verdant in the sun, of strange beasts no man had tamed and queer fruits no man had tasted, of golden cities shining underneath strange stars.

She was not the first to dream this dream. Thousands of years before the Conquest, when the Kings of Winter still reigned in the North, Brandon the Shipwright had built an entire fleet of ships to cross the Sunset Sea. He took them west himself, never to return. His son and heir, another Brandon, burned the yards where they were built, and was known as Brandon the Burner forevermore. A thousand years later, ironmen sailing out from Great Wyk were blown off course onto a cluster of rocky islands eight days' sail to the northwest of any known shore. Their captain built a tower and a beacon there, took the name of Farwynd, and called his seat the Lonely Light. His descendants lived there still, clinging to rocks where seals outnumbered men fifty to one. Even the other ironmen considered the Farwynds mad; some named them selkies.

Brandon the Shipwright and the ironborn who came after him had both sailed the northern seas, where monstrous krakens, sea dragons, and leviathans the size of islands swam through cold grey waters, and the freezing mists hid floating mountains made of ice. Alys Westhill did not intend to voyage in their wake. She would sail her *Sun Chaser* on a more southerly course, seeking warm blue waters and the steady winds she believed would carry her across the Sunset Sea. But first she had to have a crew.

Some men laughed at her, whilst others called her mad, or cursed her to her face. "Strange beasts, aye," one rival captain told her, "and like as not, you'll end up in the belly of one." A good portion of the gold that the Sealord had paid for her stolen dragon's eggs reposed safely in the vaults of the Iron Bank of Braavos, however, and with such wealth behind her, Lady Alys was able to tempt sailors by paying thrice the wages other captains could offer. Slowly she began to gather willing hands.

Inevitably, word of her efforts came to the attention of the Lord of the Hightower. Lord Donnel's grandsons Eustace and Norman, both noted mariners in their own right, were sent to question her . . . and clap her in fetters if they felt it prudent. Instead both men signed on with her, pledging their own ships and crews to her mission. After that, sailors clambered over one another in their haste to join her crew. If the Hightowers were going, there were fortunes to be had. The *Sun Chaser* departed Oldtown on the twenty-third day of the third moon of 56 AC, making her way down Whispering Sound for the open seas in company with Ser Norman Hightower's *Autumn Moon* and Ser Eustace Hightower's *Lady Meredith.*

Their departure came not a day too soon . . . for word of Alys Westhill and her desperate search for a crew had finally reached King's Landing. King Jaehaerys saw through Lady Elissa's false name at once, and immediately sent ravens to Lord Donnel in Oldtown, commanding him to take this woman into custody and deliver her to the Red Keep for questioning. The birds came too late, however . . . or mayhaps, as some suggest even to this day, Donnel the Delayer delayed again. Unwilling to risk the king's wroth, his lordship dispatched a dozen of his own swiftest ships to chase down Alys Westhill and his grandsons, but one by one they straggled back to port, defeated. Seas are vast and ships small, and none of Lord Donnel's vessels could match the *Sun Chaser* for speed when the wind was in her sails.

When word of her escape reached the Red Keep, the king pondered long and hard on chasing after Elissa Farman himself. No ship can sail as swiftly as a dragon flies, he reasoned; mayhaps Vermithor could find her where Lord Hightower's ships could not. The very notion terrified Queen Alysanne, however. Even dragons cannot stay aloft forever, she pointed out, and such charts as existed of the Sunset Sea showed neither islands nor rocks to rest upon. Grand Maester Benifer and Septon Barth concurred, and against their opposition, His Grace reluctantly put the idea aside.

The thirteenth day of the fourth moon of 56 AC dawned cold and grey, with a blustery wind blowing from the east. Court records tell us that Jaehaerys I Targaryen broke his fast with an envoy of the Iron Bank of Braavos, who had come to collect the annual payment on the Crown's loan. It was a contentious meeting. Elissa Farman was still very much in the king's thoughts, and he had certain knowledge that her *Sun Chaser* had been built in Braavos. His Grace demanded to know if the Iron Bank had financed the building of the ship, and whether they had any knowledge of the stolen dragon eggs. The banker, for his part, denied all.

Elsewhere in the Red Keep, Queen Alysanne spent the morning with her children; Princess Daenerys had finally warmed to her brother, Aemon, though she still wanted a little sister. Septon Barth was in the library, Grand Maester Benifer in his rookery. Across the city, Lord Corbray was inspecting the men of the East Barracks of the City Watch, whilst Rego Draz entertained a young lady of negotiable virtue in his manse below the Dragonpit.

All of them would long remember what they were doing when they heard the blast of a horn ringing through the morning air. "The sound of it ran down my spine like a cold knife," the queen would say later, "though I could not have said why." In a lonely watchtower overlooking the waters of Blackwater Bay, a guard had glimpsed dark wings in the distance and sounded the alarum. He sounded the horn again as the wings grew larger, and a third time when he saw the dragon plain, black against the clouds.

Balerion had returned to King's Landing.

It had been long years since the Black Dread had last been seen in the skies above the city, and the sight filled many a Kingslander with dread, wondering if somehow Maegor the Cruel had returned from beyond the grave to mount him once again. Alas, the rider clinging to his neck was not a dead king but a dying child.

Balerion's shadow swept across the yards and halls of the Red Keep as he came down, his huge wings buffeting the air, to land in the inner ward by Maegor's Holdfast. Scarcely had he touched the ground than Princess Aerea slid from his back. Even those who had known her best during her years at court scarce recognized the girl. She was near enough to naked as to make no matter, her clothing no more than rags and tatters clinging to her arms and legs. Her hair was tangled and matted, her limbs as thin as sticks. "Please!" she cried to the knights and squires and serving men who had seen her descend. Then, as they came rushing toward her, she said, "I never," and collapsed.

Ser Lucamore Strong had been at his post on the bridge across the dry moat surrounding Maegor's Holdfast. Shoving aside the other onlookers, he lifted the princess in his arms and carried her across the castle to Grand Maester Benifer. Later he would tell anyone who would listen that the girl was flushed and burning with fever, her skin so hot he could feel it even through the enameled scale of his armor. She had blood in her eyes as well, the knight claimed, and "there was something inside her, something moving that made her shudder and twist in my arms." (He did not tell these tales for long, though. The next day, King Jaehaerys sent for him and commanded him to speak no more of the princess.)

The king and queen were sent for at once, but when they reached the maester's chambers, Benifer denied them entry. "You do not want to see her like this," he told them, "and I would be remiss if I allowed you any closer." Guards were posted at the door to keep servants away as well. Only Septon Barth was admitted, to administer the rites for the dying. Benifer did what he could for the stricken princess, giving her milk of the poppy and immersing her in a tub of ice to bring her fever down, but his efforts were to no avail. Whilst hundreds crowded into the Red Keep's sept to pray for her, Jaehaerys and Alysanne kept vigil outside the maester's door. The sun had set and the hour of the bat was at hand when Barth emerged to announce that Aerea Targaryen was dead.

The princess was consigned to the flames the very next day at sunrise, her body wrapped in fine white linen from head to toe. Grand Maester Benifer, who had prepared her for the funeral pyre, looked half dead himself, Lord Redwyne confided to his sons. The king announced that his niece had died of a fever and asked the realm to pray for her. King's Landing mourned for a few days before life resumed as before, and that was the end of it.

Mysteries remained, however. Even now, centuries later, we are no closer to knowing the truth.

More than forty men have served the Iron Throne as Grand Maester. Their journals, letters, account books, memoirs, and court calendars are our single best record of the events they witnessed, but not all of them were equally diligent. Whereas some left us volumes of letters full of empty words, never failing to note what the king ate for supper (and whether he enjoyed it), others set down no more than a half-dozen missives a year. In this regard Benifer ranks near the top, and his letters and journals provide us with detailed accounts of all that he saw, did, and witnessed whilst in service to King Jaehaerys and his uncle Maegor before him. And yet in all of Benifer's writings there is not a single word to be found concerning the return of Aerea Targaryen and her stolen dragon to King's Landing, nor the death of the young princess. Fortunately, Septon Barth was not so reticent, and it is to his own account we must now turn.

Barth wrote, "It has been three days since the princess perished, and I have not slept. I do not know that I shall ever sleep again. The Mother is merciful, I have always believed, and the Father Above judges each man justly . . . but there was no mercy and no justice in what befell our poor princess. How could the gods be so blind or so uncaring as to permit such horror? Or is it possible that there are other deities in this universe, monstrous evil gods such as the priests of Red R'hllor preach against, against whose malice the kings of men and the gods of men are naught but flies?

"I do not know. I do not want to know. If this makes me a faithless septon, so be it. Grand Maester Benifer and I have agreed to tell no one all of what we saw and experienced in his chambers as that poor child lay dying . . . not the king, nor the queen, nor her mother, nor even the archmaesters of the Citadel . . . but the memories will not leave me, so I shall set them down here. Mayhaps by the time they are found and read, men will have gained a better understanding of such evils.

"We have told the world that Princess Aerea died of a fever, and that is broadly true, but it was a fever such as I have never seen before and hope never to see again. The girl was *burning*. Her skin was flushed and red and when I laid my hand upon her brow to learn how hot she was, it was as if I had thrust it into a pot of boiling oil. There was scarce an ounce of flesh upon her bones, so gaunt and starved did she appear, but we could observe certain . . . swellings inside her, as her skin bulged out and then sunk down again, as if . . . no, not as if, for this was the truth of it . . . there were *things* inside her, living things, moving and twisting, mayhaps searching for a way out, and giving her such pain that even the milk of the poppy gave her no surcease. We told the king, as we must surely tell her mother, that Aerea never spoke, but that is a lie. I pray that I shall soon forget some of the things she whispered through her cracked and bleeding lips. I cannot forget how oft she begged for death.

"All the maester's arts were powerless against her fever, if indeed we can call such a horror by such a commonplace name. The simplest way to say it is that the poor child was cooking from within. Her flesh grew darker and darker and then began to crack, until her skin resembled nothing so much, Seven save me, as pork cracklings. Thin tendrils of smoke issued from her mouth, her nose, even, most obscenely, from her nether lips. By then she had ceased to speak, though the things within her continued to move. Her very eyes cooked within her skull and finally burst, like two eggs left in a pot of boiling water for too long.

"I thought that was the most hideous thing that I should ever see, but I was quickly disabused of the notion, for a worse horror was awaiting me. That came when Benifer and I lowered the poor child into a tub and covered her with ice. The shock of that immersion stopped her heart at once, I tell myself . . . if so, that was a mercy, for that was when the things inside her came out . . .

"The things . . . Mother have mercy, I do not know how to speak of them . . . they were . . . worms with faces . . . snakes with hands . . . twist-

ing, slimy, unspeakable things that seemed to writhe and pulse and squirm as they came bursting from her flesh. Some were no bigger than my little finger, but one at least was as long as my arm . . . oh, Warrior protect me, the *sounds* they made . . .

"They died, though. I must remember that, cling to that. Whatever they might have been, they were creatures of heat and fire, and they did not love the ice, oh no. One after another they thrashed and writhed and died before my eyes, thank the Seven. I will not presume to give them names . . . they were horrors."

The first part of Septon Barth's account ends there. But some days later he returned and resumed:

"Princess Aerea is gone, but not forgotten. The Faithful pray for her sweet soul every morn and every night. Outside the septs, the same questions are on every lip. The princess was missing for more than a year. Where could she have gone? What could have happened to her? What brought her home? Was Balerion the monster believed to haunt the Velvet Hills of Andalos? Did his flames start the fire that swept across the Disputed Lands? Could the Black Dread have flown as far as Astapor to be the 'dragon' in the pit? No, and no, and no. These are fables.

"If we put aside such distractions, however, the mystery remains. Where did Aerea Targaryen go after fleeing Dragonstone? Queen Rhaena's first thought was that she had flown to King's Landing; the princess had made no secret of her wish to return to court. When that proved wrong, Rhaena next looked to Fair Isle and Oldtown. Both made sense after a fashion, but Aerea was not to be found at either place, nor anywhere in Westeros. Others, including the queen and myself, took this to mean that the princess had flown east, not west, and would be found somewhere in Essos. The girl might well have thought the Free Cities to be beyond her mother's grasp, and Queen Alysanne in particular seemed convinced that Aerea was fleeing her mother as much as Dragonstone itself. Yet Lord Rego's agents and informers could find no hint of her across the narrow sea . . . nor even a whisper of her dragon. Why?

"Though I can offer no certain proof, I can suggest an answer. It seems to me that we have all been asking the wrong question. Aerea Targaryen was still well shy of her thirteenth nameday on the morning she slipped from her mother's castle. Though no stranger to dragons, she had never ridden one before . . . and for reasons we may never understand, she chose Balerion as her mount, instead of any one of the younger and more tractable dragons she might have claimed. Driven as she was by her conflicts with her mother, mayhaps she simply wanted a beast larger and more fearsome than Queen Rhaena's Dreamfyre. It might also have been a desire to tame the beast that had slain her father and his own dragon (though Princess Aerea had never known her father, and it is hard to know what feelings she might have had about him and his death). Regardless of her reasons, the choice was made.

"The princess might well have intended to fly to King's Landing, just as her mother suspected. It might have been her thought to seek out her twin sister in Oldtown, or to go seeking after Lady Elissa Farman, who had once promised to take her adventuring. Whatever her plans, they did not matter. It is one thing to leap upon a dragon and quite another to bend him to your will, particularly a beast as old and fierce as the Black Dread. From the very start we have asked, *Where did Aerea take Balerion?* We should have been asking, *Where did Balerion take Aerea?*

"Only one answer makes sense. Recall, if you will, that Balerion was the largest and *oldest* of the three dragons that King Aegon and his sisters rode to conquest. Vhagar and Meraxes had hatched on Dragonstone. Balerion alone had come to the island with Aenar the Exile and Daenys the Dreamer, the youngest of the five dragons they brought with them. The older dragons had died during the intervening years, but Balerion lived on, growing ever larger, fiercer, and more willful. If we discount the tales of certain sorcerers and mountebanks (as we should), he is mayhaps the only living creature in the world that knew Valyria before the Doom.

"And that is where he took the poor doomed child clinging to his back. If she went willingly I would be most surprised, but she had neither the knowledge nor the force of will to turn him.

"What befell her on Valyria I cannot surmise. Judging from the condition in which she returned to us, I do not even care to contemplate it. The Valyrians were more than dragonlords. They practiced blood magic and other dark arts as well, delving deep into the earth for secrets best left buried and twisting the flesh of beasts and men to fashion monstrous and unnatural chimeras. For these sins the gods in their wroth struck them down. Valyria is accursed, all men agree, and even the boldest sailor steers well clear of its smoking bones . . . but we would be mistaken to believe that nothing lives there now. The things we found inside Aerea Targaryen live there now, I would submit . . . along with such other horrors as we cannot even begin to imagine. I have written here at length of how the princess died, but there is something else, something even more frightening, that requires mention:

"*Balerion had wounds as well.* That enormous beast, the Black Dread, the most fearsome dragon ever to soar through the skies of Westeros, returned to King's Landing with half-healed scars that no man recalled ever having seen before, and a jagged rent down his left side almost nine feet long, a gaping red wound from which his blood still dripped, hot and smoking.

"The lords of Westeros are proud men, and the septons of the Faith and the maesters of the Citadel in their own ways are prouder still, but there is much and more of the nature of the world that we do not understand, and may never understand. Mayhaps that is a mercy. The Father made men curious, some say to test our faith. It is my own abiding sin that whenever I come upon a door I must needs see what lies upon the farther side, but certain doors are best left unopened. Aerea Targaryen went through such a door." Septon Barth's account ends there. He would never again touch upon the fate of Princess Aerea in any of his writings, and even these words would be sealed away amongst his privy papers, to remain undiscovered for almost a hundred years. The horrors he had witnessed had a profound affect upon the septon, however, exciting the very hunger for knowledge he called "my own abiding sin." It was subsequent to this that Barth began the researches and investigations that would ultimately lead him to write *Dragons, Wyrms, and Wyverns: Their Unnatural History*, a volume that the Citadel would condemn as "provocative but unsound" and that Baelor the Blessed would order expunged and destroyed.

It is likely that Septon Barth discussed his suspicions with the king as well. Though the matter never came before the small council, later that same year Jaehaerys issued a royal edict forbidding any ship suspected of having visited the Valyrian islands or sailed the Smoking Sea from landing at any port or harbor in the Seven Kingdoms. The king's own subjects were likewise forbidden from visiting Valyria, under pain of death.

Not long thereafter Balerion became the first of the Targaryen dragons to be housed in the Dragonpit. Its long brick-lined tunnels, sunk deep into the hillside, had been fashioned after the manner of caves, and were five times as large as the lairs on Dragonstone. Three younger dragons soon joined the Black Dread under the Hill of Rhaenys, whilst Vermithor and Silverwing remained at the Red Keep, close to their riders. To ascertain there would be no repetition of Princess Aerea's escape on Balerion, the king decreed that all the dragons should be guarded night and day, regardless of where they laired. A new order of guards was created for this purpose: the Dragonkeepers, seventy-seven strong and clad in suits of gleaming black armor, their helms crested by a row of dragon scales that continued, diminishing, down their backs.

Little and less need be said of the return of Rhaena Targaryen from Estermont after her daughter's death. By the time the raven reached Her Grace at Greenstone, the princess had already died and been burned. Only ashes and bones remained for her mother when Dreamfyre delivered her to the Red Keep. "It would seem that I am doomed to always come too late," she said. When the king offered to have the ashes interred on Dragonstone, beside those of King Aegon and the other dead of House Targaryen, Rhaena refused. "She hated Dragonstone," she reminded His Grace. "She wanted to fly." And so saying, she took her child's ashes high into the sky on Dreamfyre, and scattered them upon the winds.

It was a melancholy time. Dragonstone was still hers if she wanted it, Jaehaerys told his sister, but Rhaena refused that as well. "There is nothing there for me now but grief and ghosts." When Alysanne asked if she would return to Greenstone, Rhaena shook her head. "There's a ghost there as well. A kinder ghost, but no less sad." The king suggested that she remain with them at court, even offering her a seat on his small council. That made his sister laugh. "Oh, brother, you sweet man, I fear you would not like any counsel I might offer." Then Queen Alysanne took her sister's hand in hers and said, "You are still a young woman. If you like, we could find some kind and gentle lord who would cherish you as we do. You could have other children." That only served to bring a snarl to Rhaena's lips. She snatched her hand away from the queen's and said, "I fed my last husband to my dragon. If you make me take another, I may eat him myself."

The place where King Jaehaerys settled his sister Rhaena in the end was mayhaps the most unlikely seat of all: Harrenhal. Jordan Towers, one of the last lords to remain faithful to Maegor the Cruel, had died of a congestion of the chest, and Black Harren's vast ruin had passed to his last surviving son, named after the late king. All of his older brothers having perished in King Maegor's wars, Maegor Towers was the last of his line, and sickly and impoverished as well. In a castle built to house thousands, Towers dwelt alone but for a cook and three elderly men-at-arms. "The castle has five colossal towers," the king pointed out, "and the Towers boy occupies part of one. You can have the other four." Rhaena was amused by that. "One will suffice, I am sure. I have a smaller household than he does." When Alysanne reminded her that Harrenhal too was said to have ghosts, Rhaena shrugged. "They are not my ghosts. They will not trouble me."

And thus it came to pass that Rhaena Targaryen, daughter of one king, wife to two, sister to a third, spent the final years of her life in the aptly named Widow's Tower of Harrenhal, whilst across the castle yard a sickly youth named after the king who had slain the father of her children maintained his own household in the Tower of Dread. Curiously, we are told, in time Rhaena and Maegor Towers came to forge a friendship of sorts. After his death in 61 AC, Rhaena took his servants into her own household and continued to maintain them until her own death.

Rhaena Targaryen died in 73 AC, at fifty years of age. After the death of her daughter Aerea, she never again visited King's Landing or Dragonstone, nor played any part in the ruling of the realm, though she did fly to Oldtown once a year to visit with her remaining daughter, Rhaella, a septa at the Starry Sept. Her hair of gold and silver turned white before the end, and the smallfolk of the riverlands feared her as a witch. Travelers who turned up at the gates of Harrenhal in hope of hospitality were given bread and salt and the privilege of a night's shelter during those years, but not the honor of the queen's company. Those who were fortunate spoke of glimpsing her on the castle battlements, or seeing her coming and going on her dragon, for Rhaena continued to ride Dreamfyre until the end, just as she had in the beginning.

When she died, King Jaehaerys ordained that she be burned at Harrenhal and her ashes interred there. "My brother Aegon died at the hands of our uncle in the Battle Beneath the Gods Eye," His Grace said at her funeral pyre. "His wife, my sister Rhaena, was not with him at the battle, but she died that day as well." With Rhaena's death, Jaehaerys granted Harrenhal and all its lands and incomes to Ser Bywin Strong, the brother of Ser Lucamore Strong of his Kingsguard and a renowned knight in his own right.

We have wandered decades ahead of our tale, however, for the Stranger did not come for Rhaena Targaryen until 73 AC, and much and more was to pass in King's Landing and the Seven Kingdoms of Westeros before that, for both good and ill.

In 57 AC, Jaehaerys and his queen found cause to rejoice again when the gods blessed them with another son. Baelon, he was named, after one of the Targaryen lords who had ruled Dragonstone before the Conquest, himself a second son. Though smaller than his brother, Aemon, at birth, the new babe was louder and lustier, and his wet nurses complained that they had never known a child to suck so hard. Only two days before his birth, the white ravens had flown from the Citadel to announce the arrival of spring, so Baelon was immediately dubbed the Spring Prince.

Prince Aemon was two when his brother was born, Princess Daenerys four. The two were little alike. The princess was a lively, laughing child who bounced about the Red Keep day and night, "flying" everywhere on a broomstick dragon that had become her favorite toy. Mud-spattered and grass-stained, she was a trial to her mother and her maids alike, for they were forever losing track of her. Prince Aemon, on the other hand, was a very serious boy, cautious, careful, and obedient. Though he could not as yet read, he loved being read to, and Queen Alysanne, laughing, was oft heard to say that his first word had been, "Why?"

As the children grew, Grand Maester Benifer watched them closely. The wounds left by the enmity between the Conqueror's sons, Aenys and Maegor, were still fresh in the minds of many older lords, and Benifer worried lest these two boys likewise turn on one another to bathe the realm in blood. He need not have been concerned. Save mayhaps for twins, no brothers could ever have been closer than the sons of Jaehaerys Targaryen. As soon as he grew old enough to walk, Baelon followed his brother, Aemon, everywhere, and tried his best to imitate him in everything he did. When Aemon was given his first wooden sword to begin his training in arms, Baelon was judged to be too young to join him, but that did not stop him. He made his own sword from a stick and rushed into the yard anyway to begin whacking at his brother, reducing their master-at-arms to helpless laughter.

Thereafter Baelon went everywhere with his stick-sword, even to bed, to the despair of his mother and her maids. Prince Aemon was shy around the dragons at first, Benifer observed, but not so Baelon, who reportedly smote Balerion on the snout the first time he entered the Dragonpit. "He's either brave or mad, that one," old Sour Sam observed, and from that day forth the Spring Prince was also known as Baelon the Brave.

The young princes loved their sister to distraction, it was plain to see, and Daenerys delighted in the boys, "especially in telling them what to do." Grand Maester Benifer noted something else, however. Jaehaerys loved all three children fiercely, but from the moment Aemon was born, the king began to speak of him as his heir, to Queen Alysanne's displeasure. "Daenerys is older," she would remind His Grace. "She is first in line; she should be queen." The king would never disagree, except to say, "She shall be queen, when she and Aemon marry. They will rule together, just as we have." But Benifer could see that the king's words did not entirely please the queen, as he noted in his letters.

Returning once again to 57 AC, that was also the year wherein Jaehaerys dismissed Lord Myles Smallwood as Hand of the King. Though undoubtedly a leal man, and well-intentioned, his lordship had shown himself to be ill-suited to the small council. As he himself would say, "I was made to sit a horse, not a cushion." An older king and wiser, this time His Grace told his council that he did not intend to waste a fortnight hashing over half a hundred names. This time he would have the Hand he wanted: Septon Barth. When Lord Corbray reminded the king of Barth's low birth, Jaehaerys shrugged off his objections. "If his father beat out swords and shod horses, so be it. A knight needs his sword, a horse needs shoes, and I need Barth."

The new Hand of the King departed within days of his elevation, taking ship for Braavos to consult with the Sealord and the Iron Bank. He was accompanied by Ser Gyles Morrigen and six guardsmen, but only Septon Barth took part in the discussions. The purpose of his mission was a grave one: war or peace. King Jaehaerys had great admiration for the city of Braavos, Barth told the Sealord; for that reason, he had not come himself, understanding as he did the Free City's bitter history with Valyria and its dragonlords. If his Hand was not able to settle the matter at hand amicably, however, His Grace would have no choice but to come himself on Vermithor for what Barth termed "vigorous discussions." When the Sealord inquired as to what the matter at hand might be, the septon gave him a sad smile and said, "Is that how this must be played? We are speaking of three eggs. Need I say more?"

The Sealord said, "I admit to nothing. If I was in possession of such eggs, however, it could only be because I purchased them."

"From a thief."

"How shall that be proved? Has this thief been seized, tried, found guilty? Braavos is a city of laws. Who is the rightful owner of these eggs? Can they show me proof of ownership?"

"His Grace can show you proof of dragons."

That made the Sealord smile. "The veiled threat. Your king is most adroit at that. Stronger than his father, more subtle than his uncle. Yes, I know what Jaehaerys could do to us, if he chose. Braavosi have a long memory, and we remember the dragonlords of old. There are certain things that we might do to your king as well, however. Shall I enumerate? Or do you prefer the threat veiled?"

"However it please your lordship."

"As you will. Your king could burn my city down to ash, I do not doubt. Tens of thousands would die in dragonflame. Men, women, and children. I do not have the power to wreak that sort of destruction upon Westeros. Such sellswords as I might hire would flee before your knights. My fleets could sweep yours from the sea for a time, but my ships are made of wood, and wood burns. However, there is in this city a certain . . . guild, let us say . . . whose members are very skilled at their chosen profession. They could not destroy King's Landing, nor fill its streets with corpses. But they could kill . . . a few. A *well-chosen* few."

"His Grace is protected day and night by the Kingsguard."

"Knights, yes. Such as the man who waits for you outside. If indeed he is still waiting. What would you say if I were to tell you that Ser Gyles is already dead?" When Septon Barth began to rise, the Sealord waved him back to his seat. "No, please, no need to rush away. I said *what if*. I did consider it. They are *most* skilled, as I said. Had I done so, however, you might have acted unwisely, and many more good people might have died. That is not my desire. Threats make me uncomfortable. Westerosi may be warriors, but we Braavosi are traders. Let us trade."

Septon Barth settled back down. "What do you offer?"

"I do not have these eggs, of course," the Sealord said. "You cannot prove elsewise. If I *did* have them, however . . . well, until they hatch, they are but stones. Would your king begrudge me three pretty stones? Now, if I had three . . . chickens . . . I might understand his concern. I do admire your Jaehaerys, though. He is a great improvement on his uncle, and Braavos does not wish to see him so unhappy. So instead of stones, let me offer . . . gold."

And with that the real bargaining began.

There are those even today who will insist that Septon Barth was made a fool of by the Sealord, that he was lied to, cheated, and humiliated. They point to the fact that he returned to King's Landing without a single dragon's egg. This is true.

What he did bring back was not of inconsiderable value, however. At the Sealord's urging, the Iron Bank of Braavos forgave the entire remaining principal of its loan to the Iron Throne. At a stroke, the Crown's debt had been cut in half. "And all at the cost of three stones," Barth told the king.

"The Sealord had best hope that they remain stones," Jaehaerys said. "If I should hear so much as a whisper of . . . chickens . . . his palace will be the first to burn."

The agreement with the Iron Bank would have great impact for all the people of the realm over the coming years and decades, though the extent of that was not immediately apparent. The king's shrewd master of coin, Rego Draz, pored over the Crown's debts and incomes carefully after Septon Barth's return, and concluded that the coin that would previously have had to be sent to Braavos could now be safely diverted to a project the king had long wished to undertake at home: further improvements to King's Landing.

Jaehaerys had widened and straightened the streets of the city, and put down cobblestones where previously there had been mud, but much and more remained to be done. King's Landing in its present state could not compare to Oldtown, nor even Lannisport, let alone the splendid Free Cities across the narrow sea. His Grace was determined that it should. Accordingly, he set out plans for a series of drains and sewers, to carry the city's offal and nightsoil under the streets to the river.

Septon Barth drew the king's attention to an even more urgent problem: King's Landing's drinking water was fit only for horses and swine, in the opinion of many. The river water was muddy, and the king's new sewers would soon make it worse; the waters of the Blackwater Bay were brackish at the best of times, and salty at the worst. Whilst the king and his court and the city's highborn drank ale and mead and wine, these foul waters were oft the only choice for the poor. To address the problem, Barth proposed sinking wells, some inside the city proper and others to the north, beyond the walls. A series of glazed clay pipes and tunnels would carry the fresh water into the city, where it would be stored in four huge cisterns and made available to the smallfolk from public fountains in certain squares and crossroads.

Barth's scheme was costly, beyond a doubt, and Rego Draz and King Jaehaerys balked at the expense . . . until Queen Alysanne served each of them a tankard of river water at the next council meeting, and dared them to drink of it. The water went undrunk, but the wells and pipes were soon approved. Construction would require more than a dozen years, but in the end "the queen's fountains" provided clean water for Kingslanders for many generations to come.

Several years had passed since the king had last made a progress, so plans were laid in 58 AC for Jaehaerys and Alysanne to make their first visit to Winterfell and the North. Their dragons would be with them, of course, but beyond the Neck the distances were great and the roads poor, and the king had grown tired of flying ahead and waiting for his escort to catch up. This time, he decreed, his Kingsguard, servants, and retainers would go ahead of him, to make things ready for his arrival. And thus it was that three ships set sail from King's Landing for White Harbor, where he and the queen were to make their first stop.

The gods and the Free Cities had other plans, however. Even as the king's ships were beating their way north, envoys from Pentos and Tyrosh called upon His Grace in the Red Keep. The two cities had been at war for three years and were now desirous of making peace, but could not agree on where they might meet to discuss terms. The conflict had caused serious disruption to trade upon the narrow sea, to the extent that King Jaehaerys had offered both cities his help in ending their hostilities. After long discussion, the Archon of Tyrosh and the Prince of Pentos had agreed to meet in King's Landing to settle their differences, provided that Jaehaerys would act as an intermediary between them, and guarantee the terms of any resulting treaty.

It was a proposal that neither the king nor his council felt he could refuse, but it would mean postponing His Grace's planned progress to the North, and there was concern that the notoriously prickly Lord of Winterfell might take that for a slight. Queen Alysanne provided the solution. She would go ahead as planned, alone, whilst the king played host to the Prince and Archon. Jaehaerys could join her at Winterfell as soon as the peace had been concluded. And so it was agreed.

Queen Alysanne's travels began in the city of White Harbor, where tens of thousands of northerners turned out to cheer her and gape at Silverwing with awe, and a bit of terror. It was the first time any of them had seen a dragon. The size of the crowds surprised even their lord. "I had not known there were so many smallfolk in the city," Theomore Manderly is reported to have said. "Where did they all come from?"

The Manderlys were unique amongst the great houses of the North. Having originated in the Reach centuries before, they had found refuge near the mouth of the White Knife when rivals drove them from their rich lands along the Mander. Though fiercely loyal to the Starks of Winterfell, they had brought their own gods with them from the south, and still worshipped the Seven and kept the traditions of knighthood. Alysanne Targaryen, ever desirous of binding the Seven Kingdoms closer together, saw an opportunity in Lord Theomore's famously large family, and promptly set about arranging marriages. By the time she took her leave, two of her ladies-in-waiting had been betrothed to his lordship's younger sons and a third to a nephew; his eldest daughter and three nieces, meanwhile, had been added to the queen's own party, with the understanding that they would travel south with her and there be pledged to suitable lords and knights of the king's court.

Lord Manderly entertained the queen lavishly. At the welcoming feast an entire aurochs was roasted, and his lordship's daughter Jessamyn acted as the queen's cupbearer, filling her tankard with a strong northern ale that Her Grace pronounced finer than any wine she had ever tasted. Manderly also staged a small tourney in the queen's honor, to show the prowess of his knights. One of the fighters (though no knight) was revealed to be a woman, a wildling girl who had been captured by rangers north of the Wall and given to one of Lord Manderly's household knights to foster. Delighted by the girl's daring, Alysanne summoned her own sworn shield, Jonquil Darke, and the wildling and the Scarlet Shadow dueled spear against sword whilst the northmen roared in approval.

A few days later, the queen convened her women's court in Lord Manderly's own hall, a thing hitherto unheard of in the North, and more than two hundred women and girls gathered to share their thoughts, concerns, and grievances with Her Grace.

After taking leave of White Harbor, the queen's retinue sailed up the White Knife to its rapids, then proceeded overland to Winterfell, whilst Alysanne herself flew ahead on Silverwing. The warmth of her reception at White Harbor was not to be duplicated at the ancient seat of the Kings in the North, where Alaric Stark and his sons alone emerged to greet her when her dragon landed before his castle gates. Lord Alaric had a flinty reputation; a hard man, people said, stern and unforgiving, tight-fisted almost to the point of being niggardly, humorless, joyless, cold. Even Theomore Manderly, who was his bannerman, had not disagreed; Stark was well respected in the North, he said, but not loved. Lord Manderly's fool had put it elsewise. "Methinks Lord Alaric has not moved his bowels since he was twelve."

Her reception at Winterfell did nothing to disabuse the queen's fears as to what she might expect from House Stark. Even before dismounting to bend the knee, Lord Alaric looked askance at Her Grace's clothing and said, "I hope you brought something warmer than that." He then proceeded to declare that he did not want her dragon inside his walls. "I've not seen Harrenhal, but I know what happened there." Her knights and ladies he would receive when they got here, "and the king too, if he can find the way," but they should not overstay their welcome. "This is the North, and winter is coming. We cannot feed a thousand men for long." When the queen assured him that only a tenth that number would be coming, Lord Alaric grunted and said, "That's good. Fewer would be even better." As had been feared, he was plainly unhappy that King Jaehaerys had not deigned to accompany her, and confessed to being uncertain how to entertain a queen. "If you are expecting balls and masques and dances, you have come to the wrong place."

Lord Alaric had lost his wife three years earlier. When the queen expressed regret that she had never had the pleasure of meeting Lady Stark, the northman said, "She was a Mormont of Bear Isle, and no lady by your lights, but she took an axe to a pack of wolves when she was twelve, killed two of them, and sewed a cloak from their skins. She gave me two strong sons as well, and a daughter as sweet to look upon as any of your southron ladies."

When Her Grace suggested that she would be pleased to help arrange marriages for his sons to the daughters of great southern lords, Lord Stark refused brusquely. "We keep the old gods in the North," he told the queen. "When my boys take a wife, they will wed before a heart tree, not in some southron sept."

Alysanne Targaryen did not yield easily, however. The lords of the south honored the old gods as well as the new, she told Lord Alaric; most every castle that she knew had a godswood as well as a sept. And there were still certain houses that had never accepted the Seven, no more than the northmen had, the Blackwoods in the riverlands chief amongst them, and mayhaps as many as a dozen more. Even a lord as stern and flinty as Alaric Stark found himself helpless before Queen Alysanne's stubborn charm. He allowed that he would think on what she said, and raise the matter with his sons.

The longer the queen stayed, the more Lord Alaric warmed to her, and in time Alysanne came to realize that not everything that was said of him was true. He was careful with his coin, but not niggardly; he was not humorless at all, though his humor had an edge to it, sharp as a knife; his sons and daughter and the people of Winterfell seemed to love him well enough. Once the initial frost had thawed, his lordship took the queen hunting after elk and wild boar in the wolfswood, showed her the bones of a giant, and allowed her to rummage as she pleased through his modest castle library. He even deigned to approach Silverwing, though warily. The women of Winterfell were taken by the queen's charms as well, once they grew to know her; Her Grace became particularly close with Lord Alaric's daughter, Alarra. When the rest of the queen's party finally turned up at the castle gates, after struggling through trackless bogs and summer snows, the meat and mead flowed freely, despite the king's absence.

Things were not going as well at King's Landing, meanwhile. The peace talks dragged on far longer than anticipated, for the acrimony between the two Free Cities ran deeper than Jaehaerys had known. When His Grace attempted to strike a balance, both sides accused him of favoring the other. Whilst the Prince and the Archon dickered, fights began to break out between their men across the city, in inns, brothels, and wine sinks. A Pentoshi guardsman was set upon and killed, and three nights later the Archon's own galley was set afire where she was docked. The king's departure was delayed and delayed again.

In the North, Queen Alysanne grew restless with waiting, and decided to take her leave of Winterfell for a time and visit the men of the Night's Watch at Castle Black. The distance was not negligible, even flying; Her Grace landed at the Last Hearth and several smaller keeps and holdfasts on her way, to the surprise and delight of their lords, whilst a portion of her tail scrambled after her (the rest remained at Winterfell).

Her first sight of the Wall from above took Alysanne's breath away,

Her Grace would later tell the king. There had been some concern how the queen might be received at Castle Black, for many of the black brothers had been Poor Fellows and Warrior's Sons before those orders were abolished, but Lord Stark sent ravens ahead to warn of her coming, and the Lord Commander of the Night's Watch, Lothor Burley, assembled eight hundred of his finest men to receive her. That night the black brothers feasted the queen on mammoth meat, washed down with mead and stout.

As dawn broke the next day Lord Burley took Her Grace to the top of the Wall. "Here the world ends," he told her, gesturing at the vast green expanse of the haunted forest beyond. Burley was apologetic for the quality of the food and drink presented to the queen, and the rudeness of the accommodations at Castle Black. "We do what we can, Your Grace," the Lord Commander explained, "but our beds are hard, our halls are cold, and our food—"

"—is nourishing," the queen finished. "And that is all that I require. It will please me to eat as you do."

The men of the Night's Watch were as thunderstruck by the queen's dragon as the people of White Harbor had been, though the queen herself noted that Silverwing "does not like this Wall." Though it was summer and the Wall was weeping, the chill of the ice could still be felt whenever the wind blew, and every gust would make the dragon hiss and snap. "Thrice I flew Silverwing high above Castle Black, and thrice I tried to take her north beyond the Wall," Alysanne wrote to Jaehaerys, "but every time she veered back south again and refused to go. Never before has she refused to take me where I wished to go. I laughed about it when I came down again, so the black brothers would not realize anything was amiss, but it troubled me then and it troubles me still."

At Castle Black the queen saw her first wildlings. A raiding party had been taken not long before trying to scale the Wall, and a dozen ragged survivors of the fight had been confined in cages for her inspection. When Her Grace asked what was to be done with them, she was told that they would have their ears cut off before being turned loose north of the Wall. "All but those three," her escort said, pointing out three prisoners who had already lost their ears. "We'll take the heads off those three. They been caught once already." If the others were wise, he told the queen, they would take the loss of their ears as a lesson and keep to their side of the Wall. "Most don't, though," he added.

Three of the brothers had been singers before taking the black, and they took turns playing for Her Grace at night, regaling her with ballads, war songs, and bawdy barracks tunes. Lord Commander Burley himself took the queen into the haunted forest (with a hundred rangers riding escort). When Alysanne expressed the wish to see some of the other forts along the Wall, the First Ranger Benton Glover led her west atop the Wall, past Snowgate to the Nightfort, where they made their descent and spent the night. The ride, the queen decided, was as breathtaking a journey as she had ever experienced, "as exhilarating as it was cold, though the wind up there blows so strongly that I feared it was about to sweep us off the Wall." The Nightfort itself she found grim and sinister. "It is so huge the men seem dwarfed by it, like mice in a ruined hall," she told Jaehaerys, "and there is a darkness there . . . a taste in the air . . . I was so glad to leave that place."

It must not be thought that the queen's days and nights at Castle Black were entirely taken up with such idle pursuits. She was here for the Iron Throne, she reminded Lord Burley, and many an afternoon was spent with him and his officers discussing the wildlings, the Wall, and the needs of the Watch.

"Above all else, a queen must know how to listen," Alysanne Targaryen often said. At Castle Black, she proved those words. She listened, she heard, and she won the eternal devotion of the men of the Night's Watch by her actions. She understood the need for a castle between Snowgate and Icemark, she told Lord Burley, but the Nightfort was crumbling, overlarge, and surely ruinous to heat. The Watch should abandon it, she said, and build a smaller castle farther to the east. Lord Burley could not disagree . . . but the Night's Watch lacked the coin to build new castles, he said. Alysanne had anticipated that objection. She would pay for the castle herself, she told the Lord Commander, and pledged her jewels to cover the cost. "I have a good many jewels," she said.

It would take eight years to raise the new castle, which would bear the name of Deep Lake. Outside its main hall, a statue of Alysanne Targaryen stands to this very day. The Nightfort was abandoned even before Deep Lake was completed, as the queen had wished. Lord Commander Burley also renamed Snowgate castle in her honor, as Queensgate.

Queen Alysanne also wished to listen to the women of the North. When Lord Burley explained that there were no women on the Wall, she persisted . . . until finally, with great reluctance, he had her escorted to a village south of the Wall that the black brothers called Mole's Town. She would find women there, his lordship said, though most of them would be harlots. The men of the Night's Watch took no wives, he explained, but they remained men all the same, and some felt certain needs. Queen Alysanne said she did not care, and so it came to pass that she held her women's court amongst the whores and strumpets of Mole's Town . . . and there heard certain tales that would change the Seven Kingdoms forever.

Back in King's Landing, the Archon of Tyrosh, the Prince of Pentos, and Jaehaerys I Targaryen of Westeros finally put their seals to "A Treaty of Eternal Peace." That a pact was reached at all was considered somewhat of a miracle, and largely due to the king's veiled hint that Westeros itself might enter the war if an accord was not reached. (The aftermath would prove even less successful than the negotiations. On his return to Tyrosh, the Archon was heard to say that King's Landing was a "reeking sore" not fit to be called a city, whilst the magisters of Pentos were so unhappy with the terms that they sacrificed their prince to their queer gods, as is the custom of that city.) Only then was King Jaehaerys free to fly north with Vermithor. He and the queen reunited at Winterfell, after half a year apart.

The king's time at Winterfell began on an ominous note. Upon his arrival, Alaric Stark led His Grace down to the crypts below the castle to show him his brother's tomb. "Walton lies down here in darkness in no small part thanks to you. Stars and Swords, the leavings of your seven gods, what are they to us? And yet you sent them to the Wall in their hundreds and their thousands, so many that the Night's Watch was hard-pressed to feed them . . . and when the worst of them rose up, the oathbreakers you had sent us, it cost my brother's life to put them down."

"A grievous price," the king agreed, "but that was never our intent. You have my regrets, my lord, and my gratitude."

"I would sooner have my brother," Lord Alaric answered darkly.

Lord Stark and King Jaehaerys would never be fast friends; the shade of Walton Stark remained between them to the end. It was only through Queen Alysanne's good offices that they ever found accord. The queen had visited Brandon's Gift, the lands south of the Wall that Brandon the Builder had granted to the Watch for their support and sustenance. "It is not enough," she told the king. "The soil is thin and stony, the hills unpopulated. The Watch lacks for coin, and when winter comes they will lack for food as well." The answer she proposed was a New Gift, a further strip of land south of Brandon's Gift.

The notion did not please Lord Alaric; though a strong friend to the Night's Watch, he knew that the lords who presently held the lands in question would object to them being given away without their leave. "I have no doubt that you can persuade them, Lord Alaric," the queen said. And finally, charmed by her as ever, Alaric Stark agreed that, aye, he could. And so it came to pass that the size of the Gift was doubled with a stroke.

Little more need be said of the time Queen Alysanne and King Jaehaerys spent in the North. After lingering in Winterfell for another fortnight, they made their way to Torrhen's Square and thence to Barrowton, where Lord Dustin showed them the barrow of the First King and staged somewhat of a tourney in their honor, though it was a poor thing compared to the tourneys of the south. From there Vermithor and Silverwing bore Jaehaerys and Alysanne back again to King's Landing. The men and women of their retinue had a more arduous journey home, traveling overland from Barrowton back to White Harbor and taking ship from there.

Even before the others reached White Harbor, King Jaehaerys had called together his council in the Red Keep, to consider an entreaty from his queen. When Septon Barth, Grand Maester Benifer, and the others had assembled, Alysanne told them of her visit to the Wall, and the day that she had spent with the whores and fallen women of Mole's Town.

"There was a girl there," the queen said, "no older than I am as I sit before you now. A pretty girl, but not, I think, as pretty as she was. Her father was a blacksmith, and when she was a maid of fourteen years, he gave her hand in marriage to his apprentice. She was fond of the boy, and he of her, so the two of them were duly wed . . . but scarcely had they said their vows than their lord came down upon the wedding with his men-at-arms to claim his right to her first night. He carried her off to his tower and enjoyed her, and the next morning his men returned her to her husband.

"But her maidenhead was gone, together with whatever love the apprentice boy had borne her. He could not raise his hand against the lord for peril of his life, so instead he raised it against his wife. When it became plain that she was carrying the lord's child, he beat it out of her. From that day on, he never called her anything but 'whore,' until finally the girl decided that if she must be called a whore she would live as one, and made her way to Mole's Town. There she dwells until this day, a sad child, ruined . . . but all the while, in other villages, other maids are being wed, and other lords are claiming their first night.

"Hers was the worst story, but not the only one. At White Harbor, at Mole's Town, at Barrowton, other women spoke of their first nights as well. I never knew, my lords. Oh, I knew of the tradition. Even on Dragonstone, there are stories of men of mine own house, *Targaryens,* who have made free with the wives of fisherfolk and serving men, and sired children on them . . ."

"Dragonseeds, they call them," Jaehaerys said with obvious reluctance. "It is not a thing to boast of, but it has happened, mayhaps more often than we would care to admit. Such children are cherished, though. Orys Baratheon himself was a dragonseed, a bastard brother to our grandsire. Whether he was conceived of a first night I cannot say, but Lord Aerion was his father, that was well-known. Gifts were given . . ."

"Gifts?" the queen said in a voice sharp with derision. "I see no honor in any of this. I knew such things happened hundreds of years ago, I confess it, but I never dreamed that the custom endured so strongly to this day. Mayhaps I did not want to know. I closed my eyes, but that poor girl in Mole's Town opened them. *The right of the first night!* Your Grace, my lords, it is time we put an end to this. I beg you."

A silence fell after the queen had finished speaking, Grand Maester Benifer tells us. The lords of the small council shifted awkwardly in their seats and exchanged glances, until finally the king himself spoke up, sympathetic but reluctant. What the queen proposed would be difficult, Jaehaerys said. Lords grew troublesome when kings began taking things that they regarded as their own. "Their lands, their gold, their rights . . ."

". . . their wives?" Alysanne finished. "I remember our wedding, my lord. If you had been a blacksmith and me a washerwoman and some lord had come to claim me and take my maidenhead the day we took our vows, what would you have done?"

"Killed him," Jaehaerys said, "but I am not a blacksmith."

"*If*, I said," the queen persisted. "A blacksmith is still a man, is he not? What man but a coward would stand by meekly whilst another man has his way with his wife? We do not want blacksmiths killing lords, surely." She turned to Grand Maester Benifer and said, "I know how Gargon Qoherys died. Gargon the Guest. How many more such instances have there been, I wonder?"

"More than I would care to say," Benifer allowed. "They are not oft spoken of, for fear that other men might do the same, but . . ."

"The first night is an offense against the King's Peace," the queen concluded. "An offense against not only the maid, but her husband as well . . . and the wife of the lord, never forget. What do those highborn ladies do whilst their lords are out deflowering maidens? Do they sew? Sing? Pray? Were it me, I might pray my lord husband fell off his horse and broke his neck coming home."

King Jaehaerys smiled at that, but it was plain that he was becoming increasingly uncomfortable. "The right of the first night is an ancient one," he argued, though with no great passion, "as much a part of lordship as the right of pit and gallows. It is rarely used south of the Neck, I am told, but its continued existence is a lordly prerogative that some of my more truculent subjects would be loath to surrender. You are not wrong, my love, but sometimes it is best to let a sleeping dragon lie."

"We are the sleeping dragons," the queen threw back. "These lords who love their first nights are dogs. Why must they slake their lust on maidens who have only just pledged their love to other men? Have they no wives of their own? Are there no whores in their domains? Have they lost the use of their hands?"

The justiciar Lord Albin Massey spoke up then, saying, "There is more to the first night than lust, Your Grace. The practice is an ancient one, older than the Andals, older than the Faith. It goes back to the Dawn Age, I do not doubt. The First Men were a savage race, and like the wildlings beyond the Wall, they followed only strength. Their lords and kings were warriors, mighty men and heroes, and they wanted their sons to be the same. If a warlord chose to bestow his seed upon some maid on her wedding night, it was seen as . . . a sort of blessing. And if a child should come of the coupling, so much the better. The husband could then claim the honor of raising a hero's son as his own."

"Mayhaps that was so, ten thousand years ago," the queen replied, "but the lords claiming the first night now are no heroes. You have not heard the women speak of them. I have. Old men, fat men, cruel men, poxy boys, rapers, droolers, men covered with scabs, with scars, with boils, lords who have not washed in half a year, men with greasy hair and lice. These are your mighty men. I listened to the girls, and none of them felt blessed."

"The Andals never practiced the first night in Andalos," Grand Maester Benifer said. "When they came to Westeros and swept away the kingdoms of the First Men, they found the tradition in place and chose to let it remain, just as they did the godswoods."

Septon Barth spoke then, turning to the king. "Sire, if I may be so bold, I believe Her Grace has the right of this. The First Men might have found some purpose in this rite, but the First Men fought with bronze swords and fed their weirwood trees with blood. We are not those men, and it is past time we put an end to this evil. It stands against every ideal of chivalry. Our knights swear to protect the innocence of maidens . . . save for when the lord they serve wishes to despoil one, it would seem. We swear our marriage vows before the Father and the Mother, promising fidelity until the Stranger comes to part us, and nowhere in *The Seven-Pointed Star* does it say that those promises do not apply to lords. You are not wrong, Your Grace, some lords will surely grumble at this, especially in the North . . . but all the maids will thank us for it, and all the husbands and the fathers and the mothers, just as the queen has said. I know the Faithful will be pleased. His High Holiness will let his voice be heard, never doubt it."

When Barth had finished speaking, Jaehaerys Targaryen threw up his hands. "I know when I am beaten. Very well. Let it be done."

And so it came to pass that the second of what the smallfolk named Queen Alysanne's Laws was enacted: the abolition of the lord's ancient right to the first night. Henceforth, it was decreed, a bride's maidenhead would belong only to her husband, whether joined before a septon or a heart tree, and any man, be he lord or peasant, who took her on her wedding night or any other night would be guilty of the crime of rape.

As the 58th year after Aegon's Conquest drew to a close, King Jaehaerys celebrated the tenth anniversary of his coronation at the Starry Sept of Oldtown. The callow boy that the High Septon had crowned that day was long gone; his place had been taken by a man of four-and-twenty who was every inch a king. The wispy beard and mustache that His Grace had cultivated early in his reign had become a handsome golden beard, shot through with silver. His unshorn hair he wore in a thick braid that fell almost to his waist. Tall and handsome, Jaehaerys moved with an easy grace, be it on the dance floor or in the training yard. His smile, it was said, could warm the heart of any maiden in the Seven Kingdoms; his frown could make a man's blood run cold. In his sister he had a queen even more beloved than he was. "Good Queen Alysanne," the smallfolk called her, from Oldtown to the Wall. The gods had blessed the two of them with three strong children, two splendid young princes and a princess who was the darling of the realm.

In their decade of rule, they had known grief and horror, betrayal and conflict, and the death of loved ones, but they had weathered the storms and survived the tragedies and emerged stronger and better from all they had endured. Their accomplishments were undeniable; the Seven Kingdoms were at peace, and more prosperous than they had been in living memory.

It was a time for celebration and celebrate they did, with a tourney at King's Landing on the anniversary of the king's coronation. Princess Daenerys and the Princes Aemon and Baelon shared the royal box with their mother and father, and reveled in the cheers of the crowd. On the field, the highlight of the competition was the brilliance of Ser Ryam Redwyne, the youngest son of Lord Manfryd Redwyne of the Arbor, Jaehaerys's lord admiral and master of ships. In successive tilts, Ser Ryam unhorsed Ronnal Baratheon, Arthor Oakheart, Simon Dondarrion, Harys Hogg (Harry the Ham, to the commons), and two Kingsguard knights, Lorence Roxton and Lucamore Strong. When the young gallant trotted up to the royal box and crowned Good Queen Alysanne as his queen of love and beauty, the commons roared their approval.

The leaves in the trees had begun to turn russet and orange and gold, and the ladies of the court wore gowns to match. At the feast that followed the end of the tourney, Lord Rogar Baratheon appeared with his children, Boremund and Jocelyn, to be warmly embraced by the king and queen. Lords from all over the realm came to join the celebration; Lyman Lannister from Casterly Rock, Daemon Velaryon from Driftmark, Prentys Tully from Riverrun, Rodrik Arryn from the Vale, even the Lords Rowan and Oakheart, whose levies once marched with Septon Moon. Theomore Manderly came down from the North. Alaric Stark did not, but his sons came, and with them his daughter, Alarra, blushing, to take up her new duties as a lady-in-waiting to the queen. The High Septon was too ill to come, but he sent his newest septa, Rhaella, who had been Targaryen, still shy, but smiling. It was said that the queen wept for joy at the sight of her, for in her face and form she was the very image of her sister, Aerea, grown older.

It was a time for warm embraces, for smiles, for toasts and reconciliations, for renewing old friendships and making new ones, for laughter and kisses. It was a good time, a golden autumn, a time of peace and plenty.

But winter was coming.

The Long Reign

Jaehaerys and Alysanne: Policy, Progeny, and Pain

On the seventh day of the 59th year after Aegon's Conquest, a battered ship came limping up the Whispering Sound to the port of Oldtown. Her sails were patched and ragged and salt-stained, her paint faded and flaking, the banner streaming from her mast so sun-bleached as to be unrecognizable. Not until she was tied up at dock was she finally recognized in her sorry state. She was the *Lady Meredith,* last seen departing Oldtown almost three years earlier to cross the Sunset Sea.

As her crew began to disembark, throngs of merchants, porters, whores, seamen, and thieves gaped in shock. Nine of every ten men coming ashore were black or brown. Ripples of excitement ran up and down the docks. Had the *Lady Meredith* indeed crossed the Sunset Sea? Were the peoples of the fabled lands of the far west all dark-skinned as Summer Islanders?

Only when Ser Eustace Hightower himself emerged did the whispers die. Lord Donnel's grandson was gaunt and sun-burned, with lines on his face that had not been there when he sailed. A handful of Oldtown men were with him, all that remained of his original crew. One of his grandsire's customs officers met him on the dock and a quick exchange ensued. The *Lady Meredith*'s crew did not simply look like Summer Islanders; they *were* Summer Islanders, hired on in Sothoryos ("at ruinous wages," Ser

Eustace complained) to replace the men he'd lost. He would require porters, the captain said. His holds were bulging with rich cargo . . . but not from lands beyond the Sunset Sea. "That was a dream," he said.

Soon enough Lord Donnel's knights turned up, with orders to escort him to the Hightower. There, in his grandsire's high hall with a cup of wine in hand, Ser Eustace Hightower told his tale. Lord Donnel's scribes scribbled as he spoke, and within days the story had spread all over Westeros, by messenger, bard, and raven.

The voyage had begun as well as he could have hoped, Ser Eustace said. Once beyond the Arbor, Lady Westhill had steered her *Sun Chaser* south by southwest, seeking warmer waters and fair winds, and the *Lady Meredith* and *Autumn Moon* had followed. The big Braavosi ship was very fast when the wind was in her sails, and the Hightowers had difficulties keeping pace. "The Seven were smiling on us, at the start. We had the sun by day and the moon by night, and as sweet a wind as man or maid could hope for. We were not entirely alone. We glimpsed fisherfolk from time to time, and once a great dark ship that could only have been a whaler out of Ib. And fish, so many fish . . . some dolphins swam beside us, as if they had never seen a ship before. We all thought that we were blessed."

Twelve days of smooth sailing out of Westeros, the *Sun Chaser* and her two companions were as far south as the Summer Islands, according to their best calculations, and farther west than any ship had sailed before . . . or any ship that had returned to tell of it, at least. On the *Lady Meredith* and *Autumn Moon,* casks of Arbor gold were breached to toast the accomplishment; on *Sun Chaser,* the sailors drank a spiced honey wine from Lannisport. And if any man of them was disquieted that they had not seen a bird for the past four days, he held his tongue.

The gods hate man's arrogance, the septons teach us, and *The Seven-Pointed Star* says that pride goes before a fall. It may well be that Alys Westhill and the Hightowers celebrated too loudly and too early, there in the ocean deeps, for soon after that the grand voyage began to go badly wrong. "We lost the wind first," Ser Eustace told his grandfather's court. "For almost a fortnight there was not so much as a breeze, and the ships moved only so far as we could tow them. It was discovered that a dozen casks of meat on *Autumn Moon* were crawling with maggots. A small enough thing by itself, but an ill omen. The wind finally returned one day near sunset, when the sky turned red as blood, but the look of it set men to muttering. I told them it boded well for us, but I lied. Before morning the stars were gone and the wind began to howl, and then the ocean rose."

That was the first storm, Ser Eustace said. Another followed two days later, and then a third, each worse than the one before. "The waves rose higher than our masts, and there was thunder all around, and lightning such as I had never seen before, great cracking bolts that burned the eyes. One struck the *Autumn Moon* and split her mast from the crow's nest down to the deck. In the midst of all that madness, one of my hands screamed that he had seen arms rising from the water, the last thing any captain needs to hear. We had lost all sight of *Sun Chaser* by then, all that remained was my lady and the *Moon*. The sea was washing over our decks with every rise and fall, and men were being swept over the side, clinging uselessly to lines. I saw the *Autumn Moon* founder with my own eyes. One moment she was there, broken and burning, but there. Then a wave rose up and swallowed her and I blinked and she was gone, quick as that. That was all it was, a wave, a monster of a wave, but all my men were screaming *'Kraken, kraken!'* and not a word I said would ever disabuse them.

"I will never know how we survived that night, but we did. The next morning the sea was calm again, the sun was shining, and the water was so blue and innocent a man might never know that under it my brother floated, dead with all his men. *Lady Meredith* was in sad shape, sails torn, masts splintered, nine men amongst the missing. We said prayers for the lost and set about making what repairs we could . . . and that afternoon, our crow's eye saw sails in the distance. It was *Sun Chaser*, come back to find us."

Lady Westhill had done more than simply survive the storm. She had found land. The winds and raging seas that had separated her *Sun Chaser* from the Hightowers had driven her westward, and when the dawn broke, her man in the crow's nest had espied birds circling a hazy mountain peak on the horizon. Lady Alys made toward it and came upon three small islands. "A mountain attended by two hills," as she put it. The *Lady Meredith* was in no fit shape to sail, but with the help of a tow from three boats off the *Sun Chaser* she was able to make the safety of the islands.

The two battered ships sheltered off the islands for more than a fortnight, making repairs and replenishing their stores. Lady Alys was triumphant; here was land farther to the west than any land had ever been known to be, islands that existed on no known chart. Since there were three of them, she named them Aegon, Rhaenys, and Visenya. The islands were uninhabited, but springs and streams were plentiful, so the voyagers were able to fill their casks with all the fresh water they required. There were wild pigs as well, and huge, sluggish grey lizards as big as deer, and trees heavy with nuts and fruit.

After sampling some of those, Eustace Hightower declared that they had no need to go any farther. "This is discovery enough," he said. "We have spices here I have never tasted, and these pink fruits . . . we have our fortunes here, in our hands."

Alys Westhill was incredulous. Three small islands, even the largest of them a third the size of Dragonstone, that was nothing. The true wonders lay farther west. There might be another Essos just beyond the horizon.

"Or there might be another thousand leagues of empty ocean," Ser Eustace replied. And though Lady Alys cajoled and pleaded and wove webs of words in the air, she could not move him. "Even had I wished to, my crew would not allow it," he told Lord Donnel in the Hightower. "To a man, they were convinced they had seen a giant kraken pull *Autumn Moon* beneath the sea. Had I given the command to sail on, they would have fed me to the waves and found another captain."

So the voyagers had parted ways as they left the islands. *Lady Meredith* turned back east for home, whilst Alys Westhill and her *Sun Chaser* pressed on westward, chasing the sun. Eustace Hightower's voyage home would prove to be nigh as perilous as his voyage out had been. There were more storms to be weathered, though none as terrible as the one that had claimed his brother's ship. The prevailing winds were against them, forcing them to tack and tack again. They had taken three of the great grey lizards on board, and one bit his steersman, whose leg turned green and had to be removed. A few days later, they encountered a pod of leviathans. One of them, a huge white bull larger than a ship, had slammed into *Lady Meredith* of a purpose, and cracked her hull. Afterward Ser Eustace had changed course, making for the Summer Islands, which he figured to be their nearest landfall. They were farther south than he had realized, however, and ended up missing the islands entirely and fetching up instead upon the coast of Sothoryos.

"We were there for a full year," he told his grandsire, "trying to make *Lady Meredith* seaworthy again, for the damage was greater than we'd thought. There were fortunes to be had there as well, though, and we were not blind to that. Emeralds, gold, spices, aye, all that and more. Strange creatures . . . monkeys that walk like men, men that howl like monkeys, wyverns, basilisks, a hundred different sorts of snakes. Deadly, all of them. Some of my men just vanished of a night. The ones who didn't began to die. One was bitten by a fly, a little prick upon his neck, nothing to fear. Three days later his skin was sloughing off, and he was bleeding from his ears and cock and arse. Drinking salt water will make a man mad, every sailor knows that, but the freshwater is no safer in that place. There are worms in it, almost too small to see, if you swallowed them they laid their eggs inside you. And the fevers . . . hardly a day went by when half my men were fit to work. We all would have perished, I think, but some Summer Islanders passing by came on us. They know that hell better than they let on, I think. With their help, I was able to get *Lady Meredith* to Tall Trees Town, and from there to home."

There ended his tale, and his great adventure.

As for Lady Alys Westhill, born Elissa of House Farman, where her adventure ended we cannot say. The *Sun Chaser* vanished into the west, still searching for the lands beyond the Sunset Sea, and was never seen again.

Except . . .

Many years later, Corlys Velaryon, the boy born on Driftmark in 53 AC, would take his ship the *Sea Snake* on nine great voyages, sailing farther than any man of Westeros had ever sailed before. On the first of those voyages, he sailed beyond the Jade Gates, to Yi Ti and the isle of Leng, and returned with such a wealth of spice and silk and jade that House Velaryon doubled its wealth from the profits of that single journey. On his second voyage, Ser Corlys sailed even farther east, and became the first Westerosi ever to reach Asshai-by-the-Shadow, the bleak black city of the shadowbinders at the edge of the world. There he lost his love and half his crew, if the tales be true . . . and there as well, in Asshai's harbor, he glimpsed an old and much weathered ship that he would swear forevermore could only have been *Sun Chaser.*

In 59 AC, however, Corlys Velaryon was a boy of six, dreaming of the sea, so we must leave him and turn back once again to the end of autumn in that fateful year, when the skies darkened, the winds rose, and winter came again to Westeros.

The winter of 59–60 AC was an exceptionally cruel one, all those who survived it agreed. The North was hit first and hardest, as crops died in the field, streams froze, and bitter winds came howling over the Wall. Though Lord Alaric Stark had commanded that half of every harvest be preserved and put aside against the coming winter, not all his bannermen had obeyed. As their larders and granaries emptied, famine spread across the land, and old men bade farewell to their children and went out into the snow to die so their kin might live. Harvests failed in the riverlands, the westerlands, and the Vale as well, and even down into the Reach. Those who had food began to hoard, and all across the Seven Kingdoms the price of bread began to rise. The price of meat rose even faster, and in the towns and cities, fruits and vegetables all but disappeared.

And then the Shivers came, and the Stranger walked the land.

The maesters knew the Shivers. They had seen its like before, a century ago, and the course of the contagion was written in their books. It was believed to have come to Westeros from across the sea, from one of the Free Cities or lands more distant still. Port cities and harbor towns always felt the hand of the disease first and hardest. Many of the smallfolk believed that it was carried by rats; not the familiar grey rats of King's Landing and Oldtown, big and bold and vicious, but the smaller black rats that could be seen swarming from the holds of ships at dock and scurrying down the ropes that held them fast. Though the guilt of rats was never proved to the satisfaction of the Citadel, suddenly every house in the Seven Kingdoms, from the grandest castle to the humblest hut, required a cat. Before the Shivers ran its course that winter, kittens were selling for as much as destriers.

The marks of the disease were well-known. It began simply enough, with a chill. Victims would complain of being cold, throw a fresh log on the fire, huddle under a blanket or a pile of furs. Some would call for hot soup, mulled wine, or, against all reason, beer. Neither blankets nor soups could stay the progress of the pestilence. Soon the shivering would begin; mild at first, a trembling, a shudder, but inexorably growing worse. Goose-prickles would march up and down the victim's limbs like conquering armies. By then the afflicted would be shivering so violently that their teeth would chatter, and their hands and feet would begin to convulse and twitch. When the victim's lips turned blue and he began to cough up blood, the end was nigh. Once the first chill was felt, the course of the Shivers was swift. Death could come within a day, and no more than one victim in every five recovered.

All this the maesters knew. What they did not know is where the Shivers came from, how to stop it, or how to cure it. Poultices were tried, and potions. Hot mustards and dragon peppers were suggested, and wine spiced with snake venom that made the lips go numb. The afflicted were immersed in tubs of hot water, some heated almost to the point of boiling. Green vegetables were said to be a cure; then raw fish; then red meat, the bloodier the better. Certain healers dispensed with the meat, and advised their patients to drink blood. Various smokes and inhalations of burning leaves were tried. One lord commanded his men to build fires all around him, surrounding himself with walls of flame.

In the winter of 59 AC, the Shivers entered from the east, and moved across Blackwater Bay and up the Blackwater Rush. Even before King's Landing, the islands off the crownlands felt the chill. Edwell Celtigar, Maegor's one-time Hand and the much despised master of coin, was the first lord to die. His son and heir followed him to grave three days later. Lord Staunton died at Rook's Rest, and then his wife. Their children, frightened, sealed themselves inside their bedchambers and barred the doors, but it did not save them. On Dragonstone, the queen's beloved Septa Edyth perished. On Driftmark, Daemon Velaryon, Lord of the Tides, recovered after being at the point of death, but his second son and three of his daughters were borne away. Lord Bar Emmon, Lord Rosby, Lady Jirelle of Maidenpool . . . the bells tolled for them all, and many lesser men and women besides.

All across the Seven Kingdoms, the noble and humble alike were struck down. The old and the young were most at risk, but men and women in the prime of their lives were not spared. The roll of those taken included the greatest of lords, the noblest of ladies, the most valiant of knights. Lord Prentys Tully died shivering in Riverrun, followed a day later by his Lady Lucinda. Lyman Lannister, the mighty Lord of Casterly Rock, was taken, together with sundry other lords of the westerlands; Lord Marbrand of Ashemark, Lord Tarbeck of Tarbeck Hall, Lord Westerling of the Crag. At Highgarden, Lord Tyrell sickened but survived, only to perish, drunk, in a fall from his horse four days after his recovery. Rogar Baratheon was untouched by the Shivers, and his son and daughter by Queen Alyssa were stricken but recovered, yet his brother Ser Ronnal died, and the wives of both his brothers.

The great port city of Oldtown was especially hard hit, losing a quarter of its population. Eustace Hightower, who had returned alive from Alys Westhill's ill-fated voyage across the Sunset Sea, survived once again, but his wife and children were not as fortunate. Nor was his grandsire, Lord of the Hightower. Donnel the Delayer could not delay death. He died shivering. So did the High Septon, twoscore of the Most Devout, and fully a third of the archmaesters, maesters, acolytes, and novices at the Citadel.

In all the realm, no place was as sorely afflicted as King's Landing was in 59 AC. Amongst the dead were two knights of the Kingsguard, old Ser Sam of Sour Hill and the good-hearted Ser Victor the Valiant, along with three lords of the council, Albin Massey, Qarl Corbray, and Grand Maester Benifer himself. Benifer had served for fifteen years through times both perilous and prosperous, coming to the Red Keep after Maegor the Cruel had decapitated his three immediate predecessors. ("An act of singular courage or singular stupidity," his sardonic successor would observe. "I would not have lasted three days under Maegor.")

All the dead would be mourned and missed, but in the immediate aftermath of their passing, the loss of Qarl Corbray was felt most grievously. With their commander dead and many of the City Watch stricken and shivering, the streets and alleys of King's Landing fell prey to lawlessness and license. Shops were looted, women raped, men robbed and killed for no crime but walking down the wrong street at the wrong time. King Jaehaerys sent forth his Kingsguard and his household knights to restore order, but they were too few, and he soon had no choice but to call them back.

Amidst the chaos, His Grace would lose another of his lords, not to the Shivers but to ignorance and hate. Rego Draz had never taken up residence in the Red Keep, though there was ample room for him there, and the king had made the offer many times. The Pentoshi preferred his own manse on the Street of Silk, with the Dragonpit looming above him atop the Hill of Rhaenys. There he could entertain his concubines without suffering the disapproval of the court. After ten years in service to the Iron Throne, Lord Rego had grown quite stout, and no longer chose to ride. Instead he moved from manse to castle and back again in an ornate gilded palanquin. Unwisely, his route took him through the reeking heart of Flea Bottom, the foulest and most lawless district of the city.

On that dire day, a dozen of Flea Bottom's less savory denizens were chasing a piglet down an alley when they chanced to come upon Lord Rego moving through the streets. Some were drunk and all were hungry—the piglet had escaped them—and the sight of the Pentoshi enraged them, for to a man they held the master of coin to blame for the high cost of bread. One wore a sword. Three had knives. The rest snatched up stones and sticks and swarmed the palanquin, driving off Lord Rego's bearers and spilling his lordship onto the ground. Onlookers said he screamed for help in words none of them could understand.

When his lordship raised his hands to ward off the blows raining down on him, gold and gemstones glittered on every finger, and the attack grew more frenzied still. A woman shouted, "He's Pentoshi. Them's the bastards brung the Shivers here." One of the men pried a stone up from the king's newly cobbled street and brought it down upon Lord Rego's head again and again, until only a red mash of blood and bone and brains remained. Thus died the Lord of Air, his skull crushed by one of the very cobblestones he had helped the king lay down. Even then, his assailants were not done with him. Before they ran, they ripped off his fine clothes and cut off all his fingers to lay claim to his rings.

When word reached the Red Keep, Jaehaerys Targaryen himself rode forth to claim the body, surrounded by his Kingsguard. So wroth was His Grace at what he saw that Ser Joffrey Doggett would say afterward,

"When I looked upon his face, for a moment it was as if I were looking at his uncle." The street was full of the curious, come out to see their king or gaze upon the bloody corpse of the Pentoshi moneychanger. Jaehaerys wheeled his horse about and shouted at them. "I would have the name of the men who did this. Speak now, and you will be well rewarded. Hold your tongues, and you will lose them." Many of the watchers slunk away, but one barefoot girl came forward, squeaking out a name.

The king thanked her, and commanded her to show his knights where this man might be found. She led the Kingsguard to a wine sink where the villain was discovered with a whore in his lap and three of Lord Rego's rings on his fingers. Under torture, he soon gave up the names of the other attackers, and they were taken one and all. One of their number claimed to have been a Poor Fellow, and cried out that he wished to take the black. "No," Jaehaerys told him. "The Night's Watch are men of honor, and you are lower than rats." Such men as these were unworthy of a clean death by sword or axe, he ruled. Instead they were hung from the walls of the Red Keep, disemboweled, and left to twist until they died, their entrails swinging loose down to their knees.

The girl who had led the king to the killers had a kinder fate. Taken in hand by Queen Alysanne, she was plunged into a tub of hot water for a scrubbing. Her clothes were burned, her head was shaved, and she was fed hot bread and bacon. "There is a place for you in the castle, if you want it," Alysanne told her when her belly was full. "In the kitchens or the stables, as you wish. Do you have a father?" The girl gave a shy nod and admitted that she did. "He was one o' them bellies you cut open. The poxy one, wi' the stye." Then she told Her Grace that she wanted to work in the kitchens. "That's where they keeps the bread."

The old year ended and a new year began, but there were few celebrations anywhere in Westeros to mark the coming of the 60th year since Aegon's Conquest. A year before great bonfires had been lit in public squares and men and women had danced around them, drinking and laughing, whilst bells rang in the new year. One year later the fires were consuming corpses, and the bells were tolling out the dead. The streets of King's Landing were empty, especially by night, the alleyways were deep in snow, and icicles hung down from the rooftops, long as spears.

Atop Aegon's High Hill, King Jaehaerys ordered the gates of the Red Keep closed and barred, and doubled the watch on the castle walls. He and his queen and their children attended sunset services at the castle sept, repaired to Maegor's Holdfast for a modest meal, and then retired to bed.

It was the hour of the owl when Queen Alysanne was awoken by her daughter shaking her gently by the arm. "Mother," Princess Daenerys said, "I'm cold."

There is no need to dwell on all that followed. Daenerys Targaryen was the darling of the realm, and all that could be done for any man was done for her. There were prayers and poultices, hot soups and scalding baths, blankets and furs and hot stones, nettle tea. The princess was six, and years past being weaned, but a wet nurse was summoned, for there were some who believed that mother's milk could cure the Shivers. Maesters came and went, septons and septas prayed, the king commanded that a hundred new ratcatchers be hired at once, and offered a silver stag for every dead rat, grey or black. Daenerys wanted her kitten, and her kitten was brought to her, though as her shivering grew more violent it squirmed from her grasp and scratched her hand. Near dawn, Jaehaerys bolted to his feet shouting that a dragon was needed, that his daughter must have a dragon, and ravens took wing for Dragonstone, instructing the Dragonkeepers there to bring a hatchling to the Red Keep at once.

None of it mattered. A day and a half after she had woken her mother from sleep complaining of feeling cold, the little princess was dead. The queen collapsed in the king's arms, shaking so violently that some feared she had the Shivers too. Jaehaerys had her taken back to her own chambers and given milk of the poppy to help her sleep. Though near exhaustion, he went next to the yard and loosed Vermithor, then flew to Dragonstone to tell them there was no need for the hatchling after all. On his return to King's Landing, he drank a cup of dreamwine and sent for Septon Barth. "How could this happen?" he demanded. "What sin did she commit? Why would the gods take her? *How could this happen?*" But even Barth, that wise man, had no answers for him.

The king and queen were not the only parents to lose a child to the Shivers; thousands of others, highborn and low, knew the same pain that winter. For Jaehaerys and Alysanne, however, the death of their beloved daughter must have seemed especially cruel, for it struck at the very heart of the Doctrine of Exceptionalism. Princess Daenerys had been Targaryen on both sides, with the blood of Old Valyria running pure through her veins, and those of Valyrian descent were not like other men. Targaryens had purple eyes and hair of gold and silver, they ruled the sky on dragons, the doctrines of the Faith and the prohibitions against incest did not apply to them . . . *and they did not get sick.*

Since Aenar the Exile first staked his claim to Dragonstone, that had been known. Targaryens did not die of pox or the bloody flux, they were not afflicted with redspots or brownleg or the shaking sickness, they would not succumb to wormbone or clotted lung or sourgut or any of the myriad pestilences and contagions that the gods, for reasons of their own, see fit to loose on mortal men and women. There was fire in the blood of the dragon, it was reasoned, a purifying fire that burned out all such plagues. It was unthinkable that a pureborn princess should die shivering, as if she were some common child.

And yet she had.

Even as they mourned for her and the sweet soul she had been, Jaehaerys and Alysanne must also have been confronting that awful realization. Mayhaps the Targaryens were not so close to gods as they had believed. Mayhaps, in the end, they too were only men.

When the Shivers finally ran its course, King Jaehaerys went back to his labors with a sadder heart. His first task was a grim one: replacing all the friends and councillors he had lost. Lord Manfryd Redwyne's eldest son, Ser Robert, was named to command the City Watch. Ser Gyles Morrigen brought forth two good knights to join the Kingsguard, and His Grace duly presented Ser Ryam Redwyne and Ser Robin Shaw with white cloaks. The able Albin Massey, his bent-backed justiciar, was not so easily replaced. To fill his seat, the king reached out to the Vale of Arryn and summoned Rodrik Arryn, the erudite young Lord of the Eyrie, who he and the queen first met as a boy of ten.

The Citadel had already sent him Benifer's successor, the sharp-tongued Grand Maester Elysar. Twenty years younger than the man whose chain he donned, Elysar had never had a thought he didn't feel the need to share. Some claimed that the Conclave had sent him to King's Landing to be rid of him.

Jaehaerys hesitated longest when it came to selecting his new lord treasurer and master of coin. Rego Draz, however despised, had been a man of great ability. "I am tempted to say you do not find such men lying about in the streets, but if truth be told, we are more like to find one there than sitting in some castle," the king told his council. The Lord of Air had never married, but he did have three bastard sons who had learned his business at his knee. Much as the king was tempted to reach out to one of them, he knew the realm would never accept another Pentoshi. "It must needs be a lord," he concluded gloomily. Familiar names were bandied once again: Lannister, Velaryon, Hightower, houses built on gold as much as steel. "They are all too proud," Jaehaerys said.

It was Septon Barth who first proposed a different name. "The Tyrells of Highgarden are descended from stewards," he reminded the king, "but the Reach is broader than the westerlands, with a different sort of wealth, and young Martyn Tyrell might prove a useful addition to this council."

Lord Redwyne was incredulous. "The Tyrells are dolts," he said. "I am sorry, Your Grace, they are my liege lords, but . . . the Tyrells are dolts, and Lord Bertrand was a sot as well."

"That is as it may be," Septon Barth admitted. "Lord Bertrand is in his grave now, however, and I am speaking of his son. Martyn is young and eager, but I will not vouch for the quality of his wits. His wife, however, is a Fossoway girl, the Lady Florence, who has been counting apples since she learned to walk. She has been keeping all the accounts at Highgarden since her marriage, and it is said she has increased House Tyrell's incomes by a third. Should we appoint her husband, she would come to court as well, I do not doubt."

"Alysanne would like that," the king said. "She enjoys the company of clever women." The queen had not been attending council since the death of Princess Daenerys. Mayhaps Jaehaerys hoped that this would help bring her back to him again. "Our good septon has never led us wrong. Let us try the dolt with the clever wife, and hope that my leal smallfolk do not beat his head in with a cobblestone."

The Seven take and the Seven give. Mayhaps the Mother Above looked down on Queen Alysanne in her grief and took pity on her broken heart. The moon had not turned twice since Princess Daenerys's death when Her Grace learned that she was once again carrying a child. With winter holding the realm in its icy grip, the queen once again chose caution and retired to Dragonstone for her lying in. Late that year, 60 AC, she was delivered of her fifth child, a daughter she named Alyssa after her mother. "An honor Her Grace would have appreciated more had she been alive," observed the new Grand Maester, Elysar . . . though not in the king's hearing.

Winter broke not long after the queen gave birth, and Alyssa proved to be a lively, healthy child. As a babe she was so like her late sister, Daenerys, that the queen oft wept to behold her, remembering the child she had lost. The likeness faded as the princess grew older, however; long-faced and skinny, Alyssa had little of her sister's beauty. Her hair was a dirty blond tangle with no hint of silver to evoke the dragonlords of old, and she had been born with mismatched eyes, one violet, the other a startling green. Her ears were too big and her smile lopsided, and when she was six playing in the yard a whack across the face from a wooden sword broke her nose. It healed crooked, but Alyssa did not seem to care. By that age, her mother had come to realize that it was not Daenerys that she took after, but Baelon.

Just as Baelon had once followed Aemon everywhere, Alyssa trailed after Baelon. "Like a puppy," the Spring Prince complained. Baelon was two years younger than Aemon, Alyssa nearly four years younger than him . . . "and a girl," which made it far worse in his eyes. The princess did not act like a girl, however. She wore boy's clothes when she could, shunned the company of other girls, preferred riding and climbing and dueling with wooden swords to sewing and reading and singing, and refused to eat porridge.

An old friend, and old adversary, returned to King's Landing in 61 AC, when Lord Rogar Baratheon rode up from Storm's End to deliver three young girls to court. Two were the daughters of his brother Ronnal, who had died shivering together with his wife and sons. The third was Lady Jocelyn, his lordship's own daughter by Queen Alyssa. The small frail babe who had come into the world during that terrible Year of the Stranger had grown into a tall young girl of solemn mien, with large dark eyes and hair black as sin.

Rogar Baratheon's own hair had gone grey, however, and the years had taken their toll of the old King's Hand. His face was pale and lined, and he had grown so gaunt that his clothes hung loose upon him, as if they had been cut for a much larger man. When he took a knee before the Iron Throne, he had trouble rising back to his feet, and required the help of a Kingsguard to stand.

He had come to ask a boon, Lord Rogar told the king and queen. Lady Jocelyn would soon be celebrating her seventh nameday. "She has never known a mother. My brother's wives looked after her as much as they were able, but they favored their own children as mothers will, and now both of them are gone. If it please you, sires, I would ask you to accept Jocelyn and her cousins as wards, to be raised here at court beside your own sons and daughters."

"It would be our honor and our pleasure," Queen Alysanne replied. "Jocelyn is our own sister, we have not forgotten. Our blood."

Lord Rogar seemed much relieved. "I would ask you to look after my son as well. Boremund will remain at Storm's End, in the charge of my brother Garon. He is a good boy, a strong boy, and he will be a great lord in time, I do not doubt, but he is only nine. As Your Graces know, my brother Borys left the stormlands some years ago. He grew sour and angry after Boremund was born, and things went from bad to worse between us. Borys was in Myr for a time, and later in Volantis, doing gods know what . . . but now he has turned up in Westeros again, in the Red Mountains. The talk is that he has joined up with the Vulture King, and is raiding his own people. Garon is an able man, and leal, but he never was a match for Borys, and Boremund is but a boy. I fear for what may befall him, and the stormlands, when I am gone."

That took the king aback. "When you are gone? Why should you be gone? Where do you mean to go, my lord?"

Lord Rogar's answering smile showed a glimpse of his old ferocity. "Into the mountains, Your Grace. My maester says that I am dying. I believe him. Even before the Shivers there was pain. It has gotten worse since. He gives me milk of the poppy, and that helps, but I use only a little. I would not sleep away what life remains to me. Nor would I die abed, bleeding out of my arse. I mean to find my brother Borys and deal with him, and with this Vulture King as well. A fool's errand, Garon calls it. He is not wrong. But when I die, I want to die with my axe in my hand, screaming a curse. Do I have your leave, Your Grace?"

Moved by his old friend's words, King Jaehaerys rose and descended from the Iron Throne to clap Lord Rogar by the shoulder. "Your brother is a traitor, and this vulture—I will not call him king—has vexed our marches long enough. You have my leave, my lord. And more than that, you have my sword."

The king was true to his word. The fight that followed is named in the histories as the Third Dornish War, but that is a misnomer, for the Prince of Dorne kept his armies well out of the conflict. The smallfolk of the time called it Lord Rogar's War, and that name is far more apt. Whilst the Lord of Storm's End led five hundred men into the mountains, Jaehaerys Targaryen took to the air, on Vermithor. "He calls himself a vulture," the king said, "but he does not fly. He hides. He should call himself the gopher." He was not wrong. The first Vulture King had commanded armies, leading thousands of men into battle. The second was no more than an upjumped raider, the minor son of a minor house with a few hundred followers who shared his taste for robbery and rape. He knew the mountains well, however, and when pursued he would simply disappear, to reappear at will. Men who came hunting him did so at their peril, for he was skilled at ambuscade as well.

None of his tricks availed him against a foe who could hunt him from above, however. Legend claimed the Vulture King had an impregnable mountain fastness, hidden in the clouds. Jaehaerys found no secret lair, only a dozen rude camps scattered here and there. One by one, Vermithor flamed them all, leaving the Vulture only ashes to return to. Lord Rogar's column, winding their way into the heights, were soon forced to abandon their horses and proceed on foot along goat tracks, up steep slopes, and through caves, whilst hidden foes rolled stones down about their heads. Yet still they came on, undaunted. As the stormlanders proceeded from the east, Simon Dondarrion, Lord of Blackhaven, led a small host of marcher knights into the mountains from the west, to seal off escape from that side. Whilst the hunters crept toward one another, Jaehaerys watched them from the sky, moving them about as once he had moved toy armies in the Chamber of the Painted Table.

In the end, they found their foes. Borys Baratheon did not know the mountain's hidden ways as the Dornish did, so he was the first to be cornered. Lord Rogar's men made short work of his own, but as the brothers came face-to-face, King Jaehaerys descended from the sky. "I would not have you named a kinslayer, my lord," His Grace told his former Hand. "The traitor is mine."

Ser Borys laughed to hear it. "Rather name me a kingslayer than him a kinslayer!" he shouted, as he rushed the king. But Jaehaerys had Blackfyre in hand, and he had not forgotten the lessons he had learned in the yard on Dragonstone. Borys Baratheon died at the king's feet, from a cut to his neck that near took his head off.

The Vulture King's turn came the new full moon. Brought to bay in a burned lair where he had hoped to find refuge, he resisted to the end,

showering the king's men with spears and arrows. "This one is mine," Rogar Baratheon told His Grace when the mountain king was led before them in fetters. At his command, the outlaw's chains were struck off and he was given a spear and shield. Lord Rogar faced him with his axe. "If he kills me, let him go free."

The Vulture proved sadly unequal to that task. Wasted and weak and wracked with pain as he was, Rogar Baratheon turned the Dornishman's attacks aside contemptuously, then clove him from shoulder to navel.

When it was done, Lord Rogar seemed weary. "It seems I will not die with axe in hand after all," he told the king sadly. Nor did he. Rogar Baratheon, Lord of Storm's End and one-time Hand of the King and Lord Protector of the Realm, died at Storm's End half a year later, in the presence of his maester, his septon, his brother Ser Garon, and his son and heir, Boremund.

Lord Rogar's War had lasted less than half a year, begun and won entirely in 61 AC. With the Vulture King eliminated, raiding fell off sharply along the Dornish Marches for a time. As accounts of the campaign spread through the Seven Kingdoms, even the most martial of lords gained a new respect for their young king. Any lingering doubts had been dispelled; Jaehaerys Targaryen was not his father, Aenys. For the king himself, the war was healing. "Against the Shivers I was helpless," he confessed to Septon Barth. "Against the Vulture, I was a king again."

In 62 AC, the lords of the Seven Kingdoms rejoiced when King Jaehaerys conferred upon his eldest the title Prince of Dragonstone, making him the acknowledged heir to the Iron Throne.

Prince Aemon was seven years of age, a boy as tall and handsome as he was modest. He still trained every morning in the yard with Prince Baelon; the two brothers were fast friends, and evenly matched. Aemon was taller and stronger, Baelon quicker and fiercer. Their contests were so spirited that they oft drew crowds of onlookers. Serving men and washerwomen, household knights and squires, maesters and septons and stableboys, they would gather in the yard to cheer on one prince or the other. One of those who came to watch was Jocelyn Baratheon, the late Queen Alyssa's dark-haired daughter, who grew taller and more beautiful with every passing day. At the feast that followed Aemon's investiture as Prince of Dragonstone, the queen sat Lady Jocelyn next to him, and the two young people were observed talking and laughing together through the evening, to the exclusion of all others.

That same year, the gods blessed Jaehaerys and Alysanne with yet another child, a daughter they named Maegelle. A gentle, selfless, and sweet-natured girl, and exceedingly bright, she soon attached herself to her sister Alyssa in much the same way that Prince Baelon had attached himself to Prince Aemon, though not entirely as happily. Now it was Alyssa's turn to bristle at having "the baby" clinging to her skirts. She evaded her as best she could, and Baelon laughed at her fury.

We have already touched upon several of Jaehaerys's achievements. As 62 AC drew near its end, the king looked ahead to the year dawning, and all the years beyond, and began to make plans for a project that would transform the Seven Kingdoms. He had given King's Landing cobblestones, cisterns, and fountains. Now he lifted his eyes beyond the city walls, to the fields and hills and bogs that stretched from the Dornish Marches to the Gift.

"My lords," he told the council, "when the queen and I go forth on our progresses, we go on Vermithor and Silverwing. When we look down from the clouds, we see cities and castles, hills and swamps, rivers and streams and lakes. We see market towns and fishing villages, old forests, mountains, moors, and meadows, flocks of sheep and fields of grain, old battlefields, ruined towers, lichyards and septs. There is much and more to see in these Seven Kingdoms of ours. Do you know what I do not see?" The king slapped the table hard. "*Roads,* my lord. I do not see roads. I see some ruts, if I fly low enough. I see some game trails, and here and there a footpath by a stream. But I do not see any proper *roads.* My lords, I will have roads!"

The building of so many leagues of road would continue throughout the rest of Jaehaerys's reign and into the reign of his successor, but it started that day in the council chambers of the Red Keep. Let it not be thought that there were no roads in Westeros before his reign; hundreds of roads crisscrossed the land, many dating back thousands of years to the days of the First Men. Even the children of the forest had paths they followed, when they moved from place to place beneath their trees.

Yet the roads as they existed were abysmal. Narrow, muddy, rutted, crooked, they wandered through hills and woods and over streams without plan or purpose. Only a handful of those streams were bridged. River fords were often guarded by men-at-arms who demanded coin or kind for the right to cross. Some of the lords whose lands the roads passed through maintained them after a fashion, but many more did not. A rainstorm would wash them out. Robber knights and broken men preyed upon the travelers who used them. Before Maegor, the Poor Fellows would provide a certain amount of protection to common folk upon the roads (when they were not robbing them themselves). After the destruction of the Stars, the realm's byways became more dangerous than ever. Even great lords traveled with an escort.

To correct all these ills in a single reign would have been impossible, but Jaehaerys was determined to make a start. King's Landing, it must be remembered, was very young as cities go. Before Aegon the Conqueror and his sisters had come ashore from Dragonstone, only a modest fishing village stood on the three hills where the Blackwater Rush flowed into Blackwater Bay. Not surprisingly, few roads of any note begin or end in modest fishing villages. The city had grown quickly in the sixty-two years since Aegon's Conquest, and a few rude roads had sprung up with it, narrow dusty tracks that followed the shore up to Stokeworth, Rosby, and Duskendale, or cut through the hills to Maidenpool. Aside from that, there was nothing. No roads connected the king's seat with the great castles and cities of the land. King's Landing was a port, far more accessible by sea than land.

That was where Jaehaerys would begin. The wood south of the river was old forest, dense and overgrown; fine for hunting, poor for travel. He commanded that a road be cut through it, to connect King's Landing with Storm's End. The same road should be continued north of the city, from the Rush to the Trident and beyond, straight along the Green Fork and through the Neck, then across the wild trackless North to Winterfell and the Wall. The *kingsroad*, the smallfolk named it—the longest and most costly of Jaehaerys's roads, the first begun, the first completed.

Others followed: the roseroad, the ocean road, the river road, the goldroad. Some had existed for centuries, in ruder form, but Jaehaerys would remake them beyond all recognition, filling ruts, spreading gravel, bridging streams. Other roads his men created anew. The cost of all this was not inconsiderable, to be sure, but the realm was prosperous, and the king's new master of coin, Martyn Tyrell—aided and abetted by his clever wife, "the apple counter"—proved almost as able as the Lord of Air had been. Mile by mile, league by league, the roads grew, for decades to come. "He bound the land together, and made of seven kingdoms, one," read the words on the plinth of the Old King's monument that stands at the Citadel of Oldtown.

Mayhaps the Seven smiled on his work as well, for they continued to bless Jaehaerys and Alysanne with children. In 63 AC the king and queen celebrated the birth of Vaegon, their fourth son and seventh child. A year later came another daughter, Daella. Three years hence, Princess Saera came into the world, red-faced and squalling. Another princess arrived in 71 AC, when the queen gave birth to her tenth child and sixth daughter, the beautiful Viserra. Though born within a decade of one another, it would be hard to conceive of four siblings so different from one another as these younger children of Jaehaerys and Alysanne.

Prince Vaegon was as unlike his elder brothers as night to day. Never robust, he was a quiet boy with wary eyes. Other children, and even some of the lords of the court, found him sour. Though no coward, he took no pleasure in the rough play of the squires and pages, or the heroics of his father's knights. He preferred the library to the yard, and could oft be found there reading.

Princess Daella, the next oldest, was delicate and shy. Easily frightened and quick to cry, she did not speak her first word until she was almost two . . . and even thereafter she was tongue-tied more oft than not. Her sister Maegelle became her guiding star, and she worshipped her mother, the queen, but her sister Alyssa seemed to terrify her, and she blushed and hid her face in the presence of the older boys.

Princess Saera, three years younger, was a trial from the very start; tempestuous, demanding, disobedient. The first word she spoke was *no*, and she said it often and loudly. She refused to be weaned until past the age of four. Even as she ran about the castle, talking more than her siblings Vaegon and Daella combined, she wanted her mother's milk, and raged and screamed whenever the queen dismissed another wet nurse. "Seven save us," Alysanne whispered to the king one night, "when I look at her I see Aerea." Fierce and stubborn, Saera Targaryen thrived upon attention and sulked when she did not receive it.

The youngest of the four, Princess Viserra, had a will of her own as well, but she never screamed and certainly never cried. *Sly* was one word used to describe her. *Vain* was another. Viserra was beautiful, all men agreed, blessed with the deep purple eyes and silver-gold hair of a true Targaryen, with flawless white skin, fine features, and a grace that was somehow eerie and unsettling in one so young. When one stammering young squire told her she was a goddess, she agreed.

We shall return to these four princelings, and the woes they visited upon their mother and their father, in due time, but for the nonce let us take a step back to 68 AC, not long after the birth of Princess Saera, when the king and queen announced the betrothal of their firstborn son, Aemon, Prince of Dragonstone, to Jocelyn Baratheon of Storm's End. There had been some thought, after the tragic death of Princess Daenerys, that Aemon should wed Princess Alyssa, the eldest of his remaining sisters, but Queen Alysanne firmly put the thought aside. "Alyssa is for Baelon," she declared. "She has been following him around since she could walk. They are as close as you and I were at their age."

Two years later, in 70 AC, Aemon and Jocelyn were joined in a ceremony that rivaled the Golden Wedding for its splendor. Lady Jocelyn at sixteen years old was one of the great beauties of the realm; a long-legged, full-breasted maid with thick straight hair that fell to her waist, black as a raven's wing. Prince Aemon was one year younger at fifteen, but all agreed that they made a handsome couple. An inch shy of six feet tall, Jocelyn would have towered over most of the lords of Westeros, but the Prince of Dragonstone had three inches on her. "There stands the future of the realm," Ser Gyles Morrigen said when he beheld the two of them side by side, the dark lady and the pale prince.

In 72 AC, a tourney was held at Duskendale in honor of young Lord Darklyn's wedding to a daughter of Theomore Manderly. Both of the young princes attended, together with their sister Alyssa, and competed in the squire's melee. Prince Aemon emerged victorious, in part by dint of hammering his brother into submission. Later he distinguished himself in the lists as well, and was awarded his knight's spurs in recognition of his skills. He was seventeen years of age. With knighthood now achieved, the prince wasted no time becoming a dragonrider as well, ascending into the sky for the first time not long after his return to King's Landing. His mount was blood-red Caraxes, fiercest of all the young dragons in the Dragonpit. The Dragonkeepers, who knew the denizens of the pit better than anyone, called him the Blood Wyrm.

Elsewhere in the realm, 72 AC also marked the end of an era in the North with the passing of Alaric Stark, Lord of Winterfell. Both of the strong sons he had once boasted of had died before him, so it fell to his grandson Edric to succeed him.

Wherever Prince Aemon went, whatever Prince Aemon did, Prince Baelon would not be far behind, as the wags at court oft observed. The truth of that was proved in 73 AC, when Baelon the Brave followed his brother into knighthood. Aemon had won his spurs at seventeen, so Baelon must needs do the same at sixteen, traveling across the Reach to Old Oak, where Lord Oakheart was celebrating the birth of a son with seven days of jousting. Arrayed as a mystery knight and calling himself the Silver Fool, the young prince overthrew Lord Rowan, Ser Alyn Ashford, both Fossoway twins, and Lord Oakheart's own heir, Ser Denys, before falling to Ser Rickard Redwyne. After helping him to his feet, Ser Rickard unmasked him, bade him kneel, and knighted him on the spot.

Prince Baelon lingered only long enough to partake of the feast that evening before galloping back to King's Landing to complete his quest and become a dragonrider. Never one to be overshadowed, he had long since chosen the dragon he wished to mount, and now he claimed her. Unridden since the death of the Dowager Queen Visenya twenty-nine years before, the great she-dragon Vhagar spread her wings, roared, and launched herself once more into the skies, carrying the Spring Prince across Blackwater Bay to Dragonstone to surprise his brother Aemon and Caraxes.

"The Mother Above has been so good to me, to bless me with so many babes, all bright and beautiful," Queen Alysanne declared in 73 AC, when it was announced that her daughter Maegelle would be joining the Faith as a novice. "It is only fitting that I give one back." Princess Maegelle was ten years of age, and eager to take the vows. A quiet, studious girl, she was said to read from *The Seven-Pointed Star* every night before sleep.

Hardly had one child departed the Red Keep than another arrived, however, for it appeared that the Mother Above was not yet done blessing Alysanne Targaryen. In 73 AC, she gave birth to her eleventh child, a son named Gaemon, in honor of Gaemon the Glorious, the greatest of the Targaryen lords who had ruled on Dragonstone before the Conquest. This time, however, the child came early, after a long and difficult labor that exhausted the queen, and made her maesters fear for her life. Gaemon was a scrawny thing as well, barely half the size his brother Vaegon had been at birth ten years earlier. The queen eventually recovered, though sad to say the child did not. Prince Gaemon died just short of the new year, not quite three moons old.

As ever, the queen took the loss of a child hard, questioning whether or not it had been through some fault of her own that Prince Gaemon had failed. Septa Lyra, her confidant since her days on Dragonstone, assured her that she was not to blame. "The little prince is with the Mother Above now," Lyra told her, "and she will care for him better than we could ever hope to, here in this world of strife and pain."

That was not the only sorrow House Targaryen was to suffer in 73 AC. It will be remembered that this was also the year that Queen Rhaena died at Harrenhal.

Near year's end, a shameful revelation came to light that shocked both court and city. The amiable and well-loved Ser Lucamore Strong of the Kingsguard, a favorite of the smallfolk, was found to have been secretly wed, despite the vows that he had sworn as a White Sword. Worse, he had taken not one but three wives, keeping each woman ignorant of the other two and fathering no fewer than sixteen children on the three of them.

In Flea Bottom and along the Street of Silk where whores and panders plied their trade, men and women of low birth and lower morals took a wicked pleasure in the fall of an anointed knight, and made bawdy japes about "Ser Lucamore the Lusty," but no laughter was heard in the Red Keep. Jaehaerys and Alysanne had been especially fond of Lucamore

Strong and were mortified to learn that he had played them both for fools.

His brothers of the Kingsguard were even angrier. It was Ser Ryam Redwyne who discovered Ser Lucamore's transgressions and brought them to the attention of the Lord Commander of the Kingsguard, who in turn brought them to the king. Speaking for his Sworn Brothers, Ser Gyles Morrigen declared that Strong had dishonored all they stood for, and requested that he be put to death.

When dragged before the Iron Throne, Ser Lucamore fell to his knees, confessed his guilt, and begged the king for mercy. Jaehaerys might well have granted him the same, but the errant knight made the fatal error of appending "for the sake of my wives and children" to his plea. As Septon Barth observed, this was tantamount to throwing his crimes in the king's face.

"When I rose against my uncle Maegor, two of his Kingsguard abandoned him to fight for me," Jaehaerys responded. "They might well have believed they would be allowed to keep their white cloaks once I'd won, perhaps even be honored with lordships and a higher place at court. I sent them to the Wall instead. I wanted no oathbreakers around me, then or now. Ser Lucamore, you swore a sacred vow before gods and men to defend me and mine with your own life, to obey me, fight for me, die for me if need be. You also swore to take no wife, father no children, and remain chaste. If you could shrug aside the second vow so easily, why should I believe that you would honor the first?"

Then Queen Alysanne spoke up, saying, "You made a mockery of your oaths as a knight of the Kingsguard, but those were not the only vows you broke. You dishonored your marriage vows as well, not once but thrice. None of these women are lawfully wed, so these children I see behind you are bastards one and all. They are the true innocents in this, ser. Your wives were ignorant of one another, I am told, but each of them must surely have known that you were a White Sword, a knight of the Kingsguard. To that extent they share your guilt, as does whatever drunken septon you found to marry you. For them some mercy may be warranted, but for you . . . I will not have you near my lord, ser."

There was no more to be said. As the false knight's wives and children wept or cursed or stood in silence, Jaehaerys commanded that Ser Lucamore be gelded forthwith, then clapped in irons and sent off to the Wall. "The Night's Watch will require vows from you as well," His Grace warned. "See that you keep them, or the next thing you lose shall be your head."

Jaehaerys left it to his queen to deal with the three families. Alysanne decreed that Ser Lucamore's sons might join their father on the Wall, if they wished. The two oldest boys chose to do so. The girls would be accepted as novices by the Faith, if that was their desire. Only one elected that path. The other children were to remain with their mothers. The first of the wives, with her children, was given over to the charge of Lucamore's brother Bywin, who had been raised to be the Lord of Harrenhal not half a year earlier. The second wife and her offspring would go to Driftmark, to be fostered by Daemon Velaryon, Lord of the Tides. The third wife, whose children were the youngest (one still on her breast), would be sent down to Storm's End, where Garon Baratheon and young Lord Boremund would see to their upbringing. None were ever again to call themselves Strong, the queen decreed; from this day they would bear the bastard names Rivers, Waters, and Storm. "For that gift, you may thank your father, that hollow knight."

The shame that Lucamore the Lusty visited on the Kingsguard and the Crown was not the only difficulty Jaehaerys and Alysanne faced in 73 AC. Let us pause now for a moment, and consider the vexing question of their seventh- and eighthborn children, Prince Vaegon and Princess Daella.

Queen Alysanne took great pride in arranging marriages, and had put together hundreds of fruitful unions for lords and ladies from one end of the realm to another, but never had she faced so much difficulty as she did whilst searching for mates for her four younger children. The struggle would torment her for years, bring about no end of conflict between her and the children (her daughters in particular), drive her and the king apart, and in the end bring her so much grief and pain that for a time Her Grace contemplated renouncing her marriage to spend the rest of her life with the silent sisters.

The frustrations started with Vaegon and Daella. Only a year apart in age, the prince and princess seemed well matched as babes, and the king and queen assumed that the two of them would eventually marry. Their older siblings Baelon and Alyssa had become inseparable, and plans were already being made for them to wed. Why not Vaegon and Daella as well? "Be sweet to your little sister," King Jaehaerys told the prince when he was five. "One day she will be your Alysanne."

As the children grew, however, it became apparent that the two of them were not ideally suited. There was no warmth between them, as the queen saw plainly. Vaegon tolerated his sister's presence, but never sought it out. Daella seemed frightened of her sour, bookish brother, who would sooner read than play. The prince thought the princess stupid; she thought him mean. "They are only children," Jaehaerys said when Alysanne brought the problem to his attention. "They will warm to one another in time." They never did. If anything, their mutual dislike only deepened.

The matter came to a head in 73 AC. Prince Vaegon was ten years old and Princess Daella nine when one of the queen's companions, new to the Red Keep, teasingly asked the two of them when they would be married. Vaegon reacted as if he had been slapped. "I would never marry her," the boy said, in front of half the court. "She can barely read. She should find some lord in need of stupid children, for that's the only sort he will ever have of her."

Princess Daella, as might be expected, burst into tears and fled the hall, with her mother, the queen, rushing after her. It fell to her sister Alyssa, at thirteen three years Vaegon's elder, to pour a flagon of wine over his head. Even that did not make the prince repent. "You are wasting Arbor gold," was all he said before stalking from the hall to change his clothing.

Plainly, the king and queen concluded afterward, some other bride must needs be found for Vaegon. Briefly, they considered their younger daughters. Princess Saera was six years old in 73 AC, Princess Viserra only two. "Vaegon has never looked twice at either one of them," Alysanne told the king. "I am not sure he is aware that they exist. Perhaps if some maester wrote about them in a book . . ."

"I shall tell Grand Maester Elysar to commence tomorrow," the king japed. Then he said, "He is only ten. He does not see girls, no more than they see him, but that will change soon. He is comely enough, and a prince of Westeros, third in line to the Iron Throne. In a few more years maidens will be fluttering around him like butterflies and blushing if he deigns to look their way."

The queen was unconvinced. *Comely* was perhaps too generous a word for Prince Vaegon, who had the silver-gold hair and purple eyes of the Targaryens, but was long of face and round of shoulder even at ten, with a pinched sour cast to his mouth that made men suspect he had recently been sucking on a lemon. As his mother, Her Grace was mayhaps blind to these flaws, but not to his nature. "I fear for any butterfly that comes fluttering round Vaegon. He is like to squash it flat beneath a book."

"He spends too much time in the library," Jaehaerys said. "Let me speak to Baelon. We will get him out into the yard, put a sword in his hand and a shield on his arm, that will set him right."

Grand Maester Elysar tells me that His Grace did indeed speak to Prince Baelon, who dutifully took his brother under his wing, marched him out into the yard, put a sword into his hand and a shield upon his arm. It did not set him right. Vaegon hated it. He was a miserable fighter, and he had a gift for making everyone around him miserable as well, even Baelon the Brave.

Baelon persisted for a year, at the king's insistence. "The more he drills, the worse he looks," the Spring Prince confessed. One day, mayhaps in an attempt to spur Vaegon into making more of an effort, he brought his sister Alyssa to the yard, shining in man's mail. The princess had not forgotten the incident of the Arbor gold. Laughing and shouting mockery, she danced around her little brother and humiliated him half a hundred times, whilst Princess Daella looked down from a window. Shamed beyond endurance, Vaegon threw down his sword and ran from the yard, never to return.

We shall return to Prince Vaegon, and his sister Daella, in due course, but let us turn now to a joyful event. In 74 AC, King Jaehaerys and Queen Alysanne were blessed again by the gods when Prince Aemon's wife, the Lady Jocelyn, presented them with their first grandchild. Princess Rhaenys was born on the seventh day of the seventh moon of the year, which the septons judged to be highly auspicious. Large and fierce, she had the black hair of her Baratheon mother and the pale violet eyes of her Targaryen father. As the firstborn child of the Prince of Dragonstone, many hailed her as next in line for the Iron Throne after her father. When Queen Alysanne held her in her arms for the first time, she was heard to call the little girl "our queen to be."

In breeding, as in so much else, Baelon the Brave was not far behind his brother Aemon. In 75 AC, the Red Keep was the site of another splendid wedding, as the Spring Prince took to bride the eldest of his sisters, Princess Alyssa. The bride was fifteen, the groom eighteen. Unlike their father and mother, Baelon and Alyssa did not wait to consummate their union; the bedding that followed their wedding feast was the source of much ribald humor in the days that followed, for the young bride's sounds of pleasure could be heard all the way to Duskendale, men said. A shyer maid might have been abashed by that, but Alyssa Targaryen was as bawdy a wench as any barmaid in King's Landing, as she herself was fond of boasting. "I mounted him and took him for a ride," she declared the morning after the bedding, "and I mean to do the same tonight. I love to ride."

Nor was her brave prince the only mount the princess was to claim that year. Like her brothers before her, Alyssa Targaryen meant to be a dragonrider, and sooner rather than later. Aemon had flown at seventeen, Baelon at sixteen. Alyssa meant to do it at fifteen. According to the tales set down by the Dragonkeepers, it was all that they could do to persuade her not to claim Balerion. "He is old and slow, Princess," they had to tell her. "Surely you want a swifter mount." In the end they prevailed, and Princess Alyssa ascended into the sky upon Meleys, a splendid scarlet she-dragon, never before ridden. "Red maidens, the two of us," the princess boasted, laughing, "but now we've both been mounted."

The princess was seldom long away from the Dragonpit after that day. Flying was the second sweetest thing in the world, she would oft say, and the very sweetest thing could not be mentioned in the company of ladies. The Dragonkeepers had not been wrong; Meleys was as swift a dragon as Westeros had ever seen, easily outpacing Caraxes and Vhagar when she and her brothers flew together.

Meanwhile, the problem of their brother Vaegon persisted, to the queen's frustration. The king had not been entirely wrong about the butterflies. As the years passed and Vaegon matured, young ladies at the court began to pay him some attention. Age, and some uncomfortable discussions with his father and his brothers, had taught the prince the rudiments of courtesy, and he did not squash any of the girls, to the queen's relief. But he took no special notice of any of them either. Books remained his only passion: history, cartography, mathematics, languages. Grand Maester Elysar, never a slave to propriety, confessed to having given the prince a volume of erotic drawings, thinking mayhaps that pictures of naked maidens comporting with men and beasts and one another might kindle Vaegon's interest in the charms of women. The prince kept the book, but showed no change in behavior.

It was on Prince Vaegon's fifteenth nameday in 78 AC, a year short of his manhood, that Jaehaerys and Alysanne broached the obvious solution to the Grand Maester. "Do you think mayhaps Vaegon might have the makings of a maester?"

"No," Elysar replied bluntly. "Can you see him instructing some lord's children how to read and write and do simple sums? Does he keep a raven in his chamber, or any sort of bird? Can you imagine him removing a man's crushed leg, or delivering a baby? All these are required of a maester." The Grand Maester paused, then said, "Vaegon is no maester . . . but he could well have the makings of an *archmaester* in him. The Citadel is the greatest repository of knowledge in the known world. Send him there. Mayhaps he will find himself in the library. That, or he'll get so lost amongst the books that you never need to concern yourselves with him again."

His words struck home. Three days later, King Jaehaerys summoned Prince Vaegon to his solar to tell him that he would be taking ship for Oldtown in a fortnight. "The Citadel will take charge of you," His Grace said. "It is for you to determine what becomes of you." The prince responded curtly, as was his wont. "Yes, Father. Good." Afterward Jaehaerys told the queen that he thought Vaegon had almost smiled.

Prince Baelon had not ceased smiling since his marriage. When not aloft, Baelon and Alyssa spent every hour together, most oft in their bedchamber. Prince Baelon was a lusty lad, for those same shrieks of pleasure that had echoed through the halls of the Red Keep on the night of their bedding were heard many another night in the years that followed. And soon enough, the much-hoped-for result appeared, and Alyssa Targaryen grew great with child. In 77 AC she gave her brave prince a son they named Viserys. Septon Barth described the boy as a "plump and pleasant lad, who laughed more than any babe I've ever known, and nursed so lustily he drank his wet nurse dry." Against all advice, his mother clapped the boy in swaddling clothes, strapped him to her chest, and took him aloft on Meleys when he was nine days old. Afterward she claimed Viserys giggled the whole while.

Bearing and delivering a child may be a joy for a young woman of ten-and-seven, like the Princess Alyssa, but it is quite another matter for one of forty, like her mother, Queen Alysanne. The joy was therefore not entirely unalloyed when Her Grace was found to be pregnant once again. Prince Valerion was born in 77 AC, after another troubled labor that saw Alysanne confined to her bed for half a year. Like his brother Gaemon four years earlier, he was a small and sickly babe, and never thrived. Half a dozen wet nurses came and went to no avail. In 78 AC, Valerion died, a fortnight short of his first nameday. The queen took his passing with resignation. "I am forty-two years old," she told the king. "You must be content with the children I have given you. I am more suited to be a grandmother than a mother now, I fear."

King Jaehaerys did not share her certainty. "Our mother, Queen Alyssa, was forty-six when she gave birth to Jocelyn," he pointed out to Grand Maester Elysar. "The gods may not be done with us."

He was not wrong. The very next year, the Grand Maester informed Queen Alysanne that she was once more with child, to her surprise and dismay. Princess Gael was born in 80 AC, when the queen was forty-four. Called "the Winter Child" for the season of her birth (and because the queen was in the winter of her childbearing years, some said), she was small, pale, and frail, but Grand Maester Elysar was determined that she would not suffer the fate of her brothers Gaemon and Valerion. Nor did she. Assisted by Septa Lyra, who watched over the babe night and day, Elysar nursed the princess through a difficult first year, until finally it seemed as if she might survive. When she reached her first nameday, still healthy if not strong, Queen Alysanne thanked the gods.

She was thankful as well that year to have finally arranged a marriage for her eighthborn child, the Princess Daella. With Vaegon settled, Daella had been next in line, but the tearful princess presented an entirely different sort of problem. "My little flower," was how the queen described her. Like Alysanne herself, Daella was small—on her toes, she stood five feet two inches—and there was a childish aspect to her that led everyone who met her to think she was younger than her age. Unlike Alysanne, she was delicate as well, in ways the queen had never been. Her mother had been fearless; Daella always seemed to be afraid. She had a kitten that she loved until he scratched her; then she would not go near a cat. The dragons terrified her, even Silverwing. The mildest scolding would reduce her to tears. Once, in the halls of the Red Keep, Daella had encountered a prince from the Summer Isles in his feathered cloak, and squealed in terror. His black skin had made her take him for a demon.

Cruel though her brother Vaegon's words had been, there was some truth to them. Daella was not clever, even her septa had to admit. She learned to read after a fashion, but haltingly, and without full comprehension. She could not seem to commit even the simplest prayers to memory. She had a sweet voice, but was afraid to sing; she always got the words wrong. She loved flowers, but was frightened of gardens; a bee had almost stung her once.

Jaehaerys, even more than Alysanne, despaired of her. "She will not even speak to a boy. How is she to marry? We could entrust her to the Faith, but she does not know her prayers, and her septa says that she cries when asked to read aloud from *The Seven-Pointed Star*." The queen always rose to her defense. "Daella is sweet and kind and gentle. She has such a tender heart. Give me time, and I will find a lord to cherish her. Not every Targaryen needs to wield a sword and ride a dragon."

In the years that followed her first flowering, Daella Targaryen drew the eye of many a young lordling, as expected. She was a king's daughter, and maidenhood had only made her prettier. Her mother was at work as well, arranging matters in every way she could to place suitable marriage prospects before the princess.

At thirteen Daella was sent to Driftmark to meet Corlys Velaryon, the grandson to the Lord of the Tides. Ten years her elder, the future Sea

Snake was already a celebrated mariner and captain of ships. Daella became seasick crossing Blackwater Bay, however, and on her return complained that "he likes his boats better than he likes me." (She was not wrong in that.)

At fourteen, she kept company with Denys Swann, Simon Staunton, Gerold Templeton, and Ellard Crane, all promising squires of her own age, but Staunton tried to make her drink wine and Crane kissed her on the lips without her leave, reducing her to tears. By year's end Daella had decided she hated all of them.

At fifteen, her mother took her across the riverlands to Raventree (in a wheelhouse, as Daella was afraid of horses), where Lord Blackwood entertained Queen Alysanne lavishly whilst his son paid court to the princess. Tall, graceful, courtly, and well-spoken, Royce Blackwood was a gifted bowman, a fine swordsman, and a singer, who melted Daella's heart with ballads of his own composition. For a short while it seemed as if a betrothal might be in the offing, and Queen Alysanne and Lord Blackwood even began to discuss wedding plans. It all fell to pieces when Daella learned that the Blackwoods kept the old gods, and she would be expected to say her vows before a weirwood. "They don't believe in *the gods*," she told her mother, horrified. "I'd go to *hell*."

Her sixteenth nameday was fast approaching, and with it her womanhood. Queen Alysanne was at her wit's end, and the king had lost his patience. On the first day of the 80th year since Aegon's Conquest, he told the queen he wanted Daella wed before the year's end. "If she wants I can find a hundred men and line them up before her naked, and she can pick the one she likes," he said. "I would sooner she wed a lord, but if she prefers a hedge knight or a merchant or Pate the Pig Boy, I am past the point of caring, so long as she picks *someone*."

"A hundred naked men would frighten her," Alysanne said, unamused.

"A hundred naked ducks would frighten her," the king replied.

"And if she will not wed?" the queen asked. "Maegelle says the Faith will not want a girl who cannot read her prayers."

"There are still the silent sisters," said Jaehaerys. "Must it come to that? *Find her someone*. Someone gentle, as she is. A kind man, who will never raise his voice or his hand to her, who will speak to her sweetly and tell her she is precious and *protect* her . . . against dragons and horses and bees and kittens and boys with boils and whatever else she fears."

"I shall do my best, Your Grace," Queen Alysanne promised.

In the end it did not require a hundred men, naked or clothed. The queen explained the king's command to Daella gently but firmly, and offered her a choice of three suitors, each of whom was eager for her hand. Pate the Pig Boy was not amongst them, it should be said; the three men that Alysanne had selected were great lords or the sons of great lords. Whichever man she married, Daella would have wealth and position.

Boremund Baratheon was the most imposing of the candidates. At eight-and-twenty, the Lord of Storm's End was the image of his father, brawny and powerful, with a booming laugh, a great black beard, and a mane of thick black hair. As the son of Lord Rogar by Queen Alyssa, he stood half-brother to Alysanne and Jaehaerys, and Daella knew and loved his sister, Jocelyn, from her years at court, which was thought to be much in his favor.

Ser Tymond Lannister was the wealthiest contender, heir to Casterly Rock and all its gold. At twenty, he was nearer to Daella's own age, and thought to be one of the handsomest men in all the realm; lithe and slender, with long golden mustachios and hair of the same hue, always clad in silk and satin. The princess would be well protected in Casterly Rock; there was no castle more impregnable in all Westeros. Weighed against Lannister gold and Lannister beauty, however, was Ser Tymond's own reputation. He was overly fond of women, it was said, and even more fond of wine.

Last of the three, and least in many eyes, was Rodrik Arryn, Lord of the Eyrie and Protector of the Vale. He had been a lord since the age of ten, a point in his favor; for the past twenty years he had served on the small council as lord justiciar and master of laws, during which time he had become a familiar figure about court, and a leal friend to both king and queen. In the Vale he had been an able lord, strong but just, affable, open-handed, loved by the smallfolk and his lords bannermen alike. In addition, he had acquitted himself well in King's Landing; sensible, knowledgeable, good humored, he was regarded as a great asset to the council.

Lord Arryn was the oldest of the three contenders, however; at six-and-thirty, he was twenty years older than the princess, and a father besides, with four children left him by his late first wife. Short and balding, with a kettle belly, Arryn was not the man most maidens dream of, Queen Alysanne admitted, "but he is the sort you asked for, a kind and gentle man, and he says that he has loved our little girl for years. I know he will protect her."

To the astonishment of every woman at the court, save mayhaps the queen, Princess Daella chose Lord Rodrik to be her husband. "He seems good and wise, like Father," she told Queen Alysanne, "and he has four children! I'm to be their new mother!" What Her Grace thought of that outburst is not recorded. Grand Maester Elysar's account of the day says only, *"Gods be good."*

Theirs would not be a long betrothal. As the king had wished, Princess Daella and Lord Rodrik were wed before year's end. It was a small ceremony in the sept at Dragonstone, attended only by close friends and kin; larger crowds made the princess desperately uncomfortable. Nor was there a bedding. "Oh, I could not bear that, I should die of shame," the princess had told her husband to be, and Lord Rodrik had acceded to her wishes.

Afterward, Lord Arryn took his princess back to the Eyrie. "My children need to meet their new mother, and I want to show the Vale to Daella. Life is slower there, and quieter. She will like that. I swear to you, Your Grace, she will be safe and happy."

And so she was, for a time. The eldest of Lord Rodrik's four children from his first wife was a daughter, Elys, three years older than her new stepmother. The two of them clashed from the first. Daella doted on the three younger children, however, and they seemed to adore her in turn. Lord Rodrik, true to his word, was a kind and caring husband who never failed to pamper and protect the bride he called "my precious princess." Such letters as Daella sent her mother (letters largely written for her by Lord Rodrik's younger daughter, Amanda) spoke glowingly of how happy she was, how beautiful the Vale, how much she loved her lord's sweet sons, how everyone in the Eyrie was so kind to her.

Prince Aemon reached his twenty-sixth nameday in 81 AC, and had proved himself more than able in both war and peace. As the heir apparent to the Iron Throne, it was felt desirable that he take a greater role in the governance of the realm as a member of the king's council. Accordingly, King Jaehaerys named the prince his justiciar and master of laws in place of Rodrik Arryn.

"I will leave the making of law to you, brother," Prince Baelon declared, whilst drinking to Prince Aemon's appointment. "I would sooner make sons." And that was just what he did, for later that same year Princess Alyssa bore her Spring Prince a second son, who was given the name Daemon. His mother, irrepressible as ever, took the babe into the sky on Meleys within a fortnight of his birth, just as she had done with his brother, Viserys.

In the Vale, however, her sister Daella was not doing near as well. After a year and a half of marriage, a different sort of message arrived at the Red Keep by raven. It was very short, and written in Daella's own uncertain hand. "I am with child," it said. "Mother, please come. I am frightened."

Queen Alysanne was frightened too, once she read those words. She mounted Silverwing within days and flew swiftly to the Vale, alighting first in Gulltown before proceeding on to the Gates of the Moon, and then skyward to the Eyrie. It was 82 AC, and Her Grace arrived three moons before Daella was due to give birth.

Though the princess professed delight that her mother had come, and apologized for sending her such a "silly" letter, her fear was palpable. She burst into tears for the slightest reason, and sometimes for no reason at all, Lord Rodrik said. His daughter Elys was dismissive, telling Her Grace, "You would think she was the first woman ever to have a baby," but Alysanne was concerned. Daella was so delicate, and she was carrying very heavy. "She is such a small girl for such a big belly," she wrote the king. "I would be frightened too, if I were her."

Queen Alysanne stayed beside the princess for the rest of her confinement, sitting by her bedside, reading her to sleep at night, and comforting her fears. "It will be fine," she told her daughter, half a hundred times. "She will be a girl, wait and see. A daughter. I know it. Everything will be fine."

She was half right. Aemma Arryn, the daughter of Lord Rodrik and

Princess Daella, came into the world a fortnight early, after a long and troubled labor. "It hurts," the princess screamed through half the night. "It hurts so much." But it is said she smiled when her daughter was laid against her breast.

Everything was far from fine, however. Childbed fever set in soon after birth. Though Princess Daella desperately wished to nurse her child, she had no milk, and a wet nurse was sent for. As her fever rose, the maester decreed that she might not even hold her babe, which set the princess to weeping. She wept until she fell asleep, but in her sleep she kicked wildly and tossed and turned, her fever rising ever higher. By morning she was gone. She was eighteen years of age.

Lord Rodrik wept as well, and begged the queen's permission to bury his precious princess in the Vale, but Alysanne refused. "She was the blood of the dragon. She will be burned, and her ashes interred on Dragonstone beside her sister Daenerys."

Daella's death tore the heart out of the queen, but as we look back, it is plain to see that it was also the first hint of the rift that would open between her and her king. The gods hold us all in their hands, and life and death are theirs to give and take away, but men in their pride look for others to blame. Alysanne Targaryen, in her grief, blamed herself and Lord Arryn and the Eyrie's maester for their parts in her daughter's demise . . . but most of all, she blamed Jaehaerys. If he had not insisted that Daella wed, that she *pick someone* before year's end . . . what harm would it have done for her to stay a little girl for another year or two or ten? "She was not old enough or strong enough to bear a child," she told His Grace back at King's Landing. "We ought never have pushed her into marriage."

It is not recorded how the king replied.

The 83rd year after Aegon's Conquest is remembered as the year of the Fourth Dornish War . . . better known amongst the smallfolk as Prince Morion's Madness, or the War of the Hundred Candles. The old Prince of Dorne had died, and his son, Morion Martell, had succeeded him in Sunspear. A rash and foolish young man, Prince Morion had long bristled at his father's cowardice during Lord Rogar's War, when knights of the Seven Kingdoms had marched into the Red Mountains unmolested whilst the Dornish armies stayed at home and left the Vulture King to his fate.

Determined to avenge this stain on Dornish honor, the prince planned his own invasion of the Seven Kingdoms.

Though he knew Dorne could not hope to prevail against the might that the Iron Throne could muster against him, Prince Morion thought that he might take King Jaehaerys unawares, and conquer the stormlands as far as Storm's End, or at very least Cape Wrath. Rather than attack by way of the Prince's Pass, he planned to come by sea. He would assemble his hosts at Ghost Hill and the Tor, load them on ships, and sail them across the Sea of Dorne to take the stormlanders by surprise. If he was defeated or driven back, so be it . . . but before he went, he swore to burn a hundred towns and raze a hundred castles, so the stormlanders might know that they could never again march into the Red Mountains with impunity. (The madness of this plan can be seen in the fact that there are neither a hundred towns nor a hundred castles on Cape Wrath, nor even a third that number.)

Dorne had not boasted any strength at sea since Nymeria burned her ten thousand ships, but Prince Morion did have gold, and he found willing allies in the pirates of the Stepstones, the sellsails of Myr, and the corsairs of the Pepper Coast. Though it took him the best part of a year, eventually the ships came straggling in, and the prince and his spearmen were loaded aboard. Morion had been weaned on the tales of past Dornish glory, and like many young Dornish lords he had seen the sun-mottled bones of the dragon Meraxes at the Hellholt. Every ship in his fleet was therefore manned with crossbowmen and equipped with massive scorpions of the sort that had felled Meraxes. If the Targaryens dared to send dragons against him, he would fill the air with bolts and kill them all.

The folly of Prince Morion's plans cannot be overstated. His hopes of taking the Iron Throne unawares were laughable, for a start. Not only did Jaehaerys have spies in Morion's own court, and friends amongst the shrewder Dornish lords, but the pirates of the Stepstones, the sellsails of Myr, and the corsairs of the Pepper Coast are none of them famed for their discretion. A few coins changing hands was all it took. By the time Morion set sail, the king had known of his attack for half a year.

Boremund Baratheon, Lord of Storm's End, had been made aware as well, and was waiting on Cape Wrath to give the Dornishmen a red welcome when they came ashore. He would never have the chance. Jaehaerys Targaryen and his sons Aemon and Baelon had been waiting as well, and as Morion's fleet beat its way across the Sea of Dorne, the dragons Vermithor, Caraxes, and Vhagar fell on them from out of the clouds. Shouts rang out, and the Dornish filled the air with scorpion bolts, but firing at a dragon is one thing, and killing it quite another. A few bolts glanced off the scales of the dragons, and one punched through Vhagar's wing, but none of them found any vulnerable spots as the dragons swooped and banked and loosed great blasts of fire. One by one the ships went up in gouts of flame. They were still burning when the sun went down, "like a hundred candles floating on the sea." Burned bodies would wash up on the shores of Cape Wrath for half a year, but not a single living Dornishman set foot upon the stormlands.

The Fourth Dornish War was fought and won in a single day. The pirates of the Stepstones, the sellsails of Myr, and the corsairs of the Pepper Coast became less troublesome for a time, and Mara Martell became the Princess of Dorne. Back in King's Landing, King Jaehaerys and his sons received a riotous welcome. Even Aegon the Conqueror had never won a war without losing a man.

Prince Baelon had another cause for celebration as well. His wife, Alyssa, was again with child. This time, he told his brother Aemon, he was praying for a girl.

Princess Alyssa was brought to bed again in 84 AC. After a long and difficult labor, she gave Prince Baelon a third son, a boy they named Aegon, after the Conqueror. "They call me Baelon the Brave," the prince told his wife at her bedside, "but you are far braver than me. I would sooner fight a dozen battles than do what you've just done." Alyssa laughed at him. "You were made for battles, and I was made for this. Viserys and Daemon and Aegon, that's three. As soon as I am well, let's make another. I want to give you twenty sons. An army of your own!"

It was not to be. Alyssa Targaryen had a warrior's heart in a woman's body, and her strength failed her. She never fully recovered from Aegon's birth, and died within the year at only four-and-twenty. Nor did Prince Aegon long survive her. He perished half a year later, still shy of his first nameday. Though shattered by his loss, Baelon took solace in the two

strong sons that she had left him, Viserys and Daemon, and never ceased to honor the memory of his sweet lady with the broken nose and mismatched eyes.

And now, I fear, we must turn our attention to one of the most troubling and distasteful chapters in the long reign of King Jaehaerys and Queen Alysanne: the matter of their ninthborn child, the Princess Saera.

Born in 67 AC, three years after Daella, Saera had all the courage that her sister lacked, along with a voracious hunger . . . for milk, for food, for affection, for praise. As a babe she did not so much cry as scream, and her ear-piercing wails became the terror of every maid in the Red Keep. "She wants what she wants and she wants it now," Grand Maester Elysar wrote of the princess in 69 AC, when she was only two. "Seven save us all when she is older. The Dragonkeepers had best lock up the dragons." He had no notion how prophetic those words would be.

Septon Barth was more reflective, as he observed the princess at the age of twelve in 79 AC. "She is the king's daughter, and well aware of it. Servants see to her every need, though not always as *quickly* as she might like. Great lords and handsome knights show her every courtesy, the ladies of the court defer to her, girls of her own age vie with one another to be her friends. All of this Saera takes as her due. If she were the king's firstborn, or better still his only child, she would be well content. Instead she finds herself the ninthborn, with six living siblings who are older than her and even more adored. Aemon is to be king, Baelon most like will be his Hand, Alyssa may be all her mother is and more, Vaegon is more learned than she is, Maegelle is holier, and Daella . . . when does a day go by when Daella is not in need of comfort? And whilst she is being soothed, Saera is being ignored. Such a fierce little thing she is, they say, she has no need of comfort. They are wrong in that, I fear. All men need comfort."

Aerea Targaryen had once been thought to be wild and willful, given to acts of disobedience, but Princess Saera's girlhood made Aerea seem a model of decorum by comparison. The border between innocent pranks, wanton mischief, and acts of malice is not always discerned by one so young, but there can be no doubt that the princess crossed it freely. She was forever sneaking cats into her sister Daella's bedchamber, knowing that she was frightened of them. Once she filled Daella's chamberpot with bees. She slipped into White Sword Tower when she was ten, stole all the white cloaks she could find, and dyed them pink. At seven, she learned when and how to steal into the kitchens to make off with cakes and pies and other treats. Before she was eleven, she was stealing wine and ale instead. By twelve, she was like as not to arrive drunk when summoned to the sept for prayer.

The king's half-witted fool, Tom Turnip, was the victim of many of her japes, and her unwitting catspaw for others. Once, before a great feast where many lords and ladies were to be in attendance, she persuaded Tom that it would be much funnier if he performed naked. It was not well received. Later, far more cruelly, she told him that if he climbed the Iron Throne he could be king, but the fool was clumsy at the best of times and prone to tremors, and the throne sliced his arms and legs to pieces. "She is an evil child," her septa said of her afterward. Princess Saera had half a dozen septas and as many bedmaids before she turned thirteen.

This is not to say that the princess was without her virtues. Her maesters affirmed that she was very clever, as bright as her brother Vaegon in her own way. She was certainly pretty, taller than her sister Daella and not half so delicate, and as strong and quick and spirited as her sister Alyssa. When she wanted to be charming, it was hard to resist her. Her big brothers Aemon and Baelon never failed to be amused by her mischief (though they never knew the worst of it), and long before she was half-grown, Saera had learned the art of getting anything she wanted from her father: a kitten, a hound, a pony, a hawk, a horse (Jaehaerys did draw a firm line at the elephant). Queen Alysanne was far less gullible, however, and Septon Barth tells us that Saera's sisters all misliked her to various degrees.

Maidenhood became her, and Saera truly came into her own after her first flowering. After all they had endured with Daella, the king and queen must have been relieved to see how eagerly Saera took to the young men of the court, and they to her. At fourteen, she told the king she meant to marry the Prince of Dorne, or perhaps the King Beyond the Wall, so she could be a queen "like Mother." That year a trader from the Summer Islands came to court. Far from shrieking at the sight of him, as Daella had, Saera said she might like to marry him too.

By fifteen she had put such idle fantasies aside. Why dream of distant monarchs when she could have as many squires, knights, and likely lords as she desired? Dozens danced attendance on her, but three soon emerged as favorites. Jonah Mooton was the heir to Maidenpool, Red Roy Connington was the fifteen-year-old Lord of Griffin's Roost, and Braxton Beesbury, called Stinger, was a nineteen-year-old knight, the finest lance in the Reach, and the heir to Honeyholt. The princess had female favorites as well: Perianne Moore and Alys Turnberry, two maids of her own age, became her dearest friends. Saera called them Pretty Peri and Sweetberry. For more than a year, the three maids and the three young lords were inseparable at every feast and ball. They hunted and hawked together too, and once sailed across Blackwater Bay to Dragonstone. When the three lords rode at rings or crossed swords in the yards, the three maids were there to cheer them on.

King Jaehaerys, who was forever entertaining visiting lords or envoys from across the narrow sea, sitting at council, or planning further roads, was well pleased. They would not need to scour the realm to find a match for Saera, when three such promising young men were here at hand. Queen Alysanne was less convinced. "Saera is clever, but not wise," she told the king. Lady Perianne and Lady Alys were pretty, vapid, empty-headed little fools from what she had seen of them, whilst Connington and Mooton were callow boys. "And I do not like this Stinger. I've heard he sired a bastard in the Reach, and another here in King's Landing."

Jaehaerys remained unconcerned. "It is not as if Saera were ever alone with any of them. There are always people about, serving men and maids, grooms and men-at-arms. What mischief can they get up to with so many eyes around them?"

He did not like the answer, when it came.

One of Saera's japes was their undoing. On a warm spring night in 84 AC, shouts and screams from a brothel called the Blue Pearl drew the notice of two men of the City Watch. The screams were coming from Tom Turnip, who was lurching helplessly in circles trying to escape from half a dozen naked whores, whilst the patrons of the house laughed uproariously and shouted on the harlots. Jonah Mooton, Red Roy Connington, and Stinger Beesbury were amongst those patrons, each one drunker than the last. They had thought it would be funny to see old Turnip do the deed, Red Roy admitted. Then Jonah Mooton laughed and said the jape had all been Saera's notion, and what a funny girl she was.

The watchmen rescued the hapless fool and escorted him back to the Red Keep. The three lords they brought before Ser Robert Redwyne, their commander. Ser Robert delivered them to the king, ignoring Stinger's threats and Connington's clumsy attempt to bribe him.

"It is never pleasant to lance a boil," Grand Maester Elysar wrote of the affair. "You never know how much pus will come out, or how badly it will smell." The pus that burst forth from the Blue Pearl would smell very badly indeed.

The three drunken lords had sobered somewhat by the time the king confronted them from atop the Iron Throne, and put up a bold front. They confessed to making off with Tom Turnip and bringing him to the Blue Pearl. None of them said a word concerning Princess Saera. When His Grace ordered Mooton to repeat what he had said about the princess, he blushed and stammered and claimed the watchmen had misheard. Jaehaerys finally ordered the three lordlings taken to the dungeons. "Let them sleep in a black cell tonight, mayhaps they will tell a different tale come morning."

It was Queen Alysanne, knowing how close Lady Perianne and Lady Alys had been to the three lords, who suggested that they be questioned as well. "Let me speak with them, Your Grace. If they see you up on the throne glaring down at them, they will be so frightened they will never say a word."

The hour was late, and her guardsmen found both girls asleep, sharing a bed in Lady Perianne's chambers. The queen had them brought before her in her solar. Their three young lords were in the dungeons, she told the girls. If they did not wish to join them, they would tell the truth. It was all she needed to say. Sweetberry and Pretty Peri stumbled over one another in their eagerness to confess. Before long both of them were weeping and pleading for forgiveness. Queen Alysanne let them plead, never saying a word. She listened, as she had done before at a hundred women's courts. Her Grace knew how to listen.

It was just a game at the start, Pretty Peri said. "Saera was teaching Alys how to kiss, so I asked if she would teach me too. The boys train at fighting every morning, why shouldn't we train at kissing? That's what girls are meant to do, isn't it?" Alys Turnberry agreed. "Kissing was sweet," she said, "and one night we started kissing with our clothes off, and that was scary but exciting. We took turns pretending we were boys. We never meant to be wicked, we were only playing. Then Saera dared me to kiss a real boy, and I dared Peri to do the same, and both of us dared Saera, but she said she would do us one better, she would kiss a man grown, a knight. That's how it began with Roy and Jonah and Stinger." Lady Perianne jumped back in then to say that afterward it was Stinger who did the training for all of them. "He has two bastards," she whispered. "One in the Reach, and one right here on the Street of Silk. Her mother is a whore at the Blue Pearl."

That was the only mention of the Blue Pearl. "Neither of the trulls knew the slightest thing concerning poor Tom Turnip, as irony would have it," Grand Maester Elysar would write afterward, "but they knew a great deal about certain other things, none of which had been their fault."

"Where were your septas during all of this?" the queen demanded when she had heard them out. "Where were your maids? And the lords, they would have been attended. Where were their grooms, their men-at-arms, their squires and serving men?"

Lady Perianne was confused by the question. "We told them to wait without," she said, in the tone of one explaining that the sun rises in the east. "They're servants, they do what you tell them. The ones who knew, they knew to keep quiet. Stinger said he'd have their tongues out if they talked. And Saera is smarter than the septas."

That was where Sweetberry broke down, and began to sob and tear at her dressing gown. She was so sorry, she told the queen, she had never wanted to be bad, Stinger made her and Saera said she was a craven, so she showed them, but now she was with child and she did not know who the father was, and *what was she to do?*

"All you can do tonight is go to bed," Queen Alysanne told her. "On the morrow we shall send a septa to you, and you can make confession of your sins. The Mother will forgive you."

"*My* mother won't," said Alys Turnberry, but she went as she was told. Lady Perianne helped her sobbing friend back to her room.

When the queen told him what she had learned, King Jaehaerys could scarce credit a word of it. Guards were sent forth, and a succession of squires, grooms, and maids were dragged before the Iron Throne for questioning. Many of them wound up in the dungeons with their masters, once their answers had been heard. Dawn had come by the time the last of them had been led away. Only then did the king and queen send for Princess Saera.

The princess surely knew that something was amiss when the Lord Commander of the Kingsguard and the Commander of the City Watch appeared together to escort her to the throne room. It was never good when the king received you whilst seated on the Iron Throne. The great hall was almost empty when she was brought in. Only Grand Maester Elysar and Septon Barth had been summoned to bear witness. They spoke for the Citadel and the Starry Sept, and the king felt a need for their guidance, but there were things like to be said that day that his other lords need never know.

It is oft said that the Red Keep has no secrets, that there are rats in the walls who hear everything and whisper in the ears of sleepers by night. Mayhaps so, for when Princess Saera came before her father, she appeared to know all that had happened at the Blue Pearl, and be not the least abashed. "I told them to do it, but I never thought they would," she said lightly. "That must have been so funny, Turnip dancing with the whores."

"Not for Tom," said King Jaehaerys from the Iron Throne.

"He is a fool," Princess Saera answered, with a shrug. "Fools are meant to be laughed at, where is the harm in that? Turnip loves it when you laugh at him."

"It was a cruel jape," said Queen Alysanne, "but just now there are other matters that concern me more. I have been speaking with your . . . ladies. Are you aware that Alys Turnberry is with child?"

It was only then that the princess came to realize that she was not there to answer for Tom Turnip, but for more shameful sins. For a moment Saera was at a loss for words, but only for a moment. Then she gasped and said, "My Sweetberry? Truly? She . . . oh, what has she done? Oh, my sweet little fool." If Septon Barth's testimony is to be believed, a tear rolled down her cheek.

Her mother was not moved. "You know perfectly well what she has done. What all of you have done. We will have the truth from you now, child." And when the princess looked to her father, she found no comfort there. "Lie to us again, and it will go very much the worse for you," King Jaehaerys told his daughter. "Your three lords are in the dungeons, you ought know, and what you say next may determine where you sleep tonight."

Saera crumbled then, and the words came tumbling out one after another in a rush, a flood that left the princess almost breathless. "She went from denial to dismissal to quibbling to contrition to accusation to justification to defiance in the space of an hour, with stops at giggling and weeping along the way," Septon Barth would write. "She never did it, they were lying, it never happened, how could they believe that, it was just a game, it was just a jape, who said that, that was not how it happened, everyone likes kissing, she was sorry, Peri started it, it was such fun, no one was hurt, no one ever told her kissing was bad, Sweetberry had dared her, she was so ashamed, Baelon used to kiss Alyssa all the time, once she started she did not know how to stop, she was afraid of Stinger, the Mother Above had forgiven her, all the girls were doing it, the first time she was drunk, she had never wanted to, it was what men wanted, Maegelle said the gods forgave all sins, Jonah said he loved her, the gods had made her pretty, it was not her fault, she would be good from now on, it will be as if it never happened, she would marry Red Roy Connington, they had to forgive her, she would never kiss a man again or do any of those other things, it wasn't her who was with child, she was their daughter, she was their little girl, she was a *princess,* if she were queen she would do as she liked, why wouldn't they believe her, they never loved her, she hated them, they could whip her if they wanted but she would never be their slave. She took my breath away, this girl. There was never a mummer in all the land who gave such a performance, but by the end she was exhausted and afraid, and her mask slipped."

"What have you done?" the king said, when at last the princess ran out of words. "Seven save us, *what have you done*? Have you given one of these boys your maidenhead? Tell me true."

"True?" said Saera. It was in that moment, with that word, that the contempt came out. "No. I gave it to all three. They all think they were the first. Boys are such silly fools."

Jaehaerys was so horrified he could not speak, but the queen kept her composure. "You are very proud of yourself, I see. A woman grown, and nearly seven-and-ten. I am sure you think you have been very clever, but it is one thing to be clever and another to be wise. What do you imagine will happen now, Saera?"

"I will be married," the princess said. "Why shouldn't I be? You were married at my age. I shall be wedded and bedded, but to whom? Jonah and Roy both love me, I could take one of them, but they are both such boys. Stinger does not love me, but he makes me laugh and sometimes makes me scream. I could marry all three of them, why not? Why should I have just one husband? The Conqueror had two wives, and Maegor had six or eight."

She had gone too far. Jaehaerys rose to his feet and descended from the Iron Throne, his face a mask of rage. "You would compare yourself to *Maegor*? Is that who you aspire to be?" His Grace had heard enough. "Take her back to her bedchamber," he told his guards, "and keep her there until I send for her again."

When the princess heard his words, she rushed toward him, crying, "Father, Father!" but Jaehaerys turned his back on her, and Gyles Morrigen caught her by the arm and wrenched her away. She would not go of her own accord, so the guards were forced to drag her from the hall, wailing and sobbing and calling for her father.

Even then, Septon Barth tells us, Princess Saera might have been forgiven and restored to favor if she had done as she was told, if she had remained meekly in her chambers reflecting on her sins and praying for forgiveness. Jaehaerys and Alysanne met all the next day with Barth and Grand Maester Elysar, discussing what was to be done with the six sinners, particularly the princess. The king was angry and unyielding, for his shame was deeply felt, and he could not forget Saera's taunting words about his uncle's wives. "She is no longer my daughter," he said more than once.

Queen Alysanne could not find it in her heart to be so harsh, however.

"She *is* our daughter," she told the king. "She must be punished, yes, but she is still a child, and where there is sin there can be redemption. My lord, my love, you reconciled with the lords who fought for your uncle, you forgave the men who rode with Septon Moon, you reconciled with the Faith, and with Lord Rogar when he tried to tear us apart and put Aerea on your throne, surely you can find some way to reconcile with your own daughter."

Her Grace's words were soft and gentle, and Jaehaerys was moved by them, Septon Barth tells us. Alysanne was stubborn and persistent and she had a way of bringing the king around to her own point of view, no matter how far apart they had been at the start. Given time, she might have softened his stance on Saera as well.

She would not have that time. That very night, Princess Saera sealed her fate. Instead of remaining in her rooms as she had been instructed, she slipped away whilst visiting the privy, donned a washerwoman's robes, stole a horse from the stables, and escaped the castle. She got halfway across the city, to the Hill of Rhaenys, but as she tried to enter the Dragonpit, she was found and taken by the Dragonkeepers and returned to the Red Keep.

Alysanne wept when she heard, for she knew her cause was hopeless. Jaehaerys was hard as stone. "Saera with a dragon," was all he had to say. "Would she have taken Balerion as well, I wonder?" This time the princess was not allowed to return to her own chambers. She was confined to a tower cell instead, with Jonquil Darke guarding her day and night, even in the privy.

Hasty marriages were arranged for her sisters in sin. Perianne Moore, who was not pregnant, was wed to Jonah Mooton. "You played a part in her ruin, you can be a part of her redemption," the king told the young lordling. The marriage proved to be a success, and in time the two became the lord and lady of Maidenpool. Alys Turnberry, who *was* pregnant, presented a harder case, as Red Roy Connington refused to marry her. "I will not pretend Stinger's bastard is my son, nor make him the heir to Griffin's Roost," he told the king, defiant. Instead Sweetberry was sent to the Vale to give birth (a girl, with bright red hair) at a motherhouse on an island in Gulltown harbor where many lords sent their natural daughters to be raised. Afterward she was married to Dunstan Pryor, the Lord of Pebble, an island off the Fingers.

Connington was given a choice between a lifetime in the Night's Watch or ten years of exile. Unsurprisingly, he chose exile and made his way across the narrow sea to Pentos, and thence to Myr, where he fell in with sellswords and other low company. Only half a year before he might have returned to Westeros, he was stabbed to death by a whore in a Myrish gambling den.

The harshest punishment was reserved for Braxton Beesbury, the proud young knight called Stinger. "I could geld you and send you to the Wall," Jaehaerys told him. "That was how I served Ser Lucamore, and he was a better man than you. I could take your father's lands and castle, but there would be no justice in that. He had no part in what you did, no more than your brothers did. We cannot have you spreading tales about my daughter, though, so we mean to take your tongue. And your nose as well, I think, so you may not find the maids quite so easy to beguile. You are far too proud of your skill with sword and lance, so we will take that away from you as well. We shall break your arms and legs, and my maesters will make certain that they heal crookedly. You will live the rest of your sorry life as a cripple. Unless . . ."

"Unless?" Beesbury was as white as chalk. "Is there a choice?"

"Any knight accused of wrongdoing has a choice," the king reminded him. "You can prove your innocence at hazard of your body."

"Then I choose trial by combat," Stinger said. He was by all accounts an arrogant young man, and sure of his skill at arms. He looked about at the seven Kingsguard standing beneath the Iron Throne in their long white cloaks and shining scale, and said, "Which of these old men do you mean for me to fight?"

"This old man," announced Jaehaerys Targaryen. "The one whose daughter you seduced and despoiled."

They met the next morning at dawn. The heir to Honeyholt was nineteen years of age, the king forty-nine, but still far from an old man. Beesbury armed himself with a morningstar, thinking mayhaps that Jaehaerys would be less accustomed to defending himself against that weapon. The king bore Blackfyre. Both men were well armored and carried shields. When the combat began, Stinger rushed hard at His Grace, seeking to overwhelm him with the speed and strength of youth, making the spiked ball whirl and dance and sing. Jaehaerys took every blow on his shield, however, contenting himself with defense whilst the younger man wore himself out. Soon enough the time arrived when Braxton Beesbury could scarce lift his arm, and then the king moved to the attack. Even the best of mail is hard-pressed to turn Valyrian steel, and Jaehaerys knew where every weak point could be found. Stinger was bleeding from half a dozen wounds when he finally fell. Jaehaerys kicked his shattered shield away, opened the visor of his helm, laid Blackfyre's point against his eye, and drove it deep.

Queen Alysanne did not attend the duel. She told the king she could not bear the thought that he might die. Princess Saera watched from the window of her cell. Jonquil Darke, her gaoler, made certain that she did not turn away.

A fortnight later, Jaehaerys and Alysanne gave another of their daughters over to the Faith. Princess Saera, who was not quite seventeen, departed King's Landing for Oldtown, where her sister Septa Maegelle was to take charge of her instruction. She would be a novice, it was announced, with the silent sisters.

Septon Barth, who knew the king's mind better than most, would later maintain the sentence was meant to be a lesson. No one could mistake Saera for her sister Maegelle, least of all her father. She would never be a septa, much less a silent sister, but she required punishment, and it was thought that a few years of silent prayer, harsh discipline, and contemplation would be good for her, that it would set her on the path to redemption.

That was not a path that Saera Targaryen cared to walk, however. The princess endured the silence, the cold baths, the scratchy roughspun robes, the meatless meals. She submitted to having her head shaved and being scrubbed with horsehair brushes, and when she was disobedient, she submitted to the cane as well. All this she suffered, for a year and a half . . . but when her chance came, in 85 AC, she seized it, fleeing from the motherhouse in the dead of night and making her way down to the docks. When an older sister came upon her during her escape, she knocked the woman down a flight of steps and leapt over her to the door.

When word of her flight reached King's Landing, it was assumed that Saera would be hiding somewhere in Oldtown, but Lord Hightower's men combed the city door to door, and no trace was found of her. It was then thought that mayhaps she would make her way back to the Red Keep, to beg pardon from her father. When she did not appear there either, the king wondered if she might not flee to her former friends, so Jonah Mooton and his wife, Perianne, were told to keep watch for her at Maidenpool. The truth did not come out until a year later, when the former princess was seen in a Lysene pleasure garden, still clad as a novice. Queen Alysanne wept to hear it. "They have made our daughter into a whore," she said. "She always was," the king replied.

Jaehaerys Targaryen celebrated his fiftieth nameday in 84 AC. The years had taken their toll on him, and those who knew him well said that he was never the same after his daughter Saera had disgraced and then abandoned him. He had grown thinner, almost gaunt, and there was more grey than gold in his beard now, and in his hair. For the first time men were calling him "the Old King" rather than "the Conciliator." Alysanne, shaken by all the losses they had suffered, withdrew more and more from the governance of the realm, and seldom came to council meetings any longer, but Jaehaerys still had his faithful Septon Barth, and his sons. "If there is another war," he told the two of them, "it will be for you to fight it. I have my roads to finish."

"He was better with roads than with daughters," Grand Maester Elysar would write later, in his customary waspish style.

In 86 AC, Queen Alysanne announced the betrothal of her daughter Viserra, fifteen years of age, to Theomore Manderly, the fierce old Lord of White Harbor. The marriage would do much and more to tie the realm together by uniting one of the great houses of the North to the Iron Throne, the king declared. Lord Theomore had won great renown as a warrior in his youth, and had proved himself a canny lord under whose rule White Harbor had prospered greatly. Queen Alysanne was very fond of him as well, remembering the warm welcome he had given her during her first visit to the North.

His lordship had outlived four wives, however, and whilst still a doughty fighter, he had grown very stout, which did little to recommend him to Princess Viserra. She had a different man in mind. Even as a little girl, Viserra had been the most beautiful of the queen's daughters. Great lords, famous knights, and callow boys had danced attendance on her all her life, feeding her vanity until it became a raging fire. Her great delight in life was playing one boy off against the other, goading them into foolish quests and contests. To win her favor for a joust, she made admiring squires swim the Blackwater Rush, climb the Tower of the Hand, or set free all the ravens in the rookery. Once she took six boys to the Dragonpit and told them she would give her maidenhead to whoever put his head in a dragon's mouth, but the gods were good that day and the Dragonkeepers put an end to that.

No squire was ever going to win Viserra, Queen Alysanne knew; not her heart, and certainly not her maidenhead. She was far too sly a child to go down the same path as her sister Saera. "She has no interest in kissing games, nor boys," the queen told Jaehaerys. "She plays with them as she used to play with her puppies, but she would no more lie with one than with a dog. She aims much higher, our Viserra. I have seen the way she preens and prances around Baelon. That is the husband she desires, and not for love of him. She wants to be the queen."

Prince Baelon was fourteen years older than Viserra, twenty-nine to her fifteen, but older lords had married younger maids, as she well knew. It had been two years since Princess Alyssa had died, yet Baelon had shown no interest in any other woman. "He married one sister, why not another?" Viserra told her closest friend, the empty-headed Beatrice Butterwell. "I am *much* prettier than Alyssa ever was, you saw her. She had a *broken nose*."

If the princess was intent on marrying her brother, the queen was equally determined to prevent it. Her answer was Lord Manderly and White Harbor. "Theomore is a good man," Alysanne told her daughter, "a wise man, with a kind heart and a good head on his shoulders. His people love him."

The princess was not persuaded. "If you like him so much, Mother, you should marry him," she said, before running to her father to complain. Jaehaerys offered her no solace. "It is a good match," he told her, before explaining the importance of drawing the North closer to the Iron Throne. Marriages were the queen's domain in any case, he said; he never interfered in such matters.

Frustrated, Viserra next turned to her brother Baelon in hopes of rescue, if court gossip can be believed. Slipping past his guards into his bedchamber one night, she disrobed and waited for him, making free with the prince's wine whilst she lingered. When Prince Baelon finally appeared, he found her drunk and naked in his bed and sent her on her way. The princess was so unsteady that she required the help of two maids and a knight of the Kingsguard to get her safely back to her own apartments.

How the battle of wills between Queen Alysanne and her headstrong fifteen-year-old daughter might finally have resolved will never be known. Not long after the incident in Baelon's bedchamber, as the queen was making arrangements for Viserra's departure from King's Landing, the princess traded clothes with one of her maids to escape the guards who had been assigned to keep her out of mischief, and slipped from the Red Keep for what she termed "one last night of laughter before I go and freeze."

Her companions were all men, two minor lordlings and four young knights, all green as spring grass and eager for Viserra's favor. One of them had offered to show the princess parts of the city that she had never seen: the pot shops and rat pits of Flea Bottom, the inns along Eel Alley and River Row where the serving wenches danced on tables, the brothels on the Street of Silk. Ale, mead, and wine all featured in the evening's frolics, and Viserra partook eagerly.

At some point, near to midnight, the princess and her remaining companions (several of the knights having become insensible from drink) decided to race back to the castle. A wild ride through the streets of the city ensued, with Kingslanders scrambling out of the way to avoid being run down and trampled. Laughter rang through the night and spirits were high until the racers reached the foot of Aegon's High Hill, where Viserra's palfrey collided with one of her companions. The knight's mare lost her footing and fell, breaking his leg beneath her. The princess was thrown from the saddle headfirst into a wall. Her neck was broken.

It was the hour of the wolf, the darkest time of the night, when it fell to Ser Ryam Redwyne of the Kingsguard to rouse the king and queen from their sleep to tell them that their daughter had been found dead in an alley at the foot of Aegon's High Hill.

Despite their differences, the loss of Princess Viserra was devastating to the queen. In the space of five years, the gods had taken three of her daughters: Daella in 82 AC, Alyssa in 84 AC, Viserra in 87 AC. Prince Baelon was greatly distraught as well, wondering if he should have spoken to his sister less brusquely the night he found her naked in his bed. Though he and Aemon were a comfort to the king and queen in their time of grief, along with Aemon's wife, the Lady Jocelyn, and their daughter, Rhaenys, it was to her own remaining daughters that Alysanne turned for solace.

Maegelle, twenty-five years of age and a septa, took leave from her sept to stay with her mother for the rest of that year, and Princess Gael, a sweet, shy child of seven, became the queen's constant shadow and support, even sharing her bed at night. The queen took strength from their presence . . . but even so, more and more she found her thoughts turning to the daughter who was not with her. Though Jaehaerys had forbidden it, Alysanne had defied his edict and secretly engaged agents to keep watch over her wayward child across the narrow sea. Saera was still in Lys, she knew from their reports, still at the pleasure garden. Now twenty years of age, she oft entertained her admirers still garbed as a novice of the Faith; there were evidently a good many Lyseni who took pleasure in ravishing innocent young women who had taken vows of chastity, even when the innocence was feigned.

It was her grief over the loss of Princess Viserra that finally drove the queen to approach Jaehaerys about Saera once again. She brought Septon Barth along with her, to speak on the virtues of forgiveness and the healing properties of time. Only when Barth had finished did Her Grace mention Saera's name. "Please," she begged the king, "it is time to bring her home. She has been punished enough, surely. She is our daughter."

Jaehaerys would not be moved. "She is a Lyseni whore," His Grace replied. "She opened her legs for half my court, threw an old woman down the steps, and tried to steal a dragon. What more do you require? Have you given any thought as to how she got to Lys? She had no coin. How do think she paid for her passage?"

The queen cringed at the harshness of his words, but still she would not yield. "If you will not bring Saera home for love of her, bring her home for love of me. I need her."

"You need her as a Dornishman needs a pit viper," Jaehaerys said. "I am sorry. King's Landing has sufficient whores. I do not wish to hear her name again." With those words, he rose to leave, but at the door he halted and turned back. "We have been together since we were children. I know you as well as you know me. Right now you are thinking that you do not need my leave to bring her home, that you can take Silverwing and fly to Lys yourself. What would you do then, visit her in her pleasure garden? Do you imagine she will fly into your arms and beg forgiveness? She is more like to slap your face. And what will the Lyseni do, if you try and make off with one of their whores? She has value to them. How much do you think it costs to lay with a Targaryen princess? At best they will demand a ransom for her. At worst they may decide to keep you too. What will you do then, shout for Silverwing to burn their city down? Would you have me send Aemon and Baelon with an army, to see if they can prise her free? You want her, yes, I hear you, you need her . . . but she does not need you, or me, or Westeros. She is dead. Bury her."

Queen Alysanne did not fly to Lys, but neither did she ever quite forgive the king for the words he spoke that day. Plans had been under way for some time for the two of them to make another progress the following year, returning to the westerlands for the first time in twenty years. Shortly after their falling out, the queen informed Jaehaerys that he should go alone. She was going back to Dragonstone, alone, to grieve for their dead daughters.

And so it was that Jaehaerys Targaryen flew to Casterly Rock and the other great seats of the west alone in 88 AC. This time he even called on Fair Isle, for the despised Lord Franklyn was safely in his grave. The king was gone far longer than had been originally intended; he had roadworks to inspect, and he found himself making unplanned stops at smaller towns and castles, delighting many a petty lord and landed knight. Prince Aemon joined him at certain castles, Prince Baelon at others, but neither could persuade him to return to the Red Keep. "It has been too long since I have seen my kingdom and listened to my people," His Grace told them. "King's Landing will do well enough in your hands, and your mother's."

When at last he had exhausted the hospitality of the westermen, he did not return to King's Landing, but moved on directly to the Reach, flying Vermithor from Crakehall to Old Oak to begin a second progress even as the first was ending. By that time, the queen's absence had been noticed, and His Grace would oft find himself seated next to some lissome maid or handsome widow at feasts, or riding beside them when hawking or hunting, but he took no notice of any of them. At Bandallon, when Lord Blackbar's youngest daughter was so bold as to seat herself in his lap and attempt to feed him a grape, he brushed her hand aside and said, "Forgive me, but I have a queen, and no taste for paramours."

For the entire year of 89 AC, the king remained on the move. At Highgarden, he was joined for a time by his granddaughter, Princess Rhaenys, who flew to his side on Meleys, the Red Queen. Together they visited the Shield Islands, where the king had never been before. Jaehaerys made a point of landing on all four Shields. It was on Greenshield, in Lord Chester's hall, that Princess Rhaenys told him of her plans to marry, and received the king's blessing. "You could not have chosen a better man," he said.

His journeys finally ended in Oldtown, where he visited with his daughter Septa Maegelle, was blessed by the High Septon and feasted by the Conclave, and enjoyed a tourney staged in his honor by Lord Hightower. Ser Ryam Redwyne again emerged as champion.

The maesters of that time referred to the estrangement betwixt the king and queen as the Great Rift. The passage of time, and a subsequent quarrel that was near as bitter, gave it a new name: the First Quarrel. That is how it is known to this day. We shall speak of the Second Quarrel in good time.

It was Septa Maegelle who bridged the Rift. "This is foolish, Father," she said to him. "Rhaenys is to be married next year, and it should be a great occasion. She will want all of us there, including both you and Mother. The archmaesters call you the Conciliator, I have heard. It is time that you conciliated."

The scolding had the desired effect. A fortnight later, King Jaehaerys returned at last to King's Landing, and Queen Alysanne returned from her own self-imposed exile on Dragonstone. What words passed between them we can never know, but for a good while afterward they were once again as close as they had been before.

In the 90th year after Aegon's Conquest, the king and queen shared one of their last good times together, as they celebrated the wedding of their eldest grandchild, Princess Rhaenys, to Corlys Velaryon of Driftmark, Lord of the Tides.

At seven-and-thirty, the Sea Snake was already hailed as the greatest seafarer Westeros had ever known, but with his nine great voyages behind him, he had come home to marry and make a family. "Only you could have won me away from the sea," he told the princess. "I came back from the ends of the earth for you."

Rhaenys, at six-and-ten, was a fearless young beauty, and more than a match for her mariner. A dragonrider since the age of thirteen, she insisted upon arriving for the wedding on Meleys, the Red Queen, the magnificent scarlet she-dragon that had once borne her aunt Alyssa. "We can go back to the ends of the earth together," she promised Ser Corlys. "But I'll get there first, as I'll be flying."

"That was a good day," Queen Alysanne would say with a sad smile, through the years that remained to her. She was fifty-four that year, but sad to say, she did not have many good days left.

It is not within the scope of this history to chronicle the endless wars, intrigues, and rivalries of the Free Cities of Essos, save where they impinge upon the fortunes of House Targaryen and the Seven Kingdoms. One such time occurred during the years 91–92 AC, during what is known as the Myrish Bloodbath. We shall not trouble you with details. Suffice it to say that in the city of Myr two rival factions vied for supremacy. There were assassinations, riots, poisonings, rapes, hangings, torture, and sea battles before one side emerged supreme. The losing faction, driven from the city, tried to establish themselves first upon the Stepstones, only to be hounded from there as well when the Archon of Tyrosh made common cause with a league of pirate kings. In their desperation, the Myrmen next turned to the island of Tarth, where their landings took the Evenstar by surprise. In a short time they had taken the entire eastern side of the island.

By that time the Myrish were little more than pirates themselves, a ragged band of rogues. Neither the king nor his council felt it would require much to drive them back into the sea. Prince Aemon would lead the assault, it was decided. The Myrmen did have some strength at sea, so the Sea Snake would first need to bring the Velaryon fleet south, to protect Lord Boremund as he crossed to Tarth with his stormlanders, to join with the Evenstar's own levies. Their combined strength would be more than sufficient to retake all of Tarth from the Myrish pirates. And if there proved to be unexpected difficulties, Prince Aemon would have Caraxes. "He does love to burn," the prince said.

Lord Corlys and his fleet set sail from Driftmark on the ninth day of the third moon of 92 AC. Prince Aemon followed a few hours later, after bidding farewell to Lady Jocelyn and their daughter, Rhaenys. The princess had just learned she was expecting, else she would have accompanied her sire on Meleys. "Into battle?" the prince said. "As if I would ever have permitted that. You have your own battle to fight. Lord Corlys will want a son, I am sure, and I would like a grandson."

Those were the last words he would ever speak to his daughter. Caraxes swiftly outdistanced the Sea Snake and his fleet, dropping down out of the sky on Tarth. Lord Cameron, the Evenstar of Tarth, had fallen back into the spine of mountains that ran down the center of his island, and established a camp in a hidden valley from which he could look down on the Myrish movements below. Prince Aemon met him there, and the two made plans together, whilst Caraxes devoured half a dozen goats.

But the Evenstar's camp was not as hidden as he hoped, and the smoke from the dragon's fires drew the eyes of a pair of Myrish scouts who were creeping through the heights unawares. One of them recognized the Evenstar as he strode through the camp at dusk, talking with Prince Aemon. The men of Myr are indifferent sailors and feeble soldiers; their weapons of choice are dirk, dagger, and crossbow, preferably poisoned. One of the Myrish scouts wound his crossbow now, behind the rocks where he was hidden. Rising, he took aim on the Evenstar a hundred yards below, and loosed his bolt. Dusk and distance made his aim less certain, and the bolt missed Lord Cameron . . . and struck Prince Aemon, standing at his side.

The iron bolt punched through the prince's throat and out the back of his neck. The Prince of Dragonstone fell to his knees and grasped the crossbow bolt, as if to pull it from his throat, but his strength was gone. Aemon Targaryen died struggling to speak, drowned on his own blood. He was thirty-seven years old.

How can my words tell of the grief that swept the Seven Kingdoms then, of the pain felt by King Jaehaerys and Queen Alysanne, of Lady Jocelyn's empty bed and bitter tears, and the way Princess Rhaenys wept to know that her father would never hold the child she was carrying? Far easier to speak of Prince Baelon's wroth, and how he came down upon Tarth on Vhagar, howling for vengeance. The Myrish ships burned as Prince Morion's ships had burned nine years earlier, and when the Evenstar and Lord Boremund descended on them from the mountains, they had nowhere to fly. They were cut down by the thousands and left to rot along the beaches, so every wave that washed ashore for days was tinged with pink.

Baelon the Brave played his part in the slaughter, with Dark Sister in his hand. When he returned to King's Landing with his brother's corpse, the smallfolk lined the streets screaming his name and hailing him as a hero. But it is said that when he saw his mother again, he fell into her arms and wept. "I slew a thousand of them," he said, "but it will not bring him back." And the queen stroked his hair and said, "I know, I know."

Seasons came and went in the years that followed. There were hot days and warm days and days when the salt wind blew bracing off the sea, there were fields of flowers in the spring, and bountiful harvests, and golden autumn afternoons, all across the realm the roads crept onward, and new bridges spanned old streams. The king took no pleasure in any of it, so far as men could tell. "It is always winter now," he said to Septon Barth one night, when he had drunk too much. Since Aemon's death, he always drank a cup or three of honeyed wine at night to help him sleep.

In 93 AC, Prince Baelon's sixteen-year-old son, Viserys, entered the Dragonpit and claimed Balerion. The old dragon had stopped growing at last, but he was sluggish and heavy and hard to rouse, and he struggled when Viserys urged him up into the air. The young prince flew thrice around the city before landing again. He had intended to fly to Dragonstone, he told his father afterward, but he did not think the Black Dread had the strength for it.

Less than a year later, Balerion was gone. "The last living creature in all the world who saw Valyria in its glory," wrote Septon Barth. Barth himself died four years later, in 98 AC. Grand Maester Elysar preceded him by half a year. Lord Redwyne had died in 89 AC, his son Ser Robert soon thereafter. New men took their places, but Jaehaerys was truly the Old King by then, and sometimes he would walk into the council chamber and think, "Who are these men? Do I know them?"

His Grace grieved for Prince Aemon until the end of his days, but the Old King never dreamed that Aemon's death in 92 AC would be like the hellhorns of Valyrian legend, bringing death and destruction down on all those who heard their sound.

The last years of Alysanne Targaryen were sad and lonely ones. In her youth, Good Queen Alysanne had loved her subjects, lords and commons alike. She had loved her women's courts, listening, learning, and doing what she could to make the realm a kinder place. She had seen more of the Seven Kingdoms than any queen before or since, slept in a hundred castles, charmed a hundred lords, made a hundred marriages. She had loved music, had loved to dance, had loved to read. And *oh,* how she had loved to fly. Silverwing had carried her to Oldtown, to the Wall, and to a thousand places in between, and Alysanne saw them all as few others ever would, looking down from above the clouds.

All these loves were lost to her in the last decade of her life. "My uncle Maegor was cruel," Alysanne was heard to say, "but age is crueler." Worn out from childbirth, travel, and grief, she grew thin and frail after Aemon's death. Climbing hills became a trial to her, and in 95 AC she slipped and fell on the serpentine steps, breaking her hip. Thereafter she walked with a cane. Her hearing began to fail as well. Music was lost to her, and when she tried to sit in council meetings with the king she could no longer understand half of what was said. She was far too unsteady to fly. Silverwing last carried her into the sky in 93 AC. When she came to earth again and climbed painfully from her dragon's back, the queen wept.

More than all of these, she had loved her children. No mother ever loved a child more, Grand Maester Benifer once told her, before the Shivers carried him away. In the last days of her life, Queen Alysanne reflected on his words. "He was wrong, I think," she wrote, "for surely the Mother Above loved my children more. She took so many of them away from me."

"No mother should ever have to burn her child," the queen had said at the funeral pyre of her son Valerion, but of the thirteen children she bore to King Jaehaerys, only three of them would survive her, Aegon, Gaemon, and Valerion died as babes. The Shivers took Daenerys at the age of six. A crossbow slew Prince Aemon. Alyssa and Daella died in childbed, Viserra drunk in the street. Septa Maegelle, that gentle soul, died in 96 AC, her arms and legs turned to stone by greyscale, for she had spent her last years nursing those afflicted with that horrible condition.

Saddest of all was the loss of Princess Gael, the Winter Child, born in 80 AC when Queen Alysanne was forty-four and thought to be well past her childbearing years. A sweet-natured girl, but frail and somewhat simpleminded, she remained with the queen long after her other children had grown and gone, but in 99 AC she vanished from court, and soon afterward it was announced that she had died of a summer fever. Only after both her parents were gone did the true tale come out. Seduced and abandoned by a traveling singer, the princess had given birth to a stillborn son, then, overwhelmed by grief, walked into the waters of Blackwater Bay and drowned.

Some say that Alysanne never recovered from that loss, for her Winter Child alone had been a true companion during her declining years. Saera still lived, somewhere in Volantis (she had departed Lys some years before, an infamous woman but a wealthy one), but she was dead to Jaehaerys, and the letters Alysanne sent her secretly from time to time all went unanswered. Vaegon was an archmaester at the Citadel. A cold and distant son, he had grown to be a cold and distant man. He wrote, as a son ought. His words were dutiful, but there was no warmth to them, and it had been years since Alysanne had last seen his face.

Only Baelon the Brave remained near her till the end. Her Spring Prince visited her as often as he could and always won a smile from her, but Baelon was the Prince of Dragonstone, Hand of the King, forever coming and going, sitting at his father's side at council, treating with the lords. "You will be a great king, even greater than your father," Alysanne told him the last time they were together. She did not know. How could she know?

After the death of Princess Gael, King's Landing and the Red Keep became unbearable to Alysanne. She could no longer serve as she once had, as a partner to the king in his labors, and the court was full of strangers whose names Alysanne could not quite recall. Seeking peace, she returned once more to Dragonstone, where she had spent the happiest days of her life with Jaehaerys, between their first and second marriages. The Old King would join her there when he could. "How is it that I am the Old King now, but you are still the Good Queen?" he asked her once. Alysanne laughed. "I am old as well, but I am still younger than you."

Alysanne Targaryen died on Dragonstone on the first day of the seventh moon in 100 AC, a full century after Aegon's Conquest. She was sixty-four years old.

Heirs of the Dragon

A Question of Succession

The seeds of war are oft planted during times of peace. So has it been in Westeros. The bloody struggle for the Iron Throne known as the Dance of the Dragons, fought from 129–131 AC, had its roots half a century earlier, during the longest and most peaceful reign that any of the Conqueror's descendants ever enjoyed, that of Jaehaerys I Targaryen, the Conciliator.

The Old King and Good Queen Alysanne ruled together until her death in 100 AC (aside from two periods of estrangement, known as the First and Second Quarrels), and produced thirteen children. Four of them—two sons and two daughters—grew to maturity, married, and produced children of their own. Never before or since had the Seven Kingdoms been blessed (or cursed, in the view of some) with so many Targaryen princelings. From the loins of the Old King and his beloved queen sprang such a confusion of claims and claimants than many maesters believe that the Dance of the Dragons, or some similar struggle, was inevitable.

This was not apparent in the early years of Jaehaerys's reign, for in Prince Aemon and Prince Baelon His Grace had the proverbial "heir and a spare," and seldom has the realm been blessed with two more able princes. In 62 AC, at the age of seven, Aemon was formally anointed Prince of

Dragonstone and heir to the Iron Throne. Knighted at seventeen, a tourney champion at twenty, he became his father's justiciar and master of laws at six-and-twenty. Though he never served his father as Hand of the King, that was only because that office was occupied by Septon Barth, the Old King's most trusted friend and "companion of my labors." Nor was Baelon Targaryen any less accomplished. The younger prince earned his knighthood at sixteen, and was wed at eighteen. Though he and Aemon enjoyed a healthy rivalry, no man doubted the love that bound them. The succession appeared solid as stone.

But the stone began to crack in 92 AC, when Aemon, Prince of Dragonstone, was slain on Tarth by a Myrish crossbow bolt loosed at the man beside him. The king and queen mourned his loss, and the realm with them, but no man was more bereft than Prince Baelon, who went at once to Tarth and avenged his brother by driving the Myrmen into the sea. On his return to King's Landing, Baelon was hailed as a hero by cheering throngs, and embraced by his father the king, who named him Prince of Dragonstone and heir to the Iron Throne. It was a popular decree. The smallfolk loved Baelon the Brave, and the lords of the realm saw him as his brother's obvious successor.

But Prince Aemon had a child: his daughter, Rhaenys, born in 74 AC, had grown into a clever, capable, and beautiful young woman. In 90 AC, at the age of sixteen, she had wed the king's admiral and master of ships, Corlys of House Velaryon, Lord of the Tides, known as the Sea Snake after the most famous of his many ships. Moreover, Princess Rhaenys was with child when her father died. By granting Dragonstone to Prince Baelon, King Jaehaerys was not only passing over Rhaenys, but also (possibly) her unborn son.

The king's decision was in accord with well-established practice. Aegon the Conqueror had been the first Lord of the Seven Kingdoms, not his sister Visenya, two years his elder. Jaehaerys himself had followed his usurping uncle Maegor on the Iron Throne, though had the order of birth alone ruled, his sister Rhaena had a better claim. Jaehaerys did not make his decision lightly; he is known to have discussed the matter with his small council. Undoubtedly he consulted Septon Barth, as he did on all important matters, and the views of Grand Maester Elysar were given much weight. All were in accord. Baelon, a seasoned knight of thirty-five, was better suited for rule than the eighteen-year-old Princess Rhaenys or her unborn babe (who might or might not be a boy, whereas Prince Baelon had already sired two healthy sons, Viserys and Daemon). The love of the commons for Baelon the Brave was also cited.

Some dissented. Rhaenys herself was the first to raise objection. "You would rob my son of his birthright," she told the king, with a hand upon her swollen belly. Her husband, Corlys Velaryon, was so wroth that he gave up his admiralty and his place on the small council and took his wife back to Driftmark. Lady Jocelyn of House Baratheon, Rhaenys's mother, was also angered, as was her formidable brother, Boremund, Lord of Storm's End.

The most prominent dissenter was Good Queen Alysanne, who had helped her husband rule the Seven Kingdoms for many years, and now saw her son's daughter being passed over because of her sex. "A ruler needs a good head and a true heart," she famously told the king. "A cock is not essential. If Your Grace truly believes that women lack the wit to rule, plainly you have no further need of me." And thus Queen Alysanne departed King's Landing and flew to Dragonstone on her dragon Silverwing. She and King Jaehaerys remained apart for two years, the period of estrangement recorded in the histories as the Second Quarrel.

The Old King and the Good Queen were again reconciled in 94 AC by the good offices of their daughter, Septa Maegelle, but never reached accord on the succession. The queen died of a wasting illness in 100 AC, at the age of four-and-sixty, still insisting that her granddaughter Rhaenys and her children had been unfairly cheated of their rights. "The boy in the belly," the unborn child who had been the subject of so much debate, proved to be a girl when born late in 92 AC. Her mother named her Laena. Two years later, Rhaenys gave her a brother, Laenor. Prince Baelon was firmly ensconced as heir apparent by then, yet House Velaryon and House Baratheon clung to the belief that young Laenor had a better claim to the Iron Throne, and some few even argued for the rights of his elder sister, Laena, and their mother, Rhaenys.

In the last years of her life, the gods dealt Queen Alysanne many cruel blows, as has previously been recounted. Her Grace knew joys as well as sorrows during the same years, however, chief amongst them her grandchildren. There were weddings as well. In 93 AC she attended the wedding of Prince Baelon's eldest son, Viserys, to Lady Aemma of House Arryn, the eleven-year-old child of the late Princess Daella (their marriage was not consummated until the bride had flowered, two years later). In 97, the Good Queen saw Baelon's second son, Daemon, take to wife Lady Rhea of House Royce, heir to the ancient castle of Runestone in the Vale.

The great tourney held at King's Landing in 98 AC to celebrate the fiftieth year of King Jaehaerys's reign surely gladdened the queen's heart as well, for most of her surviving children, grandchildren, and great-grandchildren returned to share in the feasts and celebrations. Not since the Doom of Valyria had so many dragons been seen in one place at one time, it was truly said. The final tilt, wherein the Kingsguard knights Ser Ryam Redwyne and Ser Clement Crabb broke thirty lances against each other before King Jaehaerys proclaimed them co-champions, was declared to be the finest display of jousting ever seen in Westeros.

A fortnight after the tourney's end, however, the king's old friend Septon Barth died peacefully in his sleep after serving ably as Hand of the

King for forty-one years. Jaehaerys chose the Lord Commander of his Kingsguard to take his place, but Ser Ryam Redwyne was no Septon Barth, and his undoubted prowess with a lance proved of little use to him as Hand. "Some problems cannot be solved by hitting them with a stick," Grand Maester Allar famously observed. His Grace had no choice but to remove Ser Ryam after only a year in office. He turned to his son Baelon to replace him, and in 99 AC the Prince of Dragonstone became the King's Hand as well. He performed his duties admirably; though less scholarly than Septon Barth, the prince proved a good judge of men, and surrounded himself with loyal subordinates and counselors. The realm would be well ruled when Baelon Targaryen sat the Iron Throne, lords and common folk agreed.

It was not to be. In 101 AC Prince Baelon complained of a stitch in his side whilst hunting in the kingswood. The pain worsened when he returned to the city. His belly swelled and hardened, and the pain grew so severe it left him bedridden. Runciter, the new Grand Maester only recently arrived from the Citadel after Allar was felled by a stroke, was able to bring the prince's fever down somewhat and give him some relief from agony with milk of the poppy, but his condition continued to worsen. On the fifth day of his illness, Prince Baelon died in his bedchamber in the Tower of the Hand, with his father sitting beside him, holding his hand. After opening the corpse, Grand Maester Runciter put down the cause of death as a burst belly.

All the Seven Kingdoms wept for Brave Baelon, and none more so than King Jaehaerys. This time, when he lit his son's funeral pyre, he did not even have the comfort of his beloved wife beside him. The Old King had never been so alone. And now again His Grace faced a nettlesome dilemma, for once more the succession was in doubt. With both of the heirs apparent dead and burned, there was no longer a clear successor to the Iron Throne . . . but that was not to say there was any lack of claimants.

Baelon had sired three sons by his sister Alyssa. Two, Viserys and Daemon, still lived. Had Baelon ever taken the Iron Throne, Viserys would have followed him without question, but the crown prince's tragic death at the age of four-and-forty muddied the succession. The claims of Princess Rhaenys and her daughter, Laena Velaryon, were put forward once again . . . and even if they were to be passed over on account of their sex, Rhaenys's son, Laenor, faced no such impediment. Laenor Velaryon was male, and could claim descent from Jaehaerys's elder son, whilst Baelon's boys were descended from the younger.

Moreover, King Jaehaerys still had one surviving son: Vaegon, an archmaester at the Citadel, holder of the ring and rod and mask of yellow gold. Known to history as Vaegon the Dragonless, his very existence had been largely forgotten by most of the Seven Kingdoms. Though not yet forty years of age, Vaegon was pale and frail, a bookish man devoted to alchemy, astronomy, mathematics, and other arcane arts. Even as a boy, he had never been well-liked. Few considered him a viable choice to sit the Iron Throne.

And yet it was to Archmaester Vaegon that the Old King turned now, summoning his last son to King's Landing. What passed between them remains a matter of dispute. Some say the king offered Vaegon the throne and was refused. Others assert that he only sought his counsel. Reports had reached the court that Corlys Velaryon was massing ships and men on Driftmark to "defend the rights" of his son, Laenor, whilst Daemon Targaryen, a hot-tempered and quarrelsome young man of twenty, had gathered his own band of sworn swords in support of his brother, Viserys. A violent struggle for succession was likely no matter who the Old King named to succeed him. No doubt that was why His Grace seized eagerly on the solution offered by Archmaester Vaegon.

King Jaehaerys announced his intent to convene a Great Council, to discuss, debate, and ultimately decide the matter of succession. All the great and lesser lords of Westeros would be invited to attend, together with maesters from the Citadel of Oldtown, and septas and septons to speak for the Faith. Let the claimants make their cases before the assembled lords, His Grace decreed. He would abide by the council's decision, whomever they might choose.

It was decided that the council would be held at Harrenhal, the largest castle in the realm. No one knew how many lords would come, since no such council had ever been held before, but it was thought prudent to have room for at least five hundred lords and their tails. More than a thousand lords attended. It took half a year for them to assemble (a few arrived even

as the council was breaking up). Even Harrenhal could not contain such multitudes, for each lord was accompanied by a retinue of knights, squires, grooms, cooks, and serving men. Tymond Lannister, Lord of Casterly Rock, brought three hundred men with him. Not to be outdone, Lord Matthos Tyrell of Highgarden brought five hundred.

Lords came from every corner of the realm, from the Dornish Marches to the shadow of the Wall, from the Three Sisters to the Iron Islands. The Evenstar of Tarth was there, and the Lord of the Lonely Light. From Winterfell came Lord Ellard Stark, from Riverrun Lord Grover Tully, from the Vale Yorbert Royce, regent and protector for young Jeyne Arryn, Lady of the Eyrie. Even the Dornishmen were represented; the Prince of Dorne sent his daughter and twenty Dornish knights to Harrenhal as observers. The High Septon came from Oldtown to bless the assembly. Merchants and tradesmen descended upon Harrenhal by the hundreds. Hedge knights and freeriders came in hopes of finding work for their swords, cutpurses came seeking after coin, old women and young girls came seeking after husbands. Thieves and whores, washerwomen and camp followers, singers and mummers, they came from east and west and north and south. A city of tents sprang up outside the walls of Harrenhal and along the lakeshore for leagues in each direction. For a time Harrenton was the fourth city in the realm; only Oldtown, King's Landing, and Lannisport were larger.

No fewer than fourteen claims were duly examined and considered by the lords assembled. From Essos came three rival competitors, grandsons of King Jaehaerys through his daughter Saera, each sired by a different father. One was said to be the very image of his grandsire in his youth. Another, a bastard born to a triarch of Old Volantis, arrived with bags of gold and a dwarf elephant. The lavish gifts he distributed amongst the poorer lords undoubtedly helped his claim. The elephant proved less useful. (Princess Saera herself was still alive and well in Volantis, and only thirty-four years of age; her own claim was clearly superior to those of any of her bastard sons, but she did not choose to press it. "I have my own kingdom here," she said, when asked if she meant to return to Westeros.) Another contestant produced sheafs of parchment that demonstrated his descent from Gaemon the Glorious, the greatest of the Targaryen Lords of Dragonstone before the Conquest, by way of a younger daughter and the petty lord she had married, and on for seven further generations. There was as well a strapping red-haired man-at-arms who claimed to be a bastard son of Maegor the Cruel. By way of proof he brought his mother, an aged innkeep's daughter who said that she had once been raped by Maegor. (The lords were prepared to believe the fact of rape, but not that the act had gotten her with child.)

The Great Council deliberated for thirteen days. The tenuous claims of nine lesser competitors were considered and discarded (one such, a hedge knight who put himself forward as a natural son of King Jaehaerys himself, was seized and imprisoned when the king exposed him as a liar). Archmaester Vaegon was ruled out on account of his vows and Princess Rhaenys and her daughter on account of their sex, leaving the two claimants with the most support: Viserys Targaryen, eldest son of Prince Baelon and Princess Alyssa, and Laenor Velaryon, the son of Princess Rhaenys and grandson of Prince Aemon. Viserys was the Old King's grandson, Laenor his great-grandson. The principle of primogeniture favored Laenor, the principle of proximity Viserys. Viserys had also been the last Targaryen to ride Balerion . . . though after the death of the Black Dread in 94 AC he never mounted another dragon, whereas the boy Laenor had yet to take his first flight upon his young dragon, a splendid grey-and-white beast he named Seasmoke.

But Viserys's claim derived from his father, Laenor's from his mother, and most lords felt that the male line must take precedence over the female. Moreover, Viserys was a man of twenty-four, Laenor a boy of seven. For all these reasons, Laenor's claim was generally regarded as the weaker, but the boy's mother and father were such powerful and influential figures that it could not be dismissed entirely.

Mayhaps this would be a good place to add a few additional words about his sire, Corlys of House Velaryon, Lord of the Tides and Master of Driftmark, renowned in song and story as the Sea Snake, and surely one of the most extraordinary figures of the age. A noble house with a storied Valyrian lineage, the Velaryons had come to Westeros even before the Targaryens, if their family histories can be believed, settling in the Gullet on the low-lying and fertile isle of Driftmark (so named for the driftwood that the tides brought daily to its shores) rather than its stony, smoking neighbor, Dragonstone. Though never dragonriders, the Velaryons had for centuries remained the oldest and closest allies of the Targaryens. The sea was their element, not the sky. During the Conquest, it was Velaryon ships that carried Aegon's soldiers across Blackwater Bay, and later formed the greater part of the royal fleet. Throughout the first century of Targaryen rule, so many Lords of the Tides served on the small council as master of ships that the office was widely seen as almost hereditary.

Yet even with such forebears, Corlys Velaryon was a man apart, a man as brilliant as he was restless, as adventurous as he was ambitious. It was traditional for the sons of the seahorse (the sigil of House Velaryon) to be given a taste of a seafarer's life when young, but no Velaryon before or since ever took to shipboard life as eagerly as the boy who would become the Sea Snake. He first crossed the narrow sea at the age of six, sailing to Pentos with an uncle. Thereafter Corlys made such voyages every year. Nor did he travel as a passenger; he climbed masts, tied knots, scrubbed decks, pulled oars, caulked leaks, raised and lowered sails, manned the crow's nest, learned to navigate and steer. His captains said they had never seen such a natural sailor.

At age sixteen, he became a captain himself, taking a fishing boat called the *Cod Queen* from Driftmark to Dragonstone and back. In the years that followed, his ships grew larger and swifter, his voyages longer and more dangerous. He took ships around the bottom of Westeros to visit Oldtown, Lannisport, and Lordsport on Pyke. He sailed to Lys, Tyrosh, Pentos, and Myr. He took the *Summer Maid* to Volantis and the Summer Isles, and the *Ice Wolf* north to Braavos, Eastwatch-by-the-Sea, and Hardhome before turning into the Shivering Sea for Lorath and the Port of Ibben. On a later voyage, he and the *Ice Wolf* headed north once more, searching for a rumored passage around the top of Westeros, but finding only frozen seas and icebergs big as mountains.

His most famous voyages were those he made on the ship that he designed and built himself, the *Sea Snake*. Traders from Oldtown and the Arbor oft sailed as far as Qarth in search of spice, silk, and other treasures, but Corlys Velaryon and the *Sea Snake* were the first to go beyond, passing through the Jade Gates to Yi Ti and the isle of Leng, returning with so rich a load of silk and spice that he doubled the wealth of House Velaryon in a stroke. On his second voyage in the *Sea Snake,* he sailed even farther, to Asshai-by-the-Shadow; on his third he tried the Shivering Sea instead, becoming the first Westerosi to navigate the Thousand Islands and visit the bleak, cold shores of N'ghai and Mossovy.

In the end the *Sea Snake* made nine voyages. On the ninth, Ser Corlys took her back to Qarth, laden with enough gold to buy twenty more ships and load them all with saffron, pepper, nutmeg, elephants, and bolts of the finest silk. Only fourteen of the fleet arrived safely at Driftmark, and all the elephants died at sea, yet even so the profits from that voyage were so vast that the Velaryons became the wealthiest house in the Seven Kingdoms, eclipsing even the Hightowers and Lannisters, albeit briefly.

This wealth Ser Corlys put to good use when his aged grandsire died at the age of eight-and-eighty, and the Sea Snake became Lord of the Tides. The seat of House Velaryon was Castle Driftmark, a dark, grim place, always damp and often flooded. Lord Corlys raised a new castle on the far side of the island. High Tide was built of the same pale stone as the Eyrie, its slender towers crowned with roofs of beaten silver that flashed in the sun. When the morning and evening tides rolled in, the castle was surrounded by the sea, connected to Driftmark proper only by a causeway. To this new castle, Lord Corlys moved the ancient Driftwood Throne (a gift from the Merling King, according to legend).

The Sea Snake built ships as well. The royal fleet tripled in size during the years he served the Old King as master of ships. Even after giving up that office, he continued to build, turning out merchantmen and trading galleys in place of warships. Beneath the dark, salt-stained walls of Castle Driftmark three modest fishing villages grew together into a thriving town called Hull, for the rows of ship hulls that could always be seen below the castle. Across the island, near High Tide, another village was transformed into Spicetown, its wharves and piers crowded with ships from the Free Cities and beyond. Sitting athwart the Gullet, Driftmark was closer to the narrow sea than Duskendale or King's Landing, so Spicetown soon began to usurp much of the shipping that would elsewise have made for those ports, and House Velaryon grew ever richer and more powerful.

Lord Corlys was an ambitious man. During his nine voyages on the *Sea Snake,* he was forever wanting to press onward, to go where none had gone before and see what lay beyond the maps. Though he had accomplished much and more in life, he was seldom satisfied, the men who knew him best would say. In Rhaenys Targaryen, daughter of the Old King's eldest son and heir, he had found his perfect match, a woman as spirited and beautiful and proud as any in the realm, and a dragonrider as well. His sons and daughters would soar through the skies, Lord Corlys expected, and one day one of them would sit the Iron Throne.

Unsurprisingly, the Sea Snake was bitterly disappointed when Prince Aemon died and King Jaehaerys bypassed Aemon's daughter, Rhaenys, in favor of his brother, Baelon the Spring Prince. But now, it seemed, the wheel had turned again, and the wrong could be righted. Thus did Lord Corlys and his wife, the Princess Rhaenys, arrive at Harrenhal in high state, using the wealth and influence of House Velaryon to persuade the lords assembled that their son, Laenor, should be recognized as heir to the Iron Throne. In these efforts they were joined by the Lord of Storm's End, Boremund Baratheon (uncle to Rhaenys and great-uncle to the boy Laenor), by Lord Stark of Winterfell, Lord Manderly of White Harbor, Lord Dustin of Barrowton, Lord Blackwood of Raventree, Lord Bar Emmon of Sharp Point, Lord Celtigar of Claw Isle, and others.

They were nowhere near enough. Though Lord and Lady Velaryon were eloquent and open-handed in their efforts on behalf of their son, the decision of the Great Council was never truly in doubt. By a lopsided margin, the lords assembled chose Viserys Targaryen as the rightful heir to the Iron Throne. Though the maesters who tallied the votes never revealed the actual numbers, it was said afterward that the vote had been more than twenty to one.

King Jaehaerys had not attended the council, but when word of their verdict reached him, His Grace thanked the lords for their service and gratefully conferred the style Prince of Dragonstone upon his grandson Viserys. Storm's End and Driftmark accepted the decision, if grudgingly; the vote had been so overwhelming that even Laenor's father and mother saw that they could not hope to prevail. In the eyes of many, the Great Council of 101 AC thereby established an iron precedent on matters of succession: regardless of seniority, the Iron Throne of Westeros could not pass to a woman, nor through a woman to her male descendants.

Of the last years in the reign of King Jaehaerys, little and less need be said. Prince Baelon had served his father as Hand of the King as well as Prince of Dragonstone, but after his death His Grace elected to divide those honors. As his new Hand, he called upon Ser Otto Hightower, younger brother to Lord Hightower of Oldtown. Ser Otto brought his wife and children to court with him, and served King Jaehaerys faithfully for the years remaining to him. As the Old King's strength and wits began to fail, he was oft confined to his bed. Ser Otto's precocious fifteen-year-old daughter, Alicent, became his constant companion, fetching His Grace his meals, reading to him, helping him to bathe and dress himself. The Old King sometimes mistook her for one of his daughters, calling her by their names; near the end, he grew certain she was his daughter Saera, returned to him from beyond the narrow sea.

In the year 103 AC King Jaehaerys I Targaryen died in his bed as Lady Alicent was reading to him from Septon Barth's *Unnatural History*. His

Grace was nine-and-sixty years of age, and had reigned over the Seven Kingdoms since coming to the Iron Throne at the age of fourteen. His remains were burned in the Dragonpit, his ashes interred with Good Queen Alysanne's on Dragonstone. All of Westeros mourned. Even in Dorne, where his writ had not extended, men wept and women tore their garments.

In accordance with his own wishes, and the decision of the Great Council of 101, his grandson Viserys succeeded him, mounting the Iron Throne as King Viserys I Targaryen. At the time of his ascent, King Viserys was twenty-six years old. He had been married for a decade to a cousin, Lady Aemma of House Arryn, herself a granddaughter of the Old King and Good Queen Alysanne through her mother, the late Princess Daella (d. 82 AC). Lady Aemma had suffered several miscarriages and the death of one son in the cradle over the course of her marriage (some maesters felt she had been married and bedded too young), but she had also given birth to a healthy daughter, Rhaenyra (born 97 AC). The new king and his queen both doted on the girl, their only living child.

Many consider the reign of King Viserys I to represent the apex of Targaryen power in Westeros. Beyond a doubt, there were more lords and princes claiming the blood of the dragon than at any period before or since. Though the Targaryens had continued their traditional practice of marrying brother to sister, uncle to niece, and cousin to cousin wherever possible, there had also been important matches outside the royal family, the fruit of which would play important roles in the war to come. There were more *dragons* than ever before as well, and several of the she-dragons were regularly producing clutches of eggs. Not all of these eggs hatched, but many did, and it became customary for the fathers and mothers of newborn princelings to place a dragon's egg in their cradles, following a tradition that Princess Rhaena had begun many years before; the children so blessed invariably bonded with the hatchlings to become dragonriders.

Viserys I Targaryen had a generous, amiable nature, and was well loved by his lords and smallfolk alike. The reign of the Young King, as the commons called him upon his ascent, was peaceful and prosperous. His Grace's open-handedness was legendary, and the Red Keep became a place of song and splendor. King Viserys and Queen Aemma hosted many a

feast and tourney, and lavished gold, offices, and honors on their favorites.

At the center of the merriment, cherished and adored by all, was their only surviving child, Princess Rhaenyra, the little girl the court singers dubbed "the Realm's Delight." Though only six when her father came to the Iron Throne, Rhaenyra Targaryen was a precocious child, bright and bold and beautiful as only one of dragon's blood can be beautiful. At seven, she became a dragonrider, taking to the sky on the young dragon she named Syrax, after a goddess of old Valyria. At eight, the princess was placed into service as a cupbearer . . . but for her own father, the king. At table, at tourney, and at court, King Viserys thereafter was seldom seen without his daughter by his side.

Meanwhile, the tedium of rule was left largely to the king's small council and his Hand. Ser Otto Hightower had continued in that office, serving the grandson as he had the grandsire; an able man, all agreed, though many found him proud, brusque, and haughty. The longer he served, the more imperious Ser Otto became, it was said, and many great lords and princes came to resent his manner and envy him his access to the Iron Throne.

The greatest of his rivals was Daemon Targaryen, the king's ambitious, impetuous, moody younger brother. As charming as he was hot-tempered, Prince Daemon had earned his knight's spurs at six-and-ten, and had been given Dark Sister by the Old King himself in recognition of his prowess. Though he had wed the Lady of Runestone in 97 AC, during the Old King's reign, the marriage had not been a success. Prince Daemon found the Vale of Arryn boring ("In the Vale, the men fuck sheep," he wrote. "You cannot fault them. Their sheep are prettier than their women."), and soon developed a mislike of his lady wife, whom he called "my bronze bitch," after the runic bronze armor worn by the lords of House Royce. Upon the accession of his brother to the Iron Throne, the prince petitioned to have his marriage set aside. Viserys denied the request, but did allow Daemon to return to court, where he sat on the small council, serving as master of coin from 103–104, and master of laws for half a year in 104.

Governance bored this warrior prince, however. He did better when

King Viserys made him Commander of the City Watch. Finding the watchmen ill-armed and clad in oddments and rags, Daemon equipped each man with dirk, short sword, and cudgel, armored them in black ring-mail (with breastplates for the officers) and gave them long golden cloaks that they might wear with pride. Ever since, the men of the City Watch have been known as "gold cloaks."

Prince Daemon took eagerly to the work of the gold cloaks, and oft prowled the alleys of King's Landing with his men. That he made the city more orderly no man could doubt, but his discipline was a brutal one. He delighted in cutting off the hands of pickpockets, gelding rapists, and slitting the noses of thieves, and slew three men in street brawls during his first year as commander. Before long, the prince was well-known in all the low places of King's Landing. He became a familiar sight in wine sinks (where he drank for free) and gambling pits (where he always left with more coin than when he entered). Though he sampled countless whores in the city's brothels, and was said to have an especial fondness for deflowering maidens, a certain Lysene dancing girl soon became his favorite. Mysaria was the name she went by, though her rivals and enemies called her Misery, the White Worm.

As King Viserys had no living son, Daemon regarded himself as the rightful heir to the Iron Throne, and coveted the title Prince of Dragonstone, which His Grace refused to grant him . . . but by the end of year 105 AC, he was known to his friends as the Prince of the City and to the smallfolk as Lord Flea Bottom. Though the king did not wish Daemon to succeed him, he remained fond of his younger brother, and was quick to forgive his many offenses.

Princess Rhaenyra was also enamored of her uncle, for Daemon was ever attentive to her. Whenever he crossed the narrow sea upon his dragon, he brought her some exotic gift on his return. The king had grown soft and plump over the years. Viserys never claimed another dragon after Balerion's death, nor did he have much taste for the joust, the hunt, or swordplay, whereas Prince Daemon excelled in these spheres, and seemed all that his brother was not: lean and hard, a renowned warrior, dashing, daring, more than a little dangerous.

And here we must digress to say a word about our sources, for much of what happened in the years that followed happened behind closed doors, in the privacy of stairwells, council rooms, and bedchambers, and the full truth of it will likely never be known. We have of course the chronicles laid down by Grand Maester Runciter and his successors, and many a court document as well, all the royal decrees and proclamations, but these tell only a small part of the story. For the rest, we must look to accounts written decades later by the children and grandchildren of those caught up in the events of these times; lords and knights reporting events witnessed by their forebears, third-hand recollections of aged serving men relating the scandals of their youth. Whilst these are undoubtedly of use, so much time passed between the event and the recording that many confusions and contradictions have inevitably crept in. Nor do these remembrances always agree.

Unfortunately, this is also true of the two accounts by firsthand observers that have come down to us. Septon Eustace, who served in the royal sept in the Red Keep during much of this time, and later rose to the ranks of the Most Devout, set down the most detailed history of this period. As a confidant and confessor to King Viserys and his queens, Eustace was well placed to know much and more of what went on. Nor was he reticent about recording even the most shocking and salacious rumors and accusations, though the bulk of *The Reign of King Viserys, First of His Name, and the Dance of the Dragons That Came After* remains a sober and somewhat ponderous history.

To balance Eustace, we have *The Testimony of Mushroom,* based upon the verbal account of the court fool (set down by a scribe who failed to append his name) who at various times capered for the amusement of King Viserys, Princess Rhaenyra, and both Aegons, the Second and Third. A three-foot-tall dwarf possessed of an enormous head (and, he avers, an even more enormous member), Mushroom was thought feeble-minded, so kings and lords and princes did not scruple to hide their secrets from him. Whereas Septon Eustace records the secrets of bedchamber and brothel in hushed, condemnatory tones, Mushroom delights in the same, and his *Testimony* consists of little but ribald tales and gossip, piling stabbings, poisonings, betrayals, seductions, and debaucheries one atop the other. How much of this can be believed is a question the honest histo-

rian cannot hope to answer, but it is worth noting that King Baelor the Blessed decreed that every copy of Mushroom's chronicle should be burned. Fortunately for us, a few escaped his fires.

Septon Eustace and Mushroom do not always agree upon particulars, and at times their accounts are considerably at variance with one another, and with the court records and the chronicles of Grand Maester Runciter and his successors. Yet their tales do explain much and more that might otherwise seem puzzling, and later accounts confirm enough of their stories to suggest that they contain at least some portion of truth. The question of what to believe and what to doubt remains for each student to decide.

On one point Mushroom, Septon Eustace, Grand Maester Runciter, and all our other sources concur: Ser Otto Hightower, the King's Hand, took a great dislike to the king's brother. It was Ser Otto who convinced Viserys to remove Prince Daemon as master of coin, and then as master of laws, actions the Hand soon came to regret. As Commander of the City Watch, with two thousand men under his command, Daemon waxed more powerful than ever. "On no account can Prince Daemon be allowed to ascend to the Iron Throne," the Hand wrote his brother, Lord of Oldtown. "He would be a second Maegor the Cruel, or worse." It was Ser Otto's wish (then) that Princess Rhaenyra succeed her father. "Better the Realm's Delight than Lord Flea Bottom," he wrote. Nor was he alone in his opinion. Yet his party faced a formidable hurdle. If the precedent set by the Great Council of 101 was followed, a male claimant must prevail over a female. In the absence of a trueborn son, the king's brother would come before the king's daughter, as Baelon had come before Rhaenys in 92 AC.

As for the king's own views, all the chronicles agree that King Viserys hated dissension. Though far from blind to his brother's flaws, he cherished his memories of the free-spirited, adventurous boy that Daemon had been. His daughter was his life's great joy, he often said, but a brother is a brother. Time and time again he strove to make peace between Prince Daemon and Ser Otto, but the enmity between the two men roiled endlessly beneath the false smiles they wore at court. When pressed upon the matter, King Viserys would only say that he was certain his queen would soon present him with a son. And in 105 AC, he announced to the court and small council that Queen Aemma was once again with child.

During that same fateful year, Ser Criston Cole was appointed to the Kingsguard to fill the place created by the death of the legendary Ser Ryam Redwyne. Born the son of a steward in service to Lord Dondarrion of Blackhaven, Ser Criston was a comely young knight of three-and-twenty years. He first came to the attention of the court when he won the melee held at Maidenpool in honor of King Viserys's accession. In the final moments of the fight, Ser Criston knocked Dark Sister from Prince Daemon's hand with his morningstar, to the delight of His Grace and the fury of the prince. Afterward, he gave the seven-year-old Princess Rhaenyra the victor's laurel and begged for her favor to wear in the joust. In the lists, he defeated Prince Daemon once again, and unhorsed both of the celebrated Cargyll twins, Ser Arryk and Ser Erryk of the Kingsguard, before falling to Lord Lymond Mallister.

With his pale green eyes, coal black hair, and easy charm, Cole soon became a favorite of all the ladies at court . . . not the least amongst them Rhaenyra Targaryen herself. So smitten was she by the charms of the man she called "my white knight" that Rhaenyra begged her father to name Ser Criston her own personal shield and protector. His Grace indulged her in this, as in so much else. Thereafter Ser Criston always wore her favor in the lists and became a fixture at her side during feasts and frolics.

Not long after Ser Criston donned his white cloak, King Viserys invited Lyonel Strong, Lord of Harrenhal, to join the small council as master of laws. A big man, burly and balding, Lord Strong enjoyed a formidable reputation as a battler. Those who did not know him oft took him for a brute, mistaking his silences and slowness of speech for stupidity. This was far from the truth. Lord Lyonel had studied at the Citadel as a youth, earning six links of his chain before deciding that a maester's life was not for him. He was literate and learned, his knowledge of the laws of the Seven Kingdoms exhaustive. Thrice-wed and thrice a widower, the Lord of Harrenhal brought two maiden daughters and two sons to court with him. The girls became handmaids to Princess Rhaenyra, whilst their elder brother, Ser Harwin Strong, called Breakbones, was made a captain in the gold cloaks. The younger boy, Larys the Clubfoot, joined the king's confessors.

Thus did matters stand in King's Landing late in the year 105 AC, when Queen Aemma was brought to bed in Maegor's Holdfast and died whilst giving birth to the son that Viserys Targaryen had desired for so long. The boy (named Baelon, after the king's father) survived her only by a day, leaving king and court bereft . . . save perhaps for Prince Daemon, who was observed in a brothel on the Street of Silk, making drunken japes with his highborn cronies about the "heir for a day." When word of this got back to the king (legend says that it was the whore sitting in Daemon's lap who informed on him, but evidence suggests it was actually one of his drinking companions, a captain in the gold cloaks eager for advancement), Viserys became livid. His Grace had finally had a surfeit of his ungrateful brother and his ambitions.

Once his mourning for his wife and son had run its course, the king moved swiftly to resolve the long-simmering issue of the succession. Disregarding the precedents set by King Jaehaerys in 92 and the Great Council in 101, Viserys declared his daughter, Rhaenyra, to be his rightful heir, and named her Princess of Dragonstone. In a lavish ceremony at King's Landing, hundreds of lords did obeisance to the Realm's Delight as she sat at her father's feet at the base of the Iron Throne, swearing to honor and defend her right of succession.

Prince Daemon was not amongst them, however. Furious at the king's decree, the prince quit King's Landing, resigning from the City Watch. He went first to Dragonstone, taking his paramour Mysaria with him upon the back of his dragon Caraxes, the lean red beast the smallfolk called the Blood Wyrm. There he remained for half a year, during which time he got Mysaria with child.

When he learned that his concubine was pregnant, Prince Daemon presented her with a dragon's egg, but in this he again went too far and woke his brother's wroth. King Viserys commanded him to return the egg, send his whore away, and return to his lawful wife, or else be attainted as a traitor. The prince obeyed, though with ill grace, dispatching Mysaria (eggless) back to Lys, whilst he himself flew to Runestone in the Vale and the unwelcome company of his "bronze bitch." But Mysaria lost her child during a storm on the narrow sea. When word reached Prince Daemon he spoke no syllable of grief, but his heart hardened against the king, his brother. Thereafter he spoke of King Viserys only with disdain, and began to brood day and night on the succession.

Though Princess Rhaenyra had been proclaimed her father's successor, there were many in the realm, at court and beyond it, who still hoped that Viserys might father a male heir, for the Young King was not yet thirty. Grand Maester Runciter was the first to urge His Grace to remarry, even suggesting a suitable choice: the Lady Laena Velaryon, who had just turned twelve. A fiery young maiden, freshly flowered, Lady Laena had inherited the beauty of a true Targaryen from her mother, Rhaenys, and a bold, adventurous spirit from her father, the Sea Snake. As Lord Corlys loved to sail, Laena loved to fly, and had claimed for her own no less a mount than mighty Vhagar, the oldest and largest of the Targaryen dragons since the passing of the Black Dread in 94 AC. By taking the girl to wife, the king could heal the rift that had grown up between the Iron Throne and Driftmark, Runciter pointed out. And Laena would surely make a splendid queen.

Viserys I Targaryen was not the strongest-willed of kings, it must be said; always amiable and anxious to please, he relied greatly on the counsel of the men around him, and did as they bade more oft than not. In this instance, however, His Grace had his own notion, and no amount of argument would sway him from his course. He would marry again, yes . . . but not to a twelve-year-old girl, and not for reasons of state. Another woman had caught his eye. He announced his intention to wed Lady Alicent of House Hightower, the clever and lovely eighteen-year-old daughter of the King's Hand, the girl who had read to King Jaehaerys as he lay dying.

The Hightowers of Oldtown were an ancient and noble family, of impeccable lineage; there could be no possible objection to the king's choice of bride. Even so, there were those who murmured that the Hand had risen above himself, that he had brought his daughter to court with this in mind. A few even cast doubt on Lady Alicent's virtue, suggesting she had welcomed King Viserys into her bed even before Queen Aemma's death. (These calumnies were never proved, though Mushroom repeats them in his *Testimony* and goes so far as to claim that reading was not the only service Lady Alicent performed for the Old King in his bedchamber.) In the Vale, Prince Daemon reportedly whipped the serving man who brought the news to him within an inch of his life. Nor was the Sea Snake pleased when word reached Driftmark. House Velaryon had been passed over once again, his daughter, Laena, scorned just as his son, Laenor, had been scorned by the Great Council, and his wife by the Old King back in 92 AC. Only Lady Laena herself seemed untroubled. "Her ladyship shows far more interest in flying than in boys," the maester at High Tide wrote to the Citadel.

When King Viserys took Alicent Hightower to wife in 106 AC, House Velaryon was notable for its absence. Princess Rhaenyra poured for her stepmother at the feast, and Queen Alicent kissed her and named her "daughter." The princess was amongst the women who disrobed the king and delivered him to the bedchamber of his bride. Laughter and love ruled the Red Keep that night . . . whilst across Blackwater Bay, Lord Corlys the Sea Snake welcomed the king's brother, Prince Daemon, to a war council. The prince had suffered all he could stand of the Vale of Arryn, Runestone, and his lady wife. "Dark Sister was made for nobler tasks than slaughtering sheep," he is reported to have told the Lord of the Tides. "She has a thirst for blood." But it was not rebellion that the prince had in mind; he saw another path to power.

The Stepstones, the chain of rocky islands between Dorne and the Disputed Lands of Essos, had long been a haunt of outlaws, exiles, wreckers, and pirates. Of themselves the isles were of little worth, but placed as they were, they controlled the sea lanes to and from the narrow sea, and merchant ships passing through those waters were often preyed on by their inhabitants. Still, for centuries such depredations had remained no more than a nuisance.

Ten years earlier, however, the Free Cities of Lys, Myr, and Tyrosh had put aside their ancient enmities to make common cause in a war against Volantis. After defeating the Volantenes in the Battle of the Borderland, the three victorious cities had entered into an "eternal alliance," and formed a strong new power: the Triarchy, better known in Westeros as the Kingdom of the Three Daughters (as each of the Free Cities considered itself a daughter of Valyria of old), or, more rudely, the Kingdom of the Three Whores (though this "kingdom" was without a king, being governed by a council of thirty-three magisters). Once Volantis sued for peace and withdrew from the Disputed Lands, the Three Daughters had turned their gaze westward, sweeping over the Stepstones with their combined armies and fleets under the command of the Myrish prince admiral, Craghas Drahar, who earned the sobriquet Craghas Crabfeeder when he staked out hundreds of captured pirates on the wet sands, to drown beneath the rising tide.

The conquest and annexation of the Stepstones by the Kingdom of the Three Daughters at first met with only approval from the lords of Westeros. Order had replaced chaos, and if the Three Daughters demanded a toll of any ship passing through their waters, that seemed a small price to pay to be rid of the pirates.

The avarice of Craghas Crabfeeder and his partners in conquest soon turned feelings against them, however; the toll was raised again, and yet again, soon becoming so ruinous that merchants who had once paid gladly now sought to slip past the galleys of the Triarchy as once they had the pirates. Drahar and his Lysene and Tyroshi co-admirals seemed to be vying with each other to see who was the greediest, men complained. The Lyseni became especially loathed, for they claimed more than coin from passing ships, taking off women, girls, and comely young boys to serve in their pleasure gardens and pillow houses. (Amongst those thus enslaved was Lady Johanna Swann, a fifteen-year-old niece of the Lord of Stonehelm. When her infamously niggardly uncle refused to pay the ransom, she was sold to a pillow house, where she rose to become the celebrated courtesan known as the Black Swan, and ruler of Lys in all but name. Alas, her tale, however fascinating, has no bearing upon our present history.)

Of all the lords of Westeros, none suffered so much from these practices as Corlys Velaryon, Lord of the Tides, whose fleets had made him as wealthy and powerful as any man in the Seven Kingdoms. The Sea Snake was determined to put an end to the Triarchy's rule over the Stepstones, and in Daemon Targaryen he found a willing partner, eager for the gold and glory that victory in war would bring him. Shunning the king's wedding, they laid their plans in High Tide on the isle Driftmark. Lord Velaryon would command the fleet, Prince Daemon the army. They would be greatly outnumbered by the forces of the Three Daughters . . . but the prince would also bring to battle the fires of his dragon, Caraxes, the Blood Wyrm.

It is not our purpose here to recount the details of the private war Daemon Targaryen and Corlys Velaryon waged on the Stepstones. Suffice it to say that the fighting began in 106 AC. Prince Daemon had little difficulty assembling an army of landless adventurers and second sons, and won many victories during the first two years of the conflict. In 108 AC, when at last he came face-to-face with Craghas Crabfeeder, he slew him single-handed and cut off his head with Dark Sister.

King Viserys, doubtless pleased to be rid of his troublesome brother, supported his efforts with regular infusions of gold, and by 109 AC Daemon Targaryen and his army of sellswords and cutthroats controlled all but two of the islands, and the Sea Snake's fleets had taken firm control of the waters between. During this brief moment of victory, Prince Daemon declared himself King of the Stepstones and the Narrow Sea, and Lord Corlys placed a crown upon his head . . . but their "kingdom" was far from secure. The next year, the Kingdom of the Three Daughters dispatched a fresh invasion force under the command of a devious Tyroshi captain named Racallio Ryndoon, surely one of the most curious and flamboyant rogues in the annals of history, and Dorne joined the war in alliance with the Triarchy. Fighting resumed.

Though the Stepstones were engulfed in blood and fire, King Viserys and his court remained unperturbed. "Let Daemon play at war," His Grace is reported to have said, "it keeps him out of trouble." Viserys was a man of peace, and during these years King's Landing was an endless round of feasts, balls, and tourneys, where mummers and singers heralded

the birth of each new Targaryen princeling. Queen Alicent had soon proved to be as fertile as she was pretty. In 107 AC, she bore the king a healthy son, naming him Aegon, after the Conqueror. Two years later, she produced a daughter for the king, Helaena; in 110 AC, she bore him a second son, Aemond, who was said to be half the size of his elder brother, but twice as fierce.

Yet Princess Rhaenyra continued to sit at the foot of the Iron Throne when her father held court, and His Grace began bringing her to meetings of the small council as well. Though many lords and knights sought her favor, the princess had eyes only for Ser Criston Cole, the young champion of the Kingsguard and her constant companion. "Ser Criston protects the princess from her enemies, but who protects the princess from Ser Criston?" Queen Alicent asked one day at court. The amity between Her Grace and her stepdaughter had proved short-lived, for both Rhaenyra and Alicent aspired to be the first lady of the realm . . . and though the queen had given the king not one but two male heirs, Viserys had done nothing to change the order of succession. The Princess of Dragonstone remained his acknowledged heir, with half the lords of Westeros sworn to defend her rights. Those who asked, "What of the ruling of the Great Council of 101?" found their words falling on deaf ears. The matter had been decided, so far as King Viserys was concerned; it was not an issue His Grace cared to revisit.

Still, questions persisted, not the least from Queen Alicent herself. Loudest amongst her supporters was her father, Ser Otto Hightower, Hand of the King. Pushed too far on the matter, in 109 AC Viserys stripped Ser Otto of his chain of office and named in his place the taciturn Lord of Harrenhal, Lyonel Strong. "This Hand will not hector me," His Grace proclaimed.

Even after Ser Otto had returned to Oldtown, a "queen's party" still existed at court; a group of powerful lords friendly to Queen Alicent and supportive of the rights of her sons. Against them was pitted the "party of the princess." King Viserys loved both his wife and daughter, and hated conflict and contention. He strove all his days to keep the peace between his women, and to please both with gifts and gold and honors. So long as he lived and ruled and kept the balance, the feasts and tourneys continued as before, and peace prevailed throughout the realm . . . though there were some, sharp-eyed, who observed the dragons of one party snapping and spitting flame at the dragons of the other party whenever they chanced to pass near each other.

In 111 AC, a great tourney was held at King's Landing on the fifth anniversary of the king's marriage to Queen Alicent. At the opening feast, the queen wore a green gown, whilst the princess dressed dramatically in Targaryen red and black. Note was taken, and thereafter it became the custom to refer to "greens" and "blacks" when talking of the queen's party and the party of the princess, respectively. In the tourney itself, the blacks had much the better of it when Ser Criston Cole, wearing Princess Rhaenyra's favor, unhorsed all of the queen's champions, including two of her cousins and her youngest brother, Ser Gwayne Hightower.

Yet one was there who wore neither green nor black, but rather gold and silver. Prince Daemon had at last returned to court. Wearing a crown and styling himself King of the Narrow Sea, he appeared unannounced in the skies above King's Landing on his dragon, circling thrice above the

tourney grounds . . . but when at last he came to earth, he knelt before his brother and offered up his crown as a token of his love and fealty. Viserys returned the crown and kissed Daemon on both cheeks, welcoming him home, and the lords and commons sent up a thunderous cheer as the sons of the Spring Prince were reconciled. Amongst those cheering loudest was Princess Rhaenyra, who was thrilled at the return of her favorite uncle and begged him to stay awhile.

This much is known. As to what happened afterward, here we must look to our more dubious chroniclers. Prince Daemon did remain at King's Landing for half a year, that is beyond dispute. He even resumed his seat on the small council, according to Grand Maester Runciter, but neither age nor exile had changed his nature. Daemon soon took up again with old companions from the gold cloaks, and returned to the establishments along the Street of Silk where he had been such a valued patron. Though he treated Queen Alicent with all the courtesy due her station, there was no warmth between them, and men said that the prince was notably cool toward her children, especially his nephews, Aegon and Aemond, whose birth had pushed him still lower in the order of succession.

Princess Rhaenyra was a different matter. Daemon spent long hours in her company, enthralling her with tales of his journeys and battles. He gave her pearls and silks and books and a jade tiara said once to have belonged to the Empress of Leng, read poems to her, dined with her, hawked with her, sailed with her, entertained her by making mock of the greens at court, the "lickspittles" fawning over Queen Alicent and her children. He praised her beauty, declaring her to be the fairest maid in all the Seven Kingdoms. Uncle and niece began to fly together almost daily, racing Syrax against Caraxes to Dragonstone and back.

Here is where our sources diverge. Grand Maester Runciter says only that the brothers quarreled again, and Prince Daemon departed King's Landing to return to the Stepstones and his wars. Of the cause of the quarrel, he does not speak. Others assert that it was at Queen Alicent's urging that Viserys sent Daemon away. But Septon Eustace and Mushroom tell another tale . . . or rather, two such tales, each different from the other. Eustace, the less salacious of the two, writes that Prince Daemon seduced his niece the princess and claimed her maidenhood. When the lovers were discovered abed together by Ser Arryk Cargyll of the Kingsguard and brought before the king, Rhaenyra insisted she was in love with her uncle and pleaded with her father for leave to marry him. King Viserys would not hear of it, however, and reminded his daughter that Prince Daemon already had a wife. In his wroth, he confined his daughter to her chambers, told his brother to depart, and commanded both of them never to speak of what had happened.

The tale as told by Mushroom is far more depraved, as is oft the case with his *Testimony*. According to the dwarf, it was Ser Criston Cole that the princess yearned for, not Prince Daemon, but Ser Criston was a true knight, noble and chaste and mindful of his vows, and though he was in her company day and night, he had never so much as kissed her, nor made any declaration of his love. "When he looks at you, he sees the little girl you were, not the woman you've become," Daemon told his niece, "but I can teach you how to make him see you as a woman."

He began by giving her kissing lessons, if Mushroom can be believed. From there the prince went on to show his niece how best to touch a man to bring him pleasure, an exercise that sometimes involved Mushroom himself and his alleged enormous member. Daemon taught the girl to disrobe enticingly, suckled at her teats to make them larger and more sensitive, and flew with her on dragonback to lonely rocks in Blackwater Bay, where they could disport naked all day unobserved, and the princess could practice the art of pleasuring a man with her mouth. At night he would smuggle her from her rooms dressed as a page boy and take her secretly to brothels on the Street of Silk, where the princess could observe men and women in the act of love and learn more of these "womanly arts" from the harlots of King's Landing.

Just how long these lessons continued Mushroom does not say, but unlike Septon Eustace, he insists that Princess Rhaenyra remained a maiden, for she wished to preserve her innocence as a gift for her beloved. But when at last she approached her white knight, using all she had learned, Ser Criston was horrified and spurned her. The whole tale soon came out, in no small part thanks to Mushroom himself. King Viserys at first refused to believe a word of it, until Prince Daemon confirmed the tale was true. "Give the girl to me to wife," he purportedly told his brother. "Who else would take her now?" Instead King Viserys sent him into exile, never to return to the Seven Kingdoms on pain of death. (Lord Strong, the King's Hand, argued that the prince should be put to death immediately as a traitor, but Septon Eustace reminded His Grace that no man is as accursed as the kinslayer.)

Of the aftermath, these things are certain. Daemon Targaryen returned to the Stepstones and resumed his struggle for those barren storm-swept rocks. Grand Maester Runciter and Ser Harrold Westerling both died in 112 AC. Ser Criston Cole was named the Lord Commander of the Kingsguard in Ser Harrold's place, and the archmaesters of the Citadel sent Maester Mellos to the Red Keep to take up the Grand Maester's chain and duties. Elsewise, King's Landing returned to its customary tranquillity for the best part of two years . . . until 113 AC, when Princess Rhaenyra turned sixteen, took possession of Dragonstone as her own seat, and married.

Long before any man had reason to doubt her innocence, the question of selecting a suitable consort for Rhaenyra had been of concern to King Viserys and his council. Great lords and dashing knights fluttered around her like moths around a flame, vying for her favor. When Rhaenyra visited the Trident in 112, the sons of Lord Bracken and Lord Blackwood fought a duel over her, and a younger son of House Frey made so bold as to ask openly for her hand (Fool Frey, he was called thereafter). In the west, Ser Jason Lannister and his twin, Ser Tyland, vied for her during a feast at Casterly Rock. The sons of Lord Tully of Riverrun, Lord Tyrell of Highgarden, Lord Oakheart of Old Oak, and Lord Tarly of Horn Hill paid court to the princess, as did the Hand's eldest son, Ser Harwin Strong. Breakbones, as he was called, was heir to Harrenhal, and said to be the strongest man in the Seven Kingdoms. Viserys even talked of wedding Rhaenyra to the Prince of Dorne, as a way of bringing the Dornish into the realm.

Queen Alicent had her own candidate: her eldest son, Prince Aegon, Rhaenyra's half-brother. But Aegon was a boy, the princess ten years his elder. Moreover, the two half-siblings had never gotten on well. "All the more reason to bind them together in marriage," the queen argued. Viserys did not agree. "The boy is Alicent's own blood," he told Lord Strong. "She wants him on the throne."

The best choice, king and small council finally agreed, would be Rhaenyra's cousin Laenor Velaryon. Though the Great Council of 101 had ruled against his claim, the Velaryon boy remained a grandson of Prince Aemon Targaryen of hallowed memory, a great-grandson of the Old King himself. Such a match would unite and strengthen the royal bloodline, and regain the Iron Throne the friendship of the Sea Snake with his powerful fleet.

One objection was raised: Laenor Velaryon was now nineteen years of age, yet had never shown any interest in women. Instead he surrounded himself with handsome squires of his own age, and was said to prefer their company. But Grand Maester Mellos dismissed this concern out of hand. "What of it?" he said. "I do not like the taste of fish, but when fish is served, I eat it." Thus was the match decided.

King and council had neglected to consult the princess, however, and Rhaenyra proved to be very much her father's daughter, with her own notions about whom she wished to wed. The princess knew much and more about Laenor Velaryon, and had no wish to be his bride. "My half-brothers would be more to his taste," she told the king. (The princess always took care to refer to Queen Alicent's sons as half-brothers, never as brothers.) And though His Grace reasoned with her, pleaded with her, shouted at her, and called her an ungrateful daughter, no words of his could budge her . . . until the king brought up the question of succession. What a king had done, a king could undo, Viserys pointed out. She would wed as he commanded, or he would make her half-brother Aegon his heir in place of her. At this the princess's will gave way. Septon Eustace says she fell at her father's knees and begged for his forgiveness, Mushroom that she spat in her father's face, but both agree that in the end she consented to be married.

And here again our sources differ. That night, Septon Eustace reports, Ser Criston Cole slipped into the princess's bedchamber to confess his love for her. He told Rhaenyra that he had a ship waiting on the bay, and begged her to flee with him across the narrow sea. They would be wed in

Tyrosh or Old Volantis, where her father's writ did not run, and no one would care that Ser Criston had betrayed his vows as a member of the Kingsguard. His prowess with sword and morningstar was such that he did not doubt he could find some merchant prince to take him into service. But Rhaenyra refused him. She was the blood of the dragon, she reminded him, and meant for more than to live out her life as the wife of a common sellsword. And if he could set aside his Kingsguard vows, why would marriage vows mean any more to him?

Mushroom tells a very different tale. In his version, it was Princess Rhaenyra who went to Ser Criston, not him to her. She found him alone in White Sword Tower, barred the door, and slipped off her cloak to reveal her nakedness underneath. "I saved my maidenhead for you," she told him. "Take it now, as proof of my love. It will mean little and less to my betrothed, and perhaps when he learns that I am not chaste he will refuse me."

Yet for all her beauty, her entreaties fell on deaf ears, for Ser Criston was a man of honor and true to his vows. Even when Rhaenyra used the arts she had learned from her uncle Daemon, Cole would not be swayed. Scorned and furious, the princess donned her cloak again and swept out into the night . . . where she chanced to encounter Ser Harwin Strong, returning from a night of revelry in the stews of the city. Breakbones had long desired the princess, and lacked Ser Criston's scruples. It was he who took Rhaenyra's innocence, shedding her maiden's blood upon the sword of his manhood . . . according to Mushroom, who claims to have found them in bed at break of day.

However it happened, whether the princess scorned the knight or he her, from that day forward the love that Ser Criston Cole had formerly borne for Rhaenyra Targaryen turned to loathing and disdain, and the man who had hitherto been the princess's constant companion and champion became the most bitter of her foes.

Not long thereafter, Rhaenyra set sail for Driftmark on the *Sea Snake*, accompanied by her handmaids (two of them the daughters of the Hand and sisters to Ser Harwin), the fool Mushroom, and her new champion, none other than Breakbones himself. In 114 AC, Rhaenyra Targaryen, Princess of Dragonstone, took to husband Ser Laenor Velaryon (knighted a fortnight before the wedding, since it was deemed necessary the prince consort be a knight). The bride was seventeen years old, the groom twenty, and all agreed that they made a handsome couple. The wedding was celebrated with seven days of feasts and jousting, the greatest tourney in many a year. Amongst the competitors were Queen Alicent's siblings, five Sworn Brothers of the Kingsguard, Breakbones, and the groom's favorite, Ser Joffrey Lonmouth, known as the Knight of Kisses. When Rhaenyra bestowed her garter on Ser Harwin, her new husband laughed and gave one of his own to Ser Joffrey.

Denied Rhaenyra's favor, Criston Cole turned to Queen Alicent instead. Wearing her token, the young Lord Commander of the Kingsguard defeated all challengers, fighting in a black fury. He left Breakbones with a broken collarbone and a shattered elbow (prompting Mushroom to name him "Brokenbones" thereafter), but it was the Knight of Kisses who felt the fullest measure of his wroth. Cole's favorite weapon was the morningstar, and the blows he rained down on Ser Laenor's champion cracked his helm and left him senseless in the mud. Borne bloody from the field, Ser Joffrey died without recovering consciousness six days later. Mushroom tells us that Ser Laenor spent every hour of those days at his bedside and wept bitterly when the Stranger claimed him.

King Viserys was most wroth as well; a joyous celebration had become the occasion of grief and recrimination. It was said that Queen Alicent did not share his displeasure, however; soon after, she asked that Ser Criston Cole be made her personal protector. The coolness between the king's wife and the king's daughter was plain for all to see; even envoys from the Free Cities made note of it in letters sent back to Pentos, Braavos, and Old Volantis.

Ser Laenor returned to Driftmark thereafter, leaving many to wonder if his marriage had ever been consummated. The princess remained at court, surrounded by her friends and admirers. Ser Criston Cole was not amongst them, having gone over entirely to the queen's party, the greens, but the massive and redoubtable Breakbones (or Brokenbones, as Mushroom had it) filled his place, becoming the foremost of the blacks, ever at Rhaenyra's side at feast and ball and hunt. Her husband raised no objec-

tions. Ser Laenor preferred the comforts of High Tide, where he soon found a new favorite in a household knight named Ser Qarl Correy.

Thereafter, though he joined his wife for important court events where his presence was expected, Ser Laenor spent most of his days apart from the princess. Septon Eustace says they shared a bed no more than a dozen times. Mushroom concurs, but adds that Qarl Correy oft shared that bed as well; it aroused the princess to watch the men disporting with one another, he tells us, and from time to time the two would include her in their pleasures. Yet Mushroom contradicts himself, for elsewhere in his *Testimony* he claims that the princess would leave her husband with his lover on such nights, and seek her own solace in the arms of Harwin Strong.

Whatever the truth of these tales, it was soon announced that the princess was with child. Born in the waning days of 114 AC, the boy was a large, strapping lad, with brown hair, brown eyes, and a pug nose. (Ser Laenor had the aquiline nose, silver-white hair, and purple eyes that bespoke his Valyrian blood.) Laenor's wish to name the child Joffrey was overruled by his father, Lord Corlys. Instead the child was given a traditional Velaryon name: Jacaerys (friends and brothers would call him Jace).

The court was still rejoicing over the birth of the princess's child when her stepmother, Queen Alicent, also went into labor, delivering Viserys his third son, Daeron . . . whose coloring, unlike that of Jace, testified to his dragon blood. By royal command, the infants Jacaerys Velaryon and Daeron Targaryen shared a wet nurse until weaned. It was said that the king hoped to prevent any enmity between the two boys by raising them as milk brothers. If so, his hopes proved to be sadly forlorn.

A year later, in 115 AC, there came a tragic mishap, of the sort that shapes the destiny of kingdoms: the "bronze bitch" of Runestone, Lady Rhea Royce, fell from her horse whilst hawking and cracked her skull upon a stone. She lingered for nine days before finally feeling well enough to leave her bed . . . only to collapse and die within an hour of rising. A raven was duly sent to Storm's End, and Lord Baratheon dispatched a messenger by ship to Bloodstone, where Prince Daemon was still struggling to defend his meagre kingdom against the men of the Triarchy and their Dornish allies. Daemon flew at once for the Vale. "To put my wife to rest," he said, though more like it was in the hopes of laying claim to her lands, castles, and incomes. In that he failed; Runestone passed instead to Lady Rhea's nephew, and when Daemon made appeal to the Eyrie, not only was his claim dismissed, but Lady Jeyne warned him that his presence in the Vale was unwelcome.

Flying back to the Stepstones afterward, Prince Daemon landed at Driftmark to make a courtesy call upon his erstwhile partner in conquest, the Sea Snake, and his wife, the Princess Rhaenys. High Tide was one of the few places in the Seven Kingdoms where the king's brother could be confident he would not be turned away. There his eye fell upon Lord Corlys's daughter, Laena, a maid of two-and-twenty, tall, slender, and surpassingly lovely (even Mushroom was taken with her beauty, writing that she "was almost as pretty as her brother"), with a great mane of silver-gold ringlets that fell down past her waist. Laena had been betrothed from the age of twelve to a son of the Sealord of Braavos . . . but the father had died before they could be wed, and the son soon proved a wastrel and a fool, squandering his family's wealth and power before turning up on Driftmark. Lacking a graceful means to rid himself of the embarrassment, but unwilling to proceed with the marriage, Lord Corlys had repeatedly postponed the wedding.

Prince Daemon fell in love with Laena, the singers would have us believe. Men of a more cynical bent believe the prince saw her as a way to check his own descent. Once seen as his brother's heir, he had fallen far down in the line of succession, and neither the greens nor the blacks had a place for him . . . but House Velaryon was powerful enough to defy both parties with impunity. Weary of the Stepstones, and free at last of his "bronze bitch," Daemon Targaryen asked Lord Corlys for his daughter's hand in marriage.

The exiled Braavosi betrothed remained an impediment, but not for long; Daemon mocked him to his face so savagely the boy had no choice but to call him to defend his words with steel. Armed with Dark Sister, the prince made short work of his rival, and wed Lady Laena Velaryon a fortnight later, abandoning his hardscrabble kingdom on the Stepstones. (Five other men followed him as Kings of the Narrow Sea, until the brief and bloody history of that savage sellsword "kingdom" ended for good and all.)

Prince Daemon knew that his brother would not be pleased when he heard of his marriage. Prudently, the prince and his new bride took themselves far from Westeros soon after the wedding, crossing the narrow sea on their dragons. Some said they flew to Valyria, in defiance of the curse that hung over that smoking wasteland, to search out the secrets of the dragonlords of the old Freehold. Mushroom himself reports this as fact in his *Testimony,* but we have abundant evidence that the truth was less romantic. Prince Daemon and Lady Laena flew first to Pentos, where they were feted by the city's prince. The Pentoshi feared the growing power of the Triarchy to the south, and saw Daemon as a valuable ally against the Three Daughters. From there, they crossed the Disputed Lands to Old

Volantis, where they enjoyed a similar warm welcome. Then they flew up the Rhoyne, to visit Qohor and Norvos. In those cities, far removed from the woes of Westeros and the power of the Triarchy, their welcome was less rapturous. Everywhere they went, however, huge crowds turned out for a glimpse of Vhagar and Caraxes.

The dragonriders were once again in Pentos when Lady Laena learned she was with child. Eschewing further flight, Prince Daemon and his wife settled in a manse outside the city walls as a guest of a Pentoshi magister, until such time as the babe was born.

Meanwhile, back in Westeros, Princess Rhaenyra had given birth to a second son late in the year 115 AC. The child was named Lucerys (Luke for short). Septon Eustace tells us that both Ser Laenor and Ser Harwin were at Rhaenyra's bedside for his birth. Like his brother, Jace, Luke had brown eyes and a healthy head of brown hair, rather than the silver-gilt hair of Targaryen princelings, but he was a large and lusty lad, and King Viserys was delighted with him when the child was presented at court.

These feelings were not shared by his queen. "Do keep trying," Queen Alicent told Ser Laenor, according to Mushroom, "soon or late, you may get one who looks like you." And the rivalry between the greens and blacks grew deeper, finally reaching the point where the queen and the princess could scarce suffer each other's presence. Thereafter Queen Alicent kept to the Red Keep, whilst the princess spent her days on Dragonstone, attended by her ladies, Mushroom, and her champion, Ser Harwin Strong. Her husband, Ser Laenor, was said to visit "frequently."

In 116 AC, in the Free City of Pentos, Lady Laena gave birth to twin daughters, Prince Daemon's first trueborn children. Prince Daemon named the girls Baela (after his father) and Rhaena (after her mother). The babes were small and sickly, alas, but both had fine features, silver-white hair, and purple eyes. When they were half a year old, and stronger, the girls and their mother sailed to Driftmark, whilst Daemon flew ahead with both dragons. From High Tide, he sent a raven to his brother in King's Landing, informing His Grace of the birth of his nieces and begging leave to present the girls at court to receive his royal blessing. Though his Hand and small council argued heatedly against it, Viserys consented, for the king still loved the brother who had been the companion of his youth. "Daemon is a father now," he told Grand Maester Mellos. "He will have changed." Thus were the sons of Baelon Targaryen reconciled for the second time.

In 117 AC, on Dragonstone, Princess Rhaenyra bore yet another son. Ser Laenor was at last permitted to name a child after his fallen friend, Ser Joffrey Lonmouth. Joffrey Velaryon was as big and red-faced and healthy as his brothers, but like them he had brown eyes, brown hair, and features that some at court called "common." The whispering began again. Amongst the greens, it was an article of faith that the father of Rhaenyra's sons was not her husband, Laenor, but her champion, Harwin Strong. Mushroom says as much in his *Testimony* and Grand Maester Mellos hints at it, whilst Septon Eustace raises the rumors only to dismiss them.

Whatever the truth of these allegations, there was never any doubt that King Viserys still meant for his daughter to follow him upon the Iron Throne, and her sons to follow her in turn. By royal decree, each of the Velaryon boys was presented with a dragon's egg whilst in the cradle. Those who doubted the paternity of Rhaenyra's sons whispered that the eggs would never hatch, but the birth in turn of three young dragons gave the lie to their words. The hatchlings were named Vermax, Arrax, and Tyraxes. And Septon Eustace tells us that His Grace sat Jace upon his knee atop the Iron Throne as he was holding court, and was heard to say, "One day this will be your seat, lad."

Childbirth exacted a toll on the princess; the weight that Rhaenyra gained during her pregnancies never entirely left her, and by the time her youngest boy was born, she had grown stout and thick of waist, the beauty of her girlhood a fading memory, though she was but twenty years of age. According to Mushroom, this only served to deepen her resentment of her stepmother, Queen Alicent, who remained slender and graceful at half again her age.

The sins of the fathers are oft visited on the sons, wise men have said; and so it is for the sins of mothers as well. The enmity between Queen Alicent and Princess Rhaenyra was passed on to their sons, and the queen's three boys, the Princes Aegon, Aemond, and Daeron, grew to be bitter rivals of their Velaryon nephews, resentful of them for having stolen what they regarded as their birthright: the Iron Throne itself. Though all six boys attended the same feasts, balls, and revels, and sometimes trained together in the yard under the same master-at-arms and studied under the same maesters, this enforced closeness only served to feed their mutual mislike, rather than binding them together as brothers.

Whilst Princess Rhaenyra misliked her stepmother, Queen Alicent, she became fond and more than fond of her good-sister Lady Laena. With Driftmark and Dragonstone so close, Daemon and Laena oft visited with the princess, and her with them. Many a time they flew together on their dragons, and the princess's she-dragon Syrax produced several clutches of eggs. In 118 AC, with the blessing of King Viserys, Rhaenyra announced the betrothal of her two eldest sons to the daughters of Prince Daemon and Lady Laena. Jacaerys was four and Lucerys three, the girls two. And in 119 AC, when Laena found she was with child again, Rhaenyra flew to Driftmark to attend her during the birth.

And so it was that the princess was at her good-sister's side on the third day of that accursed year 120 AC, the Year of the Red Spring. A day and a night of labor left Laena Velaryon pale and weak, but finally she gave birth to the son Prince Daemon had so long desired—but the babe was twisted and malformed, and died within the hour. Nor did his mother long survive him. Her grueling labor had drained all of Lady Laena's strength, and grief weakened her still further, making her helpless before the onset of childbed fever. As her condition steadily worsened, despite the best efforts of Driftmark's young maester, Prince Daemon flew to Dragonstone and brought back Princess Rhaenyra's own maester, an older and more experienced man renowned for his skills as a healer. Sadly, Maester Gerardys came too late. After three days of delirium, Lady Laena passed from this mortal coil. She was but twenty-seven. During her final hour, it is said, Lady Laena rose from her bed, pushed away the septas praying over her, and made her way from her room, intent on reaching Vhagar that she might fly one last time before she died. Her strength failed her on the tower steps, however, and it was there she collapsed and died. Her husband, Prince Daemon, carried her back to her bed. Afterward, Mushroom tells us, Princess Rhaenyra sat vigil with him over Lady Laena's corpse, and comforted him in his grief.

Lady Laena's death was the first tragedy of 120 AC, but it would not be the last. For this was to be a year when many of the long-simmering tensions and jealousies that had plagued the Seven Kingdoms finally came to a boil, a year when many and more would have reason to wail and grieve and rend their garments . . . though none more than the Sea Snake, Lord Corlys Velaryon, and his noble wife, Princess Rhaenys, she who might have been a queen.

The Lord of the Tides and his lady were still in mourning for their beloved daughter when the Stranger came again, to carry off their son. Ser Laenor Velaryon, husband to the Princess Rhaenyra and the putative father of her children, was slain whilst attending a fair in Spicetown, stabbed to death by his friend and companion Ser Qarl Correy. The two men had been quarreling loudly before blades were drawn, merchants at the fair told Lord Velaryon when he came to collect his son's body. Correy had fled by then, wounding several men who tried to hinder him. Some claimed a ship had been waiting for him offshore. He was never seen again.

The circumstances of the murder remain a mystery to this day. Grand Maester Mellos writes only that Ser Laenor was killed by one of his own household knights after a quarrel. Septon Eustace provides us with the killer's name and declares jealousy the motive for the slaying; Laenor Velaryon had grown weary of Ser Qarl's companionship and had grown enamored of a new favorite, a handsome young squire of six-and-ten. Mushroom, as always, favors the most sinister theory, suggesting that Prince Daemon paid Qarl Correy to dispose of Princess Rhaenyra's husband, arranged for a ship to carry him away, then cut his throat and fed him to the sea. A household knight of relatively low birth, Correy was known to have a lord's tastes and a peasant's purse, and was given to extravagant wagering besides, which lends a certain credence to the fool's version of events. Yet there was no shred of proof, then or now, though the Sea Snake offered a reward of ten thousand golden dragons for any man who could lead him to Ser Qarl Correy, or deliver the killer to a father's vengeance.

Even this was not the end of the tragedies that would mark that dreadful year. The next occurred at High Tide after Ser Laenor's funeral, when king and court made the journey to Driftmark to bear witness at his pyre, many on the backs of their dragons. (So many dragons were present that Septon Eustace wrote that Driftmark had become the new Valyria.)

The cruelty of children is known to all. Prince Aegon Targaryen was thirteen, Princess Helaena eleven, Prince Aemond ten, and Prince Daeron six. Both Aegon and Helaena were dragonriders. Helaena now flew Dreamfyre, the she-dragon who had once carried Rhaena, Maegor the Cruel's "Black Bride," whilst her brother Aegon's young Sunfyre was said to be the most beautiful dragon ever seen upon the earth. Even Prince Daeron had a dragon, a lovely blue she-dragon named Tessarion, though he had yet to ride. Only the middle son, Prince Aemond, remained dragonless, but His Grace had hopes of rectifying that, and had put forward the notion that perhaps the court might sojourn at Dragonstone after the funeral. A wealth of dragon's eggs could be found beneath the Dragonmont, and several young hatchlings as well. Prince Aemond could have his choice, "if the lad is bold enough."

Even at ten, Aemond Targaryen did not lack for boldness. The king's gibe stung, and he resolved not to wait for Dragonstone. What did he want with some puny hatchling, or some stupid egg? Right there at High Tide was a dragon worthy of him: Vhagar, the oldest, largest, most terrible dragon in the world.

Even for a son of House Targaryen, there are always dangers in approaching a dragon, particularly an old, bad-tempered dragon who has recently lost her rider. His father and mother would never allow him to go near Vhagar, Aemond knew, much less try to ride her. So he made certain they did not know, sliding from his bed at dawn whilst they still slept and stealing down to the outer yard where Vhagar and the other dragons were fed and stabled. The prince had hoped to mount Vhagar in secrecy, but as he crept up to the dragon a boy's voice rang out. "You stay away from her!"

The voice belonged to the youngest of his half-nephews, Joffrey Velaryon, a boy of three. Always an early riser, Joff had sneaked down from his bed to see his own young dragon, Tyraxes. Afraid that the boy would raise the alarm, Prince Aemond shouted at him to be quiet, then shoved him backward into a pile of dragon droppings. As Joff began to bawl, Aemond raced to Vhagar and clambered up onto her back. Later he would say that he was so afraid of being caught that he forgot to be frightened of being burned to death and eaten.

Call it boldness, call it madness, call it fortune or the will of the gods or the caprice of dragons. Who can know the mind of such a beast? We do know this: Vhagar roared, lurched to her feet, shook violently . . . then snapped her chains and flew. And the boy prince Aemond Targaryen became a dragonrider, circling twice around the towers of High Tide before coming down again.

But when he landed, Rhaenyra's sons were waiting for him.

Joffrey had run to get his brothers when Aemond took to the sky, and both Jace and Luke had come to his call. The Velaryon princelings were younger than Aemond—Jace was six, Luke five, Joff only three—but there were three of them, and they had armed themselves with wooden swords from the training yard. Now they fell on him with a fury. Aemond fought back, breaking Luke's nose with a punch, then wrenching the sword from Joff's hands and cracking it across the back of Jace's head, driving him to his knees. As the younger boys scrambled back away from him, bloody and bruised, the prince began to mock them, laughing and calling them "the Strongs." Jace at least was old enough to grasp the insult. He flew at Aemond once again, but the older boy began pummeling him savagely . . . until Luke, coming to the rescue of his brother, drew his dagger and slashed Aemond across the face, taking out his right eye. By the time the stableboys finally arrived to pull apart the combatants, the prince was writhing on the ground, howling in pain, and Vhagar was roaring as well.

Afterward, King Viserys tried to make a peace, requiring each of the boys to tender an apology to his rivals on the other side, but these courtesies did not appease their vengeful mothers. Queen Alicent demanded that one of Lucerys Velaryon's eyes should be put out, for the eye he had cost Aemond. Princess Rhaenyra would have none of that, but insisted that Prince Aemond should be questioned "sharply" until he

revealed where he had heard her sons called "Strongs." To so name them was tantamount to saying they were bastards, with no rights of succession . . . and that she herself was guilty of high treason. When pressed by the king, Prince Aemond said it was his brother Aegon who had told him they were Strongs, and Prince Aegon said only, "*Everyone* knows. Just look at them."

King Viserys finally put an end to the questioning, declaring he would hear no more. No eyes would be put out, he decreed . . . but should anyone—"man or woman or child, noble or common or royal"—mock his grandsons as "Strongs" again, their tongues would be pulled out with hot pincers. His Grace further commanded his wife and daughter to kiss and exchange vows of love and affection. But their false smiles and empty words deceived no one but the king. As for the boys, Prince Aemond said later that he lost an eye and gained a dragon that day, and counted it a fair exchange.

To prevent further conflict, and put an end to these "vile rumors and base calumnies," King Viserys further decreed that Queen Alicent and her sons would return with him to court, whilst Princess Rhaenyra confined herself to Dragonstone with her sons. Henceforth Ser Erryk Cargyll of the Kingsguard would serve as her sworn shield, whilst Breakbones returned to Harrenhal.

These rulings pleased no one, Septon Eustace writes. Mushroom demurs: one man at least was thrilled by the decrees, for Dragonstone and Driftmark lay quite close to one another, and this proximity would allow Daemon Targaryen ample opportunity to comfort his niece, Princess Rhaenyra, unbeknownst to the king.

Though Viserys I would reign for nine more years, the bloody seeds of the Dance of the Dragons had already been planted, and 120 AC was the year when they began to sprout. The next to perish were the elder Strongs. Lyonel Strong, Lord of Harrenhal and Hand of the King, accompanied his son and heir Ser Harwin on his return to the great, half-ruined castle on the lakeshore. Shortly after their arrival, a fire broke out in the tower where they were sleeping, and both father and son were killed, along with three of their retainers and a dozen servants.

The cause of the fire was never determined. Some put it down to simple mischance, whilst others muttered that Black Harren's seat was cursed and brought only doom to any man who held it. Many suspected the blaze was set intentionally. Mushroom suggests that the Sea Snake was behind it, as an act of vengeance against the man who had cuckolded his son. Septon Eustace, more plausibly, suspects Prince Daemon, removing a rival for Princess Rhaenyra's affections. Others have put forth the notion that Larys Clubfoot might have been responsible; with his father and elder brother dead, Larys Strong became the Lord of Harrenhal. The most disturbing possibility was advanced by none other than Grand Maester Mellos, who muses that the king himself might have given the command. If Viserys had come to accept that the rumors about the parentage of Rhaenyra's children were true, he might well have wished to remove the man who had dishonored his daughter, lest he somehow reveal the bastardy of her sons. Were that so, Lyonel Strong's death was an unfortunate accident, for his lordship's decision to see his son back to Harrenhal had been unforeseen.

Lord Strong had been the King's Hand, and Viserys had come to rely upon his strength and counsel. His Grace had reached the age of three-and-forty, and had grown quite stout. He no longer had a young man's vigor, and was afflicted by gout, aching joints, back pain, and a tightness in the chest that came and went and oft left him red-faced and short of breath. The governance of the realm was a daunting task; the king needed a strong, capable Hand to shoulder some of his burdens. Briefly he considered sending for Princess Rhaenyra. Who better to rule with him than the daughter he meant to succeed him on the Iron Throne? But that would have meant bringing the princess and her sons back to King's Landing, where more conflict with the queen and her own brood would have been inevitable. He considered his brother as well, until he recalled Prince Daemon's previous stints on the small council. Grand Maester Mellos suggested bringing in some younger man, and put forward several names, but His Grace chose familiarity, and recalled to court Ser Otto Hightower, the queen's father, who had filled the office before for both Viserys and the Old King.

Yet hardly had Ser Otto arrived at the Red Keep to take up the Handship than word reached court that Princess Rhaenyra had remarried, taking to husband her uncle, Daemon Targaryen. The princess was twenty-three, Prince Daemon thirty-nine.

King, court, and commons were all outraged by the news. Neither Daemon's wife nor Rhaenyra's husband had been dead even half a year; to wed again so soon was an insult to their memories, His Grace declared angrily. The marriage had been performed on Dragonstone, suddenly and secretly. Septon Eustace claims that Rhaenyra knew her father would never approve of the match, so she wed in haste to make certain he could not prevent the marriage. Mushroom puts forward a different reason: the princess was once again with child and did not wish to birth a bastard.

And thus that dreadful year 120 AC ended as it begun, with a woman laboring in childbirth. Princess Rhaenyra's pregnancy had a happier outcome than Lady Laena's had. As the year waned, she brought forth a small but robust son, a pale princeling with dark purple eyes and pale silvery hair. She named him Aegon. Prince Daemon had at last a living son of his own blood... and this new prince, unlike his three half-brothers, was plainly a *Targaryen*.

In King's Landing, however, Queen Alicent grew most wroth when she learned the babe had been named Aegon, taking that for a slight against her own son Aegon . . . which, according to *The Testimony of Mushroom,* it most certainly was.*

By all rights, the year 122 AC should have been a joyous one for House Targaryen. Princess Rhaenyra took to the birthing bed once more, and gave her uncle Daemon a second son, named Viserys after his grandsire. The child was smaller and less robust than his brother, Aegon, and his Velaryon half-brothers, but proved to be a most precocious child . . . though, somewhat ominously, the dragon's egg placed in his cradle never hatched. The greens took that for an ill omen, and were not shy about saying as much.

Later that same year, King's Landing celebrated a wedding as well. Following the ancient tradition of House Targaryen, King Viserys wed his son Aegon the Elder to his daughter Helaena. The groom was fifteen years of age; a lazy and somewhat sulky boy, Septon Eustace tells us, but possessed of more than healthy appetites, a glutton at table, given to swilling ale and strongwine and pinching and fondling any serving girl who strayed within his reach. The bride, his sister, was but thirteen. Though plumper and less striking than most Targaryens, Helaena was a pleasant, happy girl, and all agreed she would make a fine mother.

And so she did, and quickly. Barely a year later, in 123 AC, the fourteen-year-old princess gave birth to twins, a boy she named Jaehaerys and a girl called Jaehaera. Prince Aegon had heirs of his own now, the greens at court proclaimed happily. A dragon's egg was placed in the cradle of each child, and two hatchlings soon came forth. Yet all was not well with these new twins. Jaehaera was tiny and slow to grow. She did not cry, she did not smile, she did none of the things a babe was meant to do. Her brother, whilst larger and more robust, was also less perfect than was expected of a Targaryen princeling, boasting six fingers on his left hand, and six toes upon each foot.

A wife and children did little to curb the carnal appetites of Prince

* Hereafter, to avoid confusing the two princes, we will refer to Queen Alicent's son as Aegon the Elder and Princess Rhaenyra's son as Aegon the Younger.

Aegon the Elder. If Mushroom is to be believed, he fathered two bastard children the same year as the twins: a boy on a girl whose maidenhood he won at auction on the Street of Silk, and a girl by one of his mother's maidservants. And in 127 AC, Princess Helaena gave birth to his second son, who was given a dragon's egg and the name Maelor.

Queen Alicent's other sons had been growing older as well. Prince Aemond, despite the loss of his eye, had become a proficient and dangerous swordsman under the tutelage of Ser Criston Cole, but remained a wild and willful child, hot-tempered and unforgiving. His little brother, Prince Daeron, was the most popular of the queen's sons, as clever as he was courteous, and most comely as well. When he turned twelve in 126 AC, Daeron was sent to Oldtown to serve as cupbearer and squire to Lord Hightower.

That same year, across Blackwater Bay, the Sea Snake was stricken by a sudden fever. As he took to his bed, surrounded by maesters, the issue arose as to who should succeed him as Lord of the Tides and Master of Driftmark should the sickness claim him. With both his trueborn children dead, by law his lands and titles should pass to his eldest grandson, Jacaerys . . . but since Jace would presumably ascend the Iron Throne after his mother, Princess Rhaenyra urged her good-father to name instead her second son, Lucerys. Lord Corlys also had half a dozen nephews, however, and the eldest of them, Ser Vaemond Velaryon, protested that the inheritance by rights should pass to him . . . on the grounds that Rhaenyra's sons were bastards sired by Harwin Strong. The princess was not slow in answering this charge. She dispatched Prince Daemon to seize Ser Vaemond, had his head removed, and fed his carcass to her dragon, Syrax.

Even this did not end the matter, however. Ser Vaemond's younger cousins fled to King's Landing with his wife and sons, there to cry for justice and place their claims before the king and queen. King Viserys had grown extremely fat and red of face, and scarce had the strength to mount the steps to the Iron Throne. His Grace heard them out in a stony silence, then ordered their tongues removed, every one. "You were warned," he declared, as they were being dragged away. "I will hear no more of these lies."

Yet as he was descending, His Grace stumbled and reached out to right himself, and sliced his left hand open to the bone on a jagged blade protruding from the throne. Though Grand Maester Mellos washed the cut out with boiled wine and bound up the hand with strips of linen soaked in healing ointments, fever soon followed, and many feared the king might die. Only the arrival of Princess Rhaenyra from Dragonstone turned the tide, for with her came her own healer, Maester Gerardys, who acted swiftly to remove two fingers from His Grace's hand to save his life.

Though much weakened by his ordeal, King Viserys soon resumed the rule. To celebrate his recovery, a feast was held on the first day of 127 AC. The princess and the queen were both commanded to attend, with all their children. In a show of amity, each woman wore the other's color and many declarations of love were made, to the king's great pleasure. Prince Daemon raised a cup to Ser Otto Hightower and thanked him for his leal service as Hand. Ser Otto in turn spoke of the prince's courage, whilst Alicent's children and Rhaenyra's greeted one another with kisses and broke bread together at table. Or so the court chronicles record.

Yet late in the evening, after King Viserys had departed (for His Grace still tired easily), Mushroom tells us that Aemond One-Eye rose to toast his Velaryon nephews, speaking in mock admiration of their brown hair, brown eyes . . . and strength. "I have never known anyone so strong as my sweet nephews," he ended. "So let us drain our cups to these three strong boys." Still later, the fool reports, Aegon the Elder took offense when Jacaerys asked his wife, Helaena, for a dance. Angry words were exchanged, and the two princes might have come to blows if not for the intervention of the Kingsguard. Whether King Viserys was ever informed of these incidents we do not know, but Princess Rhaenyra and her sons returned to their own seat on Dragonstone the next morning.

After the loss of his fingers, Viserys I never sat upon the Iron Throne again. Thereafter he shunned the throne room, preferring to hold court in his solar, and later in his bedchamber, surrounded by maesters, septons, and his faithful fool Mushroom, the only man who could still make him laugh (says Mushroom).

Death visited the court again a short time later, when Grand Maester Mellos collapsed one night whilst he was climbing the serpentine steps. His had always been a moderating voice in council, forever urging calm and compromise whenever issues arose between the blacks and the greens. To the king's distress, however, the passing of the man he called "my trusted friend" only served to provoke a fresh dispute between the factions.

Princess Rhaenyra wanted Maester Gerardys, who had long served her on Dragonstone, elevated to replace Mellos; it was only his healing skills that had saved the king's life when Viserys cut his hand on the throne, she claimed. Queen Alicent, however, insisted that the princess and her maester had mutilated His Grace unnecessarily. Had they not "meddled," she claimed, Grand Maester Mellos would surely have saved the king's fingers as well as his life. She urged the appointment of one Maester Alfador, presently in service at the Hightower. Viserys, beset from both sides, chose neither, reminding both the princess and the queen that the choice was not his to make. The Citadel of Oldtown chose the Grand Maester, not the Crown. In due time, the Conclave bestowed the chain of office upon Archmaester Orwyle, one of their own.

King Viserys did seem to recover some of his old vigor once the new Grand Maester arrived at court. Septon Eustace tells us that this was the result of prayer, but most believed that Orwyle's potions and tinctures were more efficacious than the leechings Mellos had preferred. But such recoveries proved short-lived, and gout, chest pains, and shortness of breath continued to trouble the king. In the final years of his reign, as his health failed, Viserys left ever more of the governance of the realm to his Hand and small council. Perforce we ought to look at the members of that small council on the eve of the great events of 129 AC, for they were to play a large role in all that followed.

The King's Hand remained Ser Otto Hightower, father of the queen and uncle to the Lord of Oldtown. Grand Maester Orwyle was the newest member of the council, and was thought to favor neither blacks nor greens. The Lord Commander of the Kingsguard remained Ser Criston Cole, however, and in him Rhaenyra had a bitter foe. The aged Lord Lyman Beesbury was master of coin, in which capacity he had served almost uninterrupted since the Old King's day. The youngest councillors were the lord admiral and master of ships, Ser Tyland Lannister, brother to the Lord of Casterly Rock, and the Lord Confessor and master of whisperers, Larys Strong, Lord of Harrenhal. Lord Jasper Wylde, master of laws, known amongst the smallfolk as "Ironrod," completed the council. (Lord Wylde's unbending attitudes on matters of law earned him this sobriquet, Septon Eustace says. But Mushroom declares that Ironrod was named for the stiffness of his member, having sired twenty-nine children on four wives before the last died of exhaustion.)

As the Seven Kingdoms welcomed the 129th year after Aegon's Conquest with bonfires, feasts, and bacchanals, King Viserys I Targaryen was growing ever weaker. His chest pains had grown so severe that he could no longer climb a flight of steps, and had to be carried about the Red Keep in a chair. By the second moon of the year, His Grace had lost all appetite and was ruling the realm from his bed . . . when he felt strong enough to rule at all. Most days, he preferred to leave matters of state to his Hand, Ser Otto Hightower. On Dragonstone, meanwhile, Princess Rhaenyra was once again great with child. She too took to her bed.

On the third day of the third moon of 129 AC, Princess Helaena brought her three children to visit with the king in his chambers. The twins, Jaehaerys and Jaehaera, were six years old, their brother, Maelor, only two. His Grace gave the babe a pearl ring off his finger to play with, and told the twins the story of how their great-great-grandsire and namesake Jaehaerys had flown his dragon north to the Wall to defeat a vast host of wildlings, giants, and wargs. Though the children had heard the story a dozen times before, they listened attentively. Afterward the king sent them away, pleading weariness and a tightness in his chest. Then Viserys of House Targaryen, the First of His Name, King of the Andals, the Rhoynar, and the First Men, Lord of the Seven Kingdoms, and Protector of the Realm, closed his eyes and went to sleep.

He never woke. He was fifty-two years old, and had reigned over most of Westeros for twenty-six years.

Then the storm broke, and the dragons danced.

The Dying of the Dragons

The Blacks and the Greens

The Dance of the Dragons is the flowery name bestowed upon the savage internecine struggle for the Iron Throne of Westeros fought between two rival branches of House Targaryen during the years 129 to 131 AC. To characterize the dark, turbulent, bloody doings of this period as a "dance" strikes us as grotesquely inappropriate. No doubt the phrase originated with some singer. "The Dying of the Dragons" would be altogether more fitting, but tradition, time, and Grand Maester Munkun have burned the more poetic usage into the pages of history, so we must dance along with the rest.

There were two principal claimants to the Iron Throne upon the death of King Viserys I Targaryen: his daughter Rhaenyra, the only surviving child of his first marriage, and Aegon, his eldest son by his second wife. Amidst the chaos and carnage brought on by their rivalry, other would-be kings would stake claims as well, strutting about like mummers on a stage for a fortnight or a moon's turn, only to fall as swiftly as they had arisen.

The Dance split the Seven Kingdoms in two, as lords, knights, and smallfolk declared for one side or the other and took up arms against one another. Even House Targaryen itself was divided, when the kith, kin, and children of each of the claimants became embroiled in the fighting. Over the two years of struggle, a terrible toll was taken on the great lords of Westeros, together with their bannermen, knights, and smallfolk. Whilst the dynasty survived, the end of the fighting saw Targaryen power much diminished, and the world's last dragons vastly reduced in number.

The Dance was a war unlike any other ever fought in the long history of the Seven Kingdoms. Though armies marched and met in savage battle, much of the slaughter took place on water, and . . . especially . . . in the air, as dragon fought dragon with tooth and claw and flame. It was a war marked by stealth, murder, and betrayal as well, a war fought in shadows and stairwells, council chambers and castle yards with knives and lies and poison.

Long simmering, the conflict burst into the open on the third day of the third moon of 129 AC, when the ailing, bedridden King Viserys I Targaryen closed his eyes for a nap in the Red Keep of King's Landing and died without waking. His body was discovered by a serving man at the hour of the bat, when it was the king's custom to take a cup of hippocras. The servant ran to inform Queen Alicent, whose apartments were on the floor below the king's.

Septon Eustace, writing on these events some years later, points out that the manservant delivered his dire tidings directly to the queen, and her alone, without raising a general alarum. Eustace does not believe this was wholly fortuitous; the king's death had been anticipated for some time, he argues, and Queen Alicent and her party, the so-called greens, had taken care to instruct all of Viserys's guards and servants in what to do when the day came.

(The dwarf Mushroom suggests a more sinister scenario, whereby Queen Alicent hurried King Viserys on his way with a pinch of poison in his hippocras. It must be noted that Mushroom was not in King's Landing the night the king died, but rather on Dragonstone, in service with Princess Rhaenyra.)

Queen Alicent went at once to the king's bedchamber, accompanied by Ser Criston Cole, Lord Commander of the Kingsguard. Once they had confirmed that Viserys was dead, Her Grace ordered his room sealed and placed under guard. The serving man who had found the king's body was taken into custody, to make certain he did not spread the tale. Ser Criston returned to White Sword Tower and sent his brothers of the Kingsguard to summon the members of the king's small council. It was the hour of the owl.

Then as now, the Sworn Brotherhood of the Kingsguard consisted of seven knights, men of proven loyalty and undoubted prowess who had taken solemn oaths to devote their lives to defending the king's person and kin. Only five of the white cloaks were in King's Landing at the time of Viserys's death; Ser Criston himself, Ser Arryk Cargyll, Ser Rickard Thorne, Ser Steffon Darklyn, and Ser Willis Fell. Ser Erryk Cargyll (twin to Ser Arryk) and Ser Lorent Marbrand, with Princess Rhaenyra on Dragonstone, remained unaware and uninvolved as their brothers-in-arms went forth into the night to rouse the members of the small council from their beds.

The council convened in the queen's apartments within Maegor's Holdfast. Many accounts have come down to us of what was said and done that night. By far the most detailed and authoritative of them is Grand Maester Munkun's *The Dance of the Dragons, A True Telling*. Though Munkun's exhaustive history was not written until a generation later, and drew on many different sorts of materials, including maesters' chronicles, memoirs, stewards' records, and interviews with one hundred forty-seven surviving witnesses to the great events of these times, his account of the inner workings of the court relies upon the confessions of Grand Maester Orwyle, as set down before his execution. Unlike Mushroom and Septon Eustace, whose versions derive from rumors, hearsay, and family legend, the Grand Maester was present at the meeting and took part in the council's deliberations and decisions . . . though it must be recognized that at the time he wrote, Orwyle was most anxious to show himself in a favorable light and absolve himself of any blame for what was to follow. Munkun's *True Telling* therefore paints his predecessor in perhaps too favorable a light.

Gathering in the queen's chambers as the body of her lord husband grew cold above were Queen Alicent herself; her father, Ser Otto Hightower, Hand of the King; Ser Criston Cole, Lord Commander of the Kingsguard; Grand Maester Orwyle; Lord Lyman Beesbury, master of coin, a man of eighty; Ser Tyland Lannister, master of ships, brother to the Lord of Casterly Rock; Larys Strong, called Larys Clubfoot, Lord of Harrenhal, master of whisperers; and Lord Jasper Wylde, called Ironrod, master of laws. Grand Maester Munkun dubs this gathering "the green council" in his *True Telling.*

Grand Maester Orwyle opened the meeting by reviewing the customary tasks and procedures required at the death of a king. He said, "Septon Eustace should be summoned to perform the last rites and pray for the king's soul. A raven must needs be sent to Dragonstone at once to inform Princess Rhaenyra of her father's passing. Mayhaps Her Grace the queen would care to write the message, so as to soften these sad tidings with some words of condolence? The bells are always rung to announce the death of a king, someone should see to that, and of course we must begin to make our preparations for Queen Rhaenyra's coronation—"

Ser Otto Hightower cut him off. "All this must needs wait," he declared, "until the question of succession is settled." As the King's Hand, he was empowered to speak with the king's voice, even to sit the Iron Throne in the king's absence. Viserys had granted him the authority to rule over the Seven Kingdoms, and "until such time as our new king is crowned," that rule would continue.

"Until our new *queen* is crowned," someone said. In Grand Maester Munkun's account, the words are Orwyle's, spoken softly, no more than a quibble. But Mushroom and Septon Eustace insist it was Lord Beesbury who spoke up, and in a waspish tone.

"King," insisted Queen Alicent. "The Iron Throne by rights must pass to His Grace's eldest trueborn son."

The discussion that followed lasted nigh unto dawn, Grand Maester Munkun tells us. Mushroom and Septon Eustace concur. In their accounts, only Lord Beesbury spoke on behalf of Princess Rhaenyra. The ancient master of coin, who had served King Viserys for the majority of his reign, and his grandfather, Jaehaerys the Old King, before him, reminded the council that Rhaenyra was older than her brothers and had more Targaryen blood, that the late king had chosen her as his successor, that he had repeatedly refused to alter the succession despite the pleadings of Queen Alicent and her greens, that hundreds of lords and landed knights had done obeisance to the princess in 105 AC, and sworn solemn oaths to defend her rights. (Grand Maester Orwyle's account differs only in that he puts many of these arguments into his own mouth rather than Beesbury's, but subsequent events suggest that was not so, as we shall see.)

But these words fell on ears made of stone. Ser Tyland pointed out that many of the lords who had sworn to defend the succession of Princess Rhaenyra were long dead. "It has been twenty-four years," he said. "I myself swore no such oath. I was a child at the time." Ironrod, the master of laws, cited the Great Council of 101 and the Old King's choice of Baelon rather than Rhaenys in 92, then discoursed at length about Aegon the Conqueror and his sisters, and the hallowed Andal tradition wherein the rights of a trueborn son always came before the rights of a mere daughter. Ser Otto reminded them that Rhaenyra's husband was none other than Prince Daemon, and "we all know that one's nature. Make no mistake, should Rhaenyra ever sit the Iron Throne, it will be Lord Flea Bottom who rules us, a king consort as cruel and unforgiving as Maegor ever was. My own head will be the first cut off, I do not doubt, but your queen, my daughter, will soon follow."

Queen Alicent echoed him. "Nor will they spare my children," she declared. "Aegon and his brothers are the king's trueborn sons, with a better claim to the throne than her brood of bastards. Daemon will find some pretext to put them all to death. Even Helaena and her little ones. One of these Strongs put out Aemond's eye, never forget. He was a boy, aye, but the boy is the father to the man, and bastards are monstrous by nature."

Ser Criston Cole spoke up. Should the princess reign, he reminded them, Jacaerys Velaryon would rule after her. "Seven save this realm if we seat a bastard on the Iron Throne." He spoke of Rhaenyra's wanton ways and the infamy of her husband. "They will turn the Red Keep into a brothel. No man's daughter will be safe, nor any man's wife. Even the boys . . . we know what Laenor was."

It is not recorded that Lord Larys Strong spoke a word during this debate, but that was not unusual. Though glib of tongue when need be, the master of whisperers hoarded his words like a miser hoarding coins, preferring to listen rather than talk.

"If we do this," Grand Maester Orwyle cautioned the council, according to the *True Telling,* "it must surely lead to war. The princess will not meekly stand aside, and she has dragons."

"And friends," Lord Beesbury declared. "Men of honor, who will not forget the vows they swore to her and her father. I am an old man, but not so old that I will sit here meekly whilst the likes of you plot to steal her crown." And so saying, he rose to go.

As to what happened next, our sources differ.

Grand Maester Orwyle tells us that Lord Beesbury was seized at the door by the command of Ser Otto Hightower and escorted to the dungeons. Confined to a black cell, he would in time perish of a chill whilst awaiting trial.

Septon Eustace tells it elsewise. In his account, Ser Criston Cole forced Lord Beesbury back into his seat and opened his throat with a dagger. Mushroom charges Ser Criston with his lordship's death as well, but in his version Cole grasped the old man by the back of his collar and flung him out a window, to die impaled upon the iron spikes in the dry moat below.

All three chronicles agree on one particular: the first blood shed in the

Dance of the Dragons belonged to Lord Lyman Beesbury, master of coin and lord treasurer of the Seven Kingdoms.

No further dissent was heard after the death of Lord Beesbury. The rest of the night was spent making plans for the new king's coronation (it must be done quickly, all agreed), and drawing up lists of possible allies and potential enemies, should Princess Rhaenyra refuse to accept King Aegon's ascension. With the princess in confinement on Dragonstone, about to give birth, Queen Alicent's greens enjoyed an advantage; the longer Rhaenyra remained ignorant of the king's death, the slower she would be to move. "Mayhaps the whore will die in childbirth," Queen Alicent is reported to have said (according to Mushroom).

No ravens flew that night. No bells rang. Those servants who knew of the king's passing were sent to the dungeons. Ser Criston Cole was given the task of taking into custody such blacks as remained at court, those lords and knights who might be inclined to favor Princess Rhaenyra. "Do them no violence, unless they resist," Ser Otto Hightower commanded. "Such men as bend the knee and swear fealty to King Aegon shall suffer no harm at our hands."

"And those who will not?" asked Grand Maester Orwyle.

"Are traitors," said Ironrod, "and must die a traitor's death."

Lord Larys Strong, master of whisperers, then spoke for the first and only time. "Let us be the first to swear," he said, "lest there be traitors here amongst us." Drawing his dagger, the Clubfoot drew it across his palm. "A blood oath," he urged, "to bind us all together, brothers unto death." And so each of the conspirators slashed their palms and clasped hands with one another, swearing brotherhood. Queen Alicent alone amongst them was excused from the oath, on account of her womanhood.

Dawn was breaking over the city before Queen Alicent dispatched the Kingsguard to bring her sons Aegon and Aemond to the council. (Prince Daeron, the youngest and gentlest of her children, was in Oldtown, serving as Lord Hightower's squire.)

One-eyed Prince Aemond, nineteen, was found in the armory, donning plate and mail for his morning practice in the castle yard. "Is Aegon king?" he asked Ser Willis Fell, "or must we kneel and kiss the old whore's cunny?" Princess Helaena was breaking her fast with her children when the Kingsguard came to her . . . but when asked the whereabouts of Prince Aegon, her brother and husband, she said only, "He is not in my bed, you may be sure. Feel free to search beneath the blankets."

Prince Aegon was "at his revels," Munkun says in his *True Telling*, vaguely. *The Testimony of Mushroom* claims Ser Criston found the young king-to-be drunk and naked in a Flea Bottom rat pit, where two guttersnipes with filed teeth were biting and tearing at each other for his amusement whilst a girl who could not have been more than twelve pleasured his member with her mouth. Let us put that ugly picture down to Mushroom being Mushroom, however, and consider instead the words of Septon Eustace.

Though the good septon admits Prince Aegon was with a paramour when he was found, he insists the girl was the daughter of a wealthy trader, and well cared for besides. Moreover, the prince at first refused to be a part of his mother's plans. "My sister is the heir, not me," he says in Eustace's account. "What sort of brother steals his sister's birthright?" Only when Ser Criston convinced him that the princess must surely execute him and his brothers should she don the crown did Aegon waver. "Whilst any trueborn Targaryen yet lives, no Strong can ever hope to sit the Iron Throne," Cole said. "Rhaenyra has no choice but to take your heads if she wishes her bastards to rule after her." It was this, and only this, that persuaded Aegon to accept the crown that the small council was offering him, insists our gentle septon.

Whilst the knights of the Kingsguard were seeking after Queen Alicent's sons, other messengers summoned the Commander of the City Watch and his captains (there were seven, each commanding one of the city gates) to the Red Keep. Five were judged sympathetic to Prince Aegon's cause when questioned. The other two, along with their commander, were deemed untrustworthy, and found themselves in chains. Ser Luthor Largent, the most fearsome of the "leal five," was made the new commander of the gold cloaks. A bull of a man, nigh on seven feet tall, Largent was rumored to have once killed a warhorse with a single punch. Ser Otto being a prudent man, however, he took care to name his own son Ser Gwayne Hightower (the queen's brother) as Largent's second, instructing him to keep a wary eye on Ser Luthor for any signs of disloyalty.

Ser Tyland Lannister was named master of coin in place of the late

Lord Beesbury, and acted at once to seize the royal treasury. The Crown's gold was divided into four parts. One part was entrusted to the care of the Iron Bank of Braavos for safekeeping, another sent under strong guard to Casterly Rock, a third to Oldtown. The remaining wealth was to be used for bribes and gifts, and to hire sellswords if needed. To take Ser Tyland's place as master of ships, Ser Otto looked to the Iron Islands, dispatching a raven to Dalton Greyjoy, the Red Kraken, the daring and bloodthirsty sixteen-year-old Lord Reaper of Pyke, offering him the admiralty and a seat on the council for his allegiance.

A day passed, then another. Neither septons nor silent sisters were summoned to the bedchamber where King Viserys lay, swollen and rotting. No bells rang. Ravens flew, but not to Dragonstone. They went instead to Oldtown, to Casterly Rock, to Riverrun, to Highgarden, and to many other lords and knights whom Queen Alicent had cause to think might be sympathetic to her son.

The annals of the Great Council of 101 were brought forth and examined, and note was made of which lords had spoken for Viserys, and which for Rhaenys, Laena, or Laenor. The lords assembled had favored the male claimant over the female by twenty to one, but there had been dissenters, and those same houses were most like to lend Princess Rhaenyra their support should it come to war. The princess would have the Sea Snake and his fleets, Ser Otto judged, and like as not the other lords of the eastern shores as well: Lords Bar Emmon, Massey, Celtigar, and Crabb most like, perhaps even the Evenstar of Tarth. All were lesser powers, save for the Velaryons. The northmen were a greater concern: Winterfell had spoken for Rhaenys at Harrenhal, as had Lord Stark's bannermen, Dustin of Barrowton and Manderly of White Harbor. Nor could House Arryn be relied upon, for the Eyrie was presently ruled by a woman, Lady Jeyne, the Maiden of the Vale, whose own rights might be called into question should Princess Rhaenyra be put aside.

The greatest danger was deemed to be Storm's End, for House Baratheon had always been staunch in support of the claims of Princess Rhaenys and her children. Though old Lord Boremund had died, his son Borros was even more belligerent than his father, and the lesser storm lords would surely follow wherever he led. "Then we must see that he leads them to our king," Queen Alicent declared. Whereupon she sent for her second son.

Thus it was not a raven who took flight for Storm's End that day, but Vhagar, oldest and largest of the dragons of Westeros. On her back rode Prince Aemond Targaryen, with a sapphire in the place of his missing eye. "Your purpose is to win the hand of one of Lord Baratheon's daughters," his grandsire Ser Otto told him, before he flew. "Any of the four will do. Woo her and wed her, and Lord Borros will deliver the stormlands for your brother. Fail—"

"I will not fail," Prince Aemond blustered. "Aegon will have Storm's End, and I will have this girl."

By the time Prince Aemond took his leave, the stink from the dead king's bedchamber had wafted all through Maegor's Holdfast, and many wild tales and rumors were spreading through the court and castle. The dungeons under the Red Keep had swallowed up so many men suspected of disloyalty that even the High Septon had begun to wonder at these disappearances, and sent word from the Starry Sept of Oldtown asking after some of the missing. Ser Otto Hightower, as methodical a man as ever served as Hand, wanted more time to make preparations, but Queen Alicent knew they could delay no longer. Prince Aegon had grown weary of secrecy. "Am I a king or no?" he demanded of his mother. "If I am king, then crown me."

The bells began to ring on the tenth day of the third moon of 129 AC, tolling the end of a reign. Grand Maester Orwyle was at last allowed to send forth his ravens, and the black birds took to the air by the hundreds, spreading the word of Aegon's ascension to every far corner of the realm. The silent sisters were sent for, to prepare the corpse for burning, and riders went forth on pale horses to spread the word to the people of King's Landing, crying "King Viserys is dead, long live King Aegon." Hearing the cries, Munkun writes, some wept whilst others cheered, but most of the smallfolk stared in silence, confused and wary, and now and again a voice cried out, "Long live our queen."

Meanwhile, hurried preparations were made for the coronation. The Dragonpit was chosen as the site. Under its mighty dome were stone benches sufficient to seat eighty thousand, and the pit's thick walls, strong roof, and towering bronze doors made it defensible, should traitors attempt to disrupt the ceremony.

On the appointed day Ser Criston Cole placed the steel-and-ruby crown of Aegon the Conqueror upon the brow of the eldest son of King Viserys and Queen Alicent, proclaiming him Aegon of House Targaryen, Second of His Name, King of the Andals, the Rhoynar, and the First Men, Lord of the Seven Kingdoms, and Protector of the Realm. His mother, Queen Alicent, beloved of the smallfolk, placed her own crown upon the head of her daughter, Helaena, Aegon's wife and sister. After kissing her cheeks, the mother knelt before the daughter, bowed her head, and said, "My Queen."

How many came to see the crowning remains a matter of dispute. Grand Maester Munkun, drawing upon Orwyle, tells us that more than a hundred thousand smallfolk jammed into the Dragonpit, their cheers so loud they shook the very walls, whilst Mushroom says the stone benches were half-filled. With the High Septon in Oldtown, too old and frail to

journey to King's Landing, it fell to Septon Eustace to anoint King Aegon's brow with holy oils, and bless him in the seven names of god.

A few of those in attendance, with sharper eyes than most, might have noticed that there were but four white cloaks in attendance on the new king, not five as heretofore. Aegon II had suffered his first defections the night before, when Ser Steffon Darklyn of the Kingsguard had slipped from the city with his squire, two stewards, and four guardsmen. Under the cover of darkness they made their way out a postern gate to where a fisherman's skiff awaited to take them to Dragonstone. They brought with them a stolen crown: a band of yellow gold ornamented with seven gems of different colors. This was the crown King Viserys had worn, and the Old King Jaehaerys before him. When Prince Aegon had decided to wear the steel-and-ruby crown of his namesake, the Conqueror, Queen Alicent had ordered Viserys's crown locked away, but the steward entrusted with the task had made off with it instead.

After the coronation, the remaining Kingsguard escorted Aegon to his mount, a splendid creature with gleaming golden scales and pale pink wing membranes. "Sunfyre" was the name given this dragon of the golden dawn. Munkun tells us the king flew thrice around the city before landing inside the walls of the Red Keep. Ser Arryk Cargyll led His Grace into the torchlit throne room, where Aegon II mounted the steps of the Iron Throne before a thousand lords and knights. Shouts rang through the hall.

On Dragonstone, no cheers were heard. Instead, screams echoed through the halls and stairwells of Sea Dragon Tower, down from the queen's apartments where Rhaenyra Targaryen strained and shuddered in her third day of labor. The child had not been due for another turn of the moon, but the tidings from King's Landing had driven the princess into a black fury, and her rage seemed to bring on the birth, as if the babe inside her were angry too, and fighting to get out. The princess shrieked curses all through her labor, calling down the wrath of the gods upon her half-brothers and their mother, the queen, and detailing the torments she would inflict upon them before she would let them die. She cursed the child inside her too, Mushroom tells us, clawing at her swollen belly as

Maester Gerardys and her midwife tried to restrain her and shouting, *"Monster, monster, get out, get out, GET OUT!"*

When the babe at last came forth, she proved indeed a monster: a stillborn girl, twisted and malformed, with a hole in her chest where her heart should have been, and a stubby, scaled tail. Or so Mushroom describes her. The dwarf tells us that it was he who carried the little thing to the yard for burning. The dead girl had been named Visenya, Princess Rhaenyra announced the next day, when milk of the poppy had blunted the edge of her pain. "She was my only daughter, and they killed her. They stole my crown and murdered my daughter, and they shall answer for it."

And so the Dance began, as the princess called a council of her own. "The black council," the *True Telling* names that gathering on Dragonstone, setting it against the "green council" of King's Landing. Rhaenyra herself presided, seated between her uncle and husband, Prince Daemon, and her trusted counselor, Maester Gerardys. Her three sons were present with them, though none had reached the age of manhood (Jace was fourteen, Luke thirteen, Joffrey eleven). Two Kingsguard stood with them: Ser Erryk Cargyll, twin to Ser Arryk, and the westerman, Ser Lorent Marbrand.

Thirty knights, a hundred crossbowmen, and three hundred men-at-arms made up the rest of Dragonstone's garrison. That had always been deemed sufficient for a fortress of such strength. "As an instrument of conquest, however, our army leaves something to be desired," Prince Daemon observed sourly.

A dozen lesser lords, bannermen and vassals to Dragonstone, sat at the black council as well: Celtigar of Claw Isle, Staunton of Rook's Rest, Massey of Stonedance, Bar Emmon of Sharp Point, and Darklyn of Duskendale amongst them. But the greatest lord to pledge his strength to the princess was Corlys Velaryon of Driftmark. Though the Sea Snake had grown old, he liked to say that he was clinging to life "like a drowning sailor clinging to the wreckage of a sunken ship. Mayhaps the Seven have preserved me for this one last fight." With Lord Corlys came his wife, Princess Rhaenys, five-and-fifty, her face lean and lined, her black hair streaked with white, yet fierce and fearless as she had been at two-and-twenty. "The Queen Who Never Was," Mushroom calls her. ("What did Viserys ever have that she did not? A little sausage? Is that all it takes to be a king? Let Mushroom rule, then. My sausage is thrice the size of his.")

Those who sat at the black council counted themselves loyalists, but knew full well that King Aegon II would name them traitors. Each had already received a summons from King's Landing, demanding they present themselves at the Red Keep to swear oaths of loyalty to the new king. All their hosts combined could not match the power the Hightowers alone could field. Aegon's greens enjoyed other advantages as well. Oldtown, King's Landing, and Lannisport were the largest and richest cities in the realm; all three were held by greens. Every visible symbol of legitimacy belonged to Aegon. He sat the Iron Throne. He lived in the Red Keep. He wore the Conqueror's crown, wielded the Conqueror's sword, and had been anointed by a septon of the Faith before the eyes of tens of thousands. Grand Maester Orwyle sat in his councils, and the Lord Commander of the Kingsguard had placed the crown upon his princely head. And he was male, which in the eyes of many made him the rightful king, his half-sister the usurper.

Against all that, Rhaenyra's advantages were few. Some older lords might yet recall the oaths they had sworn when she was made Princess of Dragonstone and named her father's heir. There had been a time when she had been well loved by highborn and commons alike, when they had cheered her as the Realm's Delight. Many a young lord and noble knight had sought her favor then . . . though how many would still fight for her, now that she was a woman wed, her body aged and thickened by six childbirths, was a question none could answer. Though her half-brother had looted their father's treasury, the princess had at her disposal the wealth of House Velaryon, and the Sea Snake's fleets gave her superiority at sea. And her consort, Prince Daemon, tried and tempered in the Stepstones, had more experience of warfare than all their foes combined. Last, but far from least, Rhaenyra had her dragons.

"As does Aegon," Maester Gerardys pointed out.

"We have more," said Princess Rhaenys, the Queen Who Never Was, who had been a dragonrider longer than all of them. "And ours are larger and stronger, but for Vhagar. Dragons thrive best here on Dragonstone."

She enumerated for the council. King Aegon had his Sunfyre. A splendid beast, though young. Aemond One-Eye rode Vhagar, and the peril posed by Queen Visenya's mount could not be gainsaid. Queen Helaena's mount was Dreamfyre, the she-dragon who had once borne the Old King's sister Rhaena through the clouds. Prince Daeron's dragon was Tessarion, with her wings dark as cobalt and her claws and crest and belly scales as bright as beaten copper. "That makes four dragons of fighting size," said Rhaenys. Queen Helaena's twins had their own dragons too, but no more than hatchlings; the usurper's youngest son, Maelor, was possessed only of an egg.

Against that, Prince Daemon had Caraxes and Princess Rhaenyra Syrax, both huge and formidable beasts. Caraxes especially was fearsome, and no stranger to blood and fire after the Stepstones. Rhaenyra's three sons by Laenor Velaryon were all dragonriders; Vermax, Arrax, and Tyraxes were thriving, and growing larger every year. Aegon the Younger, eldest of Rhaenyra's two sons by Prince Daemon, commanded the young dragon Stormcloud, though he had yet to mount him; his little brother, Viserys, went everywhere with his egg. Rhaenys's own she-dragon, Meleys the Red Queen, had grown lazy, but remained fearsome when roused. Prince Daemon's twins by Laena Velaryon might yet be dragonriders too. Baela's dragon, the slender pale green Moondancer, would soon be large enough to bear the girl upon her back . . . and though her sister Rhaena's egg had hatched a broken thing that died within hours of emerging from the egg, Syrax had recently produced another clutch. One of her eggs had been given to Rhaena, and it was said that the girl slept with it every night, and prayed for a dragon to match her sister's.

Moreover, six other dragons made their lairs in the smoky caverns of the Dragonmont above the castle. There was Silverwing, Good Queen Alysanne's mount of old; Seasmoke, the pale grey beast that had been the pride and passion of Ser Laenor Velaryon; hoary old Vermithor, unridden since the death of King Jaehaerys. And behind the mountain dwelled three wild dragons, never claimed nor ridden by any man, living or dead. The smallfolk had named them Sheepstealer, Grey Ghost, and the Cannibal. "Find riders to master Silverwing, Vermithor, and Seasmoke, and we will have nine dragons against Aegon's four. Mount and fly their wild kin, and we will number twelve, even without Stormcloud," Princess Rhaenys pointed out. "That is how we shall win this war."

Lords Celtigar and Staunton agreed. Aegon the Conqueror and his sisters had proved that knights and armies could not stand against fire and blood. Celtigar urged the princess to fly against King's Landing at once, and reduce the city to ash and bone. "And how will that serve us, my lord?" the Sea Snake demanded of him. "We want to rule the city, not burn it to the ground."

"It will never come to that," Celtigar insisted. "The usurper will have no choice but to oppose us with his own dragons. Our nine must surely overwhelm his four."

"At what cost?" Princess Rhaenyra wondered. "My sons would be riding three of those dragons, I remind you. And it would not be nine against four. I will not be strong enough to fly for some time yet. And who is to ride Silverwing, Vermithor, and Seasmoke? You, my lord? I hardly think so. It will be five against four, and one of their four will be Vhagar. That is no advantage."

Surprisingly, Prince Daemon agreed with his wife. "In the Stepstones, my enemies learned to run and hide when they saw Caraxes's wings or heard his roar . . . but they had no dragons of their own. It is no easy thing for a man to be a dragonslayer. But dragons can kill dragons, and have. Any maester who has ever studied the history of Valyria can tell you that. I will not throw our dragons against the usurper's unless I have no other choice. There are other ways to use them, better ways." Then the prince laid his own strategies before the black council. Rhaenyra must have a coronation of her own, to answer Aegon's. Afterward they would send out ravens, calling on the lords of the Seven Kingdoms to declare their allegiance to their true queen.

"We must fight this war with words before we go to battle," the prince declared. The lords of the great houses held the key to victory, Daemon insisted; their bannermen and vassals would follow where they led. Aegon the Usurper had won the allegiance of the Lannisters of Casterly Rock, and Lord Tyrell of Highgarden was a mewling boy in swaddling clothes whose mother, acting as his regent, would most like align the Reach with her over-mighty bannermen, the Hightowers . . . but the rest of the realm's great lords had yet to declare.

"Storm's End will stand with us," Princess Rhaenys said. She herself was of that blood on her mother's side, and the late Lord Boremund had always been the staunchest of friends.

Prince Daemon had good reason to hope that the Maid of the Vale might bring the Eyrie to their side as well. Aegon would surely seek the support of Pyke, he judged; only with the support of the Iron Islands could Aegon hope to surpass the strength of House Velaryon at sea. But the ironmen were notoriously fickle, and Dalton Greyjoy loved blood and battle; he might easily be persuaded to support the princess.

The North was too remote to be of much import in the fight, the council judged; by the time the Starks gathered their banners and marched south, the war might well be over. Which left only the riverlords, a notoriously quarrelsome lot ruled over, in name at least, by House Tully of Riverrun. "We have friends in the riverlands," the prince said, "though not all of them dare show their colors yet. We need a place where they can gather, a toehold on the mainland large enough to house a sizable host, and strong enough to hold against whatever forces the usurper can send against us." He showed the lords a map. "Here. Harrenhal."

And so it was decided. Prince Daemon would lead the assault on Harrenhal, riding Caraxes. Princess Rhaenyra would remain on Dragonstone until she had recovered her strength. The Velaryon fleet would close off the Gullet, sallying forth from Dragonstone and Driftmark to block all shipping entering or leaving Blackwater Bay. "We do not have the strength to take King's Landing by storm," Prince Daemon said, "no more than our foes could hope to capture Dragonstone. But Aegon is a green boy, and green boys are easily provoked. Mayhaps we can goad him into a rash attack." The Sea Snake would command the fleet, whilst Princess Rhaenys flew overhead to keep their foes from attacking their ships with dragons. Meanwhile, ravens would go forth to Riverrun, the Eyrie, Pyke, and Storm's End, to gain the allegiance of their lords.

Then up spoke the queen's eldest son, Jacaerys. "*We* should bear those messages," he said. "Dragons will win the lords over quicker than ravens."

His brother Lucerys agreed, insisting that he and Jace were men, or near enough to make no matter. "Our uncle calls us Strongs, but when the lords see us on dragonback they will know that for a lie. Only *Targaryens* ride dragons." Mushroom tells us that the Sea Snake grumbled at this, insisting that the three boys were Velaryons, yet he smiled as he said it, with pride in his voice. Even young Joffrey chimed in, offering to mount his own dragon, Tyraxes, and join his brothers.

Princess Rhaenyra forbade that; Joff was but eleven. But Jacaerys was fourteen, Lucerys thirteen; bold and handsome lads, skilled in arms, who had long served as squires. "If you go, you go as messengers, not as knights," she told them. "You must take no part in any fighting." Not until both boys had sworn solemn oaths upon a copy of *The Seven-Pointed Star* would Her Grace consent to using them as her envoys. It was decided that Jace, being the older of the two, would take the longer, more dangerous task, flying first to the Eyrie to treat with the Lady of the Vale, then to White Harbor to win over Lord Manderly, and lastly to Winterfell to meet with Lord Stark. Luke's mission would be shorter and safer; he was to fly to Storm's End, where it was expected that Borros Baratheon would give him a warm welcome.

A hasty coronation was held the next day. The arrival of Ser Steffon Darklyn, late of Aegon's Kingsguard, was an occasion of much joy on Dragonstone, especially when it was learned that he and his fellow loyalists ("turncloaks," Ser Otto would name them, when offering a reward for their capture) had brought the stolen crown of King Jaehaerys the Conciliator. Three hundred sets of eyes looked on as Prince Daemon Targaryen placed the Old King's crown on the head of his wife, proclaiming her Rhaenyra of House Targaryen, First of Her Name, Queen of the Andals, the Rhoynar, and the First Men. The prince claimed for himself the style Protector of the Realm, and Rhaenyra named her eldest son, Jacaerys, the Prince of Dragonstone and heir to the Iron Throne.

Her first act as queen was to declare Ser Otto Hightower and Queen Alicent traitors and rebels. "As for my half-brothers and my sweet sister, Helaena," she announced, "they have been led astray by the counsel of evil men. Let them come to Dragonstone, bend the knee, and ask my forgiveness, and I shall gladly spare their lives and take them back into my heart, for they are of my own blood, and no man or woman is as accursed as the kinslayer."

Word of Rhaenyra's coronation reached the Red Keep the next day, to the great displeasure of Aegon II. "My half-sister and my uncle are guilty of high treason," the young king declared. "I want them attainted, I want them arrested, and I want them dead."

Cooler heads on the green council wished to parley. "The princess must be made to see that her cause is hopeless," Grand Maester Orwyle said. "Brother should not war against sister. Send me to her, that we may talk and reach an amicable accord."

Aegon would not hear of it. Septon Eustace tells us that His Grace accused the Grand Maester of disloyalty and spoke of having him thrown into a black cell "with your black friends." But when the two queens—his mother, Queen Alicent, and his wife, Queen Helaena—spoke in favor of Orwyle's proposal, the truculent king gave way reluctantly. So Grand Maester Orwyle was dispatched across Blackwater Bay under a peace banner, leading a retinue that included Ser Arryk Cargyll of the Kingsguard and Ser Gwayne Hightower of the gold cloaks, along with a score of scribes and septons, amongst them Eustace.

The terms offered by the king were generous, Munkun declares in his *True Telling*. If the princess would acknowledge him as king and make obeisance before the Iron Throne, Aegon II would confirm her in her possession of Dragonstone, and allow the island and castle to pass to her son Jacaerys upon her death. Her second son, Lucerys, would be recognized as the rightful heir to Driftmark, and the lands and holdings of House Velaryon; her boys by Prince Daemon, Aegon the Younger and Viserys, would be given places of honor at court, the former as the king's squire, the latter as his cupbearer. Pardons would be granted to those lords and knights who had conspired treasonously with her against their true king.

Rhaenyra heard these terms in stony silence, then asked Orwyle if he remembered her father, King Viserys. "Of course, Your Grace," the maester answered. "Perhaps you can tell us who he named as his heir and successor," the queen said, her crown upon her head. "You, Your Grace,"

Orwyle replied. And Rhaenyra nodded and said, "With your own tongue you admit I am your lawful queen. Why then do you serve my half-brother, the pretender?"

Munkun tells us that Orwyle gave a long and erudite reply, citing Andal law and the Great Council of 101. Mushroom claims he stammered and voided his bladder. Whichever is true, his answer did not satisfy Princess Rhaenyra.

"A Grand Maester should know the law and serve it," she told Orwyle. "You are no Grand Maester, and you bring only shame and dishonor to that chain you wear." As Orwyle protested feebly, Rhaenyra's knights stripped his chain of office from his neck and forced him to his knees whilst the princess bestowed the chain upon her own man, Maester Gerardys, "a true and leal servant of the realm and its laws." As she sent Orwyle and the other envoys on their way, Rhaenyra said, "Tell my half-brother that I will have my throne, or I will have his head."

Long after the Dance was done, the singer Luceon of Tarth would compose a sad ballad called "Farewell, My Brother," still sung today. The song purports to relate the last meeting between Ser Arryk Cargyll and his twin, Ser Erryk, as Orwyle's party was boarding the ship that would carry them back to King's Landing. Ser Arryk had sworn his sword to Aegon, Ser Erryk to Rhaenyra. In the song, each brother tries to persuade the other to change sides; failing, they exchange declarations of love and part, knowing that when next they meet it will be as enemies. It is possible that such a farewell did indeed take place that day on Dragonstone; however, none of our sources make mention of such.

Aegon II was two-and-twenty, quick to anger and slow to forgive. Rhaenyra's refusal to accept his rule enraged him. "I offered her an honorable peace, and the whore spat in my face," he declared. "What happens next is on her own head."

What happened next was war.

The Dying of the Dragons

A Son for a Son

Aegon had been proclaimed king in the Dragonpit, Rhaenyra queen on Dragonstone. All efforts at reconciliation having failed, the Dance of the Dragons now began in earnest.

On Driftmark, the Sea Snake's ships set sail from Hull and Spicetown to close the Gullet, choking off trade to and from King's Landing. Soon after, Jacaerys Velaryon was flying north upon his dragon, Vermax, his brother Lucerys south on Arrax, whilst Prince Daemon flew Caraxes to the Trident.

Let us turn first to Harrenhal.

Though large parts of Harren's great folly were in ruins, the castle's towering curtain walls still made it as formidable a stronghold as any in the riverlands . . . but Aegon the Dragon had proved it vulnerable from the sky. With its lord, Larys Strong, away in King's Landing, the castle was but lightly garrisoned. Having no wish to suffer the fate of Black Harren, its elderly castellan Ser Simon Strong (uncle to the late Lord Lyonel, great-uncle to Lord Larys) was quick to strike his banners when Caraxes lighted atop Kingspyre Tower. In addition to the castle, Prince Daemon at a stroke had captured the not-inconsiderable wealth of House Strong and a dozen valuable hostages, amongst them Ser Simon and his grandsons.

The castle smallfolk became his captives as well, amongst them a wet nurse named Alys Rivers.

Who was this woman? A serving wench who dabbled in potions and spells, says Munkun. A woods witch, claims Septon Eustace. A malign enchantress who bathed in the blood of virgins to preserve her youth, Mushroom would have us believe. Her name suggests bastard birth . . . but we know little of her father, and less of her mother. Munkun and Eustace tell us she was sired by Lord Lyonel Strong in his callow youth, making her a natural half-sister to his sons Harwin (Breakbones) and Larys (the Clubfoot). But Mushroom insists that she was much older, that she was wet nurse to both boys, perhaps even to their father a generation earlier.

Though her own children had all been stillborn, the milk that flowed so abundantly from the breasts of Alys Rivers had nourished countless babes born of other women at Harrenhal. Was she in truth a witch who lay with demons, bringing forth dead children as payment for the knowledge they gave her? Was she a simpleminded slattern, as Eustace believes? A wanton who used her poisons and potions to bind men to her, body and soul?

Alys Rivers was at least forty years of age during the Dance of the Dragons, that much is known; Mushroom makes her even older. All agree that she looked younger than her years, but whether this was simple happenstance, or achieved through her practice of the dark arts, men continue to dispute. Whatever her powers, it would seem Daemon Targaryen was immune to them, for little is heard of this supposed sorceress whilst the prince held Harrenhal.

The sudden, bloodless fall of Black Harren's seat was counted a great victory for Queen Rhaenyra and her blacks. It served as a sharp reminder of the martial prowess of Prince Daemon and the power of Caraxes, the Blood Wyrm, and gave the queen a stronghold in the heart of Westeros, to which her supporters could rally . . . and Rhaenyra had many such in the lands watered by the Trident. When Prince Daemon sent forth his call to arms, they rose up all along the rivers, knights and men-at-arms and humble peasants who yet remembered the Realm's Delight, so beloved of her father, and the way she smiled and charmed them as she made her progress through the riverlands in her youth. Hundreds and then thousands buckled on their swordbelts and donned their mail, or grabbed a pitchfork or a hoe and a crude wooden shield, and began to make their way to Harrenhal to fight for Viserys's little girl.

The lords of the Trident, having more to lose, were not so quick to move, but soon enough they too began to throw their lots in with the queen. From the Twins rode Ser Forrest Frey, the very same "Fool Frey" who had once begged for Rhaenyra's hand, now grown into a most puissant knight. Lord Samwell Blackwood, who had once lost a duel for her favor, raised her banners over Raventree. (Ser Amos Bracken, who had won that duel, followed his lord father when House Bracken declared for Aegon.) The Mootons of Maidenpool, the Pipers of Pinkmaiden Castle, the Rootes of Harroway, the Darrys of Darry, the Mallisters of Seagard, and the Vances of Wayfarer's Rest all announced their support for Rhaenyra. (The Vances of Atranta took the other path, and trumpeted their allegiance to the young king.) Petyr Piper, the grizzled Lord of Pinkmaiden, spoke for many when he said, "I swore her my sword. I'm older now, but not so old that I've forgotten the words I said, and it happens I still have the sword."

The Lord Paramount of the Trident, Grover Tully, had been an old man even at the Great Council of 101, where he spoke for Prince Viserys; though now failing, he was no less stubborn. He had favored the rights of the male claimant in 101, and the years had not changed his views. Lord Grover insisted that Riverrun would fight for young King Aegon. Yet no such word went forth. The old lord was bedridden and would not live much longer, Riverrun's maester had declared. "I would sooner the rest of us did not die with him," declared Ser Elmo Tully, his grandson. Riverrun had no defense against dragonfire, he pointed out to his own sons, and both sides in this fight rode dragons. And so whilst Lord Grover thundered and fulminated from his deathbed, Riverrun barred its gates, manned its walls, and held its silence.

Meanwhile, a very different story was playing out to the east, where Jacaerys Velaryon descended upon the Eyrie on his young dragon, Vermax, to win the Vale of Arryn for his mother. The Maiden of the Vale, Lady Jeyne Arryn, was five-and-thirty, more than twenty years his senior. Never wed, Lady Jeyne had reigned over the Vale since the death of her father and elder brothers at the hands of the Stone Crows of the hills when she was three.

Mushroom tells us that this famous maiden was in truth a highborn harlot with a voracious appetite for men, and gives us a salacious tale of how she offered Prince Jacaerys the allegiance of the Vale only if he could bring her to her climax with his tongue. Septon Eustace repeats the widespread rumor that Jeyne Arryn preferred the intimate companionship of other women, then goes on to say it was not true. In this instance, we must be grateful for Grand Maester Munkun's *True Telling,* for he alone confines himself to the High Hall of the Eyrie, rather than its bedchambers.

"Thrice have mine own kin sought to replace me," Lady Jeyne told Prince Jacaerys. "My cousin Ser Arnold is wont to say that women are too soft to rule. I have him in one of my sky cells, if you would like to ask him. Your Prince Daemon used his first wife most cruelly, it is true . . . but notwithstanding your mother's poor taste in consorts, she remains our rightful queen, and mine own blood besides, an Arryn on her mother's side. In this world of men, we women must band together. The Vale and its knights shall stand with her . . . if Her Grace will grant me one request." When the prince asked what that might be, she answered, "Dragons. I have no fear of armies. Many and more have broken themselves against my Bloody Gate, and the Eyrie is known to be impregnable. But you have descended on us from the sky, as Queen Visenya once did during the Conquest, and I was powerless to halt you. I mislike feeling powerless. Send me dragonriders."

And so the prince agreed, and Lady Jeyne knelt before him, and bade her warriors to kneel, and all swore him their swords.

Then on Jacaerys soared, north across the Fingers and the waters of the Bite. He lighted briefly at Sisterton, where Lord Borrell and Lord Sunderland did obeisance to him and pledged him the support of the Three Sisters, then flew on to White Harbor, where Lord Desmond Manderly met with him in his Merman's Court.

Here the prince faced a shrewder bargainer. "White Harbor is not unsympathetic to your mother's plight," Manderly declared. "Mine own forebears were despoiled of their birthright when our enemies drove us into exile on these cold northern shores. When the Old King visited us so long ago, he spoke of the wrong that had been done to us and promised to make redress. In pledge of that, His Grace offered the hand of his daughter Princess Viserra to my great-grandsire, that our two houses might be made as one, but the girl died and the promise was forgotten."

Prince Jacaerys knew what was being asked of him. Before he left White Harbor a compact was drawn up and signed, by the terms of which Lord Manderly's youngest daughter would be wed to the prince's brother Joffrey once the war was over.

Finally Vermax carried Jacaerys Velaryon to Winterfell, to treat with its formidable young lord, Cregan Stark.

In the fullness of time, Cregan Stark would become known as the Old Man of the North, but the Lord of Winterfell was but one-and-twenty when Prince Jacaerys came to him in 129 AC. Cregan had come into his lordship at thirteen upon the death of his father, Lord Rickon, in 121 AC. During his minority, his uncle Bennard had ruled the North as regent, but in 124 AC Cregan turned sixteen, only to find his uncle slow to surrender his power. Relations between the two grew strained, as the young lord chafed under the limits imposed upon him by his father's brother. Finally, in 126 AC, Cregan Stark rose up, imprisoned Bennard and his three sons, and took the rule of the North into his own hands. Soon after he wed Lady Arra Norrey, a beloved companion since childhood, only to have her die in 128 AC whilst giving birth to a son and heir, whom Cregan named Rickon after his father.

Autumn was well advanced when the Prince of Dragonstone came to Winterfell. The snows lay deep upon the ground, a cold wind was howling from the north, and Lord Stark was in the midst of his preparations for the coming winter, yet he gave Jacaerys a warm welcome. Snow and ice and cold made Vermax ill-tempered, it is said, so the prince did not linger long amongst the northmen, but many a curious tale came out of that short sojourn.

Munkun's *True Telling* says that Cregan and Jacaerys took a liking to each other, for the boy prince reminded the Lord of Winterfell of his own younger brother, who had died ten years before. They drank together, hunted together, trained together, and swore an oath of brotherhood, sealed in blood. This seems more credible than Septon Eustace's version, wherein the prince spends most of his visit attempting to persuade Lord Cregan to give up his false gods and accept the worship of the Seven.

But we turn to Mushroom to find the tales other chronicles omit, nor does he fail us now. His account introduces a young maiden, or "wolf girl" as he dubs her, with the name of Sara Snow. So smitten was Prince Jacaerys with this creature, a bastard daughter of the late Lord Rickon Stark, that he lay with her of a night. On learning that his guest had claimed the maidenhead of his bastard sister, Lord Cregan became most wroth, and only softened when Sara Snow told him that the prince had taken her for his wife. They had spoken their vows in Winterfell's own godswood before a heart tree, and only then had she given herself to him, wrapped in furs amidst the snows as the old gods looked on.

This makes for a charming story, to be sure, but as with many of Mushroom's fables, it seems to partake more of a fool's fevered imaginings than of historical truth. Jacaerys Velaryon had been betrothed to his cousin Baela since he was four and she was two, and from all we know of his character, it seems most unlikely that he would break such a solemn agreement to protect the uncertain virtue of some half-wild, unwashed northern bastard. If indeed there ever lived a Sara Snow, and if indeed the Prince of Dragonstone perchanced to dally with her, that is no more than other princes have done in the past, and will do on the morrow, but to talk of marriage is preposterous.

(Mushroom also claims that Vermax left a clutch of dragon's eggs at Winterfell, which is equally absurd. Whilst it is true that determining the sex of a living dragon is a nigh on impossible task, no other source mentions Vermax producing so much as a single egg, so it must be assumed that he was male. Septon Barth's speculation that the dragons change sex at need, being "as mutable as flame," is too ludicrous to consider.)

This we do know: Cregan Stark and Jacaerys Velaryon reached an accord, and signed and sealed the agreement that Grand Maester Munkun calls "the Pact of Ice and Fire" in his *True Telling*. Like many such pacts, it was to be sealed with a marriage. Lord Cregan's son, Rickon, was a year old. Prince Jacaerys was as yet unmarried and childless, but it was assumed that he would sire children of his own once his mother sat the Iron Throne. Under the terms of the pact, the prince's firstborn daughter would be sent north at the age of seven, to be fostered at Winterfell until such time as she was old enough to marry Lord Cregan's heir.

When the Prince of Dragonstone took his dragon back into the cold autumn sky, he did so with the knowledge that he had won three powerful lords and all their bannermen for his mother. Though his fifteenth nameday was still half a year away, Prince Jacaerys had proved himself a man, and a worthy heir to the Iron Throne.

Had his brother's "shorter, safer" flight gone as well, much bloodshed and grief might well have been averted.

The tragedy that befell Lucerys Velaryon at Storm's End was never planned, on this all of our sources agree. The first battles in the Dance of the Dragons were fought with quills and ravens, with threats and promises, decrees and blandishments. The murder of Lord Beesbury at the green council was not yet widely known; most believed his lordship to be languishing in some dungeon. Whilst sundry familiar faces were no longer seen about court, no heads had appeared above the castle gates, and many still hoped that the question of succession might be resolved peaceably.

The Stranger had other plans. For surely it was his dread hand behind the ill chance that brought the two princelings together at Storm's End, when the dragon Arrax raced before a gathering storm to deliver Lucerys Velaryon to the safety of the castle yard, only to find Aemond Targaryen there before him.

Borros Baratheon was a man of much different character than his father. "Lord Boremund was stone, hard and strong and unmoving," Septon Eustace tells us. "Lord Borros was the wind that rages and howls and blows this way and that." Prince Aemond had been uncertain what sort of welcome he would receive when he set out, but Storm's End welcomed him with feasts and hunts and jousting.

Lord Borros proved more than willing to entertain his suit. "I have four daughters," he told the prince. "Choose any one you like. Cass is oldest, she'll be first to flower, but Floris is prettier. And if it's a clever wife you want, there's Maris."

Rhaenyra had taken House Baratheon for granted for too long, his lordship told Aemond. "Aye, Princess Rhaenys is kin to me and mine, some great-aunt I never knew was married to her father, but the both of them are dead, and Rhaenyra . . . she's not Rhaenys, is she?" He had nothing against women, Lord Borros went on to say; he loved his girls, a daughter is a precious thing . . . but a *son,* ahhh . . . should the gods ever grant him a son of his own blood, Storm's End would pass to him, not to his sisters. "Why should the Iron Throne be any different?" And with a royal marriage in the offing . . . Rhaenyra's cause was lost, she would see that when she learned that she had lost Storm's End, he would tell her so himself . . . bow down to your brother, aye, it's for the best, his girls would fight with each other sometimes, the way girls do, but he saw to it they always made peace afterward . . .

We have no record of which daughter Prince Aemond finally decided on (though Mushroom tells us that he kissed all four, to "taste the nectar of their lips"), save that it was not Maris. Munkun writes that the prince and Lord Borros were haggling over dates and dowries on the morning Lucerys Velaryon appeared. Vhagar sensed his coming first. Guardsmen walking the battlements of the castle's mighty curtain walls clutched their spears in sudden terror when she woke with a roar that shook the very foundations of Durran's Defiance. Even Arrax quailed before that sound, we are told, and Luke plied his whip freely as he forced him down.

Mushroom would have us believe that the lightning was flashing to the east and a heavy rain falling as Lucerys leapt off his dragon, his mother's message clutched in his hand. He must surely have known what Vhagar's presence meant, so it would have come as no surprise when Aemond Targaryen confronted him in the Round Hall, before the eyes of Lord Borros, his four daughters, septon, and maester, and twoscore knights, guards, and servants. (Amongst those who witnessed the meeting was Ser Byron Swann, second son of Lord of Stonehelm in the Dornish Marches, who would have his own small part to play later in the Dance.) So here for once we need not rely entirely on Grand Maester Munkun, Mushroom, and Septon Eustace. None of them were present at Storm's End, but many others were, so we have no shortage of firsthand accounts.

"Look at this sad creature, my lord," Prince Aemond called out. "Little Luke Strong, the bastard." To Luke he said, "You are wet, bastard. Is it raining or did you piss yourself in fear?"

Lucerys Velaryon addressed himself only to Lord Baratheon. "Lord Borros, I have brought you a message from my mother, the queen."

"The whore of Dragonstone, he means." Prince Aemond strode forward and made to snatch the letter from Lucerys's hand, but Lord Borros roared a command and his knights intervened, pulling the princelings apart. One brought Rhaenyra's letter to the dais, where his lordship sat upon the throne of the storm kings of old.

No man can truly know what Borros Baratheon was feeling at that moment. The accounts of those who were there differ markedly one from the other. Some say his lordship was red-faced and abashed, as a man might be if his lawful wife found him abed with another woman. Others declare that Borros appeared to be relishing the moment, for it pleased his vanity to have both king and queen seeking his support. Mushroom (who was not there) says he was drunk. Septon Eustace (who was not there) says he was fearful.

Yet all the witnesses agree on what Lord Borros said and did. Never a man of letters, he handed the queen's letter to his maester, who cracked the seal and whispered the message into his lordship's ear. A frown stole across Lord Borros's face. He stroked his beard, scowled at Lucerys Velaryon, and said, "And if I do as your mother bids, which one of my daughters will *you* marry, boy?" He gestured at the four girls. "Pick one."

Prince Lucerys could only blush. "My lord, I am not free to marry," he replied. "I am betrothed to my cousin Rhaena."

"I thought as much," Lord Borros said. "Go home, pup, and tell the bitch your mother that the Lord of Storm's End is not a dog that she can whistle up at need to set against her foes." And Prince Lucerys turned to take his leave of the Round Hall.

But Prince Aemond drew his sword and said, "Hold, Strong. First pay the debt you owe me." Then he tore off his eye patch and flung it to the floor, to show the sapphire beneath. "You have a knife, just as you did then. Put out your eye, and I will let you leave. One will serve. I would not blind you."

Prince Lucerys recalled his promise to his mother. "I will not fight you. I came here as an envoy, not a knight."

"You came here as a craven and a traitor," Prince Aemond answered. "I will have your eye or your life, Strong."

At that Lord Borros grew uneasy. "Not here," he grumbled. "He came as an envoy. I want no blood shed beneath my roof." So his guards put themselves between the princelings and escorted Lucerys Velaryon from the Round Hall, back to the castle yard where his dragon, Arrax, was hunched down in the rain, awaiting his return.

And there it might have ended, but for the girl Maris. The secondborn daughter of Lord Borros, less comely than her sisters, she was angry with Aemond for preferring them to her. "Was it one of your eyes he took, or one of your balls?" Maris asked the prince, in tones sweet as honey. "I am *so* glad you chose my sister. I want a husband with all his parts."

Aemond Targaryen's mouth twisted in rage, and he turned once more to Lord Borros, asking for his leave. The Lord of Storm's End shrugged and answered, "It is not for me to tell you what to do when you are not beneath my roof." And his knights moved aside as Prince Aemond rushed to the doors.

Outside the storm was raging. Thunder rolled across the castle, the rain fell in blinding sheets, and from time to time great bolts of blue-white lightning lit the world as bright as day. It was bad weather for flying, even for a dragon, and Arrax was struggling to stay aloft when Prince Aemond mounted Vhagar and went after him. Had the sky been calm, Prince Lucerys might have been able to outfly his pursuer, for Arrax was younger and swifter . . . but the day was "as black as Prince Aemond's heart," says Mushroom, and so it came to pass that the dragons met above Shipbreaker Bay. Watchers on the castle walls saw distant blasts of flame, and heard a shriek cut the thunder. Then the two beasts were locked together, lightning crackling around them. Vhagar was five times the size of her foe, the hardened survivor of a hundred battles. If there was a fight, it could not have lasted long.

Arrax fell, broken, to be swallowed by the storm-lashed waters of the bay. His head and neck washed up beneath the cliffs below Storm's End three days later, to make a feast for crabs and seagulls. Mushroom claims that Prince Lucerys's corpse washed up as well, and tells us that Prince Aemond cut out his eyes and presented them to Lady Maris on a bed of seaweed, but this seems excessive. Some say Vhagar snatched Lucerys off his dragon's back and swallowed him whole. It has even been claimed that the prince survived his fall, swam to safety, but lost all memory of who he was, spending the rest of his days as a simpleminded fisherman.

The *True Telling* gives all these tales the respect they deserve . . . which is to say, none. Lucerys Velaryon died with his dragon, Munkun insists. This is undoubtedly correct. The prince was thirteen years of age. His body was never found. And with his death, the war of ravens and envoys and marriage pacts came to an end, and the war of fire and blood began in earnest.

Aemond Targaryen . . . who would henceforth be known as Aemond the Kinslayer to his foes . . . returned to King's Landing, having won the support of Storm's End for his brother Aegon, and the undying enmity of Queen Rhaenyra. If he thought to receive a hero's welcome, he was disappointed. Queen Alicent went pale when she heard what he had done, crying, "Mother have mercy on us all." Nor was Ser Otto pleased. "You only lost one eye," he is reported to have said. "How could you be so blind?" The king himself did not share their concerns, however. Aegon II welcomed Prince Aemond home with a great feast, hailed him as "the true blood of the dragon," and announced that he had made "a good beginning."

On Dragonstone, Queen Rhaenyra collapsed when told of Luke's death. Luke's young brother Joffrey (Jace was still away on his mission north) swore a terrible oath of vengeance against Prince Aemond and Lord Borros. Only the intervention of the Sea Snake and Princess Rhaenys kept the boy from mounting his own dragon at once. (Mushroom would have us believe he played a part as well.) As the black council sat to consider how to strike back, a raven arrived from Harrenhal. "An eye for an eye, a son for a son," Prince Daemon wrote. "Lucerys shall be avenged."

Let it not be forgotten: in his youth, Daemon Targaryen had been the "Prince of the City," his face and laugh familiar to every cutpurse, whore,

and gambler in Flea Bottom. The prince still had friends in the low places of King's Landing, and followers amongst the gold cloaks. Unbeknownst to King Aegon, the Hand, or the Queen Dowager, he had allies at court as well, even on the green council . . . and one other go-between, a special friend he trusted utterly, who knew the wine sinks and rat pits that festered in the shadow of the Red Keep as well as Daemon himself once had, and moved easily through the shadows of the city. To this pale stranger he reached out now, by secret ways, to set a terrible vengeance into motion.

Amidst the stews of Flea Bottom, Prince Daemon's go-between found suitable instruments. One had been a serjeant in the City Watch; big and brutal, he had lost his gold cloak for beating a whore to death whilst in a drunken rage. The other was a ratcatcher in the Red Keep. Their true names are lost to history. They are remembered (would that they were not!) as Blood and Cheese.

"Cheese knew the Red Keep better than the shape of his own cock," Mushroom tells us. The hidden doors and secret tunnels that Maegor the Cruel had built were as familiar to the ratcatcher as to the rats he hunted. Using a forgotten passageway, Cheese led Blood into the heart of the castle, unseen by any guard. Some say their quarry was the king himself, but Aegon was accompanied by the Kingsguard wherever he went, and even Cheese knew of no way in and out of Maegor's Holdfast save over the drawbridge that spanned the dry moat and its formidable iron spikes.

The Tower of the Hand was less secure. The two men crept up through the walls, bypassing the spearmen posted at the tower doors. Ser Otto's rooms were of no interest to them. Instead they slipped into his daughter's chambers, one floor below. Queen Alicent had taken up residence there after the death of King Viserys, when her son Aegon moved into Maegor's Holdfast with his own queen. Once inside, Cheese bound and gagged the Dowager Queen whilst Blood strangled her bedmaid. Then they settled down to wait, for they knew it was the custom of Queen Helaena to bring her children to see their grandmother every evening before bed.

Blind to her danger, the queen appeared as dusk was settling over the castle, accompanied by her three children. Jaehaerys and Jaehaera were six, Maelor two. As they entered the apartments, Helaena was holding his little hand and calling out her mother's name. Blood barred the door and slew the queen's guardsman, whilst Cheese appeared to snatch up Maelor. "Scream and you all die," Blood told Her Grace. Queen Helaena kept her calm, it is said. "Who are you?" she demanded of the two. "Debt collectors," said Cheese. "An eye for an eye, a son for a son. We only want the one, t' square things. Won't hurt the rest o' you fine folks, not one lil' hair. Which one you want t' lose, Your Grace?"

Once she realized what he meant, Queen Helaena pleaded with the men to kill her instead. "A wife's not a son," said Blood. "It has to be a boy." Cheese warned the queen to make a choice soon, before Blood grew bored and raped her little girl. "Pick," he said, "or we kill them all." On her knees, weeping, Helaena named her youngest, Maelor. Perhaps she thought the boy was too young to understand, or perhaps it was because the older boy, Jaehaerys, was King Aegon's firstborn son and heir, next in line to the Iron Throne. "You hear that, little boy?" Cheese whispered to Maelor. "Your momma wants you dead." Then he gave Blood a grin, and the hulking swordsman slew Prince Jaehaerys, striking off the boy's head with a single blow. The queen began to scream.

Strange to say, the ratcatcher and the butcher were true to their word. They did no further harm to Queen Helaena or her surviving children, but rather fled with the prince's head in hand. A hue and cry went up, but Cheese knew the secret passageways as the guards did not, and the killers made their escape. Two days later, Blood was seized at the Gate of the Gods trying to leave King's Landing with the head of Prince Jaehaerys hidden in one of his saddle sacks. Under torture, he confessed that he had been taking it to Harrenhal, to collect his reward from Prince Daemon. He also gave up a description of the whore he claimed had hired them: an older woman, foreign by her talk, cloaked and hooded, very pale. The other harlots called her Misery.

After thirteen days of torment, Blood was at last allowed to die. Queen Alicent had commanded Larys Clubfoot to learn his true name, so that she might bathe in the blood of his wife and children, but our sources do not say if this occurred. Ser Luthor Largent and his gold cloaks searched the Street of Silk from top to bottom, and turned out and stripped every harlot in King's Landing, but no trace of Cheese or the White Worm was

ever found. In his grief and fury, King Aegon II commanded that all the city's ratcatchers be taken out and hanged, and this was done. (Ser Otto Hightower brought one hundred cats into the Red Keep to take their place.)

Though Blood and Cheese had spared her life, Queen Helaena cannot be said to have survived that fateful dusk. Afterward she would not eat, nor bathe, nor leave her chambers, and she could no longer stand to look upon her son Maelor, knowing that she had named him to die. The king had no recourse but to take the boy from her and give him over to their mother, the Dowager Queen Alicent, to raise as if he were her own. Aegon and his wife slept separately thereafter, and Queen Helaena sank deeper and deeper into madness, whilst the king raged, and drank, and raged.

The Dying of the Dragons

The Red Dragon and the Gold

The Dance of the Dragons entered a new stage after the death of Lucerys Velaryon in the stormlands and the murder of Prince Jaehaerys before his mother's eyes in the Red Keep. For both the blacks and the greens, blood called to blood for vengeance. And all across the realm, lords called their banners, and armies gathered and began to march.

In the riverlands, raiders out of Raventree, flying Rhaenyra's banners,* crossed into the lands of House Bracken, burning crops, driving off sheep and cattle, sacking villages, and despoiling every sept they came on (the Blackwoods were one of the last houses south of the Neck who still followed the old gods).

When the Brackens gathered a strong force to strike back, Lord Samwell Blackwood surprised them on the march, taking them unawares as

* Initially both claimants to the Iron Throne flew the three-headed dragon of House Targaryen, red on black, but by the end of 129 AC, both Aegon and Rhaenyra had introduced variations to distinguish their own supporters from their foes. The king changed the color of the dragon on his banners from red to gold, to celebrate the brilliant golden scales of his dragon, Sunfyre, whilst the queen quartered the Targaryen arms with those of House Arryn and House Velaryon, in honor of her lady mother and her first husband, respectively.

they camped beneath a riverside mill. In the fight that followed, the mill was put to the torch, and men fought and died for hours bathed in the red light of the flames. Ser Amos Bracken, leading the host from Stone Hedge, cut down and slew Lord Blackwood in single combat, only to perish himself when a weirwood arrow found the eye slit of his helm and drove deep into his skull. Supposedly that shaft was loosed by Lord Samwell's sixteen-year-old sister, Alysanne, who would later be known as Black Aly, but whether this is fact or mere family legend cannot be known.

Many other grievous losses were suffered by both sides in what became known as the Battle of the Burning Mill . . . and when the Brackens finally broke and fled back unto their own lands under the command of Ser Amos's bastard half-brother, Ser Raylon Rivers, it was only to find that Stone Hedge had been taken in their absence. Led by Prince Daemon on Caraxes, a strong host made up of Darrys, Rootes, Pipers, and Freys had captured the castle by storm in the absence of so much of House Bracken's strength. Lord Humfrey Bracken and his remaining children had been made captive, along with his third wife and baseborn paramour. Rather than see them come to harm, Ser Raylon yielded. With House Bracken thus broken and defeated, the last of King Aegon's supporters in the riverlands lost heart and lay down their own swords as well.

Yet it must not be thought that the green council was sitting idle. Ser Otto Hightower had been busy as well, winning over lords, hiring sellswords, strengthening the defenses of King's Landing, and assiduously seeking after other alliances. After the rejection of Grand Maester Orwyle's peace overtures the Hand redoubled his efforts, dispatching ravens to Winterfell and the Eyrie, to Riverrun, White Harbor, Gulltown, Bitterbridge, Fair Isle, and half a hundred other keeps and castles. Riders galloped through the night to holdings closer to hand, to summon their lords and ladies to court to do fealty to King Aegon. Ser Otto also reached out to Dorne, whose ruling prince, Qoren Martell, had once warred against Prince Daemon in the Stepstones, but Prince Qoren spurned his offer. "Dorne has danced with dragons before," he said. "I would sooner sleep with scorpions."

Yet Ser Otto was losing the trust of his king, who mistook his efforts for inaction, and his caution for cowardice. Septon Eustace tells us of one occasion when Aegon entered the Tower of the Hand and found Ser Otto writing another letter, whereupon he knocked the inkpot into his grandsire's lap, declaring, "Thrones are won with swords, not quills. Spill blood, not ink."

The fall of Harrenhal to Prince Daemon came as a great shock to His Grace, Munkun tells us. Until that moment, Aegon II had believed his half-sister's cause to be hopeless. Harrenhal left His Grace feeling vulnerable for the first time. The subsequent defeats at the Burning Mill and Stone Hedge came as further blows, and made the king realize that his situation was more perilous than it had seemed. These fears deepened as ravens returned from the Reach, where the greens had believed themselves strongest. House Hightower and Oldtown were solidly behind King Aegon, and His Grace had the Arbor too . . . but elsewhere in the south, other lords were declaring for Rhaenyra, amongst them Lord Costayne of Three Towers, Lord Mullendore of Uplands, Lord Tarly of Horn Hill, Lord Rowan of Goldengrove, and Lord Grimm of Greyshield.

Loudest amongst these traitors was Ser Alan Beesbury, Lord Lyman's heir, who was demanding the release of his grandsire from the dungeon, where most believed the former master of coin to be confined. Faced with such a clamor from their own bannermen, the castellan, steward, and mother of the young Lord Tyrell of Highgarden, acting as regents for the boy, suddenly thought better of their support for King Aegon, and decided House Tyrell would take no part in this struggle. King Aegon began to drown his fears in strongwine, Septon Eustace tells us. Ser Otto sent word to his nephew, Lord Ormund Hightower, beseeching him to use the power of Oldtown to put down this rash of rebellions in the Reach.

Other blows followed: the Vale, White Harbor, Winterfell. The Blackwoods and the other riverlords streamed toward Harrenhal and Prince Daemon's banners. The Sea Snake's fleets closed Blackwater Bay, and every morning King Aegon had merchants whining at him. His Grace had no answer for their complaints, beyond another cup of strongwine. "Do something," he demanded of Ser Otto.

The Hand assured him that something *was* being done; he had hatched a plan to break the Velaryon blockade. One of the chief pillars of support for Rhaenyra's claim was her consort, yet Prince Daemon represented one of her greatest weaknesses as well. The prince had made more foes than friends during the course of his adventures. Ser Otto Hightower, who had been amongst the first of those foes, reached across the narrow sea to another of the prince's enemies, the Kingdom of the Three Daughters.

By itself, the royal fleet lacked the strength to break the Sea Snake's chokehold on the Gullet, and King Aegon's overtures to Dalton Greyjoy of Pyke had thus far failed to win the Iron Islands to his side. The combined fleets of Tyrosh, Lys, and Myr would be more than a match for the Velaryons, however. Ser Otto sent word to the magisters, promising exclusive trading rights at King's Landing if they would clear the Gullet of the Sea Snake's ships and open the sea lanes once again. To add savor to the stew, he also promised to cede the Stepstones to the Three Daughters, though in truth the Iron Throne had never claimed those isles.

The Triarchy was never quick to move, however. Lacking a true king, all important decisions in this three-headed "kingdom" were decided by the High Council. Eleven magisters from each city made up its membership, every man of them intent on demonstrating his own sagacity, shrewdness, and importance, and winning every possible advantage for his own city. Grand Maester Greydon, who wrote the definitive history of the Kingdom of the Three Daughters fifty years later, described it as "thirty-three horses, each pulling in his own direction." Even issues as timely as war, peace, and alliance were subject to endless debate . . . and the High Council was not even in session when Ser Otto's envoys arrived.

The delay did not sit well with the young king. Aegon II had run short of patience with his grandfather's prevarications. Though his mother, the Dowager Queen Alicent, spoke up in Ser Otto's defense, His Grace turned a deaf ear to her pleading. Summoning Ser Otto to the throne room, he tore the chain of office from his neck and tossed it to Ser Criston Cole. "My new Hand is a steel fist," he boasted. "We are done with writing letters."

Ser Criston wasted no time in proving his mettle. "It is not for you to plead for support from your lords, like a beggar pleading for alms," he told Aegon. "You are the lawful king of Westeros, and those who deny it are traitors. It is past time they learned the price of treason."

First to pay that price were the captive lords languishing in the dungeons under the Red Keep, men who had once sworn to defend the rights of Princess Rhaenyra and still stubbornly refused to bend the knee to King Aegon. One by one they were dragged out into the castle ward, where the King's Justice awaited them with his axe. Each man was given one final chance to swear fealty to His Grace; only Lord Butterwell, Lord Stokeworth, and Lord Rosby chose to do so. Lord Hayford, Lord Merryweather, Lord Harte, Lord Buckler, Lord Caswell, and Lady Fell valued their sworn word more than their lives, and were beheaded each in turn, along with eight landed knights and twoscore servants and retainers. Their heads were mounted on spikes above the city's gates.

King Aegon also desired to avenge the murder of his heir by Blood and Cheese by means of an attack on Dragonstone, descending on the island citadel on dragonback to seize or slay his half-sister and her "bastard sons." It took all of the green council to dissuade him. Ser Criston Cole urged a different course. The pretender princess had made use of stealth and treachery to kill Prince Jaehaerys, Cole said; let them do the same. "We will pay the princess back in her own bloody coin," he told the king. The instrument the Lord Commander of the Kingsguard chose for the king's vengeance was his Sworn Brother, Ser Arryk Cargyll.

Ser Arryk was intimately familiar with the ancient seat of House Targaryen, having visited there often during the reign of King Viserys. Many fishermen still plied the waters of Blackwater Bay, for Dragonstone depended on the sea for sustenance; it would be a simple thing to deliver Cargyll to the fishing village under the castle. From there he could make his own way to the queen. And Ser Arryk and his brother Ser Erryk were twins, identical in all respects; not even their fellows of the Kingsguard could tell the two apart, both Mushroom and Septon Eustace assert. Once clad in white, Ser Arryk should be able to move freely about Dragonstone, Ser Criston suggested; any guards who chanced to encounter him would surely mistake him for his brother.

Ser Arryk did not undertake this mission happily. Indeed, Septon Eustace tells us, the troubled knight visited the Red Keep's sept on the night he was to sail, to pray for forgiveness to our Mother Above. Yet as Kingsguard, sworn to obey king and commander, he had no choice in honor but to make his way to Dragonstone, clad in the salt-stained garb of a simple fisherman.

The true purpose of Ser Arryk's mission remains a matter of some contention. Grand Maester Munkun tells us that Cargyll had been commanded to slay Rhaenyra, putting an end to her rebellion at a stroke, whilst Mushroom insists that her sons were Cargyll's prey, that Aegon II wished to wash out the blood of his murdered son with that of his bastard nephews, Jacaerys and Joffrey "Strong."

Ser Arryk came ashore without hindrance, donned his armor and white cloak, and had no trouble gaining entrance to the castle in the guise of his twin brother, just as Criston Cole had planned. Deep in the heart of Dragonstone, however, as he was making his way to the royal apartments, the gods brought him face-to-face with Ser Erryk himself, who knew at once what his brother's presence meant. The singers tell us that Ser Erryk said, "I love you, brother," as he unsheathed his blade, and that Ser Arryk replied, "And I you, brother," as he drew his own.

The twins battled for the best part of an hour, Grand Maester Munkun says; the clash of steel on steel woke half of the queen's court, but the onlookers could only stand by helplessly and watch, for no man there could tell which brother was which. In the end, Ser Arryk and Ser Erryk dealt each other mortal wounds, and died in one another's arms with tears upon their cheeks.

Mushroom's account is shorter, saltier, and altogether nastier. The fight lasted only moments, our fool says. There were no declarations of brotherly love; each Cargyll denounced the other as a traitor as they clashed. Ser Erryk, standing above his twin on the spiral steps, struck the first mortal blow, a savage downward cut that nigh took his brother's sword arm off at the shoulder, but as he collapsed Ser Arryk grasped his slayer's white cloak and pulled him close enough to drive a dagger deep into his belly. Ser Arryk was dead before the first guards arrived, but Ser Erryk took four days to die of his gut wound, screaming in horrible pain and cursing his traitor brother all the while.

For obvious reasons, singers and storytellers have shown a marked preference for the tale as told by Munkun. Maesters and other scholars must make their own determination as to which version is more likely. All that Septon Eustace says upon the matter is that the Cargyll twins slew each other, and there we must leave it.

Back in King's Landing, King Aegon's master of whisperers, Larys Strong the Clubfoot, had drawn up a list of all those lords who gathered on Dragonstone to attend Queen Rhaenyra's coronation and sit on her black council. Lords Celtigar and Velaryon had their seats on islands; as Aegon II had no strength at sea, they were beyond the reach of his wroth. Those black lords whose lands were on the mainland enjoyed no such protection, however.

With a hundred knights and five hundred men-at-arms of the royal household, augmented by three times as many hardened sellswords, Ser Criston marched on Rosby and Stokeworth, whose lords had only recently repented of their allegiance to the queen, commanding them to prove their loyalty by adding their power to his own. Thus augmented, Cole's host advanced upon the walled harbor town of Duskendale, where they took the defenders by surprise. The town was sacked, the ships in the harbor set afire, Lord Darklyn beheaded. His household knights and garrison were given the choice between swearing their swords to King Aegon or sharing their lord's fate. Most chose the former.

Rook's Rest was Ser Criston's next objective. Forewarned of their coming, Lord Staunton closed his gates and defied the attackers. Behind his walls, his lordship could only watch as his fields and woods and villages were burned, his sheep and cattle and smallfolk put to the sword. When provisions inside the castle began to run low, he dispatched a raven to Dragonstone, pleading for succor.

The bird arrived as Rhaenyra and her blacks were mourning Ser Erryk and debating the proper response to "Aegon the Usurper's" latest attack. Though shaken by this attempt on her life (or the lives of her sons), the queen was still reluctant to attack King's Landing. Munkun (who, it must be remembered, wrote many years later) says this was because of her horror of kinslaying. Maegor the Cruel had slain his own nephew Aegon, and had been cursed thereafter, until he bled his life away upon his stolen throne. Septon Eustace claims Rhaenyra had "a mother's heart" that made her reluctant to risk the lives of her remaining sons. Mushroom alone was present for these councils, however, and the fool insists that Rhaenyra was still so griefsick over the death of her son Lucerys that she absented herself from the war council, giving over her command to the Sea Snake and his wife, Princess Rhaenys.

Here Mushroom's version seems most likely, for we know that nine days after Lord Staunton dispatched his plea for help, the sound of leathern wings was heard across the sea, and the dragon Meleys appeared above Rook's Rest. The Red Queen, she was called, for the scarlet scales that covered her. The membranes of her wings were pink, her crest, horns, and claws bright as copper. And on her back, in steel and copper armor that flashed in the sun, rode Rhaenys Targaryen, the Queen Who Never Was.

Ser Criston Cole was not dismayed. Aegon's Hand had expected this, counted on it. Drums beat out a command, and archers rushed forward, longbowmen and crossbowmen both, filling the air with arrows and quarrels. Scorpions were cranked upward to loose iron bolts of the sort that had once felled Meraxes in Dorne. Meleys suffered a score of hits, but the arrows only served to make her angry. She swept down, spitting fire to right and left. Knights burned in their saddles as the hair and hide and harness of their horses went up in flames. Men-at-arms dropped their spears and scattered. Some tried to hide behind their shields, but neither oak nor iron could withstand dragon's breath. Ser Criston sat on his white horse shouting, "Aim for the rider," through the smoke and flame. Meleys roared, smoke swirling from her nostrils, a stallion kicking in her jaws as tongues of fire engulfed him.

Then came an answering roar. Two more winged shapes appeared: the king astride Sunfyre the Golden, and his brother Aemond upon Vhagar. Criston Cole had sprung his trap, and Rhaenys had come snatching at the bait. Now the teeth closed round her.

Princess Rhaenys made no attempt to flee. With a glad cry and a crack of her whip, she turned Meleys toward the foe. Against Vhagar alone she might have had some chance, but against Vhagar and Sunfyre together, doom was certain. The dragons met violently a thousand feet above the field of battle, as balls of fire burst and blossomed, so bright that men swore later that the sky was full of suns. The crimson jaws of Meleys closed round Sunfyre's golden neck for a moment, till Vhagar fell upon them from above. All three beasts went spinning toward the ground. They struck the ground so hard that stones fell from the battlements of Rook's Rest half a league away.

Those closest to the dragons did not live to tell the tale. Those farther off could not see for the flame and smoke. It was hours before the fires guttered out. But from those ashes, only Vhagar rose unharmed. Meleys was dead, broken by the fall and ripped to pieces upon the ground. And Sunfyre, that splendid golden beast, had one wing half torn from his body, whilst his royal rider had suffered broken ribs, a broken hip, and burns that covered half his body. His left arm was the worst. The dragon-flame had burned so hot that the king's armor had melted into his flesh.

A body believed to be Rhaenys Targaryen was later found beside the carcass of her dragon, but it was so blackened that no one could be sure it was her. Beloved daughter of Lady Jocelyn Baratheon and Prince Aemon Targaryen, faithful wife to Lord Corlys Velaryon, mother and grandmother, the Queen Who Never Was lived fearlessly, and died amidst blood and fire. She was fifty-five years old.

Eight hundred knights and squires and common men lost their lives that day as well. Another hundred perished not long after, when Prince Aemond and Ser Criston Cole took Rook's Rest and put its garrison to death. Lord Staunton's head was carried back to King's Landing and mounted above the Old Gate . . . but it was the head of the dragon Meleys, drawn through the city on a cart, that awed the crowds of smallfolk into silence. Septon Eustace tells us that thousands left King's Landing afterward, until the Dowager Queen Alicent ordered the city gates closed and barred.

King Aegon II did not die, though his burns brought him such pain that some say he prayed for death. Carried back to King's Landing in a closed litter to hide the extent of his injuries, His Grace did not rise from his bed for the rest of the year. Septons prayed for him, maesters attended him with potions and milk of the poppy, but Aegon slept nine hours out of every ten, waking only long enough to take some meagre nourishment before he slept again. None was allowed to disturb his rest, save his mother

the Queen Dowager and his Hand, Ser Criston Cole. His wife never so much as made the attempt, so lost was Helaena in her own grief and madness.

The king's dragon, Sunfyre, too huge and heavy to be moved, and unable to fly with his injured wing, remained in the fields beyond Rook's Rest, crawling through the ashes like some great golden wyrm. In the early days he fed himself upon the burned carcasses of the slain. When those were gone, the men Ser Criston had left behind to guard him brought him calves and sheep.

"You must rule the realm now, until your brother is strong enough to take the crown again," the King's Hand told Prince Aemond. Nor did Ser Criston need to say it twice, writes Eustace. And so one-eyed Aemond the Kinslayer took up the iron-and-ruby crown of Aegon the Conqueror. "It looks better on me than it ever did on him," the prince proclaimed. Yet Aemond did not assume the style of king, but named himself only Protector of the Realm and Prince Regent. Ser Criston Cole remained Hand of the King.

Meanwhile, the seeds Jacaerys Velaryon had planted on his flight north had begun to bear fruit, and men were gathering at White Harbor, Winterfell, Barrowton, Sisterton, Gulltown, and the Gates of the Moon. Should they join their strength to that of the riverlords assembling at Harrenhal with Prince Daemon, even the strong walls of King's Landing might not be able to withstand them, Ser Criston warned the new Prince Regent.

The tidings from the south were ominous as well. Obedient to his uncle's entreaties, Lord Ormund Hightower had issued forth from Oldtown with a thousand knights, a thousand archers, three thousand men-at-arms, and uncounted thousands of camp followers, sellswords, freeriders, and rabble, only to find himself set upon by Ser Alan Beesbury and Lord Alan Tarly. Though commanding far fewer men, the two Alans harassed him day and night, raiding his camps, murdering his scouts, setting fires in his line of march. Farther south, Lord Costayne had issued forth from Three Towers to fall upon Hightower's baggage train. Worse, reports had reached his lordship that a host equal in size to his own was descending on the Mander, led by Thaddeus Rowan, Lord of Goldengrove. Lord Ormund had therefore decided he could not proceed without support from King's Landing. "We have need of your dragons," he wrote.

Supremely confident in his own prowess as a warrior and the might of his dragon, Vhagar, Aemond was eager to take the battle to the foe. "The whore on Dragonstone is not the threat," he said. "No more than Rowan and these traitors in the Reach. The danger is my uncle. Once Daemon is dead, all these fools flying our sister's banners will run back to their castles and trouble us no more."

East of Blackwater Bay, Queen Rhaenyra was also faring badly. The death of her son Lucerys had been a crushing blow to a woman already broken by pregnancy, labor, and stillbirth. When word reached Dragonstone that Princess Rhaenys had fallen, angry words were exchanged between the queen and Lord Velaryon, who blamed her for his wife's death. "It should have been you," the Sea Snake shouted at Her Grace. "Staunton sent to you, yet you left it to my wife to answer and forbade your sons to join her." For all the castle knew that the princes Jace and Joff had been eager to fly with Princess Rhaenys to Rook's Rest with their own dragons.

"Only I could lighten Her Grace's heart," Mushroom claims in his *Testimony*. "In this dark hour, I became the queen's counselor, setting aside my fool's sceptre and pointed hat to lend her all my wisdom and compassion. Unbeknownst to all, it was the jester who ruled them now, an invisible king in motley."

These are large claims for a small man, and ones not borne out by any of our other chroniclers, no more than by the facts. Her Grace was far from alone. Four living sons remained to her. "My strength and my consolation," the queen called them. Aegon the Younger and Viserys, Prince Daemon's sons, were nine and seven, respectively. Prince Joffrey was but eleven . . . but Jacaerys, Prince of Dragonstone, was on the cusp of his fifteenth nameday.

It was Jace who came to the fore now, late in the year 129 AC. Mindful of the promise he had made to the Maiden of the Vale, he ordered Prince Joffrey to fly to Gulltown with Tyraxes. Munkun suggests that Jace's desire to keep his brother far from the fighting was paramount in this decision. This did not sit well with Joffrey, who was determined to prove himself in battle. Only when told that he was being sent to defend the

Vale against King Aegon's dragons did his brother grudgingly consent to go. Rhaena, the thirteen-year-old daughter of Prince Daemon by Laena Velaryon, was chosen to accompany him. Known as Rhaena of Pentos, for the city of her birth, she was no dragonrider, her hatchling having died some years before, but she brought three dragon's eggs with her to the Vale, where she prayed nightly for their hatching.

Lady Rhaena's twin, Baela, remained on Dragonstone. Long betrothed to Prince Jacaerys, she refused to leave him, insisting that she would fight beside him on her own dragon . . . though Moondancer was too small to bear her weight. Though Baela also announced her intent to marry Jace at once, no wedding was ever held. Munkun says the prince did not wish to wed until the war was over, whilst Mushroom claims Jacaerys was already married to Sara Snow, the mysterious bastard girl from Winterfell.

The Prince of Dragonstone also had a care for the safety of his half-brothers, Aegon the Younger and Viserys, aged nine and seven. Their father, Prince Daemon, had made many friends in the Free City of Pentos during his visits there, so Jacaerys reached across the narrow sea to the prince of that city, who agreed to foster the two boys until Rhaenyra had secured the Iron Throne. In the waning days of 129 AC, the young princes boarded the cog *Gay Abandon*—Aegon with Stormcloud, Viserys clutching his egg—to set sail for Essos. The Sea Snake sent seven of his warships with them as escort, to see that they reached Pentos safely.

Prince Jacaerys soon brought the Lord of the Tides back into the fold by naming him the Hand of the Queen. Together he and Lord Corlys began to plan an assault upon King's Landing.

With Sunfyre wounded near Rook's Rest and unable to fly, and Tessarion with Prince Daeron in Oldtown, only two mature dragons remained to defend King's Landing . . . and Dreamfyre's rider, Queen Helaena, spent her days in darkness, weeping, and surely could not be counted as a threat. That left only Vhagar. No living dragon could match Vhagar for size or ferocity, but Jace reasoned that if Vermax, Syrax, and Caraxes were to descend on King's Landing, even "that hoary old bitch" would be unable to withstand them.

Mushroom was less certain. "Three is more than one," the dwarf claims to have told the Prince of Dragonstone, "but four is more than three, and six is more than four, even a fool knows that." When Jace pointed out that Stormcloud had never been ridden, that Moondancer was but a hatchling, that Tyraxes was far away in the Vale with Prince Joffrey, and demanded to know where Mushroom proposed to find more dragons, the dwarf tells us he laughed and said, "Under the sheets and in the woodpiles, wherever you Targaryens spilled your silver seed."

House Targaryen had ruled Dragonstone for more than two hundred years, since Lord Aenar Targaryen first arrived from Valyria with his dragons. Though it had always been their custom to wed brother to sister and cousin to cousin, young blood runs hot, and it was not unknown for men of the house to seek their pleasures amongst the daughters (and even the wives) of their subjects, the smallfolk who lived in the villages below the Dragonmont, tillers of the land and fishers of the sea. Indeed, until the reign of King Jaehaerys, the ancient right to the first night had been invoked mayhaps more oft on Dragonstone than anywhere else in the Seven Kingdoms, though Good Queen Alysanne would surely have been shocked to hear it.

Though the first night was greatly resented elsewhere, as Queen Alysanne had learned in her women's counsels, such feelings were muted upon Dragonstone, where Targaryens were rightly regarded as being closer to gods than the common run of men. Here, brides thus blessed upon their wedding nights were envied, and the children born of such unions were esteemed above all others, for the Lords of Dragonstone oft celebrated the birth of such with lavish gifts of gold and silk and land to the mother. These happy bastards were said to have been "born of dragonseed," and in time became known simply as "seeds." Even after the end of the right of the first night, certain Targaryens continued to dally with the daughters of innkeeps and the wives of fishermen, so seeds and the sons of seeds were plentiful on Dragonstone.

It was to them that Prince Jacaerys turned, at the urging of his fool, vowing that any man who could master a dragon would be granted lands and riches and dubbed a knight. His sons would be ennobled, his daughters wed to lords, and he himself would have the honor of fighting beside the Prince of Dragonstone against the pretender Aegon II Targaryen and his treasonous supporters.

Not all those who came forward in answer to the prince's call were seeds, nor even the sons or grandsons of seeds. A score of the queen's own household knights offered themselves as dragonriders, amongst them the Lord Commander of her Queensguard, Ser Steffon Darklyn, along with squires, scullions, sailors, men-at-arms, mummers, and two maids. "The Sowing of the Seeds," Munkun names the triumphs and tragedies that ensued (crediting the notion to Jacaerys himself, not Mushroom). Others prefer "the Red Sowing."

The most unlikely of these would-be dragonriders was Mushroom himself, whose *Testimony* speaks at length of his attempt to mount old Silverwing, judged to be the most docile of the masterless dragons. One of the dwarf's more amusing tales, it ends with Mushroom running across the ward of Dragonstone with the seat of his pantaloons on fire, and nigh drowning when he leapt into a well to quench the flames. Unlikely, to be sure . . . but it does provide a droll moment in what was otherwise a ghastly business.

Dragons are not horses. They do not easily accept men upon their backs, and when angered or threatened, they attack. Munkun's *True Telling* tells us that sixteen men lost their lives during the Sowing. Three times that number were burned or maimed. Steffon Darklyn was burned to death whilst attempting to mount the dragon Seasmoke. Lord Gormon Massey suffered the same fate when approaching Vermithor. A man called Silver Denys, whose hair and eyes lent credence to his claim to be descended from a bastard son of Maegor the Cruel, had an arm torn off by Sheepstealer. As his sons struggled to staunch the wound, the Cannibal descended on them, drove off Sheepstealer, and devoured father and sons alike.

Yet Seasmoke, Vermithor, and Silverwing were accustomed to men and tolerant of their presence. Having once been ridden, they were more accepting of new riders. Vermithor, the Old King's own dragon, bent his neck to a blacksmith's bastard, a towering man called Hugh the Hammer or Hard Hugh, whilst a pale-haired man-at-arms named Ulf the White (for his hair) or Ulf the Sot (for his drinking) mounted Silverwing, beloved of Good Queen Alysanne. And Seasmoke, who had once borne Laenor Velaryon, took onto his back a boy of ten-and-five known as

Addam of Hull, whose origins remain a matter of dispute amongst historians to this day.

Addam and his brother, Alyn (one year younger), had been born to a woman named Marilda, the pretty young daughter of a shipwright. A familiar sight about her father's shipyards, the girl was better known as Mouse, for she was "small, quick, and always underfoot." She was still sixteen when she gave birth to Addam in 114 AC, and barely eighteen when Alyn followed in 115. Small and quick as their mother, these bastards of Hull were both silver of hair and purple of eye, and soon proved to have "sea salt in their blood" as well, growing up in their grandsire's shipyard and going to sea as ship's boys before the age of eight. When Addam was ten and Alyn nine, their mother inherited the yards upon her own father's death, sold them, and used the coin to take to the sea herself as the mistress of a trading cog she named *Mouse*. A canny trader and daring captain, by 130 AC Marilda of Hull owned seven ships, and her bastard sons were always serving on one or the other.

That Addam and Alyn were dragonseed no man who looked upon them could doubt, though their mother steadfastly refused to name their father. Only when Prince Jacaerys put out the call for new dragonriders did Marilda at last break her silence, claiming both boys were the natural sons of the late Ser Laenor Velaryon.

They had his look, it was true, and Ser Laenor had been known to visit the shipyard in Hull from time to time. Nonetheless, many on Dragonstone and Driftmark were skeptical of Marilda's claim, for Laenor Velaryon's disinterest in women was well remembered. None dared name her liar, however . . . for it was Laenor's own father, Lord Corlys himself, who brought the boys to Prince Jacaerys for the Sowing. Having outlived all of his children and suffered the betrayal of his nephews and cousins, the Sea Snake seemed more than eager to accept these newfound grandsons. And when Addam of Hull mounted Ser Laenor's dragon, Seasmoke, it seemed to prove the truth of his mother's claims.

It should not surprise us, therefore, that Grand Maester Munkun and Septon Eustace both dutifully assert Ser Laenor's parentage . . . but Mushroom, as ever, dissents. In his *Testimony,* the fool puts forth the notion that "the little mice" had been sired not by the Sea Snake's son, but by the Sea

Snake himself. Lord Corlys did not share Ser Laenor's erotic predispositions, he points out, and the Hull shipyards were like unto a second home to him, whereas his son visited them less frequently. Princess Rhaenys, his wife, had the fiery temperament of many Targaryens, Mushroom says, and would not have taken kindly to her lord husband fathering bastards on a girl half her age, and a shipwright's daughter besides. Therefore his lordship had prudently ended his "shipyard trysts" with Mouse after Alyn's birth, commanding her to keep her boys far from court. Only after the death of Princess Rhaenys did Lord Corlys at last feel able to bring his bastards safely forward.

In this instance, it must be said, the tale told by the fool seems more likely than the versions offered by septon and maester. Many and more at Queen Rhaenyra's court must surely have suspected the same. If so, they held their tongues. Not long after Addam of Hull had proved himself by flying Seasmoke, Lord Corlys went so far as to petition Queen Rhaenyra to remove the taint of bastardy from him and his brother. When Prince Jacaerys added his voice to the request, the queen complied. Addam of Hull, dragonseed and bastard, became Addam Velaryon, heir to Driftmark.

Yet that did not write an end to the Red Sowing. More, and worse, was yet to come, with dire consequences for the Seven Kingdoms.

Dragonstone's three wild dragons were less easily claimed than those that had known previous riders, yet attempts were made upon them all the same. Sheepstealer, a notably ugly "mud brown" dragon hatched when the Old King was still young, had a taste for mutton, swooping down on shepherd's flocks from Driftmark to the Wendwater. He seldom harmed the shepherds, unless they attempted to interfere with him, but had been known to devour the occasional sheep dog. Grey Ghost dwelt in a smoking vent high on the eastern side of the Dragonmont, preferred fish, and was most oft glimpsed flying low over the narrow sea, snatching prey from the waters. A pale grey-white beast, the color of morning mist, he was a notably shy dragon who avoided men and their works for years at a time.

The largest and oldest of the wild dragons was the Cannibal, so named because he had been known to feed on the carcasses of dead dragons, and descend upon the hatcheries of Dragonstone to gorge himself on newborn hatchlings and eggs. Coal black, with baleful green eyes, the Cannibal had made his lair on Dragonstone even before the coming of the Targaryens, some smallfolk claimed. (Grand Maester Munkun and Septon Eustace both found this story most unlikely, as do I.) Would-be dragontamers had made attempts to ride him a dozen times; his lair was littered with their bones.

None of the dragonseeds were fool enough to disturb the Cannibal (any who were did not return to tell their tales). Some sought the Grey Ghost, but could not find him, for he was ever an elusive creature. Sheepstealer proved easier to flush out, but he remained a vicious, ill-tempered beast, who killed more seeds than the three castle dragons together. One who hoped to tame him (after his quest for Grey Ghost proved fruitless) was Alyn of Hull. Sheepstealer would have none of him. When he stumbled from the dragon's lair with his cloak aflame, only his brother's swift action saved his life. Seasmoke drove the wild dragon off as Addam used his own cloak to beat out the flames. Alyn Velaryon would carry the scars

of the encounter on his back and legs for the rest of his long life. Yet he counted himself fortunate, for he lived. Many of the other seeds and seekers who aspired to ride upon Sheepstealer's back ended in Sheepstealer's belly instead.

In the end, the brown dragon was brought to heel by the cunning and persistence of a "small brown girl" of six-and-ten, who delivered him a freshly slaughtered sheep every morning, until Sheepstealer learned to accept and expect her. Munkun sets down the name of this unlikely dragonrider as Nettles. Mushroom tells us the girl was a bastard of uncertain birth called Netty, born to a dockside whore. By any name, she was black-haired, brown-eyed, brown-skinned, skinny, foul-mouthed, fearless . . . and the first and last rider of the dragon Sheepstealer.

Thus did Prince Jacaerys achieve his goal. For all the death and pain it caused, the widows left behind, the burned men who would carry their scars until the day they died, four new dragonriders had been found. As 129 AC drew to a close, the prince prepared to fly against King's Landing. The date he chose for the attack was the first full moon of the new year.

Yet the plans of men are but playthings to the gods. For even as Jace laid his plans, a new threat was closing from the east. The schemes of Otto Hightower had borne fruit; meeting in Tyrosh, the High Council of the Triarchy had accepted his offer of alliance. Ninety warships swept from the Stepstones under the banners of the Three Daughters, bending their oars for the Gullet . . . and as chance and the gods would have it, the Pentoshi cog *Gay Abandon,* carrying two Targaryen princes, sailed straight into their teeth.

The escorts sent to protect the cog were sunk or taken; the *Gay Abandon* captured. The tale reached Dragonstone only when Prince Aegon arrived desperately clinging to the neck of his dragon, Stormcloud. The boy was white with terror, Mushroom tells us, shaking like a leaf and stinking of piss. Only nine, he had never flown before . . . and would never fly again, for Stormcloud had been terribly wounded as he fled the *Gay Abandon,* arriving with the stubs of countless arrows embedded in his belly, and a scorpion bolt through his neck. He died within the hour, hissing as the hot blood gushed black and smoking from his wounds.

Aegon's younger brother, Prince Viserys, had no way of escaping from the cog. A clever boy, he hid his dragon's egg and changed into ragged, salt-stained clothing, pretending to be no more than a common ship's boy, but one of the real ship's boys betrayed him, and he was made a captive. It was a Tyroshi captain who first realized whom he had, Munkun writes, but the admiral of the fleet, Sharako Lohar of Lys, soon relieved him of his prize.

The Lysene admiral divided his fleet for the attack. One pincer was to enter the Gullet south of Dragonstone, the other to the north. In the early morning hours of the fifth day of the 130th year since Aegon's Conquest, battle was joined. Sharako's warships swept in with the rising sun behind them. Hidden by the glare, they took many of Lord Velaryon's galleys unawares, ramming some and swarming aboard others with ropes and grapnels. Leaving Dragonstone unmolested, the southern squadron fell upon the shores of Driftmark, landing men at Spicetown and sending fire ships into the harbor to set ablaze the ships coming out to meet them. By mid-morning Spicetown was burning, whilst Myrish and Tyroshi troops battered at the very doors of High Tide.

When Prince Jacaerys swept down upon a line of Lysene galleys on Vermax, a rain of spears and arrows rose up to meet him. The sailors of the Triarchy had faced dragons before whilst warring against Prince Daemon in the Stepstones. No man could fault their courage; they were prepared to meet dragonflame with such weapons as they had. "Kill the rider and the dragon will depart," their captains and commanders had told them. One ship took fire, and then another. Still the men of the Free Cities fought on . . . until a shout rang out, and they looked up to see more winged shapes coming around the Dragonmont and turning toward them.

It is one thing to face a dragon, another to face five. As Silverwing, Sheepstealer, Seasmoke, and Vermithor descended upon them, the men of the Triarchy felt their courage desert them. The line of warships shattered, as one galley after another turned away. The dragons fell like thunderbolts, spitting balls of fire, blue and orange, red and gold, each brighter than the next. Ship after ship burst asunder or was consumed by flames. Screaming men leapt into the sea, shrouded in fire. Tall columns of black smoke rose up from the water. All seemed lost . . . all *was* lost . . .

Several differing tales were told afterward of how and why the dragon fell. Some claimed a crossbowman put an iron bolt through his eye, but this version seems suspiciously similar to the way Meraxes met her end, long ago in Dorne. Another account tells us that a sailor in the crow's nest of a Myrish galley cast a grapnel as Vermax was swooping through the fleet. One of its prongs found purchase between two scales, and was driven deep by the dragon's own considerable speed. The sailor had coiled his end of the chain about the mast, and the weight of the ship and the power of Vermax's wings tore a long jagged gash in the dragon's belly. The dragon's shriek of rage was heard as far off as Spicetown, even through the clangor of battle. His flight jerked to a violent end, Vermax went down smoking and screaming, clawing at the water. Survivors said he struggled to rise, only to crash headlong into a burning galley. Wood splintered, the mast came tumbling down, and the dragon, thrashing, became entangled in the rigging. When the ship heeled over and sank, Vermax sank with her.

It is said that Jacaerys Velaryon leapt free and clung to a piece of smoking wreckage for a few heartbeats, until some crossbowmen on the nearest Myrish ship began loosing quarrels at him. The prince was struck once, and then again. More and more Myrmen brought crossbows to bear. Finally one quarrel took him through the neck, and Jace was swallowed by the sea.

The Battle in the Gullet raged into the night north and south of Dragonstone, and remains amongst the bloodiest sea battles in all of history. Sharako Lohar had taken a combined fleet of ninety Myrish, Lyseni, and Tyroshi warships from the Stepstones; twenty-eight survived to limp home, all but three crewed by Lyseni. In the aftermath, the widows of Myr and Tyrosh accused the admiral of sending their fleets to destruction whilst holding back his own, beginning the quarrel that would spell the end of the Triarchy two years later, when the three cities turned against each other in the Daughters' War. But that is outside the scope of this tale.

Though the attackers bypassed Dragonstone, no doubt believing that the ancient Targaryen stronghold was too strong to assault, they exacted a grievous toll on Driftmark. Spicetown was brutally sacked, the bodies of men, women, and children butchered in the streets and left as fodder for gulls and rats and carrion crows, its buildings burned. The town would never be rebuilt. High Tide was put to the torch as well. All the treasures

the Sea Snake had brought back from the east were consumed by fire, his servants cut down as they tried to flee the flames. The Velaryon fleet lost almost a third of its strength. Thousands died. Yet none of these losses were felt so deeply as that of Jacaerys Velaryon, Prince of Dragonstone and heir to the Iron Throne.

Rhaenyra's youngest son seemed lost as well. In the confusion of battle, none of the survivors seemed quite certain which ship Prince Viserys had been on. Men on both sides presumed him dead, drowned or burned or butchered. And though his brother Aegon the Younger had fled and lived, all the joy had gone out of the boy; he would never forgive himself for leaping onto Stormcloud and abandoning his little brother to the enemy. It is written that when the Sea Snake was congratulated on his victory, the old man said, "If this be victory, I pray I never win another."

Mushroom tells us there were two men on Dragonstone that night who drank to the slaughter in a smoky tavern beneath the castle: the dragonriders Hugh the Hammer and Ulf the White, who had flown Vermithor and Silverwing into battle and lived to boast of it. "We are knights now, truly," Hard Hugh declared. And Ulf laughed and said, "Fie on that. We should be lords."

The girl Nettles did not share their celebrations. She had flown with the others, fought as bravely, burned and killed as they had, but her face was black with smoke and streaked with tears when she returned to Dragonstone. And Addam Velaryon, lately Addam of Hull, sought out the Sea Snake after the battle; what they spoke to each other even Mushroom does not say.

A fortnight later, in the Reach, Ormund Hightower found himself caught between two armies. Thaddeus Rowan, Lord of Goldengrove, and Tom Flowers, Bastard of Bitterbridge, were bearing down on him from the northeast with a great host of mounted knights, whilst Ser Alan Beesbury, Lord Alan Tarly, and Lord Owen Costayne had joined their power to cut off his retreat to Oldtown. When their hosts closed around him on the banks of the river Honeywine, attacking front and rear at once, Lord Hightower saw his lines crumble. Defeat seemed imminent . . . until a shadow swept across the battlefield, and a terrible roar resounded overhead, slicing through the sound of steel on steel. A dragon had come.

The dragon was Tessarion, the Blue Queen, cobalt and copper. On her back rode the youngest of Queen Alicent's three sons, Daeron Targaryen, fifteen, Lord Ormund's squire, that same gentle and soft-spoken lad who had once been milk brother to Prince Jacaerys.

The arrival of Prince Daeron and his dragon reversed the tide of battle. Now it was Lord Ormund's men attacking, screaming curses at their foes, whilst the queen's men fled. By day's end, Lord Rowan was retreating north with the remnants of his host, Tom Flowers lay dead and burned amongst the reeds, the two Alans had been taken captive, and Lord Costayne was dying from a wound given him by Bold Jon Roxton's black blade, the Orphan-Maker. As wolves and ravens fed upon the bodies of the slain, Ormund Hightower feasted Prince Daeron on aurochs and strongwine, and dubbed him a knight with the storied Valyrian longsword Vigilance, naming him "Ser Daeron the Daring." The prince modestly replied, "My lord is kind to say so, but the victory belongs to Tessarion."

On Dragonstone, an air of despondence and defeat hung over the black court when the disaster on the Honeywine became known to them. Lord Bar Emmon went so far as to suggest that mayhaps the time had come to bend their knees to Aegon II. The queen would have none of it, however. Only the gods truly know the hearts of men, and women are full as strange. Broken by the loss of one son, Rhaenyra Targaryen seemed to find new strength after the loss of a second. Jace's death hardened her, burning away her fears, leaving only her anger and her hatred. Still possessed of more dragons than her half-brother, Her Grace now resolved to use them, no matter the cost. She would rain down fire and death upon Aegon and all those who supported him, she told the black council, and either tear him from the Iron Throne or die in the attempt.

A similar resolve had taken root across the bay in the breast of Aemond Targaryen, ruling in his brother's name whilst Aegon lay abed. Contemptuous of his half-sister Rhaenyra, Aemond One-Eye saw a greater threat in his uncle Prince Daemon and the great host he had gathered at Harrenhal. Summoning his bannermen and council, the prince announced his intent to bring the battle to his uncle and chastise the rebellious riverlords.

He proposed to strike the riverlands from both east and west, and thus force the Lords of the Trident to fight on two fronts at once. Jason Lannister had assembled a formidable host in the western hills; a thousand armored knights, and seven times as many archers and men-at-arms. Let him descend from the high ground and cross the Red Fork with fire and sword, whilst Ser Criston Cole marched forth from King's Landing, accompanied by Prince Aemond himself on Vhagar. The two armies would converge on Harrenhal to crush the "traitors of the Trident" between them. And if his uncle emerged from behind the castle walls to oppose them, as he surely must, Vhagar would overcome Caraxes, and Prince Aemond would return to the city with Prince Daemon's head.

Not all the members of the green council favored the prince's bold stroke. Aemond had the support of Ser Criston Cole, the Hand, and that of Ser Tyland Lannister, but Grand Maester Orwyle urged him to send word to Storm's End and add the power of House Baratheon to his own before proceeding, and Ironrod, Lord Jasper Wylde, declared that he should summon Lord Hightower and Prince Daeron from the south, on the grounds that "two dragons are better than one." The Queen Dowager favored caution as well, urging her son to wait until his brother the king and his dragon, Sunfyre the Golden, were healed, so they might join the attack.

Prince Aemond had no taste for such delays, however. He had no need of his brothers or their dragons, he declared; Aegon was too badly hurt, Daeron too young. Aye, Caraxes was a fearsome beast, savage and cunning and battle-tested . . . but Vhagar was older, fiercer, and twice as large. Septon Eustace tells us that the Kinslayer was determined that this should be his victory; he had no wish to share the glory with his brothers, nor any other man.

Nor could he be gainsaid, for until Aegon II rose from his bed to take up his sword again, the regency and rule were Aemond's. True to his resolve, the prince rode forth from the Gate of the Gods within a fortnight, at the head of a host four thousand strong. "Sixteen days' march to Harrenhal," he proclaimed. "On the seventeenth, we will feast inside Black Harren's hall, whilst my uncle's head looks down from my spear." And across the realm, obedient to his command, Jason Lannister, Lord of Casterly Rock, poured down out of the western hills, descending with all his power upon the Red Fork and the heart of the riverlands. The Lords of the Trident had no choice but to turn and meet him.

Daemon Targaryen was too old and seasoned a battler to sit idly by and let himself be penned up inside walls, even walls as massive as Harrenhal's. The prince still had friends in King's Landing, and word of his nephew's plans had reached him even before Aemond had set out. When told that Aemond and Ser Criston Cole had left King's Landing, it is said Prince Daemon laughed and said, "Past time," for he had long anticipated this moment. A murder of ravens took flight from the twisted towers of Harrenhal.

On the Red Fork, Lord Jason Lannister found himself facing the Lord of Pinkmaiden, old Petyr Piper, and the Lord of Wayfarer's Rest, Tristan Vance. Though the westermen outnumbered their foes, the riverlords knew the ground. Thrice the Lannisters tried to force the crossing, and thrice they were driven back; in the last attempt, Lord Jason was dealt a mortal wound at the hand of a grizzled squire, Pate of Longleaf. (Lord Piper himself knighted the man afterward, dubbing him Longleaf the Lionslayer.) The fourth Lannister attack carried the fords, however; this time it was Lord Vance who fell, slain by Ser Adrian Tarbeck, who had taken command of the western host. Tarbeck and a hundred picked knights stripped off their heavy armor and swam the river upstream of the battle, then circled about to take Lord Vance's lines from the rear. The ranks of the riverlords shattered, and the westermen came swarming across the Red Fork by the thousands.

Meanwhile, unbeknownst to the dying Lord Jason and his bannermen, fleets of longships from the Iron Islands fell upon the shores of Lannister's domains, led by Dalton Greyjoy of Pyke. Courted by both claimants to the Iron Throne, the Red Kraken had made his choice. His ironmen could not hope to breach Casterly Rock once Lady Johanna had barred her gates, but they seized three-quarters of the ships in the harbor, sank the rest, then swarmed over the walls of Lannisport to sack the city, making off with uncounted wealth and more than six hundred women and girls, including Lord Jason's favorite mistress and natural daughters.

Elsewhere in the realm, Lord Walys Mooton led a hundred knights out of Maidenpool to join with the half-wild Crabbs and Brunes of Crackclaw Point and the Celtigars of Claw Isle. Through piney woods and mist-shrouded hills they hastened, to Rook's Rest, where their sudden appearance took the garrison by surprise. After retaking the castle, Lord Mooton led his bravest men to the field of ashes west of the castle, to put an end to the dragon Sunfyre.

The would-be dragonslayers easily drove off the cordon of guards who had been left to feed, serve, and protect the dragon, but Sunfyre himself proved more formidable than expected. Dragons are awkward creatures on the ground, and his torn wing left the great golden wyrm unable to take to the air. The attackers expected to find the beast near death. Instead they found him sleeping, but the clash of swords and thunder of horses soon roused him, and the first spear to strike him provoked him to fury. Slimy with mud, twisting amongst the bones of countless sheep, Sunfyre writhed and coiled like a serpent, his tail lashing, sending blasts of golden flame at his attackers as he struggled to fly. Thrice he rose, and thrice fell back to earth. Mooton's men swarmed him with swords and spears and axes, dealing him many grievous wounds . . . yet each blow only seemed to enrage him further. The number of the dead reached threescore before the survivors fled.

Amongst the slain was Walys Mooton, Lord of Maidenpool. When his body was found a fortnight later by his brother Manfryd, naught remained but charred flesh in melted armor, crawling with maggots. Yet nowhere on that field of ashes, littered with the bodies of brave men and the burned and bloated carcasses of a hundred horses, did Lord Manfryd find King Aegon's dragon. Sunfyre was gone. Nor were there tracks, as surely there would have been had the dragon dragged himself away. Sunfyre the Golden had taken wing again, it seemed . . . but to where, no living man could say.

Meanwhile, Prince Daemon Targaryen himself hastened south on the wings of his dragon, Caraxes. Flying above the western shore of the Gods Eye, well away from Ser Criston's line of march, he evaded the enemy host, crossed the Blackwater, then turned east, following the river downstream to King's Landing. And on Dragonstone, Rhaenyra Targaryen donned a suit of gleaming black scale, mounted Syrax, and took flight as a rainstorm lashed the waters of Blackwater Bay. High above the city the queen and her prince consort came together, circling over Aegon's High Hill.

The sight of them incited terror in the streets of the city below, for the smallfolk were not slow to realize that the attack they had dreaded was at last at hand. Prince Aemond and Ser Criston had denuded King's Landing of defenders when they set forth to retake Harrenhal . . . and the Kinslayer had taken Vhagar, that fearsome beast, leaving only Dreamfyre and a handful of half-grown hatchlings to oppose the queen's dragons. The young dragons had never been ridden, and Dreamfyre's rider, Queen Helaena, was a broken woman; the city had as well been dragonless.

Thousands of smallfolk streamed out the city gates, carrying their children and worldly possessions on their backs, to seek safety in the countryside. Others dug pits and tunnels under their hovels, dark dank holes where they hoped to hide whilst the city burned (Grand Maester Munkun tells us that many of the hidden passageways and secret subcellars under

King's Landing date from this time). Rioting broke out in Flea Bottom. When the sails of the Sea Snake's ships were seen to the east in Blackwater Bay, making for the river, the bells of every sept in the city began to ring, and mobs surged through the streets, looting as they went. Dozens died before the gold cloaks could restore the peace.

With both the Lord Protector and the King's Hand absent, and King Aegon himself burned, bedridden, and lost in poppy dreams, it fell to his mother, the Queen Dowager, to see to the city's defenses. Queen Alicent rose to the challenge, closing the gates of castle and city, sending the gold cloaks to the walls, and dispatching riders on swift horses to find Prince Aemond and fetch him back.

As well, she commanded Grand Maester Orwyle to send ravens to "all our leal lords," summoning them to the defense of their true king. When Orwyle hastened back to his chambers, however, he found four gold cloaks waiting for him. One man muffled his cries as the others beat and bound him. With a bag pulled over his head, the Grand Maester was escorted down to the black cells.

Queen Alicent's riders got no farther than the gates, where more gold cloaks took them into custody. Unbeknownst to Her Grace, the seven captains commanding the gates, chosen for their loyalty to King Aegon, had been imprisoned or murdered the moment Caraxes appeared in the sky above the Red Keep . . . for the rank and file of the City Watch still loved Daemon Targaryen, the Prince of the City who had commanded them of old.

Queen Alicent's brother Ser Gwayne Hightower, second in command of the gold cloaks, rushed to the stables, intending to sound the warning; he was seized, disarmed, and dragged before his commander, Luthor Largent. When Hightower denounced him as a turncloak, Ser Luthor laughed. "Daemon gave us these cloaks," he said, "and they're gold no matter how you turn them." Then he drove his sword through Ser Gwayne's belly and ordered the city gates opened to the men pouring off the Sea Snake's ships.

For all the vaunted strength of its walls, King's Landing fell in less than a day. A short, bloody fight was waged at the River Gate, where thirteen Hightower knights and a hundred men-at-arms drove off the gold cloaks and held out for nigh on eight hours against attacks from both within and without the city, but their heroics were in vain, for Rhaenyra's soldiers poured in through the other six gates unmolested. The sight of the queen's dragons in the sky above took the heart out of the opposition, and King Aegon's remaining loyalists hid or fled or bent the knee.

One by one the dragons made their descent. Sheepstealer lighted atop Visenya's Hill, Silverwing and Vermithor on the Hill of Rhaenys, outside the Dragonpit. Prince Daemon circled the towers of the Red Keep before bringing Caraxes down in the outer ward. Only when he was certain that the defenders would offer him no harm did he signal for his wife the queen to descend upon Syrax. Addam Velaryon remained aloft, flying Seasmoke around the city walls, the beat of his dragon's wide leathern wings a caution to those below that any defiance would be met with fire.

Upon seeing that resistance was hopeless, the Dowager Queen Alicent emerged from Maegor's Holdfast with her father, Ser Otto Hightower; Ser Tyland Lannister; and Lord Jasper Wylde the Ironrod (Lord Larys Strong was not with them. The master of whisperers had somehow contrived to disappear). Septon Eustace, a witness to what followed, tells us that Queen Alicent attempted to treat with her stepdaughter. "Let us together summon a great council, as the Old King did in days of old," said the Dowager Queen, "and lay the matter of succession before the lords of the realm." But Queen Rhaenyra rejected the proposal with scorn. "Do you mistake me for Mushroom?" she asked. "We both know how this council would rule." Then she bade her stepmother choose: yield or burn.

Bowing her head in defeat, Queen Alicent surrendered the keys to the castle and ordered her knights and men-at-arms to lay down their swords. "The city is yours, Princess," she is reported to have said, "but you will not hold it long. The rats play when the cat is gone, but my son Aemond will return with fire and blood."

Rhaenyra's men found her rival's wife, the mad Queen Helaena, locked in her bedchamber . . . but when they broke down the doors of the king's apartments, they discovered only "his bed, empty, and his chamberpot, full." Aegon II had fled. So had his children, the six-year-old Princess Jaehaera and two-year-old Prince Maelor, along with Willis Fell and Rick-

ard Thorne of the Kingsguard. Not even the Dowager Queen seemed to know where they had gone, and Luthor Largent swore none had passed through the city gates.

There was no way to spirit away the Iron Throne, however. Nor would Queen Rhaenyra sleep until she claimed her father's seat. So the torches were lit in the throne room, and the queen climbed the iron steps and seated herself where King Viserys had sat before her, and the Old King before him, and Maegor and Aenys and Aegon the Dragon in days of old. Stern-faced, still in her armor, she sat on high as every man and woman in the Red Keep was brought forth and made to kneel before her, to plead for her forgiveness and swear their lives and swords and honor to her as their queen.

Septon Eustace tells us that the ceremony went on all through that night. It was well past dawn when Rhaenyra Targaryen rose and made her descent. "And as her lord husband Prince Daemon escorted her from the hall, cuts were seen upon Her Grace's legs and the palm of her left hand," wrote Eustace. "Drops of blood fell to the floor as she went past, and wise men looked at one another, though none dared speak the truth aloud: the Iron Throne had spurned her, and her days upon it would be few."

The Dying of the Dragons

Rhaenyra Triumphant

Even as King's Landing fell to Rhaenyra Targaryen and her dragons, Prince Aemond and Ser Criston Cole were advancing on Harrenhal, whilst the Lannister host under Adrian Tarbeck swept eastward.

At Acorn Hall the westermen were checked briefly when Lord Joseth Smallwood sallied forth to join Lord Piper and the remnants of his defeated host, but Piper died in the battle that ensued (felled when his heart burst at the sight of his favorite grandson's head upon a spear, Mushroom says), and Smallwood fell back inside his castle. A second battle followed three days later, when the rivermen regrouped under a hedge knight named Ser Harry Penny. This unlikely hero died soon after, whilst slaying Adrian Tarbeck. Once more the Lannisters prevailed, cutting down the rivermen as they fled. When the western host resumed its march to Harrenhal, it was under the aged Lord Humfrey Lefford, who had suffered so many wounds that he commanded from a litter.

Little did Lord Lefford suspect that he would soon face a stiffer test, for an army of fresh foes was descending on them from the north: two thousand savage northmen, flying Queen Rhaenyra's quartered banners. At their head rode the Lord of Barrowton, Roderick Dustin, a warrior so old and hoary men called him Roddy the Ruin. His host was made up of grizzled greybeards in old mail and ragged skins, every man a seasoned warrior, every man ahorse. They called themselves the Winter Wolves. "We have come to die for the dragon queen," Lord Roderick announced at the Twins, when Lady Sabitha Frey rode out to greet them.

Meanwhile, muddy roads and rainstorms slowed the pace of Aemond's advance, for his host was made up largely of foot, with a long baggage train. Ser Criston's vanguard fought and won a short, sharp battle against Ser Oswald Wode and the Lords Darry and Roote on the lakeshore, but met no other opposition. After nineteen days on the march, they reached Harrenhal . . . and found the castle gates open, with Prince Daemon and all his people gone.

Prince Aemond had kept Vhagar with the main column throughout the march, thinking that his uncle might attempt to attack them on Caraxes. He reached Harrenhal a day after Cole, and that night celebrated a great victory; Daemon and "his river scum" had fled rather than face his wroth, Aemond proclaimed. Small wonder then that when word of the fall of King's Landing reached him, the prince felt thrice the fool. His fury was fearsome to behold.

First to suffer for it was Ser Simon Strong. Prince Aemond had no love for any of that ilk, and the haste with which the castellan had yielded Harrenhal to Daemon Targaryen convinced him the old man was a traitor. Ser Simon protested his innocence, insisting that he was a true and loyal servant of the Crown. His own great nephew, Larys Strong, was Lord of Harrenhal and King Aegon's master of whisperers, he reminded the Prince Regent. These denials only inflamed Aemond's suspicions. The Clubfoot was a traitor as well, he decided. How else would Daemon and Rhaenyra have known when King's Landing was most vulnerable? Someone on the small council had sent word to them . . . and Larys Clubfoot was Breakbones's brother, and thus an uncle to Rhaenyra's bastards.

Aemond commanded that Ser Simon be given a sword. "Let the gods decide if you speak truly," he said. "If you are innocent, the Warrior will give you the strength to defeat me." The duel that followed was utterly one-sided, all the accounts agree; the prince cut the old man to pieces, then fed his corpse to Vhagar. Nor did Ser Simon's grandsons long outlive him. One by one, every man and boy with Strong blood in his veins was dragged forth and put to death, until the heap made of their heads stood three feet tall.

Thus did the flower of House Strong, an ancient line of noble warriors boasting descent from the First Men, come to an ignoble end in the ward at Harrenhal. No trueborn Strong was spared, nor any bastard save . . . oddly . . . Alys Rivers. Though the wet nurse was twice his age (thrice, if we put our trust in Mushroom), Prince Aemond had taken her into his bed as a prize of war soon after taking Harrenhal, seemingly preferring her to all the other women of the castle, including many pretty maids of his own years.

West of Harrenhal, fighting continued in the riverlands as the Lannister host slogged onward. The age and infirmity of their commander, Lord Lefford, had slowed their march to a crawl, but as they neared the western shores of the Gods Eye, they found a huge new army athwart their path.

Roddy the Ruin and his Winter Wolves had joined with Forrest Frey, Lord of the Crossing, and Red Robb Rivers, known as the Bowman of Raventree. The northmen numbered two thousand, Frey commanded two hundred knights and thrice as many foot, Rivers brought three hundred archers to the fray. And scarce had Lord Lefford halted to confront the foe in front of him when more enemies appeared to the south, where Longleaf the Lionslayer and a ragged band of survivors from the earlier battles had been joined by the Lords Bigglestone, Chambers, and Perryn.

Caught between these two foes, Lefford hesitated to move against either, for fear of the other falling on his rear. Instead he put his back to the lake, dug in, and sent ravens to Prince Aemond at Harrenhal, begging his aid. Though a dozen birds took wing, not one ever reached the prince; Red Robb Rivers, said to be the finest archer in all Westeros, took them down on the wing.

More rivermen turned up the next day, led by Ser Garibald Grey, Lord Jon Charlton, and the new Lord of Raventree, the eleven-year-old Benjicot Blackwood. With their numbers augmented by these fresh levies, the queen's men agreed that the time had come to attack. "Best make an end to these lions before the dragons come," said Roddy the Ruin.

The bloodiest land battle of the Dance of the Dragons began the next day, with the rising of the sun. In the annals of the Citadel it is known as the Battle by the Lakeshore, but to those men who lived to tell of it, it was always the Fishfeed.

Attacked from three sides, the westermen were driven back foot by foot into the waters of the Gods Eye. Hundreds died there, cut down whilst fighting in the reeds; hundreds more drowned as they tried to flee. By nightfall two thousand men were dead, amongst them many notables, including Lord Frey, Lord Lefford, Lord Bigglestone, Lord Charlton, Lord Swyft, Lord Reyne, Ser Clarent Crakehall, and Ser Emory Hill, the Bastard of Lannisport. The Lannister host was shattered and slaughtered, but at such cost that young Ben Blackwood, the boy Lord of Raventree, wept when he saw the heaps of the dead. The most grievous losses were suffered by the northmen, for the Winter Wolves had begged the honor of leading the attack, and had charged five times into the ranks of Lannister spears. More than two-thirds of the men who had ridden south with Lord Dustin were dead or wounded.

Fighting continued elsewhere in the realm as well, though those clashes were smaller than the great battle by the Gods Eye. In the Reach, Lord Hightower and his ward, Prince Daeron the Daring, continued to win victories, enforcing the submission of the Rowans of Goldengrove, the Oakhearts of Old Oak, and the Lords of the Shield Islands, for none dared face Tessarion, the Blue Queen. Lord Borros Baratheon called his banners and assembled near six thousand men at Storm's End, with the avowed intent of marching on King's Landing . . . only to lead them south into the mountains instead. His lordship used the pretext of Dornish incursions into the stormlands to justify this, but many and more were heard to whisper that it was the dragons ahead, not the Dornishmen behind, that prompted his change of heart. Out in the Sunset Sea, the longships of the Red Kraken fell upon Fair Isle, sweeping from one end of the island to the other whilst Lord Farman sheltered behind his walls sending out pleas for help that never came.

At Harrenhal, Aemond Targaryen and Criston Cole debated how best to answer the queen's attacks. Though Black Harren's seat was too strong to be taken by storm, and the riverlords dared not lay siege for fear of

Vhagar, the king's men were running short of food and fodder, and losing men and horses to hunger and sickness. Only blackened fields and burned villages remained within sight of the castle's massive walls, and those foraging parties that ventured farther did not return. Ser Criston urged a withdrawal to the south, where Aegon's support was strongest, but the prince refused, saying "Only a craven runs from traitors." The loss of King's Landing and the Iron Throne had enraged him, and when word of the Fishfeed reached Harrenhal, the Lord Protector had almost strangled the squire who delivered the news. Only the intercession of his bedmate Alys Rivers had saved the boy's life. Prince Aemond favored an immediate attack upon King's Landing. None of the queen's dragons were a match for Vhagar, he insisted.

Ser Criston called that folly. "One against six is a fight for fools, My Prince," he declared. Let them march south, he urged once more, and join their strength to Lord Hightower's. Prince Aemond could reunite with his brother Daeron and his dragon. King Aegon had escaped Rhaenyra's grasp, this they knew, surely he would reclaim Sunfyre and join his brothers. And perhaps their friends inside the city might find a way to free Queen Helaena as well, so she could bring Dreamfyre to the battle. Four dragons could perhaps prevail against six, if one was Vhagar.

Prince Aemond refused to consider this "craven course." As regent for his brother, he might have commanded the Hand's obedience, yet he did not. Munkun says that this was because of his respect for the older man, whilst Mushroom suggests that the two men had become rivals for the affections of the wet nurse Alys Rivers, who had used love potions and philtres to inflame their passions. Septon Eustace echoes the dwarf in part, but says it was Aemond alone who had become besotted with the Rivers woman, to such an extent that he could not bear the thought of leaving her.

Whatever the reason, Ser Criston and Prince Aemond decided to part ways. Cole would take command of their host and lead them south to join Ormund Hightower and Prince Daeron, but the Prince Regent would not accompany them. Instead he meant to fight his own war, raining fire on the traitors from the air. Soon or late, "the bitch queen" would send a dragon or two out to stop him, and Vhagar would destroy them. "She dare not send *all* her dragons," Aemond insisted. "That would leave King's Landing naked and vulnerable. Nor will she risk Syrax, or that last sweet son of hers. Rhaenyra may call herself a queen, but she has a woman's parts, a woman's faint heart, and a mother's fears."

And thus did the Kingmaker and the Kinslayer part, each to his own fate, whilst at the Red Keep Queen Rhaenyra Targaryen set about rewarding her friends and inflicting savage punishments on those who had served her half-brother. Ser Luthor Largent, commander of the gold cloaks, was ennobled. Ser Lorent Marbrand was installed as Lord Commander of the Queensguard, and charged with finding six worthy knights to serve beside him. Grand Maester Orwyle was sent to the dungeons, and Her Grace wrote the Citadel to inform them that her "leal servant" Gerardys was henceforth "the only true Grand Maester." Freed from those same dungeons that swallowed Orwyle, the surviving black lords and knights were rewarded with lands, offices, and honors.

Huge rewards were posted for information leading to the capture of "the usurper styling himself Aegon II"; his daughter, Jaehaera; his son Maelor; the "false knights" Willis Fell and Rickard Thorne; and Larys Strong the Clubfoot. When that failed to produce the desired result, Her Grace sent forth hunting parties of "knights inquisitor" to seek after the "traitors and villains" who had escaped her, and punish any man found to have assisted them.

Queen Alicent was fettered at wrist and ankle with golden chains, though her stepdaughter spared her life "for the sake of our father, who loved you once." Her own father was less fortunate. Ser Otto Hightower, who had served three kings as Hand, was the first traitor to be beheaded. Ironrod followed him to the block, still insisting that by law a king's son must come before his daughter. Ser Tyland Lannister was given to the torturers instead, in hopes of recovering some of the Crown's treasure.

Lords Rosby and Stokeworth, blacks who had gone green to avoid the dungeons, attempted to turn black again, but the queen declared that faithless friends were worse than foes and ordered their "lying tongues" be removed before their executions. Their deaths left her with a nettlesome problem of succession, however. As it happened, each of the "faithless friends" left a daughter; Rosby's was a maid of twelve, Stokeworth's a girl of six. Prince Daemon proposed that the former be wed to Hard Hugh the blacksmith's son (who had taken to calling himself Hugh Hammer), the latter to Ulf the Sot (now simply Ulf White), keeping their lands black whilst suitably rewarding the seeds for their valor in battle.

But the Queen's Hand argued against this, for both girls had younger brothers. Rhaenyra's own claim to the Iron Throne was a special case, the Sea Snake insisted; her father had *named* her as his heir. Lords Rosby and Stokeworth had done no such thing. Disinheriting their sons in favor of their daughters would overturn centuries of law and precedent, and call into question the rights of scores of other lords throughout Westeros whose own claims might be seen as inferior to those of elder sisters.

It was fear of losing the support of such lords, Munkun asserts in *True Telling*, that led the queen to decide in favor of Lord Corlys rather than Prince Daemon. The lands, castles, and coin of Houses Rosby and Stokeworth were awarded to the sons of the two executed lords, whilst Hugh Hammer and Ulf White were knighted and granted small holdings on the isle of Driftmark.

Mushroom tells us that Hammer celebrated by beating one of the queen's household knights to death in a brothel on the Street of Silk when the two men quarreled over the maidenhood of a young virgin, whilst White rode drunkenly through the alleys of Flea Bottom, clad in naught but his golden spurs. These are the sorts of tales that Mushroom loves to tell, and their veracity cannot be ascertained . . . but beyond a doubt, the people of King's Landing soon grew to despise both of the queen's new-made knights.

Even less loved, if that be possible, was the man Her Grace chose as her lord treasurer and master of coin: her longtime supporter Bartimos Celtigar, Lord of Claw Isle. Lord Celtigar seemed well suited for the office: staunch and unwavering in his support of the queen, he was unrelenting, incorruptible, and ingenious, all agreed, and very wealthy in the bargain. Rhaenyra had dire need of such a man, for she found herself in desperate need of coin. Though the Crown had been flush with gold upon the passing of King Viserys, Aegon II had seized the treasury along with the crown, and his master of coin, Tyland Lannister, had shipped off three-quarters of the late king's wealth "for safekeeping." King Aegon had spent every penny of the portion kept in King's Landing, leaving only empty vaults for his half-sister when she took the city. The rest of Viserys's treasure had been entrusted to the Hightowers of Oldtown, the Lannisters of Casterly Rock, and the Iron Bank of Braavos, and was beyond the queen's grasp.

Lord Celtigar set out at once to redress the problem; to do so, he restored the selfsame taxes that his ancestor Lord Edwell had once enacted during the regency of Jaehaerys I and piled on many a new levy besides. Taxes on wine and ale were doubled, port fees tripled. Every shopkeeper within the city walls was assessed a fee for the right to keep his doors open. Innkeeps were required to pay one silver stag for each bed in their inns. The entry and exit fees that the Lord of Air had once assessed were brought back and tripled. A tax on property was decreed; rich merchants in their manses or beggars in hovels, all must pay, depending on how much land they took up. "Not even whores are safe," the smallfolk told each other. "The cunt tax will be next, and then the tail tax. The rats must pay their share."

In truth the weight of Lord Celtigar's exactions fell heaviest on merchants and traders. When the Velaryon fleet had closed the Gullet, a great many ships found themselves trapped at King's Landing. The queen's new master of coin now assessed heavy fees on all such before he would allow them to sail. Some captains protested that they had already paid the required duties, taxes, and tariffs, and even produced papers as proof, but Lord Celtigar dismissed their claims. "Paying coin to the usurper is proof of naught but treason," he said. "It does not decrease the duties owed to our gracious queen." Those who refused to pay, or lacked the means, had their ships and cargoes seized and sold.

Even executions became a source of coin. Henceforth, Celtigar decreed, traitors, rebels, and murderers would be beheaded within the Dragonpit, and their corpses fed to the queen's dragons. All were welcome to bear witness to the fate that awaited evil men, but each must pay three pennies at the gates to be admitted.

Thus did Queen Rhaenyra replenish her coffers, at grievous cost. Neither Aegon nor his brother, Aemond, had ever been much loved by the people of the city, and many Kingslanders had welcomed the queen's return . . . but love and hate are two faces of the same coin, as fresh heads began appearing daily upon the spikes above the city gates, accompanied by ever more exacting taxes, the coin turned. The girl that they once cheered as the Realm's Delight had grown into a grasping and vindictive woman, men said, a queen as cruel as any king before her. One wit named Rhaenyra "King Maegor with teats," and for a hundred years thereafter "Maegor's Teats" was a common curse amongst Kingslanders.

With the city, castle, and throne in her possession, defended by no fewer than six dragons, Rhaenyra felt secure enough to send for her sons. A dozen ships set sail from Dragonstone, carrying the queen's ladies, her "beloved fool" Mushroom, and her son Aegon the Younger. Rhaenyra made the boy her cupbearer, so he might never be far from her side. Another fleet set out from Gulltown with Prince Joffrey, the last of the queen's three sons by Laenor Velaryon, together with his dragon Tyraxes. (Prince Daemon's daughter Rhaena remained in the Vale as a ward of Lady Arryn, whilst her twin, the dragonrider Baela, divided her days between Driftmark and Dragonstone.) Her Grace began to make plans for a lavish celebration to mark Joffrey's formal installation as Prince of Dragonstone and heir to the Iron Throne.

Even the White Worm came to court; the Lysene harlot Mysaria emerged from the shadows to take up residence in the Red Keep. Though never officially seated with the queen's small council, the woman now known as Lady Misery became the mistress of whisperers in all but name, with eyes and ears in every brothel, alehouse, and pot shop in King's Landing, and in the halls and bedchambers of the mighty as well. Though the years had thickened the body that had been so lithe and lissome, Prince Daemon remained in her thrall, and called upon her every evening . . . with Queen Rhaenyra's apparent blessing. "Let Daemon slake his hungers where he will," she is reported to have said, "and we shall do the same." (Septon Eustace suggests somewhat waspishly that Her Grace's own hungers were slaked largely with sweetmeats, cakes, and lamprey pie, as Rhaenyra grew ever more stout during her days in King's Landing.)

In the fullness of her victory, Rhaenyra Targaryen did not suspect how few days remained to her. Yet every time she sat the Iron Throne, its cruel blades drew fresh blood from her hands and arms and legs, a sign that all could read. Septon Eustace claims the queen's fall began at an inn called the Hogs Head in the town of Bitterbridge on the north bank of the Mander, near the foot of the old stone bridge that gave the town its name.

With Ormund Hightower besieging Longtable some thirty leagues to the southwest, Bitterbridge was crowded with men and women fleeing before his advancing host. The widowed Lady Caswell, whose lord husband had been beheaded by Aegon II at King's Landing when he refused to renounce the queen, had closed her castle gates, turning away even anointed knights and lords when they came to her seeking refuge. South of the river the cookfires of the broken men could be seen through the trees by night, whilst the town sept sheltered hundreds of wounded. Every inn was full, even the Hogs Head, a dismal sty of a hostelry. So when a man appeared from the north with a staff in one hand and a small boy on his back, the innkeep had no room for him . . . until the traveler pulled a silver stag from his purse. Then the innkeep allowed that he and his son might bed down in his stables, provided he first mucked them out. The traveler agreed, setting aside his pack and cloak as he went to work with spade and rake amidst the horses.

The avarice of innkeeps, landlords, and their ilk is well-known. The proprietor of the Hogs Head, a scoundrel who went by the name Ben Buttercakes, wondered if there might be more silver stags where there had been one. As the traveler worked up a sweat, Buttercakes offered to slake his thirst with a tankard of ale. The man accepted and accompanied the innkeep into the Hogs Head's common room, little suspecting that his host had instructed his stableboy, known to us only as Sly, to search his pack for silver. Sly found no coin within, but what he did find was far more precious . . . a heavy cloak of fine white wool bordered in snowy satin, wrapped about a dragon's egg, pale green with sworls of silver. For the traveler's "son" was Maelor Targaryen, the younger son of King Aegon II, and the traveler was Ser Rickard Thorne of the Kingsguard, his sworn shield and protector.

Ben Buttercakes got no joy from his deceit. When Sly burst into the common room with cloak and egg in hand, shouting of his discovery, the traveler threw the dregs of his tankard into the innkeep's face, ripped his longsword from its sheath, and opened Buttercakes from neck to groin. A

few of the other drinkers drew swords and daggers of their own, but none were knights, and Ser Rickard cut his way through them. Abandoning the stolen treasures, he scooped up his "son," fled to the stables, stole a horse, and burst from the inn, hell-bent for the old stone bridge and the south side of the Mander. He had come so far, and surely knew that safety lay only thirty leagues farther on, where Lord Hightower sat encamped beneath the walls of Longtable.

Thirty leagues had as well been thirty thousand, alas, for the road across the Mander was closed, and Bitterbridge belonged to Queen Rhaenyra. A hue and cry went up. Other men took horse in pursuit of Rickard Thorne, shouting, "Murder, treason, murder."

Hearing the shouts, the guards at the foot of the bridge bade Ser Rickard halt. Instead he tried to ride them down. When one man grasped his horse's bridle, Thorne took his arm off at the shoulder and rode on. But there were guards on the south bank too, and they formed a wall against him. From both sides men closed in, red-faced and shouting, brandishing swords and axes and thrusting with long spears, as Thorne turned this way and that, wheeling his stolen mount in circles, seeking some way through their ranks. Prince Maelor clung to him, shrieking.

It was the crossbows that finally brought him down. One bolt took him in the arm, the next through the throat. Ser Rickard tumbled from the saddle and died upon the bridge, with blood bubbling from his lips and drowning his last words. To the end he clung to the boy he had sworn to defend, until a washerwoman called Willow Pound-Stone tore the weeping prince from his arms.

Having slain the knight and seized the boy, however, the mob did not know what to do with their prize. Queen Rhaenyra had offered a great reward for his return, some recalled, but King's Landing was long leagues away. Lord Hightower's army was much closer. Perhaps he would pay even more. When someone asked if the reward was the same whether the boy was alive or dead, Willow Pound-Stone clutched Maelor tighter and said no one was going to hurt her new son. (Mushroom tells us the woman was a monster thirty stone in weight, simpleminded and half-mad, who'd earned her name pounding clothes clean in the river.) Then Sly came shoving through the crowd, covered in his master's blood, to declare the

prince was his, as he'd been the one to find the egg. The crossbowman whose bolt had slain Ser Rickard Thorne made a claim as well. And so they argued, shouting and shoving above the knight's corpse.

With so many present on the bridge, it is not surprising that we have many differing accounts of what befell Maelor Targaryen. Mushroom tells us that Willow Pound-Stone clutched the boy so tightly that she broke his back and crushed him to death. Septon Eustace does not so much as mention Willow, however. In his account, the town butcher hacked the prince into six pieces with his cleaver, so all those fighting over him could have a piece. Grand Maester Munkun's *True Telling* says that the boy was torn limb from limb by the mob, but names no names.

All we know for certain is that by the time Lady Caswell and her knights appeared to chase off the mob, the prince was dead. Her ladyship went pale at the sight of him, Mushroom tells us, saying, "The gods will curse us all for this." At her command, Sly the stableboy and Willow Pound-Stone were hanged from the center span of the old bridge, along with the man who had owned the horse Ser Rickard had stolen from the inn, who was (wrongly) thought to have assisted Thorne's escape. Ser Rickard's corpse, wrapped in his white cloak, Lady Caswell sent back to King's Landing, together with Prince Maelor's head. The dragon's egg she sent to Lord Hightower at Longtable, in the hopes it might assuage his wroth.

Mushroom, who loved the queen well, tells us that Rhaenyra wept when Maelor's small head was placed before her as she sat the Iron Throne. Septon Eustace, who loved her little, says rather that she smiled, and commanded that the head be burned, "for he was the blood of the dragon." Though no announcement of the boy's death was made, word of his demise nonetheless spread throughout the city. And soon another tale was told as well, one that claimed Queen Rhaenyra had the prince's head delivered to his mother, Queen Helaena, in a chamberpot. Though the story had no truth in it, soon it was on every pair of lips in King's Landing. Mushroom puts this down as the Clubfoot's work. "A man who gathers whispers can spread them just as well."

Beyond the city walls, fighting continued throughout the Seven Kingdoms. Faircastle fell to Dalton Greyjoy, and with it Fair Isle's last resistance to the ironborn. The Red Kraken claimed four of Lord Farman's daughters as salt wives and gave the fifth ("the homely one") to his brother Veron. Farman and his sons were ransomed back to Casterly Rock for their weights in silver. In the Reach, Lady Merryweather yielded Longtable to Lord Ormund Hightower; true to his word, his lordship did no harm to her or hers, though he did strip her castle of its wealth and every scrap of food, feeding his thousands with her grain as he broke his camp and marched on to Bitterbridge.

When Lady Caswell appeared on the ramparts of her castle to ask for the same terms Lady Merryweather had received, Hightower let Prince Daeron give the answer: "You shall receive the same terms you gave my nephew Maelor." Her ladyship could only watch as Bitterbridge was sacked. The Hogs Head was the first building put to the torch. Inns, guild halls, storehouses, the homes of the mean and the mighty, dragonflame consumed them all. Even the sept was burned, with hundreds of wounded still within. Only the bridge remained untouched, as it was required to cross the Mander. The people of the town were put to the sword if they tried to fight or flee, or were driven into the river to drown.

Lady Caswell watched from her walls, then commanded that her gates be thrown open. "No castle can be held against a dragon," she told her garrison. When Lord Hightower rode up, he found her standing atop the gatehouse with a noose about her neck. "Have mercy on my children, lord," she begged, before throwing herself down to hang. Mayhaps that moved Lord Ormund, for her ladyship's young sons and daughter were spared and sent in chains to Oldtown. The men of the castle garrison received no mercy but the sword.

In the riverlands, Ser Criston Cole abandoned Harrenhal, striking south along the western shore of the Gods Eye, with thirty-six-hundred men behind him (death, disease, and desertion had thinned the ranks that had ridden forth from King's Landing). Prince Aemond had already departed, flying Vhagar.

The castle stood empty no more than three days before Lady Sabitha Frey swooped down to seize it. Inside she found only Alys Rivers, the wet nurse and purported witch who had warmed Prince Aemond's bed during his days at Harrenhal, and now claimed to be carrying his child. "I have the dragon's bastard in me," the woman said, as she stood naked in the godswood with one hand upon her swollen belly. "I can feel his fires licking at my womb."

Nor was her babe the only fire kindled by Aemond Targaryen. No longer tied to castle or host, the one-eyed prince was free to fly where he would. It was war as Aegon the Conqueror and his sisters had once waged it, fought with dragonflame, as Vhagar descended from the autumn sky again and again to lay waste to the lands and villages and castles of the riverlords. House Darry was the first to know the prince's wroth. The men bringing in the harvest burned or fled as the crops went up in flame, and Castle Darry was consumed in a firestorm. Lady Darry and her younger children survived by taking shelter in vaults under the keep, but her lord husband and his heir died on their battlements, together with twoscore of his sworn swords and bowmen. Three days later, it was Lord Harroway's Town left smoking. Lord's Mill, Blackbuckle, Buckle, Claypool, Swynford, Spiderwood . . . Vhagar's fury fell on each in turn, until half the riverlands seemed ablaze.

Ser Criston Cole faced fires as well. As he drove his men south through the riverlands, smoke rose up before him and behind him. Every village that he came to he found burned and abandoned. His column moved through forests of dead trees where living woods had been just days before, as the riverlords set blazes all along his line of march. In every brook and pool and village well, he found death: dead horses, dead cows, dead men, swollen and stinking, befouling the waters. Elsewhere his scouts came across a ghastly tableaux where armored corpses sat beneath the trees in rotting raiment, in a grotesque mockery of a feast. The feasters were men who had fallen in the Fishfeed, skulls grinning under rusted helms as their green and rotted flesh sloughed off their bones.

Four days out of Harrenhal, the attacks began. Archers hid amongst the trees, picking off outriders and stragglers with their longbows. Men died. Men fell behind the rear guard and were never seen again. Men fled, abandoning their shields and spears to fade into the woods. Men went over to the enemy. In the village commons at Crossed Elms, another of the ghastly feasts was found. Familiar with such sights by now, Ser Criston's outriders grimaced and rode past, paying no heed to the rotting dead . . . until the corpses sprang up and fell upon them. A dozen died before they realized it had all been a ploy, the work (as was learned later) of a Myrish sellsword in the service of Lord Vance, a former mummer called Black Trombo.

All this was but prelude, for the Lords of the Trident had been gathering their forces. When Ser Criston left the lake behind, striking out overland for the Blackwater, he found them waiting atop a stony ridge; three hundred mounted knights in armor, as many longbowmen, three thousand archers, three thousand ragged rivermen with spears, hundreds of northmen brandishing axes, mauls, spiked maces, and ancient iron swords. Above their heads flew Queen Rhaenyra's banners. "Who are they?" a squire asked when the foe appeared, for they showed no arms but the queen's.

"Our death," answered Ser Criston Cole, for these foes were fresh, better fed, better horsed, better armed, and they held the high ground, whilst his own men were stumbling, sick, and dispirited.

Calling for a peace banner, King Aegon's Hand rode out to treat with them. Three came down from the ridge to meet him. Chief amongst them was Ser Garibald Grey in his dented plate and mail. Pate of Longleaf was with him, the Lionslayer who had cut down Jason Lannister, together with Roddy the Ruin, bearing the scars he had taken at the Fishfeed. "If I strike my banners, do you promise us our lives?" Ser Criston asked the three of them.

"I made my promise to the dead," Ser Garibald replied. "I told them I would build a sept for them out of traitors' bones. I don't have near enough bones yet, so . . ."

Ser Criston answered, "If there is to be battle here, many of your own will die as well." The northman Roderick Dustin laughed at these words, saying, "That's why we come. Winter's here. Time for us to go. No better way to die than sword in hand."

Ser Criston drew his longsword from its scabbard. "As you will it. We can begin here, the four of us. One of me against the three of you. Will that be enough to make a fight of it?"

But Longleaf the Lionslayer said, "I'll want three more," and up on the ridge Red Robb Rivers and two of his archers raised their longbows.

Three arrows flew across the field, striking Cole in belly, neck, and breast. "I'll have no songs about how brave you died, Kingmaker," declared Longleaf. "There's tens o' thousands dead on your account." He was speaking to a corpse.

The battle that followed was as one-sided as any in the Dance. Lord Roderick raised a warhorn to his lips and sounded the charge, and the queen's men came screaming down the ridge, led by the Winter Wolves on their shaggy northern horses and the knights on their armored destriers. With Ser Criston dead upon the ground, the men who had followed him from Harrenhal lost heart. They broke and fled, casting aside their shields as they ran. Their foes came after, cutting them down by the hundreds. Afterward Ser Garibald was heard to say, "Today was butchery, not battle." Mushroom, upon hearing a report of his words, dubbed the fight the Butcher's Ball, and so it has been known ever since.

It was about this same time that one of the more curious incidents of the Dance of the Dragons occurred. Legend has it that during the Age of Heroes, Serwyn of the Mirror Shield slew the dragon Urrax by crouching behind a shield so polished that the beast saw only his own reflection. By this ruse, the hero crept close enough to drive a spear through the dragon's eye, earning the name by which we know him still. That Ser Byron Swann, second son of the Lord of Stonehelm, had heard this tale we cannot doubt. Armed with a spear and a shield of silvered steel and accompanied only by his squire, he set out to slay a dragon just as Serwyn did.

But here confusion arises, for Munkun says it was Vhagar that Swann meant to kill, to put an end to Prince Aemond's raids . . . but it must be remembered that Munkun draws largely on Grand Maester Orwyle for his version of events, and Orwyle was in the dungeons when these things occurred. Mushroom, at the queen's side in the Red Keep, says rather that it was Rhaenyra's Syrax that Ser Byron approached. Septon Eustace does not note the incident at all in his own chronicle, but years later, in a letter, suggests this dragonslayer hoped to kill Sunfyre . . . but this is certainly mistaken, since Sunfyre's whereabouts were unknown at this time. All three accounts agree that the ploy that won undying fame for Serwyn of the Mirror Shield brought only death for Ser Byron Swann. The dragon—whichever one it was—stirred at the knight's approach and unleashed his fire, melting the mirrored shield and roasting the man crouched behind it. Ser Byron died screaming.

On Maiden's Day in the year 130 AC, the Citadel of Oldtown sent forth three hundred white ravens to herald the coming of winter, but Mushroom and Septon Eustace agree that this was high summer for Queen Rhaenyra Targaryen. Despite the disaffection of the Kingslanders, the city and crown were hers. Across the narrow sea, the Triarchy had begun to tear itself to pieces. The waves belonged to House Velaryon. Though snows had closed the passes through the Mountains of the Moon, the Maiden of the Vale had proven true to her word, sending men by sea to join the queen's hosts. Other fleets brought warriors from White Harbor, led by Lord Manderly's own sons, Medrick and Torrhen. On every hand Queen Rhaenyra's power swelled whilst King Aegon's dwindled.

Yet no war can be counted as won whilst foes remain unconquered. The Kingmaker, Ser Criston Cole, had been brought down, but somewhere in the realm Aegon II, the king he had made, remained alive and free. Aegon's daughter, Jaehaera, was likewise at large. Larys Strong the Clubfoot, the most enigmatic and cunning member of the green council, had vanished. Storm's End was still held by Lord Borros Baratheon, no friend of the queen. The Lannisters had to be counted amongst Rhaenyra's enemies as well, though with Lord Jason dead, the greater part of the chivalry of the west slain or scattered at the Fishfeed, and the Red Kraken harrying Fair Isle and the west shore, Casterly Rock was in considerable disarray.

Prince Aemond had become the terror of the Trident, descending from the sky to rain fire and death upon the riverlands, then vanishing, only to strike again the next day fifty leagues away. Vhagar's flames reduced Old Willow and White Willow to ash, and Hogg Hall to blackened stone. At Merrydown Dell, thirty men and three hundred sheep died by dragonflame. The Kinslayer then returned unexpectedly to Harrenhal, where he burned every wooden structure in the castle. Six knights and twoscore men-at-arms perished trying to slay his dragon, whilst Lady Sabitha Frey only saved herself from the flames by hiding in a privy. She fled back to the Twins soon after . . . but her prize captive, the witch woman Alys Rivers, escaped with Prince Aemond. As word of these attacks spread, other lords looked skyward in fear, wondering who might be next. Lord Mooton of Maidenpool, Lady Darklyn of Duskendale, and Lord Blackwood of Raventree sent urgent messages to the queen, begging her to send them dragons to defend their holdings.

Yet the greatest threat to Rhaenyra's reign was not Aemond One-Eye, but his younger brother, Prince Daeron the Daring, and the great southron army led by Lord Ormund Hightower.

Hightower's host had crossed the Mander and was advancing slowly on King's Landing, smashing the queen's loyalists wherever and whenever they encountered them, and forcing every lord who bent the knee to add their strength to his own. Flying Tessarion ahead of the main column, Prince Daeron had proved invaluable as a scout, warning Lord Ormund of enemy movements. Oft as not, the queen's men would melt away at the first glimpse of the Blue Queen's wings. Grand Maester Munkun tells us that the southron host numbered more than twenty thousand as it crept upriver, almost a tenth of them mounted knights.

Cognizant of all these threats, Queen Rhaenyra's Hand, old Lord Corlys Velaryon, suggested to Her Grace that the time had come to talk. He urged the queen to offer pardons to Lords Baratheon, Hightower, and Lannister if they would bend their knees, swear fealty, and offer hostages to the Iron Throne. The Sea Snake proposed to let the Faith take charge of Dowager Queen Alicent and Queen Helaena, so that they might spend the remainder of their lives in prayer and contemplation. Helaena's daughter, Jaehaera, could be made his own ward, and in due time be married to Prince Aegon the Younger, binding the two halves of House Targaryen together once again. "And what of my half-brothers?" Rhaenyra demanded, when the Sea Snake put this plan before her. "What of this false king Aegon, and the kinslayer Aemond? Would you have me pardon them as well, they who stole my throne and slew my sons?"

"Spare them, and send them to the Wall," Lord Corlys answered. "Let them take the black and live out their lives as men of the Night's Watch, bound by sacred vows."

"What are vows to oathbreakers?" Queen Rhaenyra demanded. "Their vows did not trouble them when they took my throne."

Prince Daemon echoed the queen's misgivings. Giving pardons to rebels and traitors only sowed the seeds for fresh rebellions, he insisted. "The war will end when the heads of the traitors are mounted on spikes above the King's Gate, and not before." Aegon II would be found in time, "hiding under some rock," but they could and should bring the war to Aemond and Daeron. The Lannisters and Baratheons should be destroyed as well, so their lands and castles might be given to men who had proved more loyal. Grant Storm's End to Ulf White and Casterly Rock to Hard Hugh Hammer, the prince proposed . . . to the horror of the Sea Snake. "Half the lords of Westeros will turn against us if we are so cruel as to destroy two such ancient and noble houses," Lord Corlys said.

It fell to the queen herself to choose between her consort and her Hand. Rhaenyra decided to steer a middle course. She would send envoys to Storm's End and Casterly Rock, offering fair terms and pardons . . . *after* she had put an end to the usurper's brothers, who were in the field against her. "Once they are dead, the rest will bend the knee. Slay their dragons, that I might mount their heads upon the walls of my throne room. Let men look upon them in the years to come, that they might know the cost of treason."

King's Landing must not be left undefended, to be sure. Queen Rhaenyra would remain in the city with Syrax, and her sons Aegon and Joffrey, whose persons could not be put at risk. Joffrey, not quite three-and-ten, was eager to prove himself a warrior, but when told that Tyraxes was needed to help his mother hold the Red Keep in the event of an attack, the boy swore solemnly to do so. Addam Velaryon, the Sea Snake's heir, would also remain in the city, with Seasmoke. Three dragons should suffice for the defense of King's Landing; the rest would be going into battle.

Prince Daemon himself would take Caraxes to the Trident, together with the girl Nettles and Sheepstealer, to find Prince Aemond and Vhagar and put an end to them. Ulf White and Hard Hugh Hammer would fly to Tumbleton, some fifty leagues southwest of King's Landing, the last leal stronghold between Lord Hightower and the city, to assist in the defense of the town and castle and destroy Prince Daeron and Tessarion. Lord Corlys suggested that mayhaps the prince might be taken alive and held as hostage. But Queen Rhaenyra was adamant. "He will not remain a boy forever. Let him grow to manhood, and soon or late he will seek to revenge himself upon my own sons."

Words of these plans soon reached the ears of the Dowager Queen, filling her with terror. Fearing for her sons, Queen Alicent went to the Iron Throne upon her knees, to plead for peace. This time the Queen in Chains put forth the notion that the realm might be divided; Rhaenyra would keep King's Landing and the crownlands, the North, the Vale of Arryn, all the lands watered by the Trident, and the isles. To Aegon II would go the stormlands, the westerlands, and the Reach, to be ruled from Oldtown.

Rhaenyra rejected her stepmother's proposal with scorn. "Your sons might have had places of honor at my court if they had kept faith," Her Grace declared, "but they sought to rob me of my birthright, and the blood of my sweet sons is on their hands."

"Bastard blood, shed at war," Alicent replied. "My son's sons were innocent boys, cruelly murdered. How many more must die to slake your thirst for vengeance?"

The Dowager Queen's words only fanned the fire of Rhaenyra's wroth. "I will hear no more lies," she warned. "Speak again of bastardy, and I will have your tongue out." Or so the tale is told by Septon Eustace. Munkun says the same in his *True Telling*.

Here again Mushroom differs. The dwarf would have us believe that Rhaenyra ordered her stepmother's tongue torn out at once, rather than merely threatening this. It was only a word from Lady Misery that stayed her hand, the fool insists; the White Worm proposed another, crueler punishment. King Aegon's wife and mother were taken in chains to a certain brothel, and there sold to any man who wished to have his pleasure of them. The price was high; a golden dragon for Queen Alicent, three dragons for Queen Helaena, who was younger and more beautiful. Yet Mushroom says there were many in the city who thought that cheap for carnal knowledge of a queen. "Let them remain there until they are with child," Lady Misery is purported to have said. "They speak of bastards so freely, let them each have one for their very own."

Though the lusts of men and the cruelty of women can never be gainsaid, we put no credence in Mushroom here. That such a tale was told in the wine sinks and pot shops of King's Landing cannot be doubted, but it may be that its provenance was later, when King Aegon II was seeking justification for the cruelty of his own acts. It must be remembered that the dwarf told his stories long years after the events that he related, and might have misremembered. Let us speak no more of the Brothel Queens, therefore, and return once more to the dragons as they flew to battle. Caraxes and Sheepstealer went north, Vermithor and Silverwing southwest.

On the headwaters of the mighty Mander stood Tumbleton, a thriving market town and the seat of House Footly. The castle overlooking the town was stout but small, garrisoned by no more than forty men, but thousands more had come upriver from Bitterbridge, Longtable, and farther south. The arrival of a strong force of riverlords swelled their numbers further, and stiffened their resolve. Fresh from their victory at the

Butcher's Ball came Ser Garibald Grey and Longleaf the Lionslayer, with the head of Ser Criston Cole upon a spear, Red Robb Rivers and his archers, the last of the Winter Wolves, and a score of landed knights and petty lords whose lands lay along the banks of the Blackwater, amongst them such men of note as Moslander of Yore, Ser Garrick Hall of Middleton, Ser Merrell the Bold, and Lord Owain Bourney.

All told, the forces gathered under Queen Rhaenyra's banners at Tumbleton numbered near nine thousand, according to the *True Telling*. Other chroniclers make the number as high as twelve thousand, or as low as six, but in all these cases, it seems plain that the queen's men were greatly outnumbered by Lord Hightower's. No doubt the arrival of the dragons Vermithor and Silverwing with their riders was most welcome by the defenders of Tumbleton. Little could they know the horrors that awaited them.

The how and when and why of what has become known as the Treasons of Tumbleton remain a matter of much dispute, and the truth of all that happened will likely never be known. It does appear that certain of those who flooded into the town, fleeing before Lord Hightower's army, were actually part of that army, sent ahead to infiltrate the ranks of the defenders. Beyond question, two of the Blackwater men who had joined the riverlords on their march south—Lord Owain Bourney and Ser Roger Corne—were secret supporters of King Aegon II. Yet their betrayals would have counted for little, had not Ser Ulf White and Ser Hugh Hammer also chosen this moment to change their allegiance.

Most of what we know of these men comes from Mushroom. The dwarf is not reticent in his assessment of the low character of these two dragonriders, painting the former as a drunkard and the latter as a brute. Both were cravens, he tells us; it was only when they saw Lord Ormund's host with spearpoints glittering in the sun and its line of march stretching back for long leagues that they decided to join him rather than oppose him. Yet neither man had hesitated to face storms of spears and arrows off Driftmark. It may be that it was the thought of attacking Tessarion that gave them pause. In the Gullet, all the dragons had been on their own side. This too may be possible . . . though both Vermithor and Silverwing were older and larger than Prince Daeron's dragon, and would therefore have been more likely to prevail in any battle.

Others suggest it was avarice, not cowardice, that led White and Hammer to betrayal. Honor meant little and less to them; it was wealth and power they lusted for. After the Gullet and the fall of King's Landing, they had been granted knighthood . . . but they aspired to be lords and scorned the modest holdings bestowed on them by Queen Rhaenyra. When Lords Rosby and Stokeworth were executed, it was proposed that White and Hammer be given their lands and castles through marriage to their daughters, but Her Grace had allowed the traitors' sons to inherit instead. Then Storm's End and Casterly Rock were dangled before them, but these rewards as well the ungrateful queen had denied them.

No doubt they hoped that King Aegon II might reward them better, should they help return the Iron Throne to him. It might even be that certain promises were made to them in this regard, possibly through Lord Larys the Clubfoot or one of his agents, though this remains unproven and unprovable. As neither man could read nor write, we shall never know what drove the Two Betrayers (as history has named them) to do what they did.

Of the Battle of Tumbleton we know much and more, however. Six thousand of the queen's men formed up to face Lord Hightower in the field, under the command of Ser Garibald Grey. They fought bravely for a time, but a withering rain of arrows from Lord Ormund's archers thinned their ranks, and a thunderous charge by his heavy horse broke them, sending the survivors running back toward the town walls. There Red Robb Rivers and his bowmen stood, covering the retreat with their own longbows.

When most of the survivors were safe inside the gates, Roddy the Ruin and his Winter Wolves sallied forth from a postern gate, screaming their terrifying northern war cries as they swept around the left flank of the attackers. In the chaos that ensued, the northmen fought their way through ten times their own number to where Lord Ormund Hightower sat his warhorse beneath King Aegon's golden dragon and the banners of Oldtown and the Hightower.

As the singers tell it, Lord Roderick was bloody from head to heel as he came on, with splintered shield and cracked helm, yet so drunk with battle that he did not even seem to feel his wounds. Ser Bryndon Hightower, Lord Ormund's cousin, put himself between the northman and his liege, taking off the Ruin's shield arm at the shoulder with one terrible blow of his longaxe . . . yet the savage Lord of Barrowton fought on, slaying both Ser Bryndon and Lord Ormund before he died. Lord Hightower's banners toppled, and the townsfolk gave a great cheer, thinking the tide of battle turned. Even the appearance of Tessarion across the field did not dismay them, for they knew they had two dragons of their own . . . but when Vermithor and Silverwing climbed into the sky and loosed their fires upon Tumbleton, those cheers changed to screams.

It was the Field of Fire writ small, Grand Maester Munkun wrote.

Tumbleton went up in flame: shops, homes, septs, people, all. Men fell burning from gatehouse and battlements, or stumbled shrieking through the streets like so many living torches. Outside the walls, Prince Daeron swooped down upon Tessarion. Pate of Longleaf was unhorsed and trampled, Ser Garibald Grey pierced by a crossbow bolt, then engulfed by dragonflame. The Two Betrayers scourged the town with whips of flame from one end to the other.

Ser Roger Corne and his men chose that moment to show their true colors, cutting down defenders on the town gates and throwing them open to the attackers. Lord Owain Bourney did the same within the castle, driving a spear through the back of Ser Merrell the Bold.

The sack that followed was as savage as any in the history of Westeros. Tumbleton, that prosperous market town, was reduced to ash and embers. Thousands burned, and as many died by drowning as they tried to swim the river. Some would later say they were the fortunate ones, for no mercy was shown the survivors. Lord Footly's men threw down their swords and yielded, only to be bound and beheaded. Such townswomen as survived the fires were raped repeatedly, even girls as young as eight and ten. Old men and boys were put to the sword, whilst the dragons fed upon the twisted, smoking carcasses of their victims. Tumbleton was never to recover; though later Footlys would attempt to rebuild atop the ruins, their

"new town" would never be a tenth the size of the old, for the smallfolk said the very ground was haunted.

One hundred sixty leagues to the north, other dragons soared above the Trident, where Prince Daemon Targaryen and the small brown girl called Nettles were hunting Aemond One-Eye without success. They had based themselves at Maidenpool, at the invitation of Lord Manfryd Mooton, who lived in terror of Vhagar descending on his town. Instead Prince Aemond struck at Stonyhead, in the foothills of the Mountains of the Moon; at Sweetwillow on the Green Fork and Sallydance on the Red Fork; he reduced Bowshot Bridge to embers, burned Old Ferry and Crone's Mill, destroyed the motherhouse at Bechester, always vanishing back into the sky before the hunters could arrive. Vhagar never lingered, nor did the survivors oft agree on which way the dragon had flown.

Each dawn Caraxes and Sheepstealer flew from Maidenpool, climbing high above the riverlands in ever-widening circles in hopes of espying Vhagar below . . . only to return defeated at dusk. The *Chronicles of Maidenpool* tell us Lord Mooton made so bold as to suggest that the dragonriders divide their search, so as to cover twice the ground. Prince Daemon refused. Vhagar was the last of the three dragons that had come to Westeros with Aegon the Conqueror and his sisters, he reminded his lordship. Though slower than she had been a century before, she had grown nigh as large as the Black Dread of old. Her fires burned hot enough to melt stone, and neither Caraxes nor Sheepstealer could match her ferocity. Only together could they hope to withstand her. And so he kept the girl Nettles by his side, day and night, in sky and castle.

Yet was fear of Vhagar the only reason Prince Daemon kept Nettles close to him? Mushroom would have us believe it was not. By the dwarf's account, Daemon Targaryen had come to love the small brown bastard girl, and had taken her into his bed.

How much credence can we give the fool's testimony? Nettles was no more than ten-and-seven, Prince Daemon nine-and-forty, yet the power young maidens exert over older men is well-known. Daemon Targaryen was not a faithful consort to the queen, we know. Even our normally reticent Septon Eustace writes of his nightly visits to Lady Mysaria, whose bed he oft shared whilst at court . . . with the queen's blessing, purportedly. Nor should it be forgotten that during his youth, every brothel keeper in King's Landing knew that Lord Flea Bottom took an especial delight in maidens, and kept aside the youngest, prettiest, and more innocent of their new girls for him to deflower.

The girl Nettles was young, beyond a doubt (though perhaps not as young as those the prince had debauched in his youth), but it seems doubtful that she was a true maiden. Growing up homeless, motherless, and penniless on the streets of Spicetown and Hull, she would most likely have surrendered her innocence not long after her first flowering (if not before), in return for half a groat or a crust of bread. And the sheep she fed to Sheepstealer to bind him to her . . . how would she have come by those, if not by lifting her skirts for some shepherd? Nor could Netty truly be called pretty. "A skinny brown girl on a skinny brown dragon," writes Munkun in his *True Telling* (though he never saw her). Septon Eustace says her teeth were crooked, her nose scarred where it had once been slit for thieving. Hardly a likely paramour for a prince, one would think.

Against that we have *The Testimony of Mushroom* . . . and in this case, the *Chronicles of Maidenpool* as set down by Lord Mooton's maester. Maester Norren writes that "the prince and his bastard girl" supped together every night, broke their fast together every morning, slept in adjoining bedchambers, that the prince "doted upon the brown girl as a man might dote upon his daughter," instructing her in "common courtesies" and how to dress and sit and brush her hair, that he made gifts to her of "an ivory-handled hairbrush, a silvered looking glass, a cloak of rich brown velvet bordered in satin, a pair of riding boots of leather soft as butter." The prince taught the girl to wash, Norren says, and the maidservants who fetched their bath water said he oft shared a tub with her, "soaping her back or washing the dragon stink from her hair, both of them as naked as their namedays."

None of this constitutes proof that Daemon Targaryen had carnal knowledge of the bastard girl, but in light of what followed we must surely judge that more likely than most of Mushroom's tales. Yet however these dragonriders spent their nights, it is a certainty that their days were spent prowling the skies, hunting after Prince Aemond and Vhagar without success. So let us leave them for the nonce, and turn our gaze briefly across Blackwater Bay.

It was about this time that a battered merchant cog named *Nessaria* came limping into the harbor beneath Dragonstone to make repairs and take on provisions. She had been returning from Pentos to Old Volantis when a storm drove her off course, her crew said . . . but to this common song of peril at sea, the Volantenes added a queer note. As *Nessaria* beat westward, the Dragonmont loomed up before them, huge against the setting sun . . . and the sailors spied two dragons fighting, their roars echoing off the sheer black cliffs of the smoking mountain's eastern flanks. In every tavern, inn, and whorehouse along the waterfront the tale was told, retold, and embroidered, till every man on Dragonstone had heard it.

Dragons were a wonder to the men of Old Volantis; the sight of two in battle was one the men of *Nessaria* would never forget. Those born and bred on Dragonstone had grown up with such beasts . . . yet even so, the sailors' story excited interest. The next morning some local fisherfolk took their boats around the Dragonmont and returned to report seeing the burned and broken remains of a dead dragon at the mountain's base. From the color of its wings and scales, the carcass was that of Grey Ghost. The dragon lay in two pieces, and had been torn apart and partially devoured.

On hearing this news Ser Robert Quince, the amiable and famously obese knight whom the queen had named castellan of Dragonstone upon her departure, was quick to name the Cannibal as the killer. Most agreed, for the Cannibal had been known to attack smaller dragons in the past, though seldom so savagely. Some amongst the fisherfolk, fearing that the killer might turn upon them next, urged Quince to dispatch knights to the beast's lair to put an end to him, but the castellan refused. "If we do not trouble him, the Cannibal will not trouble us," he declared. To be certain of that, he forbade fishing in the waters beneath the Dragonmont's eastern face, where the vanquished dragon's body lay rotting.

His decree did not satisfy his restless charge, Baela Targaryen, Prince Daemon's daughter by his second wife, Laena Velaryon. At ten-and-four, Baela was a wild and willful young maiden, more boyish than ladylike, and very much her father's daughter. Though slim and short of stature, she knew naught of fear, and lived to dance and hawk and ride. As a younger girl she had oft been chastised for wrestling with squires in the yard, but of late she had taken to playing kissing games with them instead. Not long after the queen's court removed to King's Landing (whilst leaving Lady Baela on Dragonstone), Baela had been caught allowing a kitchen scullion to slip his hand inside her jerkin. Ser Robert, outraged, had sent the boy to the block to have the offending hand removed. Only the girl's tearful intercession had saved him.

"She is overly fond of boys," the castellan wrote Baela's father, Prince Daemon, after that incident, "and should be married soon, lest she surrender her virtue to someone unworthy of her." Even more than boys, however, Lady Baela loved to fly. Since first riding her dragon Moondancer into the sky not half a year past, she had flown every day, ranging freely to every part of Dragonstone and even across the sea to Driftmark.

Always eager for adventure, the girl now proposed to find the truth of what had happened on the other side of the mountain for herself. She had no fear of the Cannibal, she told Ser Robert. Moondancer was younger and faster; she could easily outfly the other dragon. But the castellan forbade her taking any such risk. The garrison was given strict instructions; Lady Baela was not to leave the castle. When caught attempting to defy his command that very night, the angry maiden was confined to her chambers.

Though understandable, this proved in hindsight to be unfortunate, for had Lady Baela been allowed to fly she might have spied the fishing boat that was even then making its way around the island. Aboard was an aged fisherman called Tom Tanglebeard, his son Tom Tangletongue, and two "cousins" from Driftmark, left homeless when Spicetown was destroyed. The younger Tom, as handy with a tankard as he was clumsy with a net, had spent a deal of time buying drinks for Volantene sailors and listening to their accounts of the dragons they had seen fighting. "Grey and gold they was, flashing in the sun," one man said . . . and now, in defiance of Ser Robert's prohibition, the two Toms were intent on delivering their "cousins" to the stony strand where the dead dragon sprawled burned and broken, so they might seek after his slayer.

Meanwhile, on the western shore of Blackwater Bay, word of battle and betrayal at Tumbleton had reached King's Landing. It is said the Dowager Queen Alicent laughed when she heard. "All they have sowed, now shall they reap," she promised. On the Iron Throne, Queen Rhaenyra grew pale and faint, and ordered the city gates closed and barred; henceforth, no one was to be allowed to enter or leave King's Landing. "I will have no turncloaks stealing into my city to open my gates to rebels," she proclaimed. Lord Ormund's host could be outside their walls by the morrow or the day after; the betrayers, dragon-borne, could arrive even sooner than that.

This prospect excited Prince Joffrey. "Let them come," the boy announced, flush with the arrogance of youth and eager to avenge his fallen brothers. "I will meet them on Tyraxes." Such talk alarmed his mother. "You will not," she declared. "You are too young for battle." Even so, she allowed the boy to remain as the black council discussed how best to deal with the approaching foe.

Six dragons remained in King's Landing, but only one within the walls of the Red Keep: the queen's own she-dragon, Syrax. A stable in the outer ward had been emptied of horses and given over for her use. Heavy chains bound her to the ground. Though long enough to allow her to move from stable to yard, the chains kept her from flying off riderless. Syrax had long grown accustomed to chains; exceedingly well-fed, she had not hunted for years.

The other dragons were kept in the Dragonpit. Beneath its great dome, forty huge undervaults had been carved from the bones of the Hill of Rhaenys in a great ring. Thick iron doors closed these man-made caves at either end, the inner doors fronting on the sands of the pit, the outer opening to the hillside. Caraxes, Vermithor, Silverwing, and Sheepstealer had made their lairs there before flying off to battle. Five dragons remained: Prince Joffrey's Tyraxes, Addam Velaryon's pale grey Seasmoke, the young dragons Morghul and Shrykos, bound to Princess Jaehaera (fled) and her twin, Prince Jaehaerys (dead) . . . and Dreamfyre, beloved of Queen Helaena. It had long been the custom for at least one dragonrider to reside at the pit, so as to be able to rise to the defense of the city should the need arise. As Rhaenyra preferred to keep her sons by her side, that duty fell to Addam Velaryon.

But now voices on the black council were raised to question Ser Addam's loyalty. The dragonseeds Ulf White and Hugh Hammer had gone over to the enemy . . . but were they the only traitors in their midst? What of Addam of Hull and the girl Nettles? They had been born of bastard stock as well. Could they be trusted?

Lord Bartimos Celtigar thought not. "Bastards are treacherous by nature," he said. "It is in their blood. Betrayal comes as easily to a bastard as loyalty to trueborn men." He urged Her Grace to have the two baseborn dragonriders seized immediately, before they too could join the enemy with their dragons. Others echoed his views, amongst them Ser Luthor Largent, Commander of her City Watch, and Ser Lorent Marbrand, Lord Commander of her Queensguard. Even the two White Harbor men, that fearsome knight Ser Medrick Manderly and his clever, corpulent brother Ser Torrhen, urged the queen to mistrust. "Best take no chances," Ser Torrhen said. "If the foe gains two more dragons, we are lost."

Only Lord Corlys and Grand Maester Gerardys spoke in defense of the dragonseeds. The Grand Maester said that they had no proof of any disloyalty on the parts of Nettles and Ser Addam; the path of wisdom was to seek such proof before making any judgments. Lord Corlys went much further, declaring that Ser Addam and his brother, Alyn, were "true Velaryons," worthy heirs to Driftmark. As for the girl, though she might be dirty and ill-favored, she had fought valiantly in the Battle of the Gullet. "As did the two betrayers," Lord Celtigar countered.

The Hand's impassioned protests and the Grand Maester's cool caution both proved to be in vain. The queen's suspicions had been aroused. "Her Grace had been betrayed so often, by so many, that she was quick to believe the worst of any man," Septon Eustace writes. "Treachery no longer had the power to surprise her. She had come to expect it, even from those she loved the most."

It might be so. Yet Queen Rhaenyra did not act at once, but rather sent for Mysaria, the harlot and dancing girl who was her mistress of whisperers in all but name. With her skin as pale as milk, Lady Misery appeared before the council in a hooded robe of black velvet lined with blood-red silk, and stood with head bowed humbly as Her Grace asked whether she thought Ser Addam and Nettles might be planning to betray them. Then the White Worm raised her eyes and said in a soft voice, "The girl has already betrayed you, my queen. Even now she shares your husband's bed, and soon enough she will have his bastard in her belly."

Then Queen Rhaenyra grew most wroth, Septon Eustace writes. In a voice as cold as ice, she commanded Ser Luthor Largent to take twenty gold cloaks to the Dragonpit and arrest Ser Addam Velaryon. "Question him sharply, and we will learn if he is true or false, beyond a doubt." As to the girl Nettles, "She is a common thing, with the stink of sorcery upon her," the queen declared. "My prince would ne'er lay with such a low creature. You need only look at her to know she has no drop of dragon's blood in her. It was with spells that she bound a dragon to her, and she has done the same with my lord husband." So long as he was in the girl's thrall, Prince Daemon could not be relied upon, Her Grace went on. Therefore, let a command be sent at once to Maidenpool, but only for the eyes of Lord Mooton. "Let him take her at table or abed and strike her head off. Only then shall my prince be freed."

And thus did betrayal beget more betrayal, to the queen's undoing. As Ser Luthor Largent and his gold cloaks rode up Rhaenys's Hill with the queen's warrant, the doors of the Dragonpit were thrown open above them, and Seasmoke spread his pale grey wings and took flight, smoke rising from his nostrils. Ser Addam Velaryon had been forewarned in time to make his escape. Balked and angry, Ser Luthor returned at once to the Red Keep, where he burst into the Tower of the Hand and laid rough hands on the aged Lord Corlys, accusing him of treachery. Nor did the old man deny it. Bound and beaten, but still silent, he was taken down into the dungeons and thrown into a black cell to await trial and execution.

The queen's suspicion fell upon Grand Maester Gerardys as well, for like the Sea Snake he had defended the dragonseeds. Gerardys denied having any part in Lord Corlys's betrayal. Mindful of his long leal service to her, Rhaenyra spared the Grand Maester the dungeons, but chose instead to dismiss him from her council and send him back to Dragonstone at once. "I do not think you would lie to my face," she told Gerardys, "but I cannot have men around me that I do not trust implicitly, and when I look at you now all I can recall is how you prated at me about the Nettles girl."

All the while tales of the slaughter at Tumbleton were spreading through the city . . . and with them, terror. King's Landing would be next, men told one another. Dragon would fight dragon, and this time the city would surely burn. Fearful of the coming foe, hundreds tried to flee, only to be turned back at the gates by the gold cloaks. Trapped within the city walls, some sought shelter in deep cellars against the firestorm they feared was coming, whilst others turned to prayer, to drink, and the pleasures to be found between a woman's thighs. By nightfall, the city's taverns, brothels, and septs were full to bursting with men and women seeking solace or escape, and trading tales of horror.

'Twas in this dark hour that there rose up in Cobbler's Square a certain itinerant brother, a barefoot scarecrow of a man in a hair shirt and roughspun breeches, filthy and unwashed and smelling of the sty, with a begging bowl hung round his neck on a leather thong. A thief he had been, for where his right hand should have been was only a stump covered by ragged leather. Grand Maester Munkun suggests he might have been a Poor Fellow; though that order had long been outlawed, wandering Stars still haunted the byways of the Seven Kingdoms. Where he came from we cannot know. Even his name is lost to history. Those who heard him preach, like those who would later record his infamy, knew him only as the Shepherd. Mushroom names him "the Dead Shepherd," for he claims the man was as pale and foul as a corpse fresh-risen from its grave.

Whoever or whatever he might have been, this one-handed Shepherd rose up like some malign spirit, calling down doom and destruction on

Queen Rhaenyra to all who came to hear. As tireless as he was fearless, he preached all night and well into the following day, his angry voice ringing across Cobbler's Square.

Dragons were unnatural creatures, the Shepherd declared, demons summoned from the pits of the seven hells by the fell sorceries of Valyria, "that vile cesspit where brother lay with sister and mother with son, where men rode demons into battle whilst their women spread their legs for dogs." The Targaryens had escaped the Doom, fleeing across the seas to Dragonstone, but "the gods are not mocked," and now a second doom was at hand. "The false king and the whore queen shall be cast down with all their works, and their demon beasts shall perish from the earth," the Shepherd thundered. All those who stood with them would die as well. Only by cleansing King's Landing of dragons and their masters could Westeros hope to avoid the fate of Valyria.

Each hour his crowds grew. A dozen listeners became a score and then a hundred, and by break of dawn thousands were crowding into the square, shoving and pushing as they strained to hear. Many clutched torches, and by nightfall the Shepherd stood amidst a ring of fire. Those who tried to shout him down were savaged by the crowd. Even the gold cloaks were driven off when forty of them attempted to clear the square at spearpoint.

A different sort of chaos reigned in Tumbleton, sixty leagues to the southwest. Whilst King's Landing quailed in terror, the foes they feared had yet to advance a foot toward the city, for King Aegon's loyalists found themselves leaderless, beset by division, conflict, and doubt. Ormund Hightower lay dead, along with his cousin Ser Bryndon, the foremost knight of Oldtown. His sons remained back at the Hightower a thousand leagues away, and were green boys besides. And whilst Lord Ormund had dubbed Daeron Targaryen "Daeron the Daring" and praised his courage in battle, the prince was still a boy. The youngest of Queen Alicent's sons, he had grown up in the shadow of his elder brothers, and was more used to following commands than giving them. The most senior Hightower remaining with the host was Ser Hobert, another of Lord Ormund's cousins, hitherto entrusted only with the baggage train. A man "as stout as he was slow," Hobert Hightower had lived sixty years without distinguishing himself, yet now he presumed to take command of the host by right of his kinship to Queen Alicent.

Lord Unwin Peake, Ser Jon Roxton the Bold, and Lord Owain Bourney stepped forward as well. Lord Peake could boast descent from a long line of famous warriors, and had a hundred knights and nine hundred men-at-arms beneath his banners. Jon Roxton was as feared for his black temper as for his black blade, the Valyrian steel sword called Orphan-Maker. Lord Owain the Betrayer insisted that his cunning had won them Tumbleton, that only he could take King's Landing. None of the claimants was powerful and respected enough to curb the bloodlust and avarice of the common soldiers. Whilst they squabbled over precedence and plunder, their own men joined freely in the orgy of looting, rape, and destruction.

The horrors of those days cannot be gainsaid. Seldom has any town or city in the history of the Seven Kingdoms been subject to as long or as cruel or as savage a sack as Tumbleton after the Treasons. Without a strong lord to restrain them, even good men can turn to beasts. So was it here. Bands of soldiers wandered drunkenly through the streets robbing every home and shop, and slaying any man who tried to stay their hands. Every woman was fair prey for their lust, even crones and little girls. Wealthy men were tortured unto death to force them to reveal where they had hidden their gold and gems. Babes were torn from their mothers' arms and impaled upon the points of spears. Holy septas were chased naked through the streets and raped, not by one man but by a hundred; silent sisters were violated. Even the dead were not spared. Instead of being given honorable burial, their corpses were left to rot, fodder for carrion crows and wild dogs.

Septon Eustace and Grand Maester Munkun both assert that Prince Daeron was sickened by all he saw and commanded Ser Hobert Hightower to put a stop to it, but Hightower's efforts proved as ineffectual as the man himself. It is in the nature of smallfolk to follow where their lords lead, and Lord Ormund's would-be successors had themselves fallen victim to avarice, bloodlust, and pride. Bold Jon Roxton became enamored of the beautiful Lady Sharis Footly, the wife of the Lord of Tumbleton, and claimed her as a "prize of war." When her lord husband protested, Ser Jon cut him nigh in two with Orphan-Maker, saying, "She can make widows too," as he tore the gown from the weeping Lady Sharis. Only two days later, Lord Peake and Lord Bourney argued bitterly at a war council, until Peake drew his dagger and stabbed Bourney through the eye, declaring, "Once a turncloak, ever a turncloak," as Prince Daeron and Ser Hobert looked on, horror-struck.

Yet the worst crimes were those committed by the Two Betrayers, the baseborn dragonriders Hugh Hammer and Ulf White. Ser Ulf gave himself over entirely to drunkenness, "drowning himself in wine and flesh." Mushroom says he raped three maidens every night. Those who failed to please were fed to his dragon. The knighthood that Queen Rhaenyra had conferred on him did not suffice. Nor was he surfeit when Prince Daeron named him Lord of Bitterbridge. White had a greater prize in mind: he desired no less a seat than Highgarden, declaring that the Tyrells had played no part in the Dance, and therefore should be attainted as traitors.

Ser Ulf's ambitions must be accounted modest when compared to those of his fellow turncloak, Hugh Hammer. The son of a common blacksmith, Hammer was a huge man, with hands so strong that he was said to be able to twist steel bars into torcs. Though largely untrained in the art of war, his size and strength made him a fearsome foe. His weapon of choice was the warhammer, with which he delivered crushing, killing blows. In battle he rode Vermithor, once the mount of the Old King himself; of all the dragons in Westeros, only Vhagar was older or larger.

For all these reasons, Lord Hammer (as he now styled himself) began to dream of crowns. "Why be a lord when you can be a king?" he told the men who began to gather round him. And talk was heard in camp of a prophecy of ancient days that said, "When the hammer shall fall upon the dragon, a new king shall arise, and none shall stand before him." Whence came these words remains a mystery (not from Hammer himself, who could neither read nor write), but within a few days every man at Tumbleton had heard them.

Neither of the Two Betrayers seemed eager to help Prince Daeron press an attack on King's Landing. They had a great host, and three dragons besides, yet the queen had three dragons as well (as best they knew), and would have five once Prince Daemon returned with Nettles. Lord Peake preferred to delay any advance until Lord Baratheon could bring up his power from Storm's End to join them, whilst Ser Hobert wished to fall back to the Reach to replenish their fast-dwindling supplies. None seemed concerned that their army was shrinking every day, melting away like morning dew as more and more men deserted, stealing off for home and harvest with all the plunder they could carry.

Long leagues to the north, in a castle overlooking the Bay of Crabs, another lord found himself sliding down a sword's edge as well. From King's Landing came a raven bearing the queen's message to Manfryd Mooton, Lord of Maidenpool: he was to deliver her the head of the bastard girl Nettles, who had been judged guilty of high treason. "No harm is to be done my lord husband, Prince Daemon of House Targaryen," Her Grace commanded. "Send him back to me when the deed is done, for we have urgent need of him."

Maester Norren, keeper of the *Chronicles of Maidenpool,* says that when his lordship read the queen's letter he was so shaken that he lost his voice. Nor did it return to him until he had drunk three cups of wine. Thereupon Lord Mooton sent for the captain of his guard, his brother, and his champion, Ser Florian Greysteel. He bade his maester to remain as well. When all had assembled, he read to them the letter and asked them for their counsel.

"This thing is easily done," said the captain of his guard. "The prince sleeps beside her, but he has grown old. Three men should be enough to subdue him should he try to interfere, but I will take six to be certain. Does my lord wish this done tonight?"

"Six men or sixty, he is still Daemon Targaryen," Lord Mooton's brother objected. "A sleeping draught in his evening wine would be the wiser course. Let him wake to find her dead."

"The girl is but a child, however foul her treasons," said Ser Florian, that old knight, grey and grizzled and stern. "The Old King would never have asked this of any man of honor."

"These are foul times," Lord Mooton said, "and it is a foul choice this queen has given me. The girl is a guest beneath my roof. If I obey, Maidenpool shall be forever cursed. If I refuse, we shall be attainted and destroyed."

To which his brother answered, "It may be we shall be destroyed whatever choice we make. The prince is more than fond of this brown child, and his dragon is close at hand. A wise lord would kill them both, lest the prince burn Maidenpool in his wroth."

"The queen has forbidden any harm to come to him," Lord Mooton reminded them, "and murdering two guests in their beds is twice as foul as murdering one. I should be doubly cursed." Thereupon he sighed and said, "Would that I had never read this letter."

And up spoke Maester Norren, saying, "Mayhaps you never did."

What was said after that the *Chronicles of Maidenpool* do not tell us. All we know is that the maester, a young man of two-and-twenty, found Prince Daemon and the girl Nettles at their supper that night, and showed them the queen's letter. "Weary after a long day of fruitless flight, they were sharing a simple meal of boiled beef and beets when I entered, talking softly with each other, of what I cannot say. The prince greeted me politely, but as he read I saw the joy go from his eyes, and a sadness descended upon him, like a weight too heavy to be borne. When the girl asked what was in the letter, he said, 'A queen's words, a whore's work.' Then he drew his sword and asked if Lord Mooton's men were waiting outside to take them captive. 'I came alone,' I told him, then foreswore myself, declaring falsely that neither his lordship nor any other man of Maidenpool knew what was written on the parchment. 'Forgive me, My Prince,' I said. 'I have broken my maester's vows.' Prince Daemon sheathed his sword, saying, 'You are a bad maester, but a good man,' after which he bade me leave them, commanding me to 'speak no word of this to lord nor love until the morrow.'"

How the prince and his bastard girl spent their last night beneath Lord Mooton's roof is not recorded, but as dawn broke they appeared together in the yard, and Prince Daemon helped Nettles saddle Sheepstealer one last time. It was her custom to feed him each day before she flew; dragons bend easier to their rider's will when full. That morning she fed him a black ram, the largest in all Maidenpool, slitting the ram's throat herself.

Her riding leathers were stained with blood when she mounted her dragon, Maester Norren records, and "her cheeks were stained with tears." No word of farewell was spoken betwixt man and maid, but as Sheepstealer beat his leathery brown wings and climbed into the dawn sky, Caraxes raised his head and gave a scream that shattered every window in Jonquil's Tower. High above the town, Nettles turned her dragon toward the Bay of Crabs, and vanished in the morning mists, never to be seen again at court or castle.

Daemon Targaryen returned to the castle just long enough to break his fast with Lord Mooton. "This is the last that you will see of me," he told his lordship. "I thank you for your hospitality. Let it be known through all your lands that I fly for Harrenhal. If my nephew Aemond dares face me, he shall find me there, alone."

Thus Prince Daemon departed Maidenpool for the last time. When he had gone, Maester Norren went to his lord to say, "Take the chain from my neck and bind my hands with it. You must needs deliver me to the queen. When I gave warning to a traitor and allowed her to escape, I became a traitor as well." Lord Mooton refused. "Keep your chain," his lordship said. "We are all traitors here." And that night, Queen Rhaenyra's quartered banners were taken down from where they flew above the gates of Maidenpool, and the golden dragons of King Aegon II raised in their stead.

No banners flew above the blackened towers and ruined keeps of Harrenhal when Prince Daemon descended from the sky to claim the castle for his own. A few squatters had found shelter in the castle's deep vaults and undercellars, but the sound of Caraxes's wings sent them fleeing. When the last of them was gone, Daemon Targaryen walked the cavernous halls of Harren's seat alone, with no companion but his dragon. Each night at dusk he slashed the heart tree in the godswood to mark the passing of another day. Thirteen marks can be seen upon that weirwood still; old wounds, deep and dark, yet the lords who have ruled Harrenhal since Daemon's day say they bleed afresh every spring.

On the fourteenth day of the prince's vigil, a shadow swept over the castle, blacker than any passing cloud. All the birds in the godswood took to the air in fright, and a hot wind whipped the fallen leaves across the yard. Vhagar had come at last, and on her back rode the one-eyed Prince Aemond Targaryen, clad in nightblack armor chased with gold.

He had not come alone. Alys Rivers flew with him, her long hair streaming black behind her, her belly swollen with child. Prince Aemond circled twice about the towers of Harrenhal, then brought Vhagar down in the outer ward, with Caraxes a hundred yards away. The dragons glared balefully at each other, and Caraxes spread his wings and hissed, flames dancing across his teeth.

The prince helped his woman down from Vhagar's back, then turned to face his uncle. "Nuncle, I hear you have been seeking us."

"Only you," Daemon replied. "Who told you where to find me?"

"My lady," Aemond answered. "She saw you in a storm cloud, in a mountain pool at dusk, in the fire we lit to cook our suppers. She sees much and more, my Alys. You were a fool to come alone."

"Were I not alone, you would not have come," said Daemon.

"Yet you are, and here I am. You have lived too long, Nuncle."

"On that much we agree," Daemon replied. Then the old prince bade Caraxes bend his neck, and climbed stiffly onto his back, whilst the young prince kissed his woman and vaulted lightly onto Vhagar, taking care to fasten the four short chains between belt and saddle. Daemon left his own chains dangling. Caraxes hissed again, filling the air with flame, and Vhagar answered with a roar. As one the two dragons leapt into the sky.

Prince Daemon took Caraxes up swiftly, lashing him with a steel-tipped whip until they disappeared into a bank of clouds. Vhagar, older and much the larger, was also slower, made ponderous by her very size, and ascended more gradually, in ever widening circles that took her and her rider out over the waters of the Gods Eye. The hour was late, the sun was close to setting, and the lake was calm, its surface glimmering like a sheet of beaten copper. Up and up she soared, searching for Caraxes as Alys Rivers watched from atop Kingspyre Tower in Harrenhal below.

The attack came sudden as a thunderbolt. Caraxes dove down upon Vhagar with a piercing shriek that was heard a dozen miles away, cloaked by the glare of the setting sun on Prince Aemond's blind side. The Blood Wyrm slammed into the older dragon with terrible force. Their roars echoed across the Gods Eye as the two grappled and tore at one another,

dark against a blood-red sky. So bright did their flames burn that fisherfolk below feared the clouds themselves had caught fire. Locked together, the dragons tumbled toward the lake. The Blood Wyrm's jaws closed about Vhagar's neck, her black teeth sinking deep into the flesh of the larger dragon. Even as Vhagar's claws raked his belly open and Vhagar's own teeth ripped away a wing, Caraxes bit deeper, worrying at the wound as the lake rushed up below them with terrible speed.

And it was then, the tales tell us, that Prince Daemon Targaryen swung a leg over his saddle and leapt from one dragon to the other. In his hand was Dark Sister, the sword of Queen Visenya. As Aemond One-Eye looked up in terror, fumbling with the chains that bound him to his saddle, Daemon ripped off his nephew's helm and drove the sword down into his blind eye, so hard the point came out the back of the young prince's throat. Half a heartbeat later, the dragons struck the lake, sending up a gout of water that was said to have been as tall as Kingspyre Tower.

Neither man nor dragon could have survived such an impact, the fisherfolk who saw it said. Nor did they. Caraxes lived long enough to crawl back onto the land. Gutted, with one wing torn from his body and the waters of the lake smoking about him, the Blood Wyrm found the strength to drag himself onto the lakeshore, expiring beneath the walls of Harrenhal. Vhagar's carcass plunged to the lake floor, the hot blood from the gaping wound in her neck bringing the water to a boil over her last resting place. When she was found some years later, after the end of the Dance of the Dragons, Prince Aemond's armored bones remained chained to her saddle, with Dark Sister thrust hilt-deep through his eye socket.

That Prince Daemon died as well we cannot doubt. His remains were never found, but there are queer currents in that lake, and hungry fish as well. The singers tell us that the old prince survived the fall and afterward made his way back to the girl Nettles, to spend the remainder of his days at her side. Such stories make for charming songs, but poor history. Even Mushroom gives the tale no credence, nor shall we.

It was upon the twenty-second day of the fifth moon of the year 130 AC when the dragons danced and died above the Gods Eye. Daemon Targaryen was nine-and-forty at his death; Prince Aemond had only turned twenty. Vhagar, the greatest of the Targaryen dragons since the passing of Balerion the Black Dread, had counted one hundred eighty-one years upon the earth. Thus passed the last living creature from the days of Aegon's Conquest, as dusk and darkness swallowed Black Harren's accursed seat. Yet so few were on hand to bear witness that it would be some time before word of Prince Daemon's last battle became widely known.

The Dying of the Dragons

Rhaenyra Overthrown

Back in King's Landing, Queen Rhaenyra was finding herself ever more isolated with every new betrayal. The suspected turncloak Addam Velaryon had fled before he could be put to the question. His flight had proved his guilt, the White Worm murmured. Lord Celtigar concurred and proposed a punishing new tax on any child born out of wedlock. Such a tax would not only replenish the Crown's coffers, but might also rid the realm of thousands of bastards.

Her Grace had more pressing concerns than her treasury, however. By ordering the arrest of Addam Velaryon, she had lost not only a dragon and a dragonrider, but her Queen's Hand as well . . . and more than half the army that had sailed from Dragonstone to seize the Iron Throne was made up of men sworn to House Velaryon. When it became known that Lord Corlys languished in a dungeon under the Red Keep, they began to abandon her cause by the hundreds. Some made their way to Cobbler's Square to join the throngs gathered round the Shepherd, whilst others slipped through postern gates or over the walls, intent on making their way back to Driftmark. Nor could those who remained be trusted. That was proved when two of the Sea Snake's sworn swords, Ser Denys Woodwright and Ser Thoron True, cut their way into the dungeons to free their lord. Their plans were betrayed to Lady Misery by a whore Ser Thoron had been bedding, and the would-be rescuers were taken and hanged.

The two knights died at dawn, kicking and writhing against the walls of the Red Keep as the nooses tightened round their necks. That very day, not long after sunset, another horror visited the queen's court. Helaena Targaryen, sister, wife, and queen to King Aegon II and mother of his children, threw herself from her window in Maegor's Holdfast to die impaled upon the iron spikes that lined the dry moat below. She was but one-and-twenty.

After half a year of captivity, why should Aegon's queen choose this night to end her life? Mushroom asserts that Helaena was with child after her days and nights of being sold for a common whore, but this explanation is only as creditable as his tale of the Brothel Queens, which is to say, not creditable at all. Grand Maester Munkun believes the horror of seeing Ser Thoron and Ser Denys die drove her to the act, but if the young queen knew the two men it could only have been as gaolers, and there is no evidence that she was a witness to their hanging. Septon Eustace suggests that Lady Mysaria, the White Worm, chose this night to tell Helaena of the death of her son Maelor, and the grisly manner of his passing, though what motive she would have had for doing so, beyond simple malice, is hard to fathom.

Maesters may argue about the truth of such assertions . . . but on that fateful night, a darker tale was being told in the streets and alleys of King's Landing, in inns and brothels and pot shops, even holy septs. Queen Helaena had been murdered, the whispers went, as her sons had been before her. Prince Daeron and his dragons would soon be at the gates, and with them the end of Rhaenyra's reign. The old queen was determined that her young half-sister should not live to revel in her downfall, so she had sent Ser Luthor Largent to seize Helaena with his huge rough hands and fling her from the window onto the spikes below.

Whence came this poisonous calumny, one might ask (for a calumny it most certainly is)? Grand Maester Munkun places it at the door of the Shepherd, for thousands heard him decry both crime and queen. But did he originate the lie, or was he merely giving echo to words heard from other lips? The latter, Mushroom would have us believe. A slander so vile could only have been the work of Larys Strong, the dwarf asserts . . . for the Clubfoot had never left King's Landing (as would soon be revealed), but only slipped into its shadows, from whence he continued to plot and whisper.

Could Helaena's death have been murder? Possibly . . . but it seems unlikely Queen Rhaenyra was behind it. Helaena Targaryen was a broken creature who posed no threat to Her Grace. Nor do our sources speak of any special enmity between them. If Rhaenyra were intent on murder, surely it would have been the Dowager Queen Alicent flung down onto the spikes. Moreover, at the time of Queen Helaena's death, we have abundant proof that Ser Luthor Largent, the purported killer, was eating with three hundred of his gold cloaks at the barracks by the Gate of the Gods.

All the same, the rumor of Queen Helaena's "murder" was soon on the lips of half King's Landing. That it was so quickly believed shows how utterly the city had turned against their once-beloved queen. Rhaenyra was hated; Helaena had been loved. Nor had the common folk of the city forgotten the cruel murder of Prince Jaehaerys by Blood and Cheese, and the terrible death of Prince Maelor at Bitterbridge. Helaena's end had been mercifully swift; one of the spikes took her through the throat and she died without a sound. At the moment of her death, across the city atop the Hill of Rhaenys, her dragon, Dreamfyre, rose suddenly with a roar that shook the Dragonpit, snapping two of the chains that bound her. When Dowager Queen Alicent was informed of her daughter's passing, she rent her garments and pronounced a dire curse upon her rival.

That night King's Landing rose in bloody riot.

The rioting began amidst the alleys and wynds of Flea Bottom, as men and women poured from the wine sinks, rat pits, and pot shops by the hundreds, angry, drunken, and afraid. From there the rioters spread throughout the city, shouting for justice for the dead princes and their murdered mother. Carts and wagons were overturned, shops looted, homes plundered and set afire. Gold cloaks attempting to quell the disturbances were set upon and beaten bloody. No one was spared, of high birth or low. Lords were pelted with rubbish, knights pulled from their saddles. Lady Darla Deddings saw her brother Davos stabbed through the eye when he tried to defend her from three drunken ostlers intent on raping her. Sailors unable to return to their ships attacked the River Gate and fought a pitched battle with the City Watch. It took Ser Luthor Largent and four hundred spears to disperse them. By then the gate had been hacked half to pieces and a hundred men were dead or dying, a quarter of them gold cloaks.

No such rescuers came for Lord Bartimos Celtigar, whose walled manse was defended only by six guardsmen and a few hastily armed servants. When rioters came swarming over the walls, these dubious defenders threw down their weapons and ran, or joined the attackers. Arthor Celtigar, a boy of fifteen, made a brave stand in a doorway, sword in hand, and kept the howling mob at bay for a few moments . . . until a treacherous serving girl let the rioters in through a back way. The brave lad was slain by a spear thrust through the back. Lord Bartimos himself fought his way to the stables, only to find all his horses dead or stolen. Taken, the queen's despised master of coin was bound to a post and tortured until he revealed where all his wealth was hidden. Then a tanner called Wat announced that his lordship had failed to pay his "cock tax," and must yield his manhood to the Crown as forfeit.

At Cobbler's Square the sounds of the riot could be heard from every quarter. The Shepherd drank deep of the anger, proclaiming that the day of doom was nigh at hand, just as he had foretold, and calling down the wroth of the gods upon "this unnatural queen who sits bleeding on the Iron Throne, her whore's lips glistening and red with the blood of her sweet sister." When a septa in the crowd cried out, pleading for him to save the city, the Shepherd said, "Only the Mother's mercy can save you, but you drove your Mother from this city with your pride and lust and avarice. Now it is the Stranger who comes. On a dark horse with burning eyes he comes, a scourge of fire in his hand to cleanse this pit of sin of demons and all who bow before them. Listen! Can you hear the sound of burning hooves? He comes! He comes!!"

The crowd took up the cry, wailing, *"He comes! He comes!!"* as a thousand torches filled the square with pools of smoky yellow light. Soon enough the shouts died away, and through the night the sound of iron hooves on cobblestones grew louder. "Not one Stranger, but five hundred," Mushroom says in his *Testimony*.

The City Watch had come in strength, five hundred men clad in black ringmail, steel caps, and long golden cloaks, armed with short swords, spears, and spiked cudgels. They formed up on the south side of the square, behind a wall of shields and spears. At their head rode Ser Luthor Largent upon an armored warhorse, a longsword in his hand. The mere sight of him was enough to send hundreds streaming away into the wynds and alleys and side streets. Hundreds more fled when Ser Luthor ordered the gold cloaks to advance.

Ten thousand remained, however. The press was so thick that many who might gladly have fled found themselves unable to move, pushed and shoved and trod upon. Others surged forward, locked arms, and began to shout and curse, as the spears advanced to the slow beat of a drum. "Make way, you bloody fools," Ser Luthor roared at the Shepherd's lambs. "Go home. No harm will come to you. Go home. We only want this Shepherd."

Some say the first man to die was a baker, who grunted in surprise when a spearpoint pierced his flesh and he saw his apron turning red. Others claim it was a little girl, trodden under by Ser Luthor's warhorse. A rock came flying from the crowd, striking a spearman on the brow. Shouts and curses were heard, sticks and stones and chamber pots came raining down from rooftops, an archer across the square began to loose his shafts. A torch was thrust at a watchman, and quick as that his golden cloak was burning.

On the far side of Cobbler's Square, the Shepherd was bundled away by his acolytes. "Stop him," Ser Luthor shouted. "Seize him! Stop him!" He spurred his horse, cutting his way through the throng, and his gold cloaks followed, discarding their spears to draw swords and cudgels. The Shepherd's followers were screaming, falling, running. Others produced weapons of their own, dirks and daggers, mauls and clubs, broken spears and rusted swords.

The gold cloaks were large men, young, strong, disciplined, well armed and well armored. For twenty yards or more their shield wall held, and

they cut a bloody road through the crowd, leaving dead and dying all around them. But they numbered only five hundred, and ten thousand had gathered to hear the Shepherd. One watchman went down, then another. Suddenly smallfolk were slipping through the gaps in the line. Screaming curses, the Shepherd's flock attacked with knives and stones, even teeth, swarming over the City Watch and around their flanks, attacking from behind, flinging tiles down from roofs and balconies.

Battle turned to riot turned to slaughter. Surrounded on all sides, the gold cloaks found themselves hemmed in and swept under, with no room to wield their weapons. Many died on the points of their own swords. Others were torn to pieces, kicked to death, trampled underfoot, hacked apart with hoes and butcher's cleavers. Even the fearsome Ser Luthor Largent could not escape the carnage. His sword torn from his grasp, Largent was pulled from his saddle, stabbed in the belly, and bludgeoned to death with a cobblestone, his helm and head so crushed that it was only by its size that his body was recognized when the corpse wagons came the next day.

During that long night, Septon Eustace tells us, the Shepherd held sway over half the city, whilst strange lords and kings of misrule squabbled o'er the rest. Hundreds of men gathered round Wat the Tanner, who rode through the streets on a white horse, brandishing Lord Celtigar's severed head and bloody genitals and declaring an end to all taxes. In a brothel on the Street of Silk, the whores raised up their own king, a pale-haired boy of four named Gaemon, supposedly a bastard of the missing King Aegon II. Not to be outdone, a hedge knight named Ser Perkin the Flea crowned his own squire Trystane, a stripling of sixteen years, declaring him to be a natural son of the late King Viserys. Any knight can make a knight, and when Ser Perkin began dubbing every sellsword, thief, and butcher's boy who flocked to Trystane's ragged banner, men and boys appeared by the hundreds to pledge themselves to his cause.

By dawn, fires were burning throughout the city, Cobbler's Square was littered with corpses, and bands of lawless men roamed Flea Bottom, breaking into shops and homes and laying rough hands on every honest person they encountered. The surviving gold cloaks had retreated to their barracks, whilst gutter knights, mummer kings, and mad prophets ruled the streets. Like the roaches they resembled, the worst of these fled before the light, retreating to hidey-holes and cellars to sleep off their drunks, divvy up their plunder, and wash the blood off their hands. The gold cloaks at the Old Gate and the Dragon Gate sallied forth under the command of their captains, Ser Balon Byrch and Ser Garth the Harelip, and by midday had managed to restore some semblance of order to the streets north and east of Rhaenys's Hill. Ser Medrick Manderly, leading a hundred White Harbor men, did the same for the area northeast of Aegon's High Hill, down to the Iron Gate.

The rest of King's Landing remained in chaos. When Ser Torrhen Manderly led his northmen down the Hook, they found Fishermonger's Square and River Row swarming with Ser Perkin's gutter knights. At the River Gate, "King" Trystane's ragged banner flew above the battlements, whilst the bodies of the captain and three of his serjeants hung from the gatehouse. The remainder of the "Mudfoot" garrison had gone over to Ser Perkin. Ser Torrhen lost a quarter of his men fighting his way back to the Red Keep . . . yet escaped lightly compared to Ser Lorent Marbrand, who led a hundred knights and men-at-arms into Flea Bottom. Sixteen returned. Ser Lorent, Lord Commander of the Queensguard, was not amongst them.

By evenfall, Rhaenyra Targaryen found herself sore beset on every side, her reign in ruins. "The queen wept when they told her how Ser Lorent died," Mushroom testifies, "but she raged when she learned that Maidenpool had gone over to the foe, that the girl Nettles had escaped, that her own beloved consort had betrayed her, and she trembled when Lady Mysaria warned her against the coming dark, that this night would be worse than the last. At dawn, a hundred men attended her in the throne room, but one by one they slipped away or were dismissed, until only her sons and I remained with her. 'My faithful Mushroom,' Her Grace called me, 'would that all men were true as you. I should make you my Hand.' When I replied that I would sooner be her consort, she laughed. No sound was ever sweeter. It was good to hear her laugh."

Munkun's *True Telling* says naught of the queen laughing, only that Her Grace swung from rage to despair and back again, clutching so desperately at the Iron Throne that both her hands were bloody by the time the sun set. She gave command of the gold cloaks to Ser Balon Byrch, captain at the Iron Gate, sent ravens to Winterfell and the Eyrie pleading for more aid, ordered that a decree of attainder be drawn up against the Mootons of Maidenpool, and named the young Ser Glendon Goode Lord Commander of the Queensguard (though only twenty, and a member of the White Swords for less than a moon's turn, Goode had distinguished himself during the fighting in Flea Bottom earlier that day. It was he who brought back Ser Lorent's body, to keep the rioters from despoiling it).

Though the fool Mushroom does not figure in Septon Eustace's account of the Last Day, nor in Munkun's *True Telling,* both speak of the queen's sons. Aegon the Younger was ever at his mother's side, yet seldom spoke a word. Prince Joffrey, ten-and-three, donned squire's armor and begged the queen to let him ride to the Dragonpit and mount Tyraxes. "I want to fight for you, Mother, as my brothers did. Let me prove that I am as brave as they were." His words only deepened Rhaenyra's resolve, however. "Brave they were, and dead they are, the both of them. My sweet boys." And once more, Her Grace forbade the prince to leave the castle.

With the setting of the sun, the vermin of King's Landing emerged once more from their rat pits, hidey-holes, and cellars, in even greater numbers than the night before.

On Visenya's Hill, an army of whores bestowed their favors freely on any man willing to swear his sword to Gaemon Palehair ("King Cunny" in the vulgar parlance of the city). At the River Gate, Ser Perkin feasted his gutter knights on stolen food and led them down the riverfront, looting wharves and warehouses and any ship that had not put to sea, even as Wat the Tanner led his own mob of howling ruffians against the Gate of the Gods. Though King's Landing boasted massive walls and stout towers, they had been designed to repel attacks from outside the city, not from within its walls. The garrison at the Gate of the Gods was especially weak, as their captain and a third of their number had died with Ser Luthor Largent in Cobbler's Square. Those who remained, many wounded, were easily overcome. Wat's followers poured out into the countryside, streaming up the kingsroad behind Lord Celtigar's rotting head . . . toward where, not even Wat seemed certain.

Before an hour had passed, the King's Gate and the Lion Gate were open as well. The gold cloaks at the first had fled, whilst the "lions" at the other had thrown in with the mobs. Three of the seven gates of King's Landing were open to Rhaenyra's foes.

The most dire threat to the queen's rule proved to be within the city, however. At nightfall, the Shepherd had appeared once more to resume his preaching in Cobbler's Square. The corpses from last night's fighting had been cleared away during the day, we are told, but not before they had been looted of their clothes and coin and other valuables, and in some cases of their heads as well. As the one-handed prophet shrieked his curses at "the vile queen" in the Red Keep, a hundred severed heads looked up at him, swaying atop tall spears and sharpened staffs. The crowd, Septon Eustace says, was twice as large and thrice as fearful as the night before. Like the queen they so despised, the Shepherd's "lambs" were looking to the sky with dread, fearing that King Aegon's dragons would arrive before the night was out, with an army close behind them. No longer believing that the queen could protect them, they looked to their Shepherd for salvation.

But that prophet answered, "When the dragons come, your flesh will burn and blister and turn to ash. Your wives will dance in gowns of fire, shrieking as they burn, lewd and naked underneath the flames. And you shall see your little children weeping, weeping till their eyes do melt and slide like jelly down their faces, till their pink flesh falls black and crackling from their bones. The Stranger comes, *he comes, he comes,* to scourge us for our sins. Prayers cannot stay his wroth, no more than tears can quench the flame of dragons. Only blood can do that. Your blood, my blood, *their* blood." Then he raised his right arm and jabbed the stump of his missing hand at Rhaenys's Hill behind him, at the Dragonpit black against the stars. "There the demons dwell, up there. *Fire and blood, blood and fire.* This is their city. If you would make it yours, first must you destroy them. If you would cleanse yourself of sin, first must you bathe in dragon's blood. For only blood can quench the fires of hell."

From ten thousand throats a cry went up. *"Kill them! Kill them!"* And like some vast beast with ten thousand legs, the lambs began to move, shoving and pushing, waving their torches, brandishing swords and knives and other, cruder weapons, walking and running through the streets and alleys toward the Dragonpit. Some thought better and slipped away to home, but for every man who left, three more appeared to join these dragonslayers. By the time they reached the Hill of Rhaenys, their numbers had doubled.

High atop Aegon's High Hill across the city, Mushroom watched the attack unfold from the roof of Maegor's Holdfast with the queen, her sons, and members of her court. The night was black and overcast, the torches so numerous that "it was as if all the stars had come down from the sky to storm the Dragonpit," the fool says.

As soon as word had reached her that the Shepherd's savage flock was on the march, Rhaenyra sent riders to Ser Balon at the Old Gate and Ser Garth at the Dragon Gate, commanding them to disperse the lambs, seize the Shepherd, and defend the royal dragons . . . but with the city in such turmoil, it was far from certain that the riders had won through. Even if they had, what loyal gold cloaks remained were too few to have any hope of success. "Her Grace had as well commanded them to halt the Blackwater in its flow," says Mushroom. When Prince Joffrey pleaded with his mother to let him ride forth with their own knights and those from White Harbor, the queen refused. "If they take that hill, this one will be next," she said. "We will need every sword here to defend the castle."

"They will kill the *dragons,*" Prince Joffrey said, anguished.

"Or the dragons will kill them," his mother said, unmoved. "Let them burn. The realm will not long miss them."

"Mother, what if they kill *Tyraxes*?" the young prince said.

The queen did not believe it. "They are vermin. Drunks and fools and gutter rats. One taste of dragonflame and they will run."

At that the fool Mushroom spoke up, saying, "Drunks they may be, but a drunken man knows not fear. Fools, aye, but a fool can kill a king. Rats, that too, but a thousand rats can bring down a bear. I saw it happen once, down there in Flea Bottom." This time Queen Rhaenyra did not laugh. Bidding her fool to hold his tongue or lose it, Her Grace turned back to the parapets. Only Mushroom saw Prince Joffrey go sulking off (if his *Testimony* can be believed) . . . and Mushroom had been told to hold his tongue.

It was only when the watchers on the roof heard Syrax roar that the prince's absence was noted. That was too late. "No," the queen was heard to say, "I forbid it, I *forbid* it," but even as she spoke her dragon flapped up from the yard, perched for half a heartbeat atop the castle battlements, then launched herself into the night with the queen's son clinging to her back, a sword in hand. "After him!" Rhaenyra shouted. "All of you, every man, every boy, to horse, *to horse,* go after him. Bring him back, bring him back, he does not know. My son, my sweet, my son . . ."

Seven men did ride down from the Red Keep that night, into the madness of the city. Munkun tells us they were men of honor, duty bound to obey their queen's commands. Septon Eustace would have us believe that their hearts had been touched by a mother's love for her son. Mushroom names them dolts and dastards, eager for some rich reward, and "too dull to believe that they might die." For once it may be that all three of our chroniclers have the truth of it, at least in part.

Our septon, our maester, and our fool do agree upon their names. The Seven Who Rode were Ser Medrick Manderly, the heir to White Harbor; Ser Loreth Lansdale and Ser Harrold Darke, knights of the Queensguard; Ser Harmon of the Reeds, called Iron-Banger; Ser Gyles Yronwood, an exiled knight from Dorne; Ser Willam Royce, armed with the famed Valyrian sword Lamentation; and Ser Glendon Goode, Lord Commander of the Queensguard. Six squires, eight gold cloaks, and twenty men-at-arms rode with the seven champions as well, but their names, alas, have not come down to us.

Many a singer has made many a song of the Ride of the Seven, and many a tale has been told of the perils they faced as they fought their way across the city, whilst King's Landing burned around them and the alleys of Flea Bottom ran red with blood. Certain of those songs even have some truth to them, but it is beyond our purview to recount them here. Songs are sung of Prince Joffrey's last flight as well. Some singers can find glory even in a privy, Mushroom tells us, but it takes a fool to speak the truth. Though we cannot doubt the prince's courage, his act was one of folly.

We shall not pretend to any understanding of the bond between dragon and dragonrider; wiser heads have pondered that mystery for centuries. We do know, however, that dragons are not horses, to be ridden by any man who throws a saddle on their back. Syrax was the queen's dragon. She had never known another rider. Though Prince Joffrey was known to her by sight and scent, a familiar presence whose fumbling at her chains excited no alarm, the great yellow she-dragon wanted no part of him astride her. In his haste to be away before he could be stopped, the prince had vaulted onto Syrax without benefit of saddle or whip. His intent, we must presume, was either to fly Syrax into battle or, more likely, to cross the city to the Dragonpit and his own Tyraxes. Mayhaps he meant to loose the other pit dragons as well.

Joffrey never reached the Hill of Rhaenys. Once in the air, Syrax twisted beneath him, fighting to be free of this unfamiliar rider. And from below, stones and spears and arrows flew at him from the hands of the Shepherd's blood-soaked lambs, maddening the dragon even further. Two hundred feet above Flea Bottom, Prince Joffrey slid from the dragon's back and plunged to the earth.

Near a juncture where five alleys came together, the prince's fall came to its bloody end. He crashed first onto a steep-pitched roof before rolling off to fall another forty feet amidst a shower of broken tiles. We are told that the fall broke his back, that shards of slate rained down about him like knives, that his own sword tore loose of his hand and pierced him through the belly. In Flea Bottom, men still speak of a candlemaker's daughter named Robin who cradled the broken prince in her arms and gave him comfort as he died, but there is more of legend than of history in that tale. "Mother, forgive me," Joffrey supposedly said with his last breath . . . though men still argue whether he was speaking of his mother, the queen, or praying to the Mother Above.

Thus perished Joffrey Velaryon, Prince of Dragonstone and heir to the Iron Throne, the last of Queen Rhaenyra's sons by Laenor Velaryon . . . or the last of her bastards by Ser Harwin Strong, depending on which truth one chooses to believe.

The mob was not long in falling on his corpse. The candlemaker's daughter Robin, if she ever existed, was driven off. Looters tore the boots from the prince's feet and the sword from his belly, then stripped him of his fine, bloodstained clothes. Others, still more savage, began ripping at his body. Both of his hands were cut off, so the scum of the street might

claim the rings on his fingers. The prince's right foot was hacked through at the ankle, and a butcher's apprentice was sawing at his neck to claim his head when the Seven Who Rode came thundering up. There amidst the stinks of Flea Bottom, a battle was waged in the mud and blood for possession of Prince Joffrey's body.

The queen's knights at last reclaimed the boy's remains, save for his missing foot, though three of the seven fell in the fighting. The Dornishman, Ser Gyles Yronwood, was pulled from his horse and bludgeoned to death, whilst Ser Willam Royce was felled by a man who leapt down from a rooftop to land upon his back (his famed sword, Lamentation, was torn from his hand and carried off, never to be found again). Most grievous of all was the fate of Ser Glendon Goode, attacked from behind by a man with a torch, who set his long white cloak afire. As the flames licked at his back, his horse reared in terror and threw him, and the mob swarmed over him, tearing him to pieces. Only twenty years of age, Ser Glendon had been Lord Commander of the Queensguard for less than a day.

And even as blood flowed in the alleys of Flea Bottom, another battle raged round the Dragonpit above, atop the Hill of Rhaenys.

Mushroom was not wrong: swarms of starving rats do indeed bring down bulls and bears and lions, when there are enough of them. No matter how many the bull or bear might kill, there are always more, biting at the great beast's legs, clinging to its belly, running up its back. So it was that night. The Shepherd's rats were armed with spears, longaxes, spiked clubs, and half a hundred other kinds of weapons, including both longbows and crossbows.

Gold cloaks from the Dragon Gate, obedient to the queen's command, issued forth from their barracks to defend the hill, but found themselves unable to cut through the mobs, and turned back, whilst the messenger sent to the Old Gate never arrived. The Dragonpit had its own contingent of guards, the Dragonkeepers, but those proud warriors were only seven-and-seventy in number, and fewer than fifty had the watch that night. Though their swords drank deep of the blood of the attackers, the numbers were against them. When the Shepherd's lambs smashed through the doors (the towering main gates, sheathed in bronze and iron, were too strong to assault, but the building had a score of lesser entrances) and came clambering through windows, the Dragonkeepers were overwhelmed, and soon slaughtered.

Mayhaps the attackers hoped to take the dragons within whilst they slept, but the clangor of the assault made that impossible. Those who lived to tell tales afterward speak of shouts and screams, the smell of blood in the air, the splintering of oak-and-iron doors beneath crude rams and the blows of countless axes. "Seldom have so many men rushed so eagerly onto their funeral pyres," Grand Maester Munkun wrote, "but a madness was upon them." There were four dragons housed within the Dragonpit. By the time the first of the attackers came pouring out onto the sands, all four were roused, awake, and angry.

No two chronicles agree on how many men and women died that night beneath the Dragonpit's great dome: two hundred or two thousand, be that as it may. For every man who perished, ten suffered burns and yet survived. Trapped within the pit, hemmed in by walls and dome and bound by heavy chains, the dragons could not fly away, or use their wings to evade attacks and swoop down on their foes. Instead they fought with horns and claws and teeth, turning this way and that like bulls in a Flea Bottom rat pit . . . but these bulls could breathe fire. "The Dragonpit was transformed into a fiery hell where burning men staggered screaming through the smoke, the flesh sloughing from their blackened bones," writes Septon Eustace, "but for every man who died, ten more appeared, shouting that the dragons must needs die. One by one, they did."

Shrykos was the first dragon to succumb, slain by a woodsman known as Hobb the Hewer, who leapt onto her neck, driving his axe down into the beast's skull as Shrykos roared and twisted, trying to throw him off. Seven blows did Hobb deliver with his legs locked round the dragon's neck, and each time his axe came down he roared out the name of one of the Seven. It was the seventh blow, the Stranger's blow, that slew the dragon, crashing through scale and bones into the beast's brain . . . if Eustace is to be believed.

Morghul, it is written, was slain by the Burning Knight, a huge brute of a man in heavy armor who rushed headlong into the dragon's flame with spear in hand, thrusting its point into the beast's eye repeatedly even as the dragonflame melted the steel plate that encased him and devoured the flesh within.

Prince Joffrey's Tyraxes retreated back into his lair, we are told, roasting so many would-be dragonslayers as they rushed after him that its entrance was soon made impassable by their corpses. But it must be recalled that each of these man-made caves had two entrances, one fronting onto the sands of the pit, the other opening onto the hillside. It was the Shepherd himself who directed his followers to break through the "back door." Hundreds did, howling through the smoke with swords and spears and axes. As Tyraxes turned, his chains fouled, entangling him in a web of steel that fatally limited his movement. Half a dozen men (and one woman) would later claim to have dealt the dragon the mortal blow (like his master, Tyraxes suffered further indignity even in death, as the Shepherd's followers sliced the membranes from his wings and tore them into ragged strips to fashion dragonskin cloaks).

The last of the four pit dragons did not die so easily. Legend has it that Dreamfyre had broken free of two of her chains at Queen Helaena's death. The remaining bonds she burst now, tearing the stanchions from the walls as the mob rushed her, then plunging into them with tooth and claw, ripping men apart and tearing off their limbs even as she loosed her terrible fires. As others closed about her she took wing, circling the cavernous interior of the Dragonpit and swooping down to attack the men below. Tyraxes, Shrykos, and Morghul killed scores, there can be little doubt, but Dreamfyre slew more than all three of them combined.

Hundreds fled in terror from her flames . . . but hundreds more, drunk or mad or possessed of the Warrior's own courage, pushed through to the attack. Even at the apex of the dome, the dragon was within easy reach of archer and crossbowman, and arrows and quarrels flew at Dreamfyre wherever she went, at such close range that some few even punched through her scales. Whenever she lighted, men swarmed to the attack, driving her back into the air. Twice the dragon flew at the Dragonpit's great bronze gates, only to find them closed and barred and defended by ranks of spears.

Unable to flee, Dreamfyre returned to the attack, savaging her tormentors until the sands of the pit were strewn with charred corpses, and the very air was thick with smoke and the smell of burned flesh, yet still the spears and arrows flew. The end came when a crossbow bolt nicked one of the dragon's eyes. Half-blind, and maddened by a dozen lesser wounds, Dreamfyre spread her wings and flew straight up at the great dome above in a last desperate attempt to break into the open sky. Already weakened by blasts of dragonflame, the dome cracked under the force of impact, and a moment later half of it came tumbling down, crushing both dragon and dragonslayers under tons of broken stone and rubble.

The Storming of the Dragonpit was done. Four of the Targaryen dragons lay dead, though at hideous cost. Yet the Shepherd was not yet triumphant, for the queen's own dragon remained alive and free . . . and as the burned and bloody survivors of the carnage in the pit came stumbling from the smoking ruins, Syrax descended upon them from above.

Mushroom was amongst those watching with Queen Rhaenyra on the roof of Maegor's Holdfast. "A thousand shrieks and shouts echoed across

the city, mingling with the dragon's roar," he tells us. "Atop the Hill of Rhaenys, the Dragonpit wore a crown of yellow fire, burning so bright it seemed as if the sun was rising. Even the queen trembled as she watched, the tears glistening on her cheeks. Never have I seen a sight more terrible, more glorious."

Many of the queen's companions on the rooftop fled, the dwarf tells us, fearing that the fires would soon engulf the entire city, even the Red Keep atop Aegon's High Hill. Others took themselves to the castle sept to pray for deliverance. Rhaenyra herself wrapped her arms about her last living son, Aegon the Younger, clutching him fiercely to her bosom. Nor would she loose her hold upon him . . . until that dread moment when Syrax fell.

Unchained and riderless, Syrax might have easily flown away from the madness. The sky was hers. She could have returned to the Red Keep, left the city entirely, taken wing for Dragonstone. Was it the noise and fire that drew her to the Hill of Rhaenys, the roars and screams of the dying dragons, the smell of burning flesh? We cannot know, no more than we can know why Syrax chose to descend upon the Shepherd's mobs, rending them with tooth and claw and devouring dozens, when she might as easily have rained fire on them from above, for in the sky no man could have harmed her. We can only report what happened, as Mushroom, Septon Eustace, and Grand Maester Munkun have set it down for us.

Many a conflicting tale is told of the death of the queen's dragon. Munkun credits Hobb the Hewer and his axe, though this is almost certainly mistaken. Could the same man truly have slain two dragons on the same night and in the same manner? Some speak of an unnamed spearman, "a blood-soaked giant" who leapt from the Dragonpit's broken dome onto the dragon's back. Others relate how a knight named Ser Warrick Wheaton slashed a wing from Syrax with a Valyrian steel sword (Lamentation, most like). A crossbowman named Bean would claim the kill afterward, boasting of it in many a wine sink and tavern, until one of the queen's loyalists grew tired of his wagging tongue and cut it out.

Possibly all these worthies (save Hobb) played some role in the dragon's demise . . . but the tale most oft heard in King's Landing named the

Shepherd himself as the dragonslayer. As others fled, the story went, the one-handed prophet stood fearless and alone against the ravening beast, calling on the Seven for succor, till the Warrior himself took form, thirty feet tall. In his hand was a black blade made of smoke that turned to steel as he swung it, cleaving the head of Syrax from her body. And so the tale was told, even by Septon Eustace in his account of these dark days, and so the singers sang for many years thereafter.

The loss of both her dragon and her son left Rhaenyra Targaryen ashen and inconsolable, Mushroom tells us. Attended only by the fool, she retreated to her chambers whilst her counselors conferred. King's Landing was lost, all agreed; they must needs abandon the city. Reluctantly, Her Grace was persuaded to leave the next day, at dawn. With the Mud Gate in the hands of her foes, and all the ships along the river burned or sunk, Rhaenyra and a small band of followers slipped out through the Dragon Gate, intending to make their way up the coast to Duskendale. With her rode the brothers Manderly, four surviving Queensguard, Ser Balon Byrch and twenty gold cloaks, four of the queen's ladies-in-waiting, and her last surviving son, Aegon the Younger.

Mushroom remained behind, along with other members of the court, amongst them Lady Misery and Septon Eustace. Ser Garth the Harelip, captain of the gold cloaks at the Dragon Gate, was charged with the defense of the castle, a task for which the Harelip proved to have little appetite. Her Grace had not been gone half a day when Ser Perkin the Flea and his gutter knights appeared outside the gates, demanding that the castle yield. Though outnumbered ten to one, the queen's garrison might still have resisted, but Ser Garth chose instead to strike Rhaenyra's banners, open his gates, and trust to the mercy of the foe.

The Flea proved to have no mercy. Garth the Harelip was dragged before him and beheaded, along with twenty other knights still loyal to the queen, amongst them Ser Harmon of the Reeds, the Iron-Banger, who had been one of the Seven Who Rode. Nor was the mistress of whisperers, Lady Mysaria of Lys, spared on account of her sex. Taken whilst attempting to flee, the White Worm was whipped naked through the city, from the Red Keep to the Gate of the Gods. If she were still alive by the time they reached the gate, Ser Perkin promised, she would be spared and allowed to go. She made it only half that distance, dying on the cobblestones with hardly a patch of her pale white skin left upon her back.

Septon Eustace feared for his own life. "Only the Mother's mercy saved me," he writes, though it seems more likely that Ser Perkin did not wish to provoke the enmity of the Faith. The Flea also freed all the prisoners found in the dungeons below the castle, amongst them Grand Maester Orwyle and the Sea Snake, Lord Corlys Velaryon. Both were on hand the next day to bear witness as Ser Perkin's gangling squire Trystane mounted the Iron Throne. So too was the Queen Dowager, Alicent of House Hightower. Down in the black cells, Ser Perkin's men even found King Aegon's former master of coin, Ser Tyland Lannister, still alive . . . though Rhaenyra's torturers had blinded him, pulled out his fingernails and toenails, cut off his ears, and relieved him of his manhood.

King Aegon's master of whisperers, Larys Strong the Clubfoot, fared much better. The Lord of Harrenhal emerged intact from wherever he had been hiding. Like a man risen from the grave, he came striding through the halls of the Red Keep as if he had never left them, to be greeted warmly by Ser Perkin the Flea and take a place of honor at the side of his new "king."

The queen's flight brought no peace to King's Landing. "Three kings reigned over the city, each on his own hill, yet for their unfortunate subjects there was no law, no justice, no protection," says the *True Telling*. "No man's home was safe, nor any maiden's virtue." This chaos endured for more than a moon's turn.

Maesters and other scholars writing of this time oft take their cue from Munkun and speak of the Moon of the Three Kings (other scholars prefer the Moon of Madness), but this is a misnomer, as the Shepherd never claimed kingship, styling himself a simple son of the Seven. Yet it cannot be denied that he held sway over tens of thousands from the ruins of the Dragonpit.

The heads of the five dragons that his followers had slain had been set up on posts, and every night the Shepherd would appear amongst them to preach. With the dragons dead and the threat of immolation no longer imminent, the prophet turned his wroth upon the highborn and wealthy. Only the poor and humble would ever see the halls of the gods, he declared; lords and knights and rich men would be cast down in their pride and avarice to hell. "Cast off your silks and satins, and clothe your nakedness in roughspun robes," he told his followers. "Throw away your shoes, and walk barefoot through the world, as the Father made you." Thousands obeyed. But thousands more turned away, and each night the crowds that came to hear the prophet grew smaller.

At the other end of the Street of the Sisters, Gaemon Palehair's queer kingdom blossomed atop Visenya's Hill. The court of this four-year-old bastard king was made up of whores, mummers, and thieves, whilst gangs of ruffians, sellswords, and drunkards defended his "rule." One decree after another came down from the House of Kisses where the child king had his seat, each more outrageous than the last. Gaemon decreed that girls should henceforth be equal with boys in matter of inheritance, that the poor be given bread and beer in times of famine, that men who had lost limbs in war must afterward be fed and housed by whichever lord they had been fighting for when the loss took place. Gaemon decreed that husbands who beat their wives should themselves be beaten, irrespective of what the wives had done to warrant such chastisement. These edicts were almost certainly the work of a Dornish whore named Sylvenna Sand, reputedly the paramour of the little king's mother Essie, if Mushroom is to be believed.

Royal decrees also issued forth from atop Aegon's High Hill, where Ser Perkin's catspaw Trystane sat the Iron Throne, but those were of a very different nature. The squire king began by repealing Queen Rhaenyra's unpopular taxes and dividing the coin in the royal treasury amongst his own followers. He followed that with a general cancellation of debt, raised threescore of his gutter knights to the ranks of the nobility, and answered "King" Gaemon's promise of free bread and beer for the starving by granting the poor the right to take rabbits, hares, and deer from the kingswood as well (though not elk nor boar). All the while, Ser Perkin the Flea was recruiting scores of surviving gold cloaks to Trystane's banner. With their swords he took control of the Dragon Gate, the King's Gate, and the

Lion Gate, giving him four of the city's seven gates and more than half of the towers along its walls.

In the early days after the queen's flight, the Shepherd was by far the most powerful of the city's three "kings," but as the nights passed, the number of his followers continued to dwindle. "The smallfolk of the city woke as if from a bad dream," Septon Eustace wrote, "and like sinners waking cold and sober after a night of drunken debauchery and revel, they turned away in shame, hiding their faces from one another and hoping to forget." Though the dragons were dead and the queen fled, such was the power of the Iron Throne that the commons still looked to the Red Keep when hungry or afraid. So as the power of the Shepherd waned on the Hill of Rhaenys, the power of King Trystane Truefyre (as he now styled himself) waxed atop Aegon's High Hill.

Much and more was happening at Tumbleton as well, and it is there we must next turn our gaze. As word of the unrest at King's Landing reached Prince Daeron's host, many younger lords grew anxious to advance upon the city at once. Chief amongst them were Ser Jon Roxton, Ser Roger Corne, and Lord Unwin Peake . . . but Ser Hobert Hightower counseled caution, and the Two Betrayers refused to join any attack unless their own demands were met. Ulf White, it will be recalled, wished to be granted the great castle of Highgarden with all its lands and incomes, whilst Hard Hugh Hammer desired nothing less than a crown for himself.

These conflicts came to a boil when Tumbleton learned belatedly of Aemond Targaryen's death at Harrenhal. King Aegon II had not been seen nor heard from since the fall of King's Landing to his half-sister Rhaenyra, and there were many who feared that the queen had put him secretly to death, concealing the corpse so as not to be condemned as a kinslayer. With his brother Aemond slain as well, the greens found themselves kingless and leaderless. Prince Daeron stood next in the line of succession. Lord Peake declared that the boy should be proclaimed as Prince of Dragonstone at once; others, believing Aegon II dead, wished to crown him king.

The Two Betrayers felt the need of a king as well . . . but Daeron Targaryen was not the king they wanted. "We need a strong man to lead us, not a boy," declared Hard Hugh Hammer. "The throne should be mine."

When Bold Jon Roxton demanded to know by what right he presumed to name himself a king, Lord Hammer answered, "The same right as the Conqueror. A dragon." And truly, with Vhagar dead at last, the oldest and largest living dragon in all Westeros was Vermithor, once the mount of the Old King, now that of Hard Hugh the bastard. Vermithor was thrice the size of Prince Daeron's she-dragon Tessarion. No man who glimpsed them together could fail to see that Vermithor was a far more fearsome beast.

Though Hammer's ambition was unseemly in one born so low, the bastard undeniably possessed some Targaryen blood and had proved himself fierce in battle and open-handed to those who followed him, displaying the sort of largesse that draws men to leaders as a corpse draws flies. They were the worst sort of men, to be sure: sellswords, robber knights, and like rabble, men of tainted blood and uncertain birth who loved battle for its own sake and lived for rapine and plunder. Many had heard the prophecy that the hammer would smash the dragon, and took it to mean that Hard Hugh's triumph was foreordained.

The lords and knights of Oldtown and the Reach were offended by the arrogance of the Betrayer's claim, however, and none more so than Prince Daeron Targaryen himself, who grew so wroth that he threw a cup of wine into Hard Hugh's face. Whilst Lord White shrugged this off as a waste of good wine, Lord Hammer said, "Little boys should be more mannerly when men are speaking. I think your father did not beat you often enough. Take care I do not make up for his lack." The Two Betrayers took their leave together, and began to make plans for Hammer's coronation. When seen the next day, Hard Hugh was wearing a crown of black iron, to the fury of Prince Daeron and his trueborn lords and knights.

One such, Ser Roger Corne, made so bold as to knock the crown off Hammer's head. "A crown does not make a man a king," he said. "You should wear a horseshoe on your head, blacksmith." It was a foolish thing to do. Lord Hugh was not amused. At his command, his men forced Ser Roger to the ground, whereupon the blacksmith's bastard nailed not one but three horseshoes to the knight's skull. When Corne's friends tried to intervene, daggers were drawn and swords unsheathed, leaving three men dead and a dozen wounded.

That was more than Prince Daeron's loyalist lords were prepared to suffer. Lord Unwin Peake and a somewhat reluctant Hobert Hightower summoned eleven other lords and landed knights to a secret council in the cellar of a Tumbleton inn, to discuss what might be done to curb the arrogance of the baseborn dragonriders. The plotters agreed that it would be a simple matter to dispose of White, who was drunk more oft than not and had never shown any great prowess at arms. Hammer posed a greater danger, for of late he was surrounded day and night by lickspittles, camp followers, and sellswords eager for his favor. It would serve them little to kill White and leave Hammer alive, Lord Peake pointed out; Hard Hugh must needs die first. Long and loud were the arguments in the inn beneath the sign reading "the Bloody Caltrops," as the lords discussed how this might best be accomplished.

"Any man can be killed," declared Ser Hobert Hightower, "but what of the dragons?" Given the turmoil at King's Landing, Ser Tyler Norcross said, Tessarion alone should be enough to allow them to retake the Iron Throne. Lord Peake replied that victory would be a deal more certain with Vermithor and Silverwing. Marq Ambrose suggested that they take the city first, then dispose of White and Hammer after victory had been secured, but Richard Rodden insisted such a course would be dishonorable. "We cannot ask these men to shed blood with us, then kill them." Bold John Roxton settled the dispute. "We kill the bastards now," he said. "Afterward, let the bravest of us claim their dragons and fly them into battle." No man in that cellar doubted that Roxton was speaking of himself.

Though Prince Daeron was not present at the council, the Caltrops (as the conspirators became known) were loath to proceed without his consent and blessing. Owen Fossoway, Lord of Cider Hall, was dispatched under cover of darkness to wake the prince and bring him to the cellar, that the plotters might inform him of their plans. Nor did the once-gentle prince hesitate when Lord Unwin Peake presented him with warrants for the execution of Hard Hugh Hammer and Ulf White, but eagerly affixed his seal.

Men may plot and plan and scheme, but they had best pray as well, for no plan made by man has ever withstood the whims of the gods above.

Two days later, on the very day the Caltrops planned to strike, Tumbleton woke in the black of night to screams and shouts. Outside the town walls, the camps were burning. Columns of armored knights were pouring in from north and west, wreaking slaughter, the clouds were raining arrows, and a dragon was swooping down upon them, terrible and fierce.

Thus began the Second Battle of Tumbleton.

The dragon was Seasmoke, his rider Ser Addam Velaryon, determined to prove that not all bastards need be turncloaks. How better to do that than by retaking Tumbleton from the Two Betrayers, whose treason had stained him? Singers say Ser Addam had flown from King's Landing to the Gods Eye, where he landed on the sacred Isle of Faces and took counsel with the Green Men. The scholar must confine himself to known fact, and what we know is that Ser Addam flew far and fast, descending on castles great and small whose lords were loyal to the queen, to piece together an army.

Many a battle and skirmish had already been fought in the lands watered by the Trident, and there was scarce a keep or village that had not paid its due in blood . . . but Addam Velaryon was relentless and determined and glib of tongue, and the riverlords knew much and more of the horrors that had befallen Tumbleton. By the time Ser Addam was ready to descend on Tumbleton, he had near four thousand men at his back.

Benjicot Blackwood, the twelve-year-old Lord of Raventree, had come forth, as had the widowed Sabitha Frey, Lady of the Twins, with her father and brothers of House Vypren. Lords Stanton Piper, Joseth Smallwood, Derrick Darry, and Lyonel Deddings had scraped together fresh levies of greybeards and green boys, though all had suffered grievous losses in the autumn's battles. Hugo Vance, the young lord of Wayfarer's Rest, had come, with three hundred of his own men plus Black Trombo's Myrish sellswords.

Most notably of all, House Tully had joined the war. Seasmoke's descent upon Riverrun had at last persuaded that reluctant warrior, Ser Elmo Tully, to call his banners for the queen, in defiance of the wishes of his bedridden grandsire, Lord Grover. "A dragon in one's courtyard does wonders to resolve one's doubts," Ser Elmo is reported to have said.

The great host encamped about the walls of Tumbleton outnumbered the attackers, but they had been too long in one place. Their discipline had grown lax (drunkenness was endemic in the camp, Grand Maester Munkun says, and disease had taken root as well), the death of Lord Ormund Hightower had left them without a leader, and the lords who wished to command in his place were at odds with one another. So intent were they upon their own conflicts and rivalries that they had all but forgotten their true foes. Ser Addam's night attack took them completely unawares. Before the men of Prince Daeron's army even knew they were in a battle, the enemy was amongst them, cutting them down as they staggered from their tents, as they were saddling their horses, struggling to don their armor, buckling their sword belts.

Most devastating of all was the dragon. Seasmoke came swooping down again and yet again, breathing flame. A hundred tents were soon afire, even the splendid silken pavilions of Ser Hobert Hightower, Lord Unwin Peake, and Prince Daeron himself. Nor was the town of Tumbleton reprieved. Those shops and homes and septs that had been spared the first time were engulfed in dragonflame.

Daeron Targaryen was in his tent asleep when the attack began. Ulf White was inside Tumbleton, sleeping off a night of drinking at an inn called the Bawdy Badger that he had taken for his own. Hard Hugh Hammer was within the town walls as well, in bed with the widow of a knight slain during the first battle. All three dragons were outside the town, in fields beyond the encampments.

Though attempts were made to wake Ulf White from his drunken slumber, he proved impossible to rouse. Infamously, he rolled under a table and snored through the entire battle. Hard Hugh Hammer was quicker to respond. Half-dressed, he rushed down the steps to the yard, calling for his hammer, his armor, and a horse, so he might ride out and mount Vermithor. His men rushed to obey, even as Seasmoke set the stables ablaze. But Lord Jon Roxton had claimed Lord Footly's bedchamber along with Lord Footly's wife, and was already in the yard.

When he spied Hard Hugh, Roxton saw his chance, and said, "Lord Hammer, my condolences." Hammer turned, glowering. "For what?" he demanded. "You died in the battle," Bold Jon replied, drawing Orphan-

Maker and thrusting deep into Hammer's belly, before opening the bastard from groin to throat.

A dozen of Hard Hugh's men came running in time to see him die. Even a Valyrian steel blade like Orphan-Maker little avails a man when it is one against ten. Bold Jon Roxton slew three before he was slain in turn. It is said that he died when his foot slipped on a coil of Hugh Hammer's entrails, but perhaps that detail is too perfectly ironic to be true.

Three conflicting accounts exist as to the manner of death of Prince Daeron Targaryen. The best known claims that the prince stumbled from his pavilion with his nightclothes afire, only to be cut down by the Myrish sellsword Black Trombo, who smashed his face in with a swing of his spiked morningstar. This version was the one preferred by Black Trombo, who told it far and wide. The second version is more or less the same, save that the prince was killed with a sword, not a morningstar, and his slayer was not Black Trombo, but some unknown man-at-arms who like as not did not even realize whom he had killed. In the third alternative, the brave boy known as Daeron the Daring did not even make it out at all, but died when his burning pavilion collapsed upon him. That is the version preferred by Munkun's *True Telling,* and by us.*

In the sky above, Addam Velaryon could see the battle turning into a rout below him. Two of the three enemy dragonriders were dead, but he would have had no way of knowing that. He could doubtless see the enemy dragons, however. Unchained, they were kept beyond the town walls, free to fly and hunt as they would; Silverwing and Vermithor oft coiled about one another in the fields south of Tumbleton, whilst Tessarion slept and fed in Prince Daeron's camp to the west of the town, not a hundred yards from his pavilion.

Dragons are creatures of fire and blood, and all three roused as the battle bloomed around them. A crossbowman let fly a bolt at Silverwing, we are told, and twoscore mounted knights closed on Vermithor with

* Whatever the manner of his death, it is beyond dispute that Daeron Targaryen, youngest son of King Viserys I by Queen Alicent, died at the Second Battle of Tumbleton. The feigned princes who appeared during the reign of Aegon III, using his name, have been conclusively shown to be imposters.

sword and lance and axe, hoping to dispatch the beast whilst he was still half-asleep and on the ground. They paid for that folly with their lives. Elsewhere on the field, Tessarion threw herself into the air, shrieking and spitting flame, and Addam Velaryon turned Seasmoke to meet her.

A dragon's scales are largely (though not entirely) impervious to flame; they protect the more vulnerable flesh and musculature beneath. As a dragon ages, its scales thicken and grow harder, affording even more protection, even as its flames burn hotter and fiercer (where the flames of a hatchling can set straw aflame, the flames of Balerion or Vhagar in the fullness of their power could and did melt steel and stone). When two dragons meet in mortal combat, therefore, they will oft employ weapons other than their flame: claws black as iron, long as swords, and sharp as razors, jaws so powerful they can crunch through even a knight's steel plate, tails like whips whose lashing blows have been known to smash wagons to splinters, break the spine of heavy destriers, and send men flying fifty feet in the air.

The battle between Tessarion and Seasmoke was different.

History calls the struggle between King Aegon II and his half-sister Rhaenyra the Dance of the Dragons, but only at Tumbleton did the dragons ever truly dance. Tessarion and Seasmoke were young dragons, nimbler in the air than their older kin. Time and time again they rushed one another, only to have one or the other veer away at the last instant. Soaring like eagles, stooping like hawks, they circled, snapping and roaring, spitting fire, but never closing. Once, the Blue Queen vanished into a bank of cloud, only to reappear an instant later, diving on Seasmoke from behind to scorch his tail with a burst of cobalt flame. Meanwhile, Seasmoke rolled and banked and looped. One instant he would be below his foe, and suddenly he would twist in the sky and come around behind her. Higher and higher the two dragons flew, as hundreds watched from the roofs of Tumbleton. One such said afterward that the flight of Tessarion and Seasmoke seemed more mating dance than battle. Perhaps it was.

The dance ended when Vermithor rose roaring into the sky.

Almost a hundred years old and as large as the two young dragons put together, the bronze dragon with the great tan wings was in a rage as he took flight, with blood smoking from a dozen wounds. Riderless, he knew not friend from foe, so he loosed his wroth on all, spitting flame to right and left, turning savagely on any man who dared to fling a spear in his direction. One knight tried to flee before him, only to have Vermithor snatch him up in his jaws, even as his horse galloped on. Lords Piper and Deddings, seated together atop a low rise, burned with their squires, servants, and sworn shields when the Bronze Fury chanced to take note of them.

An instant later, Seasmoke fell upon him.

Alone of the four dragons on the field that day, Seasmoke had a rider. Ser Addam Velaryon had come to prove his loyalty by destroying the Two Betrayers and their dragons, and here was one beneath him, attacking the men who had joined him for this fight. He must have felt duty bound to protect them, though surely he knew in his heart that his Seasmoke could not match the older dragon.

This was no dance, but a fight to the death. Vermithor had been flying no more than twenty feet above the battle when Seasmoke slammed into him from above, driving him shrieking into the mud. Men and boys ran in terror or were crushed as the two dragons rolled and tore at one another. Tails snapped and wings beat at the air, but the beasts were so entangled that neither was able to break free. Benjicot Blackwood watched the struggle from atop his horse fifty yards away. Vermithor's size and weight were too much for Seasmoke to contend with, Lord Blackwood told Grand Maester Munkun many years later, and he would surely have torn the silver-grey dragon to pieces . . . if Tessarion had not fallen from the sky at that very moment to join the fight.

Who can know the heart of a dragon? Was it simple bloodlust that drove the Blue Queen to attack? Did the she-dragon come to help one of the combatants? If so, which? Some will claim that the bond between a dragon and dragonrider runs so deep that the beast shares his master's loves and hates. But who was the ally here, and who the enemy? Does a riderless dragon know friend from foe?

We shall never know the answers to those questions. All that history tells us is that three dragons fought amidst the mud and blood and smoke of Second Tumbleton. Seasmoke was first to die, when Vermithor locked his teeth into his neck and ripped his head off. Afterward the bronze dragon tried to take flight with his prize still in his jaws, but his tattered wings could not lift his weight. After a moment he collapsed and died. Tessarion, the Blue Queen, lasted until sunset. Thrice she tried to regain the sky, and thrice failed. By late afternoon she seemed to be in pain, so Lord Blackwood summoned his best archer, a longbowman known as Billy Burley, who took up a position a hundred yards away (beyond the range of the dying dragon's fires) and sent three shafts into her eye as she lay helpless on the ground.

By dusk, the fighting was done. Though the riverlords lost less than a hundred men, whilst cutting down more than a thousand of the men from Oldtown and the Reach, Second Tumbleton could not be accounted a complete victory for the attackers, as they failed to take the town. Tumbleton's walls were still intact, and once the king's men had fallen back inside and closed their gates, the queen's forces had no way to make a breach, lacking both siege equipment and dragons. Even so, they wreaked great slaughter on their confused and disorganized foes, fired their tents, burned or captured almost all their wagons, fodder, and provisions, made off with three-quarters of their warhorses, slew their prince, and put an end to two of the king's dragons.

At moonrise the riverlords abandoned the field to the carrion crows, fading back into the hills. One of them, the boy Ben Blackwood, carried with him the broken body of Ser Addam Velaryon, found dead beside his dragon. His bones would rest at Raventree Hall for eight years, but in 138 AC his brother, Alyn, would have them returned to Driftmark and entombed in Hull, the town of his birth. On his tomb is engraved a single word: *LOYAL*. Its ornate letters are supported by carvings of a seahorse and a mouse.

On the morning after the battle, the Conquerors of Tumbleton looked out from the town walls to find their foes gone. The dead were strewn all around the city, and amongst them sprawled the carcasses of three dragons. One remained: Silverwing, Good Queen Alysanne's mount in days of old, had taken to the sky as the carnage began, circling the battlefield for

hours, soaring on the hot winds rising from the fires below. Only after dark did she descend, to land beside her slain cousins. Later, singers would tell of how she thrice lifted Vermithor's wing with her nose, as if to make him fly again, but this is most like a fable. The rising sun would find her flapping listlessly across the field, feeding on the burned remains of horses, men, and oxen.

Eight of the thirteen Caltrops lay dead, amongst them Lord Owen Fossoway, Marq Ambrose, and Bold Jon Roxton. Richard Rodden had taken an arrow to the neck and would die the next day. Four of the plotters remained, amongst them Ser Hobert Hightower and Lord Unwin Peake. And though Hard Hugh Hammer had died, and his dreams of kingship with him, the second Betrayer remained. Ulf White had woken from his drunken sleep to find himself the last dragonrider, and possessed of the last dragon.

"The Hammer's dead, and your boy as well," he is purported to have told Lord Peake. "All you got left is me." When Lord Peake asked him his intentions, White replied, "We march, just how you wanted. You take the city, I'll take the bloody throne, how's that?"

The next morning, Ser Hobert Hightower called upon him, to thrash out the details of their assault upon King's Landing. He brought with him two casks of wine as a gift, one of Dornish red and one of Arbor gold. Though Ulf the Sot had never tasted a wine he did not like, he was known to be partial to the sweeter vintages. No doubt Ser Hobert hoped to sip the sour red whilst Lord Ulf quaffed down the Arbor gold. Yet something about Hightower's manner—he was sweating and stammering and too hearty by half, the squire who served them testified later—pricked White's suspicions. Wary, he commanded that the Dornish red be set aside for later, and insisted Ser Hobert share the Arbor gold with him.

History has little good to say about Ser Hobert Hightower, but no man can question the manner of his death. Rather than betray his fellow Caltrops, he let the squire fill his cup, drank deep, and asked for more. Once he saw Hightower drink, Ulf the Sot lived up to his name, putting down three cups before he began to yawn. The poison in the wine was a gentle one. When Lord Ulf went to sleep, never to awaken, Ser Hobert lurched to his feet and tried to make himself retch, but too late. His heart stopped within the hour. "No man ever feared Ser Hobert's sword," Mushroom says of him, "but his wine cup was deadlier than Valyrian steel."

Afterward Lord Unwin Peake offered a thousand golden dragons to any knight of noble birth who could claim Silverwing. Three men came forth. When the first had his arm torn off and the second burned to death, the third man reconsidered. By that time Peake's army, the remnants of the great host that Prince Daeron and Lord Ormund Hightower had led all the way from Oldtown, was falling to pieces, as deserters fled Tumbleton by the score with all the plunder they could carry. Bowing to defeat, Lord Unwin summoned his lords and serjeants and ordered a retreat.

The accused turncloak Addam Velaryon, born Addam of Hull, had saved King's Landing from the queen's foes . . . at the cost of his own life. Yet the queen knew nothing of his valor. Rhaenyra's flight from King's Landing had been beset with difficulty. At Rosby, she found the castle gates barred at her approach, by the command of the young woman whose claim she had passed over in favor of a younger brother. Young Lord Stokeworth's castellan granted her hospitality, but only for a night. "They will come for you," he warned the queen, "and I do not have the power to resist them." Half of her gold cloaks deserted on the road, and one night her camp was attacked by broken men. Though her knights beat off the attackers, Ser Balon Byrch was felled by an arrow, and Ser Lyonel Bentley, a young knight of the Queensguard, suffered a blow to the head that cracked his helm. He perished raving the following day. The queen pressed on toward Duskendale.

House Darklyn had been amongst Rhaenyra's strongest supporters, but the cost of that loyalty had been high. Lord Gunthor had lost his life in the queen's service, as had his uncle Steffon. Duskendale itself had been sacked by Ser Criston Cole. Small wonder then that Lord Gunthor's widow was less than overjoyed when Her Grace appeared at her gates. Only the intercession of Ser Harrold Darke persuaded Lady Meredyth to allow the queen within her walls at all (the Darkes were distant kin to the

Darklyns, and Ser Harrold had once served as a squire to the late Ser Steffon), and only upon the condition that she would not remain for long.

Once safely behind the walls of the Dun Fort, overlooking the harbor, Rhaenyra commanded Lady Darklyn's maester to send word to Grand Maester Gerardys on Dragonstone, asking that a ship be sent at once to take her home. Three ravens flew, the town chronicles assert . . . yet as the days passed, no ship appeared. Nor did any reply return from Gerardys on Dragonstone, to the queen's fury. Once again she began to question her Grand Maester's loyalty.

The queen had better fortune elsewhere. From Winterfell, Cregan Stark wrote to say that he would bring a host south as soon as he could, but warned that it would take some time to gather his men "for my realms are large, and with winter upon us, we must needs bring in our last harvest, or starve when the snows come to stay." The northman promised the queen ten thousand men, "younger and fiercer than my Winter Wolves." The Maiden of the Vale promised aid as well, when she replied from her winter castle, the Gates of the Moon . . . but with the mountain passes closed by snow, her knights would need to come by sea. If House Velaryon would send its ships to Gulltown, Lady Jeyne wrote, she would dispatch an army to Duskendale at once. If not, she must needs hire ships from Braavos and Pentos, and for that she would need coin.

Queen Rhaenyra had neither gold nor ships. When she had sent Lord Corlys to the dungeons she had lost her fleet, and she had fled King's Landing in terror of her life, without so much as a coin. Despairing and fearful, Her Grace walked the castle battlements of Duskendale weeping, growing ever more grey and haggard. She could not sleep and would not eat. Nor would she suffer to be parted from Prince Aegon, her last living son; day and night, the boy remained by her side, "like a small pale shadow."

When Lady Meredyth made it plain that the queen had overstayed her welcome, Rhaenyra was forced to sell her crown to raise the coin to buy passage on a Braavosi merchantman, the *Violande*. Ser Harrold Darke urged her to seek refuge with Lady Arryn in the Vale, whilst Ser Medrick Manderly tried to persuade her to accompany him and his brother Ser Torrhen back to White Harbor, but Her Grace refused them both. She was adamant on returning to Dragonstone. There she would find dragon's eggs, she told her loyalists; she must have another dragon, or all was lost.

Strong winds pushed the *Violande* closer to the shores of Driftmark than the queen might have wished, and thrice she passed within hailing distance of the Sea Snake's warships, but Rhaenyra took care to keep well out of sight. Finally the Braavosi put into the harbor below the Dragonmont on the eventide. The queen had sent a raven from Duskendale to give notice of her coming, and found an escort waiting as she disembarked with her son Aegon, her ladies, and three Queensguard knights (the gold cloaks who had ridden with her from King's Landing stayed at Duskendale, whilst the Manderlys remained aboard the *Violande,* bound for White Harbor).

It was raining when the queen's party came ashore, and hardly a face was to be seen about the port. Even the dockside brothels appeared dark and deserted, but Her Grace took no notice. Sick in body and spirit, broken by betrayal, Rhaenyra Targaryen wanted only to return to her own seat, where she imagined that she and her son would be safe. Little did the queen know that she was about to suffer her last and most grievous treachery.

Her escort, forty strong, was commanded by Ser Alfred Broome, one of the men left behind when Rhaenyra had launched her attack upon King's Landing. Broome was the most senior of the knights at Dragonstone, having joined the garrison during the reign of the Old King. As such, he had expected to be named as castellan when Rhaenyra went forth to seize the Iron Throne . . . but Ser Alfred's sullen disposition and sour manner inspired neither affection nor trust, Mushroom tells us, so the queen had passed him over in favor of the more affable Ser Robert Quince. When Rhaenyra asked why Ser Robert had not come to meet her, Ser Alfred replied that the queen would be seeing "our fat friend" at the castle.

And so she did . . . though Quince's charred corpse was burned beyond all recognition when they came upon it. Only by his size did they know him, for Ser Robert had been enormously fat. They found him hanging from the battlements of the gatehouse beside Dragonstone's steward, captain of the guard, master-at-arms . . . and the head and upper torso of Grand Maester Gerardys. Everything below his ribs was gone, and the Grand Maester's entrails dangled down from within his torn belly like so many burned black snakes.

The blood drained from the queen's cheeks when she beheld the bodies, but young Prince Aegon was the first to realize what they meant. "Mother, flee," he shouted, but too late.

Ser Alfred's men fell upon the queen's protectors. An axe split Ser Harrold Darke's head before his sword could clear its scabbard, and Ser Adrian Redfort was stabbed through the back with a spear. Only Ser Loreth Lansdale moved quickly enough to strike a blow in the queen's defense, cutting down the first two men who came at him before being slain himself. With him died the last of the Queensguard. When Prince Aegon snatched up Ser Harrold's sword, Ser Alfred knocked the blade aside contemptuously.

The boy, the queen, and her ladies were marched at spearpoint through the gates of Dragonstone to the castle ward. There (as Mushroom put it so memorably many years later) they found themselves face-to-face with "a dead man and a dying dragon."

Sunfyre's scales still shone like beaten gold in the sunlight, but as he sprawled across the fused black Valyrian stone of the yard, it was plain to see he was a broken thing, he who had been the most magnificent dragon ever to fly the skies of Westeros. The wing all but torn from his body by Meleys jutted at an awkward angle, whilst fresh scars along his back still smoked and bled when he moved. Sunfyre was coiled in a ball when the queen and her party first beheld him. As he stirred and raised his head, huge wounds were visible along his neck, where another dragon had torn chunks from his flesh. On his belly were places where scabs had replaced scales, and where his right eye should have been was only an empty hole, crusted with black blood.

One must ask, as Rhaenyra surely did, how this had come to pass.

We now know much and more that the queen did not. For that we must be grateful to Grand Maester Munkun, for it was his *True Telling,* based in large part on the account of Grand Maester Orwyle, that revealed how Aegon II came to Dragonstone.

It was Lord Larys Strong the Clubfoot, who spirited the king and his children out of the city when the queen's dragons first appeared in the skies above King's Landing. So as not to pass through any of the city gates, where they might be seen and remembered, Lord Larys led them out through some secret passage of Maegor the Cruel, of which only he had knowledge.

It was Lord Larys who decreed the fugitives should part company as well, so that even if one were taken, the others might win free. Ser Rickard Thorne was commanded to deliver two-year-old Prince Maelor to Lord Hightower. Princess Jaehaera, a sweet and simple girl of six, was put in the charge of Ser Willis Fell, who swore to bring her safely to Storm's End. Neither knew where the other was bound, so neither could betray the other if captured.

And only Larys himself knew that the king, stripped of his finery and clad in a salt-stained fisherman's cloak, had been concealed amongst a load of codfish on a fishing skiff in the care of a bastard knight with kin on Dragonstone. Once she learned the king was gone, the Clubfoot reasoned, Rhaenyra was sure to send men hunting after him . . . but a boat leaves no trail upon the waves, and few hunters would ever think to look for Aegon on his sister's own island, in the very shadow of her stronghold. All this Grand Maester Orwyle had from Lord Strong's own lips, Munkun tells us.

And there Aegon might have remained, hidden yet harmless, dulling his pain with wine and hiding his burn scars beneath a heavy cloak, had Sunfyre not made his way to Dragonstone. We may ask what drew him back to the Dragonmont, for many have. Was the wounded dragon, with his half-healed broken wing, driven by some primal instinct to return to his birthplace, the smoking mountain where he had emerged from his egg? Or did he somehow sense the presence of King Aegon on the island, across long leagues and stormy seas, and fly there to rejoin his rider? Septon Eustace goes so far as to suggest that Sunfyre sensed Aegon's desperate *need*. But who can presume to know the heart of a dragon?

After Lord Walys Mooton's ill-fated attack drove him from the field of ash and bone outside Rook's Rest, history loses sight of Sunfyre for more than half a year (certain tales told in the halls of the Crabbs and Brunes suggest the dragon might have taken refuge in the dark piney woods and caves of Crackclaw Point for some of that time). Though his torn wing had mended enough for him to fly, it had healed at an ugly angle, and it remained weak. Sunfyre could no longer soar, nor remain in the air for long, but must needs struggle to fly even short distances. The fool Mushroom, cruelly, says that whereas most dragons moved through the sky like eagles, Sunfyre had become no more than "a great golden fire-breathing chicken, hopping and fluttering from hill to hill."

Yet this "fire-breathing chicken" crossed the waters of Blackwater Bay . . . for it was Sunfyre that the sailors on the *Nessaria* had seen attacking Grey Ghost. Ser Robert Quince had blamed the Cannibal . . . but Tom Tangletongue, a stammerer who heard more than he said, had plied the Volantenes with ale, making note of all the times they mentioned the attacker's golden scales. The Cannibal, as he knew well, was black as coal. And so the Two Toms and their "cousins" (a half-truth, as only Ser Marston shared their blood, being the bastard son of Tom Tanglebeard's sister by the knight who took her maidenhead) set sail in their small boat to seek out Grey Ghost's killer.

The burned king and the maimed dragon each found new purpose in the other. From a hidden lair on the desolate eastern slopes of the Dragonmont, Aegon ventured forth each day at dawn, taking to the sky again for the first time since Rook's Rest, whilst the Two Toms and their cousin Marston Waters returned to the other side of the island to seek out men willing to help them take the castle. Even on Dragonstone, long Queen Rhaenyra's seat and stronghold, they found many who misliked the queen for reasons both good and ill. Some grieved for brothers, sons, and fathers slain during the Sowing or during the Battle of the Gullet, some hoped for plunder or advancement, whilst others believed a son must come before a daughter, giving Aegon the better claim.

The queen had taken her best men with her to King's Landing. On its island, protected by the Sea Snake's ships and its high Valyrian walls, Dragonstone seemed unassailable, so the garrison Her Grace left to defend it was small, made up largely of men judged to be of little other use: greybeards and green boys, the halt and slow and crippled, men recovering from wounds, men of doubtful loyalty, men suspected of cowardice. Over them Rhaenyra placed Ser Robert Quince, an able man grown old and fat.

Quince was a steadfast supporter of the queen, all agree, but some of the men under him were less leal, harboring certain resentments and grudges for old wrongs, real or imagined. Prominent amongst them was Ser Alfred Broome. Broome proved more than willing to betray his queen in return for a promise of lordship, lands, and gold should Aegon II regain the throne. His long service with the garrison allowed him to advise the king's men on Dragonstone's strengths and weaknesses, which guards could be bribed or won over, and which must needs be killed or imprisoned.

When it came, the fall of Dragonstone took less than an hour. Men traduced by Broome opened a postern gate during the hour of ghosts to allow Ser Marston Waters, Tom Tangletongue, and their men to slip into the castle unobserved. While one band seized the armory and another took Dragonstone's leal guardsmen and master-at-arms into custody, Ser Marston surprised Grand Maester Gerardys in his rookery, so no word of the attack might escape by raven. Ser Alfred himself led the men who burst into the castellan's chambers to surprise Ser Robert Quince. As Quince struggled to rise from his bed, Broome drove a spear into his huge pale belly. Mushroom, who knew both men well, says Ser Alfred misliked and resented Ser Robert. This may well be believed, for the thrust was delivered with such force that the spear went out Ser Robert's back, through the featherbed and straw mattress, and into the floor beneath.

Only in one respect did the plan go awry. As Tom Tangletongue and his ruffians smashed down the door of Lady Baela's bedchamber to take her prisoner, the girl slipped out her window, scrambling across rooftops and down walls until she reached the yard. The king's men had taken care to send guards to secure the stable where the castle dragons had been kept, but Baela had grown up in Dragonstone, and knew ways in and out that they did not. By the time her pursuers caught up with her, she had already loosed Moondancer's chains and strapped a saddle onto her.

So it came to pass that when King Aegon II flew Sunfyre over Dragonmont's smoking peak and made his descent, expecting to make a triumphant entrance into a castle safely in the hands of his own men, with the queen's loyalists slain or captured, up to meet him rose Baela Targaryen, Prince Daemon's daughter by the Lady Laena, as fearless as her father.

Moondancer was a young dragon, pale green, with horns and crest and wingbones of pearl. Aside from her great wings, she was no larger than a warhorse, and weighed less. She was very quick, however, and Sunfyre, though much larger, still struggled with a malformed wing and had taken fresh wounds from Grey Ghost.

They met amidst the darkness that comes before the dawn, shadows in the sky lighting the night with their fires. Moondancer eluded Sunfyre's flames, eluded his jaws, darted beneath his grasping claws, then came around and raked the larger dragon from above, opening a long smoking wound down his back and tearing at his injured wing. Watchers below said that Sunfyre lurched drunkenly in the air, fighting to stay aloft, whilst Moondancer turned and came back at him, spitting fire. Sunfyre answered with a furnace blast of golden flame so bright it lit the yard below like a second sun, a blast that took Moondancer full in the eyes. Like as not, the young dragon was blinded in that instant, yet still she flew on, slamming into Sunfyre in a tangle of wings and claws. As they fell, Moondancer struck at Sunfyre's neck repeatedly, tearing out mouthfuls of flesh, whilst the elder dragon sank his claws into her underbelly. Robed in fire and smoke, blind and bleeding, Moondancer beat her wings desperately as she tried to break away, but all her efforts did was slow their fall.

The watchers in the yard scrambled for safety as the dragons slammed into the hard stone, still fighting. On the ground, Moondancer's quickness proved of little use against Sunfyre's size and weight. The green dragon soon lay still. The golden dragon screamed his victory and tried to rise again, only to collapse back to the ground with hot blood pouring from his wounds.

King Aegon had leapt from the saddle when the dragons were still twenty feet from the ground, shattering both legs. Lady Baela stayed with Moondancer all the way down. Burned and battered, the girl still found the strength to undo her saddle chains and crawl away as her dragon coiled in her final death throes. When Alfred Broome drew his sword to

slay her, Marston Waters wrenched the blade from his hand. Tom Tangletongue carried her to the maester.

Thus did King Aegon II win the ancestral seat of House Targaryen, but the price he paid for it was dire. Sunfyre would never fly again. He remained in the yard where he had fallen, feeding on the carcass of Moondancer, and later on sheep slaughtered for him by the garrison. And Aegon II lived the rest of his life in great pain . . . though to his honor, when Grand Maester Gerardys offered him milk of the poppy, he refused. "I shall not walk that road again," he said. "Nor am I such a fool as to drink any potion you might prepare for me. You are my sister's creature."

At the king's command, the chain that Princess Rhaenyra had torn from Grand Maester Orwyle's neck and given to Gerardys was now used to hang him. He was not given the quick end of a hard fall and a broken neck, but rather a slow strangulation, kicking as he gasped for air. Thrice, when he was almost dead, Gerardys was let down and allowed to catch a breath, only to be hauled up again. After the third time, he was disemboweled and dangled before Sunfyre so the dragon might feast upon his legs and innards, but the king commanded that enough of the Grand Maester be saved so "he might greet my sweet sister on her return."

Not long after, as the king lay in the Stone Drum's great hall, his broken legs bound and splinted, the first of Queen Rhaenyra's ravens arrived from Duskendale. When Aegon learned that his half-sister would be returning on the *Violande,* he commanded Ser Alfred Broome to prepare a "suitable welcome" for her homecoming.

All of this is known to us now. None of this was known to the queen when she stepped ashore into her brother's trap.

Septon Eustace (who had no love for the queen) tells us Rhaenyra laughed when she beheld the ruin of Sunfyre the Golden. "Whose work is this?" he has her saying. "We must thank him." Mushroom (who had much love for the queen) tells a different tale. In his account, Rhaenyra says, "How has it come to this?" Both accounts agree that the next words were spoken by the king. "Sister," he called down from a balcony. Unable to walk, or even stand, he had been carried there in a chair. The hip shattered at Rook's Rest had left Aegon bent and twisted, his once-handsome features had grown puffy from milk of the poppy, and burn scars covered

half his body. Yet Rhaenyra knew him at once, and said, "Dear brother. I had hoped that you were dead."

"After you," Aegon answered. "You are the elder."

"I am pleased to know that you remember that," Rhaenyra answered. "It would seem we are your prisoners . . . but do not think that you will hold us long. My leal lords will find me."

"If they search the seven hells, mayhaps," the king made answer, as his men tore Rhaenyra from her son's arms. Some accounts say it was Ser Alfred Broome who had hold of her arm, others name the two Toms, Tanglebeard the father and Tangletongue the son. Ser Marston Waters stood witness as well, clad in a white cloak, for King Aegon had named him to his Kingsguard for his valor.

Yet neither Waters nor any of the other knights and lords present in the yard spoke a word of protest as King Aegon II delivered his half-sister to his dragon. Sunfyre, it is said, did not seem at first to take any interest in the offering, until Broome pricked the queen's breast with his dagger. The smell of blood roused the dragon, who sniffed at Her Grace, then bathed her in a blast of flame, so suddenly that Ser Alfred's cloak caught fire as he leapt away. Rhaenyra Targaryen had time to raise her head toward the sky and shriek out one last curse upon her half-brother before Sunfyre's jaws closed round her, tearing off her arm and shoulder.

Septon Eustace tells us that the golden dragon devoured the queen in six bites, leaving only her left leg below the shin "for the Stranger." Elinda Massey, youngest and gentlest of Rhaenyra's ladies-in-waiting, supposedly gouged out her own eyes at the sight, whilst the queen's son Aegon the Younger watched in horror, unable to move. Rhaenyra Targaryen, the Realm's Delight and Half-Year Queen, passed from this veil of tears upon the twenty-second day of the tenth moon of the 130th year after Aegon's Conquest. She was thirty-three years of age.

Ser Alfred Broome argued for killing Prince Aegon as well, but King Aegon forbade it. Only ten, the boy might yet have value as a hostage, he declared. Though his half-sister was dead, she still had supporters in the field who must needs be dealt with before His Grace could hope to sit the Iron Throne again. So Prince Aegon was manacled at neck, wrist, and ankle, and led down to the dungeons under Dragonstone. The late queen's ladies-in-waiting, being of noble birth, were given cells in Sea Dragon Tower, there to await ransom.

"The time for hiding is done," King Aegon II declared. "Let the ravens fly that the realm may know the pretender is dead, and their true king is coming home to reclaim his father's throne."

The Dying of the Dragons

The Short, Sad Reign of Aegon II

"The time for hiding is done," King Aegon II declared on Dragonstone, after Sunfyre had feasted on his sister. "Let the ravens fly that the realm may know the pretender is dead, and their true king is coming home to reclaim his father's throne."

Yet even true kings may find some things more easily proclaimed than accomplished. The moon would wax and wane and wax again before Aegon II took his leave of Dragonstone.

Between him and King's Landing lay the isle of Driftmark, the whole breadth of Blackwater Bay, and scores of prowling Velaryon warships. With the Sea Snake a "guest" of Trystane Truefyre in King's Landing and Ser Addam dead at Tumbleton, command of the Velaryon fleets now rested with Addam's brother, Alyn, the younger son of Mouse, the shipwright's daughter, a boy of fifteen . . . but would he be friend or foe? His brother had died fighting for the queen, but that same queen had made their lord a captive and was herself dead. Ravens were dispatched to Driftmark offering House Velaryon pardon for all its past offenses if Alyn of Hull would present himself on Dragonstone and swear allegiance . . . but until and unless an answer was received, it would be folly for Aegon II to try to cross the bay by ship and risk capture.

Nor did His Grace wish to sail to King's Landing. In the days following his half-sister's death, the king still clung to the hope that Sunfyre might recover enough strength to fly again. Instead the dragon only seemed to weaken further, and soon the wounds in his neck began to stink. Even the smoke he exhaled had a foul smell to it, and toward the end he would no longer eat.

On the ninth day of the twelfth moon of 130 AC, the magnificent golden dragon that had been King Aegon's glory died in the outer yard of Dragonstone where he had fallen. His Grace wept, and gave orders that his cousin Lady Baela be brought up from the dungeons and put to death. Only when her head was on the block did he repent, when his maester reminded him that the girl's mother had been a Velaryon, the Sea Snake's own daughter. Another raven took wing for Driftmark, this time with a threat: unless Alyn of Hull presented himself within a fortnight to do homage to his rightful liege, his cousin the Lady Baela would lose her head.

On the western shores of Blackwater Bay, meanwhile, the Moon of the Three Kings came to a sudden end when an army appeared outside the walls of King's Landing. For more than half a year the city had lived in fear of Ormund Hightower's advancing host . . . but when the assault came, it came not from Oldtown by way of Bitterbridge and Tumbleton, but up the kingsroad from Storm's End. Borros Baratheon, on hearing of the queen's death, had left his newly pregnant wife and four daughters to strike north through the kingswood with six hundred knights and four thousand foot.

When the Baratheon vanguard was seen across the Blackwater Rush, the Shepherd commanded his followers to rush the river to keep Lord Borros from coming ashore. But only hundreds now came to listen to this beggar who'd once preached to tens of thousands, and few obeyed. Atop Aegon's High Hill, the squire now calling himself King Trystane Truefyre stood on the battlements with Larys Strong and Ser Perkin the Flea, gazing at the swelling ranks of stormlanders. "We do not have the strength to oppose such a host, sire," Lord Larys told the boy, "but perhaps words can succeed where swords must fail. Send me to parley with them." And so the Clubfoot was dispatched across the river under a flag of truce, accompanied by Grand Maester Orwyle and the Dowager Queen Alicent.

The Lord of Storm's End received them in a pavilion on the edge of the kingswood, as his men felled trees to build rafts for the river crossing. There Queen Alicent received the glad news that her grandaughter Jaehaera, the only surviving child of her son Aegon and daughter Helaena, had been delivered safely to Storm's End by Ser Willis Fell of the Kingsguard. The Dowager Queen wept tears of joy.

Betrayals and betrothals followed, until an accord was reached between Lord Borros, Lord Larys, and Queen Alicent, with Grand Maester Orwyle as witness. The Clubfoot promised that Ser Perkin and his gutter knights would join the stormlanders in restoring King Aegon II to the Iron Throne, on the condition that all of them save the pretender Trystane would be pardoned for any and all offenses, including high treason, rebellion, robbery, murder, and rape. Queen Alicent agreed that her son King Aegon would make Lady Cassandra, Lord Borros's eldest daughter, his new queen. Lady Floris, another of his lordship's daughters, was to be betrothed to Larys Strong.

The problem posed by the Velaryon fleet was discussed at some length. "We must bring the Sea Snake into this," Lord Baratheon is reported to have said. "Perhaps the old man would like a new young wife. I have two daughters not yet spoken for."

"He is traitor thrice over," Queen Alicent said. "Rhaenyra could never have taken King's Landing but for him. His Grace my son will not have forgotten. I want him dead."

"He will die soon enough in any case," replied Lord Larys Strong. "Let us make our peace with him now, and make what use of him we can. Once all is safely settled, if we have no further need of House Velaryon, we can always lend the Stranger a hand."

And so it was agreed, most shamefully. The envoys returned to King's Landing, and the stormlanders soon followed, crossing the Blackwater Rush without incident. Lord Borros found the city walls unmanned, the gates undefended, the streets and squares empty save for corpses. As he climbed Aegon's High Hill with his banner-bearer and household shields, he saw the ragged banners of the squire Trystane hauled down from the gatehouse battlements, and the golden dragon banner of King Aegon II raised in their stead. Queen Alicent herself emerged from the Red Keep to bid him welcome, with Ser Perkin the Flea beside her. "Where is the pretender?" Lord Borros asked, as he dismounted in the outer ward. "Taken and in chains," replied Ser Perkin.

Seasoned by countless border clashes with the Dornish and his recent victorious campaign against a new Vulture King, Lord Borros Baratheon wasted no time in restoring order to King's Landing. After a night of quiet celebration in the Red Keep, he rode forth the next day against Visenya's Hill and the "Cunny King," Gaemon Palehair. Columns of armored knights climbed the hill from three directions, riding down the street scum, sellswords, and drunkards who had gathered round the little king and putting them to rout. The young monarch, who had celebrated his fifth nameday only two days previous, was carried back to the Red Keep slung over the back of a horse, chained and weeping. His mother walked behind him, clutching the hand of the Dornishwoman Sylvenna Sand and leading a long column of whores, witch women, cutpurses, sneaks, and sots, the surviving remnants of the Palehair "court."

The Shepherd's turn came the next night. Forewarned by the fate of the whores and their little king, the prophet had called upon his "barefoot army" to assemble around the Dragonpit, and defend the Hill of Rhaenys "with blood and iron." But the Shepherd's star had fallen. Fewer than three hundred came in answer to his call, and many of those fled when the assault began. Lord Borros led his knights up the hill from the west, whilst Ser Perkin and his gutter knights climbed the steeper southern slope from Flea Bottom. Crashing through the thin ranks of defenders into the ruins of the Dragonpit, they found the prophet amongst the dragon heads (now far gone in rot), surrounded by a ring of torches, still preaching of doom and devastation. When he spied Lord Borros on his warhorse, the Shepherd pointed his stump at him and cursed him. "We shall meet in hell before this year is done," the begging brother proclaimed. Like Gaemon Palehair, he was taken alive and carried back to the Red Keep bound in chains.

Thus did peace return to King's Landing, after a fashion. In the name of her son, "our true king, Aegon, Second of His Name," Queen Alicent proclaimed a curfew, making it unlawful to be on the city streets after dark. The City Watch was re-formed under the command of Ser Perkin the Flea to enforce the curfew, whilst Lord Borros and his stormlanders manned the city's gates and battlements. Pulled down from their three hills, the three false "kings" languished in the dungeons, awaiting the true king's return. That return hinged upon the Velaryons of Driftmark, however. Behind the walls of the Red Keep, the Dowager Queen Alicent and Lord Larys Strong had offered the Sea Snake his freedom, a full pardon for his treasons, and a place on the king's small council if he would bend his knee to Aegon II as his king and deliver them the swords and sails of Driftmark. The old man had proved to be surprisingly intractable, however. "My knees are old and stiff and do not bend easily," Lord Corlys responded, before setting forth terms of his own. He wanted pardons not only for himself, but for all those who had fought for Queen Rhaenyra, and demanded further that Aegon the Younger be given Princess Jaehaera's hand in marriage, so the two of them might jointly be proclaimed King Aegon's heirs. "The realm has been split asunder," he said. "We must needs join it back together." Lord Baratheon's daughters did not interest him, but he wanted Lady Baela freed at once.

Queen Alicent was outraged by Lord Velaryon's "arrogance," Munkun tells us, especially his demand that Queen Rhaenyra's Aegon be named as heir to her own Aegon. She had suffered the loss of two of her three sons and her only daughter during the Dance, and could not bear the thought that any of her rival's sons should live. Angrily, Her Grace reminded Lord Corlys that she had twice proposed terms of peace to Rhaenyra, only to have her overtures rejected with scorn. It fell to Lord Larys the Clubfoot to pour oil on the troubled waters, calming the queen with a quiet reminder of all they had discussed in Lord Baratheon's tent, and persuading her to consent to the Sea Snake's proposals.

The next day Lord Corlys Velaryon, the Sea Snake, knelt before Queen Alicent as she sat upon the lower steps of the Iron Throne, as proxy for her son, and there pledged the king his loyalty and that of his house. Before the eyes of gods and men, the Queen Dowager granted him and his a royal pardon, and restored him to his old place on the small council, as admiral and master of ships. Ravens went forth to Driftmark and Dragonstone to announce the accord . . . and not a day too soon, for they found young Alyn Velaryon gathering his ships for an attack on Dragonstone, and King Aegon II preparing once again to behead his cousin Baela.

In the waning days of 130 AC, King Aegon II returned at last to King's Landing, accompanied by Ser Marston Waters, Ser Alfred Broome, the Two Toms, and Lady Baela Targaryen (still in chains, for fear she might attack the king if freed). Escorted by twelve Velaryon war galleys, they sailed upon a battered old trading cog named *Mouse,* owned and captained by Marilda of Hull. If Mushroom may be trusted, the choice of vessel was deliberate. "Lord Alyn might have shipped the king home aboard *Lord Aethan's Glory* or *Morning Tide* or even *Spicetown Girl,* but he wanted him seen to be creeping into the city on a mouse," the dwarf says. "Lord Alyn was an insolent boy and did not love his king."

The king's return was far from triumphant. Still unable to walk, His Grace was brought through the River Gate in a closed litter, and carried up Aegon's High Hill to the Red Keep through a silent city, past deserted streets, abandoned homes, and looted shops. The steep, narrow steps of the Iron Throne proved impossible for him as well; henceforth, the restored king must needs hold court from a carved, cushioned wooden seat at the base of the true throne, with a blanket across his twisted, shattered legs.

Though in great pain, the king did not retreat to his bedchamber again, nor avail himself of dreamwine or milk of the poppy, but immediately set to pronouncing judgment upon the three "dayfly kings" who had ruled King's Landing during the Moon of Madness. The squire was the first to face his wroth, and was sentenced to die for high treason. A brave boy, Trystane was at first defiant when dragged before the Iron Throne, until he saw Ser Perkin the Flea standing with the king. That took the heart from him, says Mushroom, but even then the youth did not plead his innocence nor beg for mercy, but asked only that he might be made a knight before he died. This boon King Aegon granted, whereupon Ser Marston Waters dubbed the lad (his fellow bastard) Ser Trystane Fyre ("Truefyre," the name the boy had bestowed upon himself, being deemed presumptuous), and Ser Alfred Broome struck his head off with Blackfyre, the sword of Aegon the Conqueror.

The fate of the Cunny King, Gaemon Palehair, was kinder. Having just turned five, the boy was spared on account of his youth and made a ward of the Crown. His mother, Essie, who had presumed to style herself Lady Esselyn during her son's brief reign, confessed under torture that Gaemon's father was not the king, as she had previously claimed, but rather a silver-haired oarsman off a trading galley from Lys. Being lowborn and unworthy of the sword, Essie and the Dornish whore Sylvenna Sand were hanged from the battlements of the Red Keep, together with twenty-seven other members of "King" Gaemon's court, an ill-favored assortment of thieves, drunkards, mummers, beggars, whores, and panders.

Lastly King Aegon II turned his attention to the Shepherd. When brought before the Iron Throne for judgment, the prophet refused to repent his crimes or admit to treason, but thrust the stump of his missing hand at the king and told His Grace, "We shall meet in hell before this year is done," the same words he had spoken to Borros Baratheon upon his capture. For that insolence, Aegon had the Shepherd's tongue torn out with hot pincers, then condemned him and his "treasonous followers" to death by fire.

On the last day of the year, two hundred forty-one "barefoot lambs," the Shepherd's most fervid and devoted followers, were covered with pitch and chained to poles along the broad cobbled thoroughfare that ran eastward from Cobbler's Square up to the Dragonpit. As the city's septs rang their bells to signal the end of the old year and the coming of the new, King Aegon II proceeded along the street (thereafter known as Shepherd's Way, rather than Hill Street as before) in his litter, whilst his knights rode to either side, setting their torches to the captive lambs to light his way. Thus did His Grace continue up the hill to the very top, where the Shepherd himself was bound amongst the heads of the five dragons. Supported by two of his Kingsguard, King Aegon rose from his cushions, tottered to the pole where the prophet had been chained, and set him aflame with his own hand.

"Rhaenyra the Pretender was gone, her dragons dead, the mummer kings all fallen, and yet the realm knew not peace," Septon Eustace wrote soon after. With his half-sister slain and her only surviving son a captive at his own court, King Aegon II might reasonably have expected the remaining opposition to his rule to melt away . . . and mayhaps it might have done so if His Grace had heeded Lord Velaryon's counsel and issued a general pardon for all those lords and knights who had espoused the queen's cause.

Alas, the king was not of a forgiving mind. Urged on by his mother, the Queen Dowager Alicent, Aegon II was determined to exact vengeance upon those who had betrayed and deposed him. He started with the crownlands, sending forth his own men and the stormlanders of Borros Baratheon against Rosby, Stokeworth, and Duskendale and the surrounding keeps and villages. Though the lords thus accosted, through their stewards and castellans, were quick to lower Rhaenyra's quartered banner and raise Aegon's golden dragon in its stead, each in turn was brought in chains to King's Landing and forced to do obeisance before the king. Nor were they freed until they had agreed to pay a heavy ransom, and provide the Crown with suitable hostages.

This campaign proved a grave mistake, for it only served to harden the hearts of the late queen's men against the king. Reports soon reached King's Landing of warriors gathering in great numbers at Winterfell, Barrowton, and White Harbor. In the riverlands, the aged and bedridden Lord Grover Tully had finally died (of apoplexy from having his house fight against the rightful king at Second Tumbleton, Mushroom says), and his grandson Elmo, now at last the Lord of Riverrun, had called the lords of the Trident to war once more, lest he suffer the same fate as Lords Rosby, Stokeworth, and Darklyn. To him gathered Benjicot Blackwood of Raventree, already a seasoned warrior at three-and-ten; his fierce young aunt, Black Aly, with three hundred bows; Lady Sabitha Frey, the merciless and grasping Lady of the Twins; Lord Hugo Vance of Wayfarer's Rest; Lord Jorah Mallister of Seagard; Lord Roland Darry of Darry; aye, and even Humfrey Bracken, Lord of Stone Hedge, whose house had hitherto supported King Aegon's cause.

Even more grave were the tidings from the Vale, where Lady Jeyne Arryn had assembled fifteen hundred knights and eight thousand men-at-arms, and sent envoys to the Braavosi to arrange for ships to bring them down upon King's Landing. With them would come a dragon. Lady Rhaena of House Targaryen, brave Baela's twin, had brought a dragon's egg with her to the Vale . . . an egg that had proved fertile, bringing forth a pale pink hatchling with black horns and crest. Rhaena named her Morning.

Though years would need to pass before Morning grew large enough to be ridden to war, the news of her birth nonetheless was of great concern to the green council. If the rebels could flaunt a dragon and the loyalists could not, Queen Alicent pointed out, smallfolk might see their foes as more legitimate. "I need a dragon," Aegon II said when he was told.

Aside from Lady Rhaena's hatchling, only three living dragons remained in all of Westeros. Sheepstealer had vanished with the girl Nettles, but was thought to be somewhere in Crackclaw Point or the Mountains of the Moon. The Cannibal still haunted the eastern slopes of the Dragonmont. Silverwing at last report had departed the desolation at Tumbleton for the Reach, and was said to have made her lair on a small, stony isle in the middle of Red Lake.

Queen Alysanne's silvery she-dragon had accepted a second rider, Borros Baratheon pointed out. "Why not a third? Claim the dragon and your crown is secure." But Aegon II was as yet unable to walk or stand, much less mount and ride a dragon. Nor was His Grace strong enough for a long journey across the realm to Red Lake, through regions infested with traitors, rebels, and broken men.

That answer was no answer, plainly. "Not Silverwing," His Grace declared. "I will have a new Sunfyre, prouder and fiercer than the last." So ravens were sent to Dragonstone, where the eggs of the Targaryen dragons, some so old they had turned to stone, were kept under guard in undervaults and cellars. The maester there chose seven (in honor of the gods) that he deemed most promising, and sent them to King's Landing. King Aegon kept them in his own chambers, but none yielded a dragon. Mushroom tells us His Grace sat on a "large purple and gold egg" for a day and a night, hoping to hatch it, "but it had as well been a purple and gold turd for all the good it did."

Grand Maester Orwyle, free of the dungeons and once more adorned with his chain of office, gives us a detailed look inside the restored green council during this troubled time, when fear and suspicion held sway even within the Red Keep. At the very time when unity was most desperately required, the lords around King Aegon II found themselves deeply divided, and unable to agree on how best to deal with the gathering storm.

The Sea Snake favored reconciliation, pardon, and peace.

Borros Baratheon scorned that course as weakness; he would defeat these traitors in the field, he declared to king and council. All he required was men; Casterly Rock and Oldtown should be commanded to raise fresh armies at once.

Ser Tyland Lannister, the blind master of coin, proposed to sail to Lys or Tyrosh and engage one or more sellsword companies (Aegon II did not lack for coin, as Ser Tyland had placed three-quarters of the Crown's wealth safely in the hands of Casterly Rock, Oldtown, and the Iron Bank of Braavos before Queen Rhaenyra seized the city and the treasury).

Lord Velaryon saw such efforts as futile. "We do not have the time. Children sit in the seats of power at Oldtown and Casterly Rock. We will find no more help there. The best free companies are bound by contract to Lys, Myr, or Tyrosh. Even if Ser Tyland could prise them loose, he could not bring them here in time. My ships can keep the Arryns from our door, but who will stop the northmen and the lords of the Trident? They are already on the march. We must make terms. His Grace should absolve them of all their crimes and treasons, proclaim Rhaenyra's Aegon his heir, and marry him at once to Princess Jaehaera. It is the only way."

The old man's words fell upon deaf ears, however. Queen Alicent had reluctantly agreed to the betrothal of her granddaughter to Rhaenyra's son, but she had done so without the king's consent. Aegon II had other ideas. He wished to marry Cassandra Baratheon at once, for "she will give me strong sons, worthy of the Iron Throne." Nor would he allow Prince Aegon to wed his daughter, and perhaps sire sons who might muddy the succession. "He can take the black and spend his days at the Wall," His Grace decreed, "or else give up his manhood and serve me as a eunuch. The choice is his, but he shall have no children. My sister's line must end."

Even that was thought to be too gentle a course by Ser Tyland Lannister, who argued for the immediate execution of Prince Aegon the Younger.

"The boy will remain a threat so long as he draws breath," Lannister declared. "Remove his head, and these traitors will be left with neither queen nor king nor prince. The sooner he is dead, the sooner this rebellion will end." His words, and those of the king, horrified Lord Velaryon. The aged Sea Snake, "thunderous in his wroth," accused king and council of being "fools, liars, and oathbreakers," and stormed from the chamber.

Borros Baratheon then offered to bring the king the old man's head, and Aegon II was on the point of giving consent when Lord Larys Strong spoke up, reminding them that young Alyn Velaryon, the Sea Snake's heir, remained beyond their reach on Driftmark.

"Kill the old snake and we lose the young one," the Clubfoot said, "and all those fine swift ships of theirs as well." Instead, he said, they must move at once to make amends with Lord Corlys, so as to keep House Velaryon on their side. "Give him his betrothal, Your Grace," he urged the king. "A betrothal is not a wedding. Name Young Aegon your heir. A prince is not a king. Look back at the history and count how many heirs never lived to sit the throne. Deal with Driftmark in due course, when your foes are vanquished and your tide is at the full. That day is not yet come. We must bide our time and speak to him gently."

Or so his words have come down to us, from Orwyle by way of Munkun. Neither Septon Eustace nor the fool Mushroom was present at the council. Yet Mushroom speaks of it all the same, saying, "Was there ever a man as devious as the Clubfoot? Oh, he would have made a splendid fool, that one. The words dripped from his lips like honey from a comb, and never did poison taste so sweet."

The enigma that is Larys Strong the Clubfoot has vexed students of history for generations, and is not one we can hope to unravel here. Where did his true loyalty lie? What was he about? He wove his way all through the Dance of the Dragons, on this side and that side, vanishing and reappearing, yet somehow always surviving. How much of what he said and did was ruse, how much was real? Was he just a man who sailed with the prevailing wind, or did he know where he was bound when he set out? So may we ask, but none will answer. The last Strong keeps his secrets.

We do know that he was sly, secretive, yet plausible and pleasant when need be. His words swayed the king and council in their course. When

Queen Alicent demurred, wondering aloud how Lord Corlys could possibly be won back after all that had been said that day, Lord Strong replied, "That task you may leave to me, Your Grace. His lordship will listen to me, I daresay."

And so he did. For though none knew it at the time, the Clubfoot went directly to Sea Snake when the council was dismissed, and told him of the king's intent to grant him all he had requested and murder him later, when the war was done. And when the old man would have stormed out sword in hand to exact a bloody vengeance, Lord Larys soothed him with soft words and smiles. "There is a better way," he said, counseling patience. And thus did he spin his webs of deceit and betrayal, setting each against the other.

Whilst plots and counterplots swirled around him, and enemies closed in from every side, Aegon II remained oblivious. The king was not a well man. The burns he'd suffered at Rook's Rest had left scars that covered half his body. Mushroom says they had rendered him impotent as well. Nor could he walk. His leap from Sunfyre's back at Dragonstone had broken his right leg in two places, and shattered the bones in his left. The right had healed well, Grand Maester Orwyle records; not so the left. The muscles of that leg had atrophied, the knee stiffening, the flesh melting away until only a withered stick remained, so twisted that Orwyle thought His Grace might do better were it cut away entirely. The king would not hear of it, however. Instead he was carried hither and yon by litter. Only toward the end did he regain the strength to walk with the aid of a crutch, dragging his bad leg behind him.

In constant pain during the last half year of his life, Aegon seemed to take pleasure only in contemplating his forthcoming marriage. Even the capers of his fools never made him laugh, we are told by Mushroom, the foremost of those fools . . . though "His Grace did smile from time to time at my sallies, and liked to keep me by his side to lighten his melancholy and help him dress." Though no longer himself capable of sexual congress due to his burns, according to the dwarf, Aegon still felt carnal urges, and would often watch from behind a curtain as one of his favorites coupled with a serving girl or lady of the court. Most often Tom Tangletongue performed this task for him, we are told; at other times certain knights of the household took the place of dishonor, and thrice Mushroom himself was pressed into service. After these sessions, the fool says, the king would weep for shame and summon Septon Eustace to grant him absolution. (Eustace says nothing of this in his own account of Aegon's final days.)

During this time King Aegon II also commanded that the Dragonpit be restored and rebuilt, commissioned two huge statues of his brothers Aemond and Daeron (he decreed they should be larger than the Titan of Braavos, and covered in gold leaf), and held a public burning of all the decrees and proclamations issued by the "dayfly kings" Trystane Truefyre and Gaemon Palehair.

Meanwhile, his enemies were on the march. Down the Neck came Cregan Stark, Lord of Winterfell, with a great host at his back (Septon Eustace speaks of "twenty thousand howling savages in shaggy pelts," though Munkun lowers that to eight thousand in his *True Telling*), even as the Maiden of the Vale sent off her own army from Gulltown: ten thousand men, under the command of Lord Leowyn Corbray and his brother Ser Corwyn, who bore the famous Valyrian blade called Lady Forlorn.

The most immediate threat, however, was that posed by the men of the Trident. Near six thousand of them had gathered at Riverrun when Elmo Tully called his banners. Sadly, Lord Elmo himself had expired on the march after drinking some bad water, after only nine-and-forty days as Lord of Riverrun, but the lordship had passed to his eldest son, Ser Kermit Tully, a wild and headstrong youth eager to prove himself as a warrior. They were six days' march from King's Landing, moving down the kingsroad, when Lord Borros Baratheon led his stormlanders forth to meet them, his strength bolstered by levies from Stokeworth, Rosby, Hayford, and Duskendale, along with two thousand men and boys from the stews of Flea Bottom, hastily armed with spears and iron pot helms.

The two armies came together two days from the city, at a place where the kingsroad passed between a wood and a low hill. It had been raining heavily for days, and the grass was wet, the ground soft and muddy. Lord Borros was confident of victory, for his scouts had told him that the rivermen were led by boys and women. It was nigh unto dusk when he spied the enemy, yet he ordered an immediate attack . . . though the road ahead was a solid wall of shields, and the hill to its right bristled with archers. Lord Borros led the charge himself, forming his knights into a wedge and thundered down the road at the heart of the foe, where the silver trout of Riverrun floated on its blue and red banner beside the quartered arms of the dead queen. His foot advanced behind them, beneath King Aegon's golden dragon.

The Citadel names the clash that followed the Battle of the Kingsroad. The men who fought it named it the Muddy Mess. By any name, the last battle of the Dance of the Dragons would prove to be a one-sided affair. The longbows on the hill shot the horses out from under Lord Borros's knights as they charged, bringing down so many that less than half his riders ever reached the shield wall. Those that did found their ranks disordered, their wedge broken, their horses slipping and struggling in the soft mud. Though the stormlanders wreaked great havoc with lance and sword and longaxe, the riverlords held firm, as new men stepped up to fill the place of those who fell. When Lord Baratheon's foot came crashing into the fray, the shield wall swayed and staggered back, and seemed as if it might break . . . until the wood to the left of the road erupted with shouts and screams, and hundreds more rivermen burst from the trees, led by that mad boy Benjicot Blackwood, who would this day earn the name Bloody Ben, by which he would be known for the rest of his long life.

Lord Borros himself was still ahorse in the middle of the carnage. When he saw the battle slipping away, his lordship bade his squire sound his warhorn, signaling his reserve to advance. Upon hearing the horn, however, the men of Rosby, Stokeworth, and Hayford let fall the king's golden dragons and remained unmoving, the rabble from King's Landing scattered like geese, and the knights of Duskendale went over to the foe, attacking the stormlanders in the rear. Battle turned to rout in half a heartbeat, as King Aegon's last army shattered.

Borros Baratheon perished fighting. Unhorsed when his destrier was felled by arrows from Black Aly and her bowmen, he battled on afoot, cutting down countless men-at-arms, a dozen knights, and the Lords Mallister and Darry. By the time Kermit Tully came upon him, Lord Borros was dead upon his feet, bareheaded (he had ripped off his dented helm), bleeding from a score of wounds, scarce able to stand. "Yield, ser," called the Lord of Riverrun to the Lord of Storm's End, "the day is ours." Lord Baratheon answered with a curse, saying, "I'd sooner dance in hell than wear your chains." Then he charged . . . straight into the spiked iron ball at the end of Lord Kermit's morningstar, which took him full in the face in a grisly spray of blood and bone and brain. The Lord of Storm's End died in the mud along the kingsroad, his sword still in his hand.*

When the ravens brought word of the battle back to the Red Keep, the green council hurriedly convened. All of the Sea Snake's warnings had proved true. Casterly Rock, Highgarden, and Oldtown had been slow to reply to the king's demand for more armies. When they did, they offered excuses and prevarications in the place of promises. The Lannisters were

* As the gods would have it, seven days later at Storm's End his lady wife gave birth to the son and heir that Lord Borros had so long desired. His lordship had left instructions that the babe was to be named Aegon if a boy, in honor of the king. But upon learning of her lord's death in battle, Lady Baratheon named the child Royce, after her own father.

embroiled in their war against the Red Kraken, the Hightowers had lost too many men and had no capable commanders, little Lord Tyrell's mother wrote to say that she had reason to doubt the loyalty of her son's bannermen, and "being a mere woman, am not myself fit to lead a host to war." Ser Tyland Lannister, Ser Marston Waters, and Ser Julian Wormwood had been dispatched across the narrow sea to seek after sellswords in Pentos, Tyrosh, and Myr, but none had yet returned.

King Aegon II would soon stand naked before his enemies, all of the king's men knew. Bloody Ben Blackwood, Kermit Tully, Sabitha Frey, and their brothers-in-victory were preparing to resume their advance upon the city, and only a few days behind them came Lord Cregan Stark and his northmen. The Braavosi fleet carrying the Arryn host had departed Gulltown and was sailing toward the Gullet, where only young Alyn Velaryon stood in its way . . . and the loyalty of Driftmark could not be relied upon.

"Your Grace," the Sea Snake said, when the rump of the once proud green council had assembled, "you must surrender. The city cannot endure another sack. Save your people and save yourself. If you abdicate in favor of Prince Aegon, he will allow you to take the black and live out your life with honor on the Wall."

"Will he?" King Aegon said. Munkun tells us he sounded hopeful.

His mother entertained no such hope. "You fed his mother to your dragon," she reminded her son. "The boy saw it all."

The king turned to her desperately. "What would you have me do?"

"You have hostages," the Queen Dowager replied. "Cut off one of the boy's ears and send it to Lord Tully. Warn them he will lose another part for every mile they advance."

"Yes," Aegon II said. "Good. It shall be done." He summoned Ser Alfred Broome, who had served him so well on Dragonstone. "Go and see to it, ser." As the knight took his leave, the king turned to Corlys Velaryon. "Tell your bastard to fight bravely, my lord. If he fails me, if any of these Braavosi pass the Gullet, your precious Lady Baela shall lose some parts as well."

The Sea Snake did not plead, or curse, or threaten. He nodded stiffly, rose, and took his leave. Mushroom says he exchanged a look with the Clubfoot as he went, but Mushroom was not present, and it seems most unlikely that a man as seasoned as Corlys Velaryon would act so clumsily at such a moment.

For Aegon's day was done, though he had yet to grasp it. The turncloaks in his midst had put their plans in motion the moment they learned of Lord Baratheon's defeat upon the kingsroad.

As Ser Alfred Broome crossed the drawbridge to Maegor's Holdfast, where Prince Aegon was being held, he found Ser Perkin the Flea and six of his gutter knights barring his way. "Move aside, in the king's name," Broome demanded.

"We have a new king now," answered Ser Perkin. He put a hand upon Ser Alfred's shoulder . . . then shoved him hard, sending him staggering off the drawbridge onto the iron spikes below, where he writhed and twisted for two days as he died.

In that same hour, Lady Baela Targaryen was being spirited away to safety by agents of Lord Larys the Clubfoot. Tom Tangletongue was surprised in the castle yards as he was leaving the stables, and beheaded forthwith. "He died as he had lived, stammering," says Mushroom. His father Tom Tanglebeard was absent from the castle, but they found him in a tavern on Eel Alley. When he protested that he was "just a simple fisherman, come to have an ale," his captors drowned him in a cask of same.

All this was done so neatly, swiftly, and quietly that the people of King's Landing had little or no inkling of what was happening behind the walls of the Red Keep. Even within the castle itself, no alarum went up. Those who had been marked down for death were killed, whilst the rest of the court went about their business, undisturbed and unawares. Septon Eustace tells us that twenty-four men were killed, whilst Munkun's *True Telling* says twenty-one. Mushroom claims to have witnessed the murder of the king's food taster, a grossly fat man named Ummet, and asserts that he was forced to hide in a barrel of flour to escape the same fate, emerging the next night "floured from head to heels, so white the first serving girl to see me took me for Mushroom's ghost." (This smells of story. Why would the plotters wish to kill a fool?)

Queen Alicent was arrested on the serpentine steps as she made her way back to her chambers. Her captors wore the seahorse of House Velaryon upon their doublets, and though they slew the two men guarding her, they did no harm to the Dowager Queen herself, nor to her ladies. The Queen in Chains was chained again and taken to the dungeons, there to await the pleasure of the new king. By then the last of her sons was already dead.

After the council meeting, King Aegon II was carried down to the yard by two strong squires. There he found his litter waiting, as was customary; his withered leg made steps too difficult for him, even with a crutch. Ser Gyles Belgrave, the Kingsguard knight commanding his escort, testified afterward that His Grace seemed unusually fatigued as he was helped into the litter, his face "grey and ashen, sagging," yet instead of asking to be carried back to his chambers, he told Ser Gyles to take him to the castle sept. "Perhaps he sensed his end was near," Septon Eustace wrote, "and wished to pray for forgiveness for his sins."

A cold wind was blowing. As the litter set off, the king closed the curtains against the chill. Inside, as always, was a flagon of sweet Arbor red, Aegon's favorite wine. The king availed himself of a small cup as the litter crossed the yard.

Ser Gyles and the litter bearers had no notion aught was amiss until they reached the sept, and the curtains did not open. "We are here, Your Grace," the knight said. No answer came, but only silence. When a second query and a third produced the same, Ser Gyles Belgrave threw back the curtains, and found the king dead upon his cushions. "There was blood upon his lips," the knight said. "Elsewise he might have been sleeping."

Maesters and common men alike still debate which poison was used, and who might have put it in the king's wine. (Some argue that only Ser Gyles himself could have done so, but it would be unthinkable for a knight of the Kingsguard to take the life of the king he had sworn to protect. Ummet, the king's food taster whose murder Mushroom claims to have seen, seems a more likely candidate.) Yet whilst the hand that poisoned the Arbor red will never be known, we can have no doubt that it was done at the behest of Larys Strong.

Thus perished Aegon of House Targaryen, the Second of His Name, firstborn son of King Viserys I Targaryen and Queen Alicent of House

Hightower, whose reign proved as brief as it was bitter. He had lived four-and-twenty years and reigned for two.

When the vanguard of Lord Tully's host appeared before the walls of King's Landing two days later, Corlys Velaryon rode out to greet them with Prince Aegon somber at his side. "The king is dead," the Sea Snake announced gravely, "long live the king."

And across Blackwater Bay, in the Gullet, Lord Leowyn Corbray stood at the prow of a Braavosi cog and watched a line of Velaryon warships haul down the golden dragon of the second Aegon and raise in its place the red dragon of the first, the banner that all the Targaryen kings had flown until the Dance began.

The war was over (though the peace that followed would soon prove to be far from peaceful).

On the seventh day of the seventh moon of the 131st year after Aegon's Conquest, a date deemed sacred to the gods, the High Septon of

Oldtown pronounced the marriage vows as Prince Aegon the Younger, eldest son of Queen Rhaenrya by her uncle Prince Daemon, wed Princess Jaehaera, the daughter of Queen Helaena by her brother King Aegon II, thereby uniting the two rival branches of House Targaryen and ending two years of treachery and carnage.

The Dance of the Dragons was done, and the melancholy reign of King Aegon III Targaryen had begun.

Aftermath

The Hour of the Wolf

The smallfolk of the Seven Kingdoms speak of King Aegon III Targaryen as Aegon the Unlucky, Aegon the Unhappy, and (most often) the Dragonbane, when they remember him at all. All these names are apt. Grand Maester Munkun, who served him for a good part of his reign, calls him the Broken King, which fits him even better. Of all the men ever to sit the Iron Throne, he remains perhaps the most enigmatic: a shadowy monarch who said little and did less, and lived a life steeped in grief and melancholy.

The fourthborn son of Rhaenyra Targaryen, and her eldest by her uncle and second husband, Prince Daemon Targaryen, Aegon came to the Iron Throne in 131 AC and reigned for twenty-six years, until his death of consumption in 157 AC. He took two wives and fathered five children (two sons and three daughters), yet seemed to find little joy in either marriage or fatherhood. In truth, he was a singularly joyless man. He did not hunt or hawk, rode only for travel, drank no wine, and was so disinterested in food that he often had to be reminded to eat. Though he permitted tourneys, he took no part in them, either as competitor or spectator. As a man grown, he dressed simply, most oft in black, and was known to wear a hair shirt under the velvets and satins required of a king.

That was many years later, however, after Aegon III had come of age and taken the rule of the Seven Kingdoms into his own hand. In 131 AC, as his reign began, he was a boy of ten; tall for his age, it was said, with "silver hair so pale that it was almost white, and purple eyes so dark that they were almost black." Even as a lad, Aegon smiled seldom and laughed less, says Mushroom, and though he could be graceful and courtly at need, there was a darkness within him that never went away.

The circumstances under which the boy king began his reign were far from auspicious. The riverlords who had broken Aegon II's last army at the Battle of the Kingsroad marched to King's Landing prepared for battle. Instead Lord Corlys Velaryon and Prince Aegon rode forth to meet them under a peace banner. "The king is dead, long live the king," Lord Corlys said, as he yielded up the city to their mercy.

Then as now, the riverlords were a fractious, quarrelsome lot. Kermit Tully, Lord of Riverrun, was their liege lord, and nominally commander of their host . . . but it must be remembered that his lordship was but nineteen years of age, and "green as summer grass," as the northmen might say. His brother Oscar, who had slain three men during the Muddy Mess and been knighted on the battlefield afterward, was still greener, and cursed with the sort of prickly pride so common in second sons.

House Tully was unique amongst the great houses of Westeros. Aegon the Conqueror had made them the Lords Paramount of the Trident, yet in many ways they continued to be overshadowed by many of their own bannermen. The Brackens, the Blackwoods, and the Vances all ruled wider domains and could field much larger armies, as could the upstart Freys of the Twins. The Mallisters of Seagard had a prouder lineage, the Mootons of Maidenpool were far wealthier, and Harrenhal, even cursed and blasted and in ruins, remained a more formidable castle than Riverrun, and ten times the size besides. The undistinguished history of House Tully had only been exacerbated by the character of its last two lords . . . but now the gods had brought a younger generation of Tullys to the fore, a pair of proud young men determined to prove themselves, Lord Kermit as a ruler and Ser Oscar as a warrior.

Riding beside them, from the banks of the Trident to the gates of King's Landing, was an even younger man: Benjicot Blackwood, Lord of

Raventree. Bloody Ben, as his men had taken to calling him, was only thirteen, an age at which most highborn boys are still squires, grooming their master's horses and scouring the rust from their mail. Lordship had fallen to him early, when his father Lord Samwell Blackwood had been slain by Ser Amos Bracken at the Battle of the Burning Mill. Despite his youth, the boy lord had refused to delegate authority to older men. At the Fishfeed he had famously wept at the sight of so many dead, yet he did not flinch from battle afterward, but rather sought it out. His men had helped to drive Criston Cole from Harrenhal by hunting down his foragers, he had commanded the center at Second Tumbleton, and during the Muddy Mess he had led the flank attack from the woods that had broken Lord Baratheon's stormlanders and won the day. Clad for court, it was said, Lord Benjicot was very much a boy, tall for his age but slight of build, with a sensitive face and a shy, self-effacing manner; clad in mail-and-plate, Bloody Ben was an altogether different man, and one who had seen more of the battlefield at thirteen than most men do in their entire lives.

There were, to be sure, other lords and famous knights amongst the host that Corlys Velaryon confronted outside the Gate of the Gods that day in 131 AC, all of them older and some of them wiser than Bloody Ben Blackwood and the brothers Tully, yet somehow the three youths had emerged from the Muddy Mess as the undoubted leaders. Bound by battle, the three had become so inseparable that their men began referring to them collectively as "the Lads."

Amongst their supporters were two extraordinary women: Alysanne Blackwood, called Black Aly, a sister to the late Lord Samwell Blackwood, and thus aunt to Bloody Ben, and Sabitha Frey, the Lady of the Twins, the widow of Lord Forrest Frey and mother of his heir, a "sharp-featured, sharp-tongued harridan of House Vypren, who would sooner ride than dance, wore mail instead of silk, and was fond of killing men and kissing women," according to Mushroom.

The Lads knew Lord Corlys Velaryon only by reputation, but that reputation was formidable. Having arrived at King's Landing with the expectation that they would need to besiege the city or take it by storm, they were delighted (if surprised) to have it presented to them as on a gilded platter . . . and to learn that Aegon II was dead (though Benjicot Blackwood and his aunt both expressed disquiet about the manner of his death, for poison was regarded as a coward's weapon, and lacking in honor). Glad cries rang down the field as word of the king's death spread, and one by one the Lord of the Trident and their allies came forward to bend their knees before Prince Aegon and hail him as their king.

As the riverlords rode through the city, smallfolk cheered them from rooftops and balconies, and pretty girls scampered forward to shower their saviors with kisses (like mummers in a farce, says Mushroom, suggesting all this had been devised by Larys Strong). The gold cloaks lined the streets, lowering their spears as the Lads rode by. Within the Red Keep, the Lads found the dead king's body laid out upon a bier beneath the Iron Throne, with his mother, Queen Alicent, weeping beside it. What remained of Aegon's court had gathered in the hall, amongst them Lord Larys Strong the Clubfoot, Grand Maester Orwyle, Ser Perkin the Flea, Mushroom, Septon Eustace, Ser Gyles Belgrave and three other Kingsguard, and sundry lesser lords and household knights. Orwyle spoke for them, hailing the riverlords as deliverers.

Elsewhere in the crownlands and along the narrow sea, the dead king's remaining loyalists were yielding too. The Braavosi landed Lord Leowyn Corbray at Duskendale, with half the power that Lady Arryn had sent down from the Vale; the other half disembarked at Maidenpool under his brother, Ser Corwyn Corbray. Both towns welcomed the Arryn hosts with feasts and flowers. Stokeworth and Rosby fell bloodlessly, hauling down the golden dragon of Aegon II to raise the red dragon of Aegon III. Dragonstone's garrison proved more stubborn, barring their gates and vowing defiance. They held out for three days and two nights. On the third night the castle's grooms, cooks, and serving men took up arms and rose against the king's men, slaughtering many as they slept and delivering the rest in chains to young Alyn Velaryon.

Septon Eustace tells us that a "strange euphoria" took hold of King's Landing; Mushroom simply says that "half the city was drunk." The corpse of King Aegon II was consigned to the flames, in the hopes that all the ills and hatreds of his reign might be burned away with his remains. Thousands climbed Aegon's High Hill to hear Prince Aegon proclaim that peace was at hand. A lavish coronation was planned for the boy, to be followed by his wedding to the Princess Jaehaera. A cloud of ravens rose from the Red Keep, summoning the poisoned king's remaining loyalists in Oldtown, the Reach, Casterly Rock, and Storm's End to King's Landing to do homage to their new monarch. Safe conducts were given, full pardons promised. The realm's new rulers found themselves divided on the question of what to do with the Dowager Queen Alicent, but elsewise all seemed in accord, and good fellowship reigned . . . for the best part of a fortnight.

The "False Dawn," Grand Maester Munkun names it in his *True Telling*. A heady time, no doubt, but short-lived . . . for when Lord Cregan Stark arrived before King's Landing with his northmen, the frolics ended, and the happy plans came crashing down. The Lord of Winterfell was twenty-three, only a few years older than the Lords of Raventree and Riverrun . . . yet Stark was a man and they were boys, as all those who saw them together seemed to sense. The Lads shrank in his presence, Mushroom says. "Whenever the Wolf of the North stalked into a room, Bloody Ben would recall that he was but three-and-ten, whilst Lord Tully and his brother blustered and stammered and flushed red as their hair."

King's Landing had welcomed the riverlords and their men with feasts and flowers and honors. Not so the northmen. There were more of them, for a start: a host twice as large as those the Lads had led, and with a fearsome repute. In their mail shirts and shaggy fur cloaks, their features hidden behind thick tangles of beard, they swaggered through the city like so many armored bears, says Mushroom. Most of what King's Landing knew of northmen they had learned from Ser Medrick Manderly and his brother Ser Torrhen; courtly men, well-spoken, handsomely clad, well disciplined, and *godly*. The Winterfell men did not even honor the true gods, Septon Eustace notes with horror. They scorned the Seven, ignored the feast days, mocked the holy books, showed no reverence to septon or septa, worshipped trees.

Two years past, Cregan Stark had made a promise to Prince Jacaerys. Now he had come to make good his pledge, though Jace and the queen his mother were both dead. "The North remembers," Lord Stark declared when Prince Aegon, Lord Corlys, and the Lads bid him welcome. "You come too late, my lord," the Sea Snake told him, "for the war is done, and the king is dead." Septon Eustace, who stood witness to the meeting, tells us that the Lord of Winterfell "gazed upon the old Lord of the Tides with eyes as grey and cold as a winter storm, and said, 'By whose hand and at whose word, I wonder?' For the savages had come for blood and battle, as we would all learn shortly, to our sorrow."

The good septon was not wrong. Others had started this war, Lord Cregan was heard to say, but he meant to finish it, to continue south and destroy all that remained of the greens who had placed Aegon II on the Iron Throne and fought to keep him there. He would reduce Storm's End first, then cross the Reach to take Oldtown. Once the Hightower had fallen, he would take his wolves north along the shores of the Sunset Sea to visit Casterly Rock.

"A bold plan," Grand Maester Orwyle said cautiously, when he heard it. Mushroom prefers "madness," but adds, "they called Aegon the Dragon mad when he spoke of conquering all Westeros." When Kermit Tully pointed out that Storm's End, Oldtown, and Casterly Rock were as strong as Stark's own Winterfell (if not stronger) and would not fall easily (if at all), and young Ben Blackwood echoed him and said, "Half your men will die, Lord Stark," the grey-eyed Wolf of Winterfell replied, "They died the day we marched, boy."

Like the Winter Wolves before them, most of the men who had marched south with Lord Cregan Stark did not expect to see their homes again. The snows were already deep beyond the Neck, the cold winds rising; in keeps and castles and humble villages throughout the North, the great and small alike prayed to their carved wooden god-trees that this winter might be short. Those with fewer mouths to feed fared better in the dark days, so it had long been the custom in the North for old men, younger sons, the unwed, the childless, the homeless, and the hopeless to leave hearth and home when the first snows fell, so that their kin might live to see another spring. Victory was secondary to the men of these winter armies; they marched for glory, adventure, plunder, and most of all, a worthy end.

Once more it fell to Corlys Velaryon, Lord of the Tides, to plead for peace, pardon, and reconciliation. "The killing has gone on too long," the old man said. "Rhaenyra and Aegon are dead. Let their quarrel die with them. You speak of taking Storm's End, Oldtown, and Casterly Rock, my lord, but the men who held those seats were slain in battle, every one. Small boys and suckling babes sit in their places now, no threat to us. Grant them honorable terms, and they will bend the knee."

But Lord Stark was no more inclined to listen to such talk than Aegon II and Queen Alicent had been. "Small boys become large men in time," he replied, "and a babe sucks down his mother's hate with his mother's milk. Finish these foes now, or those of us not in our graves in twenty years will rue our folly when those babes strap on their father's swords and come seeking after vengeance."

Lord Velaryon would not be moved. "King Aegon said the same and died for it. Had he heeded our counsel and offered peace and pardon to his foes, he might be sitting with us here today."

"Is that why you poisoned him, my lord?" asked the Lord of Winterfell. Though Cregan Stark had no personal history with the Sea Snake, for good or ill, he knew that Lord Corlys had served Rhaenyra as Queen's Hand, that she had imprisoned him on suspicion of treason, that he had been freed by Aegon II and accepted a seat upon his council . . . only, it would seem, to help bring about his death by poison. "Small wonder you are called the Sea Snake," Lord Stark went on. "You may slither this way and that way but, oh, your fangs are venomous. Aegon was an oathbreaker, a kinslayer, and a usurper, yet still a king. When he would not heed your craven's counsel, you removed him as a craven would, dishonorably, with poison . . . and now you shall answer for it."

Then Stark's men burst into the council chambers, disarmed the guardsmen at the door, pulled the aged Sea Snake from his chair, and dragged him to the dungeons. There he would soon be joined by Larys Strong the Clubfoot, Grand Maester Orwyle, Ser Perkin the Flea, and Septon Eustace, along with half a hundred others, both highborn and low, that Stark found cause to mistrust. "I was myself tempted to return to my cask of flour," Mushroom says, "but thankfully I proved too small for the wolf to notice."

Not even the Lads were spared Lord Cregan's wroth, though they were ostensibly his allies. "Are you babes in swaddling clothes, to be cozened by flowers and feasts and soft words?" Stark berated them. "Who told you the war was done? The Clubfoot? The Snake? Why, because they wish it done? Because you won your little victory in the mud? Wars end when the defeated bend the knee and not before. Has Oldtown yielded? Has Casterly Rock returned the Crown's gold? You say you mean to marry the prince to the king's daughter, yet she remains at Storm's End, beyond your reach. So long as she remains free and unwed, what is to stop Baratheon's widow from crowning the girl queen, as Aegon's heir?"

When Lord Tully protested that the stormlanders were beaten, and did not have the strength to field another army, Lord Cregan reminded them of the three envoys that Aegon II had sent across the narrow sea "any of whom might return upon the morrow with thousands of sellswords." Queen Rhaenyra had believed herself victorious after taking King's Landing, the northman said, and Aegon II thought that he had ended the war by feeding his sister to a dragon. Yet queen's men had remained, even after the queen herself was dead, and "Aegon is reduced to bones and ashes."

The Lads found themselves overmatched. Cowed, they gave way, and agreed to join their own power to Lord Stark's when he marched against Storm's End. Munkun says they did so willingly, convinced that the wolf lord had the right of it. "Flush with victory, they wanted more," he writes in the *True Telling*. "They hungered for more glory, for the fame that young men dream of that can only be won in battle." Mushroom takes a more cynical view, and suggests that the young lordlings were simply terrified of Cregan Stark.

The result was the same. "The city was his, to do with as he wished," Septon Eustace says. "The northman had taken it without drawing a sword or loosing an arrow. Be they king's men or queen's men, stormlanders or seahorses, riverlords or gutter knights, highborn or low, common soldiers deferred to him as if they had been born to his service."

For six days King's Landing trembled on the edge of a sword. In the pot shops and wine sinks of Flea Bottom, men placed wagers on how long the Clubfoot, the Sea Snake, the Flea, and the Dowager Queen would keep their heads. Rumors swept the city, one after the other. Some said that Lord Stark planned to take Prince Aegon back to Winterfell and wed him to one of his own daughters (an obvious falsehood, as Cregan Stark had no trueborn daughters at this time), others that Stark meant to put the boy to death so that he might marry Princess Jaehaera and claim the Iron Throne himself. The northmen would burn the city's septs and force King's Landing to return to the worship of the old gods, septons declared. Others whispered that the Lord of Winterfell had a wildling wife, that he threw his enemies into a pit of wolves to watch them be devoured.

The mood of euphoria had vanished; once more, fear ruled the city streets. A man who claimed to be the Shepherd reborn rose up from the gutters, calling down destruction on the godless northerners. Though he looked nothing like the first Shepherd (he had two hands, for a start), hundreds flocked to hear him speak. A brothel on the Street of Silk burned down when a quarrel over a certain whore between one of Lord Tully's men and one of Lord Stark's set off a bloody melee between their friends and brothers-in-arms. Even the highborn were not safe in the more unsavory parts of the city. The younger son of Lord Hornwood, a bannerman to Lord Stark, vanished with two companions whilst roistering in Flea Bottom. They were never found and may have ended in a bowl of brown, if Mushroom can be believed.

Soon thereafter word reached the city that Leowyn Corbray had left Maidenpool and was making for King's Landing, accompanied by Lord Mooton, Lord Brune, and Ser Rennifer Crabb. Ser Corwyn Corbray departed Duskendale at the same time to join his brother on the march. With him rode Clement Celtigar, old Lord Bartimos's son and heir, and Lady Staunton, the widow of Rook's Rest. On Dragonstone, young Alyn Velaryon was demanding the release of Lord Corlys (this much was true), and threatening to descend upon King's Landing with his ships if the old man was harmed (half-true). Other rumors claimed the Lannisters were on the march, the Hightowers were on the march, Ser Marston Waters had landed with ten thousand sellswords from Lys and Old Volantis (all without truth). And the Maiden of the Vale had set sail from Gulltown, with Lady Rhaena Targaryen and her dragon (true).

As armies marched and swords were sharpened, Lord Cregan Stark sat within the Red Keep, conducting his inquiries into the murder of King Aegon II even as he planned his campaign against the dead king's remaining supporters. Prince Aegon, meanwhile, found himself confined to

Maegor's Holdfast with no companions save the boy Gaemon Palehair. When the prince demanded to know why he was not free to come and go, Stark replied that it was for his own safety. "This city is a nest of vipers," Lord Cregan told him. "There are liars, turncloaks, and poisoners in this court who would murder you as quick as they did your uncle to secure their own power." When Aegon protested that Lord Corlys, Lord Larys, and Ser Perkin were friends, the Lord of Winterfell replied that false friends were more dangerous to a king than any foe, that the Snake, the Clubfoot, and the Flea had saved him only to make use of him, so they might rule Westeros in his name.

With the infallibility of hindsight, we now look back through the centuries and say the Dance was done, but this seemed less certain to those who lived through its dark and dangerous aftermath. With Septon Eustace and Grand Maester Orwyle languishing in dungeons (where Orwyle had begun writing his confessions, the text that would provide Munkun

with the foundation on which he would build his monumental *True Telling*), only Mushroom remains to take us beyond the court chronicles and royal edicts. "The great lords would have given us another two years of war," the fool declares in his *Testimony,* "it was the women who made the peace. Black Aly, the Maiden of the Vale, the Three Widows, the Dragon Twins, 'twas them who brought the bloodshed to an end, and not with swords or poison, but with ravens, words, and kisses."

The seeds cast into the wind by Lord Corlys Velaryon during the False Dawn had taken root and borne sweet fruit. One by one the ravens returned, bearing answers to the old man's peace offers.

Casterly Rock was the first to respond. Lord Jason Lannister had left six children when he died in battle: five daughters and one son, Loreon, a boy of four. Rule in the west had therefore passed to his widow, Lady Johanna, and her father, Roland Westerling, Lord of the Crag. With the Red Kraken's longships still menacing their coasts, the Lannisters were more concerned with defending Kayce and retaking Fair Isle than with renewing the struggle for the Iron Throne. Lady Johanna agreed to all the Sea Snake's terms, promising to come herself to King's Landing to do obeisance to the new king on his coronation, and deliver two daughters to the Red Keep, to serve as companions to the new queen (and as hostages to ensure her future loyalty). She agreed as well to restore that portion of the royal treasury that Tyland Lannister had sent west for safekeeping, providing that Ser Tyland himself was granted pardon. In return, she asked only that the Iron Throne "command Lord Greyjoy to crawl back to his islands, restore Fair Isle to its rightful lords, and free all the women he has carried off, or at the least all those of noble birth."

Many of the men who had survived the Battle on the Kingsroad had made their way back to Storm's End afterward. Hungry, weary, wounded, they drifted home alone or in small groups, and Lord Borros Baratheon's widow, the Lady Elenda, had only to look at them to realize they had lost their taste for battle. Nor did she wish to put her newborn son, Royce, at risk, for that little lord at her breast was the future of House Baratheon. Though it is said that her eldest daughter, the Lady Cassandra, wept bitter tears when she learned she was not to be a queen, Lady Elenda soon agreed to terms. Still weak from her labor, she could not come to the city herself for the coronation, she wrote, but she would send her own lord father to do homage in her stead, and three of her daughters to serve as hostages. They would be accompanied by Ser Willis Fell, together with his "precious charge," the eight-year-old Princess Jaehaera, the last living child of King Aegon II and the new king's bride-to-be.

Last to respond was Oldtown. The wealthiest of the great houses that had rallied to King Aegon II, the Hightowers remained in some ways the most dangerous, for they were capable of raising large new armies quickly from the streets of Oldtown, and with their own warships and those of their close kin, the Redwynes of the Arbor, they could float a significant fleet as well. Moreover, one-quarter of the Crown's gold still rested in deep vaults beneath the Hightower, gold that could easily have been used to buy new alliances and hire sellsword companies. Oldtown had the power to renew the war; all that was lacking was the will.

Lord Ormund had only recently taken a second wife when the Dance began, his first having died some years before in childbed. Upon his death at Tumbleton, his lands and title passed to his eldest son, Lyonel, a youth of fifteen on the cusp of manhood. The second son, Martyn, was a squire to Lord Redwyne on the Arbor; the third was fostering at Highgarden as a companion to Lord Tyrell and cupbearer to his lady mother. All three were children of Lord Ormund's first marriage. When Lord Velaryon's terms were put to Lyonel Hightower, it is said, the young lord ripped the parchment from his maester's hand and tore it into shreds, swearing to write his reply in the Sea Snake's blood.

His lord father's young widow had other notions, however. Lady Samantha was the daughter of Lord Donald Tarly of Horn Hill and Lady Jeyne Rowan of Goldengrove, both houses that had taken up arms for the queen during the Dance. Fierce and fiery and beautiful, this strong-willed girl had no intention of giving up her place as the Lady of Oldtown and mistress of the Hightower. Lyonel was but two years her junior, and (Mushroom says) had been infatuated with her since first she came to Oldtown to wed his father. Whereas previously she had fended off the boy's halting advances, now Lady Sam (as she would be known for many a year) yielded to them, allowing him to seduce her, and afterward promising to marry him ... but only if he would make peace, "for I would surely die of grief should I lose another husband."

Faced with a choice between "a dead father, cold in the ground, and a living woman, warm and willing in his arms, the boy showed surprising sense for one so highborn, and chose love over honor," says Mushroom. Lyonel Hightower capitulated, agreeing to all the terms put forth by Lord Corlys, including the return of the Crown's gold (to the fury of his cousin, Ser Myles Hightower, who had stolen a good part of that gold, though that tale need not concern us here). A great scandal ensued when the young lord then announced his intention to marry his father's widow, and the reigning High Septon ultimately forbade the marriage as a form of incest, but even that could not keep these young lovers apart. Thereafter refusing to wed, the Lord of the Hightower and Defender of Oldtown kept the Lady Sam by his side as his paramour for the next thirteen years, fathering six children on her, and finally taking her as his wife when a new High Septon came to power in the Starry Sept and reversed the ruling of his predecessor.*

Let us leave the Hightower now and return once more to King's Landing, where Lord Cregan Stark found all his plans for war undone by the Three Widows. "Other voices were making themselves heard as well, gentler voices that echoed softly through the halls of the Red Keep," says Mushroom. The Maiden of the Vale had arrived from Gulltown, bringing her own ward, the Lady Rhaena Targaryen, with a dragon on her shoulder. The smallfolk of King's Landing, who not a year before had slaughtered every dragon in the city, now became rapturous at the sight of one. Lady Rhaena and her twin sister, Baela, became the darlings of the city overnight. Lord Stark could not confine them to the castle, as he had Prince Aegon, and he soon learned that he could not control them either. When

* This is the tale as Mushroom tells it, in any case. Munkun's *True Telling* ascribes a different cause to Lord Lyonel's change of heart, however. It must be recalled that the Hightowers, as rich and powerful as they were, were bannermen sworn to House Tyrell of Highgarden, where his lordship's brother Garmund was a page. The Tyrells had taken no part in the Dance (ruled as they were by a little lord in swaddling clothes), but now at last they bestirred themselves, forbidding Lord Lyonel to raise a host or go to war without their leave. Should he disobey, his brother would pay for that defiance with his life ... for every ward is also a hostage, as a wise man once said. Or so Grand Maester Munkun avers.

they demanded to be allowed to see "our beloved brother," Lady Arryn gave them her support, and the Wolf of Winterfell yielded ("somewhat grudgingly," says Mushroom).*

The False Dawn had come and gone, and now the Hour of the Wolf (as Grand Maester Munkun names it) was waning too. The situation and the city were both slipping from the hands of Cregan Stark. When Lord Leowyn Corbray and his brother arrived in King's Landing and joined the ruling council, adding their voices to those of Lady Arryn and the Lads, the Wolf of Winterfell oft found himself at odds with all of them. Here and there throughout the realm a few stubborn loyalists still flew Aegon II's golden dragon, but they were of little significance; the Dance was done, the others all agreed, it was time to make the peace and set the realm to rights.

On one point Lord Cregan remained adamant, however; the king's killers must not go unpunished. Unworthy as King Aegon II might have been, his murder was high treason, and those responsible must answer for it. So fierce was his demeanor, so unyielding, that the others gave way before him. "Let it be on your head, Stark," Kermit Tully said. "I want no part of this, but I will not have it said that Riverrun stood in the way of justice."

No lord had the right to put another lord to death, so it was first necessary for Prince Aegon to make Lord Stark the King's Hand, with full authority to act in his name. This was done. Lord Cregan did all the rest, whilst the others stood aside. He did not presume to sit the Iron Throne, but on a simple wooden bench beneath it. One by one the men suspected of having played a part in the poisoning of King Aegon II were brought before him.

Septon Eustace was the first brought up, and the first released; there was no proof against him. Grand Maester Orwyle was less fortunate, for he had confessed under torture to having given the poison to the Clubfoot. "My lord, I did not know what it was for," Orwyle protested. "Nor

* The meeting did not go as well as the twins might have hoped, however. The prince paled at the sight of Lady Rhaena's dragon, Morning, and commanded the northmen guarding him to "get that wretched creature out of my sight."

did you ask," Lord Stark replied. "You did not wish to know." The Grand Maester was judged to be complicit and sentenced to death.

Ser Gyles Belgrave was also put down for death; if he had not put the poison in the king's wine himself, he had allowed it to happen through carelessness or willful blindness. "No knight of the Kingsguard should outlive his king when that king dies by violence," Stark declared. Three of Belgrave's Sworn Brothers had been present at King Aegon's death and were similarly condemned, though their complicity in the plot could not be proved (the three Kingsguard who were not in the city were judged innocent).

Twenty-two lesser personages were also found to have played some part in King Aegon's murder. His Grace's litter-bearers were amongst them, along with the king's herald, the keeper of the royal wine cellars, and the serving man whose task it was to make certain the king's flagon was always full. All were marked down for death. So too were the men who had put the king's food taster Ummet to the sword (Mushroom himself gave evidence against them), together with those responsible for cutting down Tom Tangletongue and drowning his father in ale. Most of these were gutter knights, sellswords, masterless men-at-arms, and scum of the streets who had been granted their dubious knighthood by Ser Perkin the Flea during the turmoil. To a man, each of them insisted that they had been acting on Ser Perkin's orders.

Of the Flea's own guilt there could be no doubt. "Once a turncloak, ever a turncloak," Lord Cregan said. "You rose up in rebellion against your lawful queen and helped drive her from this city to her death, raised up your own squire in her place, then abandoned him to save your worthless hide. The realm will be a better place without you." When Ser Perkin protested that he had been pardoned for those crimes, Lord Stark replied, "Not by me."

The men who had seized the Queen Dowager upon the serpentine steps had worn the seahorse badge of House Velaryon, whilst those who had freed Lady Baela Targaryen from her imprisonment had been in service to Lord Larys Strong. Queen Alicent's captors had slain her guards and were thus condemned to death, but an impassioned plea from Lady Baela herself spared her rescuers from a similar fate, though they too had bloodied their swords by cutting down the king's men posted at her door. "Not even the tears of a dragon could melt the frozen heart of Cregan Stark, men said rightly," Mushroom tells us, "but when Lady Baela brandished a sword and declared that she would cut off the hand of any man who sought to harm the men who had saved her, the Wolf of Winterfell smiled for all to see, and allowed that if her ladyship was so fond of these dogs, he would permit her to keep them."

The last to face the Judgment of the Wolf (as Munkun dubs these proceedings in the *True Telling*) were the two great lords at the heart of the conspiracy: Larys Strong the Clubfoot, Lord of Harrenhal, and Corlys Velaryon, the Sea Snake, Master of Driftmark and Lord of the Tides.

Lord Velaryon did not attempt to deny his guilt. "What I did, I did for the good of the realm," the old man said. "I would do the same again. The madness had to end." Lord Strong proved less forthcoming. Grand Maester Orwyle had testified that he gave the poison to his lordship, and Ser Perkin the Flea swore that he had been the Clubfoot's man, acting entirely on his orders, but Lord Larys would neither confirm nor deny the accusations. When Lord Stark asked if he had anything to say in his own defense, he said only, "When was a wolf ever moved by words?" And thus Lord Cregan Stark, Hand of the Uncrowned King, declared the Lords Velaryon and Strong to be guilty of murder, regicide, and high treason, and decreed that they must pay for their crimes with their lives.

Larys Strong had always been a man who went his own way, kept his own counsel, and changed allegiances as other men changed cloaks. Once condemned, he stood friendless; not a voice was raised in his defense. It was quite otherwise with Corlys Velaryon, however. The old Sea Snake had many friends and admirers. Even men who had fought against him during the Dance spoke up for him now . . . some out of affection for the old man, no doubt, others from concern for what his young heir, Alyn, might do should his beloved grandsire (or sire) be put to death. When Lord Stark proved unyielding, some of them sought to circumvent him by appealing to the king to be, Prince Aegon himself. Foremost amongst them were his half-sisters, Baela and Rhaena, who reminded the prince that he would have lost an ear and perhaps more if Lord Corlys had not acted as he did. "Words are wind," says *The Testimony of Mushroom*, "but a strong wind can topple mighty oaks, and the whispering of pretty girls can change the destiny of kingdoms." Aegon not only agreed to spare the Sea Snake, but went so far as to restore him to his offices and honors, including a place on the small council.

The prince was but ten years of age, however, and not yet a king. Uncrowned, and not yet anointed as king, His Grace's decrees carried no weight in law. Even after his coronation, he would remain subject to a regent or regency council until his sixteenth nameday. Therefore, Lord Stark would have been well within his rights to pay no heed to the prince's commands and proceed with the execution of Corlys Velaryon. He chose not to do so, a decision that has intrigued scholars ever since. Septon Eustace suggests that "the Mother moved him to mercy that night," though Lord Cregan did not worship the Seven. Eustace further suggests that the northman was loath to provoke Alyn Velaryon, fearing his strength at sea, but this seems singularly at odds with all we know of Stark's character. A new war would not have dismayed him; indeed, at times he seemed to seek it.

It is Mushroom who provides the most lucid explanation for this surprising leniency in the Wolf of Winterfell. It was not the prince who swayed him, the fool claims, nor the looming threat of the Velaryon fleets, nor even the entreaties of the twins, but rather a bargain struck with Lady Alysanne of House Blackwood.

"A lean tall creature was this wench," says the dwarf, "thin as a whip and flat-chested as a boy, but long of leg and strong of arm, with a mane of thick black curls that tumbled down past her waist when loosed." Huntress, horse-breaker, and archer without peer, Black Aly had little of a woman's softness about her. Many thought her to be of that same ilk as Sabitha Frey, for they were oft in one another's company, and had been known to share a tent whilst on the march. Yet in King's Landing, whilst accompanying her young nephew Benjicot at court and council, she had met Cregan Stark and conceived a liking for the stern northman.

And Lord Cregan, a widower these past three years, had responded in kind. Though Black Aly was no man's queen of love and beauty, her fearlessness, stubborn strength, and bawdy tongue struck a chord for the Lord of Winterfell, who soon began to seek out her company in hall and yard.

"She smells of woodsmoke, not of flowers," Stark told Lord Cerwyn, said to be his closest friend.

And so when Lady Alysanne came to ask that he let the prince's edict stand, he listened. "Why would I do that?" Lord Stark purportedly asked when she had made her plea.

"For the realm," she answered.

"It is better for the realm that traitors die," he said.

"For the honor of our prince," said she.

"The prince is a child. He ought not have meddled in this. It is Velaryon who brought dishonor on him, for now it will be said until the end of days that he came to his throne by murder."

"For the sake of peace," said Lady Alysanne, "for all those who will surely die should Alyn Velaryon seek vengeance."

"There are worse ways to die. Winter has come, my lady."

"For me, then," said Black Aly. "Grant me this boon, and I shall never ask another. Do this, and I shall know that you are as wise as you are strong, as kind as you are fierce. Give me this, and I shall give you whatever you may choose to ask of me."

Mushroom says Lord Cregan scowled at that. "What if I ask you for your maidenhead, my lady?"

"I cannot give you what I do not have, my lord," she answered. "I lost my maidenhead in the saddle when I was three-and-ten."

"Some would say that you squandered on a horse a gift that by rights should have belonged to your future husband."

"Some are fools," Black Aly answered, "and she was a good horse, better than most husbands I have seen."

Her answer pleased Lord Cregan, who laughed aloud and said, "I shall try to remember that, my lady. Aye, I'll grant your boon."

"And in return?" she asked.

"All I ask is all of you, forever," the Lord of Winterfell said solemnly. "I claim your hand in marriage."

"A hand for a head," said Black Aly, grinning . . . for Mushroom tells us this was her intent all along. "Done." And it was.

The morning of the executions dawned grey and wet. All those con-

demned to die were brought up from the dungeons in chains to the Red Keep's outer ward. There they were forced to their knees whilst Prince Aegon and his court looked on.

As Septon Eustace led the doomed men in prayer, beseeching the Mother to have mercy on their souls, rain began to fall. "It rained so hard, and Eustace droned on so long, that we began to fear the prisoners might drown before their heads could be cut off," says Mushroom. At last the prayer concluded, and Lord Cregan Stark unsheathed Ice, the Valyrian greatsword that was the pride of his house, for the savage custom of the North decreed that the man who passed the sentence must also wield the sword, that their blood might be upon his hands alone.

Be he a high lord or common headsman, seldom had any man faced so many executions as Cregan Stark did that morning in the rain. Yet it came undone in a trice. The condemned had drawn lots to see who would be the first to die, and the choice had fallen on Ser Perkin the Flea. When

Lord Cregan asked that cunning rogue if he had any final words, Ser Perkin declared that he wished to take the black. A southron lord might or might not have honored his request, but the Starks are of the North, where the needs of the Night's Watch are held in high regard.

And when Lord Cregan bade his men haul the Flea onto his feet, the other prisoners saw the road to deliverance, and echoed his request. "All of them began to shout at once," Mushroom says, "like a chorus of drunks bellowing out the words of a song they half remember." Gutter knights and men-at-arms, litter-bearers, serving men, heralds, the keeper of the wine cellars, three White Swords of the Kingsguard, every man of them suddenly evinced a deep desire to defend the Wall. Even Grand Maester Orwyle joined the desperate chorus. He too was spared, for the Night's Watch needs men of the quill as well as men of the sword.

Only two men died that day. One was Ser Gyles Belgrave, of the Kingsguard. Unlike his Sworn Brothers, Ser Gyles refused the chance to exchange his white cloak for black. "You were not wrong, Lord Stark," he said when his turn came. "A knight of the Kingsguard should not outlive his king." Lord Cregan took his head off with a single swift swing of Ice.

Next (and last) to die was Lord Larys Strong. When asked if he wished to take the black, he said, "No, my lord. I'll be going to a warmer hell, if it please you . . . but I do have one last request. When I am dead, hack off my clubfoot with that great sword of yours. I have dragged it with me all through life, let me be free of it in death at least." This boon Lord Stark granted him.

Thus perished the last Strong, and a proud and ancient house came to its end. Lord Larys's remains were given over to the silent sisters; years later, his bones would find their final resting place at Harrenhal . . . save for his clubfoot. Lord Stark decreed that it should be buried separately in a pauper's field, but before that could be done, it disappeared. Mushroom tells us it was stolen and sold to some sorcerer, who used it in the casting of his spells. (The selfsame tale is told of the foot torn off Prince Joffrey's leg in Flea Bottom, which makes the veracity of both suspect, unless we are meant to believe that all feet are possessed of malign powers.)

The heads of Lord Larys Strong and Ser Gyles Belgrave were mounted on either side of the Red Keep's gates. The other condemned were returned to their cells to languish until arrangements could be made to send them to the Wall. The final line in the history of the woeful reign of King Aegon II Targaryen had been written.

Cregan Stark's brief service as the Hand of the Uncrowned King ended the next day, when he returned his chain of office to Prince Aegon. He might easily have remained King's Hand for years, or even claimed the regency until young Aegon came of age, but the south held no interest for him. "The snows are falling in the North," he announced, "and my place is at Winterfell."

Under the Regents

The Hooded Hand

Cregan Stark had stepped down as Hand of the King and announced his intention to return to Winterfell, but before he could take his leave of the south he faced a thorny problem.

Lord Stark had marched south with a great host, made up in large part of men unwanted and unneeded in the North, whose return would bring great hardship and mayhaps even death for the loved ones they had left behind. Legend (and Mushroom) tells us that it was Lady Alysanne who suggested an answer. The lands along the Trident were full of widows, she reminded Lord Stark; women, many burdened with young children, who had sent their husbands off to fight with one lord or another, only for them to fall in battle. With winter at hand, strong backs and willing hands would be welcome in many a hearth and home.

In the end, more than a thousand northmen accompanied Black Aly and her nephew Lord Benjicot when they returned to the riverlands after the royal wedding. "A wolf for every widow," Mushroom japed, "he will warm her bed in winter, and gnaw her bones come spring." Yet hundreds of marriages were made at the so-called Widow Fairs held at Raventree, Riverrun, Stoney Sept, the Twins, and Fairmarket. Those northmen who did not wish to marry instead swore their swords to lords both great and small as guards and men-at-arms. A few, sad to say, did turn to outlawry and met evil ends, but for the most part, Lady Alysanne's matchmaking was a great success. The resettled northmen not only strengthened the riverlords who welcomed them, particularly House Tully and House Blackwood, but also helped revive and spread the worship of the old gods south of the Neck.

Other northerners chose to seek new lives and fortunes across the narrow sea. A few days after Lord Stark stepped down as the King's Hand, Ser Marston Waters returned alone from Lys, whence he had been sent to hire sellswords. He gladly accepted a pardon for his past crimes, and reported that the Triarchy had collapsed. On the point of war, the Three Daughters were hiring free companies as fast as they could form, at wages he could not hope to match. Many of Lord Cregan's northmen saw this as an opportunity. Why return to a land gripped by winter to freeze or starve when there was gold to be had across the narrow sea? Not one but two free companies were birthed as a result. The Wolf Pack, commanded by Hallis Hornwood, called Mad Hal, and Timotty Snow, the Bastard of Flint's Finger, was made up entirely of northmen, whilst the Stormbreakers, financed and led by Ser Oscar Tully, included men from every part of Westeros.

Even as these adventurers prepared to take their leave of King's Landing, others were arriving from every point of the compass for Prince Aegon's coronation and the royal wedding. From the west came Lady Johanna Lannister and her father, Roland Westerling, Lord of the Crag; from the south, twoscore Hightowers from Oldtown, led by Lord Lyonel and the redoubtable Lady Samantha, his father's widow. Though forbidden to wed, their passion for one another had become common knowledge by this time, and so great a scandal that the High Septon refused to travel with them, arriving three days later in the company of the Lords Redwyne, Costayne, and Beesbury.

Lady Elenda, the widow of Lord Borros, remained at Storm's End with her infant son, but sent her daughters Cassandra, Ellyn, and Floris to represent House Baratheon. (Maris, the fourth daughter, had joined the silent sisters, Septon Eustace informs us. In Mushroom's account, this was done after her lady mother had her tongue removed, but that grisly detail can be safely discounted. The persistent belief that the silent sisters are tongueless is no more than a myth; it is piety that keeps the sisters silent, not red-hot pincers.) Lady Baratheon's father, Royce Caron, Lord of Nightsong and Lord of the Marches, escorted the girls to the city, and would remain with them as their guardian.

Alyn Velaryon came ashore as well, and the Manderly brothers returned once more from White Harbor with a hundred knights in blue-green cloaks. Even from across the narrow sea they came, from Braavos and Pentos, all three of the Daughters, Old Volantis. From the Summer Isles appeared three tall black princes in feathered cloaks, whose splendor was a wonder to behold. Every inn and stable in King's Landing was soon full, whilst outside the walls a city of tents and pavilions arose for those unable to find accommodations. A great deal of drinking and fornication took place, claims Mushroom; a great deal of prayer and fasting and good works, reports Septon Eustace. The tavernkeepers of the city waxed fat and happy for a time, as did the whores of Flea Bottom, and their sisters in the fine houses along the Street of Silk, though the common people complained about the noise and stink.

A desperate, fragile air of forced fellowship hung over King's Landing in the days leading up to the wedding, for many of those crowding cheek by jowl into the city's wine sinks and pot shops had stood upon opposite sides of battlefields a year ago. "If only blood can wash out blood, King's Landing was full of the unwashed," says Mushroom. Yet there was less fighting in the streets than most expected, with only three men killed. Mayhaps the lords of the realm had finally grown weary of war.

With the Dragonpit still largely in ruins, the wedding of Prince Aegon and Princess Jaehaera was celebrated out of doors, at the top of Visenya's Hill, where towering grandstands were erected so the men and women of the nobility might sit in comfort and enjoy an unobstructed view. The day was cold but sunny, Septon Eustace records. It was the seventh day of the seventh moon of the 131st year after Aegon's Conquest, a most auspicious date. The High Septon of Oldtown performed the rites himself, and a deafening roar went up from the smallfolk when His High Holiness declared the prince and princess one. Tens of thousands packed the streets cheering Aegon and Jaehaera as they were carried in an open litter up to the Red Keep, where the prince was crowned with a circlet of yellow gold, simple and unadorned, and proclaimed Aegon of House Targaryen, the Third of His Name, King of the Andals, the Rhoynar, and the First Men, and Lord of the Seven Kingdoms. Aegon himself placed the crown upon the head of his child bride.

Though a solemn boy, the new king was undeniably handsome, lean of face and form, with silver-white hair and purple eyes, whilst the queen was a beautiful child. Their wedding was as lavish a spectacle as the Seven Kingdoms had seen since the coronation of Aegon II in the Dragonpit. All that was lacking were dragons. There would be no triumphal flight around the city walls for this king, no majestic descent upon the castle yard. And the more observant made note of another absence. The Dowager Queen was nowhere to be seen, though as Jaehaera's grandmother, Alicent Hightower ought to have been present.

As he was still but ten years of age, the new king's first act was to name the men who would protect and defend him, and rule for him until he came of age. Ser Willis Fell, the sole survivor of the Kingsguard of King Viserys's time, was made Lord Commander of the White Swords, with Ser Marston Waters as his second. As both men were considered greens, the remaining places in the Kingsguard were filled with blacks. Ser Tyland Lannister, recently returned from Myr, was made Hand of the King, whilst Lord Leowyn Corbray was named Protector of the Realm. The former had been a green, the latter a black. Over them would sit a council of regency, consisting of Lady Jeyne Arryn of the Vale, Lord Corlys Velaryon of Driftmark, Lord Roland Westerling of the Crag, Lord Royce Caron of Nightsong, Lord Manfryd Mooton of Maidenpool, Ser Torrhen Manderly of White Harbor, and Grand Maester Munkun, newly chosen by the Citadel to take up Grand Maester Orwyle's chain of office.

(It is reliably reported that Lord Cregan Stark was also offered a place amongst the regents, but refused. Conspicuous omissions from the council included Kermit Tully, Unwin Peake, Sabitha Frey, Thaddeus Rowan, Lyonel Hightower, Johanna Lannister, and Benjicot Blackwood, but Septon Eustace insists that only Lord Peake was truly angered by his exclusion.)

This was a council of which Septon Eustace heartily approved, "six strong men and one wise woman, seven to rule us here on earth as the Seven Above rule all men from their heaven." Mushroom was less impressed. "Seven regents were six too many," he said. "Pity our poor king." Despite the fool's misgivings, most observers seemed to feel that the reign of King Aegon III had begun on a hopeful note.

The remainder of the year 131 AC was a time of departures, as the great lords of Westeros took their leaves of King's Landing one by one to return to their own seats of power. Amongst the first to flee were two of the Three Widows who were present, after bidding tearful farewells to the daughters, son, siblings, and cousins who would remain to serve the new king and queen as companions and hostages. With Lady Sam went her paramour Lord Lyonel, riding south for Oldtown with their Hightowers, whilst Lords Rowan, Beesbury, Costayne, Tarly, and Redwyne joined to escort His High Holiness to the same destination. Cregan Stark led his much-diminished host north along the kingsroad within a fortnight of the coronation; three days later, Lord Blackwood and Lady Alysanne set out for Raventree, with a thousand of Stark's northerners as a tail. Lord Kermit Tully and his knights returned to Riverrun, whilst his brother Ser Oscar set sail with his Stormbreakers for Tyrosh and the Disputed Lands.

There was one who did not depart as planned, however. Ser Medrick Manderly had agreed to take the men bound for the Wall as far as White Harbor on his galley *North Star*. From there they were to proceed overland to Castle Black. On the morning the *North Star* was to sail, however, a count of the condemned revealed a man was missing. Grand Maester Orwyle, it seemed, had experienced a change of heart as regarded taking the black. Bribing one of his guards to loose his fetters, he had changed into a beggar's rags and disappeared into the stews of the city. Unwilling to linger any longer, Ser Medrick sentenced the guard who had freed Orwyle to take his place, and the *North Star* sought the sea.

By the end of 131 AC, Septon Eustace tells us, a "grey calm" had settled over King's Landing and the crownlands. Aegon III sat the Iron Throne when required, but elsewise was little seen. The task of defending the realm fell to the Lord Protector, Leowyn Corbray, the day-to-day tedium of rule to the blind Hand, Tyland Lannister. Once as tall and golden-haired and dashing as his twin, the late Lord Jason, Ser Tyland had been left so disfigured by the queen's torturers that ladies new to court had been known to faint at the sight of him. To spare them, the Hand took to wearing a silken hood over his head on formal occasions. This was perhaps a misjudgment, for it gave Ser Tyland a sinister aspect, and before very long the smallfolk of King's Landing began to whisper tales of the malign masked sorcerer in the Red Keep.

Ser Tyland's wits remained sharp, however. He might have been expected to have emerged from his torments a bitter man intent upon revenge, but this proved far from true. Instead the Hand claimed a curious failure of memory, insisting that he could not recall who had been black and who green, whilst demonstrating a dogged loyalty to the son of the very queen who had sent him to the torturers. Very quickly Ser Tyland achieved an unspoken dominance over Leowyn Corbray, of whom Mushroom says, "He was thick of neck and thick of wit, but never have I known a man to fart so loudly." By law, both the Hand and the Lord Protector were subject to the authority of the council of regents, but as the days passed and the moon turned and turned again, the regents convened less and less often, whilst the tireless, blind, hooded Tyland Lannister gathered more and more power to himself.

The challenges he faced were daunting, for winter had descended upon Westeros and would endure for four long years, a winter as cold and bleak as any in the history of the Seven Kingdoms. The kingdom's trade had collapsed during the Dance as well, countless villages, towns, and castles had been slighted or destroyed, and bands of outlaws and broken men haunted the roads and woods.

A more immediate problem was posed by the Dowager Queen, who refused to reconcile herself to the new king. The murder of the last of her sons had turned Alicent's heart into a stone. None of the regents wished to see her put to death, some from compassion, others for fear that such an execution might rekindle the flames of war. Yet she could not be allowed to take part in the life of the court as before. She was too apt to rain down curses on the king, or snatch a dagger from some unwary guardsman. Alicent could not even be trusted in the company of the little queen; when last allowed to share a meal with Her Grace, she had told Jaehaera to cut her husband's throat whilst he was sleeping, which set the child to screaming. Ser Tyland felt he had no choice but to confine the Queen Dowager to her own apartments in Maegor's Holdfast; a gentle imprisonment, but imprisonment nonetheless.

The Hand then set out to restore the kingdom's trade and begin the process of rebuilding. Great lords and smallfolk alike were pleased when he abolished the taxes enacted by Queen Rhaenyra and Lord Celtigar. With the Crown's gold once more secure, Ser Tyland set aside a million golden dragons as loans for lords whose holdings had been destroyed during the Dance. (Though many availed themselves of this coin, the loans did bring about a rift between the Iron Throne and the Iron Bank of Braavos.) He also ordered the construction of three huge fortified granaries, in King's Landing, Lannisport, and Gulltown, and the purchase of sufficient grain to fill them. (The latter decree drove up the price of grain sharply, which pleased those towns and lords with wheat and corn and barley to sell, but angered the proprietors of inns and pot shops, and the poor and hungry in general.)

Though he called a halt to work on the gargantuan statues of Prince Aemond and Prince Daeron that had been commissioned by Aegon II (not before the heads of the two princes had been carved), the Hand set hundreds of stonemasons, carpenters, and builders to work on the repair and restoration of the Dragonpit. The gates of King's Landing were strengthened at his command, so they might better be able to resist attacks from within the city walls as well as without. The Hand also announced the Crown's funding for the construction of fifty new war galleys. When questioned, he told the regents that this was meant to provide work for the shipyards and defend the city from the fleets of the Triarchy... but many suspected Ser Tyland's real purpose was to lessen the Crown's dependence on House Velaryon of Driftmark.

The Hand might also have been mindful of the continuing war in the west when he set the shipwrights to work. Whilst the ascent of Aegon III did mark an end to the worst of the carnage of the Dance of the Dragons, it is not wholly correct to assert that the young king's coronation brought peace to the Seven Kingdoms. Fighting continued in the west through the first three years of the boy king's reign, as Lady Johanna of Casterly Rock continued to resist the depredations of Dalton Greyjoy's ironborn in the name of her son, young Lord Loreon. The details of their war lie outside our purpose here (for those who would know more, the relevant chapters of Archmaester Mancaster's *Sea Demons: A History of the Children of the Drowned God of the Isles* are especially good). Suffice it to say that whilst the Red Kraken had proved a valuable ally to the blacks during the Dance, the coming of peace demonstrated that the ironmen had no more regard for them than for the greens.

Though he stopped short of openly declaring himself King of the Iron Isles, Dalton Greyjoy paid little heed to any of the edicts coming from the Iron Throne during these years . . . mayhaps because the king was a boy, and his Hand a Lannister. When commanded to cease his raiding, Greyjoy continued as before. Told to restore the women his ironmen had carried off, he replied that "only the Drowned God may sunder the bond between a man and his salt wives." Instructed to return Fair Isle to its former lords, he replied, "Should they come rising back up from beneath the sea, we shall gladly give them back what once was theirs."

When Johanna Lannister attempted to build a new fleet of warships to take the battle to the ironmen, the Red Kraken descended on her shipyards and put them to the torch, and made off with another hundred women in the nonce. The Hand sent an angry reproach, to which Lord Dalton replied, "The women of the west prefer men of iron to cowardly lions, it would seem, for they jump into the sea and plead with us to take them."

Across Westeros, the winds of war were blowing up the narrow sea as well. The murder of Sharako Lohar of Lys, the admiral who had presided over the Triarchy's disaster in the Gullet, proved to be the spark that engulfed the Three Daughters in flames, fanning the smoldering rivalries of Tyrosh, Lys, and Myr into open war. It is now commonly accepted that Sharako's death was a personal matter; the arrogant admiral was slain by one of his rivals for the favor of a courtesan known as the Black Swan. At the time, however, his death was seen as a political killing, and the Myrish were suspected. When Lys and Myr went to war, Tyrosh seized the opportunity to assert its dominion over the Stepstones.

To press that claim, the Archon of Tyrosh called up Racallio Ryndoon, the flamboyant captain-general who had once commanded the Triarchy's forces against Daemon Targaryen. Racallio overran the islands in a trice and put the reigning King of the Narrow Sea to death . . . only to decide to claim his crown for himself, betraying the Archon and his native city. The confused four-sided war that followed had the effect of closing the southern end of the narrow sea to trade, cutting off King's Landing, Duskendale, Maidenpool, and Gulltown from commerce with the east. Pentos, Braavos, and Lorath were similarly affected, and sent envoys to King's Landing in hopes of bringing the Iron Throne into a grand alliance against Racallio and the quarrelsome Daughters. Ser Tyland entertained them lavishly, but refused their offer. "It would be a grave mistake for Westeros to become embroiled in the endless quarrels of the Free Cities," he told the council of regents.

That fateful year 131 AC came to a close with the seas aflame both east and west of the Seven Kingdoms and blizzards descending on Winterfell and the North. Nor was the mood in King's Landing a happy one. The smallfolk of the city had already begun to grow disenchanted with their boy king and little queen, neither of whom had been seen since the wedding, and whispers about "the hooded Hand" were spreading. Though the "reborn" Shepherd had been taken by the gold cloaks and relieved of his tongue, others had risen in his place to preach of how the King's Hand practiced the forbidden arts, drank baby's blood, and was besides "a monster who hides his twisted face from gods and men."

Within the walls of the Red Keep, there were whispers about the king and queen as well. The royal marriage was troubled from the first. Both bride and groom were children; Aegon III was now eleven, Jaehaera only eight. Once wed, they had very little contact with one another save on formal occasions, and even that was rare, as the little queen was loath to leave her chambers. "Both of them are broken," Grand Maester Munkun declared in a letter to the Conclave. The girl had witnessed the murder of her twin brother at the hands of Blood and Cheese. The king had lost all four of his own brothers, then watched his uncle feed his mother to a dragon. "These are not normal children," Munkun wrote. "They have no joy in them; they neither laugh nor play. The girl wets her bed at night and weeps inconsolably when she is corrected. Her own ladies say that she is eight, going on four. Had I not laced her milk with sweetsleep before the wedding, I am convinced the child would have collapsed during the ceremony."

As for the king, the new Grand Maester went on, "Aegon shows little interest in his wife, or any other girl. He does not ride or hunt or joust, but neither does he enjoy sedentary pursuits such as reading, dancing, or singing. Though his wits seem sound enough, he never initiates a conversation, and when spoken to his answers are so curt one would think the very act of talking was painful to him. He has no friends save for the bastard boy Gaemon Palehair, and seldom sleeps through the night. During the hour of the wolf he can oft be found standing by a window, gazing up at the stars, but when I presented him with Archmaester Lyman's *Kingdoms of the Sky,* he showed no interest. Aegon seldom smiles and never laughs, but neither does he display any outward signs of anger or fear, save in regards to dragons, the very mention of which sends him into a rare rage. Orwyle was wont to call His Grace calm and self-possessed; I say the boy is dead inside. He walks the halls of the Red Keep like a ghost. Brothers, I must be frank. I fear for our king, and for the kingdom."

His fears, alas, would prove to be well founded. As bad as 131 AC had been, the next two years would be much worse.

It began on an ominous note when the former Grand Maester Orwyle was discovered in a brothel called Mother's, near the lower end of the Street of Silk. Shorn of his hair and beard and chain of office and going by the name Old Wyl, he had earned his bread by sweeping, scrubbing, inspecting patrons of the house for pox, and mixing moon tea and potions of tansy and pennyroyal for Mother's "daughters" to rid themselves of unwanted children. No one paid Old Wyl any mind until he took it upon himself to teach some of Mother's younger girls to read. One of his pupils demonstrated her new skill to a serjeant in the gold cloaks, who grew suspicious and led the old man in for questioning. The truth soon emerged.

The penalty for deserting the Night's Watch is death. Though Orwyle had not yet sworn vows, most still considered him an oathbreaker. There was no question of allowing him to take ship for the Wall. The original sentence of death that Lord Stark had pronounced on him must apply, the regents agreed. Ser Tyland did not deny this, though he pointed out that the office of King's Justice had yet to be filled, and as a blind man he was a poor choice to swing the sword himself. Using that for his pretext, the Hand instead confined Orwyle to a tower cell (large, airy, and far too comfortable, some charged) "until such time as a suitable headsman can be found." Neither Septon Eustace nor Mushroom were deceived; Orwyle had served with Ser Tyland on Aegon II's green councils, and plainly old friendship and the memory of all they had endured played some part in the Hand's decision. The former Grand Maester was even provided with quill, ink, and parchment, so that he might continue his confessions. And so he did for the best part of two years, setting down the lengthy history of the reigns of Viserys I and Aegon II that would later prove to be such an invaluable source for his successor's *True Telling*.

Less than a fortnight later, reports reached King's Landing of bands of wildlings from the Mountains of the Moon descending upon the Vale of Arryn in large numbers to raid and plunder, and Lady Jeyne Arryn left the court and sailed for Gulltown to see to the defense of her own lands and people. There were ominous stirrings along the Dornish Marches too, for Dorne had a new ruler in the person of Aliandra Martell, a brazen girl of ten-and-seven who fancied herself "the new Nymeria" and had every young lord south of the Red Mountains vying for her affections. To deal with their incursions, Lord Caron took his leave of King's Landing as well, hastening back to Nightsong in the Dornish Marches. Thus the seven regents became five. The most influential of those was plainly the Sea Snake, whose wealth, experience, and alliances made him the first amongst equals. Even more tellingly, he seemed the only man the young king was willing to trust.

For all these reasons, the realm suffered a terrible blow on the sixth day of the third moon of 132 AC, when Corlys Velaryon, Lord of the Tides, collapsed whilst ascending the serpentine steps in the Red Keep of King's Landing. By the time Grand Maester Munkun came rushing to his aid, the Sea Snake was dead. Seventy-nine years of age, he had served four kings and a queen, sailed to the ends of the earth, raised House Velaryon to unprecedented levels of wealth and power, married a princess who might have been a queen, fathered dragonriders, built towns and fleets, proved his valor in times of war and his wisdom in times of peace. The

Seven Kingdoms would never see his like again. With his passing, a great hole was torn in the tattered fabric of the Seven Kingdoms.

Lord Corlys lay in state beneath the Iron Throne for seven days. Afterward his remains were carried back to Driftmark aboard the *Mermaid's Kiss,* captained by Marilda of Hull with her son Alyn. There the battered hull of the ancient *Sea Snake* was floated once again and towed out into the deep waters east of Dragonstone, where Corlys Velaryon was buried at sea aboard the very ship that had given him his name. It was said afterward that as the hull went down, the Cannibal swept overhead, his great black wings spread in a last salute. (A moving touch, but most likely a later embroidery. From all we know of the Cannibal, he would have been more apt to eat the corpse than salute it.)

The baseborn Alyn of Hull, now Alyn Velaryon, had been the Sea Snake's chosen heir, but his succession was not uncontested. It will be recalled that in the time of King Viserys, a nephew of Lord Corlys, Ser Vaemond Velaryon, had put himself forward as the true heir to Driftmark. This rebellion cost him his head, but he left a wife and sons behind. Ser Vaemond had been the son of the elder of the Sea Snake's brothers. Five other nephews, sired by another brother, had claims as well. When they took their case before the sick and failing Viserys, they made the grievous mistake of questioning the legitimacy of his daughter's children. Viserys had their tongues removed for this insolence, though he let them keep their heads. Three of the "silent five" had died during the Dance, fighting for Aegon II against Rhaenyra . . . but two survived, together with Ser Vaemond's sons, and all came forward now, insisting that they had more right to Driftmark than "this bastard of Hull, whose mother was a mouse."

Ser Vaemond's sons Daemion and Daeron took their claim to the council in King's Landing. When the Hand and the regents ruled against them, they wisely chose to accept the decision and be reconciled with Lord Alyn, who rewarded them with lands on Driftmark on the condition that they contribute ships to his fleet. Their silent cousins chose a different course. "Lacking tongues with which to make their appeal, they preferred to argue with swords," says Mushroom. However, the plot to murder their young lord went awry when the guards at Castle Driftmark proved loyal to the Sea Snake's memory and his chosen heir. Ser Malentine was slain during the attempt; his brother captured. Condemned to death, Ser Rhogar saved his head by taking the black.

Alyn Velaryon, the bastard born of Mouse, was formally installed as Lord of the Tides and Master of Driftmark. Whereupon he set out for King's Landing to claim the Sea Snake's place amongst the regents. (Even as a boy, Lord Alyn never lacked for boldness.) The Hand thanked him and sent him home . . . understandably, as Alyn Velaryon was but sixteen in 132 AC. Lord Corlys's seat upon the council of regents had already been offered to an older and more seasoned man: Unwin Peake, Lord of Starpike, Lord of Dunstonbury, Lord of Whitegrove.

Ser Tyland had a far more pressing concern in 132 AC: the matter of succession. Whilst Lord Corlys had been old and frail, his sudden death had nonetheless served as a grim reminder that any man could die at any time, even seemingly healthy young kings like Aegon III. War, illness, accident . . . there were so many ways to die, and if the king should perish, who then would follow him?

"If he dies without an heir, we shall dance again, however much we may mislike the music," Lord Manfryd Mooton warned his fellow regents. Queen Jaehaera's claim was as strong as the king's, and stronger in the minds of some, but the notion of placing that sweet, simple, frightened child on the Iron Throne was madness, all agreed. King Aegon himself, when asked, put forward his cupbearer, Gaemon Palehair, reminding the regents that the boy had "been a king before." That was impossible as well.

In truth, there were only two claimants the realm was like to accept: the king's half-sisters Baela and Rhaena Targaryen, Prince Daemon's twin daughters by his first wife, Lady Laena Velaryon. The girls were now sixteen years of age, tall and slim and silver-haired, very much the darlings of the city. King Aegon seldom set foot outside the Red Keep after his coronation, and his little queen never left her own apartments, so for most of the past year, it had been Rhaena or Baela riding out to hunt or hawk, giving alms to the poor, receiving envoys and visiting lords with the King's Hand, serving as hostess at feasts (of which there were few), masques, and balls (of which there had been none as yet). The twins were the only Targaryens the people ever saw.

Yet even here, the council encountered difficulty and division. When Leowyn Corbray said, "Lady Rhaena would make a splendid queen," Ser Tyland pointed out that Baela had been the first from her mother's womb. "Baela is too wild," countered Ser Torrhen Manderly. "How can she rule the realm when she cannot rule herself?" Ser Willis Fell agreed. "It must be Rhaena. She has a dragon, her sister does not." When Lord Mooton answered, "Baela *flew* a dragon, Rhaena only has the hatchling," Roland Westerling replied, "Baela's dragon brought down our late king. There are many in the realm who will not have forgotten that. Crown her and we will rip all the old wounds open once again."

Yet it was Grand Maester Munkun who put an end to the debate when he said, "My lords, it makes no matter. They are both *girls*. Have we learned so little from the slaughter? We must abide by primogeniture, as the Great Council ruled in 101. The male claim comes before the female." Yet when Ser Tyland said, "And who is this male claimant, my lord? We seem to have killed them all," Munkun had no answer but to say he would research the issue. Thus the crucial question of succession remained unsettled.

This uncertainty did little to spare the twins from the fawning attentions of all the suitors, confidants, companions, and similar flatterers eager to befriend the king's presumed heirs, though the sisters reacted to these lickspittles in vastly different ways. Where Rhaena delighted in being the center of court life, Baela bristled at praise, and seemed to take pleasure in mocking and tormenting the suitors who fluttered around her like moths.

As young girls, the twins had been inseparable, and impossible to tell apart, but once parted, their experiences had shaped them in very different ways. In the Vale, Rhaena had enjoyed a life of comfort and privilege as Lady Jeyne's ward. Maids had brushed her hair and drawn her baths, whilst singers composed odes to her beauty and knights jousted for her favor. The same was true at King's Landing, where dozens of gallant young lords competed for her smiles, artists begged leave to draw or paint her, and the city's finest dressmakers sought the honor of making her gowns. And everywhere that Rhaena went came Morning, her young dragon, oft as not coiled about her shoulders like a stole.

Baela's time on Dragonstone had been more troubled, ending with fire and blood. By the time she came to court, she was as wild and willful a young woman as any in the realm. Rhaena was slender and graceful; Baela was lean and quick. Rhaena loved to dance; Baela lived to ride . . . and to fly, though that had been taken from her when her dragon died. She kept her silver hair cropped as short as a boy's, so it would not whip about her face when she was riding. Time and time again she would escape her ladies to seek adventure in the streets. She took part in drunken horse races along the Street of the Sisters, engaged in moonlight swims across the Blackwater Rush (whose powerful currents had been known to drown many a strong swimmer), drank with the gold cloaks in their barracks, wagered coin and sometimes clothing in the rat pits of Flea Bottom. Once she vanished for three days and refused to say where she had been when she returned.

Even more gravely, Baela had a taste for unsuitable companions. Like stray dogs, she brought them home with her to the Red Keep, insisting that they be given positions in the castle, or be made part of her own retinue. These pets of hers included a comely young juggler, a blacksmith's apprentice whose muscles she admired, a legless beggar she took pity on, a conjurer of cheap tricks she took for an actual sorcerer, a hedge knight's homely squire, even a pair of young girls from a brothel, twins, "like us, Rhae." Once she turned up with an entire troupe of mummers. Septa Amarys, who had been given charge of her religious and moral instruction, despaired of her, and even Septon Eustace could not seem to curb her wild ways. "The girl must be wed, and soon," he told the King's Hand, "else I fear that she may bring dishonor down upon House Targaryen, and shame His Grace, her brother."

Ser Tyland saw the sense in the septon's counsel . . . but there were perils as well. Baela did not lack for suitors. She was young, beautiful, healthy, wealthy, and of the highest birth; any lord in the Seven Kingdoms would be glad to take her for his wife. Yet the wrong choice could have grave consequences, for her husband would stand very close to the throne. An unscrupulous, venal, or overly ambitious mate might cause no end of war and woe. A score of possible candidates for Lady Baela's hand were considered by the regents. Lord Tully, Lord Blackwood, Lord Hightower (as yet unwed, though he had taken his father's widow as a paramour) were all put forth, as were a number of less likely choices, including Dalton Greyjoy (the Red Kraken boasted of having a hundred salt wives, but had never taken a rock wife), a younger brother of the Princess of Dorne, and even that rogue Racallio Ryndoon. All of them were ultimately discarded for one reason or another.

Finally the Hand and the council of regency decided to grant Lady Baela's hand in marriage to Thaddeus Rowan, Lord of Goldengrove. Rowan was no doubt a prudent choice. His second wife had died the year previous, and he was known to be seeking a suitable young maid to take her place. His virility was beyond question; he had fathered two sons on his first wife, and five more on his second. As he had no daughters, Baela would be the unquestioned mistress of his castle. His four youngest sons were still at home, and in need of a woman's hand. The fact that all Lord Rowan's offspring were male counted heavily in his favor; if he were to sire a son on Lady Baela, Aegon III would have a clear successor.

Lord Thaddeus was a bluff, hearty, cheerful man, well-liked and well-respected, a doting husband and a good father to his sons. He had fought for Queen Rhaenyra during the Dance, and had done so ably and with valor. He was proud without being arrogant, just in judgment but not vindictive, loyal to his friends, dutiful in religious matters without being excessively pious, untroubled by overweening ambition. Should the throne pass to Lady Baela, Lord Rowan would make the perfect consort, supporting her with all his strength and wisdom without seeking to dominate her or usurp her rightful place as ruler. Septon Eustace tells us that the regents were very pleased with the result of their deliberations.

Baela Targaryen, when informed of the match, did not share their pleasure. "Lord Rowan is forty years my senior, bald as a stone, with a belly that weighs more than I do," she purportedly told the King's Hand. Then she added, "I've bedded two of his sons. The eldest and thirdborn, I think it was. Not both at once, that would have been improper." Whether there is any truth to this we cannot say. Lady Baela was known to be deliberately provocative at times. If that was her purpose here, she was successful. The Hand sent her back to her rooms, posting guards at her door to make certain she remained there until the regents could convene.

Yet a day later, he discovered to his dismay that Baela had fled the castle by some secret means (later it was found she had climbed out a window, swapped clothes with a washerwoman, and walked out the front gate). By the time the hue and cry went up, she was halfway across Blackwater Bay, having hired a fisherman to carry her to Driftmark. There she sought out her cousin, the Lord of the Tides, and poured out her woes to him. A fortnight later, Alyn Velaryon and Baela Targaryen were married in the sept on Dragonstone. The bride was sixteen, the groom nearly seventeen.

Several of the regents, outraged, urged Ser Tyland to appeal to the High Septon for an annulment, but the Hand's own response was one of bemused resignation. Prudently, he had it put about that the marriage had been arranged by king and court, believing that it was Lady Baela's defiance that was the scandal rather than her choice of spouse. "The boy comes from noble blood," he assured the regents, "and I do not doubt that he will prove as loyal as his brother." Thaddeus Rowan's wounded pride was appeased by a betrothal to Floris Baratheon, a maid of fourteen years widely considered to be the prettiest of the "Four Storms," as Lord Borros's four daughters had become known. In her case, it was a misnomer. A sweet girl, if somewhat frivolous, she was to die in childbed two years later. The stormy marriage would prove to be the one made on Dragonstone, as the years would prove.

For the Hand and council of regents, Baela Targaryen's midnight flight across Blackwater Bay had confirmed all their doubts about her. "The girl is wild, willful, and wanton, as we feared," Ser Willis Fell declared mournfully, "and now she has tied herself to Lord Corlys's upjumped bastard. A snake for a sire, a mouse for a mother . . . is this to be our prince consort?" The regents were in agreement; Baela Targaryen could not be King Aegon's heir. "It must be Lady Rhaena," declared Mooton, "provided she is wed."

This time, at Ser Tyland's insistence, the girl herself was made a part of the discussions. Lady Rhaena proved to be as tractable as her sister had been willful. She would of course wed whomever the king and council wished, she allowed, though "it would please me if he was not so old he could not give me children, nor so fat that he would crush me when we are abed. So long as he is kind and gentle and noble, I know that I shall love him." When the Hand asked if she had any favorites amongst the lords and knights who had paid her suit, she confessed that she was "especially fond" of Ser Corwyn Corbray, whom she had first met in the Vale whilst a ward of Lady Arryn.

Ser Corwyn was far from an ideal choice. A second son, he had two daughters from a previous marriage. At thirty-two, he was a man, not a green boy. Yet House Corbray was ancient and honorable, Ser Corwyn a knight of such repute that his late father had given him Lady Forlorn, the Valyrian steel blade of the Corbrays. His brother Leowyn was the Protector of the Realm. That alone would have made it difficult for the regents to raise objection. And so the match was made: a quick betrothal, followed by a hasty wedding a fortnight later. (The Hand would have preferred a longer betrothal, but the regents felt it prudent for Rhaena to wed quickly, in the event that her sister was already with child.)

The twins were not the only ladies of the realm to wed in 132 AC. Later that same year, Benjicot Blackwood, Lord of Raventree, led a retinue up the kingsroad to Winterfell, to stand witness at the marriage of his aunt Alysanne to Lord Cregan Stark. With the North already in the grip of winter, the journey took thrice as long as expected. Half the riders lost their horses as the column struggled through howling snowstorms, and thrice Lord Blackwood's carts were attacked by bands of outlaws, who carried off much of the column's food and all the wedding gifts. The wedding itself was said to be splendid, however; Black Aly and her wolf pledged their troth before the heart tree in Winterfell's icy godswood. At the feast afterward, four-year-old Rickon, Lord Cregan's son by his first wife, sang a song for his new stepmother.

Lady Elenda Baratheon, the widow of Storm's End, also took a new husband that year. With Lord Borros dead and Royce an infant, Dornish incursions into the stormlands had grown more numerous, and the outlaws of the kingswood were proving troublesome. The widow felt the need of a man's strong hand to keep the peace. She chose Ser Steffon Connington, second son of the Lord of Griffin's Roost. Though twenty years younger than Lady Elenda, Connington had proved his valor during

Lord Borros's campaign against the Vulture King, and was said to be as fierce as he was handsome.

Elsewhere, men were more concerned with war than weddings. All along the Sunset Sea, the Red Kraken and his ironmen continued to raid and reave. Tyrosh, Myr, Lys, and the three-headed alliance of Braavos, Pentos, and Lorath battled one another across the Stepstones and the Disputed Lands, whilst the rogue kingdom of Racallio Ryndoon pinched shut the bottom of the narrow sea. In King's Landing, Duskendale, Maidenpool, and Gulltown, trade withered. Merchants and traders came howling to the king . . . who either refused to see them, or was not allowed to, depending on whose chronicle we trust. The spectre of famine loomed in the North, as Cregan Stark and his lords bannermen watched their food stores dwindle, whilst the Night's Watch turned back an ever-increasing number of wildling incursions from beyond the Wall.

Late that year, a dreadful contagion swept across the Three Sisters. The Winter Fever, as it was called, killed half the population of Sisterton. The surviving half, believing that the disease had come to their shores on a whaler from the Port of Ibben, rose up and butchered every Ibbenese sailor they could lay hands on, setting fire to their ships. It made no matter. When the disease crossed the Bite to White Harbor, the prayers of the septons and the potions of the maesters proved equally powerless against it. Thousands died, amongst them Lord Desmond Manderly. His splendid son Ser Medrick, the finest knight in the North, survived him by only four days before succumbing to the same affliction. As Ser Medrick had been childless, this had a further calamitous consequence, in that the lordship devolved upon his brother Ser Torrhen, who was thence forced to give up his place on the council of regents to take up the rule of White Harbor. That left four regents, where once there had been seven.

So many lords, both great and small, had perished during the Dance of the Dragons that the Citadel rightly names this time the Winter of the Widows. Never before or since in the history of the Seven Kingdoms have so many women wielded so much power, ruling in the place of their slain husbands, brothers, and fathers, for sons in swaddling clothes or still on the teat. Many of their stories have been collected in Archmaester Abelon's mammoth *When Women Ruled: Ladies of the Aftermath*. Though Abelon treats hundreds of widows, we must needs confine ourselves to fewer. Four such women played crucial parts in the history of the realm in late 132 and early 133 AC, whether for good or ill.

Foremost of these was Lady Johanna, the widow of Casterly Rock, who ruled the domains of House Lannister for her young son, Lord Loreon. She had appealed time and time again to Aegon III's Hand, her late lord husband's twin, for aid against the reavers, but none had been forthcoming. Desperate to protect her people, Lady Johanna at last donned a man's mail to lead the men of Lannisport and Casterly Rock against the foe. The songs tell of how she slew a dozen ironmen beneath the walls of Kayce, but those may be safely put aside as the work of drunken singers (Johanna carried a banner into battle, not a sword). Her courage did help inspire her westermen, however, for the raiders were soon routed and Kayce was saved. Amongst the dead was the Red Kraken's favorite uncle.

Lady Sharis Footly, the widow of Tumbleton, achieved a different sort of fame by her efforts to restore that shattered town. Ruling in the name of her infant son (half a year after Second Tumbleton, she had given birth to a lusty dark-haired boy whom she proclaimed her late lord husband's trueborn heir, though it was far more likely that the boy had been sired by Bold Jon Roxton), Lady Sharis pulled down the burned shells of shops and houses, rebuilt the town walls, buried the dead, planted wheat and barley and turnips in the fields where the camps had been, and even had the heads of the dragons Seasmoke and Vermithor cleaned and mounted and displayed in the town square, where travelers paid good coin to view them (a penny for a look, a star to touch them).

In Oldtown, relations between the High Septon and Lord Ormund's widow, the Lady Sam, continued to worsen when she ignored His High Holiness's command to remove herself from her stepson's bed and take vows as a silent sister as penance for her sins. Righteous in his wroth, the High Septon condemned the Dowager Lady of Oldtown as a shameless fornicator and forbade her to set foot in the Starry Sept until she had repented and sought forgiveness. Instead Lady Samantha mounted a warhorse and burst into the sept as His High Holiness was leading a prayer. When he demanded to know her purpose, Lady Sam replied that whilst he had forbidden her to set foot in the sept, he had said naught about her horse's hooves. Then she commanded her knights to bar the doors; if the sept was closed to her, it would be closed to all. Though he quaked and thundered and called down maledictions upon "this harlot on a horse," in the end the High Septon had no choice but to relent.

The fourth (and last, for our purposes) of these remarkable women emerged from the twisted towers and blasted keeps of Harrenhal, that vast ruin beside the water of the Gods Eye. Shunned and forgotten since Daemon Targaryen and his nephew Aemond had met there for their final flight, Black Harren's accursed seat had become a haunt of outlaws, robber knights, and broken men, who sallied forth from behind its walls to prey upon travelers, fisherfolk, and farmers. A year ago, they had been few, but of late their numbers had grown, and it was being said that a sorceress ruled over them, a witch queen of fearsome power. When these tales reached King's Landing, Ser Tyland decided it was time to reclaim the castle. This task he entrusted to a knight of the Kingsguard, Ser Regis Groves, who set out from the city with half a hundred seasoned men. At Castle Darry, he was joined by Ser Damon Darry with a like number. Rashly, Ser Regis assumed this would be more than sufficient to deal with a few squatters.

Arriving before the walls of Harrenhal, however, he found the gates closed and hundreds of armed men on the battlements. There were at least six hundred souls within the castle, a third of them men of fighting age. When Ser Regis demanded to speak to their lord, a woman emerged to treat with him, with a child beside her. The "witch queen" of Harrenhal proved to be none other than Alys Rivers, the baseborn wet nurse who had been the prisoner and then the paramour of Prince Aemond Targaryen, and now claimed to be his widow. The boy was Aemond's, she told the knight. "His bastard?" said Ser Regis. "His trueborn son and heir," Alys Rivers spat back, "and the rightful king of Westeros." She commanded the knight to "kneel before your king" and swear him his sword. Ser Regis laughed at this, saying, "I do not kneel to bastards, much less the baseborn whelp of a kinslayer and a milk cow."

What happened next remains a matter of some dispute. Some say that Alys Rivers merely raised a hand, and Ser Regis began to scream and clutch his head, until his skull burst apart, spraying blood and brains. Others insist the widow's gesture was a signal, at which a crossbowman on the battlements let fly a bolt that took Ser Regis through an eye. Mushroom (who was hundreds of leagues away) has suggested that perhaps one of the men on the walls was skilled in the use of a sling. Soft lead balls, when slung with sufficient force, have been known to cause the sort of explosive effect that Groves's men saw and attributed to sorcery.

Whatever the case, Ser Regis Groves was dead in an instant. Half a heartbeat later, the gates of Harrenhal burst open, and a swarm of howling riders charged forth. A bloody fight ensued. The king's men were put to rout. Ser Damon Darry, being well-horsed, well-armored, and well-trained, was one of the few to escape. The witch queen's minions hunted him all through the night before abandoning the chase. Some thirty-two men lived to return to Castle Darry, of the hundred that had set out.

The next day, a thirty-third made his appearance. Having been captured with a dozen others, he had been forced to watch them die by torture one by one before being turned loose to deliver a warning. "I'm to tell you what she said," he gasped, "but you can't laugh. The widow put a curse on me. Any man o' you laughs, I die." When Ser Damon assured him that no one was going to laugh at him, the messenger said, "Don't come again unless you mean to bend your knees, she says. Any man who comes near her walls will die. There's power in them stones, and the widow's woken it. Seven save us all, she has a *dragon*. I seen it."

The name of the messenger is lost to us, along with the name of the man who laughed. But someone did, one of Lord Darry's men. The messenger looked at him, stricken, then clutched at his throat and began to wheeze. Unable to draw breath, he was dead in moments. Supposedly the imprints of a woman's fingers could be seen upon his skin, as if she had been in the room, choking him.

The death of a Kingsguard knight was greatly troubling to Ser Tyland, though Unwin Peake discounted Ser Damon Darry's talk of sorcery and dragons and put down the death of Regis Groves and his men to outlaws. The other regents concurred. A stronger force would be required to root them out of Harrenhal, they concluded as that "peaceful" year of 132

AC came to its end. But before Ser Tyland could organize such an assault, or even consider who might take Ser Regis's place in Aegon's Seven, a threat far worse than any "witch queen" descended on the city. For on the third day of 133 AC, Winter Fever arrived in King's Landing.

Whether or not the fever had been born in the dark forests of Ib and brought to Westeros by a whaler, as the Sistermen believed, it was assuredly moving from port to port. White Harbor, Gulltown, Maidenpool, and Duskendale had been afflicted, each in turn; there were reports that Braavos was being ravaged as well. The first sign of the disease was a red flush of the face, easily mistaken for the bright red cheeks that many men exhibit after exposure to the frosty air of a cold winter's day. But fever followed, slight at first, but rising, ever rising. Bleeding did not help, nor garlic, nor any of the various potions, poultices, and tinctures that were tried. Packing the afflicted in tubs of snow and icy water seemed to slow the course of the fever, but did not halt it, those maesters who grappled with the disease soon found. By the second day the victim would begin to shiver violently and complain of being cold, though he might feel burning hot to the touch. On the third day came delirium and bloody sweats. By the fourth day the man was dead . . . or on the path to recovery, should the fever break. Only one man in four survived the Winter Fever. Not since the Shivers ravaged Westeros during the reign of Jaehaerys I had such a terrible pestilence been seen in the Seven Kingdoms.

In King's Landing, the first signs of the fatal flush were seen along the riverside amongst the sailors, ferrymen, fishermongers, dockers, stevedores, and wharfside whores who plied their trades beside the Blackwater Rush. Before most had even realized they were ill, they had spread the contagion throughout every part of the city, to rich and poor alike. When word reached court, Grand Maester Munkun went himself to examine some of those afflicted, to ascertain whether this was indeed the Winter Fever and not some lesser illness. Alarmed by what he saw, Munkun did not return to the castle, for fear that he himself might have been afflicted by his close contact with twoscore feverish whores and dockers. Instead he sent his acolyte with an urgent letter to the King's Hand. Ser Tyland acted immediately, commanding the gold cloaks to close the city and see that no one entered or left until the fever had run its course. He ordered the great gates of the Red Keep barred as well, to keep the disease from king and court.

The Winter Fever had no respect for gates or guards or castle walls, alas. Though the fever seemed to have grown somewhat less potent as it moved south, tens of thousands turned feverish in the days that followed. Three-quarters of those died. Grand Maester Munkun proved to be one of the fortunate fourth and recovered . . . but Ser Willis Fell, Lord Commander of the Kingsguard, was struck down. The Lord Protector, Leowyn Corbray, retired to his chambers when stricken and tried to cure himself with hot mulled wine. He died, along with his mistress and several of his servants. Two of Queen Jaehaera's maids grew feverish and succumbed, though the little queen herself remained hale and healthy. The Commander of the City Watch died. Nine days later, his successor followed him into the grave. Nor were the regents spared. Lord Westerling and Lord Mooton both grew ill. Lord Mooton's fever broke and he survived, though much weakened. Roland Westerling, an older man, perished.

One death may have been a mercy. The Dowager Queen Alicent of House Hightower, second wife of King Viserys I and mother to his sons, Aegon, Aemond, and Daeron, and his daughter Helaena, died on the same night as Lord Westerling, after confessing her sins to her septa. She had outlived all of her children and spent the last year of her life confined to her apartments, with no company but her septa, the serving girls who brought her food, and the guards outside her door. Books were given her, and needles and thread, but her guards said Alicent spent more time weeping than reading or sewing. One day she ripped all her clothing into pieces. By the end of the year she had taken to talking to herself, and had come to have a deep aversion to the color green.

In her last days the Queen Dowager seemed to become more lucid. "I want to see my sons again," she told her septa, "and Helaena, my sweet girl, oh . . . and King Jaehaerys. I will read to him, as I did when I was little. He used to say I had a lovely voice." (Strangely, in her final hours Queen Alicent spoke often of the Old King, but never of her husband,

King Viserys.) The Stranger came for her on a rainy night, at the hour of the wolf.

All these deaths were recorded faithfully by Septon Eustace, who takes care to give us the inspiring last words of every great lord and noble lady. Mushroom names the dead as well, but spends more time on the follies of the living, such as the homely squire who convinced a pretty bedmaid to yield her virtue to him by telling her he had the flush and "in four days I will be dead, and I would not die without ever knowing love." The ploy proved so successful that he returned to it with six other girls . . . but when he failed to die, they began to talk, and his scheme unraveled. Mushroom attributes his own survival to drink. "If I drank sufficient wine, I reasoned I might never know I was sick, and every fool knows that the things you do not know will never hurt you."

During those dark days, two unlikely heroes came briefly to the fore. One was Orwyle, whose gaolers freed him from his cell after many other maesters had been laid low by the fever. Old age, fear, and long confinement had left him a shell of the man that he had been, and his cures and potions proved no more efficacious than those of other maesters, yet Orwyle worked tirelessly to save those he could and ease the passing of those he could not.

The other hero, to the astonishment of all, was the young king. To the horror of his Kingsguard, Aegon spent his days visiting the sick, and often sat with them for hours, sometimes holding their hands in his own, or soothing their fevered brows with cool, damp cloths. Though His Grace seldom spoke, he shared his silences with them, and listened as they told him stories of their lives, begged him for forgiveness, or boasted of conquests, kindnesses, and children. Most of those he visited died, but those who lived would afterward attribute their survival to the touch of the king's "healing hands."

Yet if indeed there is some magic in a king's touch, as many smallfolk believe, it failed when it was needed most. The last bedside visited by Aegon III was that of Ser Tyland Lannister. Through the city's darkest days, Ser Tyland had remained in the Tower of the Hand, striving day and night against the Stranger. Though blind and maimed, he suffered no more than exhaustion almost to the last . . . but as cruel fate would have it, when the worst was past and new cases of the Winter Fever had dropped away to almost nothing, a morning came when Ser Tyland commanded his serving man to close a window. "It is very cold in here," he said . . . though the fire in the hearth was blazing, and the window was already closed.

The Hand declined quickly after that. The fever took his life in two days instead of the usual four. Septon Eustace was with him when he died, as was the boy king that he had served. Aegon took his hand as he breathed his last.

Ser Tyland Lannister had never been beloved. After the death of Queen Rhaenyra, he had urged Aegon II to put her son Aegon to death as well, and certain blacks hated him for that. Yet after the death of Aegon II, he had remained to serve Aegon III, and certain greens hated him for that. Coming second from his mother's womb, a few heartbeats after his twin brother, Jason, had denied him the glory of lordship and the gold of Casterly Rock, leaving him to make his own place in the world. Ser Tyland

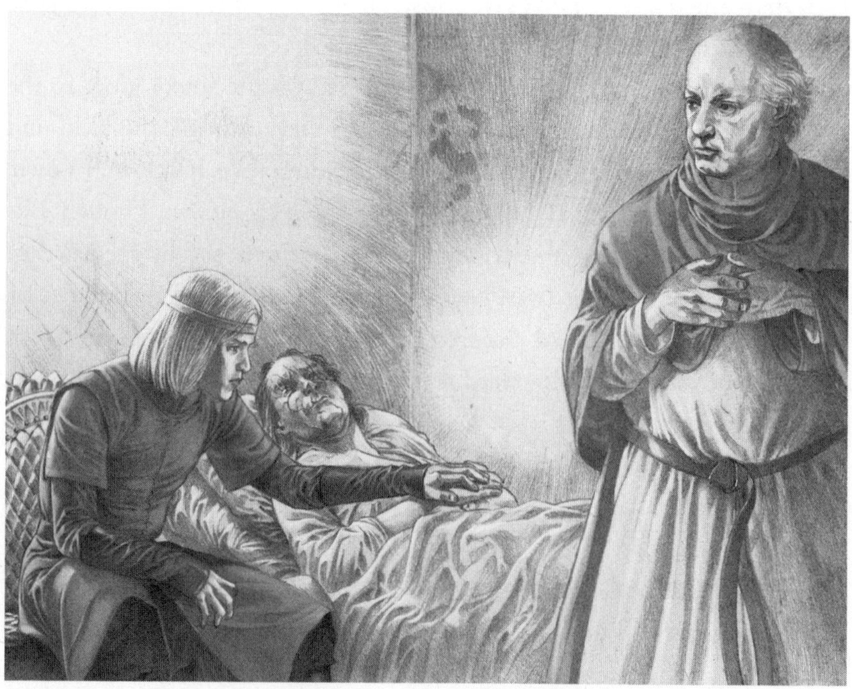

never married nor fathered children, so there were few to mourn him when he was carried off. The veil he wore to conceal his disfigured face gave rise to the tale that the visage underneath was monstrous and evil. Some called him craven for keeping Westeros out of the Daughters' War and doing so little to curb the Greyjoys in the west. By moving three-quarters of the Crown's gold from King's Landing whilst Aegon II's master of coin, Tyland Lannister had sown the seeds of Queen Rhaenyra's downfall, a stroke of cunning that would in the end cost him his eyes, ears, and health, and cost the queen her throne and her very life. Yet it must be said that he served Rhaenyra's son well and faithfully as Hand.

Under the Regents

War and Peace and Cattle Shows

King Aegon III was still a boy, well shy of his thirteenth nameday, but in the days following the death of Ser Tyland Lannister he displayed a maturity beyond his years. Passing over Ser Marston Waters, second in command of the Kingsguard, His Grace bestowed white cloaks upon Ser Robin Massey and Ser Robert Darklyn and made Massey Lord Commander. With Grand Maester Munkun still down in the city tending to victims of the Winter Fever, His Grace turned to his predecessor, instructing the former Grand Maester Orwyle to summon Lord Thaddeus Rowan to the city. "I would have Lord Rowan as my Hand. Ser Tyland thought well enough of him to offer him my sister's hand in marriage, so I know he can be trusted." He wanted Baela back at court as well. "Lord Alyn shall be my admiral, as his grandsire was." Orwyle, mayhaps hopeful of a royal pardon, hurriedly sent the ravens on their way.

King Aegon had acted without consulting his council of regents, however. Only three remained in King's Landing: Lord Peake, Lord Mooton, and Grand Maester Munkun, who came rushing back inside the Red Keep the moment Ser Robert Darklyn commanded that its gates be opened once again. Manfryd Mooton was bedridden, still recovering his strength after his battle with the fever, and asked that any decisions be postponed until Lady Jeyne Arryn and Lord Royce Caron could be summoned back from the Vale and the Dornish Marches to take part in the deliberations. His colleagues would have none of it, however, Lord Peake insisting that the former regents had given up their places on the council by departing King's Landing. With the Grand Maester's support (Munkun would later come to rue his acquiescence), Unwin Peake then set aside all of the king's appointments and arrangements, on the grounds that no boy of twelve had the judgment to decide such weighty matters himself.

Marston Waters was confirmed as Lord Commander of the Kingsguard, whilst Darklyn and Massey were commanded to surrender their white cloaks, so that Ser Marston might bestow them on knights of his own choosing. Grand Maester Orwyle was returned to his cell, to await execution. So as not to offend Lord Rowan, the regents offered him a place amongst them, and the office of justiciar and master of laws. No similar gesture was made to Alyn Velaryon, but of course there was no question of such a boy of his years, and of such uncertain lineage, serving as lord admiral. The offices of King's Hand and Protector of the Realm, previously separate, were now combined, and filled by none other than Unwin Peake himself.

Mushroom tells us that King Aegon III reacted to the decisions of his regents with a sullen silence, speaking only once, to protest the dismissal of Massey and Darklyn. "Kingsguard serve for life," the boy said, to which Lord Peake replied, "Only when they have been properly appointed, Your Grace." Elsewise, Septon Eustace tells us, the king received the decrees "courteously" and thanked Lord Peake for his wisdom, as "I am still a boy, as your lordship knows, and in want of instruction in these matters." If his true feelings were otherwise, Aegon did not choose to voice them, but instead retreated back into silence and passivity.

For the remainder of his minority, King Aegon III took little part in the rule of his realm, save for fixing his signature and seal upon such papers as Lord Peake presented him. On certain formal occasions, His Grace would be brought out to sit the Iron Throne or welcome an envoy, but elsewise he was little seen inside the Red Keep, and never beyond its walls.

It behooves us now to pause for a moment and turn our gaze upon

Unwin Peake, who would rule the Seven Kingdoms in all but name for the best part of two years, serving as Lord Regent, Protector of the Realm, and Hand of the King.

His house was amongst the oldest in the Reach, its deep roots twisting back to the Age of Heroes and the First Men. Amongst his many illustrious ancestors, his lordship could count such legends as Ser Urrathon the Shieldsmasher, Lord Meryn the Scribe, Lady Yrma of the Golden Bowl, Ser Barquen the Besieger, Lord Eddison the Elder, Lord Eddison the Younger, and Lord Emerick the Avenger. Many Peakes had served as counselors at Highgarden when the Reach was the richest and most powerful kingdom in all Westeros. When the pride and power of House Manderly became overweening, it was Lorimar Peake who humbled them and drove them into exile in the North, for which service King Perceon III Gardener granted him the former Manderly seat at Dunstonbury and its attendant lands. King Perceon's son Gwayne took Lord Lorimar's daughter as his bride as well, making her the seventh Peake maiden to sit beneath the Green Hand as Queen of All the Reach. Through the centuries, other daughters of House Peake had married Redwynes, Rowans, Costaynes, Oakhearts, Osgreys, Florents, even Hightowers.

All this had ended with the coming of the dragons. Lord Armen Peake and his sons had perished on the Field of Fire beside King Mern and his. With House Gardener extinguished, Aegon the Conqueror had granted Highgarden and the rule of the Reach to House Tyrell, the former royal stewards. The Tyrells had no blood ties to the Peakes, and no reason to favor them. And thus the slow fall of this proud house had begun. A century later, the Peakes still held three castles, and their lands were wide and well-peopled, if not particularly rich, but no longer did they command pride of place amongst the bannermen of Highgarden.

Unwin Peake was determined to redress that, and restore House Peake to its former greatness. Like his father, who had sided with the majority at the Great Council of 101, he did not believe it was a woman's place to rule over men. During the Dance of the Dragons, Lord Unwin had been amongst the fiercest of the greens, leading forth a thousand swords and spears to keep Aegon II on the Iron Throne. When Ormund Hightower fell at Tumbleton, Lord Unwin believed command of his host should have come to him, but this was denied him by scheming rivals. This he never forgave, stabbing the turncloak Owain Bourney and plotting the murders of the dragonriders Hugh Hammer and Ulf White. Foremost of the Caltrops (though this was not widely known), and one of only three still living, Lord Unwin had proved at Tumbleton that he was no man to trifle with. He would prove that again in King's Landing.

Having elevated Ser Marston Waters to command of the Kingsguard, Lord Peake now prevailed upon him to confer white cloaks on two of his own kin, his nephew Ser Amaury Peake of Starpike, and his bastard brother Ser Mervyn Flowers. The City Watch was placed under the command of Ser Lucas Leygood, the son of one of the Caltrops who had died at Tumbleton. To replace the men who had died during the Winter Fever and the Moon of Madness, the Hand bestowed gold cloaks on five hundred of his own men.

Lord Peake did not have a trusting nature, and all he had seen (and been a part of) at Tumbleton had convinced him that his enemies would bring him down if given half a chance. Ever mindful of his own safety, he surrounded himself with his own personal guard, ten sellswords loyal only to him (and the gold he lavished on them) who in due course became known as his "Fingers." Their captain, a Volantene adventurer named Tessario, had tiger stripes tattooed across his face and back, the marks of a slave soldier. Men called him Tessario the Tiger to his face, which pleased him; behind his back, they called him Tessario the Thumb, the mocking sobriquet that Mushroom had bestowed upon him.

Once secure in his own person, the new Hand began bringing his own supporters, kin, and friends to court, in place of men and women whose loyalty was less assured. His widowed aunt Clarice Osgrey was put in charge of Queen Jaehaera's household, supervising her maids and servants. Ser Gareth Long, master-at-arms at Starpike, was granted the same title at the Red Keep and tasked with training King Aegon for knighthood. George Graceford, Lord of Holyhall, and Ser Victor Risley, Knight of Risley Glade, the sole surviving Caltrops aside from Lord Peake himself, were appointed Lord Confessor and King's Justice respectively.

The Hand even went so far as to dismiss Septon Eustace, bringing in a younger man, Septon Bernard, to tend to the spiritual needs of the court and supervise His Grace's religious and moral instruction. Bernard too was of his blood, being descended from a younger sister of his great-grandsire. Once relieved of his duties, Septon Eustace departed King's Landing for Stoney Sept, the town of his birth, where he devoted himself to the writing of his great (if somewhat turgid) work, *The Reign of King Viserys, First of His Name, and the Dance of the Dragons That Came After*. Sadly, Septon Bernard preferred composing sacred music to setting down court gossip, and his writings are therefore of little interest to historians and scholars (and of less interest to those who find pleasure in sacred music, it grieves us to say).

None of these changes pleased the young king. His Grace was especially unhappy with his Kingsguard. He neither liked nor trusted the two new men, and had not forgotten the presence of Ser Marston Waters at his mother's death. King Aegon misliked the Hand's Fingers even more, if that is possible, especially their brash and foul-mouthed commander, Tessario the Thumb. That mislike turned to hatred when the Volantene slew Ser Robin Massey, one of the young knights that Aegon had wished to name to his Kingsguard, in a quarrel over a horse both men wished to buy.

The king soon developed a strong antipathy for his new master-at-arms as well. Ser Gareth Long was a skilled swordsman but a stern taskmaster, renowned at Starpike for his harshness toward the boys he instructed. Those who did not meet his standards were made to go for days without sleep, doused in tubs of iced water, had their heads shaved, and were oft beaten. None of these punishments were available to Ser Gareth in his new position. Though Aegon was a sullen student who displayed little interest in swordplay or the arts of war, his royal person was inviolate. Whenever Ser Gareth spoke to him too loudly or too harshly, the king would simply throw down his sword and shield and walk away.

Aegon seemed to have only one companion he cared about. Gaemon Palehair, his six-year-old cupbearer and food taster, not only shared all of the king's meals, but oft accompanied him to the yard, as Ser Gareth did not fail to note. As a bastard born of a whore, Gaemon counted for little in the court, so when Ser Gareth asked Lord Peake to make the lad the king's whipping boy, the Hand was pleased to do so. Thereafter any misbehavior, laziness, or truculence on King Aegon's part resulted in

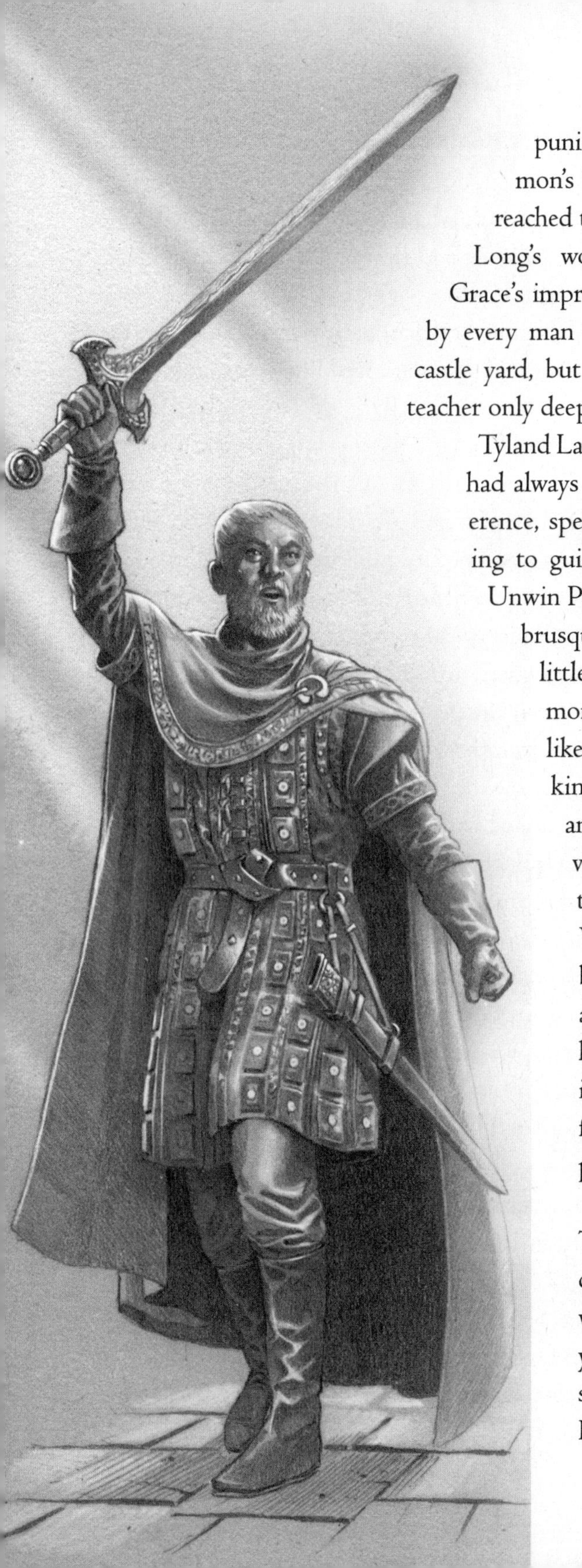

punishment for his friend. Gaemon's blood and Gaemon's tears reached the king as none of Gareth Long's words ever had, and His Grace's improvement was soon marked by every man who watched him in the castle yard, but the king's mislike of his teacher only deepened.

Tyland Lannister, blind and crippled, had always treated the king with deference, speaking to him gently, seeking to guide rather than command. Unwin Peake made a sterner Hand; brusque and hard, he showed little patience with the young monarch, treating him "more like a sulky boy than like a king" in Mushroom's words, and making no effort to involve His Grace in the day-to-day rule of his kingdom. When Aegon III retreated back into silence, solitude, and a brooding passivity, his Hand was pleased to ignore him, save on certain formal occasions when his presence was required.

Rightly or wrongly, Ser Tyland Lannister was perceived as having been a weak and ineffectual Hand, yet somehow also sinister, scheming, even monstrous. Lord Unwin Peake came to the Handship determined to demonstrate his strength and rectitude. "This Hand is not blind, nor veiled, nor crippled," he announced before king and court. "This Hand can still wield a sword." And so saying, he drew his longsword from its scabbard and raised it high so all might see it. Whispers flew about the hall. It was no common blade that his lordship held, but one forged of Valyrian steel: Orphan-Maker, last seen in the hands of Bold Jon Roxton as he laid about at Hard Hugh Hammer's men in a yard at Tumbleton.

The Feast Day of Our Father Above is a most propitious day for making judgments, the septons teach us. In 133 AC, the new Hand decreed that it should be a day when those who had previously been judged would at last be punished for their crimes. The city gaols were crowded to bursting, and even the deep dungeons below the Red Keep were near full. Lord Unwin emptied them. The prisoners were marched or dragged out to the square before the Red Keep's gates, where thousands of Kingslanders gathered to see them receive their due. With the somber young king and his stern Hand looking down from the battlements, the King's Justice set to work. As there was too much work for one sword alone, Tessario the Thumb and his Fingers were tasked with aiding him.

"It would have gone more quickly if the Hand had sent to the Street of Flies for butchers," Mushroom observes, "for it was butcher's work they were about, hacking and cleaving." Forty thieves had their hands removed. Eight rapers were gelded, then marched naked to the riverside with their genitals hung about their necks, to be put aboard ships for the Wall. A suspected Poor Fellow who preached that the Seven sent the Winter Fever to punish House Targaryen for incest had his tongue removed. Two pox-riddled whores were mutilated in unspeakable ways for passing the pox to dozens of men. Six servants found guilty of stealing from their masters had their noses slit; a seventh, who cut a hole in a wall to peek upon his master's daughters in their nakedness, had the offending eye plucked out as well.

Next came the murderers. Seven were brought forth, one an innkeep who had been killing certain of his guests (those he judged would not be missed) and stealing their valuables since the Old King's time. Where the other murderers were hanged straightaway, he had his hands hacked off and burned before his eyes, then he was hung by a noose and disemboweled as he strangled.

Last came the three most prominent prisoners, the ones that the mob had been waiting for: yet another "Shepherd Reborn," the captain of a Pentoshi merchantman who had been accused and found guilty of bringing the Winter Fever from Sisterton to King's Landing, and the former Grand Maester Orwyle, a convicted traitor and a deserter from the Night's Watch. The King's Justice, Ser Victor Risley, attended to each of them himself. He removed the heads of the Pentoshi and the false Shepherd with his headsman's axe, but Grand Maester Orwyle was granted the honor of dying by the sword, in view of his age, high birth, and long service.

"When Our Father's Feast was done and the mob before the gates dispersed, the King's Hand was well satisfied," wrote Septon Eustace, who would depart for Stoney Sept the next day. "Would that I could write that the smallfolk returned to their homes and hovels to fast and pray and beg forgiveness for their own sins, but that would be far from the truth. Flush with blood, they sought out dens of sin instead, and the city's alehouses, wine sinks, and brothels were crowded unto bursting, for such is the wickedness of men." Mushroom says the same, though in his own way. "Whenever I see a man put to death, I like to have a flagon and a woman afterward, to remind myself that I am still alive."

King Aegon III stood atop the gatehouse battlements throughout the Feast of Our Father Above, and never spoke nor looked away from the bloodletting below. "The king had as well been made of wax," observed Septon Eustace. Grand Maester Munkun echoes him. "His Grace was present, as was his duty, yet somehow he seemed far away as well. Some of the condemned turned to the battlements to shout out cries for mercy, but the king never seemed to see them, nor hear their desperate words. Make no mistake. This feast was served to us by the Hand, and 'twas he who gorged upon it."

By midyear the castle, city, and king were all firmly in the grasp of the new Hand. The smallfolk were quiet, the Winter Fever had receded, Queen Jaehaera hid in seclusion in her chambers, King Aegon trained in the yard by morning and stared at the stars by night. Beyond the walls of

King's Landing, however, the woes that had afflicted the realm these past two years had only worsened. Trade had withered away to nothing, war continued in the west, famine and fever ruled much of the North, and to the south the Dornishmen were growing bolder and more troublesome. It was past time the Iron Throne showed its power, Lord Peake decided.

Construction had been completed on eight of the ten great warships commissioned by Ser Tyland, so the Hand resolved to begin by opening the narrow sea to trade once more. To command the royal fleet, he tapped another uncle, Ser Gedmund Peake, a seasoned battler known as Gedmund Great-Axe for his favored weapon. Though justly renowned for his prowess as a warrior, Ser Gedmund had little knowledge or experience of ships, however, so his lordship also summoned the notorious sellsail Ned Bean (called Blackbean, for his thick black beard) to serve as the Great-Axe's second-in-command and advise him on all matters nautical.

The situation in the Stepstones as Ser Gedmund and Blackbean set sail was chaotic, to say the least. Racallio Ryndoon's ships had been swept from the sea for the most part, but he still ruled Bloodstone, largest of the islands, and a few smaller rocks. The Tyroshi had been on the point of overwhelming him when Lys and Myr had made peace and launched a joint attack on Tyrosh, forcing the Archon to recall his ships and swords. The three-headed alliance of Braavos, Pentos, and Lorath had lost one of its heads with the withdrawal of the Lorathi, but the Pentoshi sellswords now held all the Stepstones not in the hands of Racallio's men, and the Braavosi warships owned the waters between.

Westeros could not hope to prevail in a sea war against Braavos, Lord Unwin knew. His purpose, he declared, was to put an end to the rogue Racallio Ryndoon and his piratical kingdom and establish a presence upon Bloodstone, to ensure that never again could the narrow sea be closed. The royal fleet—comprised of the eight new warships and some twenty older cogs and galleys—was nowise large enough to accomplish this, so the Hand wrote to Driftmark, instructing the Lord of the Tides to gather "your lord grandsire's fleets and put them under the command of our good uncle Gedmund, so that he may open the sea roads once again."

This was no more than Alyn Velaryon had long desired, as the Sea Snake had before him, though when he read the message the young lord bristled and declared, "They are my fleets now, and Baela's monkey is more suited to command them than Nuncle Gedmund." Even so, he did as he was bid, bringing together sixty war galleys, thirty longships, and more than a hundred cogs and great cogs to meet the royal fleet as it swept out from King's Landing. As the great war fleet passed through the Gullet, Ser Gedmund sent over Blackbean to Lord Alyn's flagship, *Queen Rhaenys,* with a letter authorizing him to take command of the Velaryon squadrons, "so that they may benefit from his many years of experience." Lord Alyn sent him back. "I would have hanged him," he wrote to Ser Gedmund, "but I am loath to waste good hempen rope on a bean."

In winter, strong north winds oft prevail upon the narrow sea, so the fleet made splendid time on its voyage south. Off Tarth, another dozen longships rowed out to further swell their ranks, commanded by Lord Bryndemere the Evenstar. The tidings that his lordship brought proved less welcome, however. The Sealord of Braavos, the Archon of Tyrosh, and Racallio Ryndoon had made common cause; they would rule the Stepstones jointly, and only such ships as were licensed to trade by Braavos or Tyrosh would be allowed to pass. "What of Pentos?" Lord Alyn wanted to know. "Discarded," the Evenstar informed him. "A pie split three ways offers larger slices than one cut into quarters."

Gedmund Great-Axe (who had been so seasick during the voyage that the sailors had named him Gedmund Green-Sick) decided that the King's Hand should be informed of this new alignment amongst the warring cities. The Evenstar had already sent a raven to King's Landing, so Peake decreed that the fleet would remain at Tarth until a reply was received. "That will lose us any hope of taking Racallio by surprise," argued Alyn Velaryon, but Ser Gedmund proved adamant. The two commanders parted angrily.

The next day when the sun rose, Blackbean woke Ser Gedmund to inform him that the Lord of the Tides was gone. The entire Velaryon fleet had slipped off during the night. Gedmund Great-Axe snorted. "Run back to Driftmark, I'd venture," he said. Ned Bean agreed, calling Lord Alyn "a scared boy."

They could not have been more wrong. Lord Alyn had taken his ships south, not north. Three days later, whilst Gedmund Great-Axe and his royal fleet still lingered off the coast of Tarth waiting on a raven, battle was joined amongst the rocks, sea stacks, and tangled waterways of the Stepstones. The attack caught the Braavosi unawares, with their grand admiral and twoscore of his captains feasting on Bloodstone with Racallio Ryndoon and the envoys from Tyrosh. Half of the Braavosi ships were taken, burned, or sunk whilst still at anchor or tied to a dock, others as they raised sail and tried to get under way.

The fight was not entirely bloodless. The *Grand Defiance*, a towering Braavosi dromond of four hundred oars, fought her way past half a dozen smaller Velaryon warships to gain the open sea, only to find Lord Alyn himself bearing down on her. Too late, the Braavosi tried to turn to face her attacker, but the huge dromond was ponderous in the water and slow to answer, and *Queen Rhaenys* struck her broadside with every oar churning water.

The *Queen*'s prow smashed into the side of the great Braavosi ship "like a great oaken fist," one observer wrote later, splintering her oars, crashing through her planks and hull, toppling her masts, cutting the massive dromond almost in two. When Lord Alyn shouted to his rowers to back them off, the sea rushed into the gaping wound the *Queen* had made, and the *Grand Defiance* went down in mere moments, "and with it, the Sealord's swollen pride."

Alyn Velaryon's victory was complete. He lost three ships in the Stepstones (one, sadly, was the *True Heart,* captained by his cousin Daeron, who perished when she sank), whilst sinking more than thirty and capturing six galleys, eleven cogs, eighty-nine hostages, vast amounts of food, drink, arms, and coin, and an elephant meant for the Sealord's menagerie. All this the Lord of the Tides brought back to Westeros, along with the name that he would carry for the rest of his long life: Oakenfist. When Lord Alyn sailed *Queen Rhaenys* up the Blackwater Rush and rode in through the River Gate on the back of the Sealord's elephant, tens of thousands lined the city streets shouting his name and clamoring for a glimpse of their new hero. At the gates of the Red Keep, King Aegon III himself appeared to welcome him.

Once within the walls, however, it was a different story. By the time Alyn Oakenfist reached the throne room, the young king had somehow vanished. Instead Lord Unwin Peake scowled down at him from atop the Iron Throne, and said, "You fool, you thrice-damned fool. If I dared, I would have your bloody head off."

The Hand had good cause to be so wroth. However loudly the mob might cheer for Oakenfist, their bold young hero's rash attack had left the realm in an untenable position. Lord Velaryon might have captured a score of Braavosi ships and an elephant, but he had not taken Bloodstone, nor any of the other Stepstones; the knights and men-at-arms such a conquest would have required had been aboard the larger ships of the royal fleet that he abandoned off the shores of Tarth. The destruction of Racallio Ryndoon's pirate kingdom had been Lord Peake's objective; instead, Racallio appeared to have emerged stronger than ever. The last thing the Hand desired was war with Braavos, richest and most powerful of the

Nine Free Cities. "Yet that is what you have given us, my lord," Peake thundered. "You have given us a war."

"And an elephant," Lord Alyn answered insolently. "Pray, do not forget the elephant, my lord."

The remark drew nervous titters even from Lord Peake's own handpicked men, Mushroom tells us, but the Hand was not amused. "He was not a man who liked to laugh himself," the dwarf says, "and he liked being laughed at even less."

Though other men might fear to provoke Lord Unwin's enmity, Alyn Oakenfist was secure in his own strength. Though barely a man grown, and bastard born as well, he was wed to the king's half-sister, had all the power and wealth of House Velaryon at his command, and had just become the darling of the smallfolk. Lord Regent or no, Unwin Peake was not so mad as to imagine he could safely harm the hero of the Stepstones.

"All young men suspect they are immortal," Grand Maester Munkun writes in the *True Telling,* "and whenever a young warrior tastes the heady wine of victory, suspicion becomes certainty. Yet the confidence of youth counts for little against the cunning of age. Lord Alyn might smile at the Hand's rebukes, but he would soon be given good reason to dread the Hand's rewards."

Munkun knew whereof he wrote. Seven days after the triumphant return of Lord Alyn to King's Landing, he was honored in a lavish ceremony in the Red Keep, with King Aegon III seated on the Iron Throne and the court and half the city looking on. Ser Marston Waters, Lord Commander of the Kingsguard, dubbed him a knight. Unwin Peake, Lord Regent and Hand of the King, draped an admiral's golden chain about his neck and presented him with a silver replica of the *Queen Rhaenys* as a token of his victory. The king himself inquired if his lordship would consent to serve upon his small council, as master of ships. Lord Alyn humbly agreed.

"Then the Hand's fingers closed about his throat," says Mushroom. "The voice was Aegon's, the words Unwin's." His leal subjects in the west had long been troubled by reavers from the Iron Islands, the young king declared, and who better to bring peace to the Sunset Sea than his new admiral? And Alyn Oakenfist, that proud and headstrong youth, found he had no choice but to agree to sail his fleets around the southern end of Westeros to win back Fair Isle and end the menace of Lord Dalton Greyjoy and his ironmen.

The trap was neatly set. The voyage was perilous, and like to take a heavy toll of the Velaryon fleets. The Stepstones teemed with enemies, who would not be taken unawares a second time. Past them lay the barren coasts of Dorne, where Lord Alyn was not like to find safe harbor. And should he gain the Sunset Sea, he would find the Red Kraken waiting with his longships. If the ironmen prevailed, the power of House Velaryon would be broken for good and all, and Lord Peake need never again suffer the insolence of the boy called Oakenfist. If Lord Alyn triumphed, Fair Isle would be restored to its true lords, the westerlands would be freed from further outrage, and the lords of the Seven Kingdoms would learn the price of defying King Aegon III and his new Hand.

The Lord of the Tides made a gift of his elephant to King Aegon III as he took his leave of King's Landing. Returning to Hull to gather his fleet and take on provisions for the long journey, he said his farewells to his wife, the Lady Baela, who sent him on his way with a kiss, and the news that she was with child. "Name him Corlys, after my grandsire," Lord Alyn told her. "One day he may sit the Iron Throne." Baela laughed at that. "I will name her Laena, after my mother. One day she may ride a dragon."

Lord Corlys Velaryon had made nine famous voyages on his *Sea Snake,* it will be recalled. Lord Alyn Oakenfist would make six, upon six different ships. "My ladies," he would call them. On his voyage round Dorne to Lannisport, he sailed a Braavosi war galley of two hundred oars, captured in the Stepstones and renamed the *Lady Baela* after his young wife.

Some might think it queer for Lord Peake to send off the largest fleet in the Seven Kingdoms whilst war with Braavos threatened. Ser Gedmund Peake and the royal fleet had been recalled from Tarth to the Gullet, to guard the entrance to Blackwater Bay should the Braavosi seek to retaliate against King's Landing, but other ports and cities all up and down the narrow sea remained vulnerable, so the King's Hand dispatched fellow regent Lord Manfryd Mooton to Braavos to treat with the Sealord and return his elephant. Six other noble lords accompanied him, along with threescore knights, guardsmen, servants, scribes, and septons, six singers . . . and Mushroom, who supposedly hid in a wine cask to escape the gloom of the Red Keep and "find a place where men remembered how to laugh."

Then as now, the Braavosi were a pragmatic people, for theirs is a city of escaped slaves where a thousand false gods are honored, but only gold is truly worshipped. Profit means more than pride amongst the hundred isles. Upon arrival, Lord Mooton and his companions marveled at the Titan, and were taken to the fabled Arsenal to witness the building of a warship, completed in a single day. "We have already replaced every ship that your boy admiral stole or sank," the Sealord boasted to Lord Mooton.

Having thus demonstrated the power of Braavos, however, he was more than willing to be placated. Whilst he haggled with Lord Mooton over terms of peace, Lords Follard and Cressey spread lavish bribes amongst the city's keyholders, magisters, priests, and merchant princes. In the end, in return for a very sizable indemnity, Braavos forgave Lord Velaryon's "unwarranted transgression," agreed to dissolve her alliance with Tyrosh and break all ties with Racallio Ryndoon, and ceded the Stepstones to the Iron Throne (since the islands were held by Ryndoon and the Pentoshi at this time, the Sealord had in effect sold something that he did not own, but this was not unusual in Braavos).

The mission to Braavos proved eventful in other ways as well. Lord Follard became enamored of a Braavosi courtesan and elected to remain close to her rather than return to Westeros, Ser Herman Rollingford was killed in a duel by a bravo who took offense at the color of his doublet, and Ser Denys Harte supposedly engaged the services of the mysterious Faceless Men to kill a rival back in King's Landing, Mushroom asserts. The fool himself so amused the Sealord that he received a handsome offer to remain in Braavos. "I do confess that I was tempted. In Westeros my wit is wasted capering for a king who never smiles, but in Braavos they would love me . . . too well, I fear. Every courtesan would want me, and soon or late some bravo would take umbrage at the size of my member and prick me with his little pointy dwarf-skewer. So back to the Red Keep Mushroom scurried, and more fool me."

So it came to pass that Lord Mooton returned to King's Landing with peace in hand, but at a grievous cost. The huge indemnity demanded by the Sealord so depleted the royal treasury that Lord Peake soon found it necessary to borrow from the Iron Bank of Braavos just so the Crown might pay its debts, and that in turn required him to reinstate certain of Lord Celtigar's taxes that Ser Tyland Lannister had abolished, which angered lords and merchants alike and weakened his support amongst the smallfolk.

The last half of the year proved calamitous in other ways as well. The court rejoiced when Lady Rhaena announced that she was with child by Lord Corwyn Corbray, but joy turned to grief a moon's turn later when she miscarried. Widespread famine was reported in the North, and the Winter Fever descended on Barrowton, the first time it had ever traveled so far inland. A raider named Sylas the Grim led three thousand wildlings against the Wall, overwhelming the black brothers at Queensgate and spreading out across the Gift until Lord Cregan Stark rode forth from Winterfell, joined with the Glovers of Deepwood Motte, the Flints and Norreys of the hills, and a hundred rangers from the Night's Watch to hunt them down and put an end to them. A thousand leagues to the south, Ser Steffon Connington was hunting too, pursuing a small band of Dornish raiders across the windswept marches. But he rode too far and too fast, ignorant of what lay ahead until one-armed Wyland Wyl came down on him, and Lady Elenda found herself widowed once again.

In the west, Lady Johanna Lannister hoped to follow her victory at Kayce by striking another blow against the Red Kraken. Assembling a ragtag fleet of fishing boats and cogs beneath the walls of Feastfires, she loaded a hundred knights and three thousand men-at-arms aboard, and sent them out to sea under the cover of darkness to retake Fair Isle from the ironmen. The plan was to land them undetected on the south end of the island, but someone had betrayed them, and the longships were waiting. Lord Prester, Lord Tarbeck, and Ser Erwin Lannister commanded the ill-fated crossing. Dalton Greyjoy sent their heads to Casterly Rock afterward, calling it "payment for my uncle, though in truth he was a glutton and a drunkard, and the islands are well rid of him."

Yet all these were as naught against the tragedy that descended on the court and king. On the twenty-second day of the ninth moon of 133 AC, Jaehaera of House Targaryen, Queen of the Seven Kingdoms and the last surviving child of King Aegon II, perished at the age of ten. The little queen died just as her mother, Queen Helaena, had, throwing herself from a window in Maegor's Holdfast onto the iron spikes that lined the dry moat below. Impaled through breast and belly, she twisted in agony for half an hour before she could be lifted free, whereupon she passed from this life at once.

King's Landing grieved, as only King's Landing could. Jaehaera had been a frightened child, and from the day she donned her crown she had hidden herself away inside the Red Keep, yet the smallfolk of the city remembered her wedding, and how brave and beautiful the little girl had seemed, and so they wept, and wailed, and tore their clothes, and crowded into septs and taverns and brothels, to seek for whatever solace they could find. There the whispers soon were flying, just as they had when Queen Helaena died in similar fashion. Had the little queen truly taken her own life? Even inside the walls of the Red Keep, speculation was rampant.

Jaehaera was a lonely child, prone to weeping and somewhat simple-minded, yet she had seemed content in her own chambers with her maids and ladies, her kittens and her dolls. What could have made her mad enough or sad enough to leap from her window onto those cruel spikes? Some suggested that Lady Rhaena's miscarriage might have made her so distraught she did not wish to live. Others, of a more cynical bent, countered that it might have been jealousy over the child growing inside of Lady Baela that drove her to the act. "It was the king," whispered still others. "She loved him with all her heart, yet he paid her no mind, showed her no affection, did not even share his rooms with her."

And of course there were many who refused to believe that Jaehaera had taken her own life. "She was murdered," they whispered, "just as her mother was." But if that were true, who was the murderer?

There was no lack of suspects. By tradition, there was always a knight of the Kingsguard posted at the queen's door. It would have been a simple thing for him to slip inside and throw the child from her window. If so, surely the king himself had given the command. Aegon had tired of her weeping and wailing and wanted a new wife, men said. Or perhaps he wished to revenge himself on the daughter of the king who killed his mother. The boy was dour and gloomy, no one truly knew his nature. Tales of Maegor the Cruel were freely told.

Others blamed one of the little queen's companions, Lady Cassandra Baratheon. The eldest of the "Four Storms," Lady Cassandra had been briefly betrothed to King Aegon II during the last year of his life (and possibly to his brother Aemond One-Eye before that). Disappointment had turned her sour, her detractors said; once her father's heir at Storm's End, she found herself of little account in King's Landing, and bitterly resented having to care for the weepy, feeble-witted child queen whom she blamed for all her woes.

One of the queen's bedmaids also came under suspicion, when it was found that she had stolen two of Jaehaera's dolls and a pearl necklace. A serving boy who had spilled soup on the little queen the year before, and been beaten for it, was accused. Both of these were put to question by the Lord Confessor, and finally declared innocent (though the boy died under questioning and the girl lost a hand for theft). Even holy servants of the Seven were not above suspicion. A certain septa in the city had once been heard to say that the little queen ought never to have children, for simpleminded women produced simpleminded sons. The gold cloaks brought her in as well, and she vanished into a dungeon.

Grief makes men mad. With hindsight, we can say for a fair certainty that none of these played any role in the sad death of the little queen. If indeed Jaehaera Targaryen was murdered (and there is no shred of proof of that), it was surely done at the behest of the only truly plausible culprit: Unwin Peake, Lord Regent, Lord of Starpike, Lord of Dunstonbury, Lord of Whitegrove, Protector of the Realm, and Hand of the King.

Lord Peake was known to have shared his predecessor's concerns about the succession. Aegon III had no children, nor any living siblings (so far as it was known), and any man with eyes could see that the king was not like to get an heir from his little queen. Unless he did, the king's half-sisters remained his nearest kin, but Lord Peake was not about to allow a woman to ascend the Iron Throne, after having so recently fought and bled to prevent that very thing. If either of the twins produced a son, to be sure, the boy would at once become first in the order of succession... but Lady Rhaena's pregnancy had ended in miscarriage, which left only the child growing inside Lady Baela on Driftmark. The thought that the crown might pass to "the whelp of a wanton and a bastard" was more than Lord Unwin Peake was prepared to stomach.

Were the king to sire an heir of his own body, that calamity might be averted... but before that could happen, Jaehaera had to be removed so Aegon could remarry. Lord Peake could not have pushed the child from the window himself, to be sure, as he was elsewhere in the city when she died... but the Kingsguard posted at the queen's door that night was Mervyn Flowers, his bastard brother.

Could he have been the Hand's catspaw? It is more than possible, particularly in light of later events, which we shall discuss in due course. Bastard born himself, Ser Mervyn was regarded by most a dutiful, if not especially heroic, member of the Kingsguard; neither champion nor hero, but a seasoned soldier and a fair hand with a longsword, a leal man who did as he was told. Not all men are as they seem, however, particularly in King's Landing. Those who knew Flowers best saw other sides of him. When not on duty, he was fond of wine, says Mushroom, who was known to have drunk with him. Though sworn to chastity, he seldom slept alone save in his cell at White Sword Tower; despite being somewhat ill-favored, he had a rough charm that washerwomen and serving girls responded to, and when in his cups would even boast of having bedded certain highborn ladies. Like many bastards, he was hot of blood and quick to anger, seeing slights where none had been intended.

Yet none of this suggested that Flowers was the sort of monster who could take a sleeping child from her bed and throw her to a grisly death. Even Mushroom, ever ready to think the worst of everyone, says as much. If Ser Mervyn had killed the queen, he would have done it with a pillow, the fool insists... before suggesting a far more sinister and likely possibility. Flowers would never have pushed the queen out that window, the dwarf claims, but he might well have stood aside to allow someone else to enter her room, if that someone were known to him . . . someone, mayhaps, like Tessario the Thumb, or one of the Fingers. Nor would Flowers have felt the need to ask their business with the little queen, not if they said they came at the Hand's behest.

So says the fool, but to be sure, all of this is fancy. The true tale of how Jaehaera Targaryen met her end will never be known. Mayhaps she did take her own life in some fit of childish despair. If murder was indeed the cause of her demise, however, for all these reasons, the man behind it could only have been Lord Unwin Peake. Yet without proof, none of this would have been damning . . . if not for what the Hand did afterward.

Seven days after the body of the little queen was consigned to the flames, Lord Unwin paid a call upon the grieving king, accompanied by Grand Maester Munkun, Septon Bernard, and Marston Waters of the Kingsguard. They had come to inform His Grace that he must put aside his mourning blacks and wed again "for the good of the realm." Moreover, his new queen had been chosen for him.

Unwin Peake had married thrice and sired seven children. Only one survived. His firstborn son had died in infancy, as had both of his daughters by his second wife. His eldest daughter had lived long enough to marry, only to die in childbirth at the age of twelve. His second son had been fostered on the Arbor, where he served Lord Redwyne as page and squire, but at the age of twelve he had drowned in a sailing mishap. Ser Titus, heir to Starpike, was the only one of Lord Unwin's sons to grow to manhood. Knighted for valor after the Battle of the Honeywine by Bold Jon Roxton, he had died only six days later in a meaningless skirmish with a band of broken men he stumbled on whilst scouting. The Hand's last surviving child was a daughter, Myrielle.

Myrielle Peake was to be Aegon III's new queen. She was the ideal choice, the Hand declared; the same age as the king, "a lovely girl, and courteous," born of one of the noblest houses in the realm, schooled by septas to read, write, and do sums. Her lady mother had been fertile, so there was no reason to think that Myrielle would not give His Grace strong sons.

"What if I do not like her?" King Aegon said. "You do not need to like her," Lord Peake replied, "you need only wed her, bed her, and father a son on her." Then, infamously, he added, "Your Grace does not like turnips, but when your cooks prepare them, you eat them, do you not?" King Aegon nodded sullenly . . . but the tale got out, as such tales always do, and the unfortunate Lady Myrielle was soon known as Lady Turnips throughout the Seven Kingdoms.

She would never be Queen Turnips.

Unwin Peake had overreached himself. Thaddeus Rowan and Manfryd Mooton were outraged that he had not seen fit to consult them; matters of such import rightly belonged to the council of regents. Lady Arryn sent a waspish note from the Vale. Kermit Tully declared the betrothal "presumptuous." Ben Blackwood questioned the haste of it; Aegon should have been allowed half a year at least to mourn his little queen. A curt missive arrived from Cregan Stark in Winterfell, suggesting that the North might look with disfavor on such a match. Even Grand Maester Munkun began to waver. "Lady Myrielle is a delightful girl, and I have no doubt that she would make a splendid queen," he told the Hand, "but we must be concerned with appearances, my lord. We who have the honor of serving with your lordship know that you love His Grace as if he were your own son, and do all you do for him and for the realm, but others may imply that you chose your daughter for more ignoble reasons . . . for power, or the glory of House Peake."

Mushroom, our wise fool, observes that there are certain doors best not opened, for "you never know what might come through." Peake had opened a queen's door for his daughter, but other lords had daughters too (as well as sisters, nieces, cousins, and even the odd widowed mother or maiden aunt) and before the door could close they all came pushing through, insisting that their own blood would make a better royal consort than Lady Turnips.

To recount all the names put forward would take more pages than we have, but a few are worthy of mention. At Casterly Rock, Lady Johanna Lannister set aside her war with the ironmen long enough to write the Hand and point out that her daughters Cerelle and Tyshara were maidens of noble birth and marriageable age. The twice-widowed Lady of Storm's End, Elenda Baratheon, put forward her own daughters, Cassandra and Ellyn. Cassandra had once been betrothed to Aegon II and was "well prepared to serve as queen," she wrote. From White Harbor came a raven from Lord Torrhen, speaking of past marriage pacts between the dragon and the merman "broken by cruel chance," and suggesting that King Aegon might put things aright by taking a Manderly for his bride. Sharis Footly, widow of Tumbleton, made so bold as to nominate herself.

Perhaps the boldest letter came from the irrepressible Lady Samantha of Oldtown, who declared that her sister Sansara (of House Tarly) "is spirited and strong, and has read more books than half the maesters in the Citadel" whilst her good-sister Bethany (of House Hightower) was "very beautiful, with smooth soft skin and lustrous hair and the sweetest manner," though also "lazy and somewhat stupid, truth be told, though some men seem to like that in a wife." She concluded by suggesting that perhaps King Aegon should marry both of them, "one to rule beside him, as Queen Alysanne did King Jaehaerys, and one to bed and breed." And in the event that both of them were "found wanting, for whatever obscure reason," Lady Sam helpfully appended the names of thirty-one other nubile maidens from Houses Hightower, Redwyne, Tarly, Ambrose, Florent, Cobb, Costayne, Beesbury, Varner, and Grimm who might be suitable as queens. (Mushroom adds that her ladyship ended with a cheeky postscript that said, "I know some pretty boys as well, should His Grace be so inclined, but I fear they could not give him heirs," but none of the other chronicles mention this effrontery, and her ladyship's letter has been lost.)

In the face of so much tumult, Lord Unwin was forced to think again. Though he remained determined to wed his daughter Myrielle to the king, he had to do so in a way that would not provoke the lords whose support he needed. Bowing to the inevitable, he mounted the Iron Throne and said, "For the good of his people, His Grace must take another wife, though no woman will ever replace our beloved Jaehaera in his heart. Many have been put forward for this honor, the fairest flowers of the realm. Whichever girl King Aegon weds shall be the Alysanne to his Jaehaerys, the Jonquil to his Florian. She will sleep by his side, birth his children, share his labors, soothe his brow when he is sick, grow old with him. It is only fitting therefore that we allow the king himself to make this choice. On Maiden's Day we shall have a ball, the like of which King's Landing has not seen since the days of King Viserys. Let the maidens come from every corner of the Seven Kingdoms and present themselves before the king, that His Grace may choose the one best suited to share his life and love."

And so the word went out, and a great excitement took hold of the court and city, and spread out across the realm. From the Dornish Marches to the Wall, doting fathers and proud mothers looked at their nubile daughters and wondered if she might be the one, and every highborn maid in Westeros began to primp and sew and curl her hair, thinking, "Why not me? I might be the queen."

Yet even before Lord Unwin had ascended the Iron Throne, he had sent a raven to Starpike summoning his daughter to the city. Though Maiden's Day was yet three moons away, his lordship wanted Myrielle at court, in hopes that she might befriend and beguile the king, and thus be chosen on the night of the ball.

That much is known; what follows now is rumor. For it was said that even as he awaited the arrival of his own daughter, Unwin Peake also set in motion sundry secret plots and plans designed to undermine, defame, distract, and besmirch those damsels he deemed his daughter's most likely rivals. The suggestion that Cassandra Baratheon had pushed the little queen to her death was heard again, and the misdeeds of certain other young maidens, real or imagined, became common gossip about court. Ysabel Staunton's fondness for wine was bruited about, the tale of Elinor Massey's deflowering was told and retold, Rosamund Darry was said to be concealing six nipples under her bodice (supposedly because her mother had lain with a dog), Lyra Hayford was accused of having smothered an infant brother in a fit of jealousy, and it was put about that the "three Jeynes" (Jeyne Smallwood, Jeyne Mooton, and Jeyne Merryweather) liked to dress in squire's garb and visit the brothels along the Street of Silk, to kiss and fondle the women there as if the three of them were boys.

All these calumnies reached the king's ears, some from Mushroom's own lips, for the fool confesses to having been paid "handsomely" to poison Aegon III against these maids and others. The dwarf was much in His Grace's company following the death of Queen Jaehaera. Though his japes could not dispel the king's gloom, they delighted Gaemon Palehair, so Aegon oft summoned him for the boy's sake. In his *Testimony,* Mushroom says Tessario the Thumb gave him a choice between "silver or steel," and "to my shame, I bade him sheath his dagger and seized that sweet fat purse."

Nor were words the only means by which Lord Unwin sought to win his secret war for the king's heart, if the whispers can be believed. A groom was found abed with Tyshara Lannister not long after the ball had been announced; though Lady Tyshara claimed the lad had climbed in her window uninvited, Grand Maester Munkun's examination revealed her maidenhead was broken. Lucinda Penrose was set upon by outlaws whilst hawking along Blackwater Bay, not half a day's ride from the castle. Her hawk was killed, her horse was stolen, and one of the men held her down whilst another slit her nose open. Pretty Falena Stokeworth, a vivacious girl of eight who had sometimes played at dolls with the little queen, took a tumble down the serpentine steps and broke her leg, whilst Lady Buckler and both her daughters drowned when the boat that was carrying them across the Blackwater foundered and sank. Some men began to talk of a "Maiden's Day curse," whilst others wiser in the ways of power saw unseen hands at work and held their tongues.

Were the Hand and his minions responsible for these tragedies and misfortunes, or were they happenstance? In the end it would not matter. Not since the reign of King Viserys had there been a ball of any sort in King's Landing, and this would be a ball like none other. At tourneys, fair maidens and high ladies vied for the honor of being named the queen of love and beauty, but such reigns lasted only for a night. Whichever maid King Aegon chose would reign over Westeros for a lifetime. The highborn descended on King's Landing from keeps and castles in every part of the Seven Kingdoms. In an effort to limit their numbers, Lord Peake decreed that the contest would be limited to maidens of noble blood under thirty years of age, yet even so, more than a thousand nubile girls crowded into the Red Keep on the appointed day, a tide far too great for the Hand to stem. Even from across the sea they came; the Prince of Pentos sent a daughter, the Archon of Tyrosh a sister, and the daughters of ancient houses set sail from Myr and even Old Volantis (though, sadly, none of the Volantene girls ever arrived at King's Landing, being carried off by corsairs from the Basilisk Isles on the way).

"Each maid seemed lovelier than the last," Mushroom says in his *Testimony*, "sparkling and spinning in their silks and jewels, they made a dazzling sight as they made their way to the throne room. It would be hard to picture anything more beautiful, unless perhaps all of them had arrived naked." (One did, for all intents and purposes. Myrmadora Haen, daughter of a magister of Lys, turned up in a gown of translucent blue-green silk that matched her eyes, with only a jeweled girdle underneath. Her appearance sent a ripple of shock through the yard, but the Kingsguard barred her from the hall until she changed into less revealing garb.)

No doubt these maidens dreamed sweet dreams of dancing with the king, charming him with their wit, exchanging coy glances over a cup of wine. But there was to be no dancing, no wine, no opportunity for conversation, be it witty or dull. The gathering was not truly a ball in the ordinary sense. King Aegon III sat atop the Iron Throne, clad in black with a golden circlet round his head and a gold chain at his throat, as the maidens paraded beneath him one by one. As the king's herald announced the name and lineage of each candidate, the girl would curtsy, the king would nod down at them, and then it would be time for the next girl to be presented. "By the time the tenth girl was presented, the king had doubtless forgotten the first five," Mushroom says. "Their fathers could well have sneaked them back into the queue for another go-round, and some of the more cunning likely did."

A handful of the braver maidens made so bold as to address the king, in an attempt to make themselves more memorable. Ellyn Baratheon asked His Grace if he liked her gown (her sister later put it about that her question was, "Do you like my breasts?" but there is no truth to that). Alyssa Royce told him she had come all the way from Runestone to be with him today. Patricia Redwyne went her one better by declaring that her party had traveled from the Arbor, and had thrice been forced to beat back attacks by outlaws. "I shot one with an arrow," she declared proudly. "In the arse." Lady Anya Weatherwax, aged seven, informed His Grace that her horse's name was Twinklehoof and she loved him very much, and asked if His Grace had a good horse too. ("His Grace has a hundred horses," Lord Unwin answered impatiently.) Others ventured compliments about his city, his castle, and his clothes. A northern maid named Barba Bolton, daughter of the Dreadfort, said, "If you send me home, Your Grace, send me home with food, for the snows are deep and your people are starving."

The boldest tongue belonged to a Dornishwoman, Moriah Qorgyle of Sandstone, who rose from her curtsy smiling and said, "Your Grace, why not climb down from there and kiss me?" Aegon did not answer her. He answered none of them. He gave each maid a nod, to acknowledge that he had heard them. Then Ser Marston and the Kingsguard saw them on their way.

Music wafted over the hall all through the night, but could scarce be heard over the shuffle of footsteps, the din of conversation, and from time to time the faint, soft sound of weeping. The throne room of the Red Keep is a cavernous chamber, larger than any hall in Westeros save Black Harren's, but with more than a thousand maids on hand, each with her own retinue of parents, siblings, guards, and servants, it soon became too crowded to move, and suffocatingly hot, though outside a winter wind was blowing. The herald charged with announcing the name and lineage of each of the fair maidens lost his voice and had to be replaced. Four of the hopefuls fainted, along with a dozen mothers, several fathers, and a septon. One stout lord collapsed and died.

"The Maiden's Day Cattle Show," Mushroom would name the ball afterward. Even the singers who had made so much of it beforehand found little to sing about as the event unfolded, and the king himself appeared ever more restless as the hours passed and the parade of maids continued. "All this," says Mushroom, "was just as the Hand desired. Each time His Grace frowned, shifted in his seat, or gave another weary nod, the likelihood of his choosing Lady Turnips increased, Lord Unwin reasoned."

Myrielle Peake had arrived in King's Landing almost a moon's turn before the ball, and her father had made certain that she spent part of every day in the king's company. Brown of hair and eye, with a broad, freckled face and crooked teeth that made her shy with her smiles, Lady Turnips was four-and-ten, one year older than Aegon. "She was no great beauty," Mushroom says, "but she was fresh and pretty and pleasant, and His Grace did not seem averse to her." During the fortnight leading up to Maiden's Day, the dwarf tells us, Lord Unwin had arranged for Myrielle to share half a dozen suppers with the king. Called upon to entertain dur-

ing those long awkward meals, Mushroom tells us that King Aegon said little as they ate, but "seemed more comfortable with Lady Turnips than he had ever been with Queen Jaehaera. Which is to say, not comfortable at all, but he did not seem to find her presence distasteful. Three days before the ball, he gave her one of the little queen's dolls. 'Here,' he said as he thrust it at her, 'you can have this.' Not quite the words that innocent young maidens dream of hearing, perhaps, but Myrielle took the gift as a token of affection, and her father was most pleased."

Lady Myrielle brought the doll with her when she made her own appearance at the ball, cradling it in her arms as if it were a babe. She was not the first to be presented (that honor went to the daughter of the Prince of Pentos), nor the last (Henrietta Woodhull, daughter of a landed knight from the Paps). Her father had seen to it that she came before the king late in the first hour, far enough back so he could not be accused of giving her pride of place, but far enough forward so King Aegon would still be reasonably fresh. When His Grace greeted Lady Myrielle by name and said not only, "It was good of you to come, my lady," but also, "I am pleased you like the doll," her father surely took heart, believing that all his careful scheming had borne fruit.

Yet it would all be undone in a trice by the king's half-sisters, the very twins whose succession Unwin Peake had been so determined to prevent. Fewer than a dozen maids remained, and the press had thinned considerably, when a sudden trumpet blast heralded the arrival of Baela Velaryon and Rhaena Corbray. The doors to the throne room were thrown open, and the daughters of Prince Daemon entered upon a blast of winter air. Lady Baela was great with child, Lady Rhaena wan and thin from her miscarriage, yet seldom had they seemed more as one. Both were dressed in gowns of soft black velvet with rubies at their throats, and the three-headed dragon of House Targaryen on their cloaks.

Mounted on a pair of coal black chargers, the twins rode the length of the hall side by side. When Ser Marston Waters of the Kingsguard blocked their path and demanded they dismount, Lady Baela slashed him across the cheek with her riding crop. "His Grace my brother can command me. You cannot." At the foot of the Iron Throne they reined up. Lord Unwin rushed forward, demanding to know the meaning of this. The twins paid him no more heed than they would a serving man. "Brother," Lady Rhaena said to Aegon, "if it please you, we have brought your new queen."

Her lord husband, Ser Corwyn Corbray, brought the girl forward. A gasp went through the hall. "Lady Daenaera of House Velaryon," boomed out the herald, somewhat hoarsely, "daughter of the late and lamented Daeron of that house and his lady wife, Hazel of House Harte, also departed, a ward of Lady Baela of House Targaryen and Alyn the Oakenfist of House Velaryon, Lord Admiral, Master of Driftmark, and Lord of the Tides."

Daenaera Velaryon was an orphan. Her mother had been carried off by the Winter Fever; her father had died in the Stepstones when his *True Heart* went down. His own father had been that Ser Vaemond beheaded by Queen Rhaenyra, but Daeron had been reconciled with Lord Alyn and had died fighting for him. As she stood before the king that Maiden's Day, clad in pale white silk, Myrish lace, and pearls, her long hair shining in the torchlight and her cheeks flush with excitement, Daenaera was but six years old, yet so beautiful she took the breath away. The blood of Old Valyria was strong in her, as is oft seen in the sons and daughters of the seahorse; her hair was silver laced with gold, her eyes as blue as a summer sea, her skin as smooth and pale as winter snow. "She sparkled," Mushroom says, "and when she smiled, the singers in the gallery rejoiced, for they knew that here at last was a maid worthy of a song." Daenaera's smile transformed her face, men agreed; it was sweet and bold and mischievous, all at once. Those who saw it could not fail to think, "Here is a bright, sweet, happy little girl, the perfect antidote to the young king's gloom."

When Aegon III returned her smile and said, "Thank you for coming, my lady, you look very pretty," even Lord Unwin Peake surely must have known that the game was lost. The last few maidens were brought forward hurriedly to do their turns, but the king's desire to put an end to the parade was so palpable that poor Henrietta Woodhull was sobbing as she curtsied. As she was led away, King Aegon summoned his young cupbearer, Gaemon Palehair. To him was given the honor of making the announcement. "His Grace will marry Lady Daenaera of House Velaryon!" Gaemon shouted happily.

Caught in a snare of his own making, Lord Unwin Peake had no choice but to accept the king's decision with as much grace as he could muster. In a council meeting the next day, however, he gave vent to his wroth. By choosing for his bride a girl of six, "this sulky boy" had thwarted the entire purpose of the marriage. It would be years before the girl was old enough to bed, and even longer until she could hope to produce a trueborn heir. Until such time the succession would remain clouded. The foremost duty of a regency was to guard the king against the follies of youth, he declared, "follies such as this." For the good of the realm, the king's choice must be set aside, so that His Grace might marry "a suitable maid of child-bearing age."

"Such as your daughter?" asked Lord Rowan. "I think not." Nor were his fellow regents more sympathetic. For once, the council remained adamant, defying the Hand's wishes. The marriage would proceed. The betrothal was announced the next day, as scores of disappointed maidens streamed out the city gates for home.

King Aegon III Targaryen wed Lady Daenaera on the last day of the 133rd year since Aegon's Conquest. The crowds that lined the streets to cheer the royal couple were significantly smaller than those who had come out for Aegon and Jaehaera, for the Winter Fever had carried off almost a fifth of the population of King's Landing, but those who did brave the day's bitter winds and snow flurries were delighted with their new queen, charmed by her happy waves, flushed cheeks, and shy, sweet smiles. Ladies Baela and Rhaena, riding just behind the royal litter, were greeted with exuberant cheers as well. Only a few took note of the King's Hand farther back, with "his face as grim as death."

Under the Regents

The Voyage of Alyn Oakenfist

Let us leave King's Landing for a time, and turn back the calendar to speak of Lady Baela's lord husband Alyn Oakenfist on his epic voyage to the Sunset Sea.

The trials and triumphs of the Velaryon fleet as it made its way around "the arse of Westeros" (as Lord Alyn was wont to call it) could fill a mighty tome all by themselves. For those seeking the details of the voyage, Maester Bendamure's *Six Times to Sea: Being an Account of the Great Voyages of Alyn Oakenfist* remains the most complete and authoritative source, though the vulgar accounts of Lord Alyn's life called *Hard as Oak* and *Bastard Born* are colorful and engrossing in their ways, albeit unreliable. The former was written by Ser Russell Stillman, who squired for his lordship as a youth and was later knighted by him before losing a leg during Oakenfist's fifth voyage, the latter by a woman known only as Rue, who may or may not have been a septa, and may or may not have become one of his lordship's paramours. We shall not echo their work here, save in the broadest strokes.

Oakenfist displayed considerably more caution on his return to the Stepstones than he had on his previous visit. Wary of the ever-shifting alliances and studied treacheries of the Free Cities, he sent scouts ahead in the guise of fishing boats and merchantmen to discover what awaited him. They reported that the fighting on the islands had largely died away, with a resurgent Racallio Ryndoon holding Bloodstone and all the isles to the south, whilst Pentoshi sellswords in the hire of the Archon of Tyrosh controlled those rocks to the north and east. Many of the channels between the islands were closed by booms, or blocked by the hulks of ships sunk during Lord Alyn's attack. Such waterways as remained open were controlled by Ryndoon and his rogues. Lord Alyn was thus confronted with a simple choice; he must needs fight his way past "Queen Racallio" (as the Archon had named him) or treat with him.

Little has been written in the Common Tongue about this strange and extraordinary adventurer, Racallio Ryndoon, but in the Free Cities his life has been the subject of two scholarly studies and uncounted numbers of songs, poems, and vulgar romances. In his native city, Tyrosh, his name remains anathema to men and women of good blood to this very day, whilst being revered by thieves, pirates, whores, drunkards, and their ilk.

Surprisingly little is known of his youth, and much of what we believe we know is false or contradictory. He was six-and-a-half feet tall, supposedly, with one shoulder higher than another, giving him a stooped posture and a rolling gait. He spoke a dozen dialects of Valyrian, suggesting that he was highborn, but he was infamously foul-mouthed too, suggesting that he came from the gutters. In the fashion of many Tyroshi, he was wont to dye his hair and beard. Purple was his favorite color (hinting at the possibility of a tie to Braavos), and most accounts of him make mention of long curling purple hair, oft streaked with orange. He liked sweet scents and would bathe in lavender or rosewater.

That he was a man of enormous ambition and enormous appetites seems clear. He was a glutton and a drunkard when at leisure, a demon when in battle. He could wield a sword with either hand, and sometimes fought with two at once. He honored the gods: all gods, everywhere. When battle threatened, he would throw the bones to choose which god to placate with a sacrifice. Though Tyrosh was a slave city, he hated slavery, suggesting that perhaps he himself had come from bondage. When wealthy (he gained and lost several fortunes) he would buy any slave girl who caught his eye, kiss her, and set her free. He was open-handed with his men, claiming a share of plunder no greater than the least of them. In Tyrosh, he was known to toss gold coins to beggars. If a man admired something of his, be it a pair of boots, an emerald ring, or a wife, Racallio would press it on him as a gift.

He had a dozen wives and never beat them, but would sometimes command them to beat him. He loved kittens and hated cats. He loved pregnant women, but loathed children. From time to time he would dress in women's clothes and play the whore, though his height and crooked back and purple beard made him more grotesque than female to the eye. Sometimes he would burst out laughing in the thick of battle. Sometimes he would sing bawdy songs instead.

Racallio Ryndoon was mad. Yet his men loved him, fought for him, died for him. And for a few short years, they made him a king.

In 133 AC, in the Stepstones, "Queen" Racallio was at the height of his power. Alyn Velaryon could perhaps have brought him down, but it would have cost him half his strength, he feared, and he would have need of every man if he were to have any hope of defeating the Red Kraken. He therefore chose talk instead of battle. Detaching his *Lady Baela* from the fleet, he sailed her into Bloodstone beneath a parley flag, to try to arrange free passage for his ships through Ryndoon's waters.

Ultimately he succeeded, though Racallio kept him for more than a fortnight in his sprawling wooden fortress on Bloodstone. Whether Lord Alyn was a captive or a guest was never quite clear, even to his lordship himself, for his host was as changeable as the sea. One day he would hail Oakenfist as a friend and brother-in-arms, and urge him to join him in an attack on Tyrosh. The next he would throw the bones to see if he should put his guest to death. He insisted that Lord Alyn wrestle with him in a mud pit behind his fort, whilst hundreds of jeering pirates looked on. When he beheaded one of his own men accused of spying for the Tyroshi, Racallio presented Lord Alyn with the head as a token of their fellowship, but the very next day he accused his lordship of being in the Archon's hire himself. To prove his innocence, Lord Alyn was forced to kill three Tyroshi prisoners. When he did, the "Queen" was so delighted with him that he sent two of his wives to Oakenfist's bedchamber that night. "Give them sons," Racallio commanded. "I want sons as brave and strong as you." Our sources are at odds as to whether or not Lord Alyn did as he was bid.

In the end Ryndoon allowed that the Velaryon fleet might pass, for a price. He wanted three ships, an alliance writ on sheepskin and signed in blood, and a kiss. Oakenfist gave him the three least seaworthy ships in his fleet, an alliance writ on parchment and signed in maester's ink, and the promise of a kiss from Lady Baela, should the "Queen" visit them on Driftmark. That proved sufficient. The fleet sailed through the Stepstones.

More trials awaited them, however. The next was Dorne. The Dornishmen were understandably alarmed with the sudden appearance of the large Velaryon fleet in the waters off Sunspear. Lacking any strength at sea themselves, however, they chose to regard Lord Alyn's coming as a visit rather than an attack. Aliandra Martell, Princess of Dorne, came out to meet with him, accompanied by a dozen of her current favorites and suitors. The "new Nymeria" had just celebrated her eighteenth nameday, and was reportedly much taken with the young, handsome, dashing "Hero of the Stepstones," the bold admiral who had humbled the Braavosi. Lord Alyn required fresh water and provisions for his ships, whilst Princess Aliandra required services of a more intimate nature. *Bastard Born* would have us believe that he provided them, *Hard as Oak* that he did not. We do know that the attentions the flirtatious Dornish princess lavished upon him much displeased her own lords, and angered her younger siblings, Qyle and Coryanne. Nonetheless, Lord Oakenfist got fresh casks of water, enough food to see them through to Oldtown and the Arbor, and charts showing the deadly whirlpools that lurked along the southern coast of Dorne.

Even so, it was in Dornish waters that Lord Velaryon suffered his first losses. A sudden storm blew up as the fleet was making its way past the drylands west of Salt Shore, scattering the ships and sinking two. Farther west, near the mouth of the Brimstone River, a damaged galley put in to take aboard fresh water and make certain repairs, and was attacked under the cover of darkness by bandits, who slaughtered her crew and looted her supplies.

Those losses were more than made good when Lord Oakenfist reached Oldtown, however. The great beacon atop the Hightower guided *Lady Baela* and the fleet up Whispering Sound to the harbor, where Lyonel Hightower himself came forth to meet them and welcome them to his city. The courtesy with which Lord Alyn treated Lady Sam warmed Lord Lyonel to him immediately, and the two youths struck up a fast friendship that did much to put all the old enmities between the blacks and greens to rest. Oldtown would provide twenty warships for the fleet, Hightower promised, and his good friend Lord Redwyne of the Arbor would send thirty. In a stroke, Lord Oakenfist's fleet had become considerably more formidable.

The Velaryon fleet lingered overlong in Whispering Sound, waiting for Lord Redwyne and his promised galleys. Alyn Oakenfist enjoyed the hospitality of the Hightower, explored the ancient wynds and ways of Oldtown, and visited the Citadel, where he spent days poring over ancient charts and studying dusty Valyrian treatises about warship design and tactics for battle at sea. At the Starry Sept, he received the blessing of the

High Septon, who traced a seven-pointed star upon his brow in holy oil, and sent him forth to bring down the Warrior's wroth upon the ironmen and their Drowned God. Lord Velaryon was still at Oldtown when word of Queen Jaehaera's death reached the city, followed within a few short days by the announcement of the king's betrothal to Myrielle Peake. By that time, he had become close to Lady Sam as well as to Lord Lyonel, though whether he had any part in the writing of her infamous letter remains a matter of conjecture. It is known, however, that he dispatched letters to his own lady wife on Driftmark whilst at the Hightower. We do not know the contents.

Oakenfist was still a young man in 133 AC, and young men are not known for their patience. Finally he decided that he would wait no longer for Lord Redwyne, and gave the order to sail. Oldtown cheered as the Velaryon ships raised their sails and lowered their oars, sliding down the Whispering Sound one by one. Twenty war galleys of House Hightower followed, commanded by Ser Leo Costayne, a grizzled seafarer known as the Sea Lion.

Off the singing cliffs of Blackcrown where twisted towers and wind-carved stones whistled above the waves, the fleet turned north into the Sunset Sea, creeping up the western coast past Bandallon. As they passed the mouth of the Mander, the men of the Shield Islands sent forth their own galleys to join them: three ships each from Greyshield and Southshield, four from Greenshield, six from Oakenshield. Before they could move much farther north, however, another storm came down on them. One ship went down, and three more were so badly damaged that they could not proceed. Lord Velaryon regrouped the fleet off Crakehall, where the lady of the castle rowed out to meet him. It was from her that his lordship first heard of the great ball to be held on Maiden's Day.

Word had reached Fair Isle as well, and we are told that Lord Dalton Greyjoy even toyed with the idea of sending one of his sisters to vie for the queen's crown. "An iron maid upon the Iron Throne," he said, "what could be more fitting?" The Red Kraken had more immediate concerns, however. Long forewarned of the coming of Alyn Oakenfist, he had gathered his power to receive him. Hundreds of longships had assembled in the waters south of Fair Isle, and more off Feastfires, Kayce, and Lannisport. After he sent "that boy" down to the halls of the Drowned God at the bottom of the sea, the Red Kraken proclaimed, he would take his own fleet back the way that Oakenfist had come, raise his banner over the Shields, sack Oldtown and Sunspear, and claim Driftmark for his own. (Though Greyjoy was not quite three years older than his foe, he never called him anything but "that boy.") He might even take Lady Baela for a salt wife, the Lord of the Iron Islands told his captains, laughing. "'Tis true, I have two-and-twenty salt wives, but not a one with silver hair."

So much of history tells of the deeds of kings and queens, high lords, noble knights, holy septons, and wise maesters that it is easy to forget the common folk who shared these times with the great and the mighty. Yet from time to time some ordinary man or woman, blessed with neither birth nor wealth nor wit nor wisdom nor skill at arms, will somehow rise up and by some simple act or whispered word change the destiny of kingdoms. So it was on Fair Isle in that fateful year of 133 AC.

Lord Dalton Greyjoy did indeed possess two-and-twenty salt wives. Four were back on Pyke; two of those had borne him children. The others were women of the west, taken during his conquests, amongst them two of the late Lord Farman's surviving daughters, the widow of the Knight of Kayce, even a Lannister (a Lannister of Lannisport, not a Lannister of Casterly Rock). The rest were girls of humbler birth, the daughters of simple fisherfolk, traders, or men-at-arms who had somehow caught his eye, oft as not after he had slain their fathers, brothers, husbands, or other male protectors. One bore the name of Tess. Her name is all we truly know of her. Was she thirteen or thirty? Pretty or plain? A widow or a virgin? Where did Lord Greyjoy find her, and how long had she been amongst his salt wives? Did she despise him for a reaver and a raper, or love him so fiercely she went mad with jealousy?

We do not know. Accounts differ so markedly that Tess must remain forever a mystery in the annals of history. All that is known for a certainty is that on a rainy, windswept night at Faircastle, as the longships gathered below, Lord Dalton had his pleasure of her, and afterward, as he slept, Tess slipped his dagger from its sheath and opened his throat from ear to ear, then threw herself naked and bloody into the hungry sea below.

And so perished the Red Kraken of Pyke on the eve of his greatest battle . . . slain not by the sword of a foe, but by his own dagger, in the hand of one of his own wives.

Nor did his conquests long survive him. As word of his death spread, the fleet he had assembled to meet Alyn Oakenfist began to dissolve, as captain after captain slipped away for home. Dalton Greyjoy had never taken a rock wife, so his only heirs were two young sons born of the salt wives he had left on Pyke, three sisters, and several cousins, each more grasping and ambitious than the last. By law, the Seastone Chair passed to the eldest of his salt sons, but the boy Toron was not yet six and his mother, as a salt wife, could not hope to act as regent for him as a rock wife might have. A struggle for power was inevitable, a truth the ironborn captains saw well as they raced back toward their isles.

Meanwhile, the smallfolk of Fair Isle and such knights as still remained on the island rose up in red rebellion. The ironmen who had lingered when their kinsmen fled were dragged from their beds and hacked to death or set upon on the docks, their ships swarmed over and set ablaze. In the space of three days, hundreds of reavers suffered ends as cruel, bloody, and sudden as those they had inflicted on their prey, until only Faircastle remained in the ironborn hands. The garrison, composed in large part of the Red Kraken's close companions and brothers-in-battle, held out stubbornly under the sly Alester Wynch and the roaring giant Gunthor Goodbrother, until the latter slew the former in a quarrel over Lord Farman's daughter Lysa, one of the salt widows.

And so it came to pass that when Alyn Velaryon arrived at last to deliver the west from the ironmen of the isles, he found himself without a foe. Fair Isle was free, the longships had fled, the fighting was done. As the *Lady Baela* passed beneath the walls of Lannisport, the bells of the city pealed in welcome. Thousands rushed from the gates to line the shore, cheering. Lady Johanna herself emerged from Casterly Rock to present Oakenfist with a seahorse wrought in gold and other tokens of Lannister esteem.

Days of celebration followed. Lord Alyn was anxious to take on provisions and depart on his long voyage home, but the westermen were loath to see him go. With their own fleet destroyed, they remained vulnerable should the ironmen return under the Red Kraken's successor, whoever he might be. Lady Johanna even went so far as to propose an attack upon the Iron Islands themselves; she would provide as many swords and spears as might be required, Lord Velaryon need only deliver them to the isles. "We should put every man of them to the sword," her ladyship declared, "and sell their wives and children to the slavers of the east. Let the seagulls and the crabs claim those worthless rocks."

Oakenfist would have none of it, but to please his hosts, he did agree that the Sea Lion, Leo Costayne, would remain at Lannisport with a third of the fleet until such time as the Lannisters, the Farmans, and the other lords of the west could rebuild sufficient warships of their own to defend against any return of the ironmen. Then he raised his sails once more and took the remainder of his fleet back out to sea, returning from whence he'd come.

Of their voyage home, we need say little. Near the mouth of the Mander, the Redwyne fleet was finally sighted, hurrying north, but they turned about after breaking bread with Lord Velaryon on the *Lady Baela*. His lordship made a brief visit to the Arbor, as Lord Redwyne's guest, and a longer one at Oldtown, where he renewed his friendships with Lord Lyonel Hightower and Lady Sam, sat with the scribes and maesters of the Citadel so they might set down the details of his voyage, was feted by the masters of the seven guilds, and received yet another blessing from the High Septon. Again he sailed along the parched, dry coasts of Dorne, this time beating eastward. Princess Aliandra was pleased at his return to Sunspear, and insisted on hearing every detail of his adventures, to the fury of her siblings and jealous suitors.

It was from her that Lord Oakenfist learned that Dorne had joined the Daughters' War, making alliance with Tyrosh and Lys against Racallio Ryndoon . . . and it was at her court at Sunspear, during the Maiden's Day feast (the very day that a thousand maidens were parading before Aegon III in King's Landing), that his lordship was approached by a certain Drazenko Rogare, one of the envoys that Lys had sent to Aliandra's court, who begged a private word. Curious, Lord Alyn agreed to listen, and the two men stepped out into the yard, where Drazenko leaned so close that his lordship said, "I feared he meant to kiss me." Instead he whispered something in the admiral's ear, a secret that changed the course of Westerosi history. The next day, Lord Velaryon returned to *Lady Baela* and gave the command to raise sail . . . for Lys.

His reasons, and what befell him in the Free City, we shall reveal in due time, but for the nonce let us turn our gaze back on King's Landing. Hope and good feeling reigned over the Red Keep as the new year dawned. Though younger than her predecessor, Queen Daenaera was a happier child, and her sunny nature did much to lighten the king's gloom . . . for a while, at the least. Aegon III was seen about the court more often than had been his wont, and even left the castle on three occasions to show his bride such sights as the city offered (though he refused to take her to the Dragonpit, where Lady Rhaena's young dragon, Morning, made her lair). His Grace seemed to take a new interest in his studies, and Mushroom was oft summoned to entertain the king and queen at supper ("The sound of the queen's laughter was like music to this fool, so sweet that even the king was known to smile"). Even Gareth Long, the Red Keep's despised master-at-arms, made note of a change. "We no longer have to beat the bastard boy as often as before," he told the Hand. "The boy has never lacked for strength nor speed. Now at last he is showing some modicum of skill."

The young king's new interest in the world even extended to the rule of his kingdom. Aegon III began to attend the council. Though he seldom spoke, his presence heartened Grand Maester Munkun, and seemed to please Lord Mooton and Lord Rowan. Ser Marston Waters of the Kingsguard seemed discomfited by His Grace's attendance, however, and Lord Peake took it for a rebuke. Whenever Aegon made so bold as to ask a question, Munkun tells us, the Hand would bristle and accuse him of wasting the council's time, or inform him that such weighty matters were beyond the understanding of a child. Unsurprisingly, before very long His Grace began to absent himself from the meetings, as before.

Sour and suspicious by nature, and possessed of overweening pride, Unwin Peake was a most unhappy man by 134 AC. The Maiden's Day Ball had been a humiliation, and he took the king's rejection of his daughter, Myrielle, in favor of Daenaera as a personal affront. Never fond of Lady Baela, he now had reason to mislike her sister Rhaena as well; both of them, he was convinced, were working against him, most like at the behest of Baela's husband, the insolent and rebellious Oakenfist. The twins had deliberately and with malice aforethought wrecked his own plans to secure the succession, he told his own loyalists, and by seeing to it that the king took to wife a six-year-old they had ensured that the child Baela carried would be next in line to the Iron Throne.

"If the child is a boy, His Grace will never live long enough to sire an heir of his own body," Peake said to Marston Waters once, in Mushroom's presence. Shortly thereafter, Baela Velaryon was brought to childbed and delivered of a healthy baby girl. She named the child Laena after her mother. Yet even this did not long mollify the King's Hand, for less than a fortnight later, the leading elements of the Velaryon fleet returned to King's Landing bearing a cryptic message: Oakenfist had sent them on ahead whilst he set sail for Lys to secure "a treasure beyond price."

These words inflamed Lord Peake's suspicions. What was this treasure? How did Lord Velaryon mean to "secure" it? With a sword? Was he about to start a war with Lys, as he had with Braavos? The Hand had sent the rash young admiral around the whole of Westeros to rid the court of him, yet here he was about to descend on them once more, "dripping with undeserved acclaim" and mayhaps vast wealth as well. (Gold was ever a sore point for Unwin Peake, whose own house was land poor, rich in stone and soil and pride, yet chronically short of coin.) The smallfolk saw Oakenfist as a hero, his lordship knew, the man who had humbled the proud Sealord of Braavos and the Red Kraken of Pyke, whilst he himself was resented and reviled. Even within the Red Keep, there were many who hoped that the regents might remove Lord Peake as King's Hand, and replace him with Alyn Velaryon.

The excitement occasioned by Oakenfist's return was palpable, however, so all the Hand could do was seethe. When *Lady Baela*'s sails were first seen across the waters of Blackwater Bay, with the rest of the Velaryon fleet appearing from the morning mists behind her, every bell in King's Landing commenced to toll. Thousands crowded onto the city walls to cheer the hero, just as they had at Lannisport half a year before, whilst thousands more rushed out the River Gate to line the shores. But when

the king expressed the wish to go to the docks "to thank my good-brother for his service," the Hand forbade it, insisting it would not be fitting for His Grace to go to Lord Velaryon, that the admiral must come to the Red Keep to abase himself before the Iron Throne.

In this, as in the matter of Aegon's betrothal to Myrielle Peake, Lord Unwin found himself overruled by the other regents. Over his strenuous objections, King Aegon and Queen Daenera descended from the castle in their litter, accompanied by Lady Baela and her newborn daughter; her sister Lady Rhaena with her lord husband, Corwyn Corbray; Grand Maester Munkun; Septon Bernard; the regents Manfryd Mooton and Thaddeus Rowan; the knights of the Kingsguard; and many other notables eager to meet *Lady Baela* at the docks.

The morning was bright and cold, the chronicles tell us. There, before the eyes of tens of thousands, Lord Alyn Oakenfist beheld his daughter, Laena, for the first time. After kissing his lady wife, he took the child from her and held her high for all the crowd to see, as the cheers fell like thunder. Only then did he return the girl to her mother's arms and bend his knee before the king and queen. Queen Daenaera, blushing prettily and stammering just a little, hung about his neck a heavy golden chain studded with sapphires, "b-blue as the sea where my lord has won his victories." Then King Aegon III bade the admiral rise with the words, "We are glad to have you safe home, my brother."

Mushroom says that Oakenfist was laughing as he climbed back to his feet. "Sire," he replied, "you have honored me with your sister's hand, and I am proud to be your brother by marriage. Yet I can never be your brother by blood. But there is one who is." Then with a flamboyant gesture, Lord Alyn summoned forth the treasure he had brought from Lys. Down from the *Lady Baela* emerged a pale young woman of surpassing beauty, arm in arm with a richly clad boy near the king's own age, his features hidden beneath the cowl of his embroidered cloak.

Lord Unwin Peake could no longer contain himself. "Who is this?" he demanded, pushing forward. "Who are you?" The boy threw back his cowl. As the sunlight glittered on the silver-gold hair beneath, King Aegon III began to weep, throwing himself upon this boy in a fierce embrace. Oakenfist's "treasure" was Viserys Targaryen, the king's lost brother, the youngest son of Queen Rhaenyra and Prince Daemon, presumed dead since the Battle of the Gullet, and missing for nigh unto five years.

In 129 AC, it will be recalled that Queen Rhaenyra had sent her two youngest sons to Pentos to keep them from harm's way, only to have the ship taking them across the narrow sea sail into the teeth of a war fleet from the Triarchy. Whilst Prince Aegon had escaped on his dragon, Stormcloud, Prince Viserys had been taken. The Battle of the Gullet soon followed, and when no word was heard of the young prince afterward, he was presumed dead. No one could even say for a certainty which ship he had been on.

But though many thousands died in the Gullet, Viserys Targaryen was not one of them. The ship carrying the young princeling had survived the battle and limped back home to Lys, where Viserys found himself a captive of the grand admiral of the Triarchy, Sharako Lohar. Defeat had left Sharako in disgrace, however, and the Lyseni soon found himself besieged by enemies old and new, eager to bring him down. Desperate for coin and allies, he sold the boy to a certain magister of that city named Bambarro Bazanne, in return for Viserys's weight in gold and a promise of support. The subsequent murder of the disgraced admiral brought the tensions and rivalries amongst the Three Daughters to the surface, and long-simmering resentments flared into violence with a series of murders that soon led to open war. Amidst the chaos that followed, Magister Bambarro thought it prudent to keep his prize hidden away for the nonce, lest the boy be wrested away by one of his fellow Lyseni, or rivals from another city.

Viserys was well treated during his captivity. Though forbidden to leave the grounds of Bambarro's manse, he had his own suite of rooms, shared meals with the magister and his family, had tutors to instruct him in languages, literature, mathematics, history, and music, even a master-at-arms to teach him swordsmanship, at which art he soon excelled. It is widely believed (though never proved) that Bambarro's intent was to wait out the Dance of the Dragons, and then either ransom Prince Viserys back to his mother (should Rhaenyra emerge triumphant) or sell his head to his uncle (should Aegon II prove the victor).

As Lys suffered a series of shattering defeats in the Daughters' War, however, these plans went awry. Bambarro Bazanne died in the Disputed Lands in 132 AC when the sellsword company he was leading against Tyrosh turned against him over a matter of back pay. Upon his death, it was discovered that he had been enormously in debt, whereupon his creditors seized his manse. His wife and children were sold into slavery, and his furnishings, clothing, books, and other valuables, including the captive princeling, passed into the hands of another nobleman, Lysandro Rogare.

Lysandro was the patriarch of a rich and powerful banking and trading dynasty whose bloodlines could be traced back to Valyria before the Doom. Amongst many other holdings, the Rogares owned a famous pillow house, the Perfumed Garden. Viserys Targaryen was so striking that it is said Lysandro Rogare contemplated putting him to work as a courtesan . . . until the boy identified himself. Once he knew he had a prince in hand, the magister quickly revised his plans. Instead of selling the prince's favors, he married him to his youngest daughter, the Lady Larra Rogare, who would become known in the histories of Westeros as Larra of Lys.

The chance encounter between Alyn Velaryon and Drazenko Rogare at Sunspear had provided a perfect opportunity to effect the return of Prince Viserys to his brother . . . but it is not in the nature of any Lyseni to make a gift of anything that might be sold, so it was first necessary that Oakenfist come to Lys and agree to terms with Lysandro Rogare. "The realm might have been better served had it been Lord Alyn's mother at that table rather than Lord Alyn," Mushroom observes, rightly. Oakenfist was no haggler. To secure the prince, his lordship agreed that the Iron Throne would pay a ransom of one hundred thousand golden dragons, agree not to take up arms against House Rogare or its interests for a hundred years, entrust the Rogare Bank of Lys with such funds as were presently held by the Iron Bank of Braavos, grant lordships to three of Lysandro's younger sons, and . . . above all . . . swear upon his honor that the marriage between Viserys Targaryen and Larra Rogare would not be set aside, for any cause. To all of this Lord Alyn Velaryon had agreed, and affixed his sign and seal.

Prince Viserys had been seven when he was taken from the *Gay Abandon*. He was twelve on his return in 134 AC. His wife, the beautiful young woman who had walked arm in arm with him from the *Lady Baela,* was nineteen, seven years his senior. Though two years younger than the king, Viserys was in certain ways more mature than his elder brother. Aegon III had never shown any carnal interest in either of his queens (understandably in the case of Queen Daenaera, who was yet a child), but Viserys had already consummated his own marriage, as he confided proudly to Grand Maester Munkun during the feast held to welcome him home.

The return of his brother from the dead worked a wondrous change in Aegon III, Munkun tells us. His Grace had never truly forgiven himself for leaving Viserys to his fate when he fled the *Gay Abandon* on dragonback before the Battle of the Gullet. Though only nine at the time, Aegon came from a long line of warriors and heroes and had been raised on stories of their bold deeds and daring exploits, none of which included fleeing from a battle whilst abandoning your little brother to death. Down deep, the

Broken King felt himself unworthy to sit the Iron Throne. He had not been able to save his brother, his mother, or his little queen from grisly deaths. How could he presume to save a kingdom?

Viserys's return did much to lessen the king's loneliness as well. As a boy, Aegon had worshipped his three elder half-brothers, but it was Viserys who shared his bedchamber, his lessons, and his games. "Some part of the king had died with his brother in the Gullet," wrote Munkun. "It is plain to see that Aegon's affection for Gaemon Palehair was born of his desire to replace the little brother he had lost, but only when Viserys was restored to him did Aegon seem once more alive and whole." Prince Viserys once again became King Aegon's constant companion, as he had been when they were boys together on Dragonstone, whilst Gaemon Palehair was cast aside and forgotten, and even Queen Daenaera was neglected.

The return of the lost prince resolved the question of succession as well. As the king's brother, Viserys was the undisputed heir apparent, ahead of any child born to Baela Velaryon or Rhaena Corbray, or the twins themselves. King Aegon's choice of a girl of six as his second wife no longer seemed so worrisome. Prince Viserys was a lively, likely young lad, possessed of great charm and boundless vitality. Though not as tall, as strong, or as handsome as his brother, he struck all who met him as more clever and more curious than the king . . . and his own wife was no child, but a beautiful young woman well into her childbearing years. Let Aegon have his child-bride; Larra of Lys was like to give Viserys children sooner rather than later, thereby securing the dynasty.

For all these reasons, king and court and city rejoiced at the prince's coming, and Lord Alyn Velaryon became more beloved than ever for delivering Viserys from his captivity in Lys. Their joy was not shared by the King's Hand, however. Whilst Lord Unwin declared himself delighted by the return of the king's brother, he was furious at the price Oakenfist had agreed to pay for him. The young admiral had no authority to consent to such "ruinous terms," Peake insisted; only the regents and the Hand were empowered to speak for the Iron Throne, not any "fool with a fleet."

Law and tradition were on his side, Grand Maester Munkun admitted when the Hand brought his grievances to the council . . . but the king and the smallfolk felt otherwise, and it would have been the height of folly to repudiate Lord Alyn's pact. The other regents concurred. They voted new honors for Oakenfist, confirmed the legitimacy of Prince Viserys's marriage to Lady Larra, agreed to pay her father the ransom in ten annual payments, and moved a vastly greater sum of gold from Braavos to Lys.

For Lord Unwin Peake, this seemed yet another humiliating rebuke. Coming so close on the heels of the Maiden's Day Cattle Show and the king's repudiation of his daughter, Myrielle, in favor of the child Daenaera, it was more than his pride could endure. Mayhaps his lordship thought he could bend his fellow regents to his will by threatening to resign as King's Hand. Instead the council accepted his resignation with alacrity, and appointed the bluff, honest, and well-regarded Lord Thaddeus Rowan in his place.

Unwin Peake removed himself to his seat at Starpike to brood upon the wrongs he felt he had suffered, though his aunt the Lady Clarice, his uncle Gedmund Peake the Great-Axe, Gareth Long, Victor Risley, Lucas Leygood, George Graceford, Septon Bernard, and his many other appointments did not follow him, but continued to serve in their respective offices, as did his bastard brother Ser Mervyn Flowers and his nephew Ser Amaury Peake, for Sworn Brothers of the Kingsguard serve for life. Lord Unwin even bequeathed Tessario and his Fingers to his successor; the king had his guards, he declared, and so must the Hand.

The Lysene Spring and the End of Regency

Peace reigned over King's Landing for the remainder of that year, marred only by the death of Manfryd Mooton, Lord of Maidenpool and nearly the last of King Aegon's original regents. His lordship had been failing for some time, never truly having regained his strength after the Winter Fever, so his passing excited little comment. To take his place upon the council, Lord Rowan turned to Ser Corwyn Corbray, Lady Rhaena's husband. Her sister, Lady Baela, meanwhile returned to Driftmark with Lord Alyn and their daughter. Not long after, Prince Viserys thrilled the court by announcing that the Lady Larra was with child. All of King's Landing rejoiced.

Beyond the city, however, 134 AC would not be a year to remember fondly. North of the Neck, winter still held the land in its icy fist. At Barrowton, Lord Dustin closed his gates as hundreds of starving villagers gathered beneath his walls. White Harbor fared better, for its port allowed food to be brought in from the south, but prices rose so high that good men began to sell themselves into bondage to slave traders from across the sea so their wives and children might eat, whilst worse men sold their wives and children. Even in the winter town, beneath the very walls of Winterfell, the northmen fell to eating dogs and horses. Cold and hunger carried off a third of the Night's Watch, and when thousands of wildlings walked across the frozen sea east of the Wall, hundreds more of the black brothers perished in battle.

In the Iron Islands, a savage struggle for power followed upon the death of the Red Kraken. His three sisters and the men they had married seized Toron Greyjoy, the boy upon the Seastone Chair, and put his mother to death, whilst his cousins joined with the lords of Harlaw and Blacktyde to raise up Toron's half-brother Rodrik, and the men of Great Wyk rallied to a pretender called Sam Salt, who claimed to be descended of the black line.

Their bloody three-way fight had been raging for half a year when Ser Leo Costayne descended upon them with his fleet, landing thousands of Lannister swords and spears on Pyke, Great Wyk, and Harlaw. Lord Oakenfist had refused to be a part of House Lannister's vengeance upon the ironmen, but the old Sea Lion proved more amenable to Lady Johanna's entreaties . . . swayed, mayhaps, by her promise to marry him if he delivered the Iron Islands to her son's rule. That proved beyond Ser Leo's power to achieve, however. Costayne died amidst the stony hills of Great Wyk, cut down by the hand of Arthur Goodbrother, and three-quarters of his ships were seized or sunk in those cold grey seas.

Though Lady Johanna's wish to put every ironman to the sword was frustrated, no man could doubt that the Lannisters had paid their debt by the time the fight was done. Hundreds of longships and fishing boats were burned, with as many homes and villages. The wives and children of the ironborn who had wreaked such havoc on the westerlands were put to the sword wherever they were found. Amongst the slain were nine of the Red Kraken's cousins, two of his three sisters and their husbands, Lord Drumm of Old Wyk and Lord Goodbrother of Great Wyk, as well as the Lords Volmark and Harlaw of Harlaw, Botley of Lordsport, and Stonehouse of Old Wyk. Thousands more would die of starvation before the year was done, for the Lannisters also carried off many tons of stored grain and salt fish, and despoiled that which they could not carry. Though Toron Greyjoy remained upon the Seastone Chair when his defenders beat off the Lannister assault upon the walls of Pyke, his half-brother Rodrik was taken and brought back to Casterly Rock, where Lady Johanna had him gelded and made him her son's fool.

Across the width of Westeros, another struggle for succession broke out late in the year 134, when Lady Jeyne Arryn, the Maiden of the Vale, died at Gulltown of a cold that had settled in her chest. Forty years of age, she perished in the Motherhouse of Maris on its stony island in the harbor of Gulltown, wrapped in the arms of Jessamyn Redfort, her "dear companion." On her deathbed, her ladyship dictated a last testament, naming her cousin Ser Joffrey Arryn as her heir. Ser Joffrey had served her loyally for the past ten years as Knight of the Bloody Gate, defending the Vale against the savage wildlings of the hills.

Ser Joffrey was only a fourth cousin by degree, however. Far closer by blood was Lady Jeyne's first cousin, Ser Arnold Arryn, who had twice attempted to depose her. Imprisoned after his second failed rebellion, Ser Arnold was now quite mad after long years in the Eyrie's sky cells and the dungeons under the Gates of the Moon . . . but his son Ser Eldric Arryn was sane, shrewd, and ambitious, and came forward now to press his father's claim. Many lords of the Vale rallied to his banners, insisting that long-established laws of inheritance could not be put aside by "the whim of a dying woman."

A third claimant emerged in the person of one Isembard Arryn, patriarch of the Gulltown Arryns, a still more distant branch of that great house. Having split off from their noble kin during the reign of King Jaehaerys, the Gulltown Arryns had gone into trade and grown rich. Men japed that the falcon on Isembard's arms was made of gold, and he soon became known as the Gilded Falcon. He used that wealth now, bribing lesser lords to support his claim and bringing sellswords across the narrow sea.

Lord Rowan did what he could to alleviate these woes, commanding the Lannisters to withdraw from the Iron Islands, shipping food to the North, and summoning the Arryn claimants to King's Landing to present their cases to the regents, but his efforts were largely ineffectual. The Lannisters and the Arryns alike ignored his decrees, and far too little food arrived at White Harbor to alleviate the famine. Though well-liked, neither Thaddeus Rowan nor the boy he served were feared. By year's end, many at court had begun to whisper that it was not the regents who ruled the realm, but rather the moneychangers of Lys.

Though the court and city still doted on the king's brother, that clever, gallant boy Viserys, the same could not be said for his Lysene wife. Larra Rogare had taken up residence in the Red Keep with her husband, yet in her heart she remained a lady of Lys. Though fluent in High Valyrian and the dialects of Myr, Tyrosh, and Old Volantis in addition to her own Lysene tongue, Lady Larra made no effort to learn the Common Tongue, preferring to rely upon translators to make her wishes known. Her ladies were all Lyseni, as were her servants. The gowns she wore all came from Lys, even her smallclothes; her father's ships delivered the latest Lysene fashions to her thrice a year. She even had her own protectors. Lysene swords guarded her night and day, under the command of her brother Moredo and a towering mute from the fighting pits of Meereen called Sandoq the Shadow.

All this the court and kingdom might have come to accept in time, had Lady Larra not also insisted upon keeping her own gods. She would have no part in the worship of the Seven, nor the old gods of the northmen. Her worship was reserved for certain of the manifold gods of Lys: the six-breasted cat goddess Pantera, Yndros of the Twilight who was male by day and female by night, the pale child Bakkalon of the Sword, faceless Saagael, the giver of pain.

Her ladies, her servants, and her guards would join Lady Larra at certain times in performing obeisances to these queer, ancient deities. Cats were seen coming and going from her chambers so often that men began to say they were her spies, purring at her in soft voices of all the doings of the Red Keep. It was even said that Larra herself could transform into a cat, to prowl the gutters and rooftops of the city. Darker rumors soon arose. The acolytes of Yndros could supposedly transform themselves from male to female and female to male through the act of love, and whispers went about that her ladyship oft availed herself of this ability at twilight orgies, so she might visit the brothels on the Street of Silk as a man. And every time a child went missing, the ignorant would look at one another and talk of Saagael's insatiable thirst for blood.

Even less loved than Larra of Lys were the three brothers who had come with her to King's Landing. Moredo commanded his sister's guards, whilst Lotho set about establishing a branch of the Rogare Bank atop Visenya's Hill. Roggerio, the youngest, opened an opulent Lysene pillow house called the Mermaid beside the River Gate, and filled it with parrots from the Summer Islands, monkeys from Sothoryos, and a hundred exotic girls (and boys) from every corner of the earth. Though their favors cost ten times as much as any other brothel dared to charge, Roggerio never lacked for customers. Great lords and common tradesmen alike spoke of the beauties and wonders to be found behind the Mermaid's carved and painted doors . . . including, some said, an actual mermaid. (Almost all that we know of the myriad marvels of the Mermaid comes to us from Mushroom, who alone amongst our chroniclers is willing to confess to visiting the brothel himself on many occasions and partaking of its many pleasures in sumptuously appointed rooms.)

Across the sea, the Daughters' War finally reached its end. Racallio Ryndoon fled south to the Basilisk Isles with his remaining supporters; Lys, Tyrosh, and Myr divided the Disputed Lands; and the Dornish took dominion over most of the Stepstones. The Myrish suffered the greatest losses in these new arrangements, whilst the Archon of Tyrosh and the Princess of Dorne gained the most. In Lys, ancient houses fell and many a highborn magister was cast down and ruined, whilst others rose up to seize the reins of power. Chief amongst these was Lysandro Rogare and his brother Drazenko, architect of the Dornish alliance. Drazenko's ties to Sunspear and Lysandro's to the Iron Throne made the Rogares the princes of Lys in all but name.

By the end of 134 AC, some feared they might soon rule Westeros as well. Their pride and pomp and power became the talk of King's Landing. Men began to whisper of their wiles. Lotho bought men with gold, Roggerio seduced them with perfumed flesh, Moredo frightened them into submission with steel. Yet the brothers were no more than puppets in the hands of Lady Larra; it was her and her queer Lysene gods who held their strings. The king, the little queen, the young prince . . . they were only children, blind to what was happening about them, whilst the Kingsguard and the gold cloaks and even the King's Hand had been bought and sold.

Or so the stories went. Like all such tales, they had some truth to them, well mixed with fear and falsehood. That the Lyseni were proud, grasping, and ambitious cannot be doubted. That Lotho used his bank and Roggerio his brothel to win friends to their cause goes without saying. Yet in the end they differed but little from many of the other lords and ladies of Aegon III's court, all of them pursuing power and wealth in their own ways. Though more successful than their rivals (for a time, at least), the Lyseni were only one of several factions competing for influence. Had Lady Larra and her brothers been Westerosi, they might have been admired and celebrated, but their foreign birth, foreign ways, and foreign gods made them objects of mistrust and suspicion instead.

Munkun refers to this period as the Rogare Ascendency, but that term was only ever used at Oldtown, amongst the maesters and archmaesters of the Citadel. The people who lived through it called it the Lysene Spring . . . for spring was indeed a part of it. Early in 135 AC, the Conclave sent forth its white ravens from Oldtown to herald the end of one of the longest and cruelest winters that the Seven Kingdoms had ever known.

Spring is ever a season of hope, rebirth, and renewal, and the spring of 135 AC was no different. The war in the Iron Islands came to an end, and Lord Cregan Stark of Winterfell borrowed a huge sum from the Iron Bank of Braavos to buy food and seed for his starving smallfolk. Only in the Vale did fighting continue. Furious at the refusal of the Arryn claimants to come to King's Landing and submit their dispute to the judgment of the regents, Lord Thaddeus Rowan sent a thousand men to Gulltown under the command of his fellow regent, Ser Corwyn Corbray, to restore the King's Peace and settle the matter of succession.

Meanwhile, King's Landing experienced a period of prosperity such as it had not seen in many years, in no small part thanks to House Rogare of Lys. The Rogare Bank was paying rich returns on all the monies deposited with them, leading more and more lords to entrust the Lyseni with their gold. Trade flourished as well, as ships from Tyrosh, Myr, Pentos, Braavos, and especially Lys crowded the docks along the Blackwater, offloading silks and spices, Myrish lace, jade from Qarth, ivory from Sothoryos, and many other strange and wondrous things from the ends of the earth, including luxuries seldom seen in the Seven Kingdoms before.

Other port towns shared in the bounty; Duskendale, Maidenpool, Gulltown, and White Harbor saw their trade expand as well, as did Oldtown to the south, and even Lannisport upon the sunset sea. On Driftmark, the town of Hull experienced a rebirth. Scores of new ships were built and launched, and Lord Oakenfist's mother greatly expanded her own trading fleets, and began work on a palatial manse overlooking the harbor that Mushroom dubbed the Mouse House.

Across the narrow sea, Lys itself was prospering under the "velvet tyranny" of Lysandro Rogare, who had taken on himself the style of First Magister for Life. And when his brother Drazenko married Princess Aliandra Martell of Dorne, and was named by her Prince Consort and Lord of the Stepstones, the ascendancy of House Rogare reached its apex. Men began to speak of Lysandro the Magnificent.

During the first quarter of 135 AC, two momentous events were the occasion of great joy throughout the Seven Kingdoms of Westeros. On the third day of the third moon of that year, the people of King's Landing woke to a sight that had not been seen since the dark days of the Dance: a dragon in the skies above the city. Lady Rhaena, at the age of nineteen, was flying her dragon, Morning, for the first time. That first day she circled once around the city before returning to the Dragonpit, but every day thereafter she grew bolder and flew farther.

Only once did Rhaena land Morning inside the Red Keep, however, for not even the best efforts of Prince Viserys could persuade his brother the king to come see his sister fly (though Queen Daenaera was so delighted with Morning that she was heard to say that she wanted a dragon of her own). Shortly thereafter, Morning carried Lady Rhaena across Blackwater Bay to Dragonstone where, as she said, "Dragons and those who ride them are more welcome."

Less than a fortnight later, Larra of Lys gave birth to a son, Prince Viserys's firstborn child. The mother was twenty years of age, the father only thirteen. Viserys named the child Aegon after his brother, the king, and placed a dragon's egg inside his cradle, as had become the custom with all trueborn children of House Targaryen. Aegon was anointed with the seven oils by Septon Bernard in the royal sept, and the bells of the city rang in celebration of his birth. Gifts were sent from every corner of the realm, though none so lavish as those bestowed upon the babe by his Lyseni uncles. In Lys, Lysandro the Magnificent declared a day of feasting in honor of his grandson.

Yet even in the midst of joy, whispers of discontent began to be heard. This new son of House Targaryen had been anointed into the Faith, but soon enough the city heard that his mother meant to have him blessed by her own gods as well, and rumors of obscene ceremonies in the Mermaid and blood sacrifice in Maegor's Holdfast began to be heard on the streets of King's Landing. The trouble might have ended there, with talk, but soon thereafter a series of disasters befell the realm and royal family, each following hard upon the heels of the other, until even men who mocked the gods, like Mushroom, began to question whether the Seven had turned against House Targaryen and the Seven Kingdoms in their wroth.

The first omen of the dark times to come was seen on Driftmark, when the dragon's egg presented to Laena Velaryon upon her birth quickened and hatched. Her parents' pride and pleasure quickly turned to ash, however; the dragon that wriggled from the egg was a monstrosity, a wingless wyrm, maggot-white and blind. Within moments of hatching, the creature turned upon the babe in her cradle and tore a bloody chunk from her arm. As Laena shrieked, Lord Oakenfist ripped the "dragon" off her, flung it to the floor, and hacked it into pieces.

The news of this monstrous dragonbirth and its bloody aftermath were greatly troubling to King Aegon, and soon led to angry words between His Grace and his brother. Prince Viserys still had his own dragon's egg. Though it had never quickened, the prince had kept it with him throughout his years of exile and captivity, for it held great meaning for him. When Aegon commanded that no dragon's eggs were to be allowed in his castle, Viserys grew most wroth. Yet the king's will prevailed, as it must; the egg was sent to Dragonstone, and Prince Viserys refused to speak to King Aegon for a moon's turn.

His Grace was much dismayed by the quarrel with his brother, Mushroom tells us, but what happened next left him bereft and devastated. King Aegon was enjoying a quiet supper in his solar with his little queen, Daenaera, and his friend Gaemon Palehair and the dwarf was entertaining them with a silly song about a bear that drank too much, when the bastard boy began to complain of a cramping in his gut. "Run fetch Grand Maester Munkun," the king commanded Mushroom. By the time the fool returned with the Grand Maester, Gaemon had collapsed and Queen Daenaera was moaning, "My belly hurts too."

Gaemon had long served as King Aegon's food taster as well as his cupbearer, and Munkun soon declared that both he and the little queen were the victims of poisoning. The Grand Maester gave Daenaera a powerful purgative, which most like saved her life. She retched uncontrollably throughout the night, wailing and writhing in pain, and was too drained and weak to leave her bed the next day, but she was cleansed. Munkun came too late for Gaemon Palehair, however. The boy died within the hour. Born a bastard in a brothel, "King Cunny" had reigned briefly over his kingdom on a hill during the Moon of Madness, seen his mother put to death, and served Aegon III as cupbearer, whipping boy, and friend. He was thought to be but nine years old at his death.

Afterward Grand Maester Munkun fed what remained of the supper to a cage of rats, and determined that the poison had been baked into the crust of the apple tarts. Fortunately, the king had never been especially fond of sweets (nor of any other food, if truth be told). The knights of the Kingsguard at once descended to the Red Keep's kitchens and took a dozen cooks, bakers, scullions, and serving girls into custody, delivering them to George Graceford, the Lord Confessor. Under torture, seven confessed to attempting to poison the king . . . but each account differed from the next, there was no agreement on where they got the poison, and none of the captives correctly named the dish that had been poisoned, so Lord Rowan reluctantly dismissed their confessions as "not fit to wipe my arse with." (The Hand was in a black state even before the poisoning, for he had only recently suffered his own personal tragedy when his young wife, the Lady Floris, died in childbirth.)

Though the king had spent less time with his cupbearer after his brother's return to Westeros, Gaemon Palehair's death nonetheless left Aegon inconsolable. One small good came from it, for it helped to heal the rift between the king and his brother Viserys, who broke his stubborn silence to comfort His Grace in his grief, and sat with him by the queen's bedside. That proved little enough, however. Thereafter it was Aegon who was silent, for his old gloom had settled over him once again, and he seemed to lose all interest in his court and kingdom.

The next blow fell far from King's Landing, in the Vale of Arryn, when Ser Corwyn Corbray ruled that Lady Jeyne's will must prevail and declared Ser Joffrey Arryn the rightful Lord of the Eyrie. When the other claimants proved intransigent and refused to accept his ruling, Ser Corwyn imprisoned the Gilded Falcon and his sons and executed Eldric Arryn, yet somehow Ser Eldric's mad father, Ser Arnold, eluded him and fled to Runestone, where he had served as a squire in his boyhood. Gunthor Royce, known in the Vale as the Bronze Giant, was an old man, as stubborn as he was fearless; when Ser Corwyn arrived to winkle Ser Arnold out of his sanctuary, Lord Gunthor donned his ancient bronze armor and rode out to confront him. Words grew heated, turned to curses, then to threats. When Corbray drew on Lady Forlorn—whether to strike at Royce or merely threaten him will never be known—a crossbowman on Runestone's battlements loosed a quarrel and pierced him through the breast.

Striking down one of the king's regents was an act of treason, akin to attacking the king himself. Moreover, Ser Corwyn had been uncle to Quenton Corbray, the powerful and martial Lord of Heart's Home, as well as the beloved husband to Lady Rhaena the dragonrider, goodbrother to her twin, Lady Baela, and thus by marriage kin to Alyn Oakenfist. With his death, the flames of war sprang up anew across the Vale of Arryn. The Corbrays, Hunters, Craynes, and Redforts rallied in support of Lady Jeyne's chosen heir, Ser Joffrey Arryn, whilst the Royces of Runestone and Ser Arnold, the Mad Heir, were joined by the Templetons, Tolletts, Coldwaters, and Duttons, along with the lords of the Fingers and Three Sisters. Gulltown and House Grafton remained staunch in its support of the Gilded Falcon, despite his captivity.

The answer from King's Landing was not long in coming. Lord Rowan sent one last flight of ravens to the Vale, commanding those lords supporting the Mad Heir and Gilded Falcon to lay down their arms at once, lest they provoke "the Iron Throne's displeasure." When no reply was forthcoming, the Hand took counsel with Oakenfist and made plans to bring the rebellion to an end by force.

With the coming of spring, it was thought that the high road through the Mountains of the Moon would once again be passable. Five thousand men set out up the kingsroad, under the command of Ser Robert Rowan, Lord Thaddeus's eldest son. Levies from Maidenpool, Darry, and Hayford swelled their numbers on the march, and once across the Trident they were joined by six hundred Freys and a thousand Blackwoods under Lord Benjicot himself, making them nine thousand strong entering the mountains.

A second attack was launched by sea. Rather than make use of the royal fleet commanded by Ser Gedmund Peake the Great-Axe, his predecessor's uncle, the Hand turned to House Velaryon for the required ships. Oakenfist would command the fleet himself, whilst his wife, Lady Baela, went to Dragonstone to comfort her widowed twin (and incidentally make certain that Lady Rhaena did not attempt to avenge her husband's death herself on Morning).

The army Lord Alyn was to carry to the Vale would be commanded by Lady Larra's brother Moredo Rogare, Lord Rowan announced. That Lord Moredo was a fearsome fighter, none could doubt; tall and stern, with white-blond hair and blazing blue eyes, he looked the very image of a warrior of Old Valyria, men said, and bore a longsword of Valyrian steel he called Truth.

His prowess notwithstanding, however, the Lyseni's appointment was deeply unpopular. Whilst his brothers, Roggerio and Lotho, were both fluent in the Common Tongue, Moredo's grasp of the language was limited at best, and the wisdom of putting a Lyseni in command of an army of Westerosi knights was widely questioned. Lord Rowan's enemies at court—amongst them many of the men who owed their offices to Unwin Peake—were quick to say that this was proof of what they had been whispering for half a year, that Thaddeus Rowan had sold himself to Oakenfist and the Rogares.

Such muttering might not have mattered had the assaults upon the Vale been successful. They were not. Though Oakenfist easily swept aside the Gilded Falcon's sellsails to capture the harbor at Gulltown, the attackers lost hundreds of men taking the port walls by storm, and thrice as many during the house-to-house fighting that followed. After his translator was slain during the battle in the streets, Moredo Rogare had great difficulty communicating with his own troops; the men did not understand his commands, and he did not understand their reports. Chaos ensued.

At the other end of the Vale, meanwhile, the high road through the mountains proved far less open than had been assumed. Ser Robert Rowan's host found itself struggling through deep snows in the higher passes, slowing their advance to a crawl, and time and time again their baggage train came under attack by the savages native to those mountains (descendants of the First Men driven from the Vale by the Andals thousands of years before). "They were skeletons in skins, armed with stone axes and wooden clubs," Ben Blackwood said later, "but so hungry and so desperate that they could not be deterred, no matter how many we killed." Soon the cold and the snow and the nightly attacks began to take a toll.

High in the mountains, the unthinkable happened one night as Ser Robert and his men huddled about their campfires. In the slopes above, a cave mouth was visible from the road, and a dozen men climbed up to see if it might offer them shelter from the wind. The bones scattered about the mouth of the cave might have given them pause, yet they pressed on . . . and roused a dragon.

Sixteen men perished in the fight that followed, and threescore more suffered burns before the angry brown wyrm took wing and fled deeper into the mountains with "a ragged woman clinging to its back." That was the last known sighting of Sheepstealer and his rider, Nettles, recorded in the annals of Westeros . . . though the wildlings of the mountains still tell tales of a "fire witch" who once dwelled in a hidden vale far from any road or village. One of the most savage of the mountain clan came to worship her, the storytellers say; youths would prove their courage by bringing gifts to her, and were only accounted men when they returned with burns to show that they had faced the dragon woman in her lair.

Their encounter with the dragon was not the last peril encountered by Ser Robert's host. By the time they reached the Bloody Gate, a third of them had perished in a wildling attack or died from cold or hunger. Amongst the dead was Ser Robert Rowan, crushed by a falling boulder when the clansmen toppled half a mountainside down upon the column. Bloody Ben Blackwood assumed command upon his death. Though still a half year shy of manhood, Lord Blackwood by this time had as much experience of war as men four times his age. At the Bloody Gate, the entrance to the Vale, the survivors found food, warmth, and welcome . . . but Ser Joffrey Arryn, the Knight of the Bloody Gate and Lady Jeyne Arryn's chosen successor, saw at once that the crossing had left Blackwood's men unfit for battle. Far from being a help to him in his war, they would be a burden.

Even as the fighting in the Vale of Arryn continued, the promise of the Lysene Spring suffered another grievous blow hundreds of leagues to the south, with the near-simultaneous demise of Lysandro the Magnificent in Lys and his brother Drazenko in Sunspear. Though the narrow sea lay between them, the two Rogares died within a day of each other, both under suspicious circumstances. Drazenko perished first, choking to death upon a piece of bacon. Lysandro drowned when his opulent barge sank whilst carrying him from his Perfumed Garden back to his palace. Though a few would insist that their deaths were unfortunate accidents, many more took the manner and timing of their passings as proof of a plot to bring down House Rogare. The Faceless Men of Braavos were widely believed to have been responsible for the killings; no more subtle assassins were known to exist anywhere in the wide world.

But if indeed the Faceless Men had done these deeds, at whose bidding had they acted? The Iron Bank of Braavos was suspected, as was the Archon of Tyrosh, Racallio Ryndoon, and various merchant princes and magisters of Lys known to have chafed under the "velvet tyranny" of Lysandro the Magnificent. Some went so far as to suggest that the First Magister had been removed by his own sons (he had sired six trueborn sons, three daughters, and sixteen bastards). So skillfully had the brothers been removed, however, that not even the fact of murder could be proved.

None of the offices through which Lysandro exercised his dominion over Lys were hereditary. His crab-eaten corpse had scarce been dredged up from the sea before his old enemies, false friends, and erstwhile allies began the struggle to succeed him.

Amongst the Lyseni, it is truly said, wars are fought with plots and poisons rather than with armies. For the rest of that bloody year, the magisters and merchant princes of Lys performed a deadly dance, rising and falling almost fortnightly. Oft as not their falls were fatal. Torreo Haen was poisoned with his wife, his mistress, his daughters (one being the maid whose wisp of a gown had caused such scandal at the Maiden's Day Ball), siblings, and supporters at the feast he held to celebrate his elevation to first magister. Silvario Pendaerys was stabbed through the eye leaving the Temple of Trade, whilst his brother Pereno was garroted in a pillow house as a slave girl pleasured him with her mouth. The *gonfaloniere* Moreo Dagareon was slain by his own elite guards, and Matteno Orthys, a fervent worshipper of the goddess Pantera, was mauled and partly devoured by his prized shadowcat when its cage was unaccountably left open one night.

Though Lysandro's children could not inherit his offices, his palace went to his daughter Lysara, his ships to his son Drako, his pillow house to his son Fredo, his library to his daughter Marra. All of his offspring partook of the wealth represented by the Rogare Bank. Even his bastards received shares, albeit fewer than those allotted to his trueborn sons and daughters. Effective control of the bank, however, was vested in Lysandro's eldest son, Lysaro . . . of whom it was truly written, "he had twice his father's ambition and half his father's ability."

Lysaro Rogare aspired to rule Lys, but had neither the cunning nor the patience to spend decades in the slow accumulation of wealth and power, as his father Lysandro had. With rivals dying all around him, Lysaro first moved to secure his own person by buying one thousand Unsullied from the slavers of Astapor. These eunuch warriors were renowned as the finest foot soldiers in the world, and were moreover trained to absolute obedience, so their masters need never fear defiance or betrayal.

Once surrounded by these protectors, Lysaro secured his selection as *gonfaloniere*, winning the commons with lavish entertainments and the magisters with bribes larger than any of them had ever seen before. When these expenditures exhausted his personal fortune, he began to divert gold from the bank. His intent, as he later revealed, was to provoke a short, victorious war with Tyrosh or Myr. As *gonfaloniere*, the glory of conquest would accrue to him, enabling him to win the office of first magister. By sacking Tyrosh or Myr, he would gain sufficient gold to restore the funds he had taken from the bank and leave him the richest man in Lys.

It was a fool's scheme, and it was quickly undone. Legend claims it was men in the hire of the Iron Bank of Braavos who first began suggesting that the Rogare Bank might be unsound, but regardless of who started it, such talk was soon heard all over Lys. The city's magisters and merchant princes began to demand the return of their deposits; a few at first, then more and more, until a river of gold was pouring from Lysaro's vaults . . . a river that soon enough ran dry. By that time Lysaro himself was gone. Faced with ruin, he fled Lys in the dead of night with three bed slaves, six servants, and a hundred of his Unsullied, abandoning his wife, his daughters, and his palace. Understandably alarmed, the city magisters moved at once to seize the Rogare Bank, only to discover that naught remained but a hollow shell.

The fall of House Rogare was swift and brutal. Lysaro's brothers and sisters claimed to have played no part in the despoiling of the bank, but many doubted their claims of innocence. Drako Rogare escaped to Volantis on one of his galleys whilst his sister Marra fled to the temple of Yndros in man's garb and there claimed sanctuary, but all their siblings were seized and put on trial, even the bastards. When Lysara Rogare protested, "I did not know," Magister Tigaro Moraqos replied, "You should have," and the mob roared its approval. Half the city had been ruined.

Nor was the damage confined to Lys. As word of the fall of the House of Rogare reached Westeros, lords and merchants alike soon realized the coin they had entrusted to the House of Rogare was lost. In Gulltown, Moredo Rogare moved swiftly, yielding up his command to Alyn Oakenfist and taking ship for Braavos. Lotho Rogare was arrested by Ser Lucas Leygood and his gold cloaks as he attempted to depart King's Landing; all his letters and ledgers were seized, along with every scrap of gold and silver remaining in the vaults atop Visenya's Hill. Meanwhile, Ser Marston Waters of the Kingsguard descended on the Mermaid with two of his Sworn Brothers and fifty guardsmen. The patrons of the brothel were driven into the street, many of them naked (Mushroom was amongst those so rousted, by his own admission), whilst Lord Roggerio was marched at spearpoint through a jeering crowd. At the Red Keep, the brothel keeper and the banker both were imprisoned in the Tower of the

Hand; their kinship to Prince Viserys's wife spared them the horrors of the black cells, for the nonce.

At first it was widely assumed that the Hand had ordered their arrest. With Ser Corwyn's death in the Vale, only Lord Rowan and Grand Maester Munkun remained as regents. This misapprehension lasted only a few hours, for that very evening Lord Rowan himself joined the Rogares in captivity. Nor did the Fingers, the Hand's supposed protectors, do aught to defend him. When Ser Mervyn Flowers entered the council chambers to take his lordship into custody, Tessario the Tiger ordered his men to stand aside. The only resistance was that offered by Lord Rowan's squire, who was quickly overwhelmed. "Spare the boy," Lord Thaddeus pleaded, and they did . . . but not until Flowers had cut off one of the lad's ears, "to teach him not to bare steel to the Kingsguard."

The list of those to be seized and held for trial as suspected traitors did not end there. Three of Lord Rowan's cousins and one of his nephews were also arrested, along with twoscore grooms, servants, and knights retainer in his service. All were taken unawares and yielded meekly. But when Ser Amaury Peake approached Maegor's Holdfast with a dozen men-at-arms, he found Viserys Targaryen himself upon the drawbridge, a battleaxe in hand. "It was a heavy axe, the prince a somewhat spindly boy of three-and-ten," the fool Mushroom tells us. "One doubted that the lad could even lift that axe, much less wield it."

"If you are come to take my lady wife, ser, turn and go," the young prince said, "for you shall not pass whilst I still stand."

Ser Amaury found his show of defiance more amusing than threatening. "Your lady is wanted for questioning in connection with the treason of her brothers," he told the prince.

"And who is it who wants her?" the prince demanded.

"The Hand of the King," Ser Amaury replied.

"Lord Rowan?" asked Viserys.

"Lord Rowan has been removed from office. Ser Marston Waters is the new King's Hand."

At that moment Aegon III himself stepped from the holdfast gate to stand beside his brother. "I am the king," His Grace reminded them, "and I never chose Ser Marston for my Hand."

Aegon's intervention took Ser Amaury aback, Mushroom tells us, but after a moment's hesitation he said, "Your Grace is still a boy. Until you come of age, Sire, your leal lords must make such choices for you. Ser Marston was chosen by your regents."

"Lord Rowan is my regent," the king insisted.

"No longer," said Ser Amaury. "Lord Rowan betrayed your trust. His regency is at an end."

"By whose authority?" demanded Aegon.

"The Hand of the King," said the white knight.

Prince Viserys laughed at that (for King Aegon never laughed, to Mushroom's dismay) and said, "The Hand names the regent and the regent names the Hand, and round and round and round we dance . . . but you shall not pass, ser, nor shall you touch my wife. Begone, or I promise you, every man of you shall die here."

Then Ser Amaury Peake ran short of patience. He could not allow himself to be balked by two boys, one of fifteen and one of thirteen, the elder unarmed. "Enough," he said and ordered his men to move the boys aside. "Be gentle with them, and see that they come to no harm at our hands."

"This is on your head, ser," Prince Viserys warned. He drove his axe deep into the wood of the drawbridge, scampered back, and said, "Go no farther than the axe, or you will die." The king took him by the shoulder and drew him back into the safety of the holdfast, and a shadow stepped onto the drawbridge.

Sandoq the Shadow had come from Lys with Lady Larra, a gift from her father the Magister Lysandro. Black of skin and black of hair, he stood almost seven feet tall. His face, which he oft kept hidden behind a black silk veil, was a mass of thin white scars, and his lips and tongue had been removed, leaving him both mute and hideous to look upon. It was said of him that he had been the victor of a hundred fights in the death pits of Meereen, that he had once torn out the throat of a foe with his teeth after his sword had shattered, that he drank the blood of the men he killed, that in the pits he had slain lions, bears, wolves, and wyverns with no weapon but the stones he found upon the sands.

Such tales grow in the telling, to be sure, and we cannot know how much of this, if any, is to be believed. Though Sandoq could not read or write, Mushroom tells us he was fond of music, and would oft sit in the shadows of Lady Larra's bedchamber playing sweet sad notes on a queer stringed instrument of goldenheart and ebony that stood near as tall as he did. "I could sometimes make the lady laugh, though she did not understand more than a few words of our tongue," the fool says, "but the Shadow's playing always made her weep, and strange to say she liked that better."

It was a different sort of music that Sandoq the Shadow played at the gates of Maegor's Holdfast, as Ser Amaury's guardsmen rushed at him with sword and spear. That night his chosen instruments were a tall black shield of nightwood, boiled hide, and iron, and a great curved sword with a dragonbone hilt whose dark blade shone in the torchlight with the distinctive ripples of Valyrian steel. His foes howled and cursed and shouted as they came at him, but the Shadow made no sound save with his steel, sliding through them silent as a cat, his blade whistling left and right and up and down, drawing blood with every cut, slashing through their mail as if they had been clad in parchment. Mushroom, who claims to have seen the battle from the roof above, testifies that "it did not look so much like a swordfight as like a farmer reaping grain. With every stroke more stalks would topple, but these stalks were living men who screamed and cursed as they fell." Ser Amaury's men did not lack for courage, and some lived long enough to strike blows of their own, but the Shadow, always moving, caught their blades upon his shield, then used that shield to shove them backward, off the bridge onto the hungry iron spikes below.

Let this be said of Ser Amaury Peake: his dying did not disgrace the Kingsguard. Three of his men were dead upon the drawbridge and two more were twisting on the spikes below by the time Peake slid his own blade from its scabbard. "He was clad in white scale armor under his white cloak," Mushroom tells us, "but his helm was openface and he had not brought a shield, and sorely did Sandoq make him answer for these lacks." The Shadow made a dance of it, the fool says; betwixt each fresh wound he dealt Ser Amaury, he would kill one of his remaining minions before turning back to the white knight. Yet Peake fought on with stub-

born valor, and near the end, for half a heartbeat, the gods gave him his chance when the last of the guards somehow got his hand around Sandoq's sword, and ripped it from the Shadow's grasp before he went tumbling off the bridge. From his knees, Ser Amaury staggered back to his feet and charged his unarmed foe.

Sandoq tore Viserys's battleaxe from the wood where the prince had buried it and split Ser Amaury's head and helm in half from crest to gorget. Leaving the corpse to topple onto the spikes, the Shadow paused long enough to shove the dead and dying from the drawbridge before retreating inside Maegor's Holdfast, whereupon the king commanded the bridge to be raised, the portcullis lowered, and the gates barred. The castle-within-the-castle stood secure.

And so it would remain for eighteen days.

The rest of the Red Keep was in the hands of Ser Marston Waters and his Kingsguard, whilst beyond the castle walls Ser Lucas Leygood and his gold cloaks kept a firm grip on King's Landing. Both of them presented themselves before the holdfast the next morning, to demand that the king leave his sanctuary. "Your Grace does us wrong to think we mean him harm," Ser Marston said, as the corpses of the men Sandoq had slain were brought up from the moat. "We acted only to protect Your Grace from false friends and traitors. Ser Amaury was sworn to protect you, to give his own life for yours if need be. He was your leal man, as I am. He did not deserve such a death, at the hands of such a beast."

King Aegon was unmoved. "Sandoq is no beast," he answered from the battlements. "He cannot speak, but he hears and he obeys. I commanded Ser Amaury to be gone, and he refused. My brother warned him what would happen if he stepped beyond the axe. The vows of the Kingsguard include obedience, I thought."

"We are sworn to obey the king, sire, this is so," replied Ser Marston, "and when you are a man grown, my brothers and I will gladly fall upon our swords should you command that of us. So long as you remain a child, however, we are required by oath to obey the King's Hand, for the Hand speaks with the king's voice."

"Lord Thaddeus is my Hand," Aegon insisted.

"Lord Thaddeus sold your realm to Lys and must answer for it. I will serve as your Hand until such time as his guilt or innocence can be proved." Ser Marston unsheathed his sword and went to one knee, saying, "I swear upon my sword in the sight of gods and men that none shall do you harm whilst I stand beside you."

If the Lord Commander believed those words would sway the king, he could not have been more wrong. "You stood beside me when the dragon ate my mother," Aegon answered. "All you did was watch. I will not have you watch while they kill my brother's wife." Then he left the battlements, and no words of Marston Waters could induce him to return that day, or the next, or the next.

On the fourth day Grand Maester Munkun appeared together with Ser Marston. "I beseech you, sire, end this childish folly and come out, that we may serve you." King Aegon gazed down on him, saying naught, but his brother was less reticent, commanding the Grand Maester to send forth "a thousand ravens" so the realm might know the king was being held a captive in his own castle. To this the Grand Maester made no answer. Nor did the ravens fly.

In the days that followed, Munkun made several further appeals, assuring Aegon and Viserys that all that had been done was lawful, Ser Marston went from pleas to threats to bargaining, and Septon Bernard was brought forth to pray loudly for the Crone to light the king's way back to wisdom, all to no avail. These efforts drew little or no response from the boy king beyond a sullen stubborn silence. His Grace was roused to anger only once, when his master-at-arms, Ser Gareth Long, took his turn attempting to convince the king to yield. "And if I will not, who will you punish, ser?" King Aegon shouted down at him. "You may beat poor Gaemon's bones, but you will get no more blood from him."

Many and more have wondered at the seeming forbearance of the new Hand and his allies during this stalemate. Ser Marston had several hundred men within the Red Keep, and Ser Lucas Leygood's gold cloaks numbered more than two thousand. Maegor's Holdfast was a formidable redoubt, to be sure, but it was but weakly held. Of the Lyseni who had come to Westeros with Lady Larra, only Sandoq the Shadow and six more remained at her side, the rest having gone with her brother Moredo to the Vale. A few men loyal to Lord Rowan had made their way to Maegor's before its doors were closed, but there was not a knight, a squire, or a man-at-arms amongst them, nor amongst the king's own attendants. (There was one knight of the Kingsguard within the holdfast, but Ser Raynard Ruskyn was a prisoner, having been overwhelmed and wounded by the Lyseni at the very start of the king's defiance.) Mushroom tells us that Queen Daenaera's ladies donned mail and took up spears to help make it appear that King Aegon had more defenders than he did, but this ruse could not have fooled Ser Marston and his men for long, if indeed it fooled them at all.

Thus the question must be asked: Why did Marston Waters not simply take the holdfast by storm? He had more than enough men. Whilst some would have been lost to Sandoq and the other Lyseni, even the Shadow would surely have been overwhelmed in the end. Yet the Hand held back, continuing his attempts to end the "secret siege" (as this confrontation would later become known) with words, when swords would most likely have brought it to a swift conclusion.

Some will say that Ser Marston's reluctance was simple cowardice, that he feared to face the blade of the Lysene giant Sandoq. This seems unlikely. It is sometimes put about that Maegor's defenders (the king himself in some accounts, his brother in others) had threatened to hang their captive Kingsguard at the first sign of attack . . . but Mushroom calls this "a base lie."

The most likely explanation is the simplest. Marston Waters was neither a great knight nor a good man, most scholars agree. Though bastard born, he had achieved knighthood and a modest place in the retinue of King Aegon II, but his rise would likely have ended there if not for his kinship to certain fisherfolk on Dragonstone, which led Larys Strong to choose him above a hundred better knights to hide the king during Rhaenyra's ascendancy. In the years since, Waters had climbed high indeed, becoming Lord Commander of the Kingsguard over knights of better birth and far greater renown. As the Hand of the King, he would be the most powerful man in the realm until Aegon III came of age . . . but at the crux he hesitated, weighed down by his vows and his own bastard's honor.

Unwilling to dishonor the white cloak he wore by ordering an attack upon the king he had sworn to protect, Ser Marston eschewed ladders, grapnels, and assault, and continued to put his trust in reasoned words (and perhaps in hunger, for the supplies within the holdfast could not last much longer).

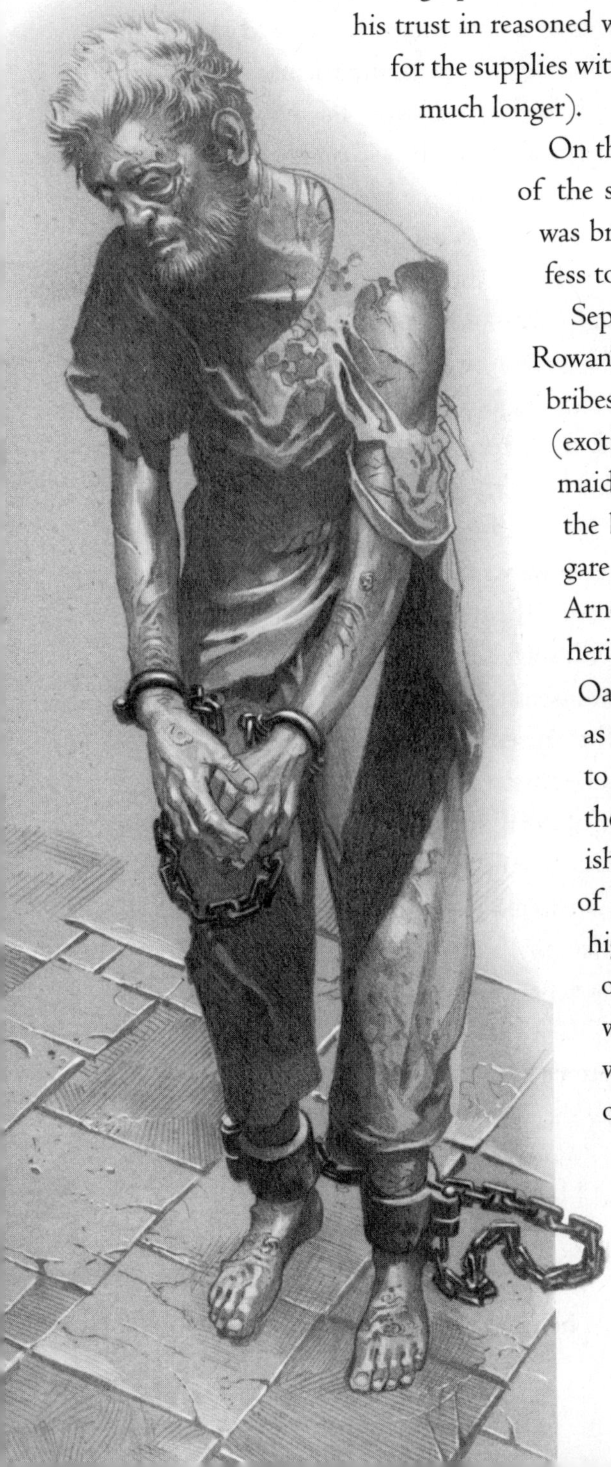

On the morning of the twelfth day of the secret siege, Thaddeus Rowan was brought forth in chains to confess to his offenses.

Septon Bernard detailed Lord Rowan's alleged crimes: he had taken bribes in the form of gold and girls (exotic creatures from the Mermaid, says Mushroom, the younger the better), had sent Moredo Rogare to the Vale to dispossess Ser Arnold Arryn of his rightful inheritance, had conspired with Oakenfist to remove Unwin Peake as the King's Hand, had helped to loot the Rogare Bank of Lys, thereby defrauding and impoverishing many "good and leal men of Westeros of noble birth and high station," had appointed his own son to a command "for which he was manifestly unworthy," leading to the death of thousands in the Mountains of the Moon.

Most terrible of all, his lordship was accused of having plotted with the three Rogares to poison

King Aegon and his queen, so as to place Prince Viserys on the Iron Throne with Larra of Lys as his queen. "The poison used is called the Tears of Lys," Bernard declared, an assertion that Grand Maester Munkun then confirmed. "Though the Seven spared you, sire," Bernard concluded, "Lord Rowan's foul plot took the life of your young friend Gaemon."

When the septon had completed his recitation, Ser Marston Waters said, "Lord Rowan has confessed to all these crimes," and beckoned to the Lord Confessor, George Graceford, to bring the prisoner forward. Manacled at ankle with heavy chains, his face so bruised and swollen as to be unrecognizable, Lord Thaddeus did not move at first, until Lord Graceford pricked him with the point of his dagger, whereupon he said in a thick voice, "Ser Marston speaks truly, Your Grace. I have confessed to all. Lotho promised me fifty thousand dragons when the deed was done, and another fifty when Viserys took the throne. The poison was given to me by Roggerio." So halting was this speech, so slurred the words, that some upon the battlements thought his lordship must be drunk, until Mushroom pointed out that all his teeth were missing.

The confession left King Aegon III bereft of speech. All that the boy could do was stand and stare, with such despair upon his face that Mushroom feared His Grace might be about to leap from the battlements onto the spikes below, to rejoin his first queen.

It fell to Prince Viserys to make answer. "And my wife, Lady Larra," he shouted down, "was she a part of this plot too, my lord?" Lord Rowan gave a heavy nod. "She was," he said. "And what of me?" asked the prince. "Aye, you as well," his lordship answered dully . . . an answer that seemed to surprise Marston Waters, whilst greatly displeasing Lord George Graceford. "And Gaemon Palehair, 'twas he who put the poison in the tart, I'll venture," Viserys went on glibly. "If it please my prince," mumbled Thaddeus Rowan. Whereupon the prince turned to the king his brother and said, "Gaemon was as guilty as the rest of us . . . of nothing," and the dwarf Mushroom called down, "Lord Rowan, was it you who poisoned King Viserys?" To which the old Hand nodded, saying, "It was, my lord. I do confess it."

The king's face grew hard. "Ser Marston," he said, "this man is my Hand and innocent of treason. The traitors here are those who tortured him to bring forth this false confession. Seize the Lord Confessor, if you love your king . . . else I will know that you are as false as he is." His words rang across the inner ward, and in that moment, the broken boy Aegon III seemed every inch a king.

To this very day, some assert that Ser Marston Waters was no more than a catspaw, a simple honest knight used and deceived by men more subtle than himself, whilst others argue that Waters was part of the plot from the beginning, but turned upon his fellows when he sensed the tide turning against them.

Whatever the truth, Ser Marston did as the king had commanded. Lord Graceford was seized by the Kingsguard and dragged away to the very dungeon he himself had ruled when he awoke that day. Lord Rowan's chains were removed, and all his knights and serving men were brought up from the dungeons into the sunlight.

It did not prove necessary to subject the Lord Confessor to torment; the sight of the instruments was all that was required for him to give up the names of the other conspirators. Amongst those he named were the late Ser Amaury Peake and Ser Mervyn Flowers of the Kingsguard, Tessario the Tiger, Septon Bernard, Ser Gareth Long, Ser Victor Risley, Ser Lucas Leygood of the gold cloaks with six of the seven captains of the city gates, and even three of the queen's ladies.

Not all surrendered peacefully. A short, savage battle was fought at the Gate of the Gods when men came for Lucas Leygood, leaving nine dead, amongst them Leygood himself. Three of the accused captains fled before they could be taken, with a dozen of their men. Tessario the Tiger chose to flee as well, but was taken in a dockside tavern near the River Gate as he was dickering with the captain of an Ibbenese whaler for passage to the Port of Ibben.

Ser Marston chose to confront Mervyn Flowers himself. "We are the both of us bastards and Sworn Brothers besides," he was heard to tell Ser Raynard Ruskyn. When told of Graceford's accusation, Ser Mervyn said, "You will be wanting my steel," drawing his longsword from its sheath and offering its hilt to Marston Waters. Yet as Ser Marston grasped it, Ser Mervyn seized his wrist, drew a dagger with his other hand, and plunged it into Waters's belly. Flowers got no farther than the stables, where a drunken man-at-arms and two young stableboys found him saddling his courser. He killed them all, but the noise brought others running, and the bastard knight was finally overwhelmed and beaten to death, still clad in the white cloak that he had shamed.

His lord commander, Ser Marston Waters, did not long outlive him. He was found in White Sword Tower in a pool of his own blood and carried to Grand Maester Munkun, who examined him and pronounced the wound mortal. Though Munkun sewed him up as best he could and gave him milk of the poppy, Waters expired that same night.

Lord Graceford had named Ser Marston as one of the conspirators as well, insisting that "that bloody turncloak" had been with them from the start, a charge Waters was no longer able to dispute. The rest of the plotters were consigned to the black cells to await trial. Some protested their innocence, whilst others claimed, as Ser Marston had, that they had acted from the honest belief that Thaddeus Rowan and the Lyseni were the traitors. A few proved more forthcoming, however. Ser Gareth Long was the most voluble, declaring loudly that Aegon III was a weakling unfit to hold a sword, much less sit the Iron Throne. Septon Bernard argued from his Faith; the Lyseni and their queer foreign gods had no place in the Seven Kingdoms. It was always intended that Lady Larra should die together with her brothers, he said, so Viserys would be free to take a proper Westerosi queen.

The frankest of the plotters was Tessario the Thumb. He had done it for gold and girls and vengeance, he said. Roggerio Rogare had banned him from the Mermaid for striking one of his whores, so he had demanded the brothel and Roggerio's manhood for his price, and these things had been promised to him. But when his inquisitors asked who had made this promise, Tessario had no answer but a grin . . . a grin that turned into a grimace, and thence a scream, when he was asked again under torture. The first name he gave was that of Marston Waters, but on further questioning he named George Graceford, and still later Mervyn Flowers. Mushroom tells us that the Tiger was on the point of giving a fourth name, mayhaps the true name, when he expired.

One name was never mentioned, though it hung over the Red Keep like a cloud. In *The Testimony of Mushroom*, the fool says plainly what few dared say at the time: that there must surely have been another conspirator, lord and master of the rest, the man who set all this in motion from afar, using the others as his catspaws. The "player in the shadows," Mushroom calls him. "Graceford was cruel but not clever, Long had courage but no cunning, Risley was a sot, Bernard a pious fool, the Thumb a bloody Volantene, worse than the Lyseni. The women were women, and the Kingsguard were used to obeying commands, not giving them. Lucas Leygood loved swaggering about in his gold cloak, and could drink and fight and fuck with the best of them, but he was no plotter. And all of them had ties to one man: Unwin Peake, Lord of Starpike, Lord of Dunstonbury, Lord of Whitegrove, once Hand of the King."

No doubt others entertained the same suspicions once the plot to kill the king had been unmasked. Several of the traitors had blood ties to the former Hand, whilst others owed him their positions. Nor was Peake a stranger to conspiracy, having once planned the murder of two dragonriders under the sign of the Bloody Caltrops. But Peake had been at Starpike during the secret siege, and none of his supposed catspaws ever spoke his name, so his involvement remained unproven, then as now.

So thick was the miasma of mistrust in the Red Keep that Aegon III did not leave Maegor's Holdfast for six more days after his brother Viserys unravelled Lord Rowan's false confession. Only when he saw Grand Maester Munkun send forth a murder of ravens, summoning twoscore leal lords to King's Landing, did His Grace allow the bridge to be lowered once again. They had run so short of food within the holdfast that Queen Daenaera cried herself to sleep at night, and two of her ladies were so weak from hunger that they had to be helped across the moat.

By the time the king emerged, Lord Graceford had named his names, many of the traitors had been seized, others had fled, and Marston Waters, Mervyn Flowers, and Lucas Leygood were dead. Soon thereafter Thaddeus Rowan once more took up residence in the Tower of the Hand . . . but it was plain to all that his lordship was in no fit state to resume his duties as the Hand of the King. The things that had been done to him in the dungeons had broken him. One moment he might seem his old self, hale and hearty, only to begin weeping uncontrollably the next. Mushroom, who could be as cruel as he was clever, would make mock of the old man, accusing him of outlandish crimes to elicit even more absurd confessions. "I do recall that one night I made him confess to the Doom of Valyria," says the dwarf in his *Testimony*. "The court roared with laughter, but as I look back upon it now, I blush for shame."

After a moon's turn, with Lord Rowan showing little or no signs of improvement, Grand Maester Munkun persuaded the king to relieve him of his office. Rowan set out for his seat at Goldengrove, promising to return to King's Landing once he had recovered his health, but he died upon the road in the company of two of his sons. For the rest of that year, the Grand Maester served as both regent and Hand, for the realm required governance and Aegon had still not reached the age of manhood. As a maester, chained and sworn to serve, Munkun did not feel it was his place to pass judgment on high lords and anointed knights, however, so the accused traitors languished in the dungeons, awaiting a new Hand.

As the old year waned and gave way to the new, lord after lord arrived in King's Landing, answering the king's summons. The ravens had done their work. Though never formally constituted as a Great Council, the gathering of the lords in 136 AC was the largest assembly of nobles in the Seven Kingdoms since the Old King had summoned the lords of the realm to Harrenhal in 101 AC. King's Landing was soon full to the point of bursting, to the delight of the city's innkeeps, whores, and merchants.

Most of those attending came from the crownlands, the riverlands, the stormlands . . . and the Vale, where Lord Oakenfist and Bloody Ben Blackwood had at last forced the Gilded Falcon, the Mad Heir, the Bronze Giant, and all their supporters to bend the knee and do homage to Joffrey Arryn as their liege (Gunthor Royce, Quenton Corbray, and Isembard Arryn were amongst those accompanying Lord Alyn to the gathering, along with Lord Arryn himself). Johanna Lannister sent a cousin and three bannermen to speak for the west, Torrhen Manderly sailed down from White Harbor with twoscore knights and cousins, and Lyonel Hightower and the Lady Sam rode up from Oldtown with a tail six hundred strong. Yet the largest retinue was that accompanying Lord Unwin Peake, who brought a thousand of his own men and five hundred sellswords. ("What ever could he be afraid of?" Mushroom quipped.)

There beneath the shadow of the empty Iron Throne (for King Aegon did not choose to come to court), the lords attempted to choose new regents to rule until His Grace could come of age. After meeting for more than a fortnight, they were no closer to accord than when they had begun. Without the strong hand of a king to guide them, some lords gave vent to old grievances, and the half-healed wounds of the Dance began to bleed afresh. The strong men had too many enemies, whilst the lesser lords were looked down upon for being poor or weak. Finally, in despair at reaching an agreement, Grand Maester Munkun proposed that three regents be chosen by lot. When Prince Viserys added his voice to Munkun's, the proposal was adopted. The lots fell to Willam Stackspear, Marq Merryweather, and Lorent Grandison, of whom it could be truly said that they were as inoffensive as they were undistinguished.

The selection of the King's Hand was a matter of more import, and one that the lords assembled were unwilling to leave to the new regents. There were those, chiefly from the Reach, who urged that Unwin Peake be asked to serve as Hand once more, but they were quickly shouted down when Prince Viserys declared that his brother would prefer a younger man, "and one less like to fill his court with traitors." Alyn Velaryon's name was also put forward, but he was deemed to be too young. Kermit Tully and Benjicot Blackwood were spurned for the same reason. Instead the lords turned to the northman, Torrhen Manderly, Lord of White Harbor . . . a man unknown to many of them, but for that very reason without enemies south of the Neck (save perhaps for Unwin Peake, whose memory was long).

"Aye, I'll do it," Lord Torrhen said, "but I'll need a man who is good with coin if I'm to deal with these Lyseni thieves and their bloody bank." Then up stood Oakenfist, to offer the name of Isembard Arryn, the Gilded Falcon of the Vale. To appease Lord Peake and his supporters, Gedmund Peake the Great-Axe was named lord admiral and master of ships (it was said that Oakenfist was more bemused than angry, and declared that the choice was a good one, as "Ser Gedmund loves paying for ships, I love sailing them"). Ser Raynard Ruskyn became Lord Commander of the Kingsguard, whilst Ser Adrian Thorne was chosen to command the gold cloaks. Formerly the captain on the Lion Gate, Thorne was the only one of Lucas Leygood's seven captains not accused of involvement in the plot.

And so it was done. All that remained was for Aegon III to put his seal to it, which he did without demur the next morning before retreating once again to the solitary splendor of his chambers.

His new Hand began at once to tend to the business of the realm. His first task was a daunting one: to sit in judgment at the trials of those accused of poisoning Gaemon Palehair and plotting treason against the king. No fewer than forty-two persons stood accused, for those named by Lord Graceford had in turn named others when questioned sharply. Sixteen had fled and eight had died, leaving eighteen to be judged. Thirteen of those had already confessed to some degree of involvement in the crimes, for the king's inquisitors were most persuasive. Five continued to insist upon their innocence, declaring that they had truly believed the treason to be Lord Rowan's, and thus had joined the plot to save His Grace from the Lyseni who meant to kill him.

The trials lasted three-and-thirty days. Prince Viserys was present throughout, often accompanied by his wife, the Lady Larra, her belly swelling with their second child, and their son Aegon with his wet nurse. King Aegon came but thrice, on the days that judgment was pronounced upon Gareth Long, George Graceford, and Septon Bernard; he showed no interest in the rest, and never asked about their fates. Queen Daenaera did not attend at all.

Ser Gareth and Lord Graceford were condemned to die, but both chose to take the black instead. Lord Manderly decreed that they should be put aboard the next ship to White Harbor, from whence they could be taken to the Wall. The High Septon had written to ask clemency for Septon Bernard "that he might atone for his sins through prayer, contemplation, and good works," so Manderly spared him from the headsman's axe. Instead Bernard was gelded and condemned to walk barefoot from King's Landing to Oldtown with his manhood hung about his neck. "If he survives, His High Holiness may make what use of him he will," the Hand decreed. (Bernard did live, and spent the rest of his life as a scribe, copying holy books at the Starry Sept under a vow of silence.)

Those gold cloaks who had been accused and taken (a number had escaped) chose to emulate Ser Gareth and Lord Graceford, taking the black in preference to losing their heads. The same choice was made by the surviving Fingers . . . but Ser Victor Risley, once the King's Justice, stood upon his right as an anointed knight to demand a trial by battle "that I may prove my innocence by wager of my body, in the sight of gods and men." Ser Gareth Long, foremost of those who had named Risley part of the plot, was duly brought back to court to face him. "You always were a bloody fool, Victor," Ser Gareth said, when his longsword was placed into his hand. The former master-at-arms dispatched the former headsman quickly, then turned with a smile to the condemned in the back of the throne room and asked, "Anyone else?"

The most troubling cases were those of the three women who stood accused, all of them highborn ladies and attendants to the queen. Lucinda Penrose (she who had been attacked whilst hawking before the Maiden's Day Ball) admitted to wanting Daenaera dead, saying, "If my nose had not been slit, it would be her serving me, not me serving her. No man will have me now, because of her." Cassandra Baratheon confessed that she had often shared her bed with Ser Mervyn Flowers, and sometimes at Ser Mervyn's behest with Tessario the Tiger, "but only when he asked it of me." When Willam Stackspear suggested that perhaps she was part of the reward the Volantene had been promised, Lady Cassandra burst into tears. Yet even her confession paled beside that of Lady Priscella Hogg, a sad and somewhat simple girl of fourteen, stout and short and plain of face, who had somehow conceived the notion that Prince Viserys would marry her if only Larra of Lys were dead. "He smiles whenever he sees me," she told the court, "and once when he passed me on the steps, his shoulder brushed against my bosom."

Lord Manderly, Grand Maester Munkun, and the regents questioned the three women closely, mayhaps (as Mushroom avers) trying to elicit the name of a fourth woman, hitherto unmentioned: Lady Clarice Osgrey, widowed aunt of Lord Unwin Peake. Lady Clarice supervised all Queen Daenaera's maids, companions, and attendants, as she did Queen Jaehaera's ladies before them, and was well acquainted with many of the confessed conspirators (Mushroom says that she and George Graceford were lovers, and suggests that her ladyship was so aroused by torture that she sometimes joined the Lord Confessor in the dungeons to assist him with his work). If she had been involved, it was likely Unwin Peake had as well. All their probing proved to no avail, however, and when Lord Torrhen asked bluntly whether Lady Clarice had been complicit, all three of the condemned women could only shake their heads.

Though unquestionably part of the conspiracy, the roles played by the three women had been comparatively minor. For that reason, and on account of their sex, Lord Manderly and the regents chose to show them mercy. Lucinda Penrose and Priscella Hogg were condemned to have their noses cut off, with the understanding that the punishment would be stayed should they give themselves to the Faith, so long as they remained true to their vows.

Cassandra Baratheon's high birth spared her the same punishment; she was, after all, the late Lord Borros's eldest child and sister to the present Lord of Storm's End, and had once been betrothed to King Aegon II. Though her mother, Lady Elenda, was not well enough to attend the trials, she had sent three of her son's bannermen to speak for Storm's End. Through them (and Lord Grandison, whose lands and keep were also of the stormlands), it was arranged for Lady Cassandra to wed a minor knight named Ser Walter Brownhill, who ruled a few hides of land on Cape Wrath from a castle oft described as being made of "mud and tree roots." Thrice bereft, Ser Walter had fathered sixteen children by his previous wives, thirteen of whom still lived. It was Lady Elenda's thought that caring for these children and any additional sons or daughters that she herself might give Ser Walter would keep Lady Cassandra from plotting any further treasons. (And so it did.)

This concluded the last of the treason trials, but the dungeons beneath the Red Keep had not as yet been emptied. The fate of Lady Larra's brothers Lotho and Roggerio remained to be decided. Though innocent of high treason, murder, and conspiracy, they still stood accused of fraud and theft; the collapse of the Rogare Bank had led to the ruination of thousands, in Westeros as well as Lys. Though bound to House Targaryen through marriage, the brothers were neither kings nor princes themselves, and their lordships were but empty courtesies, Lord Manderly and Grand Maester Munkun agreed; they would be tried and punished.

In this, the Seven Kingdoms lagged well behind the Free City of Lys, where the collapse of the Rogare Bank had led inexorably to the utter ruin of the house that Lysandro the Magnificent had built. The palace he had bequeathed to his daughter Lysara was seized, together with the manses of his other children, and all their furnishings. A handful of Drako Rogare's trading galleys learned of the house's fall in time to divert course to Volantis, but for every ship saved, nine were lost, together with their cargos and the Rogare wharves and storehouses. Lady Lysara was deprived of her gold, gems, and gowns, Lady Marra of her books. Fredo Rogare saw the magisters seize the Perfumed Garden, even as he tried to sell it. His slaves were sold, along with those of his siblings, trueborn or bastard. When that proved insufficient to pay more than a tenth of the debts left by the bank's collapse, the Rogares themselves were sold into slavery, together with their children. The daughters of Fredo and Lysaro Rogare would soon find themselves back in the Perfumed Garden where they had played as children, but as bed slaves, not proprietors.

Nor did Lysaro Rogare, architect of his family's doom, escape unscathed. He and his eunuch guards were captured in the town of Volon Therys on the Rhoyne, as they were waiting for a boat to carry them across the river. Loyal to the end, the Unsullied died to a man fighting to protect him . . . but only twenty remained with him (Lysaro had taken one hundred when he fled from Lys, but had been forced to sell most of them along the way), and they soon found themselves hemmed in and surrounded in the confused, bloody fighting by the docks. Once taken, Lysaro was sent downriver to Volantis, where the Triarchs offered him to his brother Drako, for a certain price. Drako declined and suggested the Volantenes sell him back to Lys instead. And so Lysaro Rogare was returned to Lys, chained to an oar in the belly of a Volantene slave ship.

During his trial, when asked what he had done with all the gold that he had stolen, Lysaro laughed and began to point to certain magisters in the assembly, saying, "I used it to bribe him, and him, and him, and him," picking out a dozen men before he could be silenced. It did not save him.

The men he had bought voted with the rest to condemn him (and kept the bribes as well, for the magisters of Lys put avarice ahead of honor, as is well-known).

Lysaro was sentenced to be chained naked to a pillar before the Temple of Trade, where all those despoiled by him would be allowed to whip him, the number of lashes accorded to each person to be determined by the extent of their losses. And so it was done. It is written that his sister Lysara and brother Fredo were amongst those who availed themselves of the whip, whilst other Lyseni placed wagers on the hour of his death. Lysaro expired in the seventh hour of the first day of his scourging. His bones would remain chained to the pillar for three years, until his brother Moredo pulled them down and interred them in the family crypt.

In this instance, at the least, Lysene justice proved to be considerably harsher than that of the Seven Kingdoms. Many in Westeros would gladly have seen Lotho and Roggerio Rogare suffer the same dire fate as Lysaro, for the collapse of the Rogare bank had impoverished great lords and humble tradesmen alike . . . but even those who most despised them could offer no shred of proof that either had known of their brother's depredations in Lys, or had benefited from his plundering in any way.

In the end, the banker Lotho was adjudged guilty of theft, for taking gold and gems and silver not his own, and failing to restore same on demand. Lord Manderly gave him the choice of taking the black, or having his right hand removed as if he were a common thief. "Then praise Yndros, I am left-handed," Lotho said, choosing mutilation. Nothing at all could be proved against his brother Roggerio, but Lord Manderly sentenced him to seven lashes all the same. "For what?" Roggerio demanded of him, aghast. "For being a thrice-damned Lyseni," Torrhen Manderly responded.

After the sentences had been carried out, both of the brothers left King's Landing. Roggerio closed his brothel, selling off the building, the carpets, drapes, beds, and other furnishings, even the parrots and the monkeys, using the coin thus gained to buy himself a ship, a great cog he named the *Mermaid's Daughter*. Thus was his pillow house reborn, this time with sails. For years to come, Roggerio sailed up and down the narrow sea, selling spiced wine, exotic viands, and carnal pleasure to the denizens of great ports and humble fishing villages alike. His brother Lotho, short a hand, was taken up by Lady Samantha, the paramour of Lord Lyonel Hightower, and returned with her to Oldtown. The Hightowers had not entrusted so much as a groat of their gold to the Lyseni, and thus remained one of the wealthiest houses in all Westeros, second mayhaps only to the Lannisters of Casterly Rock, and Lady Sam wished to learn how to put that gold to better use. Thus was born the Bank of Oldtown, which has made House Hightower richer still.

(Moredo Rogare, the eldest of the three brothers who had come with Lady Larra to King's Landing, was in Braavos during the trials, treating with the keyholders of the Iron Bank. Before the year was out, he would sail for Tyrosh, flush with Braavosi gold, to hire ships and swords for an attack on Lys. That is a tale for another time, however, beyond our current purview.)

King Aegon III did not once appear to sit the Iron Throne during the trials of the brothers, but Prince Viserys came every day to sit beside his wife. What Larra of Lys thought of the Hand's justice neither Mushroom nor the court chronicles can tell us, save to note that she wept when Lord Torrhen handed down his verdict.

Soon thereafter the lords began to depart, each to their own seat, and life resumed as before in King's Landing under the new regents and King's Hand . . . though more the latter than the former. "The gods chose our new regents," Mushroom observed, "and it would seem that gods are just as thick as lords." He was not wrong. Lord Stackspear loved to hawk, Lord Merryweather loved to feast, and Lord Grandison loved to sleep, and each man thought the other two were fools, but in the end it made no matter, for Torrhen Manderly proved to be an honest and able Hand, of whom it was rightly said that he was brusque and gluttonous, but fair. King Aegon never warmed to him, it is true, but His Grace did not have a trusting nature, and the events of the past year had only served to deepen his suspicions. Nor could Lord Torrhen be said to have had much regard for the king, whom he referred to as "that sullen boy" when writing to his daughter in White Harbor. Manderly did become fond of Prince Viserys, however, and doted on Queen Daenaera.

Though the northman's regency was comparatively short, it was far from uneventful. With the considerable help of the Gilded Falcon, Isembard Arryn, Manderly enacted a major reform of the taxes, providing more income for the Crown and some relief for those who could prove they had suffered losses from the plundering of the Rogare Bank. With the Lord Commander, he brought the Kingsguard up to seven once again, bestowing white cloaks upon Ser Edmund Warrick, Ser Dennis Whitfield, and Ser Agramore Cobb to fill the places of Marston Waters, Mervyn Flowers, and Amaury Peake. He formally repudiated the pact that Alyn Oakenfist had signed to secure the release of Prince Viserys, on the grounds that the agreement had been made not with the Free City of Lys, but with House Rogare, which could no longer be said to exist.

With Ser Gareth Long upon the Wall, the Red Keep had need of a new master-at-arms. Lord Manderly appointed a fine young swordsman named Ser Lucas Lothston. The grandson of a hedge knight, Ser Lucas was a patient teacher who soon became a favorite with Prince Viserys, and even won a certain grudging respect from King Aegon. For Lord Confessor, Manderly tapped Maester Rowley, a fresh-faced youth newly arrived from Oldtown, where he had studied under Archmaester Sandeman, reputedly the wisest healer in the history of Westeros. It was Grand Maester Munkun who urged that Rowley be appointed. "A man who knows how to ease pain will also know how to inflict it," he told the Hand, "but it is also important that we have a Lord Confessor who sees his work as duty, not pleasure."

On the eve of Smith's Day, Larra of Lys gave Prince Viserys a second son, a large and lusty boy that the prince named Aemon. A feast was held to celebrate, and all rejoiced at the birth of this new prince . . . save mayhaps for his year-and-a-half-old brother, Aegon, who was discovered hitting the babe with the dragon's egg that had been placed inside the cradle. No harm was done, for Aemon's howls soon brought Lady Larra running to disarm and discipline her elder son.

Soon thereafter, Lord Alyn Oakenfist grew restless, and began to make plans for the second of his six great voyages. The Velaryons had entrusted much of their gold to Lotho Rogare, and lost more than half their wealth in consequence. To restore their fortunes, Lord Alyn assembled a large fleet of merchantmen, with a dozen of his war galleys to guard them, intending to sail to Old Volantis by way of Pentos, Tyrosh, and Lys, visiting Dorne on the way home.

It is said that he and his wife quarreled before the voyage, for Lady Baela was of the blood of the dragon and quick to anger, and had heard too much talk from her lord husband about Princess Aliandra of Dorne. Yet in the end they reconciled, as they always did. The fleet set sail at midyear, led by Oakenfist in a galley he named *Bold Marilda* after his mother. Lady Baela remained on Driftmark with Lord Alyn's second child growing inside her.

The king's sixteenth nameday was drawing near. With the realm at peace, and spring in full flower, Lord Torrhen Manderly decided that King Aegon and Queen Daenaera should make a royal progress to mark his coming of age. It would be good for the boy to see the lands he ruled, the Hand reasoned, to show himself to his people. Aegon was tall and comely, and his sweet young queen could supply whatever charm the king might lack. The commons would surely love her, which could only be of benefit to the solemn young king.

The regents concurred. Plans were made for a grand progress lasting a full year, one that would take His Grace to parts of the realm that had never seen a king before. From King's Landing they would ride to Duskendale and Maidenpool, and thence take ship for Gulltown. After a visit to the Eyrie, they would return to Gulltown and sail for the North, with a stop at the Three Sisters.

White Harbor would give the king and queen a welcome such as they had never seen, Lord Manderly promised. Then they could continue north to Winterfell, perhaps even visit the Wall, before turning south again, down the kingsroad to the Neck. Sabitha Frey would host them at the Twins, they would call upon Lord Benjicot at Raventree Hall, and of course if they visited the Blackwoods they must needs spend the same amount of time with the Brackens. A few nights at Riverrun, and they would cross over the hills into the west, to visit Lady Johanna at Casterly Rock.

From there it would be down the sea road to the Reach . . . Highgarden, Goldengrove, Old Oak . . . there was a dragon at Red Lake, Aegon would not like that, but Red Lake was easily avoided . . . a visit at one of Unwin

Peake's seats might help assuage the former Hand. At Oldtown the High Septon himself could no doubt be persuaded to give the king and queen his blessing, and Lord Lyonel and Lady Sam would welcome the chance to show the king that the splendors of their city far outshone those of King's Landing. "It will be a progress such as the realm has not seen in more than a century," Grand Maester Munkun told His Grace. "Spring is a time for new beginnings, sire, and this will mark the true beginning of your reign. From the Dornish Marches to the Wall, all will know you for their king, and Daenaera for their queen."

Torrhen Manderly agreed. "It will do the lad some good to get out of this bloody castle," he declared, in Mushroom's hearing. "He can hunt and hawk, climb a mountain or two, fish for salmon in the White Knife, see the Wall. Feasts every night. It would not harm the boy to put some flesh on those bones of his. Let him try some good northern ale, so thick you can cut it with a sword."

Preparations for the king's nameday celebrations and the royal progress to follow consumed all of the attention of the Hand and the three regents in the days that followed. Lists of those lords and knights wishing to accompany the king were drawn up, torn up, and drawn up again. Horses were shod, armor polished, wagons and wheelhouses repaired and repainted, banners sewn. Hundreds of ravens flew back and forth across the Seven Kingdoms as every lord and landed knight in Westeros begged the honor of a royal visit. Lady Rhaena's desire to accompany the progress on her dragon was delicately deflected, whilst her sister Baela declared that she would come along whether she was wanted or not. Even the clothing that the king and queen would wear came in for careful thought. On the days when Queen Daenaera wore green, it was decided, Aegon would be clad in his customary black. But when the little queen wore the red-and-black of House Targaryen, the king would don a green cloak, so both colors would be seen wherever they might go.

A few matters were still under discussion when King Aegon's nameday dawned at last. A great feast was to be held that night in the throne room, and the ancient Guild of Alchemists had promised displays of pyromancy such as the realm had never seen.

It was still morning, though, when King Aegon entered the council chambers where Lord Torrhen and the regents were debating whether or not to include Tumbleton on the progress.

Four knights of the Kingsguard accompanied the young king to the council chambers. So did Sandoq the Shadow, veiled and silent, carrying his great sword. His ominous presence cast a pall in the room. For a moment even Torrhen Manderly lost his tongue.

"Lord Manderly," King Aegon said, in the sudden stillness, "pray tell me how old I am, if you would be so good."

"You are ten-and-six today, Your Grace," Lord Manderly replied. "A man grown. It is time for you to take the governance of the Seven Kingdoms into your own hands."

"I shall," King Aegon said. "You are sitting in my chair."

The coldness in his tone took every man in the room aback, Grand Maester Munkun would write years later. Confused and shaken, Torrhen Manderly prised his considerable bulk out of the chair at the head of the council table, with an uneasy glance at Sandoq the Shadow. As he held

the chair for the king, he said, "Your Grace, we were speaking of the progress—"

"There will be no progress," the king declared, as he was seated. "I will not spend a year upon a horse, sleeping in strange beds and trading empty courtesies with drunken lords, half of whom would gladly see me dead if it gained them a groat. If any man requires words with me, he will find me on the Iron Throne."

Torrhen Manderly persisted. "Sire," he said, "this progress would do much and more to win you the love of the smallfolk."

"I mean to give the smallfolk peace and food and justice. If that will not suffice to win their love, let Mushroom make a progress. Or perhaps we might send a dancing bear. Someone once told me that the commons love nothing half so much as dancing bears. You may call a halt to this feast tonight as well. Send the lords home to their own keeps and give the food to the hungry. Full bellies and dancing bears shall be my policy." Then Aegon turned to the three regents. "Lord Stackspear, Lord Grandison, Lord Merryweather, I thank you for your service. Consider yourselves free to go. I shall have no further need of regents."

"And will Your Grace have need of a Hand?" asked Lord Manderly.

"A king should have a Hand of his own choosing," said Aegon III, rising to his feet. "You have served me well, no doubt, as you served my mother before me, but it was my lords who chose you. You may return to White Harbor."

"Gladly, sire," said Manderly in a voice that Grand Maester Munkun would later call a growl. "I have not drunk a decent ale since coming to this cesspit of a castle." Whereupon he removed his chain of office and set it on the council table.

Less than a fortnight later, Lord Manderly took ship for White Harbor with a small entourage of sworn swords and servants . . . amongst them Mushroom. The fool had grown fond of the big northman, it would seem, and had eagerly accepted his offer of a place at White Harbor rather than remain with a king who seldom smiled and never laughed. "I was a fool but never such a fool as to stay with that fool," he tells us.

The dwarf would come to outlive the young king that he abandoned. The later volumes of his *Testimony,* filled with colorful accounts of his life in White Harbor, his sojourn at the court of the Sealord of Braavos, his voyage to the Port of Ibben, and his years amongst the mummers of the *Lisping Lady,* are valuable in their own right, though less useful to our purpose here . . . so, sadly, the little man with the foul tongue must pass from our story. Though never the most reliable of chroniclers, the dwarf spoke truths no one else dared speak, and was often droll besides.

Mushroom tells us that the cog that Lord Manderly and his party sailed upon was called the *Jolly Salt,* but the mood aboard the ship was far from jolly as they beat north toward White Harbor. Torrhen Manderly had never liked "that sullen boy," as his letters to his daughters make clear, nor would he ever forgive the king for the brusque manner of his dismissal, or the way His Grace "murdered" the royal progress, whose abrupt end his lordship took for a deeply humiliating personal affront.

Within moments of taking the governance of the Seven Kingdoms into his own hands, King Aegon III had made an enemy of a man who had been amongst his most leal and devoted servants.

And thus did the rule of the regents come whimpering to an end, as the broken reign of the Broken King began.

Lineages and Family Tree

The Targaryen Succession

Dated by years after Aegon's Conquest

1–37	Aegon I	the Conqueror, the Dragon
37–42	Aenys I	son of Aegon I and Rhaenys
42–48	Maegor I	the Cruel, son of Aegon I and Visenya
48–103	Jaehaerys I	the Old King, the Conciliator; Aenys's son
103–129	Viserys I	grandson of Jaehaerys
129–131	Aegon II	eldest son of Viserys [Aegon II's ascent was disputed by his half-sister Rhaenyra, ten years his elder. Both perished in the war between them, called by singers the Dance of the Dragons.]
131–157	Aegon III	the Dragonbane, Rhaenyra's son [The last of the Targaryen dragons died during the reign of Aegon III.]
157–161	Daeron I	the Young Dragon, the Boy King, eldest son of Aegon III [Daeron conquered Dorne, but was unable to hold it, and died young.]
161–171	Baelor I	the Beloved, the Blessed; septon and king, second son of Aegon III

171–172	*Viserys II*	*younger brother of Aegon III*
172–184	*Aegon IV*	*the Unworthy, eldest son of Viserys [His younger brother, Prince Aemon the Dragonknight, was champion and some say lover to Queen Naerys.]*
184–209	*Daeron II*	*the Good, Queen Naerys's son, by Aegon or Aemon [Daeron brought Dorne into the realm by wedding his sister to the Prince of Dorne.]*
209–221	*Aerys I*	*second son of Daeron II (left no issue)*
221–233	*Maekar I*	*fourth son of Daeron II*
233–259	*Aegon V*	*the Unlikely, Maekar's fourth son*
259–262	*Jaehaerys II*	*second son of Aegon the Unlikely*
262–283	*Aerys II*	*the Mad King, only son of Jaehaerys II*

Therein the line of the dragon kings ended, when Aerys II was dethroned and killed, along with his heir, the crown prince, Rhaegar Targaryen, slain by Robert Baratheon on the Trident.

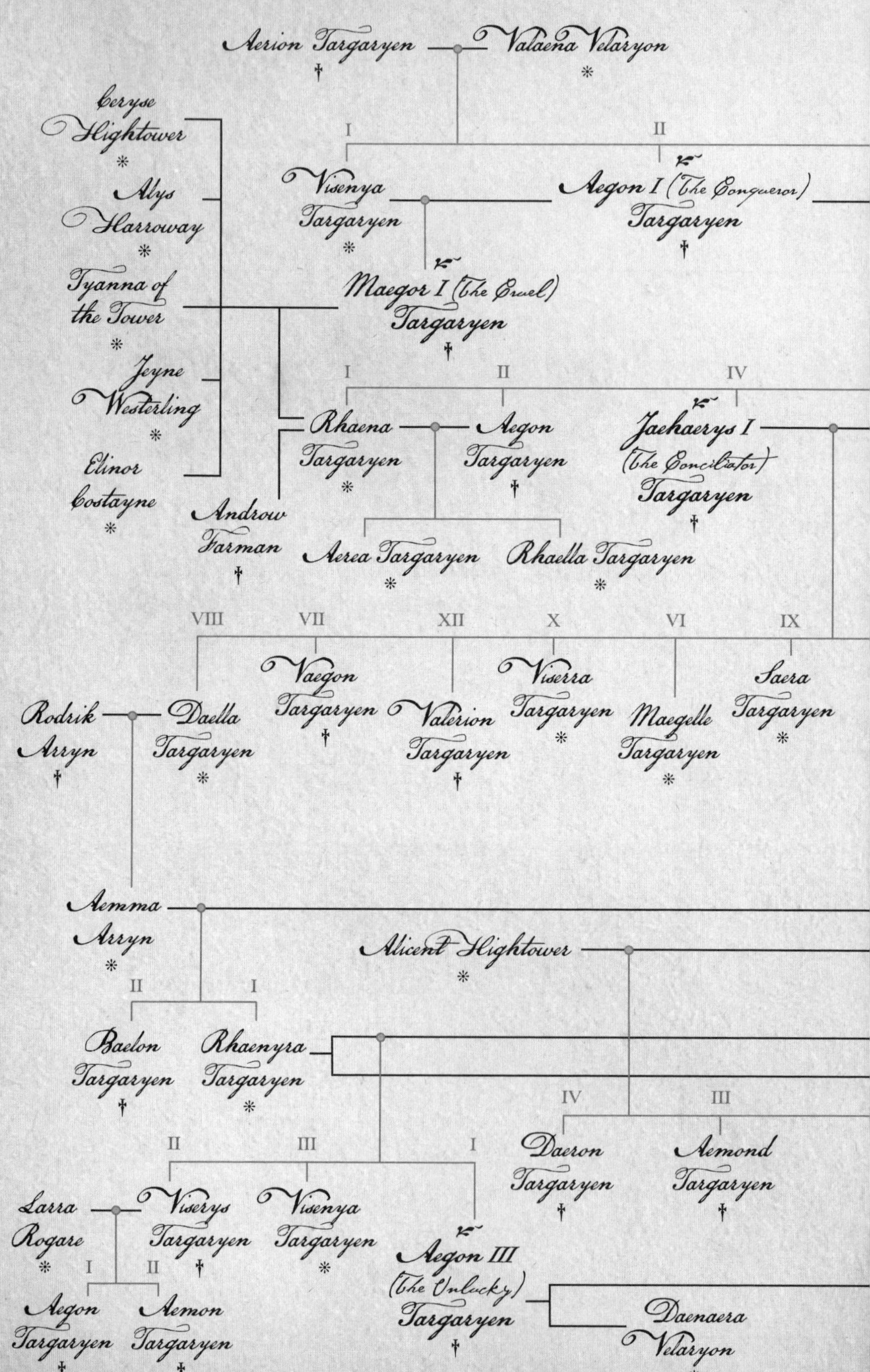

Aerion Targaryen
Valaena Velaryon
Cerysе Hightower
Alys Harroway
Tyanna of the Tower
Jeyne Westerling
Elinor Costayne
I
II
Visenya Targaryen
Aegon I (The Conqueror) Targaryen
Maegor I (The Cruel) Targaryen
I
II
IV
Rhaena Targaryen
Aegon Targaryen
Jaehaerys I (The Conciliator) Targaryen
Androw Farman
Aerea Targaryen
Rhaella Targaryen
VIII
VII
XII
X
VI
IX
Vaegon Targaryen
Viserra Targaryen
Saera Targaryen
Rodrik Arryn
Daella Targaryen
Valerion Targaryen
Maegelle Targaryen
Aemma Arryn
Alicent Hightower
II
I
Baelon Targaryen
Rhaenyra Targaryen
IV
III
Daeron Targaryen
Aemond Targaryen
II
III
I
Larra Rogare
Viserys Targaryen
Visenya Targaryen
Aegon III (The Unlucky) Targaryen
I
II
Aegon Targaryen
Aemon Targaryen
Daenaera Velaryon

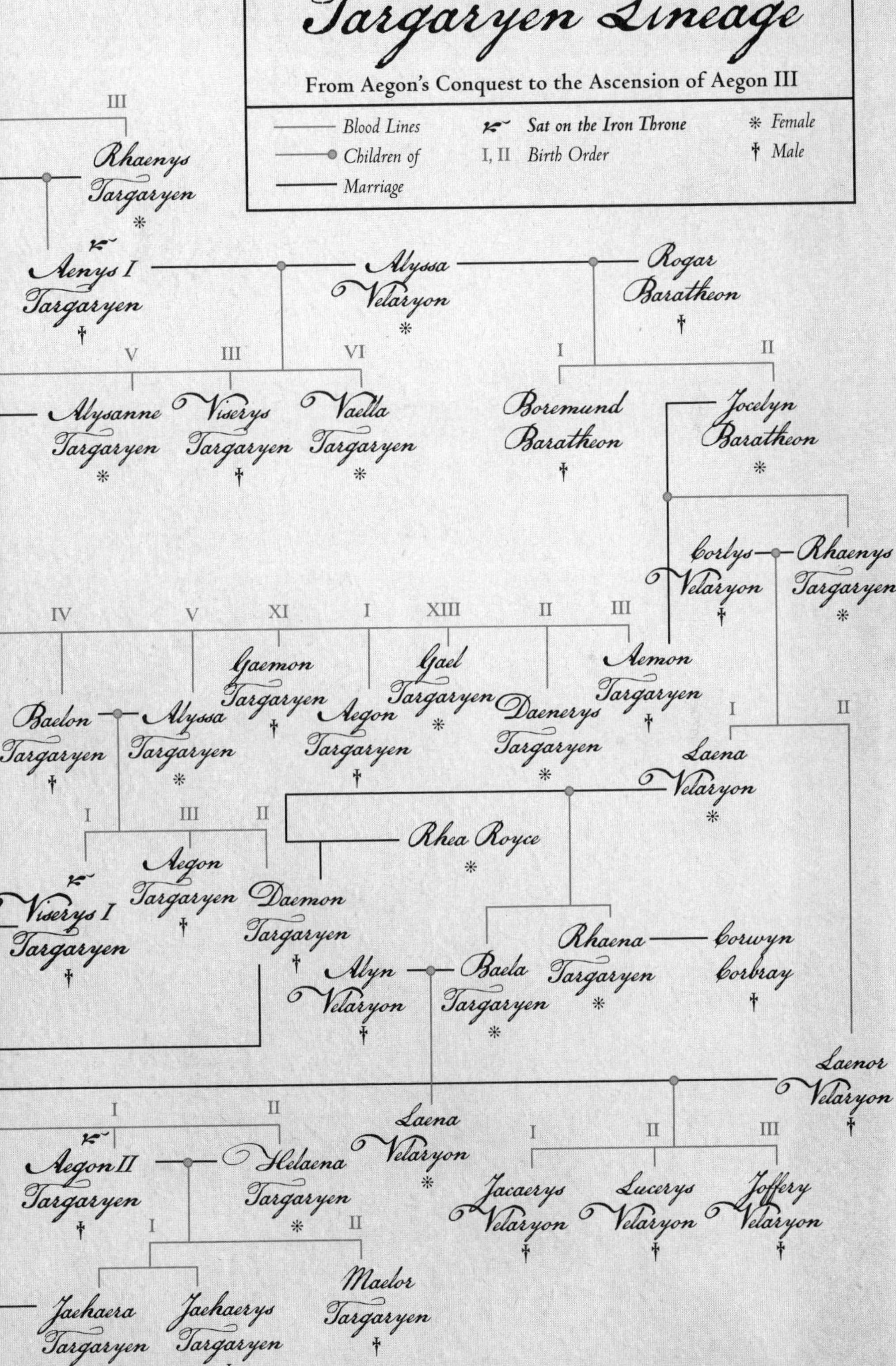
Targaryen Lineage
From Aegon's Conquest to the Ascension of Aegon III
Blood Lines
Children of
Marriage
Sat on the Iron Throne
I, II Birth Order
Female
Male
III
Rhaenys Targaryen
Aenys I Targaryen
Alyssa Velaryon
Rogar Baratheon
V
III
VI
I
II
Alysanne Targaryen
Viserys Targaryen
Vaella Targaryen
Boremund Baratheon
Jocelyn Baratheon
Corlys Velaryon
Rhaenys Targaryen
IV
V
XI
I
XIII
II
III
Gaemon Targaryen
Gael Targaryen
Aemon Targaryen
Baelon Targaryen
Alyssa Targaryen
Aegon Targaryen
Daenerys Targaryen
I
II
Laena Velaryon
I
III
II
Rhea Royce
Aegon Targaryen
Viserys I Targaryen
Daemon Targaryen
Rhaena Targaryen
Corwyn Corbray
Alyn Velaryon
Baela Targaryen
Laenor Velaryon
I
II
Laena Velaryon
I
II
III
Aegon II Targaryen
Helaena Targaryen
I
II
Jacaerys Velaryon
Lucerys Velaryon
Joffery Velaryon
Maelor Targaryen
Jaehaera Targaryen
Jaehaerys Targaryen

A Conversation Between George R. R. Martin and Dan Jones

The following questions and answers represent an edited transcript of an event that took place at the Emmanuel Centre in London in August 2019, during which George R. R. Martin was interviewed onstage by historian, journalist, and television presenter Dan Jones (author of *The Plantagenets, The Templars,* and *Crusaders*).

Dan Jones: Ladies and gentlemen, thank you for that amazing welcome for a man who really does need no introduction. I'm going to go ahead and say it—one of my favorite authors, one of the great American authors, one of the great fantasy, history, horror . . . you name the genre, he's done it. He's mastered in this book, *Fire & Blood,* the narrative nonfiction history form, which is infuriating for me because I've based my entire career on doing that.

Cast your mind back, if you will, a quarter of a century now. Take us back to when you started thinking about Westeros. Did you expect that it would end up with awards and multimillion sales all over the world?

George R. R. Martin: Uh . . . No! No, and for a long time it didn't look as though it would. When I speak to young writers—and I'm sure there are some people in this auditorium who dream of writing themselves, are writing themselves, maybe even submitting stories and novels—I always stress what an uncertain profession it is. If you're someone who needs security, don't become a writer. It's a profession for gamblers. You can be very hot one minute and the next minute your publisher has dropped you and your agent isn't returning your calls. And all you can do, I think—what I've always tried to do throughout my career—is write the best book you can, and turn it over to your agent and your publisher, hope they do a good job of getting it out, and hope that the audience finds it and likes it.

A Game of Thrones came along after I'd already been in the business for quite some time. I sold my first story in 1971. I didn't start writing *A Game of Thrones* until 1991, so I was already twenty years in as a writer—a novelist and also a television writer/producer. And it came out in '96. Publishers paid me quite a substantial sum of money for it, but then when it first came out it did not set the world on fire. It did okay, but it wasn't the breakthrough bestseller that people thought it would be. But it built. Promotion is great, advertising is great—you need all of those to really help launch a book—but the best is word of mouth. The people that read the first book told their friends about it and those friends told other friends and people started discussing it online in the primitive version of the Internet back then. And finally, when the second book came out it did better than the first one and that was the first book of mine to hit any bestseller list. We were on the *New York Times* bestseller list with the second book. We were on at number thirteen for one week and then we were off the list. But the third book did better than that. The fourth book debuted at number one on the *New York Times* list and stayed there for a while. And then the TV show came along—after that I kind of moved into the bestseller list permanently and built a nice guesthouse there. So it's really fans telling other fans and people sharing that builds up the momentum.

But no, I had no idea that it would ever be this big. I hoped that the books would be well received, that they would sell well enough for me to continue to write them, and that people would like them, and thankfully they have.

DJ: As you said, by that point you'd written extensively in the science fiction genre, you'd written some horror if you think about *Fevre Dream*, you'd worked in television as a writer and a producer. Where did this world come from? I was reading a letter by Tolkien this week, which he wrote in the 1950s about his fantasy world of elves and hobbits and so on, and

Tolkien said in the letter, "This stuff began with me. I mean, I do not remember a time when I was not building it. I've been at it since I could write." Was that your experience with this material? Had you been percolating it for years or did it come to you in a sort of flash? What was the process?

GRRM: I published my first novel in 1977—a science fiction novel, *Dying of the Light*—followed by three more novels. The first three of them had done increasingly well. The fourth novel, *The Armageddon Rag,* although it got me quite a substantial advance, was a commercial failure, so I had to go out into Hollywood for ten years. I did not have any immediate script assignments in television or film, so I thought, "Okay, it's been a few years since I wrote a novel. I will begin one." I started writing a science fiction novel called *Avalon,* which was part of my Thousand Worlds future history that I'd written a lot of stories about in the '70s, and it was going well—I'd been thinking about that one, percolating that one for some years—but then one day, suddenly, this chapter came to me almost preformed in my head, and it was the chapter where Bran finds the direwolf pups in the summer snow. And it came to me so vividly that I knew I had to write it. So I put *Avalon* on the side, I put it back in a drawer, and I sat down to write this chapter. I didn't know what it was part of—was it a standalone short story, was it part of a book? By the time I finished that chapter (it only took me two or three days) I already knew what the next chapter had to be, so I went on and I wrote that, and I wrote the one after that.

So, it all started building for me in the summer of 1991 and I think I wrote about a hundred pages that summer. And then Hollywood kicked up again. Suddenly my agent sold a television pilot for me, so I put *A Game of Thrones* in the drawer as well and went out and did a pilot, and then I did some backup scripts for the pilot, and then I did another pilot, I wrote for a feature film . . . None of them ever got made. It was like three years until I returned to *A Game of Thrones.* But, you know, when I did, it was like I'd put it down yesterday, which was huge for me, *huge* for me! Because periodically I take out those pages of *Avalon* that I also put aside in '91 and they are ice cold. I have no idea where I was going or what I was doing—it's all faded away. But it did not do that on *A Game of Thrones.* The book had such claws in me, so deep—the characters, I guess I'd been thinking about them in the back of my head all those intervening years when I'd been doing other stuff, so I got right back into it in '93 and '94 and then we sold it. And the rest is imaginary history.

DJ: So is that where it starts for you? With the characters first, and then you build the world around them? Did it start with the Starks in this case?

GRRM: In that case it started with a scene, and as I wrote the scene I learned who the characters were. I mean, I knew—it's hard to remember now after all these years, something like almost thirty years—but I knew that the protagonist of that scene had to be a young boy, who wouldn't really quite understand everything that was going on and I knew he was part of a large family. I knew I wanted the direwolf pups "found in the summer snow." That phrase was there right from the beginning. I don't know where it came from but I knew that it was the *summer* snows. And that put me on a line to the unsteadiness of the seasons, and there's something wrong in this world with our normal seasons, that you're getting snow in the middle of summer.

I've often said that there are two types of writers, two archetypes if you will: the architect and the gardener.

The architect writes books the way an architect plans a house. An architect knows how many rooms there are going to be and what the roof is going to be like and where the plumbing goes and where the bathrooms are. And how is it heated? Is it forced air heated, is it baseboard heated, is it electrical? He knows everything! It's all there on blueprints, all planned before a single board is purchased or a single nail is driven.

The gardener digs a hole in the ground and throws in a seed and waters it and he hopes something comes up. Now, he knows generally what's going to come up. He knows whether he planted an acorn for an oak tree or a tomato plant to get some tomatoes for the summer. But there's a lot of details he doesn't know. It may not grow at all. It may grow a little and then die. It may go wild. A chipmunk may eat it during the night. You don't know.

Obviously, I don't think that any writer's a hundred percent architect or a hundred percent gardener, but I'm at least ninety-seven percent gardener. And I think I have that in common with Tolkien. When he set out to write The Lord of the Rings, it was supposed to be a sequel to *The Hobbit*. "Let's have another hobbit story, another little adventure of the hobbits like the one you did with Bilbo." And he said the tale grew in the telling, and indeed it did—it grew to something much bigger than he thought when he started out, and mine has done that same thing.

DJ: Going back to *A Game of Thrones*—when you read those first chapters that you've described writing in the early nineties, I was very struck with how much of the history of this world you seemed to have already written: things that are recounted in greater depth and detail in *Fire & Blood*—Aegon's conquest, the beginning, how did this world come about, what were its major political turning points. And that reflected, it seems to me as a reader, through even the early Dunk and Egg stuff—"The Hedge Knight"—again, we've got this really strong sense of the history of the realm, of the Blackfyre Rebellion sort of hanging in the background. How much of that history did you have to map out as you went along in order to fill out the world?

GRRM: Well, I knew none of it when I began. It has been a simultaneous process. I wrote that first chapter and names came to me, I had some vague sense. And then, when I wrote the second chapter, the king is coming—where is he coming from? At some point in that process, I said, "Hmm. I'd better have a map." So I got out a piece of typing paper and initially I found a map of Ireland and turned it upside down and put that in. But I said, "Well, I don't want it to be too visible, so I'll change some of it. And then I can't fit it all on this map, so I'll need another piece of typing paper." So, you've got the south on one piece and the north on the other. I gradually filled them in as I went, and it was the same with the kings. People occasionally mention "the king" or "the old king" and "Aegon the Conqueror"—well, I'd better sit down at some point and figure out who these kings are, so I won't contradict myself. I made up a list of however many Targaryen kings there are and dates for them, trying to vary them. And at first it was just a list of names, but as I got deeper and deeper into it, even as I'm writing about the present-day characters, the past characters, the background characters, are achieving more and more reality in my head and the world got progressively more complicated.

DJ: We've had some questions, which I'm going to feed in throughout this conversation (some are from people in the audience, some of them are from social media followers), and one of them sort of pertains to what you're talking about. "How is your workspace organized to write A Song of Ice and Fire? Do you have a corkboard like in police investigations, where you've noted all the Targaryens and all the Freys?" Give us a physical sense of how you write and where you write.

GRRM: Well, I don't have a corkboard. I have maps now, because there's been a beautiful map book called *The Lands of Ice and Fire,* so I've printed out those large-scale maps and I keep them around me so I can refer to the maps from time to time. Most of the stuff is actually in my head. I do have computer files with timelines on them that I put together over the years, and bits of this and bits of that, that I can consult.

It is sometimes a daunting task, more so nowadays than when I began back in 1991, because the world has become so much bigger and has become so much more complex. In many ways I followed the template of Tolkien. If you look at The Lord of the Rings, everything begins in the Shire with the hobbits, and then as they leave the Shire they get to Rivendell, they meet some more people—they pick up Strider, they pick up the rest of the Fellowship—but then from that point they start to split up. First they split into two groups, and then the two groups split into three groups, etcetera. I followed more or less the same map. If you look at *A Game of Thrones,* everybody except Dany is together in Winterfell in the beginning—all the viewpoint characters are there—but then they start splitting. Dany is still off by herself on another continent, but some of my people go to King's Landing, some of them stay in Winterfell, and then the people who go to King's Landing get separated from each other and they go to different places. And every time a character goes off on a different tangent they meet other supporting characters, so at this point

I'm really writing not a novel but twelve intertwined novels, and each character is in a different place with their own antagonist, their own friends, their own secondary and tertiary characters surrounding them. And, yes, that is very difficult to keep in my head. I maybe should have organized it all better when I began, back in 1991, but I never thought it would get to that. Remember, I'd written four novels before this: *The Armageddon Rag, Fevre Dream, Windhaven* (with Lisa Tuttle), *Dying of the Light*. I never had any problems keeping those characters in my head; I didn't need corkboards or anything—I just remembered it all. I had no idea, though, when I got into this, the size that it would eventually become. Fortunately, it's the age of computers—we have search and replace functions and I can load up my gigantic file and say "What did I ever say about this character?" and I go through. Even then I make mistakes, and my fans, like you people (and even more obsessive people elsewhere), are always eager to point out whenever I've made a mistake. I have particular trouble with the color of people's eyes. And, rather famously, I have a horse who changes gender between the first and second books. It's hard to do a search and replace for the sex of a horse. But these errors do sneak in.

DJ: Do you ever find you've sort of painted yourself into a corner and you've set up a part of the world that then impedes your storytelling?

GRRM: Yeah, that is the disadvantage of being a gardener. You know, the architect never finds himself building closed rooms that go nowhere, but the gardener sometimes traipses down the branch and finds himself sitting all the way out at the end, realizing he can't get from that branch to anywhere else. So, sometimes I do go down byways and say, "No, I think I took the wrong turn back like three chapters ago. Let me rewrite these chapters," or, in one case "remove these chapters." I never destroy them, I keep them on my computer in case I see a way to put them in later. There's always that. Rather famously, from the last book in the series that was published, *A Dance with Dragons,* I had a chapter where Tyrion was moving down the river on the *Shy Maid*—I wrote this chapter where he meets a character called the Shrouded Lord. And it's a really good chapter. I mean, I like some chapters more than others—this is a terrific chapter. But it is an absolute dead end. Well, I don't know if it's a dead end, but it introduces like three additional layers of complication that I didn't think I actually needed. But I liked it so much I kept trying to fit it in. I first presented it straight, and then I said, "Oh, I can't fit it in. I'll present it as a dream—Tyrion has a dream and he dreams that this happened to him and it has portent." And then I split it up into like eight dreams and in every Tyrion chapter he dreamed a little bit of it. And finally I gave up and said, "I can't. I have to rip out all this stuff. I doesn't do me any good." Some day, maybe, I'll publish that lost chapter as a little standalone.

DJ: There's a question here from somebody I think may be in the audience who says, "Are there any scenes in A Song of Ice and Fire that you look back on and smile because they were just so much fun to write?" Are there any? You've mentioned the first scene with Bran. Are there any that really just give you a tingle when you look back on them?

GRRM: There are certainly scenes that I remember, but they tend not to be the ones that are fun to write—they tend to be, actually, the ones that are painful to write. The hardest thing I ever wrote was the Red Wedding scene in *A Storm of Swords*. And I knew that was coming. I was enough of an architect there that I was building toward that scene—I'd been building toward that scene since the first book—but when I actually reached that scene it was too painful to write—I couldn't write it. It occurs about two thirds of the way through *A Storm of Swords*. I skipped over it and I wrote the scenes that follow. I finished the entire book and I hadn't written that scene yet. That was the last thing I wrote for *A Storm of Swords*. I had to go back and make myself write it. And still . . . Emotionally, you become attached to these characters. I know I have the reputation for gleefully killing some of them, but that's not entirely deserved. Sometimes it's very painful for me to kill them. They're my children, for good or ill. So, that was a tough scene to write.

If I write something that I'm particularly proud of—that I think is a good piece of writing that is vivid and evocative—then that gives me pleasure, but it might not necessarily be the scenes that you guys would particularly enjoy. Some of them are just quiet things: I have to describe this landscape and I sweat and rewrite it and rewrite it and I finally get it. "Yeah, this is a great description of three guys riding through a grassy meadow." I've gotten the sights and the sounds and the smells of the scene right, to put you there. But it's not necessarily anything that ordinary readers will ever think about—"Oh my god, there was such a beautiful description of the grassy meadow on page 314."

DJ: At what point did you start to write outside the confines of A Song of Ice and Fire? I'm thinking here of the Dunk and Egg, "Hedge Knight" stuff, because that was published quite early. Was that conceived as part of this story that just didn't fit? How did that come about?

GRRM: That was Robert Silverberg's fault. Robert Silverberg decided he was going to do an anthology called *Legends,* which consisted of original stories. He wanted ten fantasy writers each writing a story in their fantasy world—an original story, never before published. He was offering what was quite a substantial advance, I think a record advance for a story in any anthology. And his lineup was amazing—Terry Pratchett and Stephen King were going to be in this, and Anne McCaffrey, and all of the best-selling fantasy writers. I was just getting into my series then. I really didn't belong in that number, but I knew that I wanted to be in this book. So, when he invited me to be in this book I gleefully accepted. And then I had a think. "Well, what am I gonna write for this book?" I'm still in the middle of writing *A Clash of Kings*—the only book out then was *A Game of Thrones.* "Am I gonna write a story about Tyrion or Arya or Jon Snow? No, I can't do that. I have to save that for the book. I have to do a prequel." So I started thinking about my history and what would be a good area to write in and I came up with the Dunk and Egg stuff.

I was particularly attracted to the whole story being built around a tournament. I love medieval tournaments—reading about them, writing about them. There are, of course, some of them in the main books, but this was an opportunity, in a time of peace not war, to look at a medieval tournament with all its pageantry, the jousting and the combat, and reveal a little of Westerosi history.

And like many other things, it grew. I gardened it, I started it, and suddenly it was all there. Actually, I was so long doing it that Bob tried to throw me out of the book. I was late delivering *A Clash of Kings*, which everybody knew about, and he had gotten a lot of money for this anthology and he wanted to deliver it on the deadline. So, all the stories were due at the end of the year—on December 31—and he said, "George, I hear you're still late for the book. I can't afford for my book to be late, so I'm dropping you from the book and we're going to replace you." And I said, "No, you're not. We have a contract here and I'm not late yet. You may think I'm going to be late but I'm not late yet, so you have to keep me in the book." So that's why *Legends* actually has eleven stories in it, not the original ten. He actually replaced me and found another guy, but I refused to be replaced and I wrote the story and goddammit I got it to him on December 31, which is the same time that I understand that like five of the stories came in, so I'm not the only writer who pushes things. And actually I think that story was one of the best decisions I ever made, because there was a real jump in my sales figures between *A Game of Thrones* and *A Clash of Kings*, and I think that story in *Legends* had a lot to do with it. I've had a lot of people come up to me over the ensuing years and say, "I'd never heard of you. I bought *Legends* because there was a new Stephen King story in it, but I loved your story and I started reading your stuff," or "I'd never heard of you, but I bought *Legends* for the Terry Pratchett story and then I read your story and it was great." So I think I gained a lot of readers by being in *Legends*.

DJ: Do you plan to do any more of them?

GRRM: I do. I've written three to date and I think I need to write another . . . I don't know, nine or something like that. But I have pretty well their entire lives in my head and of course all those things will become more detailed as I write them. But first I have to finish this book *The Winds of Winter* . . . I have to finish that and then I can write another Dunk and Egg story. And then I write *A Dream of Spring*. And then I write another Dunk and Egg story. At some point in there I have to write the second part of *Fire & Blood*, so I have my work cut out for me. Why am I talking to you here? I should be at home writing.

DJ: Let's start talking about history. First of all, I want to ask you about the history of the real world and its influence on your writing of this material about Westeros. You spoke earlier about turning a map of Ireland upside down. There are very evident influences of medieval history, but not only medieval history, on your work. Tell us a bit about how that's fed into your vision.

GRRM: Well, I've always loved history. Back when I was in college, I was a journalism major, history was my minor. And even before college I loved reading histories—popular histories and historical fiction. I have thought about writing historical fiction from time to time—there are certain periods that I love—but the problem with writing historical fiction is that you have to do all this damn research and you're stuck with the history the way it actually happened. Mostly. Unless your name is Quentin Tarantino and you can make up an ending of *Inglourious Basterds* that's completely different from what the audience expects. But for the most part you are stuck. I like the freedom of modeling my books on history, taking influences from history, but in fantasy I can make it come out differently. I can make it take a left turn when everybody is expecting it to take a right. I can do the unexpected and the revelation. And I can make it bigger. I like to say I take the things in history and I turn them up to eleven—if any of you know your *Spinal Tap,* you always have to turn it up to eleven . . . or to twenty-seven!

In 1981, my first visit to the UK, I was visiting my friend Lisa Tuttle with whom I wrote *Windhaven* and we took a car and we drove around for a while. One place we stopped was Hadrian's Wall. It had an amazing influence on me. We got there just at sunset—most of the tour buses had left, so we had it pretty much to ourselves. I went up on the wall and stood there and looked off to the north and tried to imagine I was a Roman legionary in the first century, standing on the wall and wondering what was going to come out of the hills. You know, they thought it was the end of the world. Now, I know, being a twentieth-century American, that what would actually come out of the hills would be Scotsmen, but I thought there could be a more terrifying answer. But that moment always stuck with me. And many years later, when I was writing what became *A*

Game of Thrones, I wanted a wall. I went way past Hadrian's and made it 700 feet high and made out of ice. And the things coming out of the forest and the hills to the north were a good deal scarier. That's something you can do with fantasy.

DJ: Every time that a season of *Game of Thrones* would be about to come on television in the UK, someone from a newspaper would ring me up and say, "Hey, we've got this great idea! Can you write an essay about how *Game of Thrones* is really just the Wars of the Roses?" And I'd say, "Yeah. Sure. Pay me. Of course." There's a secondary industry in George R. R. Martin material and I'm part of it. Stark and Lannister, York and Lancaster—there are all of these links. How much was it drawn from the Wars of the Roses? How much was that just convenient material for you to suck into this world?

GRRM: Well, there was certainly an inspiration, and probably the Wars of the Roses was the single greatest historical inspiration, but I'd read a lot of popular history. I also read the history of the Crusades and the Albigensian Crusade and the Hundred Years' War, and of course a lot of Nigel Tranter books—historical fiction about the history of Scotland, which always end badly. The history of Scotland is singularly bloody. If you think *Game of Thrones* is violent, read some Scottish history.

DJ: You draw on Scottish history for the Red Wedding, of course.

GRRM: Yes. The Red Wedding is loosely based on the Black Dinner, as they called it, but again, of course, I turned it up to eleven. And then David and Dan got hold of it for the TV show and turned it up to fourteen. You can always turn it up a little more.

The Black Dinner is an interesting case. I say I love history, but I always want to make it clear that I'm not a professional historian. The histories that I read and the histories that I love are what are called popular histories, they're not academic histories. The Black Dinner of Scotland—there was an enmity between the Earl of Douglas, the Black Douglas as he was called, and the King of Scotland. So the king invited the Earl of Douglas, gave him safe passage to come to the castle and discuss it. The earl was young—only eighteen or nineteen years old—and he brought his even younger brother who was like fifteen years old with him, and they had a lovely dinner with the King of Scotland. And then at the end of it they started playing this very sonorous beat and some servants entered with a covered platter, underneath which was a black boar's head, which was the symbol of death, and then they took the earl and his fourteen- or fifteen-year-old brother out and they beheaded both of them in the yard. It's a great story, and I went from that and I constructed the Red Wedding. Of course, that's the story in myth and in popular legend, but then if you read an academic history it says none of that ever happened—they did execute the earl but there was no sonorous beat, there was no black boar's head, all that stuff was invented later. And maybe it was, but whoever invented it was a pretty good storyteller, because I like the popular version of it much better than I like the boring academic version.

DJ: Let's talk about the history of Westeros, because *Fire & Blood* is your latest book and it is, as I said at the beginning, a masterpiece of popular history, and you can tell how steeped you are in the form because of the way you've constructed this book. Tell us why you chose to do this, pulling together earlier writings, some of them quite substantial, on the history of Westeros. Why put this together now?

GRRM: As you know, as I was writing the books I would have people think about or refer to things that had happened in history occasionally. It's actually in the novels—references to dead kings, references to legendary knights and so forth, of the past. At a certain point, my publishers said, "We want to publish a concordance, we want to publish a world book, because you've got all this history." And again, I was in the middle of writing novels and I said, "Yeah, well, that's a great idea, I'd love it. It has to be heavily illustrated, I want lots of gorgeous fantasy art in it." I love illustrated books, I always have since I was a kid reading Robin Hood and King Arthur books illustrated by people like Howard Pyle and N. C. Wyeth. Gorgeous books! I cut my teeth on those. So, I wanted my books done the same way. I said, "I have little bits of history in my head that I haven't had an opportunity to put in the novels yet, but I'll include them too, as sidebars."

So, we hired Elio García and Linda Antonsson, who are two of my uber-fans—they run the Westeros website, which is the oldest and the biggest of the websites devoted to Westeros and the books—and they were supposed to organize all of the historical references that were already in the novels, assemble everything and write a rough account of it. And then I would go in and I would polish that rough account and then I would put in these sidebars, which were material that had never appeared. We were supposed to have fifty thousand words of prose and then the rest would be art—art on every page, gorgeous art. By the time Elio and Linda had assembled everything we already had seventy thousand words of prose and then I wrote three hundred and fifty thousand words of sidebars. My publisher said, "Wait, wait! We can't do this. There won't be art on every page—we've already spent the whole art budget—there'll be art every twenty pages." So we ripped out all my sidebars and we got the book together. It was published a few years ago—*The World of Ice & Fire,* a very nice book!

DJ: A beautiful book!

GRRM: But then I had all of these leftover sidebars that were a history of various Targaryen kings, and I could have written more—I was only halfway through writing the sidebars when I realized how long they were. So, at a certain point, when we realized that *Game of Thrones* the TV show was winding down, but that there might be successor TV shows, I said to my publishers, "Well, we've always been talking about doing this history book . . ." (which I was calling the GRRMarillion, as a play on Tolkien) ". . . should I finish *Winds* first? Because the GRRMarrillion is almost complete, at least up to Aegon—the regency of Aegon III. And it includes material in it that is going to be the basis of some of these successor shows, so maybe we should get it out first, before the shows." And they agreed, so they said, "Yeah, finish that one and then go back to *The Winds of Winter.*" So, I sat down to finish that one—I polished all of the material I'd written, I expanded a few of the sidebars. But then I had to write, particularly, Jaehaerys I, Jaehaerys the Conciliator. I'd skipped over him in the sidebars, because he was the old king—he reigned for fifty-five years—and I had just sort of written "fifty-five years of peace and prosperity." That was the big hole in this book. And I said, "Well, I can't just have two sentences on Jaehaerys—he ran for fifty-five years. Fifty-five years of peace and prosperity is pretty dull, though. There must have been something that happened during that!" And I started inventing all the things that happened during Jaehaerys's reign. All of his children, who were trouble in many different ways, and conspiracies, and the roughness when he first took over things. But I loved it and I finished all of that, and I finally got the whole book done too, through the regency of Aegon III, and I'm very pleased with it. It's different—it's not a conventional novel, it is imaginary history. My real influence on this was Thomas Costain's A History of the Plantagenets, which if any of you haven't read, go out and find a copy in the used bookstore. It's wonderfully written, it's full of great, great stories, most of which academic historians have probably disproved by now. But they're still terrific stories, and the Plantagenets were a family that were equally as interesting as the Targaryens—they lacked only dragons, otherwise they would be right up there. So, that was my influence and I tried to do that in this imagined history book.

DJ: Costain is the second best book ever written about the Plantagenets, actually . . . There are some great scenes! Aegon's Conquest at the beginning of the book—would I be right in saying a sort of version of the Norman conquest of England in 1066, but on dragonback?

GRRM: With dragons, yes!

DJ: Do you have any particular favorite characters or episodes? I mean, the Dance of the Dragons forms, in a sense, the core part of the book.

GRRM: Well, I have a lot of affection for Mushroom.

DJ: Say a little bit about Mushroom and link it, if you wouldn't mind, to the process of writing fake history, because this is something that really struck me, that you've done so skillfully with this book. Explain who Mushroom is, maybe.

GRRM: Well, Mushroom is a dwarf, but he's not a well-born one like Tyrion, he's a dwarf of lowly birth who's the fool at the court during the events leading up to, and during much of, the Dance of the Dragons and its aftermath. He's a jester. There were actually a number of jesters in the Middle Ages, of course. You've probably seen them in many movies—fools, jesters, as they were called. Some of them were very, very clever men, who could do all sorts of witticisms and jokes, who could juggle and ride unicycles, and do other colorful things. Some of them were people who were physically deformed, who were dwarfs or hunchbacks. The people of the Middle Ages found that wonderfully amusing. So, Mushroom is a dwarf, but he's of the clever sort, and he's an observer.

Fire & Blood is not actually written by me, you see—it's written by Archmaester Gyldayn of the Citadel. He's writing a history, and like anyone writing history he has to go back to primary sources. I had a lot of fun with that, because when he gets to the Dance of the Dragons he has a number of primary sources, but three of them are most major. He has Grand Maester Orwyle's official court records, he has the septon of King's Landing and the Red Keep, who of course is a religious figure—so he interprets everything as the will of the gods, and what was a sin, what wasn't a sin—and he has Mushroom, who was semiliterate and couldn't actually write anything, but who told his story in later years to the equivalent of a monk, who wrote it all down. And Mushroom's story, of course, is always the most scandalous, scurrilous, filthy version of events, all of which had to do with people betraying each other and poisoning each other, having similar types of fun—sleeping in places they shouldn't sleep. I loved the idea, since this was a fake history, of not telling it as an omniscient historian sitting down to say "this is what actually happened." I loved the idea of telling it as a historian in-world who's trying to figure out what happened, but he's looking at his primary sources and he's finding contradictory accounts.

This was impressed on me many years ago, long before *A Game of Thrones* began. I was writing a novel that was never completed or published. It was

Black and White and Red All Over, a novel about 1890s journalism in New York City, when there were fourteen competing daily newspapers, one of which was the *New York World,* owned and operated by Joseph Pulitzer, the great, great journalist for whom the Pulitzer Prize is named. The New York World Building, which no longer exists but which was down on Park Row, which is where all the newspapers were built, was the tallest building in the world at its time. It had a golden dome on the top. It was a very memorable building. It was built right next to *The Sun,* a competing paper, but it was so high that the people said Pulitzer could lean out and spit on *The Sun* if he wanted, spit straight down at the smaller building next to him. The thing is, when I tried to research the World Building—the tallest building in the world—how many stories was it exactly? I found three different, contradictory citations—it was twenty stories tall or sixteen, I think, or fifteen. And that really impressed on me. This is 1890 I'm looking at—this is like yesterday in comparable things—this is a simple, factual question, how many stories were in this building, and I'm getting three different accounts. If they can't even get that right, what's the odds that they know what happened to . . . Charlemagne? The odds are astronomical!

So a modern historian or someone like Archmaester Gyldayn has to sort through these stories and decide which he believes, which he doesn't believe. I had a lot of fun being able to tell Mushroom's accounts, which are probably all turned up to thirty-seven, and then the duller accounts, but I didn't have to just stick to the duller accounts—I could give all three, and that was a great deal of fun.

DJ: The second volume of *Fire & Blood* won't come out anytime soon but could you give us an idea of some elements that it will contain? We go up to the reign of Aegon the Unlucky here—what are some of the highlights of the putative next volume of this?

GRRM: Well, this book only goes up to the regency of Aegon and ends when Aegon III actually reaches manhood and takes control, so I have his reign to cover, which includes the deaths of the last dragons. Although Aegon III is called the Dragonbane, there are still three or four dragons kicking around when he takes the crown and there are none by the time he's over, so that's one thing I was going to cover—why and what happens there—and some of the troubles and rebellions of his reign. And then, ultimately, his children, who are fairly interesting. He has five, one of whom is Daeron I, the Young Dragon, who conquers Dorne. He's a fourteen-year-old Alexander the Great kind of hero-king figure, but he dies young. And then his brother Baelor takes over, and Baelor is very religious, he's more of a Saint Louis kind of figure—a little extreme in his religiosity. Among other things, he imprisons his three sisters—in luxurious imprisonment in the Red Keep, in the Maidenvault. But he doesn't like them walking around the court because they tempt him. They have breasts and things underneath their clothes and he finds that very disturbing to contemplate, so he hides them away. So, I'll tell their stories and I'll tell Baelor's story. And then, after him, we get the brief reign of Viserys II, and then his son Aegon IV, Aegon the Unworthy, takes over, and he's a very colorful figure. I obviously drew on Henry VIII for him—Henry VIII had six wives, Aegon the Unworthy had nine mistresses. And they all exist in my head, I know who they all were and what happened to each of them—who had their heads chopped off and who had affairs, so there's a lot of cool material there. And then you get into the Blackfyre Rebellions, of which there were five. I've referred to them frequently so I'll get all the details on the Blackfyre Rebellions in. And ultimately we'll get to the Mad King and Robert's Rebellion, and that's where I'll draw it to a close.

DJ: I do have one more question for you. In this book we have many, many dragons and many, many Valyrian steel swords. If you could ride one dragon and wield one sword, which would it be?

GRRM: If I could ride on one dragon I might as well go with the biggest, which would be Balerion the Black Dread. He's the megadragon in this early book. He's the only one who remembers Valyria, up to a certain point, because he was brought over from Valyria a little before the Doom of Valyria. He's the biggest and meanest of the dragons that exists.

If I could wield only one sword, I don't think it would be any of the

Targaryen swords, it would be Dawn, the sword wielded by the Sword of the Morning, the heir of House Dayne of Starfall, which is made from the metal from a fallen star. Who knows what magical property fallen stars bring to earth?

DJ: Well, I think you've got a little bit of fallen star in you. I'm very sorry that we have to go, but it has been, I think you'll all agree, an enormous privilege and an utter joy and a pleasure to have with us the one and only George R. R. Martin. Give him a big hand!

GRRM: Thank you!

The full video is readily available online.

About the Author

George R. R. Martin is the #1 *New York Times* bestselling author of many novels, including those of the acclaimed series A Song of Ice and Fire—*A Game of Thrones, A Clash of Kings, A Storm of Swords, A Feast for Crows,* and *A Dance with Dragons*—as well as related works such as *Fire & Blood, A Knight of the Seven Kingdoms,* and *The World of Ice & Fire,* with Elio M. García, Jr., and Linda Antonsson. Other novels and collections include *Tuf Voyaging, Fevre Dream, The Armageddon Rag, Dying of the Light, Windhaven* (with Lisa Tuttle), and *Dreamsongs Volumes I* and *II.* As a writer-producer, he has worked on *The Twilight Zone, Beauty and the Beast,* and various feature films and pilots that were never made. He lives with his lovely wife, Parris, in Santa Fe, New Mexico.

georgerrmartin.com
Facebook.com/georgerrmartinofficial
Twitter: @GRRMspeaking

About the Illustrator

Doug Wheatley is a comic book artist, concept designer, and illustrator who has worked on such properties and characters as *Star Wars, Aliens,* Superman, The Incredible Hulk, and Conan the Barbarian to name just a few. Wheatley was the artist on the comic book adaptation of the film *Star Wars: Episode III: Revenge of the Sith* and contributed illustrations to *The World of Ice & Fire.*

Facebook.com/doug.wheatley
Twitter: @wheatley_doug
Instagram: @doug_wheatley